Aran

A novel by Michael P.C. Rocha

Creator of The MiddleVerse

www.middleverse.net

Published by Aeon Publishing, a division of Axis Mundi, Inc.

Aeon Publishing
106 Newport Towne Center
Newport Tennesse 37821
office.aeonpublishing@gmail.com

ISBN 979-8-218-70029-4
UPC 199284253407

Index

Aran

Preface

"Time does not forget. It does not yield to the weight of oblivion nor succumb to the erosion of memory. It is a river without end, a tide that laps at the shores of eternity, whispering the echoes of the past to those who would listen. In the infinite expanse of The MiddleVerse, where the fabric of existence is woven with the threads of countless lives, there are those who seek to preserve the truth of what was, that the future may not falter in ignorance. We are the House of Tempus, the silent watchers of the Cosmic Dance, the weavers of time's great tapestry, and the guardians of the *Echoing Archives.*

The story herein, *'The Book of Aran,'* is not merely a tale of one man's ambition, nor is it confined to the mortal struggles of a world wreathed in sand and scorched by its merciless sun. No, it is a convergence of fate, a moment in the ever-turning wheel of destiny where the shifting sands of Zarah bore witness to the forging of a legacy that would outlive the stars themselves. It is a story of unity and division, of war and peace, of the eternal struggle between order and chaos.

Aran ibn Khalid, whose name would one day become the cornerstone of a great House, was not the first to dream of uniting the fractious tribes of Zarah. Many before him had dared to stand against the winds of discord, only to be swallowed by the shifting dunes of time, their names reduced to whispers on the wind. Aran was different. He was not merely a man of vision - he was the vision itself, a flame kindled in the depths of Zarah's deserts, burning against the encroaching dark.

To those who traverse the vast corridors of history, Zarah is a paradox - a planet where life clings tenaciously to its very bones, where the people are as unyielding as the stone beneath their feet. It is a world where survival is an art, honed through millennia of hardship and tempered by the knowledge that the desert gives nothing freely. The main tribes of the Fourth Era, the Shamari, the Rasha, the Bahir, the Ulema, and the Tarek, each bore their own wisdom, their own traditions, their own unbreakable laws of survival.

But the House of Draco, ever the architect of ruin, saw in their disunity an opportunity. They came not with swords drawn but with poisoned words, with gifts that burned the hands that received them, with promises laced in chains. The tribes, blinded by their own struggles, could not see the strings being woven around them until it was nearly too late.

And so, amidst the chaos of war and deceit, Aran rose. Not with brute force alone, nor with mere words, but with the unshakable certainty that Zarah was meant for more. He saw not enemies but brothers and sisters, not fractured tribes, but the foundation of a civilisation that could stand unbowed against the forces that sought to consume them.
He understood what others could not - that unity, through understanding, was not the death of identity but its greatest expression.

This book, inscribed within the *Echoing Archives*, is not a relic of a forgotten age. It is a living testament, a ripple that continues to shape the currents of The MiddleVerse. For the past does not rest. It does not remain still. It lingers in the choices we make, in the battles yet to be fought, in the futures yet to unfold.

It is said that time favours no man, but we of the House of Tempus know the deeper truth - time favours those who understand it. Aran ibn Khalid, knowingly or not, walked the path of the Cosmic Dance. He heeded the whispers of destiny, and in doing so, he wove himself into the great pattern of The MiddleVerse. Whether his choices were his own or the design of forces greater than he could comprehend is a question best left to philosophers.

We record this story not merely for the sake of remembrance but as a beacon to those who will come after. To the rulers who would shape empires, to the warriors who would raise their banners, to the seekers who would unravel the mysteries of existence - know this: time is a fire that consumes the weak and refines the strong. Aran ibn Khalid stood before the inferno and emerged as something more.

Read, then, and remember..."
The House of Tempus, Echoing Archives, Chronaxis, the Kronos System

Prologue

Born of Sand and Blood

The desert winds of Sarim stir the sands like whispers from a distant past, carrying with them the echoes of a time when planet Zarah was young and the House of Aran had not yet risen to its present greatness. In the earliest days of the planet's formation, when the scorching sun still sculpted the land and the twin moons hung low over an arid, untouched expanse, life emerged amid the chaos, taking its first fragile steps upon the blistering stone and shifting dunes. The people who would become the Aran were not always masters of the desert, but like the land itself, they were shaped by its unforgiving nature - hardened, refined, and ultimately elevated to prominence.

From the deep chasms of history, long before the founding of Qamaria, before even the Old Weaver Kings were forgotten by most, before the first banners of Aran fluttered proudly above the desert cities, there existed only small nomadic tribes wandering the endless sands.

These tribes lived by the mercy of the land as their ancestors had for generations, their existence sustained only by their deep understanding of the desert's rhythms. It was a harsh life, for the desert gave little and demanded much. Yet, through their suffering and their perseverance, these early people came to know the desert as a teacher, a mother, and a judge. From this knowledge arose the seeds of the civilisation that would become the House of Aran.

Leander's primary, the fierce sun at the centre of the star system, had always ruled Zarah with an unforgiving grip, but it was the night, cold and clear beneath the twin moons, that offered the tribes respite from the day's harshness. Under these celestial bodies, the first ancient councils were held, small gatherings around flickering fires, where tribal elders shared their wisdom. These early tribes, though scattered and often at odds with one another, were bound by one shared belief: that the desert was alive, a living force whose will must be heeded if they were to survive.

The earliest known tribes of Zarah lived in harmony with the desert's cycles, eking out their existence from the sparse resources the land provided. They worshipped the elements - the sun, the wind, the sand, the water - and believed that these forces were divine entities that could be placated through offerings and rituals. Among these tribes were the Shamari, who lived closest to what would one day become the Kingdom

9

of Shamas, and the Arsari, who roamed the rocky highlands, where the Kingdom of Arsian would later rise. These tribes, though primitive in comparison to the later Aran kingdoms, were the first to understand the desert's true nature: its beauty and its danger, its generosity, and its cruelty.

From the blistering deserts rose the towering Solarwood trees, their reddish bark gleaming under the scorching sun. The Shamari tribe, masters of the hot sand deserts, discovered that Solarwood's durable material could withstand the heat, and it soon became the backbone of their crafts. The Moonleaf trees, with their silver trunks and pale green leaves, were worshipped by the Rasha of the cold deserts. They believed the Moonleaf captured the light of the twin moons, Anar and Nysa, and imbued their priests with divine visions.

The Tarek, nomads of the endless dunes, relied on the hardy Sand Whisper grass to weave baskets and thatch roofs. Meanwhile, the Shamari harvested the sweet Moonmelon from oasis groves, its water-rich flesh a blessing during droughts.
The tribes also learned to coexist with the desert's creatures. The Bahir, who lived near the rocky deserts, revered the Dune Stalkers - six-legged predators with exoskeletons that shimmered under the desert sun. Hunting these creatures was a rite of passage, and their claws became symbols of status and power. The Shamari told stories of the Sand Serpents, ancient guardians of the dunes that emerged in times of peril. Their scaled hides were said to glow with an otherworldly light, reflecting the desert's fury.

Legend speaks of Ashira of the Sands, who became a revered shamaness of the zafiri tribe. It was said that she communed directly with the desert. Ashira, through her visions, foretold the coming of a great leader - a unifier who would rise from the sands to bring the tribes together under one banner. Her prophecies would be remembered through the centuries, becoming the foundation of the House of Aran's belief in destiny and divine will.
Yet, as with all things in the desert, peace was fleeting. The tribes, while united by their reverence for the desert, were often torn apart by the constant struggle for survival. Resources were scarce, and the cruel harshness of life in Zarah bred fierce competition. Water, the most precious of all resources, was often the cause of bloody conflict. The 'Wars of the Oases', as they would later be called, became the defining struggle of the early tribes. The largest oases, which sustained the

greatest numbers of people and animals, became battlegrounds where rival tribes clashed in brutal combat.

At the end of Zarah's Fourth Age, called the Age of the Shattered Thrones, amid the chaos, one man rose to prominence - a warrior named Aran ibn Khalid, later known as King Aran I, the first ruler of what would become the House of the same name. Born of the Tarek tribe, he was a man of vision and determination. Aran believed that the tribes could not continue their endless cycles of war and bloodshed. To survive in the desert, they needed unity. Still, this unity could not be achieved through force alone - it required a shared purpose, a common identity that transcended tribal loyalty. To this end, Aran ibn Khalid began his great journey across the deserts of Zarah, seeking to unite the tribes not through conquest but through diplomacy and wisdom.
Aran's journey became the subject of legend, and the tales of his travels are still told in the courts of Qamar and Shamas to this day.
He travelled to the colder deserts of the north, where he met with the Rasha tribe, who lived in the 'shadow of the twin moons' and held the secret of water extraction from the crystalline sands. He crossed the scorching southern deserts, where the future kingdom of Shamas would one day thrive, to meet the Shamari, the masters of solar energy and heat-resistant technology. Along the way, he gathered followers - warriors, artisans, and mystics - who believed in his vision of a united Zarah.
It was at the site of the Great Oasis of Qamar, a place of breathtaking beauty in the heart of the cold desert, that Aran ibn Khalid made his stand. Here, he established his first permanent settlement - a city of tents that would later become the sprawling capital of Qamaria. The Great Oasis of Qamar, with its crystal-clear waters and lush palm groves, became the heart of his still fledgling kingdom. It was here that Aran ibn Khalid called the first Council of the Desert, a gathering of tribal leaders from across Zarah. The council marked the beginning of the Great Desert Unification, a process that would take decades to achieve its full completion but would forever change the course of Zarah's history.

The unification of the tribes under Aran was not won through conquest, but through vision, patience, and the quiet force of undeniable truth. Many leaders resisted, clinging to the independence their ancestors had safeguarded for generations. They saw unity as a chain, a threat to their ways. Aran, however, did not come as a conqueror, but as a builder, offering something greater than survival.

In the subtropical deserts to the south, the Shamari, masters of solar forges and water purification, stood as a barrier to his dream. Their leader, Karim al-Shamar, a man of sharp mind and sharper instinct, saw Aran not as an enemy, but as an anomaly - a man who spoke of peace yet commanded the loyalty of warriors. When the time came for confrontation, Aran did not raise a blade. Instead, he walked into the heart of the Shamari stronghold unarmed, bringing with him the knowledge of the Bahir's sandstorm prediction methods and the Rasha's water-harvesting techniques. He laid them before Karim, not as bargains, but as proof of what could be achieved together.

For three nights, they spoke. Aran did not demand allegiance - he illuminated a future where the tribes thrived, not as rivals, but as kin. He spoke of cities where solar mirrors would power forges, where oasis water would be shared instead of fought over, where the knowledge of one tribe would elevate all.

In the end, it was not the strength of his warriors that won the Shamari, but the strength of his vision. One by one, the remaining tribes saw what Karim had seen - that unity was not a loss, but a rebirth.

With the unification of the tribes complete, Aran ibn Khalid was crowned King Aran I, the first monarch of the House of Aran. His reign, though turbulent at first, eventually marked the beginning of a new era for the people of Zarah - a time of peace, prosperity, and cultural flourishing. It was also a time of great challenge, as the House of Draco played their hand in trying to reshape the reality of Zarah and its peoples by meddling with powers they probably should have not. But despite the Draconian interference, under his leadership, the newly unified kingdom began to build the great cities that would define the future of Zarah.

During these troublesome times, Qamaria, the new capital city, became a beacon of learning, art, and spirituality. Its towering citadel, built from the very stone of the desert, stood as a symbol of the strength and resilience of the Aran people. The Royal Gardens, a vast oasis filled with exotic plants and animals from across Zarah, became a centre of cultural life, where poets, musicians, and artists gathered to create works of unparalleled beauty.

At the base of the Crimson Cliffs stands the great statue of Aran himself, its immense form casting a long shadow over the bustling oasis city of Qamaria. The king's outstretched arm seems to beckon travellers and conquerors alike, a silent challenge to those who would dare to test the mettle of his descendants.

King Aran I's legacy was not just one of political unification, but of cultural renaissance. He encouraged the study of the desert's mysteries, leading to advancements in desert technologies, including irrigation systems, solar power, and sandstorm prediction. His reign saw the establishment of the Priesthood of the Sun, a powerful spiritual order tasked with maintaining the balance between the people and the desert. The priesthood, at the time led by the enigmatic High Priestess Amara al-Rasha, named after the queen of legend, became a central institution in their society, guiding both the spiritual and temporal affairs of the kingdom.

As was mentioned previously, long before the House of Aran ascended to the heights of power it now occupies, the deserts of Zarah were inhabited by a patchwork of nomadic tribes, remnants from the time of the Old Kings, each with their own beliefs, customs, and struggles. These tribes were as diverse as the deserts they wandered, bound by a single truth: survival in Zarah's arid expanse was neither a right nor a guarantee. It was earned, day by day, through grit, cunning, and an almost mystical attunement to the land.

The legends of these early tribes have been passed down through millennia, immortalized in songs, carvings, and tales whispered around campfires under the star-laden skies. In order to truly understand the House of Aran, one must journey far back to a time, when the deserts had not yet been tamed, when the people had no kingdoms, and the sands themselves were believed to be alive with ancient spirits.

In the age before cities, fortresses, and kingdoms, the people of Zarah lived in small, mobile clans that roamed the deserts in search of sustenance. Water was life, and those who could find it wielded tremendous power. The tribes had names now long lost to history, though some persist in ancient lore: the Tarek, the Rasha, the Bahir, the Ulema, the Shamari, and the oldest of all, the elusive Qarr. Each tribe carved out an existence in the harsh deserts, mastering different elements of survival, from finding hidden oases to reading the shifting sands for signs of an oncoming storm or any unwelcome creatures.

The Tarek, known for their unmatched skill in navigating the endless dunes of the Hot Sand Deserts, were believed to be able to 'speak' with the desert itself. Their shamans would interpret the movement of the dunes, reading them like a vast text written by the winds. They claimed that the sands spoke of the past, revealing lost cities and ancient paths that only the chosen could uncover. They developed a tradition of carving Solarwood talismans, believed to channel the desert's guidance, which were passed down through generations.

Tarek legends tell of a time when they stumbled upon the First Oasis, a place so vast and abundant with water that it was said to have been created by the gods themselves. When they attempted to settle there, the sands shifted violently, burying the oasis beneath tons of rock and earth, as if the desert had rejected them.

The Rasha, meanwhile, were masters of the cold deserts near the poles, where the air was thin and the crystalline sands shimmered under the pale light of the moons. They were people of quiet endurance, their survival hinged on their knowledge of rare plant life and the migration patterns of the animals that could withstand the freezing nights and scorching days. The Rasha believed that the moons held sway over the desert, that they controlled the tides of sand just as a distant ocean was governed by lunar cycles. They were deeply spiritual people, their lives shaped by lunar phases, and their numinous leaders - often women, known as Moon Seers - guided the tribe with visions they claimed were sent by the twin moons, Anar and Nysa.

The Bahir tribe roamed the rocky Black Dunes, where jagged cliffs and deep ravines made travel treacherous. These same rocky deserts and its surrounding lands would one day be home to the future kingdoms of Sayf and Arsian. The Bahir were the most militaristic of the early tribes, renowned for their warrior culture and the fortresses they carved into the sides of mountains and cliffs. The Bahir tribe believed the desert to be a battlefield, not between men but between life and death itself. Their warriors, known to be fierce, trained from a young age to fight both their enemies and the desert itself, honing their bodies and minds in relentless conditions. They wore cloaks woven from the silk-like fibres of Sand Weaver spiders, combining elegance and practicality. Bahir old folklore tells of the Trial of the Blade, where warriors proved their strength by defeating a Dune Stalker single-handedly. The Bahir would later play a crucial role in the eventual unification of the tribes, but in this ancient time, they were more often a scourge upon their neighbours, launching raids for water and resources, claiming that only the strong deserved to survive the harsh conditions of Zarah's deserts.

The Ulema, a nomadic tribe of the subtropical deserts, relied on the fertile oases to sustain their people. They believed that oases were sacred, guarded by unseen forces. Their priests performed rituals under the towering Solarwood trees, using their fragrant incense to summon blessings.

However, among all the early tribes, none were more enigmatic than the Qarr, a nomadic people who believed they were descended directly from Zarah's sands themselves. They did not build settlements or fortresses, nor did they farm or domesticate animals as other tribes eventually learned to do. Instead, they lived entirely in harmony with the desert, moving constantly, never staying in one place long enough to disrupt the natural order. The Qarr spoke of a Great Silence, a mystical force they believed lay beneath the sands, an ancient power that governed the balance of life and death. They claimed to hear this silence in the howling of the desert winds, in the shifting of the dunes, and in the stillness of the night. Millennia later, Yaran and Qamarian scholars speculated that during the time of the Qarr tribe, at the birth of Zarah's Second Age, they were still able to communicate with the Primordials - forces of creation, bound to intrinsic elements of existence. The Qarr were both feared and revered by other tribes, for they possessed knowledge of hidden water sources and survival techniques that no one else could replicate. Legends say that the Qarr disappeared into the desert without a trace, vanishing into the sands when the times of change approached. They are not part of this tale.

While Zarah's deserts posed countless challenges, they also inspired innovation. The early tribes harnessed the environment's resources to develop technologies that set them apart.

The Shamari devised early irrigation systems, creating channels to collect rainwater during the brief subtropical downpours. The Rasha perfected the art of extracting water from frozen sands, using ancient techniques still considered sacred by their descendants.

The Shamari's mastery of Solarwood extended to their early, innovative, experiments with solar technology. In time, they learned to build sun mirrors, reflecting and concentrating sunlight to heat their homes during the cold desert nights.

The Tarek tribe developed instruments using Sand Whisper grass and animal bones to detect changes in wind patterns. These simple tools allowed them to anticipate sandstorms, giving them a crucial advantage during migrations.

Among the earliest legends of Zarah's tribes is the myth of the Sand Serpents, the Uramaki, colossal creatures said to dwell beneath the desert's surface. These serpents were said to be as long as rivers, moving unseen beneath the sands, their presence always felt but never fully revealed. According to the myth, they were born of the desert itself, emerging in times of great need or great disaster, when the balance of the land was threatened. The Tarek saw these serpents as guardians of the land, ancient beings entrusted with preserving the sands from those who sought to take more than they were given.

One of the most famous stories involving the Sand Serpents tells of Iram the Bold, a Bahir warrior who sought to unite the tribes under his command by force. Iram believed that by controlling all the water sources in the desert, he could crown himself as the ruler of Zarah. He gathered a massive force and began conquering tribe after tribe, claiming their oases and cutting off water supplies to those who did not submit to his rule. As Iram's ambition grew, so too did the desert's discontent.

One night, when Iram and his forces camped near the largest oasis in Arsian country, the ground beneath them began to tremble. At first, they mistook it for a distant sandstorm. As the tremors deepened, the dunes themselves began to undulate - swelling and collapsing like waves upon a restless Yaran ocean. Before anyone could react, a massive serpent, its wide body and its scales glinting in the moonlight, erupted from the ground. Its guttural hiss was said to have shaken the moons from the sky.

The serpent, later named Uramak, laid waste to Iram's forces - swiftly swallowing men, horses, and entire tents in a single, monstrous sweep. In the chaos, Iram attempted to fight the creature, but his curved blade shattered against its scales like glass. The serpent encircled the oasis, its vast coils tightening like the grip of the desert itself. Then, with a single, cataclysmic plunge, it vanished beneath the sands - taking the oasis, and all who remained, with it. Iram's army was destroyed, and he himself was never seen again.

The tribes, witnessing this display of the desert's wrath, took it as a sign that no man could control the sands, and thus, the first attempt to unite Zarah ended in disaster. The mythical tale of Uramak serves as both a cautionary tale and a reminder of the desert's power, a story passed down through the generations to teach that the desert cannot be tamed by force, it is to be respected and understood.

Years later, the oasis was rediscovered, and an elderly Tarek shaman proclaimed it sacred, naming it the Oasis of Shadows. The tribes agreed to never claim it for themselves, and it became a neutral ground for gatherings, a symbol of the desert's dominion over its people.

For the early tribes, survival was not just a matter of physical endurance but a spiritual journey as well. One of the most sacred traditions was the Wanderers' Rite, a ritual undertaken by young members of the tribes as they came of age. This rite of passage required the individual to venture alone into the desert with nothing but a small pouch of water, a blade, and their wits. The goal was not to conquer the desert but to survive within it - to learn its ways, and to emerge with a deeper understanding of its nature.

Many never returned. The desert does not forgive the unready, nor does it mourn the lost - it merely swallows them, leaving only whispers on the wind. Those who did return were forever changed. They were welcomed back as full members of their tribe, their survival seen as proof that they had been chosen by Zarah itself to continue their people's legacy.

The stories of these wanderers are numerous, each one adding to the rich tapestry of the planet's history. One of the most famous tales is that of Amira, of the mysterious Qarr tribe mentioned earlier, a young woman who was said to have wandered the desert for several days and nights. She did not survive through strength or cunning, but through surrender. She listened - not just to the silence, but to something deeper.

The sands, she claimed, whispered secrets to her, guiding her to hidden waters and unseen shelters in the storm. When she returned home, she carried with her a small, black smooth stone, which she said had been a gift from the desert spirits.

Amira's tale became legendary, and her stone was passed down through the generations, believed to bring good fortune to those who carried it. In time, Amira's stone became more than a keepsake - it became a relic. A symbol of the desert's blessing, enshrined in the Royal Citadel of Qamaria, by order of King Aran I, where it remains to this day, a silent testament to those who dare to listen to the sands.

The early tribes of Zarah had no idea that a shadow had already fallen over their world. An intergalactic shadow that had its claws sunken, deep into the planet's history. The House of Draco, a shadowy reptilian force known for its shape-shifting abilities and cunning manipulation, took a deeper interest in this desert world, located in The MiddleVerse's Leander star system. The Draconians, with their vast knowledge of subterfuge and infiltration, saw in Zarah not just a barren wasteland but a world ripe for exploitation - its people scattered and disunited, its resources untapped. They came not with armies, but with whispers and gifts - disguised as wandering merchants, their hands full of wonders, their hearts full of lies. They offered weapons that could harness the power of the suns, devices that could detect water buried deep beneath the sands, and other marvels that dazzled the tribes. With each exchange, the House of Draco took more than it gave, subtly influencing the tribal leaders, sowing discord where there had once been peace.

At first, the Draconians' influence was subtle, like shifting sands beneath unsuspecting feet. In time, the delicate balance between the tribes and the desert began to crumble. Conflicts that had once been minor disputes escalated into full-blown wars, as the tribes, armed with Draco technology, began to see one another as enemies rather than brothers and sisters of the sand. The Wars of the Twin Suns, a series of brutal conflicts, erupted across the desert, forever changing the political landscape of Zarah.

In the darkest of times, when the sands ran red with war, a leader rose - one who would see through their deception and remind the tribes of who they truly were. His name, as mentioned before, was Aran ibn Khalid, and his rise would mark the beginning of the end for the Draconian influence on Zarah. Though the struggle had begun long before his time, and would continue long after his legacy was forged, Aran became the fulcrum upon which centuries of resistance turned - uniting what generations had defended in isolation into a single, enduring defiance.

The desert remembers. It remembers the blood spilled upon its sands, the whispers of betrayal carried by the wind, and the long years of darkness when its people forgot who they were. Yet, in the midst of ruin, the seeds of destiny were sown. For every shadow cast, there must come a light. In time, the desert would give rise to one who would bind its fractured tribes and forge a new path forward.

Therefore, every story must have a beginning, for in order to understand a man, you must first understand the land that made him...

Zarah had always been a planet of gold and fire, of endless dunes and towering cliffs, of whispering winds that carried both prayers and curses alike. It was a world that belonged to no one and yet held dominion over all who walked its sands. A land that birthed rulers and swallowed empires without mercy, leaving behind only bones and forgotten names. Yet from this tapestry of legend and loss, from bloodlines that carried the memory of ancient glory and the wisdom of survival, would emerge the fulfilment of Ashira's prophecy. Not born to palaces, or crowned in ceremony, but shaped by the very forces that had tested his ancestors - the unforgiving desert, the weight of division, and the burning need for unity that only the truly tested could understand.

The first memories Aran had were of motion - his mother rocking him to sleep, the rhythmic sway of a steed's gait beneath him, the scent of warm leather and spice from the merchant caravans, and the rustling of tents under star-choked skies. He did not know the comfort of walls or the permanence of cities. He was born into the wind, carried across the sands by the fate of his father's trade.

Despite being a ferocious warrior himself, Khalid ibn Rashid was a man of wisdom, not war - now a merchant who dealt in knowledge as much as he did in coin. Where other traders merely sought gold, he sought understanding. He spoke the tongues of many tribes, sat at the feet of scholars, and carried with him the rarest of all treasures: stories of the past, legacies of old. Forgotten by most, but not all...

"Every man must know his own price," Khalid once told his son, Aran, as they sat before a dwindling fire in the vast emptiness of the Arsian dunes. "Some sell themselves for power. Some for silver. The wisest man does not sell himself at all - he buys the world around him with knowledge."

Aran, barely old enough to understand the weight of his father's words, simply stared at the fire, watching the embers dance like spirits in the wind. "What do you buy, father?" he asked, drinking it all in.

Khalid smiled, his weathered hands resting on his knees. "Time, my son. With it, we buy time to understand what came before us so we may know what comes after." It was in those quiet moments, among the shifting sands and endless horizons, that Aran first began to see the world not as it was, but as it could be. However, Zarah was not a planet that allowed dreams to live long, at least not those that could not withstand its tests.

By the time he was ten, Aran had travelled across its vastness more than most men would in a lifetime. He had seen the sun-scorched spires of Sarim, where the Rasha Seers spoke in riddles and moonlight. He had walked the steel-forged streets of Shamaris, where the Shamari tinkered with sun mirrors and water engines. He had watched the Bahir warlords ride through the Black Dunes, their blades singing as they carved the wind, their onyx-coloured steeds reflecting the sunlight.

Still, no matter how many cities he visited, one truth remained: Zarah was broken. The tribes lived in fear of one another, bound by grudges older than memory, divided by ancient hatreds that had turned to law. Water was hoarded, knowledge was lost, and the only thing that held power over all was war. He learned early that survival meant knowing how to walk the line between words and steel.

His mother, Zahara, taught him the healing arts, infusing her son with all the knowledge she had amassed throughout her life. His father, Khalid, taught him the arts of the blade and negotiation, two skills that didn't diverge that much from one another. He taught his son how to weigh a man's heart as one would weigh a bag of gold.

Khalid was not a man of soft hands or idle comforts. He was a proud son of the Tarek, a people who no longer had a home, a people whose name had been stripped from history.

Though he did not speak of it often, there was a fire in him that the desert itself seemed to fear. "A man must know how to defend himself, Aran." Khalid told his son, pressing a dagger into his small hands when he was no older than eight. "Because when words fail, the hand that holds the blade will decide who lives and who is forgotten."

This was not a lesson of violence but of necessity. For Zarah's deserts did not care for those who could not stand…

The night was quiet and the desert air was heavy with the scent of jasmine and dust. It was the season of the Qamarian Winds, when the dunes moved like restless spirits, shifting their forms under Anar and Nysa's watchful gaze. Aran sat beneath the twisted branches of an old Dune Ash Tree, staring out at the vast horizon, listening to the rhythmic hush of the wind as it whispered through the sands.

He had always found comfort in the desert's silence. A silence that knew no kings, no warlords, no masters. A silence untouched by greed. But that night, the silence was wrong. It was waiting. Aran could feel the weight of it, like a thousand unseen eyes watching from the darkness. He should have listened to it.

His father had always been a man of measured words and long thoughts. He was a warrior at heart, but did not crave power. Where others sought dominion, he sought understanding, travelling across Zarah's fractured lands, speaking with chieftains, merchants, and mystics alike. "Knowledge is the strongest blade, my son," he would invariably say. "Wield it well, and no one will ever rule you." Aran had never doubted that - until that night.

His father sat across from him, wrapped in the flowing robes of a Tarek elder, his weathered face illuminated by the flickering lanterns of their modest camp, his eyes troubled. "We should leave before the sun rises," Khalid said, his voice low, thoughtful. Aran frowned. "You fear something."

"Not something," Khalid murmured, gaze fixed on the sands beyond their camp. "Someone."

It had been years since Aran had seen his father like this. Wary. Uncertain. The man who had stood before warlords and spoken to them as equals now glanced over his shoulder as though he were being hunted.

"The warlords of the east do not like your vision," Aran said, cautiously. Khalid exhaled sharply. "No. They do not."

Aran's father had been meeting with the Shamari Council, seeking a fragile peace between the divided tribes. A peace that could have changed everything. Under Leander's primary unrelenting heat, peace was a dangerous ambition. "The Bahir would rather see Zarah burn than share their power with others," Aran continued. "And the House of Draco will never allow an alliance that they can not control."
His father nodded slowly. "That is why we must leave, Aran. The desert shifts, but tonight, it shifts against us." That night, for the first time, Aran felt the weight of fear in his father's voice.
Unrelenting as the threads of fate, the attack came with no warning. No war cries. No clashing steel. No thunder of hooves. Only the whisper of blades through canvas, the sharp gasp of dying men, the sudden bloom of fire licking the edge of their tents. Aran woke to the scent of burning leather and blood, his heart pounding against his ribs.
Outside, the camp was a chaos of shadows and flame - large scaled mercenaries in dark veils moving like ghosts through the wreckage, cutting down his father's men before they could even reach for their weapons. Aran reached for his own - only to feel a strong hand grab his wrist. "Run," Khalid commanded. His father's face was streaked with soot, his robes torn. "Now!"
Aran froze. "I won't leave you."
"You must!" Khalid's grip tightened. "You are not ready for this fight. But you will be. One day, you will be."
Aran clenched his teeth, his hands trembling. "Who did this?"
Khalid's dark eyes burned. "The Vulture."
Malik the Vulture was a warlord who feasted on the weak, who had sold his own people to the House of Draco in exchange for gold and power. A man who killed visionaries before they could become legends. Aran's breath turned to fire in his chest. "I won't -"
A shuddering cry split the air - one of his father's men falling beneath a mercenary's blade. Khalid's eyes softened. "Go," and then he turned - blade drawn, standing between his son and death. Aran watched, unable to help his father. He hesitated, anguish eating away at his heart - then, he ran for his life.

By the time the sun rose, the camp was nothing but ash and ruin. The bodies of his father's men lay scattered among the sands, their lifeless eyes staring at a sky that no longer belonged to them. At the heart of it all, Khalid ibn Rashid lay still, his robes stained red, the hilt of his sword still clutched in his fingers.

There was no burial. No mourning. Only Aran, kneeling before his dead father's body, his hands shaking, his heart empty. The desert does not mourn the dead, but Aran did.

From the smoke, a figure stepped forward. "Thank the moons I found you. We thought you would be dead by now." A young woman's voice - sharp, steady. His cousin, Zahira.

She had come alone, her eyes dark with grief, her hands wrapped tightly around the hilt of her dagger. She did not speak false comforts but merely looked at him and asked the only question that mattered. "What will you do now, Aran?" He stood slowly. The weight of his father's blood was heavy on his soul. "I will finish what he started."

For weeks, he wandered alone, moving deeper into Zarah's unforgiving expanse of sand and heat, guided by nothing but grief and a rage that burned deeper than the midday sun. Initially, he had pursued his father's assassins with a desperate hope of justice, but what could a grieving boy accomplish against seasoned killers? What chance did a single heart, broken and bleeding, have against the indifferent vastness of Zarah's deserts? So he walked…

He walked until his feet were raw, until the skin cracked and bled into the sand. Hunger became his close companion, thirst his only conversation, and in that profound solitude, the desert began its ancient work. It tested him, not with violence, but with something far more ruthless - with silence.

The desert whispered of his insignificance. It spoke of failure, of how he was nothing more than a transient breath, a momentary disturbance in an endless landscape. Just another grain of sand, soon to be forgotten, soon to be swallowed. Faced with his own mortality, Aran was not merely watching - he was listening.

He observed how the dunes moved - not like static land, but like living water. Shifting, breathing, and telling stories most were too impatient to hear. He learned to read the stars not as distant points of light but as a map etched across the night's dark canvas. He learned to follow the wind's subtle languages, to walk as the desert walked - patient, resolute, relentless, transformative.

Most critically, he learned to listen to the silence. Not the absence of sound, but the profound space between breaths, between heartbeats. In that silence, he found a strength that had nothing to do with vengeance and everything to do with understanding.

It was on the seventh night, as Anar and Nysa cast their silver light across the dunes, that understanding crystallized. A Nightwing circled overhead, its seven-foot wingspan cutting silently through the darkness, its feathers drinking in the moonlight until it seemed less bird than living shadow. Aran watched as it descended to a hidden spring he had not noticed - water revealed not through desperate searching, but through patient observation of the desert's own rhythms. The Nightwing had not hoarded its knowledge of water; it had simply followed its nature, and in doing so, revealed life to one who desperately needed it. The tribes, scattered and suspicious, were like that hidden spring - powerful in isolation, but life-giving when their wisdom flowed together.

When he emerged weeks later, he was no longer a boy. The desert had carved something new from his grief - a leader, a visionary.

The first thing Aran realized was that revenge was too small a solution to his father's murder. Too narrow. Too personal. His father's death was merely a symptom of a deeper wound - Zarah itself was fractured. Countless generations of tribal divisions, of petty warlords and self-serving kings had bled the land dry.

No, he would not seek to kill those who had killed his father. Instead, he would transform the very system that had made such violence possible. He would unite the tribes. Not out of sentiment, not out of personal loss, but out of a profound understanding that only together could they heal. Only together could they become more than a collection of competing fragments. "No more warlords," he whispered, and Zarah's deserts seemed to hold their breath. "No more divisions. No more blind kings," his voice grew stronger. "One people. One desert. One Zarah."

At that moment, something shifted. Not just in himself but in the landscape around him. Zarah's ancient sands had been waiting, for millennia, for someone to finally speak these words. The legend of King Aran I was only just beginning.

Chapter I

The Moon Seers' Warning

The desert winds carry many stories, but few have been told as many times or with as much reverence as the tale of Aran ibn Khalid. His name is etched into the annals of Zarah's history, not as a conqueror or a mere tribal chief, but as a visionary who united a fractured people.

After the fall of the Old Kings, the tribes of the desert were scattered like the grains of sand that covered their lands. With the exceptions of Sarim, Ryvath, and a few other kingdoms, most of Zarah remained a land of fragmented nomadic clans. Under Aran's guidance, these disparate factions were woven into a single thread, each adding its own strength to the fabric of what would become the House that would carry his name through the annals of history of The MiddleVerse.

Again, to understand the man, one must first understand the world he was born into: a world where survival was a daily battle, where alliances were fragile and short-lived, and where the shadowy influence of the House of Draco had already begun to take root amongst its institutions. Against the cosmic tide was Aran...

For he was no ordinary child, and his journey from obscurity to legend is a tale steeped in mysticism, strategy, and profound understanding of his people's deepest needs and most secret yearnings.

His origins, at first glance, were as humble as any on Zarah.

Born in the oasis town of Karash, second son to a small and humble, unremarkable family of the Tarek tribe, his early life gave no indication of the greatness that awaited him.

The Tarek, once powerful and respected as masters of the dunes, had fallen into obscurity by the time of his birth. Their shamans, who once communed with the sands, were now old and scattered, their influence waning. Karash, a town of perhaps a few hundred souls, was little more than a stopping point for traders and travellers crossing the desert wastes of Zarah.

From an early age, however, Aran displayed qualities that set him apart from the other children, even from his brother Amir. Being a few years older than Aran, Amir was already fully dedicated to martial life, therefore his younger brother's interests were of no interest to him. Amir was rash and impulsive, Aran was quiet, observant, and introspective, often found sitting at the edge of the oasis, staring out into the vast expanse of dunes. While the other boys of his age took pride in learning the arts of hunting and combat, Aran was more interested in the stories of the old shamans, the legends of his people, and the history of the desert itself.

Although he excelled at martial training, he also had a fascination with the land that seemed to transcend the simple need for survival. To him, the desert was alive - not just a sea of sand, but a living, breathing entity with a soul and will of its own.

Their mother, Zahara, was a healer known for her knowledge of herbs and ancient remedies. She often told Aran the stories her own mother had passed down to her - stories of the First Oasis, the Sand Serpents, and of the time when the Tarek could still read the shifting sands. Their father, Khalid, to the best of Aran's knowledge, was but a modest trader, eking out a living by transporting goods between oases, always worried about the survival of his family.

Though Khalid was a pragmatic man, focused on the day-to-day struggle to put food on the table, he never dismissed Aran's curiosity. In fact, to the boy's delight, Khalid often took his son with him on his trading routes, allowing the young man to see more of the deserts than most adults ever would in a lifetime.

For some reason that he could not explain, Aran always felt that his father was withholding something, some secret part of his life. As though there were certain things he avoided discussing with his family. Certain subjects like his past, what his life was like before his sons were born. "Aran, that belongs in the past," his father would always say, his tone leaving no room for argument. Despite avoiding some of his son's questions, Khalid kept taking the boy with him. Together, travelling Zarah's caravan routes.

It was during these journeys that Aran first encountered the other tribes of Zarah, and even at a young age, he understood that there was a deep, underlying connection between all of them. The Rasha, the Bahir, the Ulema, the Shamari - they were all bound by the same struggle, the same dependence on the land and its fickle generosity. But there was also mistrust, hostility, and division. The tribes fought over water, over land, over resources. Each believed that they alone had the right to survive in the desert and others were seen as trespassers.

As he watched the tribes barter, quarrel, and survive, a realization took root within him - these people were not meant to be rivals. They were meant to be a single, unbreakable force.

The years passed, and as Aran grew, it became clear that he was not just an ordinary youth with a passing interest in ancient tales. By the age of fifteen, he had already begun to form his own ideas about the future of the tribes, ideas that would have been dismissed as naive, or even dangerous, by the elders. He spoke of unity, of a time when the tribes would no longer fight over the same resources but work together to tame the deserts. He believed that the tribes' deep connection to the land could be their greatest strength, but only if they stood united. These ideas, though radical, began to take hold among his peers, especially the younger generation, who were weary of the endless cycle of conflict and hardship.

The elders, however, were not so easily swayed. They had lived through decades of war and bloodshed, and their distrust of the other tribes ran deep. The Bahir had raided their caravans, the Rasha had sabotaged their wells, and the Ulema had cheated them in trade negotiations. To them, Aran's vision of unity was a fool's dream, an idealistic fantasy with no place in the harsh reality of the desert.

It was during these formative years that Aran's first encounter with the House of Draco would occur, and along with his father's death this became an event that would shape his future and the future of Zarah in ways no one could have anticipated.

The Draconians, always subtle in their machinations, had long been observing the tribes of Zarah. They had infiltrated the highest circles of power, from the Bahir warlords to the Rasha council of seers, cunningly manipulating events from behind the scenes. They thrived on chaos, using it to further their own ends, and the fractured state of the tribes was a perfect breeding ground for their influence.

It was in Karash, during one of the rare festivals that drew travellers from across the desert, that Aran first met a 'man' who would later be revealed as a Draconian. This person, who introduced himself as Ashir, was a trader of rare and exotic goods. His wares were unlike anything Aran had ever seen - strange devices that glowed with an otherworldly light, weapons that seemed to hum with hidden power, and artefacts that Ashir claimed had been plucked from the ruins of ancient, forgotten civilizations, buried by the sands.

Aran, always curious, was naturally drawn to Ashir's stall. The trader, sensing something in the boy, took a special interest in him, offering to show items that were not on display. That night, beneath the cold gaze of the twin moons, Ashir beckoned Aran away from the festival's warmth. In the shadowed dunes, he unveiled a stone - smooth, ancient, its worn surface carved with the twisting symbol of a fractured sun. The moment Aran touched it, he felt a strange sensation. The symbols glowing, as if the stone was alive, vibrating in the palm of his hand, with a soft, mystic energy.

"That is no ordinary stone," Ashir said, as Aran held it, his voice low and conspiratorial. "It is a key." His eyes glowed with intent. "A key to what?" Aran asked. Ashir paused for a second, then locked eyes with the boy. "A key to power beyond anything you can imagine," his eyes reflecting the twin satellites. "A key to reshape reality. This came from an ancient temple, hidden deep in the caves to the north of Karash," he added. "A Draconian temple."
Aran, though intrigued, was wary. He had heard tales of the Draconians, of their deceptions and their lust for control. To his surprise, Ashir did not press him further. Instead, he offered the stone as a gift, saying that it was merely a token of goodwill, nothing more.
"You have potential," Ashir said, his eyes gleaming in the moonlight. "Great potential. I foresee that the deserts will one day bow to you. Still, you must be careful, for there are those who would see you fail." He leaned closer, placing a hand on the boy's shoulder, "farewell Aran." With that, Ashir disappeared into the night, leaving Aran with the stone and a sense of unease that he could not shake.

In the years that followed, Aran's life took a strange turn. He began to experience vivid dreams, dreams in which the desert itself seemed to speak to him. In these dreams, the sands shifted and danced, forming symbols and patterns that he could not fully understand. He saw visions of the tribes, not as enemies, but as brothers and sisters, standing together against a great and terrible force that loomed on the horizon.
At first, he dismissed these dreams as mere fantasies, the result of his overactive imagination. As they became more frequent and much more intense, he began to realize that they were something more. The desert was trying to tell him something, trying to show him a path that he had not yet considered. As the years unspooled like desert winds, the stone Ashir had given him still rested in his travelling pack, its surface now cold and lifeless, as if the years had drained it of whatever power it once held. He kept it not out of belief, but because some quiet part of him was unwilling to let it go. In its mute stillness, it whispered of paths untrodden and promises half-remembered, binding him to a hope he could neither name nor forsake.

One night, as the moons shone bright outside his tent, during one of his dreams, Aran found himself standing at the edge of a vast chasm. On the other side, he saw the tribes - united, strong, and prosperous. Between him and this vision was a swirling maelstrom of sand and shadow, a force that threatened to consume everything. As he stood there, watching the storm grow, he felt a presence behind him. Turning, he saw a figure cloaked in moonlight and gloom. An old woman, her hooded face unreadable, but her eyes gleaming with the light of truths too ancient to name.

Though her features seemed familiar - perhaps his grandmother's eyes, or the face of the old Tarek shamans from his childhood - the early signs of recognition slipped away like sand through his fingers.

"The storm is coming, Aran," she whispered, her voice like the wind itself. "But do not fret my child, for you are the key." Her words reminded him of Ashir. "A key for what?" he managed to ask.

The old woman lifted her hood, revealing a familiar face, though he could not remember where he had seen it before. "A key to reshape the foundations of Zarah," she said. "You must bring them together, Aran. You must fight the external threat and repair the old pacts." She paused. "What do you mean? What if I cannot do that?" he asked, in desperation. The woman covered her face once more. "Then Zarah will crumble, its people scattered to the winds, your father would have died for nothing, and all that will remain is dust and regret."

"Who are you?" he managed to ask, but the vision was already fading away. When Aran awoke, he knew what he had to do. He saw it with utter clarity. Either the peoples of Zarah would stand united, or they would fall.

His first attempts to gather the tribes were met, at best, with scepticism and occasionally with outright hostility. The Tarek elders, though proud of his intelligence and vision, were unwilling to risk the tribe's safety on what they saw as a hopeless cause. The other tribes were even less receptive. The Bahir warlords laughed at the idea of uniting with their enemies, the Ulema seers warned of dark omens, and the Rasha simply ignored him. Though there was one among them, a council member called Farid al-Rasha, who took a special interest in Aran and his vision, and he would make sure his scaled friends would as well…

Despite whatever setbacks he faced, Aran was nothing if not persistent. He travelled from tribe to tribe, speaking to anyone who would listen, not just the leaders but the common people - the traders, the farmers, the warriors. He told them of his vision, of a time when the tribes would no longer fight over the same dwindling resources but work together to help create a new future for all. He spoke of the desert as a living entity, one that would reward those who respected it and punish those who tried to dominate it. Nevertheless, Aran's vision was not without its obstacles, and chief among them was the growing influence of the House of Draco.

Though their presence was subtle, Aran, with ease, recognized their methods - sowing discord through bribes, subterfuge, and promises of technological superiority.

In the rocky highlands near the lands of Arsian, where one of the future six kingdoms of his House would one day reside, Aran and his followers stumbled upon a caravan of Draconian traders peddling strange devices. Among their wares were weapons capable of firing concentrated bursts of solar energy and vials of shimmering liquid that they claimed could heal any wound. Aran confronted the leader of the caravan, a sly Draconian named Malik, whose voice stirred something dark in Aran's memory. "Why fight over scraps of water and land when the Draco can give you abundance?" Malik said, holding up a vial of the liquid. "The tribes are wasting their time with your foolish dreams of unity, Aran ibn Khalid. Let us show you a better path." The veil of memory lifted.

The face before him was older, more weathered, but unmistakably that of Ashir - the trader who had given him the stone years ago.

Aran's voice was steady, but his eyes burned with conviction as he studied Malik's face, searching for confirmation of an old suspicion. "Your gifts come at a price, one that my people can not afford. Zarah will not be bought or divided." As Aran turned to leave, Malik called after him, his tone laced with venom. "The desert does not favour fools, Aran. It swallows them whole. Remember that, when your vision collapses into dust. Remember the past." Something in the way Malik said "the past" made Aran's hand instinctively tighten around the hilt of his father's blade.

Aran left the encounter with a heavier heart but greater resolve. He knew the Draco would not cease their efforts to undermine his mission, and their shadow - one that had perhaps already claimed his father - loomed ever larger over his journey.

To Aran, his travels were as much about continuing to learn as they were about uniting the tribes. In every corner of Zarah, he sought not only to bring people together but to understand the unique strengths that each region contributed to the survival of their shared homeland.

Back in the rocky deserts of Arsian, Aran was hoping to find the Bahir tribe, known for their unyielding warrior culture. He had heard tales of the awe-inspiring trials they endured. The Trial of the Blade, where young warriors duelled against the fearsome Dune Stalkers, creatures whose claws could pierce steel. They also also practised the Trial of the Scorpion. This was a test of strength, endurance, and cunning, as well as a right to challenge for leadership. The warriors who took the Trial of the Scorpion were not only tested on strength and endurance but on their ability to outthink a predator. It was said that no outsider had ever

completed it. If Aran wanted the Bahir to listen, he would have to prove himself in their own crucible. Recognizing the Bahir tribe's military prowess, Aran saw them as a possible cornerstone to his vision.
A people who could protect the unified Zarah from internal, as well as external threats.

Chapter II

Oaths of Fire and Sand

In the blistering desert of Zarah, where the sands seem endless and the horizon stretches beyond the imagination, the notion of unity was as alien to the various tribes as water flowing freely through the desert, without creating life. Yet, it was within these unforgiving Black Dunes, among the scattered clans, that Aran ibn Khalid sought to forge an alliance. It was a seemingly impossible task, fraught with dangers both seen and unseen. His mission was not born from ambition alone, but also out of necessity and a belief that survival itself hinged on bringing these scattered, hostile, factions together. However, he knew that unity, like steel, must be forged in the heat of conflict. His dream, his vision, would be tested in the flames of treachery, war, and the inexorable forces of the House of Draco, whose manipulations would threaten everything he sought to build.

Of all the tribes Aran sought to unite, the Bahir were the most feared. Known as the 'Scorpions of the Sands,' they were, partly, a nomadic people, fierce in battle and merciless in their raids. The Bahir were not known for diplomacy or negotiation. Their society was built on strength, and their leaders - warlords who had proven themselves in combat - valued little else. For Aran to convince them to consider his vision of a united Zarah, he would need more than words.

Accompanied by his longtime friend, Rafiq ibn Azim, and a very small contingent of loyal Tarek warriors, Aran finally ventured deep into Bahir territory, a treacherous journey that took him across the Black Dunes.

These dunes were an unforgiving expanse of coal-coloured sands, their shifting tides unpredictable and deadly. Even experienced, seasoned travellers avoided this region, for these dunes were said to be cursed by the spirits of those who had perished there. Despite the dangers, the Bahir thrived in this harsh landscape, their mastery of its secrets a true testament to their resilience.

As Aran studied the Bahir, he saw not just raiders, but survivors - people who had mastered the desert as no others had. If they could be turned from warriors of division to warriors of unity, then perhaps Zarah had a future beyond endless war. As Aran's group traversed the dunes, they observed signs of Bahir life - towering rock formations carved into fortresses, the remnants of ancient battles, and, most notably, the intricate patterns left by Sand Weaver spiders. These creatures spun massive underground webs, their silk harvested by the Bahir to create garments that shimmered in the sun but were as strong as armour.

The Bahir stronghold, hidden within the depths of a jagged canyon, was said to be a marvel of natural and architectural ingenuity. Shamari solar mirrors placed at the canyon's mouth reflected light into its shadowy depths, illuminating pathways and revealing the tribe's resourcefulness. As Aran approached, his resolve hardened, for deep down, he knew that this meeting could define the future of his vision.

This tribe's mastery of the desert's hidden paths was unmatched, often ambushing travellers who dared to enter their lands without permission. While they crossed the dunes, Aran's company remained ever watchful, for they knew the Bahir could strike at any moment.

The wind howled relentlessly, carrying with it grains of black sand that stung the skin like needles. The sun, hidden behind a veil of swirling dust, cast an eerie, dim light over the landscape. For days, they pressed forward, their supplies dwindling, their water running dangerously low. The weight of the journey bore down on them, but Aran's resolve remained unshaken. He knew that to win the Bahir's respect, he had to first endure the desert that had shaped them.

It was on the fifth day, as they reached the outskirts of the tribe's hidden encampment, that the attack came. Silent and swift, the Bahir warriors emerged from the dunes like shadows, their faces obscured by black veils, their swords gleaming in the dim light. Aran's company drew their weapons, but they were outnumbered and surrounded.

In the chaos of the ambush, Aran did not raise his sword. Instead, he stepped forward, his arms raised in a gesture of peace. His voice, though firm, was calm, carrying over the wind.

"I am Aran ibn Khalid, of the Tarek tribe. I come not as your enemy, but as one who seeks to end the bloodshed between our peoples."

For a moment, there was only silence. The Bahir warriors, their blades poised to strike, exchanged glances, uncertain. Then, from behind them, a figure emerged - a tall man, his armour adorned with the symbols of their ruling house. This was Kasim al-Bahir, and despite a few grey hairs signalling the passage of time, he was still the most feared warlord in the region. His eyes, cold and calculating, sized Aran up as though he were appraising a prize animal.

Kasim approached, his sword still drawn, and circled Aran slowly.

"Tell me, Aran, son of Khalid," he paused, facing his prize. "Why should we listen to the son of a forgotten tribe?" Kasim's voice was low and dangerous, each word an open challenge.

Aran met his gaze without flinching. His voice was loud and firm, so that all could hear him, though he kept its tone warm and respectful.

"Because your strength alone will not be enough when the storm comes. The desert is changing, and with it, the rules of survival. The days of raiding and warring over water and land will soon be over, whether you will it or not." He looked around. The Bahir warriors surrounding him took a step backwards and looked at their leader.

Kasim stopped pacing around him, his face expressionless. "And what storm is that?" he asked, amused.

"The storm I have seen in my dreams," Aran said, his voice steady. "A force greater than any tribe, one that will consume all of us if we remain divided. I offer you more than survival, Kasim. I offer you a place in the future of Zarah - a future where the Bahir are not feared as raiders but respected as leaders."

There was a longer pause this time. The Bahir warlord studied Aran's face, searching for any sign of weakness or deceit. Suddenly, without warning, Kasim sheathed his sword and laughed - a cold, harsh sound that echoed across the dunes. Aran felt Kasim's warriors relaxing their muscles as they lowered their weapons.

"You speak boldly, Aran, son of Khalid, son of Rashid," he said. "Unfortunately for you, words alone will not suffice to win my trust. If you truly wish to prove yourself before our tribe, to be worthy of our alliance, you must first survive the Trial of the Scorpion."

With a gesture, he ordered his warriors to leave. "However, I feel most obliged to tell you that you can die in this trial," Kasim was looking deep in Aran's eyes. "Are you ready to risk your life because of a vision? Of a dream?" Without blinking, or averting his eyes, he concluded. "Make your choice."

Aran met Kasim's gaze in silence. He was well prepared for this, fully aware of the danger he was about to face. This trial was an old rite of passage among the Bahir, reserved for those who sought to join their ranks, but most of all, for those who wished to challenge their leaders. It was a test of strength, endurance, and cunning - a brutal trial designed to break all but the strongest. Few had ever survived it, and none from outside the Bahir had ever attempted it.

For Aran, there was no choice to be made here. He had made his choices long before this moment, way back in that fateful night, when his father was murdered. Besides, refusing the trial would be to forfeit any chance of winning the Bahir tribe's allegiance. This wasn't a matter of choice but of destiny. Without hesitation, he accepted.

Clearly, the Bahir were not expecting this. The men exchanged looks of surprise, mingled with respect. They believed history would repeat itself, for most outsiders forsake this challenge when made aware of its mortal perils. Because of his unyielding bravery, and as a token of their respect for him, he was allowed to dine with Kasim and his warriors.

A simple though sumptuous repast, followed by an ancient tribal dance performed by the Bahir women. During the meal, Aran was constantly reminded of his chances of success, but he chose instead to speak of his vision for Zarah and its people. To everybody's astonishment, the man was speaking as if the trial had already been overcome. As if it was merely a matter of going through the process. He shared his vision, drank, ate, and even managed to join in the laughter.

In spite of his outward behaviour, in Aran's mind, another scenario was playing out. He knew exactly what was ahead of him, and he needed to remain focused. All of his demeanour was intended to project an image of confidence, for he knew the Bahir warriors respected that.

Aware of their customs, he knew their taunting was, in fact, a bizarre form of flattery, and he needed to reflect strength back at them.

That night, under the light of the twin moons, Aran was led deep into the desert by Kasim al-Bahir and his personal guards. After walking in utter silence for half an hour, they stopped at the edge of a small, jagged box canyon, where the ground was littered with the bones of creatures long dead. In the centre was a pit surrounded by ancient stones carved with the symbols of the Bahir's ancestors. The air was thick with tension, and the only sounds were the distant howling of the wind and the mellifluous call of the Nightwings.

Kasim stood at the edge of the pit and addressed the gathered warriors. "The Trial of the Scorpion begins now. Aran ibn Khalid will soon face the desert's wrath and prove his worth - or he will die, as all those who are unworthy have died before him."

These words did not deter Aran. He understood that the Bahir were a proud people. They were warriors, and he respected that. He would face their trial, and he would face his destiny. Aran looked Kasim straight in the eyes so the man could see there was no fear in him. The Bahirian warlord nodded and spoke directly to him. "The Trial of the Scorpion is not merely a test of bravery," Kasim declared. "It is a test of cunning, of patience, and of respect for the desert's creatures. Aran of the Tarek, if you are to earn our loyalty, you must prove yourself worthy by retrieving the Mark of the Bahir from beneath this guardian's shadow."

The mark was a small, intricately carved stone placed directly beneath the scorpion's body. To claim it, Aran would need to bravely navigate the creature's lethal pincers and venomous tail.

With that, Kasim motioned for Aran to enter the pit.

His best friend, Rafiq, shifted his stance, his hand instinctively moving to the hilts of his dual blades before he caught himself. His eyes met Aran's for the briefest moment - a silent exchange between brothers-in-arms that spoke volumes. Rafiq's jaw tightened as he forced himself to remain still among the Bahirian observers, though every muscle in his body seemed poised to intervene should the worst occur.

The first thing Aran noticed, upon entering the pit, was the absolute silence that surrounded him. The Bahirian warriors were watching intently, their breath held in collective anticipation, following his every move. Kasim, in particular, was observing him with a predatory intensity that suggested this was far more than a simple test.

At the bottom, Aran found himself surrounded by darkness. The pit was a stone throat, narrow and deep, its walls slick with moisture from an underground spring - each surface, a potential betrayal. In the centre, a large stone sat like an altar, and upon it lay the object of his trial: a Sand Scorpion of monstrous proportions.

This was no ordinary creature. Larger than any Aran had encountered in his travels, the scorpion was a living nightmare of chitin and venom. Its exoskeleton gleamed with an oily sheen, segments moving with a slow, precise, mechanical menace. The creature's pincers - each as long as a man's hand - snapped with a sound like breaking bone. Its tail, thick as a warrior's forearm, arched above its onyx body like a segmented whip, dripping with venom that could dissolve flesh. "Easier said than done," Aran muttered, his mouth dry.

The scorpion was not merely waiting - it was hunting. Its multiple eyes, each a black pearl of predatory intelligence, tracked Aran's every micro-movement. Generations of desert survival had refined this creature into a perfect killing machine. The stone beneath it was not just an object - it was bait, a trap designed to test the very limits of human skill and courage.

Aran's training kicked in. Years of studying desert creatures, of learning their rhythms and weaknesses, condensed into this moment. Still, this was different. This scorpion moved with a calculated intelligence that defied everything he knew. When he took a careful step, it mirrored him - not retreating - but positioning itself for a potential strike.

The warriors above watched in total silence. Kasim's face was a mask of stone, revealing nothing.

Sweat traced rivers down Aran's back. One mistake meant death. The scorpion's tail twitched - not a warning, but a promise. Suddenly, it lunged with impossible speed. Aran dove, feeling the wind of its stinger passing mere inches from his face. The creature's pincers snapped, catching the edge of his sleeve, tearing fabric and skin. Blood dripped. The scorpion tasted it. Now it was personal.

Aran realized this was no simple test. This was survival. The stone lay tantalizingly close, but between him and it stood a living weapon that wanted nothing more than to end his life. He would need more than skill. He would need something deeper. Something primal.

At that moment, Aran understood the true nature of the Bahir trial. It was not about retrieving a stone. It was about becoming something more than human - about finding the predator within. The scorpion prepared for its next strike - Aran smiled.

In that split second, he remembered everything his father's close friend, Barash, had taught him about reading the desert's most cunning, deadly creatures. Not just their movements but their essence. The scorpion was a creature of pure survival - each motion carefully calculated, each strike purposeful. He would use its own nature against it.

As the creature lunged, Aran didn't dodge. Instead, he moved into its strike, disrupting its calculated trajectory. His hand swept not for the stone but for the creature itself. In a move that would later become legendary among the Bahir, he seized the scorpion - not by its tail, not by its pincers, but by the precise point where its exoskeleton joined, immobilizing its most critical joint.

The scorpion thrashed. Venom splattered. For a moment, it seemed impossible that a human could hold such a creature and survive. With his free hand, Aran snatched the stone. The warriors above stopped breathing. Kasim's eyes widened - the first genuine emotion he'd shown.

In one fluid motion, Aran threw the scorpion against the pit's wall, stunning it, and simultaneously rolled away. The creature hit the stone surface with a sound like cracking chitin, momentarily disoriented.

When the dust settled, Aran stood - bloodied, breathing hard but victorious. The stone with the Bahir emblem clutched in his hand. He had not just passed the trial - he had transformed it.

Above the pit, Rafiq's rigid posture finally broke. The breath he had been holding escaped in a rush as his shoulders visibly sagged with relief. His white-knuckled grip on his dagger's hilt loosened, and a smile - common and genuine - flashed across Rafiq's face before he quickly composed himself again. Though not before Kasim al-Bahir had noticed this clear, momentary glimpse into the depth of loyalty Aran commanded from his companions. It was a loyalty that spoke volumes, louder than any oath of allegiance ever could.

When Aran emerged from the pit, stone in hand, the Bahir warriors remained silent. Kasim stepped forward, his expression unreadable. For a long moment, the warlord said nothing. Then, slowly, he nodded. "It is not so easy to impress me. No man, from outside our tribe, has ever survived the Trial of the Scorpion. You have earned my respect, Aran ibn Khalid," Kasim's voice was filled with a grudging admiration. "In spite of that, respect, although vital, is not enough to bind us to your cause. If we are to follow your lead, you must offer us something greater than survival. You must offer us victory."

Aran met Kasim's gaze and spoke the words he had long waited to utter. "The Bahir are warriors," he stepped closer, letting the silence settle like a veil between them. The crackle of the fire, the breath of the wind - everything faded. Only the weight of what was to be said remained. Kasim stood tall, waiting.

"Therefore, I offer you not gold, not promises, but what your souls truly hunger for - I offer you a war." Kasim's eyes widened, and so Aran pressed. "Your people know the deserts well - surely they know how to tell a true predator from a scavenger. Can you not see who our true enemy is? Empires fall, Kasim - my brother - not from a lack of steel, but from a loss of purpose. We already have the strength. What we lack - what I am trying to offer - is direction. A banner beneath which we all may stand - not kneel. I am not speaking of a war of conquest," Aran intoned, "but of a war to end all wars. A battle to unite Zarah, not through subjugation, but as equals. A war against Zarah's true enemy - the House of Draco."

Kasim's brow furrowed, the firelight catching the scars etched into his skin by countless years of battle. "The Draco?" he repeated, voice low. "Do you mean the outlanders who meddle in our pockets with gold and whisper into the ears of our sons?"

"They are doing more than meddling," Aran warned, "They seek to divide us altogether, to weaken us so they can take control of Zarah's wealth and power. They have already infiltrated the Rasha and the Ulema. If we do not act in unison, we will all be their pawns. Mere tools to be used and discarded, after we have fulfilled our use to them."

Kasim al-Bahir considered this for a long moment. Only the voice of the wind could be heard now, as if whispering long lost secrets, above the desert sands. Then, with a slow, deliberate motion, Kasim extended his hand, "Very well, Aran ibn Khalid. By the bones of our ancestors and the burning sands that forged us, we will stand with you. But do not forget - our loyalty is as fierce as the desert winds. Should you falter, we will be the first to tear down what you build." Kasim's words were as harsh as his tribe, but Aran could feel that he had won the man's loyalty. He grasped Kasim's hand in the ancient manner of the desert tribes, palm to palm, binding their words with flesh and blood.

Behind Aran, Rafiq smiled. The Bahir were now part of their coalition. Still, this was only the beginning of it. The other tribes would not be so easily swayed, and the Draconians were already moving their pieces on the board, preparing to strike.

In celebration of his victory and their new-found alliance, Aran was invited to stay one more day. The following evening, the Bahir hosted a grand feast in his honour. Around a roaring fire, warriors recounted tales of past trials, while musicians played haunting melodies on flutes carved from Dune Stalker bones. Aran listened intently, absorbing the Bahir's history and traditions.

As the night deepened, Kasim stood to address the gathering. "Aran, son of Khalid, has passed the Trial of the Scorpion, proving his courage and cunning. Now, we shall see if he understands the Bahir spirit."

A young warrior approached, offering Aran a ceremonial Sand Serpent cloak. The gift was symbolic. Only those who had earned the tribe's respect could wear the serpent's scales. Donning the cloak, Aran rose to address the Bahir warriors.

"You have shown me the heart of the desert," he began, his voice steady. "Now I see that the Bahir tribe is its pulse. Your strength and resilience are unmatched, but imagine what we could achieve together. The Bahir as protectors, the Shamari as innovators, the Rasha as our navigators, the Ulema as traders. We could create a Zarah united not by force, but by purpose."

The crowd murmured, their scepticism slowly giving way to pondered consideration. Kasim al-Bahir nodded, his expression thoughtful.

"Your words are bold, Aran," he said. "Boldness is what the Bahir tribe respects most. You have earned our allegiance. Though, you would do well to remember what I told you last night. If you falter, we will not forgive weakness." Behind Aran, his friend Rafiq stiffened.

Following their alliance, Aran encouraged a cultural exchange between the Bahir and the Tarek. Bahir warriors shared their old techniques for crafting armour from Dune Stalker exoskeletons, while the Tarek tribe introduced the Bahir to their irrigation methods. This exchange further strengthened the bond between the two tribes and demonstrated the practical benefits of unity.

The Bahir's craftsmen also taught Aran's followers to weave Sand Weaver silk into garments that could withstand the harshest conditions. In turn, Aran shared the Tarek's knowledge of sandstorm prediction, ensuring safer travel through the Black Dunes.

Through these exchanges, Aran's vision began to take root - not just as a political idea but as a tangible reality, with tribes learning from and supporting one another. For the first time, Aran saw his dream reflected in the people around him - not just in words, but in action.

When Yasmin, a young Bahir weaver, successfully demonstrated the Tarek irrigation technique to her clan elders, using precious water to coax green shoots from the black sand, even the most sceptical warriors nodded in recognition of the alliance's practical worth.

The tribes were no longer just surviving; they were learning, adapting, becoming something greater.

Chapter III

Serpents in the Dark

The pact with the Bahir marked a turning point in Aran's quest but, although he had secured alliances, true victory remained elusive. The allegiance with the Bahir tribe, though fierce and loyal for now, could still prove tenuous. Kasim's warning echoed in Aran's mind, reminding him that failure would not be forgiven. The stakes were higher than ever, and the next steps required far more than brute force. Diplomacy and cunning would now be Aran's primary tools as he moved to secure the other tribes, each one with its own agendas, suspicions, and grudges.

As Aran navigated the volatile world of tribal politics, the House of Draco, far from passive, was quietly preparing its own war on Zarah. Operating from the shadows, they rarely had need for armies. The Draco's primary weapons were whispers, gold, and manipulation. They sought to divide, to sabotage, and, ultimately, to control. In this delicate balance of power, the real war would be fought not on the battlefield, but in secret councils or back rooms where promises were made, and knives waited to be plunged into the backs of those who trusted too easily.

In the subtropical deserts, Aran journeyed back to the Shamari tribal settlements, from which the future kingdom of Shamas would one day rise. He was astonished by their advancements in solar energy. The Shamari's sun mirrors, large polished plates that focused sunlight into searing beams, were a testament to their ingenuity.

Aran marvelled at how they used these mirrors to purify water and power their heat-resistant forges. However, he also saw their pride in these achievements as a potential barrier to unity - they were fiercely independent and reluctant to share their knowledge.

In the coastal deserts of Yara, where Sarim stood, Aran observed the dangers of the sea. The Yaran people lived in relative harmony with the monstrous Crystalline Leviathans that roamed their waters, crafting hauntingly beautiful Ocean Pipes from the creatures' bones. Yaran leaders were reluctant to align with Aran, dismissing his warnings of a united Zarah as irrelevant to their maritime existence.

However, it was in the cold deserts of Qamar, where the sands glittered with icy crystals, that Aran felt most connected to his vision. Most from the Rasha tribe were in Sarim, but part of them lived here under the twin moons. Their lives were deeply intertwined with the celestial cycles. The Moon Seers invited Aran to partake in the Lunar Bloom Festival, where

Moonleaf incense filled the air and silver-robed dancers performed beneath the glow of Anar and Nysa. It was during this festival that a Moon Seer named Safira al-Rasha approached Aran, her voice trembling with urgency.

"The moons have whispered of your coming," she said. "They have shown us a storm rising from the core of our world to beyond the stars, a storm that will devour Zarah unless we stand together."

Her words, echoing his own visions, gave Aran the validation he had long sought, and he felt his message gaining new urgency among the gathered tribes.

Slowly, his words began to take root. As before, the younger generation, in particular, was drawn to his message of hope and unity. They were tired of the endless wars, the constant struggle for survival. They saw in Aran a chance for something different, something better.

However, the path to unity would not be easy, and the forces arrayed against Aran, both within the tribes and from the House of Draco, would stop at nothing to see him fail.

At the Great Oasis of Qamar, Aran called the first Council of the Desert. Representatives from each tribe gathered beneath the swaying palms, their faces painted with suspicion and scepticism. The Bahir tribal leader, Kasim al-Bahir, sat with arms crossed, his warriors standing behind him like statues of stone. The Shamari whispered among themselves, their expressions guarded. The Rasha sat in silence, their Moon Seers watching Aran intently.

He spoke not of conquest or dominance but of a shared purpose. "The deserts have taught us that survival is not guaranteed. It must be earned. But we cannot earn it alone - isolated from one another. The House of Draco threatens our planet, our people, and our future. United, we can repel them. Divided, we will undoubtedly fall."

Aran's words stirred murmurs among the tribal lords, but it was Safira, the Moon Seer of Sarim, who silenced them with a raised hand. "Our moons have shown me a vision," she said. "Of a Zarah united under one banner. I believe Aran ibn Khalid speaks the truth."

The Shamari leader, Karim al-Shamar, rose to his feet, adjusting his spectacles. "Words are not enough, Aran. Show us that your vision is more than a dream. Prove that you can lead us." Karim's words hung in the desert air like a blade suspended over Aran's future.

Around the oasis, tribal representatives exchanged glances - some were hopeful, others sceptical, all waiting to see if this young, visionary leader possessed more than eloquent words.

With this challenge, the council adjourned, leaving Aran with the grave, daunting task of turning his words into action.

Following the first Council of the Desert, he decided to gather his closest advisors. The wind outside the tent carried a chilling reminder that the deserts were a place of secrets and danger. Sitting around a low fire, the flickering flames cast long shadows on the canvas walls. Sura, his trusted spymaster, sat beside him. Her dark eyes, given the scarce light, matching her hair, reflected the firelight. Rafiq, his oldest friend and most trusted warrior, sat in the corner, listening, while he sharpened his steel. His cousin, Zahira, a former Tarek priestess who had renounced her ties to the order, joined them as the newest addition to his inner circle.

"We have the Bahir, the Shamari, the Ulema, and part of the Rasha," Rafiq said without looking up from his blades. "Though their loyalty feels thin. What is to be our next step?" His voice carried urgency.

Aran leaned back, his gaze lost in the flames. "We will need all of the Rasha tribe's support," his eyes unfocused. "The Bahir and the Shamari control the trade routes through the western passes and have the best archers - aside from the Rasha - and warriors in all of Zarah. If we secure them, we control the flow of supplies. However, the Yarans are merchants at heart, more concerned with profit than principles. We'll need something they can't refuse."

"Money speaks to them," Sura said, her voice as sharp as the wind outside. "Besides, they know the House of Draco offers plenty."

"Which is why we need to strike before the Draco fully secure their alliance," Zahira interjected, her tone steady, but there was a tension beneath her words. She had seen firsthand, in her former order, how the Draconians corrupted from within, and this knowledge weighed heavily on her. Rafiq stopped sharpening his swords. "The Rasha, in Yaran country, are already leaning toward the Draconians as well, aren't they?"

Zahira nodded, her expression grim. "I have heard whispers from the Ulema that the Draconians have been funnelling gold into the Rasha council, on Sarim. Promises of wealth, protection, and autonomy. They're being lured in with the false hope that they can stay neutral and play both sides. We, gathered here, know the Draconian game very well - they will consume the Rasha tribe, piece by piece."

Aran's fists clenched involuntarily. "Then we need to move fast. We are definitely not in a position to outbid the Draco with gold, but we can offer something more valuable to the Rasha. We can offer them freedom."

The idea of freedom, in these times, was a currency of its own and one that the House of Draco could never fully offer. The Rasha tribe prided themselves on their independence, and Aran thought that the notion of losing that autonomy might sway them - it had to.

Still, deep down, Aran knew this would not be enough. They needed leverage, a way to undermine the House of Draco's influence directly.

"We need to expose the Draconian deceit," he said after a long pause. "If we show the Rasha the true cost of their alliance with them, I believe they will reconsider. However, we will need hard evidence. Undeniable proof that they plan to subjugate the Rasha tribe, not partner with them." He looked around the tent.

Sura al-Rasha raised an eyebrow. "How do you propose we get this evidence? It's not like the Draconians are careless with their secrets."

Aran smiled grimly. "They may not be careless, but they are definitely ambitious. Ambition breeds greed. That breeds overconfidence, and overconfidence creates cracks. We only need to find one."

Zahira leaned forward, her eyes narrowing. "I may have a lead of sorts. When I was still with the order, I heard rumours of a Draconian agent operating within the Rasha - a spy sent to manipulate the council from within. If we can unmask this agent and expose their plot, it could turn the tide."

Aran's heart quickened at the prospect. "Do you have any idea who this agent might be?"

Zahira shook her head. "Not yet. But I know where they operate. The Rasha's capital in Yaran country - Sarim. It is where the council of the Rasha meets, and it is also where the Draconian influence on Zarah is strongest. If we are to find this agent, that is where we should start."

Aran nodded. "Sounds like a good plan to me," he bowed to his cousin, in deference. "We make for Sarim, but we need to move quietly and gather information without raising suspicion. Once we have proof, we confront the Rasha council directly."

At the time this story takes place, the city of Sarim was unlike any other municipality in Zarah. Nestled by the coast, in between the regions of Qamar and Yara, this was a city of shimmering contrasts. It was known as the Jewel of the Northeast, its silver Minare spires glistened under the sun, while intricate mosaics adorned the walls of its ornate buildings, depicting the Rasha's history and their reverence for Zarah's twin moons, Anar and Nysa.

The city bustled with life. Merchants in vibrant robes called out from their stalls, offering spices, textiles, and artefacts from across Zarah. The air was filled with the mingling scents of spices and roasted Moonmelon, a delicacy unique to the Rasha.

By night, Sarim transformed into a world of soft silver light as the moons illuminated its streets, and the hum of Lunar Bloom ceremonies echoed through the city.

At the centre of the city stood the Lunar Citadel, an awe-inspiring structure with domes made of polished Moonleaf wood that reflected the moonlight like mirrors. It was here that the Rasha Council convened, debating the future of their people under the watchful gaze of the Moon Seers.

Beneath the surface of Sarim's apparent prosperity, lay an undercurrent of unease. Whispers of Draconian dealings had spread among the populace, and the council was split between those who welcomed their gold and those who feared their influence.

The Rasha had built their wealth on controlling the eastern passes, ensuring that all trade - whether it came from the southern oases or the distant northern kingdoms - flowed through their gates.

As a result, through the centuries, Sarim had grown prosperous - its streets now bustling with merchants, craftsmen, and travellers from across the myriad deserts of Zarah.

The city's architecture also reflected its wealth. Markets overflowed with goods, cloths, spices, and precious metals, while the scent of exotic foods filled the air. Yet, beneath the surface of prosperity, there was that undercurrent of tension. The Rasha council, once a steady bastion of independence, now stood divided.

Overhearing the murmurs of street conversations, Aran and his group of companions felt the weight of history pressing down upon them.

He wondered how many rulers before him had tried - and failed - to unite Zarah. How many dreams had been undone by pride and greed? He could not allow this to be another chapter in that endless cycle. He would not.

It was into this cauldron of conflicting interests that Aran and his friends entered, disguised as simple travellers. They blended into the crowds, their faces obscured by desert veils, their weapons hidden beneath their cloaks. Though the Draconian warriors had disguised themselves as natives of Zarah, Aran recognized them at once - their eyes too sharp, too disciplined, ever watchful for signs of dissidence.

The group made their way through the maze-like streets of Sarim, avoiding the heavily guarded council district and heading instead toward the outskirts of the city, where Zahira had arranged a meeting with a contact - someone who might be able to provide them with the kind of information they needed.

Their destination was a modest tea house, known as the Whispering Sands, tucked away in a quiet alley. This place was a haven for those seeking refuge from Sarim's vibrant chaos. The interior was dimly lit, and the scent of spiced tea filled the air. A few patrons sat at low tables, speaking in hushed tones. At the far end of the room, a figure waited for them, his face hidden beneath a hood.

Zahira led the way. As they approached, the figure raised his head, revealing the weathered face of an old man, his name Jamil, a former Rasha councillor who had been forced into exile after opposing the growing Draconian influence. His eyes, sharp and calculating, betrayed years of experience in the dangerous world of Rasha politics. "Zahira," Jamil greeted her with a nod, his voice low. "You have brought allies, I see."

Zahira motioned to Aran and the others. "These are more than allies, Jamil. They are friends," she exhaled. "I must deeply apologise beforehand, for being so forward, but we are in dire need of your help," she exchanged a furtive look with her cousin. "We are looking for a Draconian agent operating within the Rasha council."

Jamil's expression darkened. He sipped his drink. "There are more than just one, I fear. The Draco have sunk their claws deep in the council. There is one in particular who holds the key to their plans - Farid al-Rasha, a councillor who has been working closely with the Draconian emissaries. He presents himself as loyal to the Rasha council, but I have seen enough to know that he is selling us to the highest bidder."

Aran frowned. "Pardon me for asking you this, Jamil, but if you know this much about his dealings with the House of Draco, then why have you not tried to expose him yourself?"

Jamil gave a bitter laugh. "Because, my young friend," Aran did not miss the sarcasm in the man's voice but remained silent, allowing him to continue. "Farid has powerful allies, both within the council as well as outside of it. Anyone who opposes him publicly ends up disgraced, or worse - dead. The council is too fractured, and Farid has positioned himself as the broker of the House of Draco's promises. If we want to bring him down, we need undeniable proof of his betrayal. Something the council cannot ignore. Remember, most do not know that they are shapeshifters."

"Do you have anything at all on him?" Rafiq asked impatiently, his hand resting on the hilt of his well sharpened dagger. He had always been more a man of action rather than words.

Composing himself, Jamil nodded nervously, a trickle of sweat dripping down his temple. "There is a meeting happening tonight, in one of the old warehouses near the harbour. Farid and a Draconian emissary called Drathis will be there to discuss the terms of their agreement. If you can infiltrate the meeting and get evidence of their collusion, it could be enough to turn the council against him."

Aran's mind raced. This was the opportunity they so desperately needed, but it was also extremely dangerous. If they were caught, it would mean certain death - not just for them, but for their entire cause.

His dream for Zarah weighed in the balance. Once more, he was faced with a hard choice. Then again, as he thought about it, there hadn't been an easy choice to make since he began to try and bring his vision to fruition. Every choice, after his father's demise, usually meant life or death. "We will take the risk," Aran finally said, his voice firm. "Where, exactly, is this meeting taking place?"

Jamil leaned in, lowering his voice to a whisper. "Follow the western road to the edge of the harbour. There's a narrow alley behind the spice market that leads to an abandoned warehouse. That is where you will find Drathis and Farid." Jamil al-Rasha wiped the sweat from his brow, with a cloth. "Be careful, Aran. They will have guards, and Draconian warriors are not to be underestimated."

"Neither are we!" Rafiq's reply came swift, his hand still resting on his dagger.

Aran stood, his resolve hardened. "We will get proof, and when we do, the Rasha will see the Draconians for what they truly are - deceivers."

As night fell over Sarim, the city's bustling markets quieted, and the streets emptied, save for a few wandering merchants and city guards patrolling the main thoroughfares.

Aran and his companions moved swiftly through the shadows, their destination clear. The warehouse loomed ahead, a hulking structure of stone and Solarwood, its windows dark and foreboding.

They approached cautiously, sticking to the narrow alleyways and avoiding the main entrances. The salt-tinged air from the nearby harbour mixed with the lingering scents of spices from the market, creating an oddly comforting backdrop to their dangerous mission.

Zahira had managed to secure a way in - a loose panel in the back wall, hidden from view. One by one, the group slipped inside, their collective movements silent and precise.

The warehouse was vast and empty, save for a few crates and barrels scattered about. The sound of voices echoed from the far end of the room, where a dim light flickered from a lantern. Aran motioned for the others to stay low as they crept closer, careful not to make a sound. Jamil's informant had revealed the existence of a ledger hidden in an upstairs office.

Upon entering, Sura moved with impressive speed. She slipped inside unnoticed and quickly found the ledger beneath a false floor. Its pages were filled with meticulous handwriting in both Rasha script and

Draconian glyphs, telling a story of systematic betrayal that made her stomach turn. It detailed every transaction, every bribe, and every shipment, implicating Farid al-Rasha as a Draco's key ally in Sarim.

Returning to her friends, she gave Aran the ledger, and from their vantage point behind a stack of crates, they could see the meeting unfold. Farid al-Rasha, tall and imposing, stood before Drathis, whose dark armour gleamed faintly in the lantern light. A few steps away, obscured in the shadows, stood a towering Draconian, a hulking mass of a warrior, observing in silence as the two figures spoke in hushed tones.

From where he stood, the conversation was barely audible, so Aran leaned forward. "...the council is already divided," Farid was saying. "However, with your support, I can secure their loyalty. The Rasha tribe will have no choice but to align itself with the House of Draco, so there will be no need for an all out open war." It appeared to Aran that Farid was struggling to get his words out. "In return, am I to trust you have promised autonomy for our people." Farid pleaded.

Drathis nodded, a cold smile curling on his now-undisguised reptilian face. "Of course," his voice dripped with venom. "The House of Draco values its allies. Still, understand this, Farid, autonomy is a luxury, not a right to be attributed dismissively." Drathis smirked. "As long as you serve our interests, your people will be free to govern themselves. Cross us, and your council will be replaced - swiftly, and without ceremony."

Farid al-Rasha hesitated for a moment, then nodded gravely. "Agreed then. I will deliver the council to you but, in return, I expect your avowed promises to be kept."

Drathis' smile widened. His hissing voice barely reached Aran's ears. "They will be... as long as you remain useful to me."

A cold fury settled in Aran's chest. Drathis' words dripped with deception, his promises as empty as the sands after a storm. If the Rasha allied with the House of Draco, they wouldn't gain autonomy - they would be enslaved in all but name. If the Rasha allied with them, they would lose everything they held dear.

Aran exchanged a glance with Zahira and Rafiq, whose hands were already wrapped around the handle of their swords. They both nodded in silent agreement. It was time to act.

Just as they prepared to move, a shadow fell across their party. Before any of them could react, a group of Draconian warriors emerged from the darkness, their weapons already drawn.

In the back of the warehouse, the hulking Draconian titan did nothing, he merely observed, his tyrian purple eyes locked on Rafiq and Aran.

A sudden prickle ran down Aran's spine. The air had changed - too still, too silent. Then, a voice cut through the darkness. "Did you really think it would be that easy?" The voice came from behind them. It was Farid, his expression smug as he stepped into view.
Aran's heart sank. They had been betrayed, and he knew exactly by whom.

Chapter IV

A Web of Betrayal

The darkness of the warehouse seemed to close in, suffocating and cold. Aran's heart pounded in his chest, the realization of betrayal settling over him like a weight that crushed his lungs. He had not foreseen this.

He trusted his cousin Zahira's judgement, and she trusted Jamil. Therefore, he had trusted the man as well. Still, he should have known better. He should have sensed that something was wrong. Farid's smug face, half-lit by the flickering lantern, was a reminder of the treachery that now surrounded them.

The Draconian warriors, sleek in their black armour, moved forward, weapons at the ready. Behind them, Drathis, a being of sharp features and cold eyes, gave a slow clap, the sound echoing eerily in the large, empty warehouse. His voice was calm, a serpent's hiss in the quiet. "Well done, Farid. As promised, you have proven your worth. The House of Draco will not forget this service."

Farid gave a shallow bow, but his eyes never left Aran's, gleaming with both triumph and a hint of uncertainty. "A necessary sacrifice, Aran. I had no choice." His voice lacked conviction, as if he was trying hard to convince himself more than anyone else. Whether the emotion was true or feigned, Aran was unsure.

His body tensed. He wanted nothing more than to leap at Farid. To drive a blade into his treacherous heart. But he knew better than that. His group was seriously outnumbered, their position compromised. Any rash move would end in certain death. Both swift and meaningless. Aran needed to think fast. He had to find a way out of this web of betrayal.

Sura, standing beside him, shifted slightly, her hand inching toward the daggers concealed at her waist. Zahira's face was unreadable, her eyes locked on Drathis. Rafiq, his twin swords drawn, but still hidden beneath his cloak, gave a nearly imperceptible nod to Aran. He stood ready, but even Rafiq, ever the fearless warrior, knew the odds were not stacked in their favour. Standing in the shadows, the massive Draconian warrior had not moved. His tyrian-purple eyes glowed as he watched - silent, calculating.

"We are not dead yet," Aran muttered under his breath, his mind working furiously to find a way out. His eyes scanned the warehouse, searching for any possible escape routes.

He finally spotted, near the back, a stack of crates leading up to a broken window. It was narrow, but it could be their only chance.

Drathis continued, his voice dripping with mockery. "Did you truly think you could outmanoeuvre the House of Draco? You are nothing but desert dwellers playing at war. This land belongs to us, and your little dream of unity will end up crumbling under our might - beneath the weight of the Weaving." Drathis trailed off, hissing these last words to himself, making it impossible for anyone else to discern them.

Aran met his gaze, forcing upon himself a calm he did not feel. "Your promises are nothing but lies. The Rasha will not bend so easily to your rule. You may think you control Zarah, but we will not be broken."

The reptilian laughed softly. It was a cold, calculated sound, devoid of emotion or empathy. "You misunderstand me, Aran ibn Khalid."

Aran's mind reeled. "How does he know my name?"

Before he could process this disturbing revelation, Drathis continued, unbothered. "We do not need to break you. People like Farid have already done that for us. Power is not always taken by force. Most times, it is simply bought. Isn't that right, Farid?" Drathis looked dismissively at the Rasha councillor.

Aran could feel Drathis' delight in tormenting the broken man. For the House of Draco, victory itself was not enough. They needed to step on their conquests. To rejoice in their misery.

Farid's face hardened at the words, a flash of discomfort passing over his features. Though silent, his clenched hands betrayed him.

It was clear he had made his choice. Though perhaps not without some regret, Aran thought.

Before Farid could respond, Drathis raised a hand, signalling his trusted warriors forward. "Enough talk. Bind them. The Rasha council will enjoy seeing these rebels brought to justice."

Aran instinctively touched the inner pocket of his tunic, feeling the shape of the small leather-bound ledger hidden there. The document contained meticulously recorded transactions between Farid and the House of Draco - damning evidence of corruption that could sway the Rasha council, if they ever made it out alive. He would need to guard this object with his life.

For a second, time stretched. The invading warriors moved in - swift, efficient, inevitable. Aran's muscles coiled. Then, he struck. In one fluid motion, he ducked beneath one of the reptilian warriors, grabbing his wrist and twisting it violently. The crack of bone was drowned by the clatter of the warrior's sword as it hit the stone floor. In the chaos, Sura unsheathed her daggers and lunged at the nearest enemy, slashing across his throat before he could raise his blade. Blood sprayed the air, and the warehouse exploded into a frenzy of movement. Still unmoving, standing against the far wall of the warehouse, the large and muscular Draconian warrior followed Rafiq and Aran's movements with great interest.

Rafiq, always a step ahead, drew his blades and engaged two Draco warriors at once, his strikes precise and lethal. Zahira, though deprived of her weapon, moved like a shadow, disarming one of the attackers with a sharp twist of her arm, then sweeping his legs out from under him. Despite the group's best efforts, it was not enough. More Draconian warriors continued to pour in from the far side of the warehouse.

Drathis, untouched by the chaos, stood calmly next to his heavily built first lieutenant. Both were watching the scene unfold with detached amusement. "He fights well. I want to meet that man in battle, one day." The ponderous Draconian was looking at Rafiq, his voice a deep low rumbling.

"You will have your chance," Drathis murmured through clenched teeth. "The other one is mine!"

Fully appraising the situation, Aran knew instantly that they could not win this fight. Not here, and certainly not under these circumstances.

"Rafiq!" he shouted over the clamour. "Get to the window!"

Rafiq, mid-duel, glanced at the broken window Aran had spotted. He understood immediately. They had to escape. Now.

Sura was already making her way toward the stack of crates, cutting down another scaled warrior as she moved. Zahira followed, quick and silent, while Rafiq forced his opponents back with a flurry of strikes before turning to cover their retreat.

Aran darted toward the crates, his heart racing. Just as he reached the base, a hand grabbed his arm. It was Farid. For the briefest of moments, something flickered in his eyes - was it regret? Perhaps doubt?

Whatever it was, it was gone before Aran could be sure.

The Rasha councillor's face was a mixture of fury and desperation, his tight grip surprisingly strong. With adrenaline rushing through his veins, Aran did not feel the ledger dropping from his pocket.

"This is not over, Aran," Farid shouted. "You cannot stop what is already set in motion."

Aran, wondering what he meant by that, twisted out of Farid's grip, his eyes cold. "Neither can you."

With a swift motion, he drove his knee into Farid's stomach, sending the man crumpling to the ground, gasping for breath.

In the shadows, Drathis and his lieutenant broke out laughing. It was a cold, guttural laugh, like the growling of some beast. Aran didn't wait. He scrambled up the crates, Sura already pulling herself through the narrow window above. Zahira followed next, her movements graceful and fluid. Rafiq was the last to ascend, his swords flashing as he blocked a final strike from a Draconian warrior before leaping to the window and pulling himself through.

Aran was right behind him, feeling Drathis' guards closing in. He hoisted himself up, squeezing through the small opening just as a blade sliced through the air where his neck had been moments before.

The group tumbled out into the night, landing in a narrow alley behind the warehouse. The cold night air hit them like a slap, but there was no time to rest. The hisses of Drathis' warriors coming from inside the warehouse grew louder. They had to escape to safety despite how feeble the chance.

"Aran, we need to move!" Rafiq urged, already sprinting down the alley. The others followed, their footsteps echoing off the stone walls.

The streets of Sarim were a labyrinth of alleys and narrow passageways, but Aran knew them well enough from his prior visits to the city. They needed to get to the outskirts, where the old ruins provided better cover from their pursuers, as well as fewer patrols.

As they ran for their lives, the city seemed to come alive with the hum of danger. Draconian infiltrators were not the only threat they needed to be aware of. In a place like Sarim, loyalty was a fickle thing, and many eyes watched from the shadows - egotistical eyes, eager to report the group's movements for a few coins of Draconian gold. Selling their souls for the lives of their own kind, not realising they were, in fact, also selling their own.

Rafiq, always pragmatic, gave Zahira an urgent look. The air was thick with tension, and the stakes had never felt higher. She was the first to break the silence as they darted through an open plaza. "We cannot keep running," she exchanged looks with Aran. "They will have the city locked down soon."

Zahira looked at her cousin, "Do you have the ledger?"

Aran checked his pockets many times over, to no avail. "I must have dropped it during the fight," he replied, cursing under his breath. The records of Farid's treachery were gone.

"It does not matter. Not now, anyway. Survival is more important. We can always gather more evidence," Zahira replied, though the worry in her eyes betrayed how crucial that ledger had been to their cause.

But it did matter to Aran. The ledger had been more than evidence - it had been proof that his instincts about Farid were right, proof that he wasn't the naive idealist his enemies claimed. Now, without it, who would believe the word of a fugitive against a sitting councillor?

Aran knew they needed to hide, and they had to do it fast. He also knew that his cousin was right. The House of Draco's influence had already spread through Sarim like a disease. If they were caught, there would be no trial and no mercy. Just a swift execution, to send a message to the rest of Zarah.

Taking in a deep breath, he asked his friends. "Any ideas?"

"I know a place," Sura said, her breath ragged but determined. "Where we first met, remember?"

Aran nodded, though he could swear he saw something other than pure loyalty, flashing in her hypnotic eyes.

"It is risky," Sura continued, "but we do not have much of a choice."

Rafiq looked sceptical. "Where is this place you speak of?"

Sura hesitated, her eyes darting toward a distant corner of the city. "The Old Quarter. There's an underground network of tunnels beneath the ruins. If we can reach it, we can lose them there."

Aside from having visited it, Aran had often heard stories about the Old Quarter, in the caravan routes while accompanying his father in his professional endeavours.

It was a part of Sarim long abandoned, said to be haunted by the ghosts of those who had perished during one of the city's many sieges. The tunnels, however... they were something else. A remnant of the city's ancient past, forgotten by most. The tunnels were a maze of twisting passages, some collapsing, others leading to hidden exits beyond the city walls.

"It is our best shot," Aran agreed, glancing at the others. Rafiq sheathed his swords and shot a glance at Aran. "It's not like we have many other options," he mused, "let us go then."

They moved quickly through the city's darkened streets, staying in the shadows and avoiding the main thoroughfares where Draconian patrols would be heaviest. As they approached their destination, the polished stone and bustling activity of central Sarim gave way to neglect and silence.

At the time our story takes place, the Old Quarter of Sarim was a desolate place, the once grand structures now reduced to crumbling ruins. Its streets were eerily quiet, save for the wind whistling through the broken windows of abandoned buildings. It was a stark contrast to the bustling heart of the city, and as they entered its shadowy streets, it felt as though they had stepped into another world entirely.

Sura led them through the winding alleys, her steps sure despite the darkness. The others followed closely, their eyes scanning for any signs of pursuit.

After several tense moments, during which they were almost caught, they arrived at the entrance to the Old Quarter. It was a half-buried doorway hidden beneath a collapsed building.

Sura knelt, brushing away the dirt and debris to reveal a set of ancient stone steps leading downward.

"This is it," she whispered, her voice barely audible in the stillness of the night. "Get in. Quick!"

Without hesitation, Aran descended first, the darkness swallowing him as he moved into the tunnel. The air was damp and musty, the walls slick with moisture. Behind him, the others followed in silence, their footsteps soft but deliberate.

The tunnel twisted and turned, and soon, it became clear to the group why the place was a refuge for those fleeing capture. The labyrinth of tunnels seemed endless, the passages leading off in all directions, some caved in, others stretching into the dark unknown.

They moved cautiously, aware that even in this sanctuary, there were dangers lurking in its shadows. The tunnels had their own reputation, of creatures moving in the dark, of bandits who used them as hideouts, and of the occasional collapse that buried unfortunate souls beneath tons of stone and earth. For now, the shadows offered safety, and that was all that mattered to the group.

After what felt like hours of walking, they stumbled upon a small, hidden chamber. It was a small space carved into the stone with enough room for them to rest. Zahira used her flint and steel to light a small torch, the flickering flame casting long shadows on the walls.

Aran slumped against the cold stone, exhaustion pulling at his limbs. Though he knew there would be no real rest waiting for them here. Not yet anyway.

They had escaped the immediate threat, yes, but the war was far from over. The House of Draco was tightening its grip on Zarah, and Farid's betrayal had only made things worse. "We need to regroup," Aran said, his voice rough. "Figure out our next move."

Rafiq nodded, but there was a grimness in his expression. "Well, we lost the evidence we had," there wasn't the slightest hint of accusation in Rafiq's voice, it was merely a statement of fact. "Farid has the council's ear. He will turn them against us, if he can." Despite not being his fault, Aran couldn't help but feel a tinge of culpability.

"Not if we can expose him first," Zahira said, her eyes gleaming with determination. "We need to find more evidence. Something that proves the House of Draco's true intentions."

Sura, still catching her breath, shot Zahira an inquisitive look. "How do you plan to do that? We are outnumbered and outmanoeuvred. Farid has the House of Draco backing him, and we are running out of allies," she further added, her brow furrowing. "Not to mention, that we are running and hiding ourselves."

Aran did not answer. Staring into the flickering flame of the torch, his mind was turning over the possibilities. They were up against forces far greater than he had anticipated. Still, there had to be a way. There always had been. "Then we find new allies," he said finally, his voice steady. "The Rasha council may be divided, but there are still those who will fight for Zarah's freedom. We just need to unite them."

It was a desperate plan, but it was the only one he could think of, given the circumstances.

The vision he had nurtured throughout his life - for Zarah and its peoples - was teetering on the edge of destruction. Yet, as long as he drew breath, and his friends were by his side, there was still hope for his dream. There, in the depths of Sarim's past, surrounded by shadows and uncertainty, hope was all they had left. For the moment, it would have to be enough.

Aran had heard stories of the Old Quarter - whispers of lost souls, of things that lurked in the dark. Though right now, the living were far more dangerous than the dead.

Chapter V

Buried Truths and Broken Chains

The air inside the tunnels was thick with moisture and the scent of old stone. Every footstep echoed off the walls, reverberating with the weight of history. As the group gathered in the small chamber, a quiet unease settled over them. The flickering light from Zahira's torch cast long, dancing shadows on the walls, giving the impression that they weren't entirely alone in the dark. For this was a place where the dead walked with the living - if not in flesh, then in memory.

Aran leaned against the wall, every muscle in his body aching from the fight and the escape. His mind, however, refused to rest. The betrayal by Jamil and Farid gnawed at him, feeding a slow burn of anger in his gut. He clenched his fists in rage. The leather of his fingerless gloves creaked. He exhaled deeply - this was no time for anger, for that would solve nothing. It was time for action. However, for that to happen, they needed to come up with a plan first.

Rafiq's voice cut through the silence. "Aran, we cannot stay here for long. Draconian warriors will search the tunnels eventually. They will end up thinking of this place."

"Oh, they will think of it, I am sure of that." Sura agreed, sitting cross-legged and rubbing her sore legs. "But they do not know it like we do," she added. "The tunnels are vast, dangerous, even for those who know the way. We will be very hard to find."

Aran nodded in agreement, his mind racing with possibilities. They had gained temporary sanctuary, but that was not nearly enough. The larger battle still loomed over them.

So It appeared, the House of Draco had taken over much of Sarim's political landscape, and with the council split and Farid playing his own dangerous game, their chances were growing slimmer by the hour.

Everyone in the group sat in silence, lost in their own thoughts. Aran kept running their options in his head. Sura sat in meditation. Rafiq, as was his custom after battle, was sharpening his blades. Zahira sat against a pillar, observing the dancing flames and the shadows they were casting on the walls - two swirling shapes, projected by the light source, seemed to be fighting each other for dominance.

Suddenly, she straightened up. "We need to move fast," Zahira's voice cut through the quiet like the edge of a well-sharpened blade through skin. "Farid's betrayal must be exposed, and we need proof that the House of Draco is corrupting the council from within."

"Zahira," Rafiq quipped, "I am grateful for your clear exposition of the obvious," he winked at her. "But what proof?" he asked, his dark eyes narrowing. "What more proof do you think we will be lucky enough to find? Farid isn't foolish enough to leave a trail. I doubt we will be able to find another ledger. He will have long covered his tracks by now."

"No, he wouldn't have. Not all of them," Zahira retorted, and her voice carried a cold certainty. "I have known people like Farid. Power makes them arrogant, and arrogance makes them reckless. He will have left something behind - we just have to find it. There will be something else, mark my words, letters, ledgers, something that ties him to the House of Draco."

Sura leaned back against the wall, her eyes thoughtful. "Alright Zahira, let us say you are right. Where do you expect us to find such proof? If it even exists, Farid will have it well-guarded. His home is a fortress, and trying to get in there would be suicide."

Silence fell once more over the group as they weighed the options.

The more Aran thought about it, the more he came to the conclusion that breaking into Farid's stronghold was indeed a dangerous idea. Nevertheless, it wasn't just his domicile that held Sarim's secrets.

As a result of his travelling years with his father, Aran knew that the city had many layers to it, and Farid wasn't the only one playing a double game in Yara's capital. "There is another way," he said, finally breaking the silence. "The House of Draco has deeper ties to Sarim than we suspected. However, If we can expose their larger network, by finding Draconian agents and their plans, we can start to unravel their schemes in the process."

Rafiq shot him a questioning glance. "What are you suggesting?"

Aran's gaze hardened. He had been silently weighing their choices, and felt confident in his decision. "Instead of running, we need to strike at the heart of Draconian operations in Sarim. The smuggling rings, the bribed officials, the hidden deals. Farid is just one piece of their web. We have to cut it at its source. They will never expect it."

Sura looked at him sharply. "Where do you plan to start? The House of Draco's influence is everywhere, and their network is hidden in plain sight. Do you think we can just walk in and expose it all?"

"No," Aran replied, shaking his head. "We cannot just walk in. Still, we may have something they do not have - knowledge of the old city." The group weighed his words, in silence. "As well as someone who might be willing to help us, in our quest." He added.

Beneath the Sarim known to most, lies the skeleton of a far older city - born in Zarah's Second Age, ten thousand years ago, its story etched deep in stone long before the desert reclaimed it, and far long before memory forgot its name. The Old Quarter, where they were now hiding in, was just one part of a sprawling underground network of tunnels, ruins, and chambers that dated back to the days when this sprawling metropolis had been a centre of power in its own right - long after the fall of the Old Kings, after the wars that tore Zarah's deserts apart.

Aran had heard these stories growing up - tales whispered by Tarek elders about the underground labyrinth that stretched for miles beneath Sarim's foundations. In those ancient days, the tunnels had served as secret passages during sieges, places where treasures and knowledge were hidden away from conquering armies. Over time, they had been abandoned, forgotten by most of the city's inhabitants, and lost to history. Though not all had forgotten about its ancient history.

During Aran's time, the tunnels were still used by those who sought to evade the law, by smugglers and thieves who trafficked in the shadows, and by those who knew that the true power of Sarim lay not in its royal palaces, but rather in its forgotten depths. The older part of the city was a place of secrets, and if the Draconians had infiltrated Sarim, their web of influence would have taken root there.

After a long silence that seemed to stretch forever, Rafiq was the first to break the quiet. "Aran, do you really think these tunnels will lead us to their agents?"

"I am sure they have used them before," his friend replied, nodding. "Farid may be working with the outlanders, but he cannot be the only one in league with them. The House of Draco has eyes and ears all over Sarim, and if they have been moving goods like weapons and supplies through the city under the council's nose, where do you think they are moving them through? These hidden tunnels are the perfect route for smuggling. If we can trace their network, maybe we can find where they are hiding their key players." Aran knew his choices were narrowing.

Every step he took brought him closer to either uniting Zarah - or losing everything. The weight of expectation sat heavy on his shoulders, but there was no turning back now.

Zahira's eyes gleamed with renewed determination. "Then we start here. The tunnels beneath us could hold more than just passageways. They might hold the evidence we need to expose their operations. If we find proof of their dealings, we can bring it to the council before it's too late."

Rafiq cut in. "You are assuming the council would believe us?"

"Not to mention, that the tunnels are a deathtrap," Sura cut in, glancing around at the shadows that loomed large on the chamber's walls. "They are full of collapsed sections, unstable ground, and worse. There are things down there that even the desert cannot explain. Stories of creatures of old magic that linger in the stones."

Aran looked at Rafiq first, then met Sura's gaze. "Do you have a better idea? After all, you were the one that suggested we come to the Old Quarter," he gave her a wink.

Rafiq nodded, in agreement with Aran. Sura, pensive, hesitated for a brief moment, then sighed. "If we are to do this, we will need someone who knows the tunnels better than any of us. You mentioned that you knew someone who could help us?"

Aran, smiling, held her gaze. "I might know someone."

He led the group to a contact he had known since childhood, an old friend of his father, a man named Barash ibn Sulaym, who had lived most of his life navigating the forgotten passageways beneath Zarah's surface. Barash was considered a ghost in the city of Sarim, a figure of rumour and mystery, feared by some but respected by most. He was a relic of the old world, someone who had survived the fall of Sarim's earlier rulers and had watched the rise of Draconian influence with wary eyes.

The night had fallen fully by the time Aran and the others found him. He was holed up in a derelict inn near the edge of the Old Quarter, a place that had long since been abandoned by the rest of the city. The inn was a ruin, its walls crumbling, the ceiling sagging under the weight of the inexorable passage of time.

Inside, Barash sat alone, his back hunched, a thick, hooded cloak, ornate with sun symbols, draped over his frail form. His eyes, however, were sharp. Too sharp for a man of his age, as they glittered with a cunning that made the group wary. Aran trusted Barash, but there was something elusive about the man as well.

"Aran," Barash greeted him with a rasping voice. "It's been a while," there was genuine worry in the man's voice. "I see you are still alive, though I can not say that I expected that, given the circumstances." He mused, yet his jest barely hid his concern.

Aran nodded, stepping forward cautiously. "We need your help, old friend. We mean to go into the old tunnels beneath Sarim."

Barash raised a thin eyebrow, an enigmatic smile playing at the corner of his lips. "The tunnels? That is a fool's errand, lad. You know what is down there as well as I do. Or have you forgotten?"

"I have not forgotten it." Aran answered, his voice hesitant but calm. "But I do not have..." he paused, looking at the ground. Raising his head, he looked Barash in the eyes. "I mean, we do not have a choice. We are running out of options," he pointed to his friends.

Barash leaned back in his chair, his bony fingers tapping idly on the table in front of him. "What makes you think I will help you? The tunnels are indeed dangerous, however, it is not just the collapses or the many creatures that might lurk down there that should worry you. There are people in those deep places who do not take kindly to intruders. If you take my meaning?" Barash's expression was unreadable.

"We are not just intruding," Zahira cut in, her voice cold. "We are also hunting." She desperately wanted revenge.

Barash's eyes flicked to her, taking her measure for a moment before he turned back to Aran. "May I ask what, exactly, are you hunting?"

"The Draco," Aran said simply. "We need to expose their network in the city, and we need someone who knows the tunnels better than anyone. Naturally, I thought of you." His eyes twinkled.

For a long moment, Barash was silent, his eyes studying Aran with an intensity that made the young warrior uncomfortable. Then, with a slow sigh, the old man stood, his joints trembling with the effort. "You're a damn fool, Aran. But I've always had a soft spot for fools. If what you intend to do means making the Draconians suffer, well... I suppose I can guide you through the dark one last time," he said, enigmatically. Aran exhaled, the tension in his chest easing slightly. Barash was a stalwart, dangerous ally, and he was the only one who could lead them where they needed to go.

With their newfound guide leading the way, the group ventured deeper into the tunnels beneath Sarim. The passageways grew narrower, more claustrophobic, as they descended into the heart of the forgotten city. The air grew colder, the light from their torches flickering against the damp walls. Every sound seemed amplified in the oppressive silence - the drip of water, the echo of their footsteps, the creak of stone settling above them.

Barash moved with surprising agility for a man of his age, navigating the twisting corridors with ease. He didn't speak much, his focus on the path ahead, but Aran could see the tension in the old man's posture. The old tunnels were dangerous, yes, but there was more to Barash's wariness. There were also old memories there, old ghosts that still lingered in the shadows.

With a shudder, Aran recalled the stories Barash used to tell him, when he was a child, after his father's demise.

Those tales had seemed like mere fantasy then, spoken by firelight to distract a grieving boy. Now, descending into their very setting, Aran realized they had been lessons in disguise - warnings of what lay beneath Zarah's surface.

As they descended, deeper under the city, Zahira fell into step beside Aran. "Do you trust him?" she asked, her voice low.

"I trust him to get us where we need to go," Aran replied, glancing at Barash's hunched figure ahead of them. "Beyond that point... my father trusted him, and Barash always did right by me, so we shall see."

Zahira nodded, her eyes scanning the walls around them. "These city tunnels are older than I thought they would be. I can feel it... the weight of history is palpable here."

"There is more than history in these stones," Aran said grimly. "There is something else living in them." he muttered, recalling Barash's childhood tales. Zahira halted but, nonetheless, held her next question inside, then she continued walking in silence, pondering on her cousin's words.

With every step, the tunnels changed. Smooth stone, slowly gave way to crumbling walls etched with strange symbols, their edges worn but still humming with a faint energy. The air grew heavier, charged with something unseen. It was as though the tunnels themselves were alive, watching them, waiting for something. Strange symbols, carved into the walls, flickered in the torchlight - ancient runes that none, aside from Barash, recognized.

The old man stopped suddenly, his head tilted as though listening to something none of the others could hear.

"What is it?" Rafiq asked, his voice tense, hand poised on the handle of one of his swords.

Barash didn't answer. Instead, he took a few careful steps forward, his fingers brushing the wall as though searching for something. Then, with a soft grunt of satisfaction, he pressed against a section of the wall, and a hidden door slid open with a low groan.

"This is where you will find what you are looking for," he said, stepping back to let them through. "But be warned, lad. What lies beyond this door is not for the faint of heart."

Aran nodded firmly, then looked at his friends. His jaw set, he turned to Barash. "We are ready!"

With that, they stepped through the doorway and into the unknown. The weight of the past pressed down on them as they ventured deeper into the labyrinth of tunnels, chasing the secrets that could bring the Draconians to their knees. "Or destroy us all in the process." Aran thought to himself. A strange unease curled in his gut. The tunnels were unfamiliar - yet something in the air, in the very stone, felt known to him. As if the past itself was watching.

Chapter VI

Whispers in the Dark

The threshold into the labyrinth of tunnels was like crossing into another world. Beyond the hidden door Barash had opened, the air felt different - thicker, cooler, and laden with an energy that made the hair on Aran's neck stand on end. This was not just an extension of the tunnels they had been navigating; it was something older, perhaps forgotten by the people but not by the land.

Zahira stepped cautiously into the dark passage ahead, her torchlight barely cutting through the gloom. The walls here were closer, more oppressive, and covered in ancient markings.

Symbols twisted in unfamiliar patterns, their meaning lost to the ages, yet they pulsed faintly in the flickering light as if whispering secrets to those who dared to read them. Leaning in, Aran felt a surge of energy under his skin - there was something familiar about these runes.

"This place," Barash began, his voice no more than a whisper. "It has been sealed for a long time," his voice was very low, as though he feared waking whatever lay beyond. "Few know of its existence, even fewer dare to enter. This is older than the city above. Much older. From a time that perhaps should not have been forgotten."

Aran moved to examine the nearest wall, running his fingers over the strange carvings. The stone was smooth and cool to the touch, but the symbols seemed to hum beneath his skin, leaving an unsettling tingle that made him pull his hand back.

The sensation lingered, a warmth that seemed to spread through his veins before fading. For a heartbeat, the symbols had felt less like mere carvings and more like... recognition. As though something in his blood remembered what his mind had forgotten.

"What is this place?" he asked while rubbing his fingers, his voice barely above a whisper. "It feels familiar," he paused, still rubbing the palm of his hand. "Like something out of a dream."

Barash looked at him with hooded eyes, his expression unreadable. "A tomb of sorts. Not for the dead," he added, studying Zahira's reaction. "It was built for knowledge long buried here. The founders of old Sarim were not the first to walk this world. Thousands of years before them came the Old Kingdoms, and even they were young when these tunnels were carved. They say the stones themselves remember and that those who listen closely can hear the voices of the past."

"Perhaps a forgotten temple?" Sura ventured, her eyes scanning the intricate carvings, with great interest. "Or a shrine?"

Barash shrugged. "Call it what you will. I am not discussing semantics," his tone was sombre now. "Names are a secondary consideration, while the function of a place is what truly matters," he sighed, the light in his eyes dimming slightly. "The old ones left their mark here, but whatever they were guarding - whether treasure, knowledge, or something darker - was hidden deep. If, indeed, the House of Draco is using these tunnels, then they are playing with forces they do not understand," he paused, pondering his next words. "If, in fact, they do understand them, then that makes them even more dangerous." Barash added, ominously.

Aran nodded firmly, his gaze already sweeping the passage ahead. "We need to press on," his tone matching Barash's. "The answers we are looking for are here. I can feel it in my bones. Whatever the Draconians are after, it is tied to this place. We have to find out what it is before they do."

Barash didn't reply, but there was a shadow in his eyes that made Aran uneasy. This was more than just ancient architecture he was showing them. The labyrinth had a history, and the old man seemed to know more than he was letting on.

As they ventured deeper, the passage opened into a larger chamber. The walls here were even more elaborately carved, covered with reliefs that depicted strange scenes. Towering figures draped in robes, their hands raised as though in command of the elements. Below them, cities burned, the skies torn asunder by violent storms. At the centre of each image was the same symbol. A circle surrounded by jagged lines like the rays of a sun but twisted in unnatural ways. Aside from Barash, it was a sigil none of them recognized, but its presence was unsettling, as though it was something not meant to be seen by mortal eyes.

Aran froze for the briefest moment. Something in his chest tightened - not quite memory, but something older. He had seen this before... or something like it. A flicker. A shape half-buried in the folds of his mind. The stone. The one Ashir had given him.

"What is this?" Rafiq asked, his voice filled with a deep mix of awe and unease, as he studied the carvings.

Zahira moved closer, tracing the outline of the central symbol. "It looks like a form of worship," she said. "Though not of gods I have ever seen mentioned in the histories. These figures... they seem more like rulers... or sorcerers."

Barash, standing in the shadows near the chamber's entrance, nodded slowly. "They say that before Sarim, before the city-states of Zarah, there were kingdoms that stretched across our world. These were empires built on magic, for lack of a better word, on the power of the elements themselves. They controlled the land, the skies, the seas. In time, their ambition grew too great, and their hunger for power tore their civilizations apart. The Old Kingdoms fell, but the technology or power they wielded did not die along with them. It was buried deep, hidden away - concealed in places like this."

Aran felt a chill run down his spine. "Now, the House of Draco is after that power," he murmured darkly.

Barash smiled grimly. "They are just the latest in a long line of fools. They think they can harness the forces the Old Kingdoms left behind, but power like this... it doesn't bend to anyone's will. It consumes them."

Zahira's eyes darkened as she turned to face Barash. "What of Farid? Is he merely a traitor, working for the House of Draco, or does he have his own ambitions?"

Barash's smile faded, replaced by a look of deep concern. "Farid... he's always been ambitious, always chasing power. Despite having those traits, I seriously doubt that he even understands what he is involved in. The Draconians are clearly using Farid, manipulating him. If he chooses to continue down this path, he will be consumed just like all the others who came before."

A heavy silence fell over the group as they absorbed Barash's words. The chamber seemed to hum with a faint, unseen presence, as though the very stones were alive with the echoes of the past.

Aran glanced again at the strange sigils, the twisted sun-like symbol that seemed to watch him from the walls - like remnants of a dream. For a brief moment, doubt gnawed at him. Could they truly stop this, or were they already too late? He quickly pushed that thought away. Fear would not save Zarah - only action could.

"We must stop them," he said finally. "Whatever the Draco are after down here, whatever they are trying to unleash - it is more dangerous than I thought. We need to find proof of their plans and take it to the Rasha council before it is too late."

Zahira nodded to her cousin, her expression grim. "How do you figure we find what we are looking for? These tunnels are vast, and if they already started working with whatever technology is buried down here, we may be walking into a trap."

"I believe we are already in the trap," Sura said quietly, glancing at Aran. "The question is how do we spring it without being caught," she threw him a wink - her eyes, a deep pool of feelings.

Barash gestured to a passage on the far side of the chamber. "There are deeper levels, going further down, older than even this one. If they are after something down here, that is where they will be." He looked at

Aran, "I am warning you, lad. What lies below us is not meant for the living. You will find yourself facing more than just warriors and traps down there. The old power... it has a way of warping what it touches." Aran's jaw tightened. He took one long look at his friends. "Then we shall face it together," he said, encouragingly, before entering.

The passage spiralled downward, leading the group deeper into the heart of the labyrinth. As they descended, the air grew colder, the walls damper. The carvings became more sparse, replaced by rough-hewn stone that spoke of a hurried construction - no longer the elegant, fluid handiwork of the old kingdoms, but something far more ancient and primal.
Barash's pace slowed, his eyes scanning the walls nervously. "We are nearing the lower levels," he said in a hushed tone. "This is where the Old Kings buried their darkest secrets."
The torches sputtered in the damp air, casting flickering shadows that danced unnaturally on the walls. There was an odd pressure in the air now, a faint hum that vibrated through the stone. It was as though the deeper they went, the more they stepped into a place where the laws of physics bent and shifted - as if free from the rules that bound them.
The tunnel they had been walking in sloped downward, widening into darkness. Then, without warning, the space opened. An enormous cavern stretched before them - vast, silent, waiting. Aran's breath caught as his eyes adjusted, and then he saw it in all its glory.
This underground chamber was massive, its ceiling lost in darkness. There it stood, at its centre, a structure alike, and yet unlike anything Aran had ever seen before. A massive black stone obelisk, rising from the ground like the spine of some ancient beast. Its surface was covered in the same twisted sun symbols they had seen in the upper chambers, but here, the carvings seemed to pulse with a faint inner light, as though the stone monolith itself was alive.
Around the obelisk, strange metallic apparatuses had been erected. Aran could see scaled figures moving between them, Draco warriors and engineers toiled in the dim light to unearth whatever lay within the obelisk's heart. They were manipulating complex machines, pipes, and wires snaking around the stone, feeding into its base.
Zahira cursed under her breath. "They have already started working on something down here. We might be too late."
Aran clenched his fists. "Not yet, it seems. If we can manage to disrupt this operation, by destroying whatever they are using to tap into the obelisk's power," he was thinking fast, "we can still stop them."

"We will have to be extremely careful," Rafiq said, his eyes narrowing as he studied the setup below. "One wrong move, and we could trigger whatever power is buried here. If what Barash said is true..."

Zahira nodded at Aran, a wary look in her eyes. "We could be dealing with forces capable of tearing the city apart," she nodded at Rafiq.

Barash stepped forward, his face pale but resolute. "What I told you is the truth, but you are right to be cautious. The obelisk... it's a conduit. A focus for the old power. Still, it is more than that. It is also a prison."

Aran shot him a sharp look. "A prison, you say?! For what?"

Barash's gaze darkened. "The Old Kings did not just rule over the five elements. They bound the spirits of their enemies - creatures of power and cunning - into these stones. The House of Draco, blinded by its unbound ambition, thinks they can use that power - moreover, they think they can control it. If they manage to break the seals on this monolith, they will unleash something far worse than they imagine."

A cold silence followed Barash's words. The weight of the situation pressed heavily on Aran's shoulders. They weren't just fighting against the ambition of the House of Draco - they were standing on the daunting precipice of something far older and more dangerous.

"We have to act now," Aran said firmly. "Zahira, Sura, try to find a way to sabotage their machinery. Rafiq and I will take out the guards. Barash, stay back and guide us from here. We cannot afford any mistakes."

The rest of the group nodded in grim agreement, yet as they split up to carry out his plan, Aran couldn't shake the feeling that they were racing against more than just Draconian schemes. They were fighting against time itself. Against forces that had been waiting for millennia to be set free. If they failed, their world would never be the same. At that moment, Aran felt that same surge of energy under his skin. Somewhere deep in the stone, something... stirred.

Chapter VII

Beneath the Shadow of Kings

The vast cavern swallowed all sound but for the steady hum of power emanating from the black obelisk. From their vantage point high on a stone ledge, Aran could see the massive chamber stretched nearly half a league in diameter, its ceiling lost in shadows, its floor swarming with Draconian workers like insects around a carcass.

He crouched in the shadows, watching the scene below, the sheer scale of what the Draco had begun was becoming horrifyingly clear. The shiny metallic apparatuses lashed to the obelisk pulsed with unnatural energy, their strange arcane mechanisms spiralling into movement as the busy Draconians worked to unlock whatever was trapped deep within the stone.

"What are they trying to extract from it?" Aran whispered to Barash, who crouched beside him, his eyes narrowed in concentration.

Barash's gaze remained fixed on the obelisk, his voice barely a breath. "It's not about extracting. The obelisks are keys. Those devices they are using... they are trying to force it open."

"Obelisks?! Do you mean to say there are more of these things?" Aran's stomach twisted. Barash, however, did not address his question. Instead, he pointed at the stone monolith.

Aran glanced down at the devices, the many wires, the glowing symbols, trying to wrap his mind around the scale of what the Draco were doing. "Keys?" he asked Barash. "You said the obelisk is a prison. What lies within?"

Barash's lips tightened, his face etched with the weight of too many ancient secrets. "When the Old Kings ruled, they didn't just conquer lands. They conquered forces. Beings. Spirits that defied the laws of the cosmos. Not demons, not gods... something in between. The Old Kings bound them, forced them into service, and, eventually, sealed them away, in these stone prisons."

"Now, the House of Draco wants to let them loose." Aran said, the heavy weight of the revelation settling over him like a shroud.

Barash nodded. "They think they can control the power of the ancients. But these creatures... they do not serve. They consume."

Before Aran could respond, the metallic shriek of one of the Draconian devices pierced the air. A low vibration ran through the floor, rippling up from deep within the earth. It felt as if the stone beneath them was alive, quivering in anticipation. Aran turned his eyes toward the obelisk, his breath catching as the sigils carved into its surface began to shift, the twisted rays of the strange sun-like symbol slowly coming to life.

"They are getting close to whatever they are after," Zahira whispered, her voice taut with urgency as she joined them in the shadows.

Aran forced himself to focus. They couldn't afford to lose control of the situation now. "We need to sabotage the devices before they go any further. Sura, Rafiq, do you think you can cut the power?"

Rafiq, his sharp eyes scanning the tangle of pipes and wires, nodded. "If we can take out the main conduit feeding those devices, we might be able to disrupt the whole operation. We will need to move fast. Once they realize what we are doing..."

"They will throw everything at us," Sura finished grimly.

For a brief second, doubt clawed at Aran once more. What if they were already too late? What if the power the House of Draco sought had already begun unravelling?

Regardless of how he felt, doubt had no place here - action did.

Aran met their eyes, steady and determined. "Then we don't give them a chance. Change of plans, Zahira, Rafiq, and Sura, you three handle the sabotage. Barash and I will take out as many of the guards as we can and cover your retreat. Once the machines are down, we get out. No heroics, everyone. The city above still needs to know what is happening down here."

"What do you mean, Barash and I?" the old man jested, his eyes glinting. "I'm still a warrior, yes, but a very old one."

"You are right," Aran replied, "just stay close to me." He faced the others. "Are you ready?" They exchanged an understanding look.

Zahira's jaw trembled, but she nodded firmly. "We will not fail."

As they split up, creeping toward their respective targets, the tension in the cavern seemed to thicken. Every step felt like a gamble with fate, every shadow a potential threat.

Aran moved swiftly and silently, Barash kept close behind him as they approached the nearest cluster of Draconian warriors. These weren't ordinary mercenaries. They were the Draconian elite guard, seasoned warriors who had seen their share of battle.

However, even the best-trained warriors were vulnerable, particularly when distracted by strange, incomprehensible forces.

Without warning, Barash moved ahead, signalling to Aran with a quick hand gesture. Two Draconians stood near a control panel, their eyes fixed on the glowing symbols rising from the obelisk. Aran watched as Barash slid through the shadows like a ghost, his movement precise, deadly. In a single swift motion, he drew a thin blade from his sleeve and pressed it to one of the guard's throats, dragging him into the darkness. Before the second could react, Barash's blade flashed again, and the reptilian warrior crumpled silently to the floor.

Aran couldn't help but marvel at Barash's ruse. The old man had clearly been fooling them. His skills were still honed to perfection, untouched by the passage of years.

Aran breathed out, his pulse steady, and moved forward to secure the area. "We have a clear path," he whispered into the darkness, his eyes scanning for any sign of movement.

Zahira, Sura, and Rafiq were already working on the devices, disabling the energy conduits with swift, steady efficiency. Still, time was running short. While Zahira and Rafiq worked deftly to dismantle one of the key apparatuses connected to the obelisk, Sura felt something stir in the air. A presence that pricked her skin and made the hair on the back of her neck stand up. The obelisk wasn't just a symbol of power. It was clearly watching them.

"The air is changing," she murmured, her voice low as she worked a metal rod into the main conduit. "We need to move faster."

"I am going as quick as I can," Rafiq muttered, his hands moving deftly over a series of complex gears. "These devices are far more advanced than anything I have ever seen before. Whoever built this, knew exactly what they were doing."

Just as Rafiq twisted the final piece free, a low, deep rumble rolled through the chamber, followed by a sudden pulse of light from the obelisk. The sigils carved into the stone flared, a brilliant crimson glow that illuminated the entire cavern. It was as though the ancient prison was awakening, its power unleashed by being tampered with.

A sharp crack split the air, and the ground shuddered violently, throwing Zahira and Rafiq to the floor. Sura drew her blades.

In the distance, the eerie, otherworldly hum intensified, and from the base of the obelisk, dark shapes began to swirl. A black mist that twisted and coiled like living smoke, taking on forms both humanoid and eldritch, monstrous. "What is this witchcraft?" Sura asked, in horror.

"We are too late!" Zahira shouted, scrambling to her feet as the mist began to spread, swallowing everything in its path.

Aran's head snapped toward the obelisk as the surge of power quickly intensified. The air around it seemed to warp, distorting as the swirling black mist bled into the cavern like an infection. Figures moved within the mist, shapes that defied reason, their forms flickering between faint shadow and substance. "What is that?" Sura repeated, gasping, her voice filled with dread as the mist crept closer.

Barash's face was pale, his eyes wide with fear. "The Old Kings didn't just bind their enemies. They trapped the fragments of their own power in these prisons. What you are seeing... it is their essence, leaking through."

The mist rolled across the floor, swallowing the first line of Draconian warriors. Their shrieks and hisses echoed through the cavern, their lives cutting short as their scaled bodies crumpled, dissolving into the mist as though they had never existed.

Aran's heart raced. "We need to fall back. Now!"

Before they could retreat, a shape stepped from the shadows - a lanky figure with sharp, angular features and dark, piercing eyes. He was clad in ornate robes, and in his hand, he held a staff of twisted black metal, the tip crowned with a fragment of the same glowing stone that powered the obelisk.

"Farid," Zahira shouted, her voice thick with anger and betrayal. Images of years of study in the Rasha Academies of Sarim flashed through her mind - how could a man who had once been a teacher to others fall so far?

Farid smiled, a slow, predatory grin that sent a chill down Aran's spine. There was something off about the way he moved, something strangely familiar in his gestures that Aran couldn't quite place.

"You have come far, Aran ibn Khalid." Farid said. "Though I am afraid this is the end of your journey - your road is spent."

Aran stepped forward, his hand tightening around his father's sword. "It does not have to be this way," he pleaded. "You are being used like a puppet on a string, and the House of Draco will promptly cast you aside the moment they have what they want from you."

Farid's smile didn't falter. "You still don't understand, do you?" His tone was one of mockery. "The Draco are not in control here. I am." The man raised his staff, and the mist shifted, coiling around him like a protective shroud. His fingers twitched around the staff, as if even his own body struggled to contain the power surging through him. The mist coiled tighter, responding to his emotions like a living thing. Was he controlling it, or was it controlling him? "The power of the Old Kings is mine now," Farid shouted. "With it, I shall reshape this world, and have all of it ordained by my will."

Aran tightened his grip on the sword. "What are you doing?! You are a fool if you think you can control that power. It will consume you."

Farid's eyes gleamed with madness. "I do not need to control it. I need only to harness it. The Old Kings knew the truth - the world, life itself, is chaotic," he looked deranged. "There is no good or evil, in life - there is only power, and those who are strong enough to wield it."

With a wave of his hand, the mist surged forward, crashing toward Aran and his companions like a living wave of death and darkness.

"Move!" Aran shouted, diving to the side as the mist slammed into the ground where he had stood seconds before.

The force of the impact sent shards of stone flying, and Aran barely had time to catch his breath before the mist swirled again, forming into a towering figure - one of the shadowy, humanoid creatures bound within the obelisk. Its eyes glowed with an unnatural red light, and it moved with a predatory grace that belied its size.

Farid's maniacal laughter echoed through the chamber. "You cannot stop me, Aran. The power of the ancients is mine now. All that remains is to sweep aside the old world and build a new one in its place." He seemed to be drunk on his newfound power. "A new dawn is coming to Zarah, and there is nothing anyone can do to stop it."

Aran scrambled to his feet, his mind racing. Farid's, erratic, unexpected behaviour didn't make any sense. The man had clearly lost all sense of reason, consumed by his unquenchable thirst.

Moreover, the mist, the ancient magic, was beyond anything they had prepared for. If they didn't act fast, the entire city, perhaps even the world, could fall.

"We need to take him down," Zahira growled, her eyes locked on Farid. "He is the one controlling the mist."

"Easier said than done," Rafiq muttered, already looking for an escape route as the mist closed in on them from all sides.

Barash stepped forward, his voice was calm despite the chaos swirling around them. "There is still a way. The obelisk is the anchor for all of this. If we destroy it, the power will collapse."

Aran's mind was whirring. Destroying the obelisk might save them from the immediate threat, but the consequences were impossible to predict. The ancient prison held powers beyond their understanding. If shattered, it could unleash something far worse.

Again, there it was - one more hard choice to be made. If they destroyed it, the mist might vanish - or it might consume everything. The choice was impossible. Hesitation, on the other hand, would kill them faster than the mist itself. Yet, there was no choice to be made here, there was only destiny at play.

Aran felt the weight of his bloodline in that moment - generations of rulers who had faced impossible choices, who had paid prices they could never fully calculate. His father had spoken of such moments when a king must choose not between right and wrong, but between one catastrophe and another. The obelisk had stood for millennia, a prison that had kept Zarah safe through its very existence. Now, he would be the one to shatter that ancient compact, to release forces that even the Old Kings had feared to destroy outright.

"Then we take it down," Aran decided, his voice grim. "Whatever it takes." The weight of command settled on his shoulders - not just from lessons his father had imparted onto him - but one he now claimed willingly, knowing full well the cost might be measured in more than just his own life. As the mist closed in, and Farid's laughter echoed through the cavern, the group prepared for one final, desperate assault.

Chapter VIII

The Shattered Throne

The peoples of Zarah had endured for thousands of years. Their legacy carved into its very bones, but their history was one written in blood and betrayal, whispered through the halls of forgotten kings.

In the bowels of Sarim, as Aran and his companions fought for survival, that history loomed over him like a curse. The very air of the chamber felt heavy with the weight of generations long gone, each one shaped by decisions not so different from the one now laid before him.

The flickering torchlight cast long shadows on the walls of the ancient chamber, illuminating intricate carvings that adorned the stone. Aran's eyes caught glimpses of the heraldry and the symbols of the past. A lion rampant, a shattered crown, and above all, the ever-present sun symbol with its twisted rays, an emblem of power, ruin, and retribution.

The obelisk in the centre of the cavern hummed with barely contained energy, and the mist that swirled around it carried the echoes of those ancient kings who had bound it in place...

Before the city of Sarim stood, before Zarah and its deserts had been divided into its current warring states, there had been a singular realm, a vast and terrifying empire that spanned the known world. Its name had been lost to time, to history, but its rulers, the Old Kings, had shaped the very fabric of reality itself.

The Old Kings were not mere mortals. It was said that they had risen from the primordial chaos that had once consumed the world, born from the very forces they had conquered.

Other legends claimed that they came from the stars, millennia ago. They spoke of their mastery over life and death, their ability to command the winds, seas, and even the passage of time. Inevitably, such power came at a heavy price. As they carved their empire into existence, they awakened forces that had long slumbered in the forgotten depths of the planet. These forces, the ancient spirits, these beings beyond mortal comprehension, rebelled against the Kings, challenging their dominion.

Wars were fought, not with armies but with the raw essence of Zarah itself. Entire cities were razed to the ground, turned to dust by the same destructive power wielded by the Old Kings and their enemies.

In the end, the Old Kings emerged victorious, but their triumph was hollow. The creatures they had fought could not be destroyed, not in any way that mortal minds could understand.

So, they devised prisons, obelisk-like structures infused with the essence of their own power, to contain the spirits. They spread these prisons across the planet, each one holding a fragment of the very same forces that had threatened to unmake the world.

However, binding such power came with its consequences.

The Old kings themselves became tethered to the very prisons they had themselves built. Slowly, their own power began to decay, the weight of their actions and the constant pull of the bound forces weakening them. Their reign, once seen as eternal, began to crumble. The great empire that had united the world fell into ruin, torn apart by internal strife and the insidious influence of the creatures still trapped within the prisons they had built.

Aran's family, though not one of the original dynasties, had risen in the wake of this collapse. They had been vassals of the Old Kings, warriors, and scholars who had served the Old Thrones loyally.

With the fall of the empire, they had seized their own destiny, claiming lands and titles in the chaos that followed. In time, they became rulers in their own right, their very name synonymous with power and stability in a world constantly teetering on the edge of destruction.

Yet, even as they built their new kingdoms, Aran's bloodline could never escape the shadow of its past. His ancestors had been part of the vile, ancient war, and the bloodlines of the Old Kings still ran through their veins, mingled with the curse of the creatures they had helped imprison. Now, countless centuries later, that same curse had come to claim their descendants…

As Aran stood before the obelisk, he could feel the pull of that history, a deep, resonant thrum that echoed in his bones. Yet, it was more than just the power of the stone prison itself, there was something personal in its call, something tied to the very blood that ran through his veins. His family had always been close to this kind of power, even if it had not been openly spoken of in generations.

It was his father who had broken that tradition, deciding he would be a mere merchant, leaving behind those ties - hoping they faded away.

"Barash," Aran said quietly, not taking his eyes off the swirling mist that now filled the chamber. "There is more to this. More to why we are here, why I have been drawn into this." These were not questions and Barash knew it.

His silence was heavy, his face lined with the weight of knowledge long kept secret. In the distance, Farid's voice punctuated these silent, short intervals. After a moment, the old warrior spoke, his voice was low and measured. Holding Aran's gaze in his. "Your bloodline," Barash sighed.

"Was not always what it is now. Your ancestors were once the right hand of the Old Kings. Advisors, warriors, yes, but also enforcers. They were the ones tasked with ensuring the obelisks remained intact, that the creatures trapped inside never escaped."

Aran's eyes flicked to Barash, his voice hard. "Why would you withhold this knowledge from me?"

Farid's voice cut in. "You are running out of time, my nosy friends." His taunt seemed to come out of the mist itself.

Barash's gaze was steady. "It was not my secret to tell, Aran. Your own father should have been the one to tell you this. What drove him to think it would be best to keep you away from such knowledge?"

He had posed the precise question Aran was asking himself.

"I can only speculate on why," Barash continued, his brow heavy. "Perhaps he believed that by doing so, you would be spared from this fate," he exhaled, readying himself for the hardest blow. "It is vital that you understand this, lad. For the Old Kings did more than merely bind those creatures. They infused part of their own power into these prisons. Your family... your bloodline is bound to that same power. That is why the House of Draco targeted you, and why Farid betrayed you to them. The blood of the Old Kings runs in your veins. You are part of this, whether you like it or not," he paused for a second, observing Aran's reaction. "Whether you want to, or not." Barash's eyes blazed, like they were fuelled by a secret promise that burned deep within.

Farid's voice echoed through the cavern. "You can not hide forever, Aran. You know I will find you, so why not face me like a man."

Aran's thoughts were focused inward, toiling with a gale of emotions, struggling to make sense of it all - Farid's scoff had no effect on him.

Barash's harsh revelations, on the other hand, hit him harder than any physical blow ever could.

For a brief moment, time stood still. It was hard for him to breathe, as if oxygen had suddenly turned to ice in his lungs, then he collapsed on the ground. The weight of his family's legacy, always present but never fully understood, now pressed down on him with crushing force. The fateful decisions of his ancestors, long buried beneath layers of history, had shaped the path that had led him here, to this moment.

Aran wondered if his father had allowed him to accompany the caravans so he might discover the truth for himself, instead of having the burden of revealing such a devastating blow.

Barash said nothing, merely observing his charge in silence.

After Farid's voice subsided once more, he caught Aran's eyes.

"They believed," he whispered, "that only those who shared the same bloodline could control the obelisks. That is why your family survived when the Old Kings fell. They became custodians of the prisons, even if they did not know it themselves."

"Why didn't we know? Why keep us in the dark, about something as monumental as this?" Zahira asked, her voice tinged with frustration and confusion. "If our bloodline was supposed to guard these things, why keep it a secret? Why?" Zahira's eyes were ablaze with emotion. Being Aran's cousin, she wasn't merely asking questions. She was demanding answers.

Barash hesitated, choosing his words carefully, his gaze distant. "Because knowledge is dangerous, my child. The ancient records were either lost or, most likely, hidden on purpose. Perhaps your ancestors believed that if the obelisks were forgotten, no one would seek to use them again," he paused, observing Zahira and Aran's reaction. Seeing the dawn of understanding coming over their faces, he concluded. "Clearly, that was a mistake on their part."

Aran clenched his fists, anger rising in his chest. "So, we have been but puppets all along? Pawns, playing a game with rules set a long time ago. Fighting for a dream, for a united, stronger Zarah, when all the while we have been nothing more than keepers of some ancient curse?"

Aran could feel his world unravelling.

"No," Barash said firmly. "You are not puppets. You are heirs to a power greater than any throne. Whether you like it or not, with that same power also comes a heavy responsibility, my boy. One that you cannot merely brush away. The consequences would be disastrous for everyone. Your bloodline was entrusted to protect this world from the forces entrapped within these monoliths. Now, that duty falls to you."

The mist began to thicken, coiling around the base of the obelisk like an ophidian creature. Farid's voice echoed through the cavern, filled with dark glee. "You see it now, don't you, Aran? The truth of your bloodline. You were always meant for this. To wield the power of the ancients. To become what the Old Kings could not."

Aran's mind raced. Farid's actions made no sense. He was a corrupt man, but this course of action was beyond his grasp for power. Far beyond his abilities. He wasn't just trying to free the spirits within the obelisk. He wanted to claim their power for himself.

Nevertheless, if what Barash just told him was true, and he knew it was, then Aran held the key to stopping this madness.

In that moment, he chose to fully accept his fate. He felt the blood of the Old Kings flow through him, and with it, the power to control the obelisk responded.

Still, control wasn't enough, for that can be lost, and it can be taken.

Aram needed to find a way to permanently erase the problem altogether. He had to destroy the prison. "Barash," he said, his voice steady despite the chaos swirling around them. "If I have, inside me, what it takes to tap into the power of the obelisk, does that mean I can use that same power to destroy it as well?"

Barash hesitated, then nodded. "Yes," he began hesitantly. "Given the circumstances, it is probably best that you do, for the alternative is to let it fall into enemy hands. However, understand this - to do so, it will take everything you have. The obelisks were built by the Old Kings, and their power is… vast. If you try to break that bond, you might not survive."

There it was again, Aran though, another hard choice to be made.

He wondered how many more would there be, before one took his life. Yet, deep down, once again, he truly felt that there was no decision to be made. There was only the inevitable unfolding of events, and his role within them. Or was it fate, as Barash had said?

Aran set his jaw. "There is no choice to be made," he spoke aloud. "I have made my choices a long time ago, and they have led me here."

Farid's laughter echoed again, and the mist surged forward, tendrils of darkness reaching for Aran and his companions. Zahira, Sura and Rafiq fought to hold it back, their weapons flashing in the dim light, but the mist was relentless, slow but certainly pushing them toward the walls of the chamber.

"There is always a choice," Farid called out, his voice dripping with pure deceit. "Join me, Aran. Together, we can rebuild this world. Together, we can be kings." No answer came his way.

In frustration, he added, with malice dripping from every syllable. "This is a one-time offer, boy. I suggest you take it."

Farid's voice sounded different now. Not at all like his own. In its texture, it began to carry threads of a serpent's hiss.

Aran found this very strange. Suspicions forming, in the back of his mind. "Could it be?"

He chose to push those daunting thoughts away, for now. His focus was on the obelisk. The carvings on its surface glowed with an otherworldly light, the twisted rays of the sun-like symbol seeming to pulse in time with his own heartbeat. He could feel the power within it, a vast and terrible force that thrummed beneath the surface, patiently waiting to be unleashed.

Aran reached out, his hand hovering mere inches from the stone. The air crackled with energy, and for a brief moment of surprise, he hesitated. This was, after all, his family's legacy. The power of the Old Kings, the very thing that had shaped that world for millennia.

His fingers trembled inches from the stone. The unbearable weight of history bore down on him.

If he shattered the obelisk, his family's legacy would end here. No more kings. No more hidden power. If he hesitated… Zarah would burn. On the other hand, if he used that power to destroy the obelisk, it would sever that connection forever. Erase the last remnants of an ancient, forgotten empire - lost forever to the sands of time.

Deep, in the confines of his soul, Aran also knew that he must. Their world had moved on from the time of the Old Kings. The power they had wielded was too dangerous, too corrupting.

If he didn't destroy the obelisk, it would consume them all. Taking a deep breath, still unsure of what to do, Aran placed his hand on the obsidian surface.

The moment his fingers touched it, a surge of energy shot through his body, like fire coursing through his veins. His vision blurred, and for a moment, he was no longer in the chamber. He was standing in a vast, empty expanse, the sky above him filled with swirling clouds of darkness. In the distance, he could see figures. Tall, regal silhouettes, shrouded in shadow. Was he looking at the Old Kings?

They stared at him, impassive, their eyes burning with cold fire.

He could feel their power inside his skin, their anger in his soul, their patient desire to break free from the prisons they had, in their haste, inadvertently, created for themselves. Without warning or filter, Aran also felt their pain - unbridled.

He did not wish to hurt them, but he wasn't here to free them either, for it was too late for that. He was here to end it - to crush his dream, before it could begin to flourish.

Steadying his breathing, drawing on the strength of his ancestors, on the blood that ran through his veins, Aran focused all of his will on the obsidian obelisk. With his hand on the aged stone, he could feel the resistance, the ancient power fighting back, but he pushed harder, forcing his way through the thick layers of history and protection that had been woven into the very monument.

Nothing, no matter how strange, in his journeys, had prepared him for this. He was operating on intuition alone, feeling his way through forces beyond comprehension.

The chamber suddenly began to shake, the ground trembling beneath their feet. Cracks appeared in the surface of the obelisk, and the mist that had filled the room recoiled as if in pain.

"Cousin!" Zahira's voice cut through the chaos. "It's working! Whatever you are doing, keep going!"

Aran doubled his efforts, yet it wasn't enough, the power of the ancient stone prison was too great. He needed to call on more than instinct. On more than luck, more than... "Focus!" Barash shouted. "Focus, Aran. Turn inward. You need to draw on the full strength of your bloodline, the legacy of your family." His friend's words cut deep. Why did they hurt so much?

Aran took a shuddering breath and thought of his father. His mother. His grandmother - the angel. He thought of his older brother... The loss, the guilt - it was still there, still raw. "Enough!"

With a final, desperate effort, he reached deep within himself, pulling on the power of his ancestors. The kingship of his bloodline surged through him, filling him with a strength he had never thought to be possible. The cracks in the obelisk widened, and with a deafening roar, the ancient stone shattered, sending shards of black stone flying in all directions.

The mist screamed in pain - hidden history bleeding profusely from it. A sound of pure agony, and then it was gone, evaporating into the air as if it had never existed. Silence filled the immense cavern.

Aran collapsed to his knees, sweat trickling down his skin, his clothes soaked, his body shaking with exhaustion.

The obelisk was broken, reduced to rubble, and with it, the power that had threatened to destroy them all - but the cost had been heavy.

The bond between his bloodline and the ancient powers appeared to have been severed, and with it, a piece of its legacy had been lost forever.

He felt hollow, as if something essential had been carved from his very soul. The weight of kingship, never fully understood until this moment, was gone - and with it, perhaps, any hope of truly uniting Zarah under a single crown.

Looking around at his friends, at the ruins of the ancient chamber, Aran feared that the planet would never be the same after this.

When the Obelisk shattered, he saw Farid feel the first tremors of his power slipping like grains of sand through his clenched fist.

He stumbled backwards, the oppressive weight of the black smoke he had summoned now surging against him, writhing with a mind of its own. It pulsed and hissed, as if recognizing a sudden vulnerability in its new master.

Aran saw Farid feel the sharp sting of betrayal as the darkness began to close around him, suffocating, pressing inward like a vice. The councillor gasped, his hands clenching his throat as if struggling for air.

Then his bones cracked. His skin rippled. The air around Farid al-Rasha shimmered like a heat mirage, distorting his form. What was once a man dissolved into something else. Something reptilian. A monster shedding its human disguise. Suddenly, without warning, Aran's worst fears were confirmed. To the rest of the group's astonishment, Farid's physical features began to morph. His fingers became clawed. His skin was now covered in scales. His overall semblance began shapeshifting back to its Draconian nature. Kael Drathis, forced, by the obelisk's destruction, to change back to his reptilian form.

"It is you." Aran shouted. "I suspected as much. Where is Farid?"

Drathis looked first at Aran, then at the others. There was pure spite in his slitted eyes - his words, venomous. "Farid was never here, you fools. He is a traitor to your world and the perfect scapegoat for us, but even he would not dare to disturb the Weaving." Drathis smirked. "No matter, it is done." As he hissed these last words, the black smoke began to swirl around him once more.

Yet, Kael Drathis had delved into the ancient tomes of forbidden power for many decades, scouring the hidden crevices of knowledge to harness the Old Kings own binding forces. The black smoke he had conjured was not simply a weapon. It was an extension of his will, so he thought, a companion crafted from the essence of fear and chaos, tempered to obey only those who mastered the Weaving's secrets.

Though it surprisingly sought now to consume him in the wake of the obelisk's destruction, Drathis' resolve remained unyielding.

With a low, guttural chant in a tongue Aran and his friends, not even Barash, could recognize, he drew his clawed hand across the air, slicing through the smoke with an invisible blade of intent.

The incantation was one Drathis had sworn never to use unless driven to the very edge of ruin, and as the words left his mouth, the air around him shimmered with a darkness deeper than shadow, a blackness that seemed to drink in the light and chill the very marrow of existence.

In spite of his best efforts, honed by decades of practice, Drathis' incantation was not working and the Primordials were clearly thrusting him out. He bared his fangs in a twisted grin, his form still flickering between human and reptilian."Small setback. No matter," he mused, aware that he could not remain here, vulnerable and drained.

Drathis hissed his final threat before fleeing the caves. "You might believe this to be a victory, Aran, son of Khalid, but the war will be mine. Zarah will be ours. The day will come, when you will look back at this moment, and realise that you should have taken my offer."

Chapter IX

The Echoes of Kings

In the aftermath of the obelisk's sundering, when Drathis' revelations still echoed through the chambers of memory, the very fabric of the world seemed altered. The obsidian monument's destruction had changed more than the physical world - it had altered Aran himself.

Where once stood a man driven by necessity, now remained a warrior burdened by the weight of ancestral sins made manifest.

In the silence that followed its destruction, a subtle shift rippled across the fabric of existence. Though the immediate danger had passed, the air felt heavy with an unspeakable tension, as though Zarah itself had drawn a breath and held it, uncertain of what would come next.

Aran, now more aware than ever of the weight his bloodline carried, could not escape the questions that haunted him.

For the future House of Aran, what had happened that day was just the beginning.

The shattered remains of the stone prison lay scattered across the chamber floor, glowing faintly in the darkness. In the cold aftermath of his battle against Drathis and the ancient powers, Aran could feel the fatigue clinging to him, not only in body but deep inside his soul.

His hands trembled as the reality of what had transpired settled upon his shoulders like a shroud. His companions were equally exhausted, their breaths shallow as they leaned against the crumbling walls, trying to comprehend the magnitude of the battle they had barely survived.

"Aran," Zahira asked, hesitantly. "What do you think Drathis meant by war? Do you think the Draconians will openly attack Zarah?"

Aran didn't answer, his mind drowning in questions. Most were related to what just happened, others to what was still to happen.

Drathis' move to shapeshift as Farid, had been a well played hand. One that had almost worked, if he had not destroyed the monolith. Farid al-Rasha, despite being a treacherous silver tongued individual, was not an evil man at his core. Ambitious, no doubt, maybe even disloyal, but certainly not evil. Not in the same manner as the Draco were. "I do not know," Aran finally answered. "Not yet anyway."

Other, more pressing questions were bursting out of him.

"Barash," he turned to face, truth be told, his eldest friend. "Drathis mentioned something called the Weaving. I wonder what it means? Have you ever heard of such a thing?"

Barash stiffened, his weathered hands clenched into fists. A flicker of something - recognition? Fear? - crossed his face before it vanished. He turned away, feigning disinterest. "Names have power, Aran. Until the right time presents itself, some questions are best left unanswered. "The Weaving," he continued, his voice dropping to barely above a whisper, "is not knowledge meant for chambers where ears may hide in shadows. When we stand beneath the open skies of Zarah, with none but trusted hearts as witness, then shall these words find voice. Until that hour, let silence be our guardian." Barash stopped abruptly, seemingly lost in thought.

Aran studied his friend's weathered features, noting how the man's jaw had set in that familiar way that meant certain doors would remain firmly closed. How many secrets did Barash carry? And why, when the world teetered on the edge of chaos, did he still insist on parcelling out truth like a miser counting coins?

The questions burned in Aran's throat, but he swallowed them. Some battles, he had learned long ago, were not won by direct assault.

Silence fell over the group. Each of them replaying in their minds the recent events. Aran couldn't help but wonder: had Barash withheld knowledge, or had he chosen to ignore the query for some unknown reason?

In the quiet that followed, a sound rose from the broken stones. A soft, almost imperceptible, hum vibrating through the chamber, neither threatening nor welcoming, but filled with the resonance of ages past. Aran closed his eyes, listening, and for a moment, he thought he could hear voices. Distant, barely audible, as though carried on a breeze from a place far removed from this world. A desert whisper, layered with countless voices, slithered through the ruins. Not made of words, but emotions - sorrow thick as blood, anger searing as fire, and regret, as vast as the deserts of Zarah.

The air pulsed around them, and Aran felt the weight of countless invisible eyes upon him. Watching. Judging. Waiting. They spoke not in words but in feelings. Those of sorrow, anger, and regret.

Here, in this place where ancient power had been bound, the ghostly veil between worlds grew thin as morning mist. The dead did not rest easy when their works cast shadows across the living, and the Old Kings had left shadows darker than any night Zarah had known.

It was the layered voices of his ancestors, who had long since passed into the forgotten realms of Zarah's history. The blood they had shed to bind the world had left an imprint, and now, that mark was speaking to him. The voices rose and fell like wind through ancient bones, each whisper a lament for choices made and prices paid.

Aran felt their sorrow seep into his own spirit - the crushing weight of crown and conscience, the terrible arithmetic of power where every victory demanded its toll in blood and tears. These were not mere echoes of the dead, but the living pain of kingship itself, passed down through generations like a hereditary curse. With a start, Aran realized that the destruction of the obelisk had not silenced them. Rather, it had merely unleashed a new form of their presence.

Barash stepped forward, his eyes dark with knowledge. "It's them, isn't it? The ones who came before? The ancients." Waving his hand through the air, he added. "I can sense it too."

Aran nodded, his face pale. "They are still here, with us. Even now, as we speak." From the corner of his eye, he noticed Sura shift.

Zahira, her gaze resolute despite the exhaustion weighing her down, stood at her cousin's side. "Do you mean the Old Kings? The ones who built this... prison?"

"Yes," Aran murmured. "But they did not just build the prisons. They bound themselves to them, to the power they were trying to control."

Barash's face twisted in a grimace. "That is the tragedy of the Old Kings. They thought they could master the forces of the cosmos and bend them to their will. Servants to their own vanity, they became slaves to the very forces they sought to control."

The reality of the situation dawned on them all, slowly but inevitably. Aran's Bloodline, from its very inception, had been entwined with this ancient power. They had not merely been rulers, but the custodians of a much darker legacy. A legacy of imprisonment, of control. In sum, a legacy of sacrifice. The destruction of the obelisk had been necessary, but it had only begun to unravel the threads that bound his family to its past.

The long journey back to the surface was filled with a silence broken only by the echo of their footsteps and the occasional groan of shifting stone. They encountered no Draconians on the way up, and the city above them, Sarim, was quiet now. Wounded from the reptilian presence, but not destroyed. Its people were weary, watching the skies with wary eyes, waiting for the next threat that might descend upon them.

Scorch marks still marred the ancient stones where draconian fire had touched them, and more than one merchant's stall remained shuttered - their owners fled or worse. The city's wounds would heal, as cities' wounds always did, but the scars would linger. Trust, once shattered, proved harder to rebuild than walls or homes.

Aran, however, had no time to rest. Questions flooded his mind faster than he could begin to address them.

After a long journey back from the depths of the Old Quarter, they emerged from the underground crypt into the Hall of Kings. Hidden in the bowels of Sarim's Royal Palace, this ancient wing had long been abandoned, its vast corridors lined with statues - monuments Aran now knew depicted the rulers of his own bloodline.

Here, in the silent company of his forebears, the weight of his family's past pressed down on him with renewed intensity.

The air itself seemed heavy with the dust of centuries, carrying within it the faint scent of old parchment and forgotten incense - offerings made to kings whose names were carved in stone but whose deeds were written in blood. Each footfall echoed with the hollow resonance of a tomb, as though the very stones remembered the weight of crowns they had once supported.

The Hall was a grand structure, its towering columns and vaulted ceiling, a testament to the might and ambition of those who had come before. Each statue was intricately carved, capturing the likenesses of kings and queens long dead, their expressions stern and unmoving. They were immortalized in stone, but their presence was far from comforting.

Aran could not help but feel their eyes upon him, judging him for the decisions he had made and the battles he had fought.

In this place, the history of his bloodline came alive, not as a mere recounting of victories and defeats, but as a living presence, pulsing with the ambitions, failures, and sacrifices of each generation. Here, Aran saw not only the glory but the curse of his bloodline. Each ruler had carried the burden of the Old Kings, whether they knew it or not, and now that burden had been passed to him.

Again, that gnawing doubt eating away at his heart. Why had his father never mentioned any of this? Moreover, how had his father escaped such a fate? Aran decided, in that moment of doubt, that he would trust his father's judgement. "Perhaps he knew what he was doing."

As they walked through the hall, taking pause to observe the royal sculptures, Barash spoke, his voice reverberating off the stone walls. "Do you know why the Hall of Kings was built?" he asked.

Aran, suddenly pulled away from his thoughts, was taken by surprise. He shook his head, as he searched for an answer. "Not beyond the obvious. To honour the rulers of my bloodline."

Barash's eyes narrowed. "Well, yes and no. This hall was built not only as a monument to honour the dead, but also as a warning. This was to be a reminder of what happens when power goes unchecked." He paused before one of the statues, a figure clad in ancient armour, its face stern and unyielding. "This is Aradas the Conqueror, your great ancestor - at the birth of Zarah's Second Age. He was the one who led the rebellion against the Old Kings, the one who first took control of Sarim, though it was not known by that name, in those days. His reign was long, filled with triumphs, but it was also marked by betrayal and bloodshed. Just as the Old Kings before him, Aradas firmly believed he could control the forces of the world. In the end, he paid the price for his pride."

Aran studied the statue, feeling a strange sense of kinship with the man it depicted. "What happened to Aradas?"

"He died alone," Barash's reply was brief, his voice heavy with meaning. "His own blood turned against him in the end - three sons who each believed themselves the rightful heir to power they could never truly possess. They came to him in the dead of night, not as assassins but as judges, convinced that patricide was justice. The crown passed through blood, as it always does, but the lesson perished with him - that the very forces we seek to master inevitably become our masters in return."

Aradas' tale struck a chord deep within Aran. There seemed to be a pattern pervading through the long bloodied history of his family. A vicious cycle of ambition, power, and inevitable ruin. Each king, in their own way, had strived to master the forces that had shaped their world, only to be undone by their own hubris. "Why does it always end this way?" he asked Barash, his voice barely above a whisper.

The old man's gaze was inscrutable. "Because power, true power, always comes with a price, my boy - a heavy price. Always, Aran! Those who, blindly, seek to take control of it should, perhaps, not so often forget that undeniable truth."

The weight of that revelation followed them from the ancient halls into the harsh light of present necessity. Each ascending step carried them further from the ancient darkness below, yet Aran felt the shadows of revelation clinging to his spirit like grave-cloth. The weight of stone above had been replaced by the weightier burden of knowledge - that terrible gift which, once received, could never be returned to ignorance's merciful embrace.

Along with the fallen obelisk, the House of Draco's conspirators - those who had worked to undermine Sarim from within - seemed to vanish into the wind, leaving the city's council feeling like it woke from a powerful incantation.

Standing, with Barash, before the Rasha council, Aran could feel the hatred seeping from Farid's eyes. He obviously could not attack him in the open and, in turn, Aran had no way of proving Farid was involved with the Draconians - with Drathis.

The chamber itself seemed to hold its breath, as though even stone and timber understood the delicate balance of accusation and proof.

To speak too freely was to invite chaos; to remain silent was to court treachery's triumph.

In such moments, wise men learned the true weight of words - and the heavier burden of those left unspoken.

Given the precarious circumstances they found themselves in, Barash and Aran explained to the council as much as they could of what had transpired so far, carefully omitting certain key parts of the story until they could find more proof of their veracity.

"There is no need to alarm them further," Barash said quietly as they left the chamber. "We lack the evidence to condemn him outright - or to prove that Drathis ever wore his face," he confessed.

Farid lingered in the shadows, his influence waning amidst the shifting tides of power. "I will have you yet, Aran Ibn Khalid. Mark my words." The thought echoed through his mind like a silent, unending chant - part curse, part vow.

Later, alone in his study, Farid penned three letters. The first bore the seal of a merchant house in the coastal city of Najra. The second carried the mark of mercenaries who asked no questions for the right price. The third... The third bore no seal at all, for its recipient dwelt in shadows deeper than any honest person should know. If Aran thought their game had ended, he would soon learn otherwise.

That same evening, when Zarah's blazing sun began to set over the horizon, casting long shadows across the city of Sarim, Aran retreated to his new chambers, seeking solace in the quiet. Yet, peace was hard to find that night.

Solitude brought no peace - only the echo of ancestral voices and the weight of expectations he had never sought. For a moment, in the privacy of his chambers, Aran allowed the mask of leadership to slip. His hands trembled as he poured mead into a chalice, not from fear but from the sheer exhaustion of carrying burdens that seemed to multiply with each passing day. He had wanted to unite the tribes to build something lasting and just, though he had never imagined that path would lead through the graveyard of his own family's sins.

How many kings before him had harboured such noble dreams, only to find them twisted by the very legacy they sought to transcend? The crown, it seemed, was both blessing and curse - offering the power to shape nations while shackling the bearer to the sins of fathers long dead. Such was the bitter arithmetic of royalty: that each generation must

answer not only for its own choices, but for the accumulated weight of those who came before.
The events of the past few days weighed heavily on his mind - made heavier still by the knowledge he had gained about his family's ancient legacy, which only served to deepen his unease.
Aran had always been proud of his family's history, that which he knew of, its humble lineage stretching back to the earliest days of the Tarek tribe. However, after recent events, that history seemed tainted to him, its glory intertwined with a darkness that he had never truly understood.
According to Barash, the Old Kings had been tyrants, yes, but they had also been something more. They inadvertently became guardians of a power that was beyond their comprehension. Aran's ancestors had inherited that burden, whether they wanted it or not, and his fate would be no different from theirs.
He sat by the window, watching the last rays of the Leander system's primary star disappear beyond the horizon, his thoughts drifting back to the obelisk - the stone prison. The innate power it contained was unlike anything he had ever felt before. It was vast, ancient, and terrifying. It had called to him, not just because of his bloodline, but because of something deeper, something intrinsic to who he was as an individual.
Nevertheless, that power was dangerous. He had seen for himself what it could do to those who sought to control it.
He thought of Drathis, of how he had tried to consume that power. Would he have succeeded if the obelisk had not been destroyed?
No matter how he spun it in his head, Aran couldn't shake the feeling that there was still more to know about this story. Deep within, he felt that the full truth of his family's legacy had yet to be revealed.
A knock at the door interrupted his thoughts. Natheless, even before it opened, Aran sensed the familiar presence - blood of his blood, sharer of his burdens, the one soul in all Zarah who understood the price of their shared heritage without need for words.
Zahira entered, her face etched with concern. She had remained a close ally throughout his quest - throughout his life. Ever since his father's death, and though she had fought alongside her cousin for years now, Aran knew that she, too, had her own doubts and fears about the future.
"We need to talk," she said, closing the door behind her.
Aran nodded, gesturing for her to sit. "I always have time for you, cousin. What's on your mind?"
She sat down, hesitating for a moment before speaking. "It's about the obelisk. I would like to ask you about what happened," her eyes locked with his, a puzzled look etched on her face as she ventured. "What did you do, down there?"

"In truth, I do not understand it myself," Aran admitted, his voice tired. "I just focused on what needed to be done," he held Zahira's hands in his. "If I had not destroyed it, we all would have died in that place. Or worse. Imagine what would happen if such a power ended up in the hands of Drathis? In the hands of his House?"

Both shuddered at the thought. "I know," she said softly, steadying her voice against the fear creeping in. "Frightening as it sounds, that is not what worries me most. It's what comes next that does." She stood straight. "We might have won the day, Aran, but Drathis will not remain idle for long. We destroyed one obelisk, yes - but if Barash's words were truly a slip of the tongue, there must be more out there. It is only logical. Moreover, if what he says is true, then you are the only one who can destroy them." As the last words left Zahira's lips, a shadow of concern passed over her face. She was, after all, the daughter of Aran's aunt - his mother's sister.

Her words lingered in the air, heavy with unspoken consequences. Aran felt the weight of responsibility settle even deeper on his shoulders. He had already suspected as much. The destruction of one obelisk had only been the beginning. Others had to exist, scattered across Zarah - each one a prison, holding back ancient forces that had once threatened to tear the world apart.

Barash wasn't the kind of man to make mistakes. His tongue did not slip by accident. He had said keys - plural. Aran was certain of it.

Now, by the legacy of his bloodline, it was his burden to find them, and to destroy them.

"Drathis was after something," Zahira continued, pulling Aran from his thoughts. "Something bigger than just the obelisk. He spoke of a greater plan - of others working with him. We need to find out what that plan is, what they are after, before it is too late."

Aran sighed, running a hand through his hair. "I understand. But they are gone. Where do you suggest we start?" She felt no sting from his words, for it was a logical question. "The world is vast," Aran reminded her, "these obelisks could be anywhere. Besides, we have other, more pressing matters to deal with. Or have you forgotten the long-term goal of a united Zarah? I know you have not forgotten how hard it will be to get the tribes to come together."

Zahira's eyes flashed with purpose. "No, I have not, my dear cousin. However, I still believe, and so should you, that these obelisks must take precedence over everything else." She ran a hand through her hair, "I have spoken with Barash about this, and he is a firm believer that we should start with the legends - the old stories, the forgotten histories. There are always grains of truth hidden in myths and old tales," she held his gaze in hers. "I have a feeling the answers we seek might lie buried in our past."

Aran nodded in agreement, though an insistent sense of dread kept gnawing at him. In the past few days, their family's history had already revealed itself to be filled with horrors, and yet, it seemed clear to him that there were still more secrets to uncover, more darkness to face - more challenges to overcome. Through it all, insistent, the voice of his ancestors whispered in the back of his mind, a constant reminder of the legacy he had inherited and the price that was yet to be paid. The price of destiny.

"Yes," Aran concurred. "I agree with you, cousin. Nevertheless, before we pursue that perilous road, we must first solidify the alliances we've so precariously secured thus far." He stood, the weight of leadership settling on his shoulders once more - becoming something of a familiar feeling. "We will ride to Qamar at first light. Would you please ask Rafiq to choose and send emissaries to the six tribes tonight. They should carry a message Informing the tribal leaders to ride like the wind and meet us there, by the Great Oasis." Zahira took in his words. Whatever her thoughts were, her reply came effortlessly. "I trust you, cousin. I will see it done."

The journey across the shifting sands proved uneventful, giving Aran too much time to contemplate the shadows that now clung to his family name. Seven days of dunes and stars, each sunset bringing them closer to a gathering without precedent.

A week later, already in Qamar, Aran presided over a gathering at the Great Oasis, an historical location chosen for its neutrality and its symbolic significance. It was the first time in history that representatives from all the major tribes assembled in one place. The Bahir, the Shamari, the Rasha, the Tarek, and the Ulema, all trying to work together. Despite recent events, Aran could not help but feel a sense of hope.

The oasis shimmered under the twin moons, its waters reflecting the glow of Anar and Nysa. Young Medjool Palms swayed gently in the night breeze, their fronds rustling like whispers of long-forgotten secrets. At the centre of the gathering stood a grand tent, its canopy woven from Sand Weaver silk and, besides the colour black, it was dyed in the colours of each tribe. Gold for the Shamari, crimson for the Bahir, silver for the Rasha, blue for the Tarek, and green for the Ulema.

Inside, the air was thick with tension. Leaders sat on cushions arranged in a circle, their expressions ranging from cautious optimism to outright scepticism. Kasim al-Bahir leaned back, his muscled arms crossed, while Karim al-Shamar tapped his fingers on his knee, clearly impatient.

Safira, the Moon Seer of the Rasha tribe, sat serenely, her silver robes shimmering in the candlelight, while Sura, Zahira and Rafiq flanked Aran, their presence a silent reminder of his friends and relatives undying support.

He rose, his gaze sweeping across the assembly. "We are not enemies to one another. We are children of the same land, shaped by the same sun, toiling with the same struggles and bound by the same fate. Our deserts do not forgive division - they demand unity. If we do not stand together, we will fall alone."

A few tribal leaders shifted in their seats. This did not go unnoticed by Aran. "Conspirators," he continued, "even now, seek to exploit our mistrust to take control of Zarah. They tried to manipulate the obelisks, to interfere with the stability of our world." More uncomfortable shifting. "I found them tampering with one of those stone monoliths, deep in the catacombs of Sarim's Old Quarter."

A nervous murmur quickly spread throughout the tent.

Unbothered by this, Aran continued. "Under the circumstances we deemed it best to be destroyed - which I did." He inhaled deeply. "Now we," he pointed at his close companions, "will continue searching for the remaining obelisks, for I am sure there are bound to be more out there. Along with this, we have also uncovered that the House of Draco is after that power. For what purpose? We do not know yet. Still, we fought them and for the moment managed to delay their plans."

Karim al-Shamar nervously adjusted his spectacles as Aran's words washed over him. Though, he was not the only one surprised by this.

"My friends," Aran pressed, "we are still discussing our course of action. Yet, I beg of you, that while we try to find a solution, you must also strive to remain united. Our enemies continue to seek, with all their might, to divide us. Therefore, my people, I beg you to stand together - united we can resist them. Together, we will thrive."

As a tangible example to bring them closer as allies, Aran chose to focus on more mundane things. He rose from his chair and gestured to the many artefacts displayed in the centre of the circle.

There was an irrigation system prototype from the Shamari tribe, a Bahir-crafted Dune Stalker blade, a Rasha Moon Seer's chart of the constellations, and a Tarek sandstorm predictor. "These are the gifts of our people, birthed by our wit - the strength that makes us who we are. Just try and imagine what we could achieve if we shared our hard-won accumulated knowledge, our tribal resources, and our shared vision." Heavy, thoughtful silence followed Aran's words.

Safira stood up, proud, her voice calm yet commanding. "The moons have shown me a Zarah united under one banner. Yet prophecy, like the desert wind, carries both promise and warning upon its breath. However, they have also shown me that before we can achieve that goal, dark times await us all," she paused, looking around. "Friends gathered here, please heed my words - we must stand united." Murmurs of agreement filled the tent. She was, after all, a respected Rasha Seer. "I, for one, believe Aran speaks the truth. We must set aside our rivalries and work together, if we are to have a prayer of surviving."

The tent fell silent, save for the whisper of wind through the palm fronds above. Karim al-Shamar's restless fingers grew still upon his knee, while Kasim al-Bahir's crossed arms slowly relaxed.

Even the most hardened sceptics, it seemed, could not entirely dismiss the weight of prophecy when spoken by one whose sight pierced the veils between worlds.

When Safira spoke of what the moons revealed, wise men listened - and fools learned wisdom or courted their doom.

Kasim narrowed his eyes, "Words are cheap, Aran. You speak boldly, of kingship, but unity is forged in action, not talk. Show us how you intend to lead, and perhaps we will follow."

Kasim's eyes held the weight of battles fought and blood spilled in defence of his people. Here was no court flatterer or merchant greedily counting coins, but a man who had earned his authority through deed rather than birth. When such men spoke, their words carried the authority of proven steel.

He looked Aran in the eyes, fearless, as he asked his next questions, those burning deep inside. "What of the obelisks you speak of? What do you intend to do about it?"

Aran nodded, his tone resolute. "Kasim, you say that I am all words and no action? Yet, I have proved you wrong before. Remember?"

Kasim looked taken aback, but still managed a smile. Aran was sure he had not forgotten the Trial of the Scorpion. "Then let my first action be one of leadership. I will return to Sarim and continue to pursue the truth about these obelisks." He pointed at those gathered, "You, in return, must promise me that you will continue working together. As I try to unravel the meaning behind my family's curse, as well as deal with these monolithic tethers, promise me that you will remain united," he looked in their eyes, "Rest assured that I will always choose death before failure. I will not so easily give up on my dream, my vision of a united Zarah. A world where all men, women and children, can live free - without exceptions."

All those present could sense the energy change in those next to them. Every lord and lady felt a surge of purpose running through their veins, as if Aran's words were coming out from the very depths of Zarah itself.

He stood up and bowed to the council, turned to his friends and left the tent.

Outside, while they were preparing their steeds for the long ride back to Sarim, Rafiq was the first to break the silence. "A speech of remarkable grace and fluency," he jested. "Do you think it will hold? Words spoken beneath stars often fade with the dawn."

Even though Rafiq was making light of things, the look of concern on his face did not go unnoticed by Aran.

"It must!" He intoned. "There is only so much one man can do, my dear friend. Sooner or later, one will need help from others. That is why we are here, on this plain of existence, brother - to help each other." Aran looked at the horizon, as he said. "The future calls, but its voice is still uncertain. Hope will guide us - but so will the shadows. Let us ride."

The stars wheeled overhead in their eternal cosmic dance, silent witnesses to the words spoken and promises made. Whether those vows would prove as enduring as the constellations themselves, only time - that most impartial of judges - would reveal. With that, they mounted their steeds and departed for Sarim.

Chapter X

The Unseen Tapestry

The morning air was thick with an eerie stillness. It had been two weeks since the Council of Qamar, as Aran stood on the highest balcony of the palace. Below, the city of Sarim stretched out, bruised but standing, its once-vibrant streets muted in the aftermath of the recent scuffles with Draconians mercenaries, while Aran had been away. A cool breeze whispered through the broken columns, carrying with it the scent of ash and distant rain. Aran's thoughts, however, were far from the present.

His gaze lingered on the horizon, where the sun barely pierced the heavy clouds. A world shrouded in uncertainty - a mirror of himself.

His mind was a labyrinth, one turn leading deeper into the enigma of his family's past, while another took him to his vision for a unified Zarah.

Since the destruction of the obelisk, the weight of his ancestry grew heavier. The realization that his bloodline was bound not just to the rulership of Sarim but to a deeper, more perilous legacy gnawed at him, the rulership of Zarah. His ancestors had walked a path that spanned several of Zarah's Ages, a road littered with forgotten oaths, even darker bargains, and sacrifices that had shaped their world.

The Hall of Kings had become a powerful reminder of that. The lined statues of his forebears stood as sentinels of history, but they also concealed layers of truth Aran had yet to fully understand.

Every king and queen of his bloodline had played a role in the grand design of the world. Their lives were woven into a tapestry so vast and ancient that its true form was still hidden. Now, as the last living heir of this bloodline, he was being drawn into the very heart of that design.

Many weeks had passed since Aran and his companions had emerged from the depths of the crypt, yet the revelations still haunted him. Clearly, the obelisk had only been the beginning. Sarim had quieted, its people nursing wounds both physical and emotional, but beneath that quietude, Aran sensed something far more profound.

A ripple through the fabric of reality itself. The obelisk had been a prison, yes, but it was also a keystone, part of a network that, he suspected, or rather felt, spanned the entire globe. Its destruction had sent powerful shockwaves, and thus Zarah was beginning to stir.

Barash had since confirmed that the fall of one obelisk would not be the end. The Old Kings scattered their power across the land, binding it to places of ancient strength.

There were more prisons hidden in the most forgotten corners of Zarah, and each one held the potential to either save or doom the planet, all depending on how it was unsealed.

Aran was no longer simply a prince thrust into destiny, he was becoming something else. He felt it in the quiet moments when the world slowed and the voices of his ancestors crept in, a murmur just below the threshold of perception. They called to him, not as mere spirits, but as part of the larger pattern. A design that had been woven long before the time of his birth.

The day after they returned to the palace, from the Council of Qamar, Barash summoned Aran to a forgotten chamber deep within Sarim's bowels. It was a place few knew existed, hidden in the deeper levels beneath layers of history, dust, and stone.

As they descended the narrow staircase, torches flickering weakly against the darkness, Barash's voice was low and sombre.

"There is something you need to see here," the old warrior-scholar whispered, "something that has been kept from you, from most of us, for countless generations. However, before I show it to you, I must first beg your forgiveness for not having told you about this before." He hesitated. "I needed to be sure that you were ready to know this."

Aran had not pressed Barash since the events in the crypt. He had thus decided that his friend would speak when he was ready to do so. Barash's knowledge of the Old Kings and their ancient power was unparalleled, and though often cryptic, Aran had grown to trust him. When they reached the base of the stairs, the young warrior could feel the weight of history pressing down upon him, thick and suffocating.

The chamber they entered was vast, far larger than he had anticipated, its walls lined with carvings that seemed to pulse with an otherworldly energy.

The air here was cold, unnaturally so, and the torches barely illuminated the edges of the room, leaving much of it in flickering shadows. In the centre stood an altar, hewn from black stone, its surface etched with symbols that Aran did not immediately recognize, yet he instinctively feared them.

"What is this place?" he asked, looking around. His voice dampened by the oppressive energy in the air, came out barely more than a whisper.

Barash's demeanour changed as he moved toward the altar. His lined, tired face seemed weighed with knowledge, threatening to escape - as if he could no longer contain it.

Holding his charge's gaze, the old promise stirring in his chest, he spoke. "My boy, the time has come for you to hear the truth of it."

Aran looked taken aback, yet he remained silent - waiting.

"This is where the first ruler of your bloodline made his pact." It hurt Barash to utter these words, when all he wished was to spare the young man from this truth - just as Khalid, the boy's father had tried.

Aran's blood ran cold at the words. He stepped closer, his eyes tracing the intricate carvings that adorned the walls.

They depicted scenes from a time long before Zarah's written history. Figures of immense power, locked in battle with creatures that defied description. Above them all loomed a personage, cloaked in shadow, its hands outstretched as if to command the very forces of creation.

"This is the origin of your predecessors' legacy," Barash continued. "Your ancestors did not merely seize power. They were given it, though at a price. Passed onto them by forces far older and far more dangerous than the Old Kings."

Aran's eyes widened. "They were given this power? By whom?"

Barash turned to face him, his eyes dark with the weight of millennia of knowledge. "By the Primordial Ones. Forces of nature that existed before the world as we know it was shaped. When the Old Kings rose to power, they did so by sealing away these entities, binding them within the obelisks you have now begun to unearth." Aran's heart pounded, a cold, alien sensation coiling through his veins.

The Primordials - whispered in legend, dismissed as myth - had not only existed, but his bloodline had been bound to them. He felt it again, a presence lurking just beyond his senses, watching - waiting. His breath quickened. He was not just the heir of a throne - he was the heir of a debt unpaid. To think that his family had been tied to them was almost incomprehensible.

Barash gestured to the altar. "This is where your ancestors made their pact. They sought power to rival the Old Kings, and in their desperation, they turned to the Primordials. The obelisks were created not only as prisons for these entities but as conduits. Keys, Aran."

He gave the young man a nod, then continued, struggling to get the words out. "Your family, your bloodline, became the guardian of these prisons, but the price of that power became far greater than their ability to fully understand its consequences."

Aran felt the impact of Barash's words like they were physical blows. The realization that his ancestors had not merely fought the Old Kings, but had drawn upon the very forces that the Kings themselves had sought to suppress, filled him with a deep unease.

Is that what Drathis was after? Harness the power of the Primordials?

His mind reeled - how could anyone believe they could control such forces? The uncertainty of the same weakness coursing through his veins haunted him. "But why?" he asked, his voice hollow. "Why would they make such a pact?"

Barash's eyes softened, but his voice was still firm. "Because, lad, they believed it was the only way to survive. The Old Kings ruled with an iron fist, and their power was absolute - undisputed. Your ancestors saw no other path but to fight fire with fire. They bound themselves to the Primordials, not realizing that in doing so, they were binding the lives of their descendants along with theirs."

Aran took a step back, the enormity of it all sinking in. His family had not just been rulers. They had been part of something much larger, sinister, something far darker. The obelisks were no mere keys or prisons. They were also a part of the balance that held the world together.

As things stood, with one of them destroyed, that balance was bound to unravel.

With a heavy heart, Barash indicated the stairs. Both returned to the surface in silence. The older man relieved of a burden he carried for so long, entrusted by Aran's father, the younger man beginning to feel the pressure of its weight.

Later that night, unable to sleep, Aran found himself in the palace's vast library, its shelves filled with ancient tomes and scrolls that held the knowledge of generations. He thought he would find solace here, among the pages of history, but now the books seemed to mock him with their silence. Every word he read felt hollow, every line a reminder of the knowledge he still lacked. Knowledge that he was in dire need of.

As he scanned the shelves, his eyes fell on a single, weathered volume tucked away in a corner. Its spine was cracked, and the lettering faded beyond recognition. Nevertheless, something about it seemed to be calling to him, so he pulled it from the shelf with trembling hands. The book was very old, far older than anything else in the library. Its pages were brittle and yellowed with age. He opened it carefully, his breath catching as he saw the first page. The text was written in a language he did not recognize, but the symbols were familiar. They were the same as those carved in the deepest chambers of Sarim's Old Quarter, the stone gifted by Ashir, as well as those carved into the black altar Barash had shown him earlier that day - a sun symbol, with distorted rays.

"The Book of Weaving," a voice came from behind Aran. He turned to see Barash standing in the doorway, his expression unreadable.

"You know what this is?" Aran asked, holding up the old book.

Barash stepped forward, his eyes lingering on the tome. "I do," his voice was heavy, as if laboured. "It is one of the few surviving records of the Weavers. They were an ancient order that served the Primordials, in

Zarah's distant past. We are talking more than ten thousand years ago, Aran... It was them who shaped the world, who wove the threads of reality into what we know today," Barash looked at his charge. The young man seemed perplexed, unsure of how to respond.

"So the legend goes," the old man added, with a twinkle in his eyes. "They also used the services from an ancient order as old as time itself, so the records state," he locked eyes with Aran. "They were called the Wardens. From their distant sanctum called the Shadowed Vale, they worked in tandem with the Weavers, aiding in binding the Primordials and entwining the Weaving into its current configuration.

Aran frowned, flipping through the pages. Obelisks, Primordials, Weavers, Wardens? His mind was spiralling.

"My ancestors... were a part of this?!" he asked, overwhelmed. It was, after all, a hard tea to swallow.

"They played their part in it," Barash said, nodding. "However, you must understand that the Weavers and the Wardens were not just alchemists or scholars. They became the architects of reality, able to manipulate the very fabric of existence. When your ancestors made their pact, they bound themselves to the Weavers' legacy. That is why the obelisks are so important. They are not just prisons, or keys, they are also anchors, holding the weave of reality together."

Aran stared at the ancient text, fingers tracing the unfamiliar symbols. How could simple structures, no matter how ancient, hold such profound significance? The idea that physical objects could anchor reality itself seemed beyond comprehension, yet something within him - perhaps the same blood that connected him to his ancestors - whispered in his heart that Barash spoke truth.

Aran's mind whirred as he tried to process this new information. "So," he began, hesitantly, "when I destroyed the obelisk, I was not just releasing the power within it. I was also unravelling part of the world?" He could not believe it. Who, in their right mind, would?

How could these old tales be true? He asked himself, struggling with such a concept. It all felt like a bad dream, a nightmare he was unable to wake up from. Yet, in the back of his mind, his recurring dreams about the future came forth - weren't they a reminder of the veracity of it all?

Barash nodded gravely, confirming his dread. "Yes, my boy. That is why destroying the obelisks is so dangerous. Each one is tied to a different aspect of the world - things like time, space, life, and death. There may be more connections we do not yet know. To destroy them is to risk unravelling the very threads that hold existence together."

Aran closed the book slowly, his hands trembling, questions bursting out of him before he could mould them. "Then why, in Zarah's name, did you let me destroy one? What am I supposed to do, Barash? If the obelisks can not be destroyed, yet they are also a threat, then what is the solution?"

The old man's gaze was steady. Aran was ready, he thought. "I told you to destroy it, because otherwise that power would end up in the hands of the House of Draco. Can you imagine if that happened?" Aran didn't have to. He knew very well just how dangerous the Draconians could be, let alone if they managed to take control of such a fundamental power.

Barash exhaled deeply. "Destruction is easy, Aran, nurturing is hard. Any fool can break a thread, but not all can create one. The Weavers understood something greater - mending the fabric of existence requires mastery. If you do not learn this, every obelisk you break will unravel reality itself." He sighed. "You must not just fight the Weaving, you must learn to wield it."

There was a long pause, as if time itself were testing its elasticity.

"Do you mean to tell me," Aran asked, half amused, half dumbfounded, "that you know the art of the weave?"

The revelation still struck him like a physical blow. Barash - his mentor, his friend - had possessed such profound knowledge all this time? Had watched him struggle without revealing this crucial piece of information?

For a moment, anger flared within him, though it was quickly replaced by a dawning realization that Barash's secrets likely ran deeper still. "By the gods," Aran whispered, "is there anything about you that is not hidden behind layers of mystery?"

Aran shook his head in disbelief. "I swear, Barash, this is the last time you will ever surprise me." The warrior, scholar, weaver, and what else, Aran wondered, was a never ending source of amazement.

"Yes," Barash's reply came swiftly, "and I will teach it to you." There was a fire burning in the old man's eyes, kindled by an old promise.

"Wait," Aran fired back. "If you can use the art of the weave, then why did you not stop Drathis and mend the obelisk yourself? Why tell me to destroy it instead?"

Barash took a moment of silence, allowing Aran time to quiet himself. "Because, my boy, there is a difference between knowing the theory and being strong enough to wield such dangerous power." Understanding dawned on Aran's face. "It must be you," Barash explained. "If I had tried to mend the Weaving, Drathis would have won. You were untrained so, under the circumstances, I made the call based on the power of your bloodline. Remember, lad, you are the last of a long line of guardians. Their abilities flow in your blood."

Aran's mind was spinning, struggling, he desperately needed time to process everything Barash had told him.

"I understand the gravity of what you are telling me," he turned fully, facing his father's friend, "and I promise that I will learn what you have to teach. However, if we are to do this, I must rest and so should you. I bid you a goodnight, my friend." He bowed, in respect.

Barash did not say a word. Before turning to leave, he looked his young student in the eyes. Was it his imagination, or did Aran see a flicker of admiration in his teacher's face? It had only lasted for a second, yet he was sure he had seen it.

The days that followed their conversation became a blur of study and training. Barash guided Aran through the ancient texts, teaching him the ways of the Weavers. It was not magic or science in the traditional sense. Yet, with time and study, it revealed itself to be something far more profound than both, a manipulation of the fundamental forces that governed reality.

Indeed, Barash was proving himself to be a box of surprises. "Well, no surprise there." Aran laughed to himself.

With his tutor's guidance, he learned to see the world not as a fixed place but as a tapestry of endless possibilities, each thread representing a different path, a different outcome. However, with this new knowledge came a heavy realization. The more he learned, the more Aran realized not only how little he knew, but also just how precarious the world's balance truly was.

The obelisks were not simply objects of power. They were keystones in the grand design of existence. To destroy them was to risk tearing apart the very fabric of reality, but to leave them intact meant leaving the Primordials' power unchecked.

It was a delicate dance, and Aran found himself walking a razor's edge.

His ancestors had made their choices, but now it was up to him to decide the future. Would he continue down the path of destruction, or would he find a way to restore the balance?

"I believed my path in life, despite its difficulty, was clear, that my destiny was transparent to me. To unify the tribes and kingdoms of Zarah. To ensure peace and prosperity for every man, woman, and child on the planet. Little did I know then," he paused, weighing his thoughts. "Yet, the more I learn now, the more I realise how much more there is still to know." Like waking from a dream, Aran was taken aback by the sound of his unconscious words reverberating in the empty chambers of his quarters.

As the days slowly turned into weeks, and those began turning into months, he began to feel the weight of his ancestors' legacy more acutely than ever before. His own heritage would not just be a mere ruling dynasty, it would be a key player in the fate of Zarah. Every decision he made, every step he took, would reverberate throughout history, shaping the course of the future. He had to free Zarah from war. There was no other choice, it was either that or he would die trying.

With the passage of time, in the back of his mind, the whispers of the Primordials grew louder, their presence a constant reminder of the power that lay just beyond his grasp. They were watching, waiting, and though Aran did not know what they wanted, he knew one thing for certain. The tapestry of his life was far from finished, and the threads that had been woven long ago were only now beginning to reveal their true pattern.

"Destiny, indeed." he thought to himself. The shield of humour, as always, patrolling the edges of his mind.

As a warm autumn gave way to a mild winter and then to the scorching heat of spring, Aran's plans began to take tangible form. Months of careful diplomacy culminated at the latest Council of the Tribes in Qamaria, where Aran formally ordered the construction of the King's Road. This construction was a monumental task, requiring cooperation from every tribe. That way, Aran was ensuring the tribes' cooperation while he dealt with the greater problems that loomed on the horizon.

The Shamari provided the engineering expertise, designing aqueducts and bridges to traverse the harshest terrains. The Bahir supplied labour and protection, their warriors guarding the work crews from sandstorms and the occasional creature attacks.

The Tarek, Aran's tribe, with their deep knowledge of the desert, charted the safest and most efficient paths, while the Ulema ensured the supply lines remained uninterrupted by utilizing their extensive trade networks.

Despite the collaboration, tensions often flared. Bahir warriors clashed with Shamari engineers over perceived slights, Tarek guides argued with Rasha merchants over the best routes. Aran, Sura and Rafiq, moved tirelessly between camps, mediating disputes, whilst reminding everyone of their shared goal.

One evening, many months later, as the road neared completion, Aran stood atop a rocky outcrop, gazing at the progress. The road stretched like a ribbon of hope across the dunes and rocky plains, connecting villages and oases that had once seemed impossibly distant. Sura joined him, her voice soft, her scent intoxicating to him. "We have done well. It is beautiful, Aran." Suddenly, a shadow came over her face. "Do you think it will be enough to hold us together?"

His gaze remained fixed on the horizon, trying to stay focused. "It is a start. Unity is not built overnight, Sura, but this road will remind them that we are stronger together. Despite how hard the future might look."

While Aran worked to unite the tribes of Zarah, and learn the secrets of the Weaving, darkness gathered elsewhere.

In the shadowed halls of the temple of Nathair, located in the southern mountain ranges of Zarah, Drathis and his advisors were reviewing reports of Aran's progress. His elongated snout curled into a sinister smile as he addressed his subordinates, with a cold, reptilian gaze.

"The tribes are rallying behind this so-called unifier, Aran ibn khalid," he hissed. "Still, unity is a fragile thing. All it takes is a single crack to shatter it. Aran took the bait with the obelisks, unbeknownst to him, giving birth to a chain of events with unpredictable consequences for his people. Now we must complete the job, on other fronts."

Drathis was enjoying the moment. This was, after all, his favourite part of the game. The planning, the plotting, the anticipation, and then the strike. The kill. The conquest. It was exhilarating.

His plan was as insidious as it was effective. He did not just send his agents - he walked among the tribes himself, his form shifting with ease, whispering poison into the ears of chieftains. A stolen shipment here, a fabricated insult there - trust unravelled like fraying cloth. Aran's dream of unity was fragile. All Drathis had to do was pull the right thread, and it would all come undone. They sabotaged segments of the King's Road, blaming rival tribes for the destruction. In one instance, they planted evidence suggesting the Rasha had stolen supplies meant for the Shamari, nearly sparking a violent conflict.

Aran's network of spies, led by Sura, uncovered the truth, but the damage had been done. Rebuilding trust took time, and the delays threatened to derail the project. Yet, Aran refused to give up. "Every setback in life is a potential lesson in disguise," he told his friends and advisors. "Therefore, every lesson brings us closer to understanding how to best overcome adversity."

Regardless of setbacks, Aran made sure that the King's Road was completed, and its inauguration was marked by a grand ceremony at the Great Oasis of Qamar. Delegates from every tribe gathered to witness the lighting of the Unity Torch, a flame carried along the length of the road by riders from each tribe, mounted on black desert steeds.

As the torch reached its final destination, Aran stood before the gathered crowd, his voice carrying over the murmuring wind. "This road is not just a path through the desert. It is a promise. One that we will stand together against all who seek to divide us. Let this flame burn as a symbol of our unity, our strength, and our future."

The crowd erupted into cheers, their voices echoing across the sands. For the first time in generations, the people of Zarah felt a spark of hope that their fractured world could truly become whole. "The bigger irony being, there are forces from outside of our world that seek to unravel it from within." Aran murmured to himself.

It was almost poetic. They had built a road to unite Zarah, yet unseen hands still pulled at its seams. Even now, something stirred beyond the horizon - watching. Waiting. And when it came, the desert itself might not be enough to stop it.

Chapter XI

The Eclipse of Kings

Beneath the cold stone of Sarim's palace, in the shadowed corners where the light of the world above barely reached, Aran could feel the weight of ages pressing down on him. The histories of his ancestors, once distant tales of valour and power, were now revealed to be far more tangled, far more dangerous than he had ever imagined. They were not merely stories of kings and battles. They were the threads and tethers that bound his bloodline to the fate of Zarah.
Several months had passed since Aran first laid eyes on the Book of Weaving. Since that day, he had spent as much time as he could poring over it. The knowledge contained within its brittle pages had opened a new door to his understanding of reality.
Yet with each revelation, the future seemed more uncertain, the path ahead more treacherous.
He had begun his new studies under Barash with a hunger to learn, to understand the 'magic', for lack of a better word, that had been hidden from him for so long. Now, as the enormity of what he was learning unfolded before him, he wondered if any mortal being should possess such knowledge. How could anyone hold such power and not be corrupted by it?
The Weavers, the Wardens, those ancient people who had once shaped reality, had left behind more than mere relics and forgotten lore. They had left a power that could bend the world, reshape it according to their will. In their absence, that power had been claimed by the kings and queens of old. However, it was not a gift but a responsibility, a burden that grew heavier with each generation.
Aran, standing now at the fulcrum of Zarah's history, knew that he could no longer simply follow the path of his forebears. He would have to carve a new way forward, one that balanced the ancient forces vying for dominance. First, in order to do so, there was another mystery to unravel. The Primordials.

He was standing before the great window of the palace's Hall of Kings, staring out over Sarim's skyline. It was late, and the city was bathed in the dim, silver light of the twin moons, their reflections broken by the rippling waters of the Elara river that wound through the city. Aran's thoughts lingered on the events of the months passed. The obelisk's destruction, the dark revelations about his ancestors, the Draco, and now, the looming presence of the Primordial Ones.

Barash had spoken of them with reverence and fear. These beings, said to be older than time itself, had once walked this world, shaping it to their whims before the Old Kings, said to have come from the stars, had risen to challenge them.

The Old Kings, being weavers themselves, had been powerful, but they had not simply cast down the Primordials. They had sealed them away, tethering them to the obelisks that Aran's ancestors had been entrusted to guard. Now, with the destruction of the first obelisk, he had unknowingly begun to unbind those chains.

But why? He couldn't help but ask himself. Why had his ancestors entered into a pact with such beings?

Was it a mere ambition that drove them, or was there something more? Aran could not shake the feeling that there was a deeper truth hidden beneath the layers of history, a truth that had been deliberately obscured.

He turned as the doors to the hall creaked open, and Barash entered, his face lined with exhaustion but his eyes sharp with purpose. His father's old friend, a warrior turned scholar, and now, once more, his tutor, had aged in recent times. The weight of the secrets they had uncovered bearing down on him as much as it did on his student.

"You called for me, my prince?" Barash asked, his voice low and respectful, his face serious, but there was always a twinkle in his eye.

Aran nodded, gesturing for Barash to join him at the window. For a moment, they stood in silence, gazing out at the city that lay sprawled beneath them.

"Tell me, Barash," Aran said finally, his voice heavy with the gravity of his thoughts. "You told me that you have studied the Primordials for most of your life. Do you believe they can be controlled?"

Barash hesitated, his brow furrowing. "Control, my lad, is a dangerous illusion to play with when it comes to beings as old and powerful as they are," he was absent-mindedly playing with a dagger between his fingers with astonishing dexterity. "The Primordials are not like the gods of our faith, who act with purpose or favour toward mortals. They are forces of nature. Chaotic, unyielding, and remain indifferent to the lives of mortals. To think anyone could control them would be akin to trying to command the Yaran tides or the desert winds. We might be able to navigate their power in order to influence them. But control them? No, I do not believe that is achievable." Barash's voice cracked as if it had reached the boundaries of the Weaving.

Aran's next question seemed only logical to him. "Then why did my ancestors enter into such a pact with them? Surely, they were aware of the risks."

Barash sighed, his expression hardened. "First, you must understand that your ancestors were desperate. During Zarah's First Age, before the rise of your bloodline, the Old Kings held dominion over the world with a grip that could not be broken by mortal means. The pact with the Primordials gave your forebears a power that could rival that of the Old Kings," he exhaled. "As you know by now, it came with a terrible price."

"And we are the ones paying that cost, but with interest." Aran muttered, almost imperceptibly.

Barash nodded, as he flipped the dagger. "Yes, but it is a debt we do not yet fully understand," he held the dagger still. "The obelisks are but one part of the equation. There is more. Something that is hidden, even from the texts I have studied. The Primordials did not merely seek to return to the world; they were bound to it by a purpose. A purpose we have yet to uncover."

Aran frowned, his thoughts turning over Barash's words. There was something elusive about the Primordials that gnawed at him, something that felt both alien and yet strangely familiar.

For a fleeting moment, something stirred in the silence. A whisper - no, he thought, not a sound, but a vibration, a hum just beneath his skin. It was ancient, patient, but it was not passive. It was watching him. Waiting...

The presence of the Primordials coiled through the air like an unseen predator, pressing against his thoughts. Not malevolent. Not benevolent. Something worse - indifferent. "We need to know more," Aran said, his voice firm. "I cannot afford to walk blindly into this - there is too much at stake. If the Primordials are half as dangerous as you say, then we must understand what they want."

Barash nodded again, but there was a hesitation in his gaze. "There may be a fast way to achieve this, my prince, but it is not without peril."

Aran turned to him, his curiosity piqued. "What do you mean, my friend? Please, speak plainly."

The old man hesitated for a moment, as though weighing whether to share what he knew. "There is a place," he said slowly, "a place that predates even the Weavers. It is said to be where the Primordials once walked freely, a place where their power still lingers. If you truly wish to understand them, you must venture there, my lad. But beware, Aran, for it is not a place for the faint of heart. It is one of the few realms on Zarah where the boundaries between our world and the Weaving are thin, where reality itself can be bent and twisted."

Aran felt a chill run down his spine, but he was not about to falter now. "Where is this place? How do I find it?"

Barash's eyes darkened. "In the old texts, it is called the Echo of Worlds. A land long forgotten, resting beyond the borders of any known kingdom of men. Few who have ventured there have returned, and the very few who have entered returned forever changed." He was observing the candle light, casting shadows around them, whilst spinning his dagger. "Your father tried…" Barash swallowed hard, his fingers still spinning the dagger between them. Too sharp, too fast. Aran caught the way Barash's hand stiffened when the blade cut his skin. The old warrior did not flinch - but he did not meet the young man's gaze either.

"My father tried what?" Aran asked, expectantly.

Barash inhaled, slowed and measured. "Nothing," he said too quickly, sheathing the blade. "I just recalled something he used to say about the difference between knowledge and wisdom."

He knew instantly that Barash was withholding something from him. Something huge. But why?

He studied the old man, but Barash remained silent. Bidding his pupil goodnight, he retired to his chambers.

Aran spent the night awake, pacing his quarters. What his tutor had proposed was a journey steeped in uncertainty, and the mysteries surrounding it continued to mount without relent. After many hours of careful thought, he resolved that, before he departed for the Echo of Worlds - should their venture falter - it would be best to establish a new ruling body in Sarim, one he trusted to govern justly in his absence.

At the heart of his vision for the unification of Zarah was the creation of a permanent Council of Tribes, sometimes also called families or clans. It would be a governing body where representatives from each major tribe could voice their concerns and guide the kingdom's direction in his absence. The council convened in the Lunar Citadel of Sarim, chosen for its central location and symbolic ties to Anar and Nysa, the moons that united Zarah's spiritual beliefs.

The council chamber was a circular hall, its walls adorned with carvings of the desert's flora and fauna - symbols drawn from each of the great tribes. Aran had commissioned its design with care, intending it to be more than a place of governance. It was to be a sanctuary of unity, a reflection of what bound them together rather than what kept them apart. Moonleaf wood pillars, sacred to the Rasha and known for their silver sheen beneath moonlight, supported a domed ceiling etched with the constellations visible from every corner of Zarah - a silent reminder to all who sat there of their shared place beneath the stars.

Each tribe contributed a representative. From the Black Dunes of Arsian country came Kasim al-Bahir, a grizzled warrior whose blunt demeanour masked a sharp tactical mind. The Shamari sent Karim al-Shamar, an old acquaintance of Aran's father and a master engineer whose innovations had revolutionized solar technology.

The Rasha were represented by Safira, the Moon Seer of Sarim, whose visions often provided guidance in moments of doubt.

The Tarek contributed with Zahira, Aran's cousin and former priestess-warrior to the Rasha, who had become a voice for justice and wisdom, in recent times. Finally, the Ulema tribe chose to send Amir al-Ulema, a trader whose knowledge of Zarah's oases was unmatched.

"Much like my father's." Aran thought to himself.

At the council's first meeting, he stood at the centre, flanked by Sura and Rafiq, while Barash sat a short distance behind them, silent and watchful, the faint curl of smoke rising from his nafas'tal bone-pipe as he observed his pupil step into the fullness of his destiny.

"This council is not merely a gathering of tribes or clans," Aran began. "It is the heart of our new kingdom. Here, we will decide our path together, as equals. No tribe's voice will be greater than another's, for our strength lies in our unity."

Kasim's stare was sharp as a blade, as honed as his sword arm. "Unity is an easy promise to make, Aran. Nevertheless, unity alone is not what wins wars. Strength does." Murmurs of agreement rippled through the chamber.

Before her cousin could respond, Zahira smoothly interjected, her voice carrying the perfect blend of deference and authority that had made her such an effective diplomat.

Sitting in the shadows, Barash smiled, his eyes twinkling.

"Strength indeed, noble Kasim," she acknowledged with a respectful inclination of her head. "Still, I ask you, where is strength found if not in unity? The Bahir sword arm is mighty indeed," she continued, gesturing to the tribal sigil on the table, "but even the fiercest warrior must, without fail, eventually sleep. It is when the Shamari stand watch while the Bahir warriors rest, when the Rasha healers tend Bahir wounds, when Ulema caravans bring supplies to Bahir outposts - that is when our true, united, strength emerges in earnest."

She turned to include the entire council with her gaze, her former training as a Rasha priestess evident in her commanding presence. "Divided, we are but isolated fingers that can be easily broken one by one. United," she closed her hand into a fist, "we become the weapon that cannot be shattered."

Several council members nodded thoughtfully. Even Kasim al-Bahir's stern expression softened slightly, grudging respect in his eyes. Aran caught Zahira's gaze, giving her a silent nod, grateful for her help redirecting the council's energy.

Kasim pressed on. "Point taken," he acquiesced, with a nod to Zahira. "However, the House of Draco plays their hand, yet we sit here, speaking of alliances while the enemy sharpens their blades. If they are the ones behind this unravelling of our world, then we are in dire need of action, not words. What do you intend to do?"

Finally, there it was, Aran thought. "Their fears are out in the open now." He stood steady, his gaze unwavering. He needed to be strong for his people - still, he chose honesty. "I do not know," he kept his voice firm, despite the doubts crawling through his thoughts.

"It makes no difference where the danger comes from," his words commanded authority now. "We shall decide together how to defend Zarah. More important than that, we will ensure that the desert's future is shaped by its people - not by outsiders. Regardless of where they come from, be it this world or some otherworldly place." There was a general murmur of appreciation for his words. "What matters is that we remain united," he emphasized. "Working as one people, together. Trust in me, for I will not fail you. But, above anything else, you must trust and not fail yourselves." Barash's eyes twinkled.

Nods of approval spread throughout the room. After that, minor issues were discussed, and the council members turned to state affairs, such as caravan routes, commerce, and the interchange of technologies among the various tribes.

In the weeks that followed, Aran watched with quiet satisfaction as the council's work bore fruit. At the western oasis, Shamari engineers worked alongside Rasha farmers, installing their solar-powered irrigation systems. "The yield will triple by next harvest," Karim had promised, his eyes alight with the possibilities of collaboration.

Meanwhile, in the training grounds outside Sarim, Bahir warriors drilled young men from all six tribes in their battle formations. "Strike as one!" Kasim's voice boomed across the sands. "When your brother falls, you stand in his place - no matter what tribe's colours he wears!"

By night, around council fires, Ulema water-finders shared their secrets with Tarek guides, mapping new routes between oases that had once been jealously guarded by tribal knowledge. These exchanges strengthened not only Zarah's infrastructure but also wove the first threads of a shared identity among people who had for generations seen each other as rivals.

"They begin to see themselves as Zarahans first, tribespeople second," Sura observed one evening, watching the mingling of colours and customs in the marketplace. Aran nodded, though he knew their unity remained fragile - vulnerable to those who thrived on division. "Let us hope our journey to the Echo does not change that." Aran said to Rafiq, as the three walked the streets of Sarim, under the twin moonlight.

Far beyond Yaran country, where Aran was, inside the ancient temple of Nathair, a lone figure stood before an ancient mirror of blackened glass. Drathis traced his clawed fingers across its surface, watching the faint, shifting images within. The Council of Tribes. The rise of Aran ibn Khalid. The Weaving, trembling with something it had not known in aeons. A cruel smile played on his snout. "You think yourself the unifier of Zarah, Aran?" he murmured. "You think you understand the game?" The mirror darkened, the images vanishing into oblivion. Drathis turned, stepping into the swirling mist of the chamber. "So be it," he whispered. "Let us see how long your unity lasts while the Weaving is torn apart before your eyes - thread by thread.

It took weeks for Aran to prepare for the perilous journey before him, and even longer to gather the courage to embark on it. Neither himself nor his friends had been out of Sarim in months, and he feared that what lay ahead was far more dangerous than any battlefield they had ever walked into. The Echo of Worlds, as Barash had described it, was a place that defied understanding. A landscape shaped not by nature but by the very forces of creation and destruction that the Primordials commanded.

He chose a small group of trusted warriors to accompany him, each one skilled and loyal to him and his cause. Sura was at his side as always, her warm, silent, presence a comfort in these uncertain times. Along with her was Rafiq, the seasoned Bahir warrior who had fought beside Aran for many years.

Barash accompanied him as well, but he asked Zahira to step back on this one, fearing for her safety. "You are a politician now, cousin. Words are your weapons. Use them well. Keep our kingdom safe and united." He squeezed her hands in his. Zahira made no effort in hiding her emotions. She held his face, kissed him tenderly on the forehead and bid them farewell.

Their journey took them far from the familiar lands of Sarim, across the deserts of the south-eastern territories and into the mountains, beyond where the future kingdom of Kartal would one day be founded.

With each step, the world around them twisted. The air crackled, charged with an unseen force, as if reality itself resisted their presence.

The sky flickered - deep purple one moment, then a golden hue so bright it burned Aran's eyes. The ground kept pulsing beneath their feet, alive, whispering of something ancient waiting in the depths.

The road to the Echo proved to be treacherous, filled with dangers both natural and unnatural. Since the shattering of the first obelisk, strange creatures, twisted by the Primordials' lingering presence, started to roam the wilds, their eyes glowing with a sickly light.

The ground itself seemed to pulse beneath their feet, as though it were alive, breathing in tandem with some ancient, unseen force.

On the seventh day, they reached the edge of the Echo. It was like nothing Aran had ever seen.

The air itself tasted different here - metallic and sweet simultaneously, like breathing liquid starlight. A constant thrumming emanated from the ground, not heard but felt, vibrating through his bones as if the earth were trying to speak in a language older than words.

The sky above was torn, fractured in places where the fabric of reality seemed to unravel, revealing glimpses of stars and distant galaxies. Things he could not comprehend.

The ground beneath their feet shifted as they walked, sometimes solid, sometimes malleable. The colours of the landscape constantly shifted from green to blue to red in a way that made Aran's head spin.

"This is it," Barash whispered, his voice barely audible over the hum around them. "We have arrived at The Echo of Worlds."

Aran stared out at the landscape, a sense of awe and dread washing over him. Here, in this place where the Primordials' power still lingered, he could feel the weight of their presence. It was a force that pressed down on him, heavy and oppressive, but it was also seductive. Calling to him in a way that made his heart race.

"What now?" Rafiq asked, his voice tense. The stout warrior had always been fearless, but even he seemed unnerved by the unnatural beauty of the Echo.

"We go deeper," Aran said, looking at Barash, his voice steady despite the fear gnawing at him. "There's something here we need to find." His tutor nodded. Rafiq's face, on the other hand, was a combination of fear and wonder.

"There is something I need to know. Something I need to learn." Aran whispered to himself, exchanging another glance with Barash.

As they ventured deeper into the Echo, the land grew increasingly alien and distorted. Time itself seemed to bend and twist around them. One moment, the sun hung low in the sky, casting long shadows across the ground, and the next, it was high above, blinding in its intensity.

The air was thick with the scent of ozone, and every step they took echoed unnaturally, as though they were walking on hollow ground.

Rafiq's weathered face had grown pale, his usual jovial manner quickly replaced by a tense alertness that spoke of battles fought against enemies that could not be cut with steel. Sura moved closer to Aran's side, not merely out of fear but also from an instinct that whispered of protective duty - though what she might protect him from in this place of twisted reality, she could not say.

Even Barash, for all his knowledge of the ancient mysteries, seemed diminished here, his confident bearing replaced by the careful steps of one walking through a predator's domain.

Aran's skin prickled with phantom sensations - for a second he felt submerged in warm Shamari waters, the next exposed to Qamaria's winds that left no trace of frost. Sounds seemed to arrive before their sources, sometimes without them: the cry of a Nightwing avian that flew past moments later, or the splash of water from a stream they never crossed. It felt like there was nothing separating them from the chasm underneath them, besides a thin layer of terra firma.

Suddenly, without warning, they found it - what Barash called "The Heart of the Echo."

It was a vast, circular clearing that seemed to breathe with an ancient, primordial energy. Towering monoliths of obsidian-black stone rose around the perimeter like silent sentinels, their surfaces etched with intricate, swirling patterns that seemed to shift and move when viewed from the corner of one's eye. Each stone stood as a guardian of some forgotten ritual, their bases rooted deep into the ground that trembled with barely contained power.

At the centre of this impossible space lay a pool of liquid that defied natural understanding - its surface a living canvas of shimmering light that moved not like water, but like liquid starlight. Each breath carried whispers of words in languages that predated speech itself, pressing against their minds like half-remembered dreams.

The iridescent surface rippled with colours that Aran had no names for, bleeding, as best he could describe them, from deep violet to a blue so intense it hurt to look at, then dissolving into vivid shades that existed between perception and dream.

The pool sang - not with voice but with pure resonance that made Aran's teeth ache and his eyes water. Its song smelled of steel and flowers, of lightning and decay. Each note pressed against his chest like a physical thing, trying to synchronize with his heartbeat, to pull him into its ancient rhythm.

He felt the pool's power as a physical entity - a presence that pressed against his skin, that wound through his veins like liquid memory. Each pulse matched the rhythm of his heart, but not in harmony - in challenge. As if the very essence of this almost intangible place was testing him, measuring his resolve, demanding to know if he was worthy of standing within its ancient bounds.

Aran's breath caught in his throat. This was more than a place. This was a moment of reckoning.

"This is it," Barash said quietly, turning to him, his voice filled with awe. "The place where the Primordials once walked."

Aran stepped forward, his eyes fixed on the pool. He could feel the pull of it, the power that lay within. It was a potential unlike anything he had ever felt before. Raw, untamed, and ancient beyond the comprehension bestowed upon his mortal coil.

For a moment, he hesitated, for he knew that once he touched the power of the Primordials, there would be no turning back. The path ahead was uncertain, fraught with danger, but it was also the only way forward. The only way to understand what his ancestors had done, and to find a way to either stop the Primordials or harness their power. Either way, he needed to do it. He had to protect his people.

The group remained silent as if frozen in place. They hung on every movement of their leader. While reality swirled and swayed around them, the whole group was still - including Aran.

"This is it," he thought, gripping his father's sword hilt, sweat trickling down his back. "After this, there is no turning back." He took one last look at Barash.

The old warrior's face was impassive, but his eyes were locked with his, as if he could guess what his charge was thinking and feeling. Aran's mind was whirring, weighing the consequences.

On the other hand, they had not come this far to turn back now.

With a deep breath, he reached out, his fingers brushing the surface of the pool. The moment he touched it, everything changed.

The world around him dissolved, the landscape of the Echo falling away as he was plunged into a vision.

This was nothing like the visions he experienced, in his recurring dreams. It was much more potent and intense than that. Without any filter, he saw his ancestors - old rulers, standing before the Primordials, their faces filled with both fear and determination.

He witnessed the forging of the pact, the sealing of the obelisks, as well as the beginning of the cycle that had endured for the last ten millennia.

Overwhelming as that was to experience, there was more. He felt in his core the truth behind the pact his forefathers had struck, the hidden cost that his ancestors had been willing to pay.

He was also given a glimpse into a possible future. One where the Primordials returned to his world, their unbridled power unleashed and the very fabric of reality torn apart. However, as far as he could perceive, there was a missing thread in the equation - Kael Drathis.

For all his ambition, he appeared to be an outsider in this celestial game. Aran saw no tether binding the Draconian warlord to the Weaving - only his hunger to exploit its unravelling. The Primordials had rejected Drathis, forcing him to play at power rather than truly wield it.

Then why? He asked himself. Why had Drathis manipulated him into shattering the first obelisk? Had Aran, in destroying it, set something in motion Drathis could not? A chilling thought gripped him.

What if Drathis didn't want control of the Weaving? What if he merely wanted Aran to be the one to destroy it? These were some of the questions, swirling in his mind while the revelations unfolded before him. Questions he would later have to carefully ponder on.

When the visions subsided, Aran staggered back, his heart pounding in his chest. Its steady, though quickened beat reverberating in his ears. He finally understood that the pact his forebears forged with the Primordials had not been made out of desperation. The cold irony was, it had been struck out of naive hope.

His ancestors had believed that by binding the Primordials, they could eventually learn to control them, to harness their power for the good of the world. "How wrong they had been."

Aran wondered if, his own dream, his vision for Zarah, would one day bring peace for its peoples, or would it instead bring about more chaos. With each passing second, one thing was becoming clearer and certain to him. Barash was right - the Primordials could not be controlled.

No matter how he looked at it, he could not understand how the Old Kings, or the Weavers, believed they could ever achieve such a thing. These were powerful forces of nature that, if ever unleashed, would bring about the end of all things, unbound and unstoppable.

Aran stood there, breathing heavily, his mind racing. He had seen the truth, but he had also been given a glimpse of the future. The choice before him was clear as fresh water. Either he continued down the path his ancestors had set, or he could find a way to break the cycle and prevent the return of the Primordials.

This was a choice that would define not only the future of his lineage, but the future of the world as well. The future of Zarah itself. What would his legacy be? One of freedom or imprisonment?

Aran, standing at the heart of the Echo, knew that the weight of that choice would haunt him for the rest of his life. He also knew deep down, as it always had been, that choices are an illusion. Regardless of what needed to be done, he would see it through. Even if doing so meant forfeiting his life.

That night, in his tent, Aran sat before his father's sword, the visions still burning behind his eyes. The pool's otherworldly song echoed in his memory, and he found himself tracing patterns in the air - movements that felt both foreign and achingly familiar. When Sura brought him his evening meal, she paused at the threshold. "You are different," she said simply. "I know," he replied, not turning from the blade's reflection. "I just hope I am still the man you believed in."

The journey back to Sarim passed in contemplative silence, each member of the expedition carrying the weight of what they had witnessed. As the familiar towers of the city appeared on the horizon, Aran felt both relief and renewed purpose. His visions in the Echo had changed him, but they had also given him clarity. The time had come to build what his ancestors could not - a kingdom united not by fear or force, but by choice and common cause.

During their second night's camp, as the twin moons cast their silver light across the desert, Aran found himself unable to sleep. The visions from the Echo lingered not as memories but as living presences in his mind. He noticed how differently his companions regarded him now - Sura's glances carried a new wariness, as though she sensed the change the Primordial pool had wrought in him. Even Barash seemed to study his student with fresh eyes, searching for signs of what the ancient power might have awakened.

When Aran raised his hand to gesture toward their water supplies, he saw his own fingers shimmer faintly in the moonlight, as though the Echo's otherworldly energy still clung to his skin. The sensation was neither pleasant nor painful - simply alien, a reminder that he was no longer quite the same man who had entered the Echo of Worlds.

In the depths of the temple of Nathair, Kael Drathis paced like a caged predator, his fingers trailing along cold stone walls etched with ancient Draconic bloodlines and forgotten conquests. The reports of Aran's progress were more than mere information - they were a poison spreading through his carefully constructed plans. "Unity," he scoffed. The word itself was a mockery. He had spent decades cultivating division, playing tribes against each other like pieces on a fractured game board. Now this upstart, this dreamer Aran, believed he could undo generations of carefully woven conflict with mere words and empty promises.

Drathis breath came in ragged bursts, a mixture of rage and something deeper - a primal fear that this young leader might actually succeed where others had failed. The tribes of Zarah had been his to manipulate, his to control. Each fracture, each betrayal, each subtle manipulation had been a stroke of his grand design. Now, this single man threatened to unravel everything.

"Dispatch the Shadow Hand," Drathis snarled, his voice a blade of pure malevolence. The temple's shadows seemed to coil around him, responding to his fury. "We will show Aran that unity is a fleeting illusion. Let us see how he deals with the Primordials while, politically, his vision for a united Zarah crumbles around him."

His lieutenant, Vhaskar, watched in silence, knowing better than to interrupt. Drathis seemed beyond reason now - a strategist consumed by the very obsession that had driven his ambitions. He would not merely defeat Aran. He would utterly destroy everything the young leader represented. The dream of unity would be crushed so completely that no one would dare imagine such a possibility again.

Yet beneath his fury, something else stirred - not regret, but a hunter's recognition of worthy prey.

Aran's methods, his careful balance of strength and mercy, represented everything Drathis had been bred to despise and destroy. The young leader's very existence was an affront to the natural order - the strong should dominate, not coddle the weak with unity and hope. This made Aran not just an enemy, but a philosophical abomination that needed to be crushed utterly. The Primordials would be Drathis' ultimate weapon, and the boy-dreamer would be the instrument of his own destruction.

The Shadow Hand infiltrated the towns and settlements, targeting key infrastructure projects like the King's Road and irrigation systems. They set fire to supply depots and spread false rumours of betrayal between the tribes. In one village near the Bahir border, they incited a revolt by claiming the Shamari had withheld vital water supplies.

Aran and the council acted swiftly to quell the unrest. Safira's moon visions revealed Drathis' hand in the chaos, and Rafiq led a contingent of warriors to uncover and neutralize the operatives. Despite the council's best efforts, the damage was done. Their chambers grew heated, arguments teetering on the edge of violence. Kasim al-Bahir slammed his fist against the table. "You expect us to believe this was all Draco trickery?" he looked furious. "Then why did Shamari warriors march on Bahir farmlands? Why were Rasha merchants caught hoarding grain?" The council could not provide a satisfactory answer.

Drathis' shapeshifting agents were doing their job, and Aran felt the foundation of unity cracking beneath him. The Shadow Hand had done more than sabotage buildings. They had planted the seeds of doubt, and those had proven themselves, time and time again, more dangerous than any sword could ever be.

Having returned to Sarim from an unsuccessful excursion to find another obelisk, Aran was present during one such antagonistic council session. When addressing the tribal leaders, his voice was firm but calm, though Zahira noticed something had changed in her cousin's bearing - a stillness that seemed to hold depths she had never perceived before, as though he carried within him distant echoes of places beyond mortal understanding. Aran's words washed over those assembled.
"The Draco seek to divide us because they fear what we can become. Do not commit the sin of forgetting that they thrive on chaos and dissidence. Particularly in situations when they are the ones pulling the strings. Every time we falter, we give them power over us. Every time we rebuild, we take that power back."
Aran looked them, one by one, in the eyes. "Rest assured, I will deal with the obelisks and, together, we shall deal with the Draco." Murmurs of approval spread through the council room. "I am giving you my all. I expect nothing less in return!" Aran's words commanded authority.
To his relief, he managed to reignite the council's resolve, and the tribes recommitted to the unity he had fought so hard to achieve.
That night, by the reflective light of Shamari mirrors, in Aran's private chambers, he and Zahira, supervised by Barash, laboured over the parchment that would become the First Edict of his House.
"The words must be perfect," Aran insisted, striking through a line for the third time. "This document will outlive us all."
Zahira nodded, her keen political mind working through each principle. "Eclectic Unity," she read aloud, testing the weight of the words. "Each tribe retains its customs, yet all contribute to Zarah's strength."
"And here," Aran pointed to the second principle, "Shared Resources. The oases, trade routes, and harvests - managed collectively for the good of all."
"The Bahir and the Ulema tribes will resist this most," Zahira cautioned. "Their lands hold the richest water sources."
"Then we must show them how their prosperity multiplies when shared," Aran answered, adding the third principle: "Defence of Zarah. A unified army, to protect us all."
"No longer will tribe fight against tribe." Zahira murmured.

Sat in the back of the room, enveloped in smoke, Barash's smile was broad - his charge had come a long way.

As dawn broke over Sarim, they completed the fourth principle - "Justice for All" - establishing the Council of Tribes as the highest court on the planet, bound to uphold the law regardless of a person's birth or station.

When Aran presented the finished edict to the council days later, the chamber fell silent as each member weighed the radical vision before them. It was not merely a document - it was the foundation stone of a new world.

The day came when the decree was finally signed, but the weight of its words hung heavy in the air. Aran scanned the faces before him - tribal leaders, warriors, merchants, mystics, leaders of men.

Some stood with pride, others with lingering doubt. "It will not hold," Kasim al-Bahir muttered under his breath. "Not under trial by fire."

Aran met his gaze, unflinching. "Then we will hold it together, brother."

Pride shone in Kasim's eyes. He extended his hand to Aran, who shook it firmly. For the first time, the council chambers did not echo with division - but with something else. Something that, at long last, felt like a nation being born.

Ironically, Aran thought, such a massive endeavour rested on his ability to repair his forebears' mistakes, whilst dealing with the Draconian threat. "A burden light as mountains." He mused internally.

In the confines of his soul, he sometimes wondered if humour wasn't, in fact, his own last line of defence.

To commemorate the official unification of the tribes, in concordance with the other tribal leaders, Aran commissioned the creation of the 'Crescent Banner', a flag that represented the tribes of Zarah's shared identity. The banner featured crescent moons, symbolizing the natural twin satellites that guided the tribes, along with six stars. Each star represented one of Zarah's major regions: Qamar, Shamas, Arsian, Sayf, Kartal and Yara.

The unveiling ceremony took place at the Great Oasis of Qamar. As the banner was raised, silence fell over the crowd - a moment of breathless uncertainty.

The wind caught the fabric, and for a moment it seemed to dance against the azure sky, its silver threads catching the light of both sun and distant mountains. The scent of Moonleaf from the oasis mixed with the clean smell of wind-blown sand, and somewhere in the crowd, a child laughed - pure and bright as crystal.

Then, like a desert breeze picking up, voices rose together, swelling into a mighty cheer. For the first time, Zarah's natives looked upon one another, not as rivals, not as divided tribes, but as one people - united in a single purpose.

Near the front of the crowd, an elderly woman caught Aran's eye. Her clothes bore the traditional markings of the Rasha tribe, yet she stood proudly beside a young man wearing Bahir colours, her grandson by marriage - Aran would later learn. As the banner unfurled above them, she took the young man's hand and raised it high alongside her own. "My husband died fighting his father," she told Aran afterwards, her weathered face solemn. "Now our families share bread and water. This is what your banner means to us."

Aran exhaled slowly, the weight in his chest lifting. This was not just a banner. It was the first thread in the tapestry of a kingdom yet to be woven. "Who knows?" He was feeling optimistic. "Maybe one day, they will see themselves as part of one House," his eyes on the horizon.

"That would be the day, indeed," Rafiq, who was standing just behind Aran, jested. "They better get along with it, because if they don't, I will make them myself," he poked Aran on the back. "Are you ready for your speech?"

Suppressing a laugh, Aran stepped on the balcony and addressed the crowd, his voice carried by the wind. "This banner is more than a symbol. It is a promise," the crowd cheered. "A promise that we will face the future together, as one people united by the desert and its spirit. My brothers and sisters, rest assured. I will not rest, until I have set us free. Free from this curse, free from the Draconians' interest in Zarah and its peoples. Free to carve our own destiny, as one people. Do not commit the sin of forgetting that our enemies thrive on chaos and disorder. Let us not give them the satisfaction."

Months went by, while the infrastructure Aran had established was being set in place. His days were spent galloping across the deserts, visiting the oases towns, making sure everything was going according to his plans. Aside from a small skirmish with a Draconian patrol in the jagged cliffs of the future kingdom of Sayf, things were going as smoothly as possible.

However, in spite of how well things seemed to be flowing, time does not wait for fools. The moment had come to address the matter of the obelisks, so Aran convened the Council of Tribes once more.

The air in the Hall of Unity was heavy with anticipation, as if the walls themselves held their breath. Inside the circular chamber, the leaders of Zarah's tribes sat around the crescent-shaped table. The table was now inlaid with the sigils of each tribe. The Crescent Banner at its centre reflected the soft glow of the new sun mirrors embedded in the chamber walls.

Aran sat at the head of the table, his posture rigid yet not unbending - a reflection of the delicate balance he had learned to maintain in his leadership. His young eyes, rimmed with the subtle lines earned from years of desert winds and sleepless nights, swept across the gathered tribal leaders. One hand rested near the intricate map spread before him, his fingers tracing the invisible lines of potential futures.

Beside him stood Barash, a figure who seemed to exist between worlds. His frame was lean and corded with muscle, wrapped in a weathered, dark robe that bore the subtle shimmer of desert threads - a garment that seemed to blur the lines between fabric and the mystical energies he commanded. Scars traced his exposed arms, each a testament to battles fought both in the physical realm and in the unseen dimensions of the Weaving.

Aside from his father, Barash was the first to introduce Aran to the ancient mysteries of their land. Months earlier, within the very bowels of Sarim, during a venture that had tested the limits of both their endurance and understanding, he had guided Aran through the treacherous paths of the Weaving.

The warrior-mystic's presence was a constant reminder of the delicate balance between physical might and spiritual insight. Where Aran brought strategic vision and political acumen, Barash brought an understanding of the deeper, more mystical currents that flowed beneath the surface of their emerging kingdom.

The first obelisk, discovered in a large underground crypt underneath the Old Quarter, had already been destroyed, after an intense battle. Its chaotic energy quelled through its destruction, along with a temporary victory against Drathis and the House of Draco.

However, the act had left several questions unanswered and certain fears were left unspoken. The room was tense in anticipation.

Now, reports based on a lead discovered by Barash, had confirmed the existence of a second obelisk in the southern mountain range, where the sands gave way to jagged peaks and hidden valleys. The council had gathered to determine their course of action.

Kasim al-Bahir, his broad frame draped in a crimson cloak, was the first to speak. He leaned forward, his powerful hands gripping the edge of the table.

"We are wasting time with debate," Kasim declared, his voice gruff.

"If it was not for Aran, the awakening of the first obelisk would have torn Sarim apart. If there is another, he should destroy it as well. The matter is settled."

Karim al-Shamar adjusted his spectacles, his frame hunched over a map of the southern mountains spread across the table. "Destroy it? What, and risk triggering another catastrophe? According to Aran and Barash, the obelisks are ancient and interconnected. Having destroyed one, we do not know what it has done to the others."

Kasim al-Bahir scoffed. Once a warrior, always a warrior. He could not stand inaction."So, we do nothing? Wait for it to wake up and tear Zarah apart, while we scratch our heads about what should be done about it?"

Zahira, seated beside Aran, raised a hand to calm the tension. Though she had recently exchanged battlefields, her past experience and measured voice carried the authority of one who had seen the dangers of the deserts first-hand. "Neither destruction nor inaction are viable paths. We must approach this with caution. The southern mountains are treacherous, and the next obelisk may be far more unstable than the first, due to the former's destruction. I, for one, trust my cousin. He has led us right, so far, has he not? It is my humble opinion that we should," she took a pause to correct herself. "That is, Aran should mend the damage done by the destruction of the first. Though that was unavoidable, I know. I was there," she added, exchanging glances with her cousin and Rafiq. Aran's loyal protector threw Zahira a wink of acknowledgement.

Safira, the Moon Seer, had been sitting quietly until now, her silver eyes distant as if peering into another realm. When she spoke, her voice was soft but resonant. "Our moons have shown me new visions of the obelisks. They are not merely keys, prisons, or tethers. They are also wounds upon the land, and wounds must either heal or fester. I agree with Zahira. Harmonization may be the only way forward. Just ask Aran, or perhaps Ba-"

Barash cleared his throat, his deep, gravelly voice filling the chamber. Though old and apparently frail, his presence was striking. His dark robes were adorned with glyphs of an ancient language, sown in colours of fire. His weathered hands carried the marks of one who had delved deeply in battle and the unknown powers of ancient history.

"Harmonization is delicate," Barash began. "The obelisks are not simply artefacts. They are conduits, tied to forces we barely comprehend. Healing requires balance, but know this - the energy within them is neither inherently good nor evil. It is nonetheless very powerful. Pending towards the intent of the weavers who last crafted its threads. Therefore, if we choose destruction, we may risk shattering that balance entirely."

Aran leaned forward. He had remained silent until now, for he wanted to feel the pulse of the council. His voice was steady, but his tone was betrayed by his inner conflict. "Safira, you said the obelisks are wounds upon the land. Unfortunately, they are more than that, they are tied to our own reality. The very fabric of our planet. The very essence of Zarah." A ripple of unease spread through the room like a sandstorm before the thunderclap.

Kasim al-Bahir's fists clenched as he rose abruptly, his chair scraping against the floor. "You expect us to just trust this new information? That these cursed monoliths must be saved? That we gamble Zarah's future on myths and whispers?!" A chorus of murmured agreements followed, voices rising, overlapping, clashing. Not for the first time, the Council felt on the verge of breaking.

Aran stood swiftly, his voice cutting through the clamour.

"Enough!" his gaze swept the room, holding each leaders's eyes. "We stand here, today, because of trust, because of unity. I do not expect blind faith from anyone - but I do expect a certain amount of wisdom." His eyes were alight with purpose.

Kasim, though supportive of his conduct, shifted uncomfortably in his chair, while Karim's hand froze over the map.

Barash's gaze met Aran's. "Both Aran and I know it to be not only possible, but also true. The obelisks are older than any kingdom of men ever raised upon Zarah. They might be older than any historical records in existence, with the exception of the Wardens' in the Shadowed Vale or the records of the lost city of Valamar. If they even still exist." Barash looked around the room. No one seemed to be willing to place much confidence in old tales and myths.

After all, he was speaking of things and places most of them had never heard of in the entirety of their lives. Despite their illiteracy, or perhaps because of it, he decided to remain focused on tangible matters. "The obelisk's influence on our world is considerable. I believe healing them is the path to take, and I have also made sure that our chosen leader is up to the task."

Aran did not miss the twinkle in his tutor's eyes, in spite of the heavy silence following his statements.

Kasim was the one who broke it, his tone sharp. "Then that is even more reason to destroy them. If these things are connected to our world and their presence is dangerous, then we can not risk leaving them intact or even try to mend them. Let us destroy their influence and be done with it. Then we can rebuild our world anew."

"What if the path of destruction unleashes something worse?" Safira countered, her keen eyes narrowing. "The moons have warned me of a storm of darkness, but they have also shown me light and hope. These obelisks may yet hold the key to understanding our plight. If they do not, I trust Aran to make the right decision when the time comes. You see," she fidgeted with the arrow heads on her quiver. "The moons have also shown me signs of one who would unite Zarah. Has he not proven, so far, to be that person?"

They were not making it easy for him. Aran ran a hand over his face, caressing his beard, frustration etched into his features. Every path felt like a gamble - with Zarah's soul as the wager. True to his nature, he chose honesty. "What if I am no different from them? The Old Kings, the Weavers, even my ancestors - each believed they could bend fate to their will. Each had left scars upon the world." He clenched his fists. "Am I leading us to salvation, or merely walking the same doomed path? Besides, if we destroy it, what if that destabilizes the others or awakens whatever slumbers beneath their power and vigilance?" Somehow unaware of it, Aran had spoken his thoughts out loud.

"I do not care," he thought, "I have got nothing to hide."

Barash placed one hand on the table and the other on Aran's shoulder. His voice was calm but firm. "Leadership is not about certainty, my prince. It is, in fact, about weighing uncertainty with wisdom," he paused, to let the words sink in, before concluding.

"The next obelisk will not wait for us to make the perfect choice. We must act."

After hours of debate, the council reached a fragile consensus, which, in truth, meant that no decision had been reached. The obelisk would be approached cautiously, and its energy would be assessed before deciding whether to harmonize or destroy it. Most left the room, but a few remained - loyal, willing to help as best they could.

Aran seemed lost in thought. "It is up to me," the realization fully formed in his mind. "It has always been up to me. If I have learned one thing on my path, that would be that choices are nothing but illusions. I will face my destiny, and what will happen will happen."

Sura spread the map of the southern mountains further across the table, pointing to the marked location of the obelisk. "The journey will not be easy. The southern range is unpredictable. There are sandstorms, hidden crevasses, and beasts that call the mountains home to contend with. We will need the best scouts and supplies to reach it."

Kasim al-Bahir cracked his knuckles, pulling Aran from his musings. "Your honesty will never cease to amaze me." Kasim was looking at Aran, with unmistakable pride. "Our warriors will lead the vanguard. Any who stand in your path shall taste desert steel and regret their folly."

A warm feeling began to spread in Aran's chest - loyalty is priceless.

Karim al-Shamar added, "The Shamari will provide the necessary equipment. We have been developing portable Sun Mirrors for energy-based defences. They should help stabilize or neutralize the obelisk's energy field if things get out of hand."

Safira al-Rasha's voice softened. "The Moon Seers will prepare protective talismans. The obelisks' energy is not merely physical. It seeps into the mind and spirit. You will need every safeguard we can provide you with."

Amir al-Ulema, the master merchant, who had remained quiet until now, finally spoke. His voice was calm but carried the weight of pragmatism. "I will ensure the supply lines between Zarah's kingdoms remain strong. Also, for your journey, food, water, and medical supplies will be sent ahead to staging points in the mountain passes. Moreover, if your expedition fails, we will need to prepare for the consequences back here in Sarim. I will take the necessary steps."

Aran nodded at Amir, happy to see the political structure he helped set in place functioning adequately. "We leave in three days," he said. "Rafiq, gather your scouts and map the safest route. Kasim, prepare your warriors. Karim, I want those Sun Mirrors ready for deployment. Safira, meet with the Moon Seers and keep studying the night sky."

To himself, he thought. "Barash and I will study the Weaving once more to see if it reveals anything new about the obelisks."

Looking around the crescent table, he concluded. "Council adjourned." The few lords and ladies remaining dispersed, conversations sprouting here and there.

Springing to his feet, Aran approached Sura privately. Before she could utter a word, looking deep into her eyes, he held her hands and said, "I know you want to come with me and, even though I would give anything for it to be otherwise, I would expect nothing else from you."

She held his gaze, her eyes searching his soul.

Holding Sura's hypnotic stare, he tried as best he could to remain objective. "I need you to stay here in my stead. I need you to work with my cousin, Zahira. If things do not go well for me, I need to know that I have people here in Sarim whom I can trust," he squeezed her hands gently, letting the gesture speak where words could not.

"Understood," Sura replied, her voice short but kind. She held his gaze a moment longer, her eyes conveying what her words did not - fear for his safety, faith in his judgement, and something deeper that remained unspoken between them. Then she squeezed his hands once, firmly, before turning away.

"Return to us, Aran," she added softly, her fingers lingering against his. "Return to me." Her voice carried the weight of unspoken words - promises made in glances, in moments of shared silence during their journeys together. For a heartbeat, Aran saw not the warrior who had stood beside him through battles, but the woman who had chosen to bind her fate to his own uncertain path.

"I will," he whispered, and for the first time in days, he truly believed it.

As each of the council members went about their evening affairs, Barash lingered behind. He approached Aran, his dark robes trailing softly over the marble floor, its embroidered orange symbols shining brightly, enhanced by the sun's dying rays. "You hesitate," Barash said, his voice low. "I know you too well."

Aran turned to face his teacher. "Because I do not know if I am making the right choice. It feels like we are standing on the edge of a precipice, and every misstep could send us tumbling into the void."

Barash nodded slowly. "That is the very nature of leadership, lad. Like a traveller facing the endless dunes, you must choose a direction without seeing what lies beyond the horizon. The obelisks are a mystery that neither you nor I can fully unravel. Or rather, I should say, through my experience, they will be better understood by you than by me. You are the one whose bloodline is tied to them, and it is up to you to make a final decision." Seeing Aran wearing the weight of it all on his face, he quickly added. "Do not fret, my boy. I have trained you well, and you have proven yourself to be a gifted learner. A quality often overlooked in kingship, as is kindness."

Aran did not deal very well with compliments. "I trust you," he said.

The old man sighed. "You can trust in me, but, above anyone else, you must trust in yourself. After all, it is a student's charge to surpass their master." He locked eyes with Aran. "Remember this - the desert has endured storms far greater. Every time, it was not the sand nor the wind that broke - but the men who stood upon it."

Barash placed a hand on the shoulder of his dearest friend's son.

"Do not fear the storm, lad. Instead, be the wind that shapes it!"

Aran exhaled deeply, his shoulders relaxing slightly. "We shall see, Barash. We shall see."

Chapter XII

The Covenant of Shadows

He stood before what had once been a colossal obelisk, the remnants of its shattered surface casting long shadows over its surroundings. Still unsure whether to harmonize them, he had begun by trying to heal this one, only to end up destroying it.

So much deliberation in the council, and it had all come down to this. He had placed his hands on the obelisk's surface, feeling the Weaving's power pulse beneath his palms. The healing had begun - threads of light weaving through the ancient stone. Then the Shamari sun mirrors, positioned to provide light, caught an errant ray. The focused beam struck the obelisk's core, and suddenly, the structure groaned. Cracks spider-webbed across its surface.

"Pull back!" Aran shouted, but it was too late. The choice was no longer his - destroy it, controlled, or let it explode and kill everyone nearby.

Barash had found clues for its whereabouts in a tome from the old kingdom, at the royal library of Sarim. Aran's heart still trembled from the vision the Weaving had granted him, the echo of the Primordials' dark whispers lingering in his mind like a haunting melody. Healing the obelisks would have been the correct decision.

Now the destruction of yet another had not merely reinforced the already broken ancient seal, but it also seemed to have set something else in motion. Or rather, allow it to continue. Something far beyond his mortal comprehension.

The ground beneath his feet felt unsteady, as if the very fabric of Zarah was responding to the fracture. Or was it just his imagination? The guilt, speaking in his stead?

It had taken them weeks to reach the site where this monolith lay. A long and quiet journey, without much incident. No sandstorms slowing their travels. Calm nights under the stars, during which Aran had plenty of time to come to a final decision. Hindsight offered little comfort now. On his side of the choice, it felt lonely.

Beside him, Rafiq stood silent, his eyes fixed on the still smoking remains of the stone tether. His friend's usual stoicism was betrayed by the tension in his jaw and the tight grip on the hilt of his dagger.

But then again, Rafiq had not felt the weight of the revelation. The truth that had been hidden for aeons. Aran saw it. Worse, he had felt it. "The obelisks..." he whispered, his voice barely audible over the wind that whipped through the now desolate plain. "By inadvertently destroying this one, I confirmed that they are not merely tools of creation. They can also be used as tethers, to create a binding that holds the Primordials at bay. Barash told me they could be used as prisons, yes… but he never clarified that small nuance." Aran paused, his thoughts turning inward. "It was always about destroying or mending. Never about containing. Either he chose not to tell me… or he does not know."

Rafiq nodded, his gaze still locked on the broken monolith. Ignoring Aran's reference to Barash, his words were as sharp as his twin blades. "A prison you chose to continue to break, my friend," he kept his eyes low, as if he was restraining himself from looking at his companion.

Aran closed his eyes - Rafiq's words rang true. The enormity of his misjudgement wrapped around him like iron chains, tightening with each breath. He should have mended it - he should have listened. Instead, he had hesitated at the precipice, and in that moment, he had chosen destruction. Now the world itself seemed to shudder in response. What if this was the beginning of the end?

Aran's hands curled into fists, but there was no time for regret.

He could only move forward, and find a way to make amends, regardless of personal cost. His mistake, during the process, was that he wasn't thinking of himself at the time, but rather of those for whom he felt responsible for.

Rafiq remained silent by his side, a living remembrance of his misstep. Because of that decision, the situation had become far worse. Desperate to find something he might have overlooked, he quickly ran the logic through his mind, trying to remember everything he had learned, so far; The Primordials were beings of immeasurable power, who had once roamed the world freely, shaping reality to their whims. The ancient pact between them and the mortal world had bound them to the Weaving, each obelisk serving as a node in the intricate network that kept their influence contained. Here and now, given his unexpected choice to destroy the second obelisk, that balance was clearly shifting. "Why did I not follow my instinct?" he cursed under his breath. Reality, however, remained indifferent to his plight. There was nothing more he could do about it now, aside from learning from his mistake.

"We must find the others," he spoke out loud, his voice firmer now. "Before it is too late. I must try to repair the wrong I have done."

The admission hung between them like a blade. Aran could feel the wrongness of his choice echoing through the Weaving itself - a discordant note in an ancient song. Each destroyed seal was a crack in reality's foundation, and he had just admitted to widening that crack with his own hands.

Rafiq finally turned to face him, his expression unreadable. He truly could not understand why Aran had destroyed it, and his friend had not explained himself yet. "What then? Do we destroy them as well, or seek to restore the seals?" it was a genuine question, without a hint of defiance. Rafiq merely wanted to understand his friend's motives.

The query hung in the air between them, its weight oppressive.

Aran didn't really have an answer to give. Not yet anyway.

That was why he hadn't explained his sudden change of course to Rafiq.

The vision he experienced, while trying to mend the obelisk, had shown him the devastation the Primordials could wreak, but it had also hinted at something else. An opportunity, a potential path to wield their power rather than be consumed by it. Something that, in and of itself, fuelled Aran's fears of inner weakness. What if he was corruptible like his forebears had been before him?

A fine line to walk on, he thought. A particular one, where the slightest imbalance could launch events with catastrophic consequences, regardless of the side he happened to fall on.

"First," Aran began, answering his friend as much as himself, "I must understand what I saw." A solution forming in his mind. "I apologize for not being clear, my friend, but I need knowledge - knowledge lost to time, hidden in the histories of the old kingdoms. We must return to Sarim." Regardless of whatever doubts eating away at him, Rafiq said nothing. He merely bowed to his friend and went about getting the company ready for their return.

However, returning to Yara's capital meant confronting not only the potential political turmoil that Aran feared had been simmering in his absence but also the deeper currents of conspiracy and betrayal within his recently unified tribes - the very foundation of his vision for Zarah and its peoples. The forces arrayed against him were not only supernatural. He had been aware, for some time now, that beside the House of Draco, rival lineages in his own kingdom were creating factions within his court and were plotting to usurp his right to rule.

He decided that for the time being, he needed to trust his allies in the council to keep things from deteriorating. His thoughts turned to Sura and Zahira. As he turned away from the ruins of yet another obelisk, Aran's musings were heavy with the knowledge that his unforeseen change of mind had brought them to the starting line - or, worse, behind it. His vision was in dire need of allies, both old and new, if it was to survive what lay ahead.

The journey back to Sarim stretched before them like an unwritten scroll. Each step away from the ruined obelisk felt like walking deeper into quicksand - the further they travelled from his mistake, the heavier it seemed to weigh upon his shoulders. Rafiq's silence during those long days spoke louder than any accusation could have, and Aran found himself studying his friend's profile against the endless dunes, searching for signs of the judgement he feared to find there.

Each day brought new weight to his shoulders as he pondered the implications of his choice. Rafiq maintained a respectful distance, allowing his friend the solitude he clearly needed. Only when the coastal winds finally carried the salt-scent of home did Aran emerge from his brooding silence.

After a long return, the city loomed on the horizon like a distant memory. Its alabaster Minare spires gleaming against the twilight sky. When the city gates loomed near, Aran felt the shift in the air - an unease that had not been there before his departure. Guards who once greeted him with eager salutes now stood rigid, hesitant, their eyes darting to one another before stepping aside. Even here, at the gates of his citadel, the poison of betrayal seemed to have crept into the cracks of his kingdom.

The scent of stone, smoke, and sea was the same, but the streets felt different - as if the city itself was holding its breath. This suspicion washed over him, stirring something deep within. Four weeks had gone by, since he had left the coastal capital in search of the second obelisk, and though he had expected the tension of returning to the court, he could not shake the feeling that something had changed in his absence.

The city was bustling with activity as Aran and his friends made their way through the crowded streets. Overhearing conversations, they gathered that the citizens were largely unaware of the growing darkness that loomed just beyond their borders. Nevertheless, there were whispers, rumours of strange occurrences in the far reaches of this future Kingdom of Yara. Rumours of shadows moving in places they should not, of unnatural storms and whispered voices carried on the wind.

Rafiq led the way toward the palace, his eyes scanning the crowd for threats. Aran followed, his mind still occupied with the Weaving and the Primordials. When they reached the gates, a figure stepped out from the shadows, her Nightwing Cloak blending seamlessly with the darkness. "What a relief. You have returned," her voice low and sharp as a blade, but warm and welcoming. It was Sura, his trusted spymaster. "And not a moment too soon, Aran. There have been... err, developments in your absence."

Aran raised an eyebrow, his fears confirmed. "Developments?"

Sura's eyes flickered toward the palace. "The Council has been busy. Barash left us two weeks ago, in search of further knowledge, and they have convened in secret many times since. Now, there are those who believe your time to claim the throne has come to an end."

Aran's jaw tightened. He had known there were few who would seek to usurp him, but the speed with which they had moved in his absence was alarming. "Who leads them?" Aran knew the answer to his own question before the words had left his lips.

Sura hesitated for a moment before confirming his suspicions. "Farid."

The name landed like a blow. Not because it surprised him, but because he had feared it all along. Aran had hoped he was wrong. But with Barash gone and his own prolonged absences, Farid had clearly seized the moment to tighten his grip on the council.

"I do not believe he will move against you directly," Sura pressed. "He would not dare, for he is too much of a coward to challenge your authority, out in the open. However, he is spreading dissent, questioning your ability to rule in the face of the growing unrest throughout the land. Myself, Zahira, Karim, Safira and a few others, have done our best to keep the tribes united, but Farid plays a dangerous game. He preys on the needs and wants of the council members, making sure to nudge their opinions in ways that favour him. If you do not act swiftly, he will make them force your hand." After a short pause, she added. "Some of us believe he might be working with the House of Draco once more."

Aran nodded, his mind racing. Because of his misjudgement, the threat from the Primordials was growing, but if he lost control of the council as well, his ability to combat that greater danger would be severely crippled. He needed to reassert his authority, but he also had to tread carefully. Farid was dangerous and cunning, and any misstep could lead to civil war. "What do you suggest, my friend?" he asked, turning to Sura.

Her eyes gleamed with a dangerous light. "I've placed trusted agents within the Council." When he tilted his head, her eyes narrowed.

"Farid is a serpent, Aran," she pressed. "If you cut off his head now, you save yourself from a thousand knives in the dark. Do you really think honour will protect you from his ambition? Tell that to the past kings who showed mercy, only to have their throats slit in their sleep."

Sura leaned in, her voice dropping lower. "Farid will not stop until you are buried. I say strike first, or die waiting." She spoke with composure, though her eyes gave her away. "Despite some of us believing he is betraying us again, most think he lost his rapport with the House of Draco, and that is why he is looking for new political alliances. Personally, I believe he is doing both. Still working for the Draco, whilst helping them destroy us from within. He keeps creating distress in the council, so we continue to fight amongst ourselves, instead of uniting against our common enemy. More reasons to eliminate him, I say." Sura's mind seemed set.

Aran shook his head, heavy with the burden of his next move. "No. If we act in secret and remove him, not only are we lowering ourselves to his level, but that will also feed the rumours that I am weak. That I cannot rule without resorting to shadows and daggers. No, Sura, we must confront him openly, and I will do it on the floor of the Council. In front of everyone."

She frowned. "That is a dangerous gamble. Farid has gathered many allies in your absence. If they stand with him-"

"No, Sura," Aran said, cutting her off, his voice hard. "I will not slink through shadows like a coward - I will stand beneath Zarah's sun and cast mine long upon the council. Let them hear me. Let them remember who I am." A surge of energy ran through his veins, the blood of the Old Kings, coursing hot. "Take me to the Council Hall."

Since the council's inception, its chambers kept evolving. Its vaulted ceiling now adorned with banners of the six kingdoms, each one a testament to Zarah's long and storied history.

The crescent-shaped table dominated the chamber, its polished Solarwood surface reflecting the flickering light from the crystal chandeliers above. Aran's seat commanded the head position, while the tribal representatives arranged themselves according to ancient protocol - the Bahir to his right, their warrior-diplomats seated with backs straight and hands never far from their ceremonial blades. Across from them, the Shamari contingent consulted quiet notes and diagrams. Farid had positioned himself at the far end of the crescent's curve, where shadows gathered thickest, flanked by those few who still wavered in their loyalties.

The air in the room was thick with tension as Aran entered, his presence commanding the attention of every tribal leader gathered around the crescent table. Farid stood up and moved to the far end of the room, his eyes narrowing as Aran approached. A cold smile dancing upon his lips, almost as if he knew a secret no one else did.

He was a tall man, his once dark hair now streaked with grey, his features sharp and angular, a long goatee adorning the tip of his chin. Farid radiated a quiet confidence, the kind of authority that came from years of political manoeuvring and double crossing. "The kind of experience that makes him an extremely dangerous political opponent." Aran mused in silence.

"Ah, our wandering king returns at last." Farid's voice was silk, smooth and almost welcoming - but the gleam in his eyes betrayed his true intent. "Forgive our concern, my liege, but we feared you had more pressing matters than the well-being of your people." He looked around, arms wide open, indicating the rest of the council members.

Aran decided to ignore the barb and took his seat at the head of the crescent table, his gaze sweeping over those assembled around it.

He could see the unease in their faces, the uncertainty. They had been swayed by Farid's rhetoric and lies, but they were not fully committed to his cause. Not yet, it seemed. There was still a chance of bringing those who had strayed back to his side - if he kept his wits about him and played his hand well.

At Farid's words 'wandering king,' Zahira's eyes blazed and she moved to stand, but Aran beckoned her to take her seat.

He stood up and addressed Farid directly, locking eyes with him.

"I have returned," Aran said, his voice calm but firm. "Upon my arrival, to my surprise, I find that much has transpired in my absence." He was looking at Farid with such intensity, the man could not hold his gaze for more than a second.

An uncomfortable silence followed. Long enough for those around the table to begin shifting in their seats.

Aran did not break it, but rather let it linger - enjoying its effects.

Finally, Farid grinned. It was a cold smile, almost reptilian in nature, for no emotion reached his eyes. "Indeed," his gaze was as cold as the winds of Qamar. "The kingdom faces growing unrest. There have been strange occurrences in the outlying regions, rumours of rebellion. The people are frightened, so naturally they look to their rulers for leadership." He took one furtive look at Aran. "You are our so-called leader, correct? Or do you disagree?"

The question was asked rhetorically, though Farid clearly took pleasure in the taunt.

In the heavy silence that followed, murmurs rippled through the chamber. After a long, uncomfortable pause, Farid continued. "Yet, you have been... absent." He let the final words slip slowly from his tongue, savouring each as if it were a rare delicacy.

Farid's tone was laced with false concern, though its poison ran deep. He had served the Rasha Council long before Aran's ascension, had watched lesser rulers fall to the same grand visions that now consumed his young opponent.

In his mind, he was saving the kingdom from yet another royal dreamer bound to lead them to ruin. That such salvation required Draconian gold was merely... pragmatic, or so he told himself. Truth be told, he had sold his soul long ago.

Aran held his gaze, unmoved, but the council was not so still.

Several members shifted uncomfortably, casting uncertain glances at one another. A few lowered their eyes, unwilling to meet the king's gaze. The minor lords, in particular, flicked their attention toward Farid, their loyalties unclear.

Others turned toward Ryvan - a powerful tribal leader known more for silence than speech during council sessions - as if waiting for a spark to ignite the chamber.

Aran had expected this. Farid's poison had seeped deep. "I have been dealing with matters of grave importance, as you all know or perhaps should," he said at last, his voice cutting through the tension like a blade. "Matters that concern the safety of Zarah itself. It has been a long and turbulent road. One I am happy to walk on, for the safety of our people. Nevertheless, I am here now and I will address these concerns you speak of."

There was a new murmur among the Council, but Farid's smile widened as if he had been expecting this. "Grave matters, you say? Yet, you leave us in the dark for weeks on end. What could possibly be more important than the welfare of your people?"

Aran knew that Farid was well aware of the reasons behind his absence, but had chosen instead to feign ignorance.

Kasim al-Bahir couldn't take it anymore. His warrior spirit and loyalty to Aran, getting the better of him. "How dare you speak to our leader in those terms." He slammed his fist on the table, startling Farid.

Zahira stood up, a look on her face of pure spite. Others began to argue amongst themselves. The situation looked like it was getting out of hand. Aran raised his, beckoning all for restraint.

The last thing he needed was for the council to invite chaos inside.

"The Weaving," he said. Not loudly, but with absolute certainty. Silence fell - not immediate, but in a slow, creeping wave. The murmurs died. The shifting ceased. The weight of his words settled over them like a desert storm on the horizon - heavy, unstoppable. Even Farid stilled. His smirk faltered, just slightly. He blinked, clearly taken aback. "The Weaving?" He did not expect Aran to address this subject so bluntly.

Farid had heard of the Weaving from Drathis and was aware of his intentions in the old crypt. He was, however, blind to the fact that the Draconian was impersonating him, at the time.

"Yes," Aran continued, his voice carrying across the chamber. "The ancient power that binds our world. As we speak, there are forces at work. Forces that have been long forgotten but are now stirring once more, underneath the sands of time. The House of Draco started tampering with them," Farid swallowed hard, his knuckles white. "Is he going to mention me?" his heart skipped a beat.

Aran, however, continued without doing so. "The obelisks that stand in the far reaches of our planet are not mere monuments. As I am sure you are all aware by now, they are seals, keeping something far more dangerous at bay."

He paused, letting his words sink in. The faces of those sitting around the crescent table were a combination of a plethora of emotions, ranging from pure fright to complete astonishment.

Deep down, Aran wanted to speak the whole truth. To let them all know of Farid's betrayal, of his involvement with Drathis. He looked at the man, and for whatever reason a memory of his younger years shook loose in his mind.

He remembered his father's words, during one of their last conversations, before he died. The same words that, he was sure, Barash used to distract him with, enough to draw blood from his spinning dagger, not wanting to disclose his previous slip.

"Knowing what to say is intelligence, my son, but knowing when to say it - that is wisdom, Aran."

He decided this was not the time to reveal Farid's betrayal to the council. After all, he had seen doubt in the man's eyes before.

The lords and ladies, sitting around the council table, exchanged uneasy glances. Their doubt was palpable.

Kasim and Safira looked at each other, concerned. Zahira was stewing in her seat - her eyes still ablaze. Farid, however, was not so easily swayed. "You expect us to believe this... tale? That the fate of the kingdom rests on these obelisks? I mean no offence, but it sounds like the ramblings of a madman." He looked at Aran, a look of pure delight on his face. Farid was clearly enjoying himself.

Aran rose to his feet, his eyes blazing with authority. "I have seen it with my own eyes. The Weaving is stirring. If another seal is broken, that might unravel our world, our reality. If that happens, everything we know, everything we hold dear, will be destroyed."

There was a long, tense silence. Finally Karim al-Shamar spoke, his voice uncertain. "If this is true... then what must we do?"

An expression of fear etched on his face as he fidgeted with his spectacles. "What can we do?" he concluded, more to himself than to the council.

Aran turned to face them. "We must prepare, as best we can. Put all our efforts into finding the remaining obelisks and ensure they are not disturbed. It should go without saying that we must also remain united.

Now, more than ever my friends, for the threat we face is far greater than any internal squabble or political ambition we might have amongst ourselves." There was a murmur of approval throughout the room. Quite a few that had doubted him looked ashamed now.

Farid's smile vanished, replaced by a look of cold fury. He knew he had lost the battle, but he was not one to be easily defeated or swept aside. "Very well, Aran Ibn Khalid," Farid said, his voice dripping with venom. "We shall see if your words hold truth. But know this - we will be watching." He looked around for supporters. "If you falter, if you fail, I will not hesitate to act in our defence."

How were some people able to lie so blatantly? Aran mused internally. How could anyone, in their right mind, put their welfare above others'? "No matter, I will prevail in the end. Zarah will be free - I will see to it, or I will die in the attempt." The words engraved in his very soul. Meeting the man's gaze, unafraid, Aran took a step forward. Slow, deliberate. Farid did not move, but Aran saw it - the tightening of his jaw, the flicker of unease behind his cold gaze.

"Do what you must, Farid al-Rasha," Aran said, his voice unshaken, absolute. "But know this - when the dust settles, and the true ruler of Zarah stands, it will be me."

Farid's smirk remained, but it was hollow now. He said nothing. He only turned, slipping back into the shadows of the council chamber.

Aran was looking at him with such intensity that the man was again forced to look away - he had won. The lords seemed appeased for now. Kasim, Safira, Sura, and a few others, exchanged looks of approval with him. Relieved, he made the decision, from now on, to follow his instincts.

The days that followed his confrontation with Farid moved swiftly. Word of his victory in the council spread through Sarim's winding streets, carried by merchants and whispered in the markets.

Aran seized this momentum, knowing that unity forged in words must now be tempered in action. Within a week of his return, he had issued the proclamation that would reshape Zarah forever - its first unified army. Within the span of three moons, what had been separate tribal forces would become something unprecedented in Zarah's history.

The creation of this fighting force was a monumental task, requiring careful diplomacy to balance the military traditions of each tribe.

The first joint council session nearly ended in bloodshed. "Our Dune Stalker blade is an extension of the soul," Kasim al-Bahir growled, slamming his fist on the table. "You cannot simply teach it like some Shamari diagram."

Karim al-Shamar adjusted his spectacles, unmoved. "In turn, your 'soul' will mean nothing when our enemies attack with projectile weapons from beyond your blade's reach."

"Enough." Aran's voice cut through the rising tension. He drew his father's blade - a hybrid creation combining Tarek craftsmanship with Shamari steel work. "We don't choose between traditions. We forge new ones." The demonstration that followed left both men silent, watching as their young leader seamlessly blended combat styles they'd thought incompatible.

After his open confrontation with Farid, Aran also convened a special council session, inviting not only tribal leaders but also their most seasoned warriors to contribute their expertise. That way, not only did it serve the army, but also ensured that Farid was kept in check.

The Bahir, once more, brought their legendary skill in close combat, training warriors in the use of the Dune Stalker blades and the art of partisan warfare. The training ground erupted in chaos as Bahir warriors clashed with Shamari engineers.

What started as a demonstration had devolved into a brawl.

"Hold!" Aran waded into the melee, physically separating two combatants. Sweat dripped from his brow as he faced the assembled warriors. "You fight each other while the House of Draco sharpens their blades. Is this the army that is supposed to defend Zarah?"

Ashamed silence fell over the field. Proud warriors avoiding each other's eyes. Then, from the back, a young Shamari engineer stepped forward. "Teach us your way, Aran. Show us how to be one."

What followed were three days of gruelling joint exercises, with Aran leading by example - learning alongside those who would fight for him, making mistakes, getting bruised, proving that unity required sacrifice from all - especially from one that leads.

From that point on, the Bahir war chants, said to strike fear into their enemies, became a unifying ritual during the army's military drills.

The Shamari engineered solar-powered weapons were presented before the council, including the new handheld mirrors capable of temporarily blinding enemies, as well as new lightweight armour, resistant to heat and projectiles.

The prototype Sand Serpent armour lay on the workshop table, a fusion of Shamari innovation and Bahir practical knowledge. Karim al-Bahir ran his fingers along the overlapping plates. "The theory is sound," he muttered, "but in practice -"

"In practice, it saved my life." Rafiq entered, still wearing a battle-tested version. Scorch marks and blade scratches told the story. "Your design, Karim - with your modifications, Kasim. Together, they work."

The two tribe leaders exchanged glances - rivals, unexpectedly becoming collaborators, step by careful step.

After that revelatory exchange, Karim al-shamar further helped devise and construct mobile fortresses, designed to withstand sandstorms while providing strategic vantage points, in battle.

The future Kartal's, at the time known as Rasha's moonlit archery techniques were incorporated into the army's training.

Under the twin moons, Safira demonstrated the Crescent Draw to a mixed group of Tarek and Bahir archers. Her movements were fluid, almost dance-like. "Feel the moon's pull," she instructed. "Let Anar and Nysa guide your aim."

A Tarek scout scoffed. "Mysticism will not help when the sand stings your eyes and wind tears at your arrows."

Safira smiled, as she nocked an arrow into her bow string. "Then, allow me to show you how mysticism handles practical concerns." She closed her eyes, spun three times, after which she released. The arrow split the Tarek's waterskin from fifty paces - in a sandstorm Karim's weather predictors had announced moments before. "The Rasha tribe does not ignore the physical world," she explained to the stunned audience. "We dance with it - we adapt."

After Safira's demonstration, the Crescent Bow was introduced into Zarah's unified army - a weapon crafted from Moonleaf wood that could fire with unmatched precision, even in the cold deserts' biting winds.

Under Aran's guidance, the Tarek tribe trained elite scouts, known as Sand Shadows, who could navigate the desert undetected. Using sandstorm predictors and camouflage techniques, they became invaluable for reconnaissance missions. The Ulema tribe secured the army's heartbeat, by managing its supply chains, ensuring that food, water, and medical supplies reached even the most remote outposts. Their trade networks allowed for rapid resupply, a critical advantage in Zarah's harsh environments.

The army's first testing ground was at the Plains of Sarim, divided by the Elara river, winding its way through the city, into the Yaran ocean. These plains had seen many battles, but never one like this. Six tribal contingents faced each other across the river, centuries of mistrust visible in their formations.

"Begin!" Aran's command echoed across the water.

What followed was orchestrated chaos. Bahir warriors charged through shallow crossings while Shamari mirrors created blinding light walls. Rasha arrows darkened the sky as Tarek scouts melted into reed beds. Ulema supply lines snaked between positions while Kartal cavalry thundered along the riverbank.

For three days, they fought - not to conquer, but to learn. Each sunset brought joint meals where yesterday's opponents shared tactics and tomorrow's allies planned counters.

By the fourth dawn, something had changed. When Aran called for the final exercise, the tribes no longer moved as six units but as one force - fluid, adaptive, united. "This," Aran declared to the assembled warriors, his voice carrying across the plain, "this is the army that will defend Zarah. Not Bahir or Shamari, not Rasha or Tarek, but Zarahan. Remember this day, for you have made history." The cheer that arose could be heard throughout Sarim itself - six tribal voices, overlaid, slowly becoming one.

The army became a symbol of unity. Warriors from all tribes trained side by side, forging bonds that transcended their ancestral rivalries. Aran continued to personally oversee the martial exercises, often joining the warriors in the scorching heat to demonstrate his commitment to their cause. "Always lead by example," his father used to say. He paused at the edge of the training ground, watching as a Bahir warrior helped a fallen Shamari engineer to his feet. They clasped forearms - desert warrior and scholar - before returning to their sparring. Six months ago, such a scene would have been unthinkable.

That night, as the moons shone over Sarim, he stood on the balcony of his chambers, staring out at the dark horizon. The weight of his responsibilities pressed heavily on his shoulders, but he knew there was no turning back. The choice had been made. Or had there ever been an alternative to begin with? No. The path before him was fraught with danger, both from within his court and from the ancient forces that stirred beneath the surface of the world, but he knew he could not give up. Ironically, through the unforeseen paths of destiny, something completely outside of his own control or desires, he was their rightful king. Because of that, he would face whatever came his way with courage and resolve. His legacy would endure. "Or would it fall?" Aran asked Anar and Nysa, now sitting in their celestial thrones, bathing Zarah in a silver light.

The next morning, in order to further protect his Kingdom from external threats, he commissioned Karim al-Shamar to oversee the construction of the Fortresses of the Crescent Cliffs - on Qamar and on the cliffs of the future kingdoms of Kartal, Sayf and Arsian. Perched atop a series of towering red cliffs near the Great Oases, the fortresses overlooked the vast deserts, serving as both military bases and as symbols of Zarah's united strength.

As if working against them, the cornerstone of the first fortress being built refused to set in properly. Three times, the foundation had shifted despite precise Shamari calculations and unyielding Bahir muscle.

"The cliff face is unstable," reported the chief engineer, frustration evident. "Perhaps we should -"

"Wait." Safira al-Rasha approached, her silver robes catching the morning light. She knelt, placing her palms against the red stone. "Every mountain has its own rhythm. You keep fighting against it instead of listening."

What followed was unprecedented in tribal culture. Tarek earth-sensors working alongside Shamari engineers, Rasha moon-readers calculating optimal construction times, and Bahir warriors learning to feel the mountain's pulse before each strike of their hammers.

When the foundation finally held, it was not through force or calculation alone, but instead through a harmony none of them had imagined possible. These fortresses were marvels of Shamari engineering. Their walls were reinforced with Solarwood, capable of withstanding the intense heat of the sun, while the towers were equipped with sun mirrors to detect and signal approaching enemies. The Bahir tribe, under Kasim's guidance, crafted the fortresses' formidable gates - massive structures carved from the bones of Crystalline Leviathans, taken from Yara's ocean. Further contributing to their magnificence, the Rasha contributed with moonlit pathways, designed to glow faintly at night to guide defenders.

Inside, these strongholds housed training grounds, barracks, and great strategy halls where Aran and his allies could convene. Called the "Halls of Unity," these chambers were built into every stronghold, where the banners of each tribe hung side by side - a living testament to their shared purpose, and to the dream that had once seemed impossible.

The House of Draco's agents, always aware of Aran's growing power, launched a calculated offensive to destabilize his fledgling kingdom. Drathis, leading the campaign, devised a three-pronged strategy: infiltration, sabotage, and direct assault.

Disguised Draconian spies spread like poison through the tribes, exploiting every old wound and lingering mistrust.

Among their deadliest was Valek - a shape-shifter of formidable cunning and a master of psychological warfare. Posing as a trusted seer among the Rasha, Valek did more than merely spread rumours - he conjured false stories, illusions so vivid that even the sharpest minds could scarcely separate dream from reality.

His whispered prophecies foretold betrayal, famine, and ruin, but were always carefully crafted to turn the Bahir against the other tribes.

Slowly, fear festered, alliances wavered, and the council teetered once more on the brink of collapse. Before that could happen, Aran and Sura, suspecting the unnatural influence, orchestrated a trap.

In the hallowed halls of the Lunar Citadel, they exposed Valek's true form under the light of the moon mirrors, revealing the scaled monstrosity lurking beneath the human mask.

Though Valek was defeated, Aran still allowed him to return to Drathis alive and unarmed - a deliberate message to the House of Draco, that their games were no longer played in secret. He knew that in Draconian culture there was no greater shame than failure.

After this defeat the Draco began targeting critical infrastructures, including the King's Road and the Fortresses of the Crescent Cliffs.

In one daring raid, they destroyed a key aqueduct near the Shamari border, cutting off water supplies to several villages.

Aran quickly dispatched Rafiq and a contingent of Sand Shadows to eliminate the saboteurs, but the damage left the smaller affected tribes questioning Aran's ability to protect them. Drathis' most brazen move was an assault on the Great Oasis of Kartal. A small contingent of cloaked Draconian warriors descended upon the sacred spring, their blades glowing in the night sky.

The conflict that followed - later known as the 'Battle of the Crimson Sands' - became Zarah's first true test as a unified force against a common foe... and an alien one, at that.

As Drathis' forces attacked, Aran quickly mobilized his own defences.

Bahir warriors surged forward to engage the enemy on the ground, their Dune Stalker blades gleaming under the moons. Shamari engineers activated their sun mirrors, blinding the Draco and forcing them to slow their attack. Rasha archers took their positions on the cliffs, their Crescent Bows relentlessly raining arrows upon the invaders. Amidst the chaos, Aran led a daring counterattack.

Riding his Desert Steed, its onyx coat reflecting the moonlight, he charged into the fray, rallying his warriors with a battle cry that echoed across the dunes. Sura and Rafiq fought relentlessly by his side, their skill and determination inspiring those toiling alongside them.

The turning point in the battle came when a group of Tarek warriors attacked Drathis' contingent from behind, disabling their cloaking devices and exposing them to the archer's arrows.

The air filled with the metallic ring of steel meeting steel and the wet sound of arrows finding their marks, while beneath it all, the desert sand drank deeply of both Zarahan and Draconian blood, turning the pale dunes crimson under the moonlight.

Overwhelmed, the remaining Draco forces retreated, their confidence shattered. The victory came at a heavy cost. Many lives were lost, and the oasis bore its scars for many weeks thereafter.

In spite of their suffering, Zarah's tribes emerged stronger, their unity forged in the crucible of war - the Crescent Banner, raised over the battlefield at dawn, a symbol of their resilience and determination.

In the aftermath, the council of tribes convened to assess the kingdom's next steps. Safira spoke first, her voice tinged with both sorrow and hope. "The House of Draco will not give up so easily. They will return, stronger and more determined. We must be ready for retribution. Let us not commit the sin of forgetting how dangerous they truly are."

Aran nodded. "This victory has shown us what we are capable of when we stand together, but it has also shown us the cost of unity. We must honour those who have fallen by ensuring that their sacrifices were not in vain." Under his guidance, the council passed a resolution to expand the kingdom's defences, including the construction of watchtowers along the King's Road and the training of additional warriors. The tribes also pledged to increase their collaboration, recognizing that only by working together could they secure Zarah's future.

As the final pledges were spoken and silence settled once more over the chamber, Aran's expression grew more grave, for he knew the trials ahead reached far beyond swords and treaties. "Bear in mind that besides the Draco, I'm still contending with the obelisks and the Weaving." He stood up, his gaze steady. Seeing concern hatched on their faces, he quickly added, "This is not the end, my friends. No matter how hard the road we still have to tread, I believe this could be the beginning of something greater. Drathis has underestimated us - but he will not make that mistake again." His voice was resolute. "In turn, neither can we underestimate their greed."

A murmur of appreciation rippled across the council chambers. Their leader was taking on the weight of his mantle. The room buzzed with anticipation as the councillors prepared to debate the next pressing matter - a subject Sarim's inner circle had been postponing for far too long.

Safira al-Rasha, Sarim's Moon Seer, stood, her silver robes catching the faint light filtering through the Moonleaf windows, her hair flowing long as the night. "As a people, we stand at a crossroads," she began, her voice resonating with quiet authority. "The House of Draco has tested us several times, and we have endured thus far. Aran has faced the kismet of his forebears - and he, too, has endured. Still, true unity requires more than mere survival. It requires a symbol. Someone for us to unite under. It requires an official leader to guide us through the challenges ahead."

The room seemed to close in around Aran. Safira's words hung heavy in the air, laden with expectation. Was this truly his fate? Somehow, it still felt alien to him. He had dreamed of a unified Zarah ever since childhood, yes, but ruling over it was an entirely different matter. A crown was not merely an honour - it was a cage.

His ancestors had worn it and fallen. The weight of their failures coiled around his thoughts like a sandstorm, familiar, relentless and blinding. What if he, too, was doomed to repeat their mistakes? He had wielded a sword in battle - but could he wield the Weaving? Could he stand against the Primordials without becoming like them? Or was the same weakness that had felled his forebears running quietly through his own veins? Aran had no answers to such questions, but he knew one thing for certain - he would rather die than fail his people. He would rule as their servant, not the other way around.

Kasim al-Bahir unfolded his muscular arms, and made a gesture of approval. "I second that motion." his hand over his chest. Karim al-Shamar nodded, his voice gruff but supportive. "Safira speaks the truth. Aran ibn Khalid has proven himself not just in battle but also in his vision for Zarah. Consider what we have achieved, since we began to follow him. It is time we officially crown him as our king."

Farid sat in the shadows, his face unreadable, but Aran saw it - the slight twitch in his fingers, the way his jaw clenched just a little too tightly. He was losing his political grip, and he knew it. The council spoke of unity, but Farid's silence was a promise. It was not over.

The council erupted into murmurs, some in agreement, others hesitant to do so. Kasim rose to his feet, and though he was past his prime, his imposing warrior figure still commanded authority. "A king, yes," he declared, "but a king who understands that his crown rests upon the will of the tribes - not above them"

Aran, who had remained silent, listening to the council's deliberations, finally rose. "If I truly am to be your king, it will not be as a ruler who commands but as a servant who leads. All through my life, I have nurtured the idea of a unified Zarah - not for power's sake, but for the betterment of its people. In my heart, I know this crown you offer me is no prize. It is a heavy responsibility. One I will humbly carry… but only if it is your will." The council raised their voices in resounding unity.

Seated in the shadows behind Aran, Barash exhaled a slow ribbon of smoke from his nafas'tal bone-pipe - in the silence that followed, his approval was understood. The verdict was clear. Zarah had found its king. Aran ibn Khalid rose to his full height, the weight of history settling upon his bones. He was no longer just a warrior, nor a dreamer of unity. He was King of Zarah.

The Great Oasis of Qamar was transformed into a site of unparalleled splendour for the coronation. Cactus silk, in the colours of the tribes, fluttered in the desert breeze, and thousands gathered under the twin moons to witness the historic event. At the centre of the oasis, a grand dais had been constructed from Solarwood and adorned with carvings of Zarah's flora and fauna. The Crescent Banner hung prominently, its crescent moons and six stars symbolizing the unity of the kingdom. As Aran ascended the dais, the cheers of thousands filled the air, but his heart pounded like a war drum. He had both dreamed and dreaded, in equal measure, this moment since childhood, and now, standing before his people, the weight of the crown felt heavier than he had ever imagined.

The shimmering Sand Weaver silk draped over his shoulders felt like a mantle of expectation. Could he truly bear it? Would he succeed where his ancestors had failed? Then his eyes met Sura's. Her gaze was steady, certain - she had always believed in him.

However, the crown's weight was nothing compared to the weight of their expectations, their hopes, their fears. Every face in that moonlit crowd represented a choice - to trust in his vision or cling to the old ways. As Zahira approached with the Crescent Crown, Aran realized he was not just accepting kingship, but the responsibility for every dream deferred, every ancient grudge, every hope for something better than what had come before.

He exhaled slowly and took the final step. His cousin was by his side. In her hands, she carried his future crown, a masterpiece forged by Shamari artisans from Moonleaf silver and inlaid with sand crystals from the Black Dunes. Safira stepped forward, her voice carrying across the crowd. "Under the gaze of Anar and Nysa, our moons, we crown Aran ibn Khalid as the sole King of Zarah. May his reign be guided by wisdom, strength, and the unity of our people."

As Zahira placed the crown upon Aran's head, the crowd erupted into cheers. The tribes knelt as one, their voices rising in a unified chant: "Long live the King of Zarah. Long live King Aran!" Behind him, Barash smiled broadly.

The coronation solidified his position, but it also brought new challenges to his rule. The tribes, while united in principle, through cunning Draconian manipulation, remained wary of one another.

Old rivalries resurfaced during council meetings, and disputes over resource allocation threatened to fracture the fragile unity.

During a heated debate, Kasim al-Bahir accused the Shamari of hoarding water supplies, while Karim al-Shamar countered by pointing out the Bahir tribes' aggressive expansion near the Black Dunes.

Aran intervened, his voice calm but firm. "We cannot afford to let old grievances blind us to the greater threat. The Draco are watching, do not forget that. They are waiting for us to falter, or worse. As we speak, they might be working in the shadows to ensure that will happen. Every argument we have, every division we allow, gives them power. Let us resolve these disputes as one people, not as divided, squabbling tribes."

To address these growing tensions, Aran established the Circle of Mediation, a group of representatives from each tribe tasked with resolving conflicts before they reached the council. This initiative, though met with initial scepticism, gradually gained support as it reduced the frequency of disputes. The timing for the convergence of these separate issues was hard to believe - but there it was.

He was fighting the House of Draco on one front, dealing with the Weaving on another, whilst trying to hold his kingdom united. He couldn't help but wonder how it would all end.

Despite whatever doubts eating at his heart, Aran continued to project outer strength to his people. He envisioned his kingdom's new capital, Qamaria, as a city that embodied unity and progress. Built against the mountains, near the Great Northern Oasis. Qamaria blended the architectural styles of all the tribes. The Bahir contributed its defensive walls, crafted from dark stone and adorned with carvings of Dune Stalkers. The Shamari designed the city's solar-powered infrastructure, including aqueducts and public baths. The Rasha built the Lunar Plaza, a circular space where festivals and council meetings could be held under the moons. At the city's heart stood the Royal Palace, a breathtaking structure with Minare spires that reached toward the sky. Its central dome, crafted from Moonleaf wood and inlaid with crystals, reflected the silver light of Anar and Nysa, symbolizing the harmony of the kingdom. Qamaria quickly became a hub of culture and innovation, attracting traders, scholars, and artisans from across Zarah. Its establishment marked the beginning of Aran's vision, a kingdom united in purpose and spirit. "We did all of this in the midst of the unravelling of the Weaving, of all things. But will it hold?" he asked Zahira, as they shared a twilight together. Her eyes glowed with respect for her king. "You will do well, cousin. I am sure of it!" Both turned to face the sunset.

They kept silent for a long time, merely watching Leander's primary finishing its daily, cosmic dance, behind the horizon.

Far away, in the ancient, shadowy halls of the Nathair temple, Drathis convened his war council. Maps of Zarah sprawled across the stone table, marked with key locations: the Great Northern Oasis, the Fortresses of the Crescent Cliffs, and the King's Road. "The desert king grows stronger with each passing cycle of the moons, and the tribes remain united under a single banner," he hissed, his voice filled with disdain. Drathis traced a hand over the map, his talons cutting deep into the old parchment, tracing the trade routes connecting the tribal lands. "Unity is their strength, but it's also their weakness. Create the right pressure, and even the strongest alliance shatters along its fault lines. For the time being, we will not break it with war. Instead, we will help it rot from the inside."

A large figure shifted in the shadows. Despite his large frame, his silhouette was barely visible in the dim blue torchlight. Drathis turned to him, his voice dropping to a whisper. "Vhaskar, it is time to put you to good use." The hulking warrior's reply came in the form of a deep, low, rumbling. His tyrian purple eyes were ablaze with cold fury.

In the aftermath of recent events, doubling their efforts, Drathis launched a campaign of psychological warfare, targeting the kingdom's morale. Draconian agents, shapeshifting as natives, spread whispers of rebellion, claiming that Aran favoured certain tribes over others. They also staged false-flag attacks, disguised as neighbouring tribe members, to sow distrust. One such incident occurred near the Ulema border, where a caravan was ambushed and left with evidence implicating the Bahir tribe. The council nearly fractured over the incident, if it wasn't for a Tarek scout discovering the truth, exposing Drathis' deception. Though his schemes were foiled, the incidents left scars. Aran knew that his greatest challenge would not be defeating the Draconians in battle but maintaining the trust of his people. All, whilst trying to deal with the obelisks, the Weaving and the Primordials.

"What a time to be alive," he said to Rafiq, sharing his worries while they drank minthe tea, overlooking the sunset bathing Zarah in a fiery glow.

"I would not have it any other way," the strong warrior replied, as he placed a hand on Aran's shoulder. "Can you imagine how boring it would be if your vision did not come with obstacles?"

Aran turned to face his friend, only to find Rafiq smiling back at him, a twinkle in his eyes. "Your friendship has been my anchor through all of this chaos, Rafiq. When crown and Weaving both threaten to consume me, you remind me who I was before either existed." He meant every word.

"Well," Rafiq replied, making light of things. "One thing is certain. If I did not have you with me, It would have been a tedious road to travel." Aran burst into laughter. "Draw your sword," he said with a smile. "Let us fence, as we used to when we were youngsters." Rafiq and Aran both drew their blades. As they crossed swords under the silver light of Anar and Nysa, laughter and steel rang through the air. For a moment, they were not warriors, kings, or soldiers - just friends, as they had been in their youth. Though, even in this mock battle, they both knew the truth. In that moment of joy, neither spoke of what they both knew - that the next time their blades met steel, it would not be in practice but in the crucible of a war that was surely coming.

Chapter XIII

The Gathering Storm

The following morning Aran woke up refreshed. The weight of impending decisions pressed against his consciousness like the desert heat, but for the first time in weeks, his mind felt clear.

His sparring session with Rafiq, the previous night, had done him good. It had focused his mind. Therefore, to fortify his alliances and counter the ever present Draconian threat, he dispatched envoys to neighbouring territories, to help the tribes bolster their defensive positions against them.

The first mission was to the Kingdom of Shamas, whose cities were renowned for their advanced solar energy technologies.

Sura led the envoy to Shamas, presenting gifts of Tarek weaponry, as well as Rasha Crescent Bows and Moonleaf incense, an extremely sought-after commodity throughout Zarah. With Karim al-Shamar serving now on the ruling council in Sarim, the new Shamasian ruler, Tariq al-Shamar, welcomed the delegation. Though he began by immediately voicing his concerns, "Aran's vision for Zarah is admirable, but the Draconian shadow reaches far, and word of the Weaving's unravelling has reached our ears," his fears laid bare, he asked. "What can you offer to assure us of our king's strength?"

Sura, ever pragmatic, replied, "the House of Draco's shadow stretches wide, but it is shallow. Together, we can forge a bond that outlasts their schemes. Trade between our nations has proven, over and over, to strengthen both our economies. You must clearly see that our combined knowledge will outshine their lies."

Tariq al-Shamar pondered on her words. After a brief moment of silence, Sura continued, "as to what regards the Weaving, our king is doing his best to face that threat and that is all we can ask from anyone, in such times." She spoke with finality. Despite his early hesitance, Tariq seemed reassured.

The alliance was formalized with the 'Treaty of the Twin Moons', ensuring the continuation of a network of alliances that would later, in Zarah's annals of history, be known as 'The Great Desert Unification'. Similar treaties were brokered with the Coastal Confederation of Yara, where the city of Sarim stood, and the Highlands of Arsian and Kartal, expanding Aran's influence and securing critical trade routes. In the several months since uniting the tribes under his banner, Aran had transformed Zarah's political landscape.

Under Aran's guidance, the cities of Sarim and Qamaria flourished as cultural centres, despite the recently unified kingdom being under threat by both the Primordials and the House of Draco. A testament, in and of itself, of the endurance of the human spirit, even against such insurmountable odds.

The city of Qamaria hosted the first Festival of Unity, a week-long celebration where tribes shared their traditions through music, dance, and storytelling. The 'Tales of the Sand Serpents' became a recurring highlight. Children and elders alike gasped as Tarek performers slithered across the sand-strewn stage, their bodies undulating in perfect mimicry of Uramak - the colossal ophidian from myth.

"Behold! The Sand Serpent rises anew!" Shouted the lead storyteller, his voice carrying across the plaza. The ancient legend, once told only around Tarek campfires, now belonged to all of Zarah.

The Bahir showcased their war dances, while the Shamari displayed their dazzling pyrotechnic light shows, illuminating the night sky with patterned explosions.

The Lunar Gardens, a collaboration between the Rasha and the Ulema, became a symbol of Qamaria's spirit. Filled with Moonleaf trees and reflective pools, the gardens served as a tranquil retreat for Qamarian citizens and visitors alike.

Artists and scholars flocked to the city, contributing to the creation of the Crescent Academy, a centre of learning that combined the scientific advancements of the Shamari with the spiritual wisdom of the Rasha. The academy quickly gained renown, attracting students from all across the planet.

From their hidden locations, the Draco kept intensifying their efforts to destabilize Zarah, furthering the effects of the Weaving and the Primordials. They did so by sending agents to infiltrate its growing institutions, the very pillars of the recently established House of Aran. One such agent of disruption was a Draconian operative named Velkara. Posing as a trader, she gained access to the Crescent Academy, in Qamaria, using her position to gather intelligence about Zarah's infrastructure, planting devices to disrupt its solar networks.

Velkara's sabotage culminated during the Festival of Unity, at night, when the city's solar grids suddenly failed, plunging Qamaria into natural darkness. Panic spread through the streets, as rumours of a Draconian assault took hold of the city.

Aran, well aware of Drathis' tactics of disruption, quickly addressed the crowd from the Lunar Plaza. His voice carried strength and reassurance.

"The House of Draco continues to seek to divide us with fear," the crowd reacted like the waves of the Yaran shores.

Murmurs of an attack could still be heard amongst the crowd.

Aran waited for those to subside, then continued, the sound of his voice commanding authority. "Still, we will not be divided. We shall remain united. Because, only together can we prevail. My people, rest assured that I will not fail you. We will be free from this foreign threat. Now," he raised his arms. "Let us carry on with the festival."

The crowd hesitated, a collective breath held tight, then slowly returned to the celebration. Drums resumed their heartbeat rhythm, the scent of Moonleaf incense and roasted meat reclaimed the air, and voices rose once more in laughter and song. Yet beneath it all ran an undercurrent of unease, quick glances cast toward the darkened corners, hands resting closer to concealed daggers.

Aran's voice had filled them with confidence, but fear, once awakened, is never so easily lulled back to sleep. Nevertheless, against all odds, they believed that their king would not fail them.

After addressing the crowd, he quietly asked Sura and Rafiq to lead a team to uncover the source of the disruption. A couple of days later, after a swift but thorough investigation, they ended up tracking Velkara to an abandoned warehouse in the outskirts of Qamaria.

During a tense confrontation, she revealed Drathis' ultimate plan. There was to be a coordinated attack on Zarah's trade routes, designed to choke the kingdom's economy and force its surrender.

Velkara's reptilian features twisted into something between a sneer and resignation as Sura's blade pressed against her throat. "Do you think capturing one agent changes anything?" she hissed, though her defiance carried an undertone of grudging respect for their efficiency.

Aran convened the Council of Tribes to coordinate a defence of the King's Road, the new lifeline of the planet's economy.

It was paramount to keep his kingdom united and ready to meet the Draconians in battle if need be, while he figured out a solution for the Primordials' threat. That did not come without its challenges, however, due to Aran's leadership skills, each tribe contributed to the effort.

The Tarek dispatched Sand Shadows to patrol the trade routes, intercepting Draconian scouts before they could report back. The Bahir established fortified checkpoints along the road, their warriors standing as unyielding sentinels against the darkness. The Rasha provided supply caravans and set up emergency waystations stocked with food, water, and medical supplies. The Shamari reinforced Sarim and Qamaria's solar lighting systems, ensuring events like the one that took place during the Festival of Unity would not happen again. The Ulema mobilized their merchants, spreading news of the kingdom's resilience, in order to reassure traders as well as maintain commerce flowing through the King's road. The peoples of Zarah were fighting back - and they would not yield to the enemy so easily.

The aftermath of Velkara's sabotage lingered like a shadow over Qamaria for weeks. As the city's defences were fortified and Shamari engineers worked tirelessly to prevent another attack, reports from Sura's network flowed in - Draconian movements along the borders had increased threefold. The council chambers in Sarim buzzed with tension day and night. Then, just before dawn on the twentieth day after the festival, what many feared finally came to pass.

Incensed by their failures, Drathis sent an emissary to Sarim with a chilling message. It was the early hours of the morning when, undisguised, the reptilian envoy, draped in dark robes and flanked by large Draconian guards from the Varros bloodline, stood before the Council of Tribes and their king. A hush fell over the chamber as councillors exchanged uneasy glances - the brazen appearance of Draconians in their sacred halls was unprecedented, a deliberate show of contempt for their protocols and boundaries.

The air itself seemed to thicken. Rafiq and Sura exchanged meaningful glances, hands unconsciously drifting toward weapon hilts.

"Aran ibn Khalid," the emissary intoned, his voice slithering like a serpent through the air. "I am Nathas, of the House of Draco," he paused, looking around the room. "You stand upon a fragile throne, built on the shifting sands of your own arrogance."

Nathas stepped forward, his slitted eyes gleaming. "Surrender your crown, and we will spare your people. Refuse, and you will watch as Zarah burns - not from war, but from the very power you claim to control," his smirk deepened. "The Weaving does not belong to you, boy. It will devour you whole."

Standing to each side of the king, Rafiq and Sura's eyes met - ready.

Pondering his next words carefully, Aran stepped forward, his gaze unwavering. "Nathas, is it? Well Nathas, do not mistake the apparent frailty of our unity for weakness. Zarah's peoples are proud and stubborn, yes, but we are also strong and resilient. We do not bow to tyrants. Go back and tell Drathis that, if he chooses to bring war to our sands, he will find only defeat."

The Draconian emissary looked taken aback. He now seemed to be pondering ordering his guards to attack the council. Aran, who was carefully studying him, did not miss this subtle change in demeanour.

"Be careful," Aran warned, his voice carrying the authority of his throne. "Do not forget where you are. Your House might be powerful in its own right, but you," he pointed his finger at the emissary. "You, on the other hand, hold no power in these halls!"

Tension was building in the room. Nathas hissed loudly, his tone was venomous as he addressed the rest of the council. "Who do you desert dwellers think you are? Just because you recently found a leader with some vision, all of a sudden you think you pose a threat to the House of Draco. We take what we want, others can either acquiesce to our demands or they can die trying to stop us," he made a gesture, an almost imperceptible nod of the head, for his guards to attack the king.

Well aware of what was about to happen, Aran raised a hand.

In a flash of a second, every Draconian had a blade to their throat.

"I warned you not to forget where you are," he ordered his elite guards, holding their blades under reptile necks, to disarm their prey. "Now, leave us. Return to Drathis and tell him that we will not be defeated so easily."

The emissary looked perplexed. Their king was allowing them to return without punishment?

The council chamber fell into tense silence, each member's hand drifting instinctively toward their weapons. The Draconian guards shifted uneasily, their reptilian eyes darting between their emissary and the desert king who defied all their expectations.

There was no worse insult one could throw at the Draco, other than forgiveness, for they saw it as weakness. "You are letting us go without retribution?" Nathas spat, making no effort to conceal his venomous tone.

"No. Or rather, yes." Aran replied. "Just not the way you think. Instead of harming you, which would not solve our problem, I will allow you to return safely to your master." The reptilian scoffed at these words.

"A gesture, I am sure, you would not extend to me." Aran quipped, though he knew it to be true.

The emissary's snout curled into a smile, his eyes cold as ice.

Aran, aware of the meaning behind the smirk, added. "Make no mistake about it. I am not letting you go out of the kindness of my heart," He declared. "I want you to deliver my message to Drathis."

Nathas' eyes narrowed. "So be it, Aran ibn Khalid, your message shall be delivered," he hissed - his tone as chilling as that of a Sand Serpent, in the night. "But know this. You will pay for every word of yours I deliver to him. In the end, we will destroy you!"

With that, accompanied by his guards, the emissary turned and left the council room, leaving the kingdom on edge.

The council met late into the afternoon, its voices filled with both determination and apprehension. "The Draco will come, and this time they will not be testing us - they will be seeking to break us," Kasim al-Bahir was the first to speak, his voice edged with steel.

Farid, who had been silent for months during council sessions, leaned forward with a smirk. "Tell me, great King of Zarah," his tone dripping with mockery, fingers drumming impatiently on the crescent table, "when the time comes - when real blood is spilled - will the people still stand with you? Or will they remember that you abandoned them to chase ghosts and myths?"

Murmurs rippled through the council. Aran's eyes locked onto Farid's. "They will," he spoke with confidence, "because I do not lead them with lies and shadows." Farid blushed. Having no response to counter Aran's statement, he sat back down, and remained silent.

Looking directly at Farid, Kasim added, "I will issue orders to my tribe, for them to reinforce our defensive positions."

"As will I." Karim al-Shamar's voice seconded Kasim's. Sura was next. Being Aran's spymaster, she had her hand on Zarah's pulse. Not much happened in the deserts without her having knowledge of its occurrence. "I will tell my agents to double their efforts in rooting out Draconian agents." Rafiq stepped forward. "Our army is strong and we will hold our own. Let them come, we will be ready!"

Safira nodded. "The moons keep showing me visions of fire and shadow, but also of hope. Our unity remains our greatest weapon. Especially during these testing times, while our king is struggling to decide what to do about the obelisks and the Weaving."

Aran kept quiet - listening. His mind racing with strategies, his heart a whirlpool of emotions.

"The Draconians think they can break us. The Primordials think they can erase us. Yet, both are underestimating our spirit. We will fortify our borders, strengthen our defences, and show them that Zarah is more than a collection of deserts. We are a force of nature to be reckoned with."

He had every intention of sharing most of these thoughts with those present. There were, however, a few things he didn't want to divulge to the council just yet. Not until he was sure they were ready to know. To the gathered crowd his words were measured. He decided this was not the time to mention the Primordials. Most of them wouldn't believe him anyway.

"My friends," Aran began. "Let us make sure our defences are well prepared and ready for whatever comes our way. If we remain steady, united, they can not break us. We are desert people, hard to the core.

Our spirit is strong and our resolve is unyielding. I trust in you to honour your duty as I will honour mine," he paused, exhaling deeply.

"I know this is not the best of times for any of you, but I must turn my attention to the Weaving and the threat it poses for all of us. For all of Zarah. I must not postpone it any longer. The Weaving is beginning to unravel. You cannot feel it like I do but, trust me, it is. I am connected to it, by blood. The time has come for me to face the mistakes made by my forebears, for I would rather die than fail them, or you." Aran looked at all council members one by one, ensuring that all of them could sense his determination. "Now, if you will excuse me," he made a gesture to stand. "I will retire. Council adjourned." As he stood, so did the other tribal leaders. Aran bowed to them and left the Crescent table. "Am I strong enough to break the cycle? Or will I become what they fear?" He thought to himself, as he walked through the silver inlaid doors.

Hours later, as the sun began its descent toward the western dunes, Aran found himself alone in the high tower of Sarim's Royal Citadel, overlooking the vast expanse of the sand dunes, under an ochre sunset. The scent of the nearby ocean flirting with his olfactory senses. Dusk descended. Below him, the city hummed with life, unaware of the titanic forces stirring just beyond the horizon, both from this dimension as well as the next. Aran had been feeling it for days - an unease in his heart, as if something paramount was about to happen. Something related to the Weaving. The vision of the Primordials clawed at his mind, a shadow that would not lift. His breath came slower, heavier, as if the very air carried the weight of the doom he had seen.

His hands curled into fists at the memory of the shattered obelisks - their destruction echoing in the Weaving - in his bones. He had seen them awakening. However, he had also made the mistake of destroying the first two. One due to ignorance, the other for lack of confidence in himself.

As he stood there, the ripples of their destruction were spreading through the Weaving like cracks in a dam. "Once the water starts seeping through, it is a matter of time before..." This train of thought was abruptly interrupted by another. It was not only the supernatural forces that threatened his reign. Though his main supporters remained loyal to him, upon looking them in the eyes, he had left the council chamber with the impression that some of the other tribal leaders were faltering in their reliability.

Had this been Drathis' plan all along? Not just to unravel the Weaving, but to unravel him as well? To push him into doubt, to make his council waver, to make his people lose faith before the first true battle was even fought? To put him in a situation where, by destroying the obelisks, he would gain a false sense of knowledge about them, thus bringing forth the unravelling of the Weaving, while Drathis' House worked in disguise to undermine Zarah's social infrastructures from within?

Farid and Ryvan had already begun whispering in the ears of certain minor tribal lords. Aran had seen it in their shifting gazes during the last council meeting - hesitation, doubt. Or worse… calculation.

Truly, an idea to stir the mind, he thought to himself.

Nevertheless, it was one that made sense. Despite everything else, there was one thing he was sure of - regardless of all the progress he had achieved in uniting the tribes, his newborn kingdom remained vulnerable.

Both from within and outside his own court, the tension was palpable. Aran had sensed that tide of suspicion and ambition swirling just beneath the surface. Farid, though thwarted in the council, a while ago, was not yet finished. The Draconian threat kept looming near, and in the halls of his palace, there were whispers. Dark rumours of his absences, of his mind being clouded by visions and distant powers. He knew these murmurs well, for they mirrored the doubts that lingered in his own heart. Was he fit to lead them? Fit to save Zarah from this apparent, looming catastrophe? Was he ready for the impending war with the Draconians? Or had his years of studying, pilgrimage, and diplomacy dulled his warrior's edge, leaving him vulnerable to forces far beyond his control?

Below in the citadel's halls, Aran knew, whispered conversations would already be taking place. Sura had warned him that morning that three minor tribal lords from the eastern settlements had sent inquiries about grain distribution, matters that would normally be handled swiftly through established channels. Now, they demanded personal audiences, testing whether their king's attention had truly turned elsewhere. Each delayed response would be noted, catalogued, and shared among those who questioned his fitness to rule.

The door to the tower opened softly behind him, pulling him away from his thoughts.

He quickly turned, his hand instinctively moving to the hilt of his sword. But it was Rafiq, his steadfast companion, who entered. The powerful man's footsteps echoing in the stone chamber. "You left the council abruptly, and you have been here for hours," Rafiq said, his voice stern but not unkind. "They are growing restless."

Aran let out a long breath, turning back to the window, "I did not leave abruptly," he replied, "I left only after we had discussed matters and not before leaving instructions on how to deal with each one of them." Rafiq remained silent. Taking notice, Aran explained himself, "I just needed some time alone to think, my friend." Looking at his brother-in-arms, he jested. "Besides, the court is always restless. It is their nature."

Rafiq stepped forward, his brow furrowing as he glanced at the fading light outside. "It is different now, Aran. You know that as well as I do. Farid and Ryvan's influence is growing with each passing day. I believe Sura was right - Farid might be working with the Draconians again. As we discussed before, during the council meetings, they have been active and their actions have had serious consequences. The lords of certain tribes are starting to listen to Farid again. They are paying heed to his web of deceit. They began questioning your absence, your secrecy. They speak of the dangers we face, but they truly don't understand them, the dangers you face," he looked at Aran. "The dangers looming over us all."

"They do not need to understand," Aran replied, his voice hardening. "Not yet anyway. They need to remain focused on the Draconian threat. On striving to remain united. Besides, when the time comes, they will know the whole truth. They will not be able to run from it."

"What is that truth? What are we facing?" Rafiq asked expectantly.

He studied Aran in silence, his grip tightening on the hilt of his dagger. "I trust you," he said, his voice steady, "but I also know the Weaving does not let go easily. It took your ancestors. I will not let it take you."

Aran closed his eyes, the vision flashing before him once more. The shattered obelisks, the vast shadow of the Primordials, the world teetering on the edge of oblivion. "The truth is, we have another war on our hands, Rafiq. But not a war of mortals - a war of gods. The Primordials are waking, and if they are freed from the Weaving, they will consume everything in their path. Never mind the Draco, that would be like comparing the crystalline leviathans to sandfish."

Rafiq's eyes darkened. He had seen the ruins of the obelisks, had felt the tremors in the earth beneath his feet. Therefore, he had no reason to doubt Aran's words, but still, the scope of it was beyond anything he had ever imagined. "Then we must stop them. Keep destroying the obelisks, as you have done twice, before the Primordials can be freed." Rafiq had been wondering if Aran was in fact right, in destroying those stone monoliths. Perhaps that was the way to go.

"That is what I thought at first," Aran replied, turning away from the window to face his old friend. "As for the second one. I intended to mend it at first, but something happened with the solar mirrors, its energy became unstable and I feared for the safety of everyone around me. So, I ended up destroying it... Besides, it is not that simple, Rafiq. I have kept up with my studies with Barash, since his return. We have found that the binding... it was never meant to be a permanent solution. The obelisks do not just hold the Primordials. From the moment they were set in place, they became part of the fabric of our world. That being so, destroying them weakens the very reality we live in. Do you understand, my friend? If we break too many, we risk unravelling everything - the world we live in."

Rafiq 's expression tightened. A look of perplexity dawning on his visage. "Then what do we do? Mend them?! What does that even mean?" The man was a warrior, these matters were beyond his grasp.

Aran hesitated, the weight of the decision pressing down on him. "I do not know. Not yet anyway. I desperately need more answers. They might be hidden in the histories of the old kingdoms, in the ruins of the world that existed before the binding. Barash told me that there are ancient texts, forgotten lore that might hold the key to understanding how we can confront the Primordials without destroying ourselves."

Rafiq nodded, his face set in grim determination. "Then we will find them, Aran. Together. Whatever it takes. Whatever happens. I will stand by your side." He locked eyes with his childhood friend, then placed a hand on his shoulder, squeezing gently, in a gesture of reassurance.

Aran smiled faintly. Rafiq's unwavering loyalty was a rare comfort in these dark times, but even that was not enough to dispel the gnawing uncertainty. "There's more," he said quietly. "In the vision... I saw something else. Something that could be a way to fight them."

"What did you see?" Rafiq was hanging on his friend's every word.

Aran's voice dropped lower, as if speaking the words aloud would summon the very thing he feared. "It appeared to be some sort of knowledge, of incredible power, from the First Age when the Primordials walked on Zarah. Something that could be turned into a weapon, but it also felt like it was more than that. I sensed it to be more like a bond, a pact between the mortal world and the forces beyond. If I can learn it, I may be able to harness the power of the Weaving with greater control."

Rafiq's brow furrowed. "A sort of knowledge, a weapon, you say? But what kind of weapon could stand against beings like the Primordials?"

Aran shook his head. "I do not know, but our research has led me to believe that it was hidden in the Echo of Worlds."

At the mention of the Echo, Rafiq stiffened. Blood running cold in his veins. He feared no man or beast, but they had barely escaped that liminal place once, and now his friend was speaking of returning there? The Echo was a place of shadows, a reflection of their world where time and reality bled into one another. It was a dangerous place, extremely unpredictable, and filled with horrors that defied understanding. However, if what his friend was saying was true, it could also hold the key to their survival.

"We will need more than just ourselves this time," Rafiq's voice was steely. "If we are considering going back to the Echo, we are going to need powerful allies." As those last words left his throat, absent-mindedly, he looked to the north.

"I wholeheartedly agree," Aran replied, his mind already racing through the names of those who might join their cause. "But not just any allies, Rafiq. We need people who understand the old ways, those who have studied ancient histories, and the Weaving. Upon his return, Barash told me that there are scholars in the northern kingdom, priests in the mountains who still honour the old faith. That is where he went, in search of answers, when he left us last time. If I know Barash, I believe they will be expecting our arrival."

Rafiq's expression darkened, his eyes facing the very north Aran was suggesting venturing into. "When you say they," Rafiq's voice was low, "Do you mean the northern kingdom? The kingdom of Ryvath?"

Aran nodded. The kingdom of Ryvath had long been one of the great powers in the north, a line steeped in the old traditions and magic of the world, going back thousands of years. Their relationship with the rest of Zarah had been tenuous at best and, at worst, fraught with open hostility. However, if there were any in the world who still understood the mysteries of the Weaving, it was them. They desperately needed to find a way to benefit from their knowledge.

"Isn't it ironic how destiny is never played along a straight line?" Aran mused to himself. Never, upon attempting to achieve his vision, trying to unite the tribes and kingdoms of Zarah, did he dream that road would have led him here - fighting for the very fabric of the world they lived in.

A sudden gust of wind tore through the chamber, rattling the cactus-silk shutters. Aran froze, the hairs on his arms rising. The Weaving was shifting again. He could feel it inside him - like a whisper threading through his veins. "I have thought this through to the point of exhaustion, and I do not see any other way. If we are to stop the Primordials, I need the knowledge the Ryvath tribe possesses. If we wait any longer, we may be too late," he confessed, the weight of his visions pressing against his chest.

Rafiq's jaw tightened, but he nodded firmly. Looking his king, his lifetime friend, directly in the eyes, his only words were, "Then we shall go north." His voice was steady and determined.

Aran placed, in turn, a hand on Rafiq's shoulder, the gesture now one of gratitude. An attempt to convey without words, how much his friendship and loyalty meant to him. "Thank you, my friend. Now, go prepare the men. We leave at dawn."

As Leander's primary commenced its daily dance across the undulating dunes, it cast forth a radiant tapestry of amber and saffron that suffused the ancient citadel of Sarim. Such radiance spilt like molten gold through the cityscape and its weathered stone, transforming every surface it touched into a canvas of ethereal luminescence. "How resplendent," Aran thought to himself. "Dawn - the sun's own paean to Zarah." It truly was an ephemeral masterpiece, rendered in light and shadow.

Beneath this auroral mantle, three magnificent obsidian steeds stood proud, their lustrous coats catching the dawn's nascent rays like liquid onyx. These noble beasts, bred from the finest bloodlines of the desert realms, bore their distinguished riders with regal grace. Aran himself sat astride his steed, flanked by his ever-faithful companion, Rafiq, to his right, and Sura, his steadfast friend, to his left.

Their horses' coats rippled with each movement, a mesmerizing dance of light upon darkness, as though the very stars of night had been captured in their gleaming flanks. Their proud necks arched with practised nobility, while their eyes, keen as polished jet, surveyed the gathering warriors below. The steeds' muscles, honed by countless leagues across the singing sands, tensed and relaxed beneath their riders, charged with the restless energy that always heralded the dawn of great journeys.

From their elevated position, Aran and his companions observed their assembled company in contemplative silence, the weight of their impending embassy to Ryvath heavy in the morning air. The horses shifted in perfect synchronicity, their silver-shod hooves leaving precise crescents in the dawn-kissed sand. They were a mirror of their riders' own unspoken brotherhood, forged through years of shared triumphs and tribulations.

Yet beneath this celestial pageantry, Aran's warriors stood in contemplative disquiet, their hearts harbouring that peculiar admixture of anticipation and trepidation that precedes all great ventures. Each polished piece of their sand-serpent scale armour reflected the dawn's glory, while within their breasts stirred that ancient tension known to all who had stood upon the precipice of destiny.

Though he had summoned them as their king, Aran had made certain every man in the company knew exactly what they were signing up for. Taking one last look at Sarim, Aran turned to Rafiq. "Let us go. Please give the order for departure."

As the company formed their mounted column, Kasim al-Bahir approached Aran's obsidian steed, his weathered face grave with unspoken concerns. "My king," he said quietly, his voice pitched for Aran's ears alone, "I have sent word to my brothers in the outer

settlements. They will watch the trade routes in your absence." He paused, his calloused hand resting on the horse's flank. "But know that some among the council grow... restless. Return swiftly, with whatever answers you seek. The kingdom needs its king present, not just in spirit." Aran met the older man's eyes, seeing there the same unwavering loyalty that had first drawn the tribes together.
"I will return, Kasim. And when I do, Zarah will be stronger for what I have learned."

The journey northward was long and gruelling, the roads winding through treacherous mountain passes and over desolate plains. With each day that passed, Aran felt the weight of his decisions like a stone upon his chest. The long, cold nights gnawed at his resolve, and in the solitude of campfires, he found himself tracing the hilt of his father's sword, as if it could ground him.
He knew that returning to Sarim with the answers he sought would not only determine the fate of his future kingdom but also solidify his place in history - either as the king who saved Zarah or the one who doomed it.
As the days stretched into weeks, the group's numbers began to dwindle. Some of his warriors fell to bandit attacks, while others simply abandoned the quest, unwilling to face the dangers that lay ahead. Aran allowed them to leave without repercussions, but he pressed on - setting the example, driven by the certainty that failure was not an option.
For weeks, they rode through landscapes that seemed carved by increasingly alien hands - first the familiar amber dunes giving way to grey stone, then to peaks that clawed at storm-heavy skies.
The third week brought them closer, where the mountain winds carried voices of the ancient dead. There, as they navigated treacherous ledges slick with cold stone, two of his finest Tarek warriors - men who had stood with him since the first tribal gathering - simply vanished in the night, leaving only their weapons behind. Whether taken by the Draco or driven to despair by homesickness, Aran could not say.
What he could feel, however, was how the Weaving's influence grew thinner with each northward mile, as if the very fabric of reality wore threadbare in these forgotten reaches.
Finally, after what felt like an eternity, they reached the borders of the northern kingdom of Ryvath.
Following three weeks of hard travel, the landscape began to change dramatically. The air was colder, the skies darker. Snow capped the jagged peaks of the mountains, and the land itself seemed to exude an ancient, primal energy.

Aran felt that there, the influence of the Weaving was different, and the old magic of the world still lingered in the shadows. "What will I find here?" he asked himself, unaware that he did so, out loud.
Sura, looking at him enigmatically, uttered two words. "Maybe, yourself." She gave him a wink, her eyes hypnotic.
On the twenty-fourth day of their journey, as winter's first frost appeared on their morning blankets, the imposing silhouette of Ryvath's mountain fortress appeared on the horizon.
The stronghold itself was carved into the side of the mountain, its towers rising like jagged teeth against the sky. As they approached the gates, Aran felt a strange sense of déjà vu, as if he had been here before - though he knew that was impossible. This place, like the Echo, seemed to exist on the border of reality, its presence both ethereal and imposing. The gates now loomed before them, hewn from black stone that seemed to drink the light. The Ryvath warriors emerged from the shadows, their dark armour blending into the mountain's gloom. Their eyes, cold and assessing, lingered on Aran for a moment too long - as if they were measuring not just his words, but his very soul. The leader of the delegation, a tall, broad-shouldered man with a scar running down the side of his face, stepped forward.
"You seek an audience with the Lord of Ryvath," the man said, his voice rough though not unwelcoming. Barash's charm seemed to not have been wasted on them.
"I do," Aran replied, meeting the man's gaze without flinching. "I am sure you have felt the shifting of the sands. My tutor, Barash, advised me to come here in search of knowledge. He believes that what I may find will help me save us all from what looms beyond the horizon."
The man studied him for a long moment, saying nothing, then nodded. "He was here himself. A fascinating man, to be sure. He warned us that you would be coming. Please, follow me," he bowed slightly.
They were led into the heart of the fortress, Aran could feel the weight of centuries pressing down on him. The halls were lined with ancient tapestries, depicting scenes of long-forgotten battles and strange rituals. The air was thick with the scent of Moonleaf incense, and faint, almost imperceptible whispers seemed to echo from the stone walls.
Finally, they entered the great hall, where the Lord of Ryvath sat upon a throne carved from black stone. He was an old man, his hair white as snow, his face lined with age and wisdom.
His eyes, however, were sharp and clear, holding depths that seemed to reflect not just centuries of accumulated wisdom, but glimpses of the very foundations upon which reality rested - as if he had gazed too long into the Weaving itself and carried its mysteries within his regard.

"Aran of Karash," the lord said, his voice resonant and commanding, each syllable deliberate as ancient ritual. "You seek knowledge of the Weaving and the Primordials. Knowledge that has not been shared with outsiders since before your great-grandfather's grandfather drew first breath."

This was not a question, so Aran remained silent, his eyes locked with the old man's, studying him. After a long, uncomfortable pause, the lord of Ryvath leaned forward and asked him. "What makes you think, Aran, son of Khalid, that we would share such secrets with you?”

Aran took a deep breath, steeling himself. "Because, if the Primordials are released, it will not just be my kingdom that suffers. It will be yours as well. All of Zarah will fall, as you well know." Aran's voice dropped to a near whisper. "I have seen it in the Weaving - lands turned to glass, the Yaran sea boiling away, the very air we breathe becoming poison. Not conquest, not subjugation, but erasure. The Primordials will not rule what we leave behind - they will unmake it entirely, returning Zarah to the formless chaos from which they first shaped it." He paused, still holding the old ruler's gaze. "The very fabric of our world will unravel." Aran was looking for any kind of reaction from the old monarch.

The Lord of Ryvath leaned in, the dim torchlight casting deep shadows across his lined face. His old gaze, still sharp as flint, fixed upon Aran's. “Knowledge is never given freely, young king,” he said, his voice a whisper of ancient echoes. “What do you offer in return?”

“I offer you an alliance,” Aran replied, his voice firm. “Together, we can confront the Primordials and restore balance to our world. I will not stand by and watch as my kingdom falls into chaos. Everything I have done to unite the desert tribes into one House will be lost. If you have the means to help, I will do everything in my power to see that your tribe is highly honoured.”

For a long moment, silence hung in the air, heavy with expectation. Finally, the lord leaned back in his throne, his eyes narrowing. “Your passion is commendable, Aran, but passion alone will not suffice you. Deeper knowledge of the Weaving always comes at a price.”

Barash had not mentioned this. The revelation struck Aran like a shifting dune beneath his feet, unsettling yet inevitable. His mind became a storm of questions. “What price?” he finally asked, his heart racing. The lord tilted his head, studying him closely.

“You seem like a very bright young man. Therefore, I am sure you have gathered by now that the knowledge you seek is not hidden in the Echo of Worlds, but rather here.” Rafiq let out a quiet sigh of relief.

“However,” the old ruler warned, “to attain the knowledge that you seek, you must first confront the spirits of the Old Kings who still guard these secrets. Brace for what comes next, for they will not give you their wisdom lightly. First, you must prove yourself worthy."

Aran swallowed hard. "How do I do that?"

"The trials of the Old Kings are almost as old as the desert itself," the lord of Ryvath intoned, his voice like the shifting of stone. "They do not test merely strength or courage - they test the weight of your soul. Your past, your failures, your hidden truths… these will rise before you as spectres. If you are not ready, they will break you." He looked deep into Aran's eyes. "Only then, if you prevail, will they grant you access to the knowledge you seek."

Aran felt a mix of dread and determination coursing through him. This was the path he had chosen, and there was no turning back now.

"I accept the challenge," he said firmly.

"Very well," the old king replied, a faint smile touching his aged lips. "But know that the trials will not prove themselves to be easy. Prepare yourself accordingly, for what lies ahead may shake you to your very core."

Aran, Sura and Rafiq were given quarters for the night, though any of them barely slept. As the hours rolled by, and he made ready for the trials ahead, Aran felt a growing sense of purpose within him. Each step he took was one closer to understanding the Weaving and, in turn, the Primordials. No matter what came his way, he would prove himself worthy, not just for his people but, more importantly, to himself.

Nevertheless, as he pondered on the trials that awaited him, he couldn't shake the feeling that the true storm was still gathering, not only within himself but all across Zarah.

In the shadows of Sarim, Farid and the Draconian conspirators were, most certainly, not idle. If Rafiq's suspicions were correct, he was plotting, gathering support among the faltering tribal lords, waiting for the moment when Aran's absence would reveal their weakness. Then he would exploit it, in Drathis' favour.

As winter crept over the land, the shadows stirred - whispering secrets, testing Aran's resolve. Deep down, he knew, without a doubt, that before this was over, he would either master the Weaving - or be broken by it.

Chapter XIV

The Trials of the Old Kings

The morning after his audience with the Lord of Ryvath, the cold mountain air seemed sharper - laden with the gravity of the task ahead. The ancient fortress seemed suspended outside of time, its towering walls encased in frost and memory, its halls echoing with the whispers of a long-forgotten past. That day, those whispers would become voices, for it was the day Aran would face the judgement of the Old Kings.

He stood in the outer courtyard with Rafiq, Sura, and a few of the northern warriors who had decided to join them after their arrival.

His breath rose in pale clouds as he steadied himself for what lay ahead - the trials that would evaluate not only his strength or resilience, but also his right to stand before history.

Each one would test a different aspect of his character. His physical prowess, his courage, his wisdom and, ultimately, his worthiness to carry the burden of the knowledge he so desperately needed.

"Are you certain about doing this?" Rafiq asked, his voice edged with concern. His hand rested on the hilt of his dagger, though they both knew steel would do little against the spirits of the past.

"I made my choice long ago," Aran replied, his tone resolute, though a flicker of doubt still gnawed at him. "Besides, if I do not do this..." he paused, catching his breath in the cold morning air. "If I do not learn and understand how to fully control the Weaving. How to contain the Primordials. Then we can forget the House of Draco, because Zarah will fall, regardless of their warmongering. This may well be our only path forward."

Rafiq sighed heavily, his gaze drifting toward the towering keep of Ryvath where the old magic still lingered like a mist. "I am not saying this to deter you, but the Old Kings were not known for their mercy. These trials could break you."

Aran turned to face his friend fully, his eyes hard. "Then I shall make sure that I endure them. The tribal leaders must know I am strong enough to lead them in this battle."

Sura stepped forward, her voice quiet but steady as she stared into his eyes. "You have already proven yourself. Time and time again. In spite of that, you should do well to remember that the Old Kings will not just test physical strength. They will delve into your heart - your past. You must be prepared to face the truth of who you are," she exchanged looks with Rafiq, then added, "do not forget, Aran, we might be able to lie to others, but never truly to ourselves."

Sura's words sent a chill down his spine, but he nodded nonetheless, taking in the advice.

The trials ahead, particularly when facing the Primordials, would not be battles of sword alone. They would be battles of the soul. He had expected as much, though the thought of facing the deepest parts of himself unsettled him more than any physical foe ever had.

They entered Ryvath's Hall of Kings, a vast, circular chamber deep within the mountain keep. The air was thick with incense and the lingering scent of some ancient power. The walls were lined with murals depicting the history of this northern kingdom and the rulers who had once reigned from this very place.

To his right stood a masterfully carved depiction of the tale of Uramak, the Sand Serpent, and to his left, a detailed carving of Amara, the legendary queen, taking flight in her Nightwing. The carvings seemed infused with life, as if history itself had awakened.

At the centre of the hall, a great stone circle lay carved into the floor, encircled by glowing runes pulsing with arcane light.

An ancient figure awaited them in the chamber - an elder priest, draped in heavy robes embroidered with the distorted sun symbols of the Old Kings. The very same symbols Aran had seen in Sarim's Old Quarter, many months ago. Could it really have been a year? Time had drifted as a river beyond his ken, its currents unmarked by mortal reckoning.

Aran studied the old man. Though the priest's eyes were clouded with age, a sharpness in his expression belied his years. The mural carvings flickered in the torchlight, as if waiting in expectance.

"King Aran," the priest intoned, his voice echoing off the stone walls. "You seek the knowledge of the Weaving, the secrets that can bind or break the Primordials. Yet, such power is not given freely. The kings of old guard it, and they will not yield it to one unworthy."

They had already told him this. Why repeat it now? Most likely due to protocol, but Aran couldn't help but wonder if it was because they suspected that unworthiness was already inside him.

"I understand," he replied, stepping into the circle. His heart pounded in his chest, but he kept his face steady. He was ready. Was he not?

The priest raised a gnarled hand, his fingers curling as he murmured a chant in the old tongue. The runes around the stone circle flared to life, casting a harsh light across the chamber.

Servants moved dexterously, lighting the ceremonial incense.

As the light grew brighter, and the scented smoke swirled around Aran, he felt a pull, a tugging sensation that seemed to draw him inward, deeper into himself, and farther away from the world around him. Though his body remained within the stone circle, his consciousness slipped free, untethered from flesh.

This was more than illusion or vision - the Old Kings would test his very essence, in a realm where thought became reality and the boundaries between memory, fear, and possibility dissolved.

The chamber blurred and faded, and suddenly, he was no longer standing in Ryvath's Hall of Kings.

He found himself in a vast field of endless twilight, the sky above him a swirling mix of violet and gold. The ground beneath his feet was soft, like the shifting sands of a dream. Ahead, rising from the horizon, were the figures of five towering thrones, each occupied by a spectral regent, their forms shimmering like ghosts caught between worlds.

These were the Old Kings, the rulers of the First Age, before the Weaving had forged Zarah to its current state, before the world had been bound to its current order.

Each king bore a crown of a different design and material. One crown of iron, one of silver, one of gold, one of crystal, and one made of burnt wood. Solarwood, it seemed to him. Their faces were obscured, but their voices rang clear as one.

"Aran of Karash," they spoke in unison, their voices layered like the rolling of distant thunder - the unfolding sound of a lightning storm. "You seek to walk the path of the Old Kings to claim the knowledge that was lost to time." There was a long pause, then the thundering voices continued. "However, before we judge you worthy or not of such power, you must prove yourself to be deserving of it."

"I stand ready," Aran shouted, though his voice felt weak in the vastness of the twilight field. "Even though I do not feel ready whatsoever," he whispered to himself. The Old Kings sat, silent, observant.

The king with the iron crown spoke first. His voice was deep, resonant with the weight of battle. "Strength." The iron king said. "The first trial is strength. In the days of old, we ruled through conquest - through force of arms. Show us that you have the strength to bear the crown."

The field shifted again, and suddenly Aran stood on the battlefield of Sarim, years earlier, during one of the bloodiest conflicts in the kingdom's history - the Battle of Al Kharan.

Aran recognized the scene instantly. This was the moment when he had led the charge against the forces of the Halithar tribe, a smaller southern realm that had risen in defiance of Sarim's rule.

The sound of clashing steel and the screams of the dying filled his ears, and Aran felt the familiar weight of his father's sword in his hand.

He looked around, and there they were, his men, fighting and dying around him.

Rafiq was at his side, his swords flashing as he cut down enemies with ruthless efficiency. Strangely, this time, a few things were different, as if taken from a delirious nightmare. The Halithar warriors were not mere men. Their forms flickered, half-seen in the twilight haze, their eyes glowing with an unnatural light. They moved with a speed and ferocity that defied reason, their weapons cutting through flesh and armour with terrifying ease.

Aran raised his sword, shouting commands to the men around him, but the battle seemed to be spiralling out of control. The enemy forces surged forward, overwhelming his lines, cutting down his warriors with brutal precision.

Suddenly, Rafiq fell beside him, a spear thrust through his chest, and Aran's heart lurched with horror. "No!" he shouted, his voice raw with desperation. His mind reeled in confusion. "Wait - Rafiq did not fall at Al Kharan. This is not how it happened."

The realization struck him even as he parried another attack.

This was no mere memory - the Old Kings had twisted his past into something new, something designed to test him beyond what he had already faced. But there was no time to dwell on it; the onslaught of the supernatural Halithar forces was relentless.

Aran kept charging forward, cutting through the enemy with all his strength. Still, it was not enough to sway the tide, for they kept coming, relentless - an endless tide of death and destruction.

Aran's men were falling, and there was nothing he could do to stop it. He shouted. "Forgive me brothers, but I cannot save you all."

Then the voice of the iron-crowned king thundered through his mind, a force that rattled his very bones. "Strength is not the measure of a single man. It is the weight of those who follow you, those who will live - or die - by your command."

Aran's breath came ragged, his muscles burned, but the words struck deeper than any blade could. He had spent years mastering the sword, but had he truly learned the cost of wielding it? After a short pause, the disembodied voice asked. "Can you bear that weight, King Aran from Karash? Are you willing to?"

Aran gritted his teeth, his muscles burning with exhaustion as he fought on. His men were dying around him, and his heart ached with the weight of their loss. He could not save them all, not even if he tried - he could not be everywhere at once. He needed to make a choice, and fast. Either to fight on the front lines or retreat and rally his remaining forces for a counterattack.

It was then that the simple realization struck him like lightning.

He could not win this battle, or any other for that matter, through sheer force alone. He had to lead, to strategize. He had to command.

With a roar of defiance, Aran sheathed his sword and turned to his surviving warriors. "Fall back!" he shouted, his deep voice cutting through the chaos. "To me! To me! Regroup!"

At first, they hesitated, unwilling to abandon the fight. Then they saw the determination in his eyes, and slowly, they began to retreat, forming a defensive line around him. Aran stood at the centre, issuing orders, directing the flow of battle with clarity harnessed from years of experience. He watched as his men rallied, their formation tightening, their defence growing stronger. Slowly, the tide of the battle turned. The enemy forces began to falter, their momentum broken by the disciplined retreat of Aran's forces. When the time was right, he led the counterattack, striking with precision and overwhelming the enemy with the strength of his united army. At that moment, he felt in his heart the weight of command.

Without warning, the battlefield started to dissolve like ink bleeding into water. One moment, Aran stood amidst the cries of the dying - the next, the field of twilight reformed around him.

The battlefield was gone, but the weight of command lingered in Aran's bones. He breathed deeply, tasting the strange metallic tang of this twilight realm. The ground beneath his feet shifted, the very fabric of reality rearranging itself as the next test formed around him.

He gasped, gripping his chest, the ghost of exhaustion lingering in his limbs. The iron-crowned king watched him in silence, then inclined his head ever so slightly. "You have passed the trial of strength," the king said. "Always remember that strength is not only found in the sword arm or in the muscles of your body, but also in the heart and mind that guides them."

Aran nodded, humbled, his heart pounding in his ears from the intensity of the trial. Rafiq's death had been an illusion, but he had not expected it to feel so real. Truth be told - he had not expected the trial to be so personal. "Maybe, yourself," he recalled Sura saying. She had a way about her, a natural, intuitive manner of cutting through the superficial, straight into his heart. "How many more of her clues have I missed, and how many more will I?" He chuckled, but knew he couldn't lower his guard. There were more trials ahead, more obstacles to overcome. This had only been the first of several.

His mind on Sura, Aran steeled himself for what would come next.

In the distance, the thrones stood, all five kings were observing him in silence. Time, in this place, seemed to stretch, as vast as eternity itself.

He had questions he wanted to ask, burning in his throat, but decided it would be best to wait.

As the silence stretched into the vastness of the twilight realm, the second king, adorned with an ornate silver crown, spoke. His voice was not deep or resonant, but smooth - a whisper like a gentle breeze over calm waters.

"Wisdom," the silver king began. "The second trial is founded on insight. In the days of old, we ruled through power but lacked the wisdom that knowledge should bring. Prove to us that, beyond strength, you possess the wisdom to rule your people justly."

After a moment of silence, his voice heavy with unspoken judgement, the king asked. "Wisdom, Aran - do you possess it?"

Before he had time to process the question, the acrid smoke of battle dissolved into the musty sweetness of ancient parchment, reality reshaping itself around him.

He found himself standing in a vast library, its shelves filled with ancient tomes and scrolls, towering high above him. The air was thick with the scent of old parchment and the quiet hum of arcane energy. Before him stood a figure of a woman dressed in flowing robes, her face was partly obscured by a hood.

"You look just like my m-" he tried to say, but she raised a hand, beckoning silence.

The resemblance unsettled him deeply. His mother had been gone for years, but her face remained carved in his memory. This woman's eyes held the same knowing depth, her gesture the same quiet authority that had guided his childhood. Was this a trick of the Old Kings, using his memories against him? Or something deeper - a connection to the wisdom passed through his bloodline?

In her other hand she was holding a scroll, her voice was soft but firm as she spoke, further reminding Aran of his own progenitor.

"The Weaving is a complex and dangerous force, one that can shape worlds or destroy them. You are here because you seek to control it, my child, but do you understand the true nature of what you seek?"

Aran hesitated, unsure of how to respond. He had learned much about the Weaving during his tutelage under Barash but, the truth was, he did not fully understand the complexity of its depths yet.

In many of its facets, the Weaving remained a mystery to him - a force passed down through the Ages, through bloodline, its origins shrouded in myth and legend. And yet, its secrets continued to elude him - as if mocking his efforts.

The weight of her question hung in the air between them. Just as Aran gathered his thoughts to answer, suddenly, the woman shifted her stance. She held out the scroll to him, accompanied with a warning. "To master the Weaving is to walk the edge of oblivion," she intoned, her voice distant, layered as though a hundred generations spoke in unison. "Every king who has sought this knowledge has paid its price. Some in blood. Others with their very souls."

A chill settled into Aran's bones, deeper than the mountain air. The parchment in her outstretched hand seemed to pulse, alive with unseen power. Was this wisdom - or a trap?" Why could he not shake the unnerving feeling that this was his mother?

He reached out, his hand hovering over the scroll. He could feel the weight of the decision pressing down on him. The knowledge contained within this very document could be the key to defeating the Primordials, to saving his unified kingdom.

"But at what cost, and for whom?" he pondered. This and numerous other questions were flashing through his mind, as his hand hovered over the scroll. No matter the consequences he would face, in order to save Zarah, he was more than willing to pay the ultimate price - his life.

When his fingers brushed the parchment, a sudden rush of images flooded his mind. Visions of the past, of the ancient kings who had wielded the power of the Weaving and the terrible destruction they had wrought. He saw cities reduced to ash, entire kingdoms torn apart by the uncontrolled use of its power. In the heart of it all, stood the Primordials, vast and terrible, their power unleashed upon the world.

Aran recoiled, his mind reeling from the intensity of the visions.

The Old Kings, in their unchecked vanity and hubris, had recklessly used the power of the Weaving to achieve their own egotistical goals and ambitions, without regard for the lives of others or, what's more, for the repercussions of their own choices. Now, it was time for him to make his own and pay its price.

The visions shattered around him, leaving him breathless, trembling. The Weaving - it was not a tool, not a weapon. It was a living current, untamed and eternal. It had never been meant to be controlled, only understood. The kings before him had grasped at its power like greedy hands reaching for fire - and they had burned for it.

To use it heedlessly would be to invite an inevitable disaster.

Aran looked at his mother, his decision clear in his mind. "I will seek the knowledge of the Weaving, but I swear on our forebears that I will not repeat their mistakes, nor will I use it without caution. The power it holds is too great to be wielded carelessly, I know that now. I will respect its limits, and if I fail, I will find another way to defeat the Primordials. You have my word." He waited expectantly for her reply.

She regarded him for a long time, then gently nodded. "You have passed the trial of wisdom, Aran, son of Khalid." The library trembled, the scrolls fluttering like restless birds. A whisper curled through the air, its source unseen, unfathomable. "However, wisdom alone will not save you, my child."

The woman faded away as the king wearing the gold crown stepped into the library. His crown seemed forged not from earthly metal but from something richer, as though the very sun had been melted down to adorn his brow. His robes were embroidered with threads of starlight, and his eyes burned with an intensity that pierced the soul.

The library dissolved, replaced by the golden sands of Zarah's dunes. These were not the familiar deserts Aran came to know so well, throughout his life. No. This was a nightmare given form. The sun blazed down like an unforgiving eye, and before him stretched a battlefield soaked in the blood of his people. Worse - he saw them fall. Kasim al-Bahir, his once-unbreakable dune stalker blade shattered at his feet. Sura, her fierce, piercing green eyes staring lifelessly at the sky. Safira, her Crescent Bow, broken in her grasp. His cousin, Zahira, was slaughtered at his feet. The banners of Zarah, torn and burning, fluttered in the wind as the House of Draco stood victorious - Drathis' laughter echoing like the tolling of funeral bells.

Aran stumbled backwards, his breath shallow. "No. This is not real."

"It could be," came the voice of the golden-crowned king, stepping forward. His face was stern, devoid of mercy. "You fear failure, Aran ibn Khalid. You fear it more than death itself. You wear Zarah's crown, but do you understand the cost of wearing it? What if this is to be the price of your reign?"

Aran clenched his fists. "I will not allow it to happen. I cannot!"

The king's gaze burned into him. "Will you not? Or is this the path already set in motion, long before you were born? You fear the weakness in your blood, the whisper of ambition, the hunger for power. What if the path to victory means becoming what you despise the most?"

A shadow moved across the battlefield. Aran turned on the spot. He couldn't believe his eyes, for what he saw made him question his own sanity. He was looking at himself. Rather, it was another version of himself, one clad in black armour. His eyes were cold and empty, standing upon the ruins of the House he had worked so hard to build.

This future-Aran raised his blade, and ordered his people to kneel before him, not as a king, but as a tyrant.

"You fear this most of all, do you not?" The golden king whispered. "That you are not a protector, but a conqueror in disguise?"

Aran's breath came in short, ragged bursts. His chest tightened, as though unseen hands were crushing his ribs. The image of himself - merciless, clad in black, ruling over a conquered wasteland - seared into his mind like a hot brand. He clenched his fists, fingernails biting into his palms. "No," he whispered, then louder. "I will not become that!" his voice cracked, but it held firm. "I did not forge Zarah's unity for conquest - I did it to protect them."

"Then prove it!" the king challenged. "Do not let your fear control you, when you should be the one controlling it. Master yourself."

Aran took a deep breath, trying to focus his mind. He could not allow his consternation to be his master. In that moment, something else shifted in him. The battlefield trembled. The visions of his fallen loved ones flickered, their pain fading. Aran stepped forward, rejecting fear, rejecting weakness. "I accept the burden of my choices and I will not let fear rule me."

"Good," the king exhaled. "Fear is for those who know, with all certainty, what the future will bring. No one alive has ever been in that position. Fear does have its use, to a certain degree, but for the most part it profits man nothing." As Aran's surroundings began to swirl around him once more, he heard the voice say. "You have passed the trial of fear." When the smoke dissipated, Aran found himself in the twilight field, facing the Old Kings.

The king that bore the crown of crystal spoke next. Each facet of his diadem reflected countless images of Aran - versions of himself that were twisted, broken, or exalted in glory. His robes shimmered like the surface of a still lake, rippling with the weight of unseen futures.

The field began to morph. Aran now stood in the Lunar Citadel of Sarim. The council chamber was alive with debate, but the faces around the table were filled with looks of accusation. Kasim al-Bahir slammed a fist on the table. "We have to act now! The Draco are regrouping. Either we strike first, or we die waiting!"

Safira's voice was calm but firm. "If we attack, we risk losing everything. We must protect our people, not march them into war."

The worst came when Sura stepped forward. "Aran, you must choose," she said. "You can not serve two masters. Make your decision, will it be Zarah, or your own conscience? Which will it be?"

Then he saw them - two distinct futures laid bare before him. One path showed him choosing the safety of Zarah, abandoning Sura to capture or death. In this vision, he became a wise and beloved king, but his heart was scarred, carrying the weight of her loss forever.

The other path showed him choosing her, saving her at the cost of Zarah's future. The council was torn apart, and the Draco, led by Drathis, descended upon a weakened kingdom, its defences crumbling.

The crystal-crowned king spoke, his voice heavy with sorrow.

"Loyalty is the virtue of kings, but so is sacrifice, as so many regents seem to forget. What are you willing to give up for your duty?"

Aran clenched his jaw. "Surely, there must be another way."

The crystal king's gaze bore into him. "There might not be one. To rule is to carry the burden of responsibility."

Aran exhaled slowly. "Then I would choose Zarah. But mark my words - I will never stop searching for another path. I would rather sacrifice myself, for I will never accept the sacrifice of others in my stead."

The crystal king remained silent for a long time. His presence began to fade, but when he finally spoke, his words were unexpectedly kind. "You have shown your true character, Aran ibn Khalid. A king should always be ready and willing to sacrifice himself ahead of his charge. You have passed the trial of selflessness." Before Aran could blink, the scene shifted once more, and darkness engulfed him.

The last king sat further back in the shadows. This one wore the crown of burnt wood, its jagged edges blackened as if consumed by an unholy fire. His presence was suffocating to bear, a pitiless void that seemed to drink in what light there was left around him. When the smoke faded, Aran was standing at the edge of a cliff. Below him stretched a ruined Zarah, its dunes dark with spilt blood. The wind howled, not with the voice of the desert, but with the whispers of the fallen - Kasim, Sura, Safira, their voices layered over one another in a chorus of despair. A shattered Crescent Banner lay half-buried in the sand. When he tried to move, the shadows clung to him, pulling him downward, toward the graves of those he had failed to save.

The king's voice emerged from the shadows. It was jagged, like the cracking of burning wood. "Honour is a fine thing, king of Zarah, but tell me, what of your mistakes?" The shadows shifted, and Aran saw them - the moments he regretted. The times he had doubted his own people. The decisions where his hesitation had cost lives. The warriors who had perished because he had chosen wrongly.

"Do you think you are deserving of leadership?" the shadow king whispered. Aran's throat tightened. "I do not know." He truly did not.

The king tilted his head. "That is the correct answer. That is the honest response of a man who understands the burden of command. You have proven yourself to be worthy of your charge. Only those who do not seek power are deserving of its weight. You have passed the trial of power."

The darkness faded, leaving Aran in the twilight field. The shadow king stepped aside, to reveal the others. "You are not a perfect king. You probably never will be. However, if you continue to bear your past with open eyes, you may yet come very close to being one."

The Old Kings looked upon Aran with approval. When they spoke, it was in unison, "We have tested your mettle and its quality withstood our scrutiny."

By the time the trials were complete, Aran felt as though he had been torn apart and rebuilt from the inside out. He had faced his past, his fears, and his flaws, coming victorious on the other end, and in doing so, he had proven himself worthy in the eyes of the Old Kings.

He stood before the thrones once more. The kings regarded him with solemn approval. "You have passed our trials, Aran of Karash," they spoke in unison. "You have shown strength, wisdom, courage, loyalty, and honour. The knowledge you seek is yours." The iron-crowned king leaned forward, his gaze piercing Aran's soul. "You can now access the Echo of Worlds through the obelisks and the Weaving. No longer must you journey physically to that realm, but understand this: such power is a labyrinth that has consumed far greater minds than yours."

Aran felt a surge of emotions - fear and relief braided together, sharp as a blade's edge. The knowledge of the Weaving was no gift but a burden. A responsibility that demanded everything and promised nothing but the risk of losing oneself in infinite possibilities.

The shadows around the thrones seemed to pulse with unspoken warnings. Ever since they merged with the Weaving over ten millennia ago, the Old Kings had seen kingdoms rise and crumble, and in their eyes, Aran read the true cost of forbidden knowledge.

The iron-crowned king spoke again, his voice grave. "Beware, Aran. The knowledge you now possess is a double-edged sword. Use it wisely, or it may consume you."

With that final warning, the thrones and the twilight field began to fade. The world crumbled around him - sand dissolving into mist, shadows curling back into the void. A sudden weight pressed upon his chest, and his breath hitched. Then, the scent of incense, the cool stone beneath his knees. He blinked. The dim glow of the runes greeted him, flickering like dying embers. The voices of the Old Kings faded, replaced by the worried whispers of Rafiq and Sura. He was back.

Both rushed to his side, their faces lined with concern. "What happened?" Sura asked, her voice tight with worry. "You remained completely silent and still, like a newly raised statue, in the middle of the stone circle. We were getting worried."

She exchanged a glance with Rafiq, whose face remained mostly expressionless, with but a small tremble in his lips betraying his, otherwise, stoic posture.

Aran took a deep breath, steadying himself. The trials had felt so real, so physical, yet somehow, it all happened within himself. "I passed the trials. The Old Kings have granted me the knowledge I sought."

Sura's eyes narrowed. "What did you learn?" Her hypnotic eyes bore into his.

Aran looked at her, his expression hard. "I found out that the Weaving is far more dangerous than I ever imagined. That defeating the Primordials will require more than just power. It will require wisdom and restraint, but also sacrifice."

Her expression darkened. "Sacrifice?" Sura whispered, pensively. He could tell she was reading into the deeper meanings of his words. Aran was taken aback by how easily she could pierce his defences. Seeing the mark of concern lined upon her face, he quickly added. "Do not fret for now, I shall explain things later."

Sura looked at him inquisitively. Rafiq nodded, though his brow furrowed with concern. "So, what do we do now?"

Aran straightened, his resolve firm. "Now, we return to Sarim. There is much to prepare, and the time for battle draws near. I fear that Drathis has not been resting."

Even as he spoke, he couldn't shake the feeling that, despite how hard the trials had been, they had only been the beginning. The true test was still to come. Could he face the Primordials and the Draconians simultaneously? Could he wage wars on two fronts. A whirlwind of doubts was brewing in Aran's soul.

He turned to bow, in respect, to the lord of Ryvath, only to find the old man smiling. "I hope we have been helpful, king of Zarah."

Far away, in the Yaran coast, Drathis stood on the bridge of the Shadow's Maw, the salt air thick with the scent of war. Below, his captains barked orders, steel clashing as warriors tested their blades. He did not hear them. His cold, slitted eyes were fixed on the horizon - on Sarim. "They believe they are strong now," he murmured, more to himself than to his captains. "But unity is a fragile thing, a blade balanced on a trembling hand." He let the silence stretch before turning to his officers. "First, we cut their trade. Then we starve them. Then we turn them against each other. When the sand is red with their own blood, then we strike. Let the boy-king chase shadows in ancient halls while I reshape his kingdom in his absence."

Drathis' plan involved three simultaneous attacks. First he intended to create a naval blockade along Zarah's coastal routes, targeting the trade ships vital to the kingdom's economy. Second on his list was an assault on the Fortresses of the Crescent Cliffs, key strongholds protecting Zarah. Last, but not least, the deployment of infiltrators to sow chaos within the Council of Tribes, turning their unity into division.

Informed of this by Sura's network of spies, the Council of Tribes met in an emergency session at the Lunar Citadel in Sarim. The mood was tense, the air thick with anticipation. Aran was away and the tension in the room was palpable. It crackled in the council chamber like a brewing storm.

Kasim al-Bahir slammed his fist against the table. "Our king is absent while the Draconians gather at our shores! We must act now!" There was no hint of accusation in his voice, it was merely a statement of fact. If Aran was away, he had good reasons for it.

Karim al-Shamar's eyes narrowed. "And charge blindly into battle? You would have us fight without strategy, without preparation?"

"They seek to choke our trade and starve us into submission. We cannot allow this. I say it's better to fight than to wait and watch our lands crumble!" Kasim retorted, his mind as sharp as his blade.

Safira raised a hand, her voice calm but cutting through the storm. "Enough. If we turn on each other, we have already lost. We must hold until Aran returns. Trust in his plan."

Kasim al-Bahir leaned forward, his fists clenched. "Our king might not be here, but we are not defenceless without him. He organised the kingdom's defences impeccably. Let them come. The Bahir have fought worse foes, along the Black Dunes."

Karim al-Shamar shook his head. "Bravado will not save us, Kasim. We need strategy. We need our king. If the Draconians disrupt our solar grids, we will lose more than solar power, we will lose the backbone of our survival."

Safira, the Moon Seer, replied calmly. "Anar and Nysa have shown me a path, but it is shrouded in uncertainty. To succeed, we must rely not only on strength but on trust. Have trust in our king. If he is not here now, rest assured he has good reasons to be absent. He is out there, risking his life, trying to find answers on how to repair the Weaving. Surely, a subject of such importance takes precedence over the Draco threat, especially when he left instructions on how to defend ourselves." She looked admonishingly around the crescent table. "You all should do well to remember that."

Kasim nodded in approval. "The Draco would have us at each other's throats before their ships ever reach our shores." His voice softened, his hands unclenching as he looked at each council member in turn. "Our tribes have stood separate for generations, but Aran has given us something more precious than gold - he has given us unity. I will not see it squandered while he risks his life for our future. Our strengths are Zarah's strengths now. Together, we shield our home."

Despite Aran's absence, the council, under Safira and Kasim, devised a multi-layered strategy.

The Rasha, with their expertise in maritime navigation, would lead the defence against the Draco's blockade, supported by Yara's coastal fleet. The Bahir and Shamari would fortify the Fortresses of the Crescent Cliffs, ensuring they remained unassailable strongholds. Finally, Tarek scouts and Ulema merchants would try to root out Draco infiltrators, preserving the council's unity.

Chapter XV

The Looming of Fate

Aran's journey back to Sarim was both calm and silent. The northern mountains receded behind him and his company as they descended into the vast plains that stretched before them.

The night winds were cold, biting with the memory of the trials he had endured within the ancient halls of Ryvath. But a deeper chill lingered in his bones - the weight of what was to come.

The Primordials would not wait for him to marshal his strengths. They would move soon, and when they did, Zarah would tremble.

As they rode through the wild lands of Sarim, Aran's thoughts were consumed by the hard-earned knowledge passed onto him by the Old Kings. The Weaving, ancient and terrible, was a power that could change the course of the coming war. But what would be the cost?

That question, more than any other, kept consuming his thoughts.

The idea of succumbing to such power terrified him more than sacrificing himself to save Zarah and its peoples.

The visions he had experienced so far, the echoes of past rulers who had lost themselves to the Primordial forces, haunted him.

He now had the means to shape the Weaving, to bend it toward his will. On the other hand, directly because of that, every choice in that realm would carry dire consequences for the planet, and the balance between salvation and ruin had never felt so precarious.

When Sarim's gates finally loomed on the horizon, towering beneath the fading twilight, a knot tightened in Aran's chest. It was, by all means, the same city he had left more than a month ago, yet it was different - transformed by the looming spectre of war.

Smoke curled from blacksmith forges, filling the salty air with the scent of scorched metal and burning coal.

The rhythmic clang of hammers against steel was like a heartbeat, steady, and unrelenting. Warriors drilled in tight formations, their eyes shadowed with exhaustion yet fierce with determination.

The city hummed with urgency, but beneath it, Aran sensed something deeper - fear, tension, the brittle edge of a people standing on the precipice of war.

He exhaled, steadying himself. "Did they follow my instructions?" he wondered, though he already knew the answer.

Sarim was bracing for battle, and it would stand or fall with him. War had come to his door, not just in name but in spirit and flesh. The people understood this reality well, and were preparing accordingly for it.

Rafiq rode beside him, the silent pillar of strength he had always been. He glanced at Aran, his weathered face set in lines of determination. Though he said nothing, his hand rested reassuringly on his dagger - a warrior's promise that whatever came, they would face it together. Like always, he sensed the gravity of his friend's thoughts without needing them voiced.

Sura followed closely, her gaze ever watchful, her mind undoubtedly racing through the same dark possibilities as Aran was. Behind them rode a small contingent of northern warriors who had pledged themselves to Aran's cause after his triumph in Ryvath. These were fierce warriors, loyal to the core, and highly skilled - much needed allies in the days ahead.

As they were passing through the marketplace, Aran couldn't help picking up on conversations. "The western traders speak of strange lights in the sky," whispered the spice merchant to her neighbour. "And my cousin in the border villages says the ground itself trembles at night." The baker shook his head grimly. "My grain stores run low, but the tribal lords demand more for our army. How are we to feed our children if this continues?"

When the party crossed the threshold into the heart of the city, they were met by Captain Toren al-Tarek, the grizzled second in command of Sarim's armies, left in charge by Rafiq, in his absence.

Toren's face was lined by time, by recent as well as old battles, but his eyes gleamed with sharp intelligence. "My liege," he greeted, bowing deeply. "You return to us at a crucial hour. The Draco are amassing forces to attack us on multiple fronts. The smaller tribes have begun to send their forces to our borders. Though not all are united in purpose."

Aran dismounted. "What do you mean, Captain? Speak plainly."

Toren's expression darkened. "The Halithar, our old rivals turned allies in defeat, have refused our summons. They claim that the Primordials are but myths, tales spun by those who wish to seize power for themselves. They have remained isolated thus far, so I gather they remain ignorant to the larger threat. Their forces remain in the south, fortified and unwilling to march for us."

"The Halithar..." Aran's voice trailed off, remembering the bloody conflicts of years past. Old wounds festered in the south, it seemed. Though Aran had defeated them in battle before, the Halithar were not easily broken. Because of that, their reluctance to join him was now proving itself to be dangerous, not only for themselves, but everyone else as well. Without unity, his kingdom could not stand against the forces that were gathering beyond the mountains.

"What of the other smaller tribes?" Sura asked, her tone sharp.

"The Vari sent aid," Toren replied, his voice grim. "Though only a token force. Their leader, Juras al-Vari, is old and cautious now, more concerned with maintaining his wealth and territory than joining a desperate war. They fear losing, far more than they fear our enemies."

Aran clenched his jaw, his mind racing. The political landscape of his unified kingdom had always been fragile, but now, on the brink of the House of Draco's attack, it seemed to be crumbling.

The alliances he had painstakingly forged over the course of his life were fracturing under the weight of fear and greed. The Draco were not making things easy.

"What of the council, what of Farid?" Aran asked, his voice low but laced with ire and frustration.

Toren hesitated, his eyes flicking toward the council chambers as if their walls could whisper. "The council met in your absence. They devised a strategy, yes, but divisions fester beneath the surface," he exhaled sharply. "Farid has been... persuasive. He speaks in hushed tones, but his words carry weight. He sows doubt, whispers that you are not saving Zarah but dooming it - that your dealings with the Weaving have stirred forces best left untouched."

Aran's jaw tightened. "And the council listens?"

"Some do." Toren's expression darkened. "Fear is a powerful tool, my king, and he has used it well to his favour. Now, some minor tribal lords whisper that the House of Draco and the Primordials stir because of your actions, not despite them."

Rafiq's eyes narrowed. "Fools. They cannot see the danger even when it's standing at their doorstep."

Aran held up his hand in appeasement. "They are afraid. Fear clouds judgement, my friend, remember that. In any case, we cannot afford to wait for them to see reason. If the council does not act, we must find a way to unite the minor tribes ourselves."

"But how?" Rafiq asked, stepping forward. "If the Halithar tribe refused to march, other smaller clans may follow in their footsteps."

Aran was silent for a moment, staring out at the Yaran capital.

He had known from the beginning that this war would be as much a battle of wills as it was a clash of swords. The Draco and the Primordials were not the only enemies he faced, he also had to contend with the ambitions and fears of the other tribal lords of Zarah.

"There is one way," Aran said finally, his voice heavy with resolve. "We must remind all of the Council of what is at stake. They do not fear what lays ahead because they do not understand the full extent of the threat we face. If we can show them… if they can see for themselves what we have seen, perhaps they will unite, if nothing else, out of fear."

"How do you suppose we do that?" Rafiq asked, his brow furrowed. "The Primordials are not exactly something we can summon at will."

"No," Aran replied, turning to face his closest advisor. "However, the obelisks are, so to speak. The Weaving that binds Zarah to the Echo of Worlds runs through them. If I can unlock their secrets, I can show the council the truth. Show them the vision I saw in Ryvath."

Sura's eyes widened. "Does that mean you intend to use the Weaving?"

Aran nodded, though he still felt reticent. "It is dangerous, I know. However, if what I learned so far is real, we are running out of options. If the council remains divided, if the tribes do not stand united, Sarim and Qamaria will fall, and the rest of Zarah will follow suit."

Rafiq folded his arms, his expression thoughtful. "According to you, as well as Barash, the obelisks are scattered, some in lands held by those who are still our enemies, others lay beyond that. It will be no easy task to find them or reach them, let alone use them."

"That is why we must act quickly," Aran replied. "Something happened to me during the trials in Ryvath. Because of it, I can feel the energy coming from the obelisks now - I can sense it inside me. So, here is what I propose. I will go for the third one myself. It lies in the valley of Erythmar, deep within the cliffs, in the southern oases. If I can awaken it, I might be able to connect it to the rest and use the Weaving to project the vision to the council."

Sura stepped forward, her eyes gleaming with determination. She held Aran's gaze in hers. "If you are going, I shall go with you."

Rafiq followed suit. "As will I." He winked at his friend.

Aran smiled, grateful for their unwavering support. "Then it is settled. We shall go for the obelisks. Nevertheless, before we do that, we must not neglect the imminent Draconian threat," he said firmly, looking at Rafiq, Sura and Toren. "Let us go. I must address the council."

Minutes later, he stood once more before the assembled tribal lords, their faces a mixture of fear, doubt, and calculation. The council chamber, at times, a place of measured debate, now crackled again with tension.

"The Draco are merely the first wave," Aran explained, his voice steady despite the hostile glares from Farid's supporters. "Behind them come forces that will consume all we have worked so hard to build."

Farid al-Rasha rose slowly, his rich robes rustling. "Yet we have seen only the Draco. This... Weaving you speak of remains conveniently unseen." He smirked. "Indeed, my lord, we must address the threats we can see and evaluate." Farid's tone was measured, reasonable. "The House of Draco gathers strength while we speak of... other matters. Perhaps our focus should remain on the battles we know we face." He paused, letting his words settle. "After all, it was only after your return from the northern mountains that these attacks intensified, was it not?"

Murmurs rippled through the chamber, and Aran felt the weight of suspicion settling upon him - Farid was repaying him poorly for his earlier leniency.

"Would you have us prepare for phantoms while real enemies gather at our gates?" Farid pressed, his voice silken with false concern.

Rafiq stepped forward, hand resting on the hilt of his dagger.

"Watch your words carefully, Farid. They border on treason."

Aran raised his hand, silencing his friend. "I do not ask for blind faith. I ask only that you remember who has led you through darkness before. When compared to the unravelling of the Weaving, the House of Draco is but a nuisance. However, I say that we either prepare for both, or prepare for nothing at all."

The council session ended with no clear resolution, its divergence of opinions seemed to be running deeper than ever. Aran's shoulders sagged as the council chamber emptied, leaving him alone with the echoing weight of unspoken doubts.

While his kingdom braced for war with the Draco, he found himself increasingly isolated. His days were consumed by council meetings, strategy sessions, and inspections of the kingdom's defences. At night, he sat alone atop the Council Tower, the stars in the firmament, cold and distant. Indifferent to the troubles brewing below.

He traced the constellations absently, searching for meaning in their ancient patterns, but they offered no guidance. His people expected certainty, yet all he had were more questions.

Had he done enough to protect them? Or had he led them down a path from which there was no return?

The weight of Zarah's crown felt heavier than ever.

He longed for the certainty of his father's steel in his hand, the simplicity of battle. Yet, this war - this war was fought in shadows, in whispers, in doubt and deceit. Aran was drowning in all three.

Sura, ever his closest ally, noticed the strain. "You should not carry this burden alone," she said one evening as they stood atop the Council room - Leander's primary bathing Sarim in colours of fire.

"That is my charge," Aran replied, his voice tinged with exhaustion. "The kingdom depends on me. On me, Sura. If I falter, everything we have built will collapse." His eyes searched for hers.

Sura placed a hand on his face. "You are not alone, Aran. The council, the tribes, despite their hesitation, I am sure they will stand with you. Trust in them as you have asked them to trust in you."

Her words, insightful as always, brought him some comfort. Still, on a deeper level than Sura, Aran knew that the path ahead would test them all in ways they had never dared to imagine. Some of the minor tribes still remained unfaithful and he feared for the safety of what he had worked so hard to build.

That unsettling feeling manifested itself without delay. The following week, under Drathis' orders, the Draco launched their attack on the coastal city of Najra, a vital trade hub part of the lands of Yara.

Under the cover of darkness, a fleet of cloaked warships unleashed a barrage of solar disruptor blasts, crippling the city's reflecting defences. The night sky blazed with terrible light as the disruptor blasts cut through Najra's outer defences like fire through parchment. Citizens fled screaming through streets suddenly illuminated by the unnatural glow, their shadows sharp and desperate against stone walls. Fathers fought, while mothers clutched children to their breasts. The elders who could neither fight nor run, prayed in doorways as the city trembled under the assault.

Admiral Zarus al-Rasha's response was swift and calculated. His shallow-draft vessels, built for navigating Yara's coastal waters, proved their worth against the House of Draco's deep-sea warships. As the enemy fleet pursued them into the narrow straits, Zarus executed a centuries-old Rasha tactic - the Serpent's Embrace.

His ships formed a loose line, appearing to flee in panic. The Draco took the bait, following them into waters they didn't know, where hidden rocks and shifting sandbars waited like teeth. As the lead Draco ships struggled against the treacherous shallows, Zarus's fleet wheeled about in perfect coordination.

Meanwhile, Sura's infiltration team had reached the flagship. The explosive charges they planted didn't just disable the ship's cloaking system - they created a beacon of fire that lit the entire enemy fleet for the Rasha archers positioned along the clifftops. As the fleet's outline shimmered into view, they fired salvo after salvo of explosive arrows, reducing it to a blazing wreck.

Najra's victory was hard-won, but it was carved from blood and ruin. Dozens of ships burned in the harbour, their blackened husks still smouldering. The once-proud trade hub had become a graveyard of shattered buildings, its streets littered with debris and the wounded. Aran walked among the wreckage, his boots crunching over broken glass and scorched stone. A child sat beside the ruins of a collapsed home, staring blankly at the remnants of her world. He knelt before her, offering a hand, but she did not move. The Draco had not just attacked the city. They had torn through its very soul.

A young Tarek warrior, his arm bound in bloodied linen, looked up as Aran passed. "My lord," he called weakly, "is it true what they say? That worse things than the House of Draco are coming?" His eyes held fear, but also hope - the kind of desperate faith common people place in their leaders when the world grows dark.

Aran turned to the gathered survivors, his voice steady but edged with steel. "This is what the House of Draco brings - destruction and despair." He looked at the crowd gathering around him. "Zarah does not bow. We do not break. We will rebuild. We will endure," he took the child's face in his hands, and looked her in the eyes. "We will make them pay."

The journey back to Sarim was sombre, the weight of Najra's destruction heavy on every mind. Yet even as Aran grappled with the cost of victory, new troubles were already taking root in Yara's capital. Word reached them before they crossed the gates - whispers of discord, of suspicion spreading like plague through the markets and council halls. In the aftermath Draconian infiltrators, posing as traders and advisors, began spreading false rumours throughout Sarim and Qamaria. They claimed the Bahir tribe was planning to seize control of the council, that the Shamari were withholding critical supplies, and that Aran ruled from Sarim and Qamaria because he favoured the Rasha and the Shamari over the other tribes. Tensions reached a breaking point when a fight broke out in the Lunar Plaza between Bahir warriors and Shamari engineers. Aran intervened personally, standing between the two groups as their weapons were drawn.

"Enough!" he commanded, his voice cutting through the chaos. "This is exactly what the House of Draco wants us to do - to fight amongst ourselves while they plot to take over what remains. We are not each other's enemies. We are brothers and sisters of Zarah. Never forget that. Remember who we are." Aran's words defused the conflict, but the incident underscored the fragility of his kingdom's unity.

One night, Safira approached Aran with a vision she had experienced during her meditations. "I have seen the desert ablaze with fire, the moons obscured by smoke. I have seen the Primordials rising." Though her face showed fear, her words carried hope. "I also saw a light - a beacon rising from the sands, uniting the tribes against the darkness."

Aran was listening intently. "What do you think it means?"

Safira, sensing his inner struggle, smiled faintly. "Do not put too much pressure on yourself, my liege. Others can help you bring your vision to fruition," she paused, reading his demeanour, "It simply means that even in the face of devastation, there is always hope, Aran. Remember that hope lies in us, in our unity, our strength, our faith in one another, and ultimately, yes, it lies in your leadership."

Safira's words stayed with Aran as he prepared for the battles to come. He spent that night in seclusion with Barash, debating his course of action once he found the next obelisk.

"I think you have learned enough thus far to trust your instinct," his tutor told him with confidence. "I trust you to make the right decision when the time comes. The Ryvath warriors that joined our ranks told me you did splendidly in the trials. I believe you are ready."

Aran, who knew Barash well, asked with a faint smile, "Why do I sense that you are not coming with me on this one?"

"Because I am not," the old man replied, his tone growing sombre. "I am needed here, lad. We are all facing more threats than any of us fully understand." As he spoke, Barash paused, studying Aran's face - the slight tension in his jaw - the flicker of doubt behind his steady eyes. The mask of confidence was strong, but Barash had known him too long not to see the cracks. "Do not worry," he added gently, "for when it truly matters, I shall be there by your side."

Aran exhaled, the weight in his chest easing slightly. He hadn't realized how badly he'd needed to hear those words. Just knowing Barash would not abandon him gave him strength.

"Now, make your preparations to leave in the morning," Barash continued, the moment of vulnerability passed. "The time has come for you to face the Primordials."

Aran knew that he couldn't avoid it any longer. Even though he felt more needed to be done, here at home, he knew that the kingdom was protected for now. He had, after all, taken all the necessary measures to ensure that they would endure in his absence. He issued instructions for preparations to be made for his departure and retired for the night. The following morning, Aran, along with his trusted companions set out for Erythmar.

The sun barely crested the horizon as they rode through the oases of Sarim. The journey would be long, and danger seemed to lurk in every shadow.

The first day's travel took them through familiar territory - the outer reaches of Sarim's influence where shepherds still tended their flocks and traders moved in small, well-guarded caravans. As they pushed deeper into the equatorial deserts, the landscape began to change in subtle, disturbing ways.

The oases beyond Yaran country, as well as the Medjool Palms that populated their dunes and bodies of water, had grown wild in recent times, due to the current unsteadiness of the Weaving. Now, rumours of strange creatures, twisted by the Primordials' influence, were rumoured to have spread like wildfire through the wilderness. In spite of that, they managed to cross these water holes swiftly, without encountering any such beings.

They rode in silence during the daytime, the weight of their mission pressing on each of them. At night, gathered around campfires, they shared their musings. As the days went by, the further they travelled through Zarah's deserts, the more unsettling the atmosphere became. In some oases, the Karna trees had become grotesque imitations of their former selves - twisted, gnarled things that stretched unnaturally toward the sky, their bark blackened as though burned from within. Their branches tangled together like skeletal fingers, weaving a suffocating canopy that devoured the sunlight. The air beneath them was heavy, stagnant, abundant with the cloying scent of damp rot and something else - something wrong. Something that had never before been seen in the planet's recorded history. The air was thick, and the damp ground decayed. Even the soil beneath their mounts' hooves seemed to yield unnaturally, as though the very earth was corrupted at its core.

Then came the sound - a distant howl, low and guttural, echoing through the twisted canopy. Not an animal's cry, nor the wind's whisper, but something deeper, hungrier. It was followed by another, closer this time.

"What was that?" Sura whispered, her voice barely audible. Even Rafiq, hardened by war, stiffened, his hand drifting toward his sword hilt. Aran exhaled slowly, willing his heart to steady. "Pray we do not find out," Rafiq murmured. In the silence that followed, his words felt less like a prayer and more like a plea.

Having crossed that haunted place, many days later, they found themselves in the equatorial rocky deserts, where the Kingdom of Sayf would one day be established. Located in the central highlands. These regions are defined by jagged cliffs, vast stone plateaus, and deep canyons with vast plains. Water exists here, in the form of rivers, and these areas have long oases, extending for miles.

As twilight deepened over the canyons, the desert wind carried with it the scent of Solarwood smoke and distant spices. Aran and his companions crested a low ridge and came upon a small cluster of tents nestled in the lee of a sandstone outcrop - a humble encampment of desert dwellers, their fires glowing soft and golden in the gathering dark.

The caravan's leader, an older man with sun-cracked skin and wary eyes, stepped forward in greeting, offering water and shelter with quiet reverence. It was clear they knew who stood before them, though none dared speak it aloud.

While the adults murmured among themselves, eyes flicking toward Aran with equal parts, hope, and uncertainty, a young girl slipped through the circle of firelight. She couldn't have been more than eight, her hair braided with tiny charms of bone and bronze, her feet bare and dusted with sand.

She looked up at him, not with fear, but with wide-eyed wonder. "Are you the king who fights the monsters?"

Her father moved quickly, hand outstretched to hush her, but Aran raised a hand, halting him gently. "I try to," he replied simply. "Though sometimes the monsters are harder to find than we think."

The girl's father bowed his head, clearly torn between apology and pride. "Forgive her, my lord," he said, his voice low and hoarse from years of desert wind. "She hears stories whispered by the fires - of a king who walks the dunes with blades of starlight and serpents that vanish into sand. We never expected to meet you in the flesh."

Aran looked at the man - not with distance, but with the quiet burden of a ruler who had heard such words before, and never quite believed he deserved them.

"She has the right to ask," he replied, his gaze shifting to the child, who now hid shyly behind her father's robes. "If I do not face the monsters in your stead, then what use is a crown at all?"

The man's expression softened. He placed a hand atop his daughter's head, and for a moment, the desert wind stilled.

As they took their leave, the girl's father pressed his hand to his heart in the old gesture of respect. "May the stars light your path, my lord," he said quietly. "And may you find what you seek in the deep places."

The words followed them as they rode away, and Aran found himself thinking of all the children across Zarah who looked to the horizon with hope and fear in equal measure. The weight of their trust in him felt heavier than any armour.

"We should make camp soon," Rafiq pointed, as the sun dipped low in the sky, casting long shadows across the landscape.

Aran nodded. "We can stop by the river ahead," he replied. "From there, we still have a day's ride to the valley of Erythmar."

The twin moons hung high in the firmament by the time they reached the river. By setting up camp near the banks of the rushing stream, the sound of the water provided a momentary reprieve from the oppressive silence of the recently sprung, desert forest they crossed previously.

Aran sat by the fire, staring into the flames, watching the lighter embers levitate into the night sky. His thoughts drifted back to the trials he had faced in Ryvath. The weight of the knowledge he now carried felt like a physical burden, pressing down on him with every step.

Sura sat down beside him, her face illuminated by the dancing flames. "You are brooding again." She settled beside him, close enough that he could feel the warmth radiating from her. "More than usual, I mean." She added, with a smile.

The sound of Rafiq sharpening his blades, punctuated the silences.

Aran looked at her, then back at the swaying flames, "There is much to think about." His words came out heavy - Sura merely observed.

Aran exhaled, the weight of her words pressing down on him. Then, he looked at her - truly looked at her, as though seeing her for the first time. "Yes," he admitted. "I have seen what happens when the Weaving is misused. The visions showed me what the Primordials could do. What I could do, if I lost control."

Sura was silent for a long moment. Then, with quiet certainty, she reached for his hand and squeezed it once. "Then don't," she said simply. "You are not alone in this. You never have been." She nodded, her gaze thoughtful, "I know the Draco are in the back of your mind, and though we know how dangerous they are, at this precise moment you are not concerned about them. You are thinking about Ryvath, are you not? About the Primordials? Concerned about what it might cost you, in the end."

Most of that had been a statement, but Aran knew precisely what she wanted to know. He had been sensing in her an aptitude for the unseen, a certain untapped potential. "Who knew?" he thought to himself.

The sound of sharpening steel melded with the crackling fire, creating a hypnotic effect on the senses.

"Yes," he admitted. "The Weaving is a powerful force, but it is also extremely unpredictable. I have been shown what happens when it is misused. The vision I had in Ryvath... it showed me the destruction the Primordials can bring, if the weaver loses control. It also showed me how fragile the balance is. One wrong move, and we could lose everything we hold dear."

Sura remained silent for a long time, pondering Aran's words. When she finally spoke, it was soft, but firm. "As I have stated many times, we stand with you. Whatever happens, we will face it together. You know that, right?" As she spoke, her eyes seemed to catch the firelight strangely, holding depths that hadn't been there before. "I've been... sensing things lately." She hesitated, searching for words. "When you speak of the Weaving, something in me responds to it. Like an echo answering a call."

Aran studied her face, noting the uncertainty there. "What kind of things?"

"Dreams that feel like memories. Visions of places I've never been." She shook her head. "It started after Ryvath. After our return."

Aran smiled in confirmation, though the weight in his chest remained. He appreciated her insightful words, her unyielding trust - both were invaluable to him. Still, deep down, he knew that the burden of leadership was one he would have to carry alone. No one else could make the choices that lay ahead - no one else could decide the fate of this world. Although he suspected that Drathis would have a difference of opinion on the matter - there it was again, humour, his last line of defence.

The trio remained in silence for hours, observing the flames, lost in thought, until, one by one, they all fell asleep.

The following morning, Leander's primary greeted Zarah with its habitual intensity. Aran was already saddling their steeds when his companions awoke, his movements precise but hurried. "We must depart now," he said without looking up. "Time works against us on multiple fronts. Drathis will not wait for our convenience, and every day we delay gives him the opportunity to exploit our divisions. We should attend the next obelisk and return to Sarim as fast as we can. For even if I manage to heal its energies, there is still a very long journey back home, and I foresee we will be needed there before long."

They spent the following hours traversing canyons and plateaus, passing through natural tunnels that cut through the high mesas.

They finally reached the hidden valley of Erythmar a few hours after the sun had passed its zenith in the sky.

The valley revealed itself gradually, like a secret being whispered. Towering cliff walls, carved smooth by aeons of wind and sand, formed a natural amphitheatre around the ancient monument. The air itself felt different here - thicker, charged with an energy that made their steeds restless and their skin prickle. There, in the centre of it all, stood the obelisk.

It was larger than Aran had expected - many times the height of a man - but it was not its size that commanded attention. The black stone seemed to drink in the afternoon light, creating a pocket of shadow that defied the desert sun. Around its base, the sand had been fused into glass, forming intricate patterns that spiral outward like frozen ripples in water.

"This is it," Rafiq and Sura spoke in unison, their voices hushed with awe.

When Aran neared the stone monolith, still mounted on his stygian steed, the Weaving surged through him, an electric rush that filled his veins with something vast and terrible - power, pure and unfiltered, called to him.

As he dismounted, the Weaving stirred within him like a sleeping giant awakening. Even from a distance, he could feel the obelisk's pull - not physical, but something deeper. It called to the power he had awakened in Ryvath, recognizing him as surely as he recognized it.

He took a step forward, then stopped. The whispers were already beginning - not words, exactly, but promises spoken in a language older than thought. Power. Control. The ability to reshape the world according to his will.

Aran's jaw clenched as he fought the sensation. The pull was undeniable, almost overwhelming, but he had learned caution in the trials of the Old Kings. Whatever connection he was about to forge with this ancient monument, it would change everything. And once begun, there would be no turning back.

He stood there, poised between certainty and the unknown, knowing that his next choice would determine not just his fate but the fate of all Zarah. He placed his hand on the cold stone, and the familiar energy coursed through him, filling him with a sense of power - but also with dread.

Chapter XVI

The Awakening

Night had fallen. Anar and Nysa began their celestial dance in the heavens. Aran had spent the last hour with his arm outstretched, touching the obelisk, familiarising himself with its energy - the stone hummed beneath his palm. It felt ice-cold, then unnaturally warm, pulsing with ancient energy that seemed to seep into his bloodstream.

It was as though the ancient rock, untouched by time and forgotten by most, held the memory of aeons.

The Weaving thrummed just beneath its surface, coiling around him in invisible threads, waiting.

No, they were begging to be pulled. The energy felt alive, restless, as if the dormant power within the obelisk recognized Aran's touch, gently whispering long-forgotten secrets and looming danger.

The air around them grew thick, almost oppressive, as if the very atmosphere in the valley of Erythmar recognized the presence of an awakened king.

Sura and Rafiq stood a few paces behind, their eyes locked on Aran's figure.

They, too, could feel the raw energy swirling through the space around them, but for Aran, it was far more than a sensation - it was a dialogue. One that stretched back to the primeval roots of the Weaving itself, and his ancestors' connection to it.

This was the third obelisk he had encountered, but it was the first time he had attempted to draw upon their full power. Before Ryvath, he had only understood the Weaving as something Barash spoke of in hushed tones - a legend of the Old Kings. Nothing he could put his faith into. Now, he knew better. The Weaving was not a tool to be used lightly - it was a living, cosmic, force that demanded respect. A power deeply intertwined with the very existence of the world, its bones and ancient pacts. For a moment, Aran hesitated. Could he truly control this power? Could anyone?

The decision as to what to do next weighed heavily on him, and the memories of the vision he had seen in Ryvath resurfaced. He saw the great halls in flames, the world fracturing under the weight of some raw uncontrolled power, and the Primordials walking the planet once more, bringing with them devastation and madness.

He needed to be certain, yet certainty felt like a luxury he could not afford - time was running out, fast. "I must do this," he said quietly, his voice nearly lost to the wind.

Sura stepped forward, her hand resting on the hilt of her dagger. "Are you sure you can control it?" Aran did not answer, he seemed to be lost in thought. She studied him closely. "You know," she hesitated, "I have been feeling a pull towards the art of the weave, and have been familiarising myself with the subject, spending many hours reading what Barash indicated you should." Sura was clearly worried about him. "The ancient texts speak of the Weaving," she continued, "as a living entity, not merely a tool. The Old Kings who tried to bend it completely to their will always paid a terrible price. It has broken some very strong men throughout our ancient history. Men who thought they could wield it and instead became its victims."

Aran acknowledged this but did not turn to face her. "We do not have other options. If I do nothing, The Primordials will rise and everything will be lost. Do you not see? The council must see the truth, and the tribes must remain united. If they do not, then everything we have fought for, all we have bled as one people, will have been for nothing."

Rafiq grunted in agreement. "If anyone can master this power, I believe it to be you, Aran. But be careful, brother. If I have understood this correctly, the obelisks hold more than just knowledge. The Weaving is tied to the Primordials. You know what that means."

Aran did know. The Primordials were not simply beings of myth, they were forces of creation and destruction. Bound by ancient pacts, they had retreated from the world, but their influence remained in the echoes of the Weaving. Each obelisk was a conduit, a focal point where the power of the Weaving met the material world, and somewhere, far beyond their comprehension, the Primordials were watching.

Aran took a deep breath, closing his eyes. He allowed the sensations around him to swell, focusing not on the fear or doubt but on the rhythm of the Weaving itself. Slowly, he began to reach out, tugging at the threads that flowed through the obelisk, intertwining them into a pattern. One that would allow him to connect with the other obelisks, and through the grid they were part of, directly to the Council of Sarim.

The stone beneath his palm grew warmer, and the hum of energy turned into a low, resonant pulse. The ground trembled, sending ripples through the valley. Sura and Rafiq exchanged uneasy glances, but they stayed where they were, held by an unwavering trust in their friend's abilities. Nevertheless, they were both ready to intervene if Aran's strength appeared to falter.

The obelisk's surface did not just glow - it bled light, a searing pulse that seemed to twist the very air around them. The ground trembled, stones cracking as if reality itself were resisting Aran's will.

Shadows elongated, twisting into shapes that should not be. The Weaving was no longer passive; it was alive, shifting and restless, a force both ancient and unknowable.

Aran felt the Echo of Worlds claw at him, dragging his consciousness beyond the material plane. His breath caught as he glimpsed things moving in the liminal space between dimensions - whispers that weren't words, shapes that weren't fully formed. Something watched him from the void - then, it pushed back.

Aran's mind expanded, his consciousness stretching outward across the vast distances of Zarah. He could feel the presence of the other obelisks, each one a distant beacon of power, waiting to be unlocked. More than that, he could feel the eyes of the council, their uncertainty and fear, their divided loyalties.

He saw the tribes that had already sent their forces to Sarim, and those who hesitated, unsure if they would follow a king who dabbled in powers beyond their mortal understanding.

He also felt something else, a presence, ancient and cold, stirring in the dark corners of the Weaving. It was subtle, almost imperceptible, but unmistakable - the Primordials were watching him.

Aran tightened his grip on the threads of the Weaving, entwining them tighter, binding the obelisks together in a vast network of power. He needed to show the council the truth, to make them understand what was at stake. He had to make them see the vision he had seen.

The destruction, the chaos, the end of the world as they knew it.

As he delved deeper into the Weaving, something pushed back. The presence he felt, whatever it was, resisted his control, fighting against him, trying to unravel the pattern he had created. The obelisk pulsed violently, the light flickering as the ground beneath them shook harder.

Sura stepped forward, an expression of alarm flashing across her face. "Aran, stop! You are losing control!"

Still, he couldn't stop; he couldn't let go. For if he did, the Weaving would collapse and everything would be lost. The opportunity to mend its unravelling, to keep the tribes united and save Zarah, would be lost.

He gritted his teeth, forcing himself to hold on, to push back against this mysterious presence, trying to unravel his work. Sweat dripped down his face as the strain of maintaining the connection grew unbearable. "I cannot falter. I must... hold on!"

Aran's voice sounded like thunder, echoing across the valley. He doubled his efforts, in one last desperate attempt to harmonize this stone tether with all the others spread across the planet.

Suddenly, the resistance vanished. The presence withdrew, slipping away into the shadows of the Weaving, leaving behind a strange, hollow silence. The obelisk's light stabilized, the pulsing slowing to a steady, rhythmic beat.

Aran exhaled sharply, his body trembling from the effort - he had done it. He had connected the obelisks and, through them, the vision he saw in Ryvath had reached the council. Despite his success, there was something about the experience that left him unsettled.

The presence he had felt had not been a random fragment of the Weaving - it had been deliberate and purposeful. Something had been watching him, and it had chosen to withdraw, but not before making its presence known.

Aran turned to face Sura and Rafiq, who had been watching him with concern. "It is done. The council will see what I witnessed in Ryvath. They will be forced to understand now."

Rafiq raised an eyebrow, clearly unconvinced. "What if they do not?" He asked. "What if they are made to think this to be just another one of your tricks? You know just how blinding ignorance can be, further fuelled by Farid's persuasiveness."

"They will have no choice but to believe," Aran replied, his voice steadier than he felt. "The vision is real. They will not only see the truth, but they will also feel it," he concluded enigmatically.

"Anything else?" Rafiq asked, looking intently at his friend.

"What do you mean?" Aran didn't want to tell them about the presence he had felt. He did not want to worry his friends any more than it was necessary. However, he knew far too well that if anyone deserved his full honesty, it was them. "Very well," he began as Rafiq and Sura straightened up. "I felt a presence watching through the Weaving - not a natural part of it, but something foreign. Something ancient that was using the Weaving as a window to observe us. Some external force that wanted me to know about it. It revealed itself, almost breaking me. Then, without warning, it vanished. The presence felt... calculating. Not hostile, not yet, but studying me, studying us. As if measuring our capability to resist."

"It must have feared your roar." Rafiq quipped. He was happy to see his jest bring a smile to his friend's face.

Sura's gaze, on the other hand, was piercing - as though she could see the doubt lurking beneath Aran's confident façade. "What about the presence you felt? Do you have any idea what it was?"

Aran hesitated. "I do not know. But it is gone now," he seemed to be thinking fast. "Whatever it was, it was not ready to face us yet," he jokingly added, not wanting to further alarm his friends.

Throwing Sura an admonishing glance, Rafiq turned to Aran and grunted. "Let us hope it stays that way."

Aran wasn't so sure of that. The presence he had felt was not gone; it was merely waiting, biding its time. The Primordials were stirring, and soon, they would act. Indifferent to his best efforts, the Weaving was becoming more fragile than ever, and next time one misstep would be enough to unravel everything.

They mounted their steeds and rode back toward Sarim, the obelisk's glow fading behind them as they left the valley of Erythmar. Aran's mind churned with the events of the day, but there was no time to dwell on the mysteries of the Weaving.

The council would see his vision soon, "Like some supernatural apparition, hovering above the Crescent table." Aran could not help but smile, imagining the faces of those who didn't believe him. Then the real challenge would begin. As they rode away, Aran couldn't shake the feeling that something was watching them.

Their departure from Erythmar was sombre, each lost in their own thoughts about what had transpired at the obelisk. The first few days of travel passed in relative silence, each mile carrying them further from the ancient stone but not from its implications. By the time they reached the southern desert expanses, they could no longer see the mountains behind them, but Aran could still feel the echo of power in his veins.

A week after they left Erythmar, the southern desert still stretched before them, an endless expanse of golden dunes and broken lands, shimmering under Zarah's, cruel, primary star. The journey back north was proving itself to be harder than the way down. "Or maybe I am just tired," Aran mused to himself. The deserts felt different, as if some alien entity was messing with their primal energies. "Alien entity," he thought. "Well, take your pick - the Draco or the Primordials? Which is more alien to Zarah, to you?"

An uncanny howl echoed in the distance. The steeds neighed and the trio shivered, wondering what creature could make such a sound.

The Weaving had been severely damaged by his earlier mistakes, there was no doubt about that. However, despite how much guilt he was willing to pile on himself, its threads were also being tangled by forces beyond his mortal comprehension.

The obelisk in Erythmar had been key in stabilizing the Weaving at least for now, but Aran could still feel its lingering tremors in the world around him, like desert sands shifting beneath unseen energy tides. Something had changed and, despite his best efforts, he was sure it had not been for the better.

For many days, they travelled northward, their steeds moving swiftly across the dunes. The desert heat pressed down upon them like an incandescent hand of domination, the air thick with the scent of sunbaked stone and distant salt from the Veil of Mirari, a dried seabed located in this area.

The grit of sand between his teeth, the relentless heat pressing against his skin like a physical weight, and the taste of salt on the wind reminded Aran that the desert itself was as much an enemy as any Draconian.

The silence between them was heavy, but not uncomfortable. They had fought together, bled together, and now each step toward Sarim carried the weight of all they had endured as a unit.

Rafiq broke the silence first. "So, does anyone want to try to explain what actually happened back in Erythmar? Sura, you have been dabbing in old literature, have you not? Care to enlighten me?"

She threw him a steely look but couldn't maintain it for long, breaking into a smile. She winked at Rafiq and, still smiling, suggested, "Maybe Aran would be kind enough to enlighten us?"

Aran exhaled, adjusting the reins of his onyx steed. "I have told you both before. I felt an external presence in the Weaving. It wanted me out, so I pushed myself beyond what I ever thought possible. I was almost sure that the strain was going to kill me, but suddenly it disappeared, just like it had appeared. I think it merely wanted me to be aware of its existence. Once it vanished, that allowed me to mend what I had broken myself," he looked down at the ground, deep in thought, "I did manage to mend it, at least in part. The problem is that I do not know how long it will hold. We must find the other obelisks, otherwise I fear the end might be nigh, for all of us."

Sura, riding beside him, asked with genuine interest, her tone hesitant. "What you were able to do… what do you think that means for us?"

Aran glanced at her, his expression unreadable. "It means that nothing is certain, my friends. Our world is… shifting. The deserts feel different, as if they are waking up to something they do not yet understand." He looked, yearningly, at the horizon. "Neither can I." He kept this last thought to himself, his fear of failure, as always, was present.

Rafiq snorted. "Perfect. Just what we needed - deserts with a mind of their own. Perhaps next the rocks will grow legs and chase us."

Aran smiled faintly, but the weight of the journey ahead remained. The Weaving had been temporarily mended, but its scars had not healed.

Sura spoke again, her voice softer now. "Back in Erythmar, when you touched the obelisk... you did not just mend the Weaving, did you? You saw other things?" Her words sat in between a statement and a question.

She was, indeed, intuitive to the core, reading his mind like an open book. A splendid woman to be sure, and an invaluable companion to have by his side, no doubt. While Rafiq was dear to him through years of shared friendship and battle, Aran found himself increasingly aware of how Sura's presence affected him in ways that went beyond mere companionship - stirring feelings he hadn't expected to find amidst their perilous journey.

Aran hesitated to answer. The visions he experienced still clawed at the edges of his mind. Besides the foreboding threat of what the Primordials could bring, he also saw fractured images of the past, of old kings from his bloodline, long dead now. He witnessed their mistakes dripping down through history, and the Weaving was now unravelling, only for their debt to be paid by their, yet unborn, progeny. He saw Images of unwritten futures and of shadows deeper than the night sky stretching over Zarah.

The sound of their steeds' hooves hitting the ground was playing as a counterpoint to their conversation. "I saw echoes," he admitted. "Memories trapped in the Weaving. Warnings. Remnants of those who came before us."

Rafiq exhaled. "Let me guess. None of it was good."

Aran looked ahead at the endless dunes, his expression darkening. "No. None of it was good," he said, with a sigh.

That night, they made camp at the base of a ruined outpost, its walls eroded by centuries of sandstorms. The fire flickered between them, casting shadows against the cracked stone.

Sura cleaned her daggers absent-mindedly. "We are too exposed."

Rafiq leaned back, hands behind his head. "We are in the middle of the desert. Who, do you think, is going to find us here?"

Suddenly, a blade whispered through the air, embedding itself in the sand just inches from Rafiq's outstretched legs.

In an instant, the three of them were on their feet. Shapes were moving in the darkness between the Medjool palms. Aran couldn't believe his eyes. They were clad in Draconian desert armour! Their reptilian eyes glinting like slitted rubies in the firelight.

"How about them?" Sura muttered, drawing her blades.

Aran rolled forward, seizing his sword as the first Draconian lunged in. Their blades clashed, sparks flying as steel met steel. The Draconian was large and strong, his strikes brutal, but Aran fought with precision, dodging, parrying, and driving his knee into his attacker's ribs.

Sura engaged two smaller warriors at once, her movements were a blur. One of the warriors swung a serrated blade at her, but she ducked low, spinning and sweeping his legs out from under him before slashing a dagger across his throat. The second, at first taken aback by her speed, charged, but she sidestepped him, slashing under his outstretched arm. Mortally wounded, he crumpled to the ground.

Rafiq, armed with his well sharpened twin swords, fought as if all this was but a well planned choreography. Spinning, weaving, his blades flashing in the firelight. He easily sidestepped a spear thrust, grabbing the Draconian by the wrist and twisting hard, breaking bone before driving a sword into his foe's chest. "Damn lizards," he took pleasure in seeing the light fade from his enemy's eyes.

A Draconian assassin, hidden in the shadow, leapt from the ruins, his dagger aimed for Aran's spine, but Sura saw him first.

"Aran!" she shouted. Her voice carried threads of a deeper, veiled emotion. Aran turned just in time to catch the assassin's wrist, but the blade still sliced across his shoulder, finding a gap in his armour. Gritting his teeth, he drove his sword through his opponent's ribs.

The last of the Draconians tried to retreat, but Rafiq was faster. He threw his dagger, catching the enemy between the shoulder blades. The warrior collapsed, and silence returned to the desert.

Aran exhaled, wiping blood from his blade. "Well, Rafiq. You were saying?"

The sturdy warrior groaned, as he wiped his blades clean. "I'm never saying anything ever again." A smile dawned on his face, and both men burst out laughing, in a much-needed cathartic moment of levity.

Sura nudged the nearest Draconian corpse with her boot. "They were obviously expecting to catch us off guard and, most certainly, were not expecting us to put up a fight this fierce. Probably scouts," clarity was dawning on her, "or assassins sent by Drathis to eliminate us before we reached Sarim."

Aran observed the insignia on their armour. It wasn't the standard Draconian crest. This warrior bore the mark of the Silent Claw, Drathis' elite strike force. "Yes. They knew exactly who we were," he murmured. "And they knew exactly where to find us. Drathis was behind this." The fire kept them warm, but none of them slept that night.

Two weeks had gone by, since they left Erythmar. Having crossed the central highlands once more, on their way back to Sarim, they were travelling again through sandy deserts. After a hard day's ride, they finally reached a small oasis, surrounded by Moonleaf trees, its emerald waters glistened under the sun. They drank cautiously and refilled their flasks, letting their desert steeds quench their thirst and rest in the shade of the trees. After a few hours of rest, twilight was upon them, so they decided to make camp for the night. The air was thick, unnatural, as if the desert itself was holding its breath.

"Do you think it could have been just a random patrol?" Sura asked expectantly.

"I do not think so," Aran was thinking fast. "After all, they wore his seal," an idea was forming in his mind. "I believe it was Drathis, but how could he know where we were? We have not been followed, not that we could spot it anyway," his mind drifted elsewhere, trying to make sense of it all, so he missed the signs, the deadly silence that surrounded them.

Rafiq, who had spent the day in introspection, was honing his blades.

"Why does this place feel so... wrong?" The sound of steel being sharpened stopped abruptly.

The silence around them became so palpable it felt oppressive.

Suddenly, they all felt it. A deep, pulsing disturbance beneath the sand, as if something was moving underneath them. Something big. The oasis erupted, as though it was in the throes of a desert storm.

The sand erupted in a violent explosion, revealing not a creature but an aberration of nature. The sand serpent's scales were blackened and cracked, as if its body had been half-formed from the desert itself. Its eyes were wrong, glowing with an eerie, pulsating light, appearing as though something else was looking through them.

It moved unnaturally, its body coiling and jerking like it were being controlled by invisible strings. When it opened its mouth, its fangs weren't just long - they were warped, stretching and shifting like molten glass, as though the very Weaving had twisted its flesh into something unholy. Its body was so broad, it cast shadows over the oasis.

The creature's scales rasped against the sand with a sound like steel being dragged across stone, and the air filled with its putrid breath - a smell of decay and something else, something alien.

Sura barely had time to scream before the creature struck, its jaws snapping shut just where her left leg had been a second before.

"Move!" Aran shouted, rolling away as the serpent coiled and lunged at him, its mouth wide enough to swallow them whole.

His mind sharpened, instincts taking over. "Sura! The eyes!" He barked, already moving. She didn't hesitate - her daggers flashed through the air, striking the beast's glowing pupils.

It shrieked, rearing back, and Aran seized the opening. "Rafiq! Go for the throat!"

Rafiq didn't need to be told twice. He jumped, twin blades flashing and plunged them deep into the creature's exposed flesh. The serpent convulsed, its body writhing violently. The scales of sand serpents are generally very hard. In fact, some of the tribes, after going through their rite of passage, which is facing these things, fashion their hides into resistant armour.

Unfortunately for the trio, the Weaving's corruption had turned this one's scales even more resistant to ordinary weapons, and they didn't have any desert scorpion's poisoned tip arrows. "What I would not give for just one of those," Aran cursed himself, "Straight into its belly would be enough to put it to sleep."

Writhing in pain from Rafiq's attack, the serpent turned on Sura, its muscular tail whipping toward her with deadly speed.

"Look out!" Aran shouted, diving forward. The force of his tackle knocked Sura aside, but the tail still slammed into his ribs, sending him splashing into the water, bruised.

Rafiq seized the moment. Grabbing a burning log from the campfire, he hurled it into the serpent's open maw. The beast shrieked, rearing back in agony.

Aran, drenched and gasping for air, forced himself up. For a flash of a second, he saw the serpent's weakness, exposed by the burning log Rafiq had thrown. The fire had burned away part of its warped scales, exposing the flesh beneath. But he was too far away. "Rafiq!" he shouted, pointing at the beast. "Go for the burned spot. There!"

With a cry, the proud Bahir warrior ran towards the beast, vaulting over his steed and leapt high, driving both swords deep into the serpent's throat, as it was coming in for the kill. His cut ran deep.

The creature convulsed, its coils thrashing as it let out a final, deafening screech before collapsing. Its ruin smashed through trees and bushes. Rafiq rolled with the fall.

For a long moment, everything became still. Aran wiped sweat from his brow, exhaling. He turned to Sura and Rafiq, their faces marked with exhaustion, but also triumph. "We should be dead," Sura muttered, shaking her head.

"Yet here we stand," Rafiq grinned, resting his swords on his shoulders. Aran looked between them, his chest tightening - not with fear, but with something else. Pride. They had fought as one, against both enemies and the unknown forces of the Weaving itself. No matter what lay ahead, he knew this much: he was not alone.

Then Rafiq muttered, "I am so done with this desert." They laughed, a breathless chuckle, covered in sand and blood, but victorious. Sarim was still far away - but they would reach it together.

Chapter XVII

A Storm Brews Within

The city of Sarim was cloaked in a muted haze as Aran, Sura, and Rafiq approached its towering walls. Brought by its present king to become a symbol of unity, but now it appeared to be a fractured capital. Its people divided, the council uncertain. When Aran, flanked by his two friends, entered the city through the familiar gates, the whispers of unrest hung in the air, lingering like the distant echo of a gathering storm. The great banners of the united tribes flew above the city's battlements, but even those emblems of power and pride seemed muted, as though the weight of looming catastrophe had drained them of their colours and the city of its vitality.

For all the grandeur that Sarim projected outwardly, the trio could easily sense the disquiet that stirred within its walls. The marketplace, usually bustling with traders from every corner of Zarah, was subdued. People moved with a quiet urgency, as though anticipating the unravelling of something far greater than their mundane minds could grasp. Even Aran's presence, always welcomed as a sign of hope and stability, now caused a ripple of anxiety, for the people of Sarim had begun to disperse rumours of what was happening. Of the ancient pacts that had been breached and the forces that stirred beneath the surface of their world.

Rafiq, always ready to lighten the mood, leaned over and whispered to Sura. "They could not possibly have heard of our slithering friend, could they?" She repressed a nervous laugh, then looked at Aran.

As they rode toward the palace, his thoughts turned inward to the power he had drawn from the obelisk, and to the presence he had felt observing him in the Weaving. No matter how hard he tried, he could not get rid of it, the memory of that encounter was fresh in his mind, its implications unsettling. The Primordials were no longer a distant myth. They had awakened once again and, when they chose to act, no force in the world would be able to stand against them. None?! Well... maybe. But that still remained to be seen. Yet, even as this looming threat pressed down upon him, he could not ignore the more immediate dangers. His kingdom was divided once more, the Draco had clearly been at work from within his infrastructure and he suspected that mysterious presence in the Weaving to be a Primordial.

These were hard times indeed. His rule being undermined by the House of Draco, right in the midst of the unravelling of the Weaving.

"What more can happen?" He rhetorically asked himself, as they rode through the streets of the city, heading towards the Royal Citadel.

When they crossed the central courtyard of the palace, Aran could already see the growing factions in the faces of those who awaited. The Bahir, the Rasha, the Ulema, the Tarek and the other main tribes were standing with him. However, the smaller Yrith tribe, bold and stubborn, had aligned themselves with Farid, who had openly questioned Aran's methods of dealing with the Weaving.

The Sylenna, another smaller clan hailing from the southern regions of Zarah, pragmatic and ever-calculating, remained neutral, waiting for a sign that the balance of power would shift one way or another, before committing.

There were others too, minor lords, and a few of the most powerful tribal leaders. Most were loyal, a few were plotting, but all of them were waiting for him to make a move.

Inside the grand hall, the council had already gathered. The long stone chamber had never felt more oppressive, with its vaulted ceiling and tapestries depicting the flora and fauna of Zarah. Now they also depicted victories of the Old Kings, overseen by Barash at Aran's request, before he left for the valley of Erythmar.

The echoes of footsteps, murmurs of the assembled nobility, and the occasional clank of sword scabbards on armour, reverberated off the walls, creating a cacophony of tension. Aran took his place at the head of the crescent table, his hands resting on the cold, intricately-carved Solarwood, as he surveyed the faces of those before him.

He allowed the smaller tribes to speak first. It was his way of maintaining political balance, making sure none felt inferior or superior to their peers.

"Your Grace," lord Iram al-Yrith began, his voice laced with Farid's influence, barely masking the challenge within. "During your absence, the House of Draco has struck us again. We managed to keep them at bay, at great cost to our own. However, stranger things are happening all around us. It feels as though our very reality is unravelling before our eyes," lord Iram paused, looking around the room. "It actually is much worse than that. We have received troubling reports, rumours of your use of the Weaving's power, of ancient magics that are best left undisturbed. Now, the obelisks have shown us chaos? Here before the Council?! We must understand your intent."

Kasim al-Bahir shifted forward in his seat, mirrored by Safira and Karim al-Shamar. The king made a quick gesture, understood by them as a request for silence - he would handle this himself.

He met Iram al-Yrith's gaze steadily. Aran knew this moment would come. The time for candour, for disclosure. "Before we discuss anything

else, let me say that I am happy to hear that, while I have been away, you were able to thwart yet another Draco incursion. I trust you followed the protocols I put in place?”
He looked around the room, observing the reactions. His cousin, Zahira, gave him a reassuring nod. Barash, silent in the corner, observed with calm wisdom - he trusted his king to handle the situation.
“Now,” Aran continued. “Regarding the unravelling of the Weaving and the obelisks’ connection to it? What you, with levity, labelled as rumours, are in fact truths that have been hidden from us for aeons of time. The Weaving is not merely a tool to be feared or used at one's discretion. It is the very foundation of our world. The obelisks are part of this web - this net. They are tied to pacts far more ancient than the kingdoms we define as old. These are the pacts that were broken.”
“Broken you say, but by whom?” Iram al-Yrith pressed, his eyes narrowing. “By you? By the Draco? Maybe by the actions of your ancestors?”
The later question carried with it the threads of insult, of accusation. Aran chose to ignore this. This was not the time for inner conflict. It was time for mutual understanding and consensus. He gathered himself and pressed on. “It was broken by forces far older than any of us,” his voice cold, despite his best efforts. “Forces that even now stir in the dark corners of the Weaving. The Primordials,” Aran paused for a moment, allowing the room to catch up to the gravity of the situation. Murmurs spread through the council. “The Primordials?“ a voice asked, in astonishment.
“The creatures from myth?” Other voices whispered.
“Yes,” Aran’s response confirmed their worst fears. “The entities our forebears told us about, as bedtime stories.”
Finally, there it was. The truth, raw and naked. "Now," he spoke with finality, “we shall see what you are all made of, what truly matters to you the most. Will it be survival or power? Selflessness or egotism?" Aran’s words were embedded in truth, and those present felt them, deep within - some tribal lords shifted in their seats, while others, discreetly covered their faces, in shame.
The mere mention of the Primordials’ name was enough to send a ripple of discomfort through the chamber. It was a name heard by most here, at one time or another in their lives, but a name that, until now, had only been spoken of in ancient texts, bedtime stories and old wives tales. A concept of power so immense that even speaking it aloud seemed to summon danger. Lords and ladies exchanged uneasy glances, and the silence that followed was thick with apprehension.

Lady Sylenna was a tribal leader from the south-western regions of Zarah. Her sharp features and calculating eyes gave her the appearance of a viper waiting to strike - fitting for one whose tribe had survived generations by pledging loyalty to whoever held power longest. Sylenna was neither friend nor foe; she was simply practical.
She spoke next. "If these Primordials are as powerful as the old stories suggest, then why should we believe they would concern themselves with our petty affairs now? What could we, as mere mortals, possibly offer or deny them?" Barash and Aran exchanged wary looks.
Safira rose, her eyes ablaze. "Have you learned nothing so far? Have you not been warned by myself, as well as by our king, countless times, in this very council room?" She did not wait for an answer, for she did not need one - Anar and Nysa had shown her the truth. "Trust in our king, for he is the one our moons have shown me. The one who will lead us to liberty. Freedom to chart our own destiny, as one people." A charged silence transformed the room.
Aran, silently, beckoned Safira to take her seat. Listening to her, one would think she was speaking of another man. Could he really accomplish what she was promising them, or would he be weak and corruptible, like his forebears had been?
Lady Sylenna shifted nervously in her seat. Her demeanour reminded Aran of the Sand Serpent he had recently encountered. "Our slithering friend," Rafiq had called it. "Very well," he thought, "she asked for it."
Leaning forward, he kept his voice low and deliberate. "Because, milady, the Weaving is breaking. The balance that has been held for millennia is faltering. If it collapses, it will not be a question of what they want, but rather the question of whether any of us will survive."
There was a murmur of discontent from some of the lords assembled. The Weaving was a mystery to most, an abstract concept best left in the hands of scholars and myth-makers. Still, here was their king, speaking of it as though it were something they must all contend with.
Farid, who had been silently sitting in a corner, saw his opportunity. His voice dripped with venom. "You would have us believe," he interjected, "that you alone can restore this balance? That we must follow you, without question, into this madness? While the Draco are probably right now, planning to attack us again?" he asked, with delight.
Aran felt the sting of Farid's words. His fake unsureness reeked of betrayal, but Aran kept his composure nonetheless. "I have seen the vision," he said, his voice calm but unyielding. "I have felt the presence of the Primordials. They are stirring, and they will not be ignored. Unfortunately, we do not have the luxury of debate, or of having a choice on the matter. If we do not act now. If we do not remain united.

Then we will all be swept away when the Weaving collapses. The Draco are but a nuisance, when compared to the threat the Primordials represent."

"What of the obelisks?" Lord Iram al-Yrith demanded again. "You have drawn upon their power, yes? What assurances can you give us that you will not use that power against us?"

It was Sura who answered, stepping forward. "Think of what you are saying. You speak as if the obelisks are weapons to be wielded against men. They are not. Do you not understand? They are anchors, ballasts that keep the Weaving stable. Aran's connection to them is the only thing that stands between us and total catastrophe."

The council room fell silent once more. Aran could see the doubt in their eyes, the uncertainty. These were men and women who had lived their lives according to the rules of the desert, its politics and power struggles, where alliances were forged in the fire of ambition, and trust was a fragile commodity. To them, the Weaving was a distant myth, a thing of scholars and ancient kings. Aran knew better, for he had felt its power, and he had seen what would happen if it was left unchecked.

"You do not need to trust me," he said finally, his voice hardening. "However, you should trust the truth of what you have seen with your own eyes. What I have shown you through the Weaving itself."

There was a long pause. Almost everyone fidgeted in their seats. It was Farid who broke the silence. "What proof do we have that what you have shown us was not an illusion?"

Instead of acquiescing to such a ludicrous enquiry, Aran asked a question in turn. "What possibly could I gain by doing such a thing?"

Farid's reply was swift. "Keeping your precious throne, of course."

Aran mastered his anger as best he could. "Have we fought, bled, and sacrificed - only to turn on each other at the final hour?" His voice was low, but it carried through the hall like distant thunder. "The Weaving has shown us the truth. I will restate that you do not have to trust me, but you should trust yourselves. If you ignore it, we will all burn."

Lord Iram sprang to his feet, fists clenched at his sides. Clearly, Farid had gotten to him. "What if we chose not to believe or heed your warning? If we choose to reject this path you have shown us, what then?"

Aran rose from his seat, looked at everyone in turn, and then locked eyes with lord Iram. "Then you will have doomed us all."

His words hung in the air, heavy with finality. The council shifted uneasily, their faces pale as the gravity of the situation sank in. They could no longer deny that something far greater than the House of Draco's attacks, or their own inner petty squabbles, was at play.

The Primordials were rising, and the balance of their world hung by a thread.

"You will need more than words to unite all the tribes," Lady Sylenna said after a long pause. "Nevertheless, if the vision is as dire as you have shown us, then you must act swiftly. The other obelisks," she asked, "there are more, yes?" The urgency, in her voice, was unmistakable - fear had struck her core.

Aran nodded patiently. "Yes, there are more, scattered across Zarah," he had told them this before. "Each one is tied to a different aspect of the Weaving. If we are to stabilize it, we must secure them all."

"What if the House of Draco interferes?" Farid asked, nonsensically, in one last desperate attempt to disrupt Aran's reasoning. The man's voice was dripping with hate - he felt alone and without allies.

Farid was a man whose political manoeuvring was in the throes of death. He knew that he couldn't defeat the king in combat, and now he had just lost another battle. Which brought Aran's win count up to three, their first clash was physical, the last two had been political. Without support from the House of Draco, he was nothing more than a silver tongued weakling, grasping for power.

In spite of his betrayal, Aran knew this was a time for unity, not for division. He would not turn against his people, no matter their own, personal choices.

He would give Farid one last chance at redemption. Meeting the man's gaze, the weight of his responsibility pressing down on him. "Then we fight, Farid." All the colour left the turncoat's face. "But not as rivals," Aran continued, still looking him in the eyes. "Instead, we shall fight as one people. United for a common goal."

Farid blanched, as though the blood had fled his veins, leaving only dread behind. He anticipated anger from Aran, maybe even frustration, but not this. This display of benevolence was, if nothing else, extremely unexpected. Was the king extending him the hand of forgiveness?

Despite his own betrayal, almost leading to Aran's death, the man still found absolution in his heart. Floored by the gesture, Farid said nothing. For a fleeting moment, shame and something like gratitude flickered across his face - emotions quickly masked by his practised neutrality. He sat down in shame and remained mute for the rest of the meeting, his plans momentarily derailed by unexpected mercy. Barash, sitting in his corner, did nothing to hide a smile of satisfaction.

The council room was heavy with silence, each lord and lady weighing the enormity of what the king was asking of them. However, because of the truth of it, in the end, they had very little choice. The storm was indeed coming, and whether they believed in the Weaving or not, the truth was undeniable. Something ancient was waking, and it would not be stopped by politics or its fragile, illusory power.

After such a long silence, Lady Sylenna was the first to speak, her voice was steady but grim. "Very well, my king. We will unite under your banner," Lady Sylenna drew herself up to her full height. "We will now, not follow you blindly. Yet, if the balance tips too far, if the Weaving is lost, then you will have led us all to ruin." Aran nodded, accepting the warning but offering one of his own. "Then let us make sure that we remain united and make certain that ruin does not come to us."

The council meeting was adjourned for a few hours, but no one left their seat. Conversations began to break out throughout the room.

Aran was staring at the fading light outside the great arched windows. He had won their cooperation for now, but the real battle was still ahead. He was sure that Drathis was bound to attack again, the obelisks needed to be secured, and the Primordials would not sit idly by, while he attempted to restore balance to the Weaving.

Even as he prepared for the battles to come, one thought insisted on lingering in his mind - the external presence that manifested itself in the Valley of Erythmar, the one that had retreated but had not entirely disappeared. It was still out there, waiting - watching. Aran knew that when it returned, it would not do so quietly.

As the council adjourned, Aran knew the respite would be brief. The threats they faced - both mystical and martial - would not wait for political consensus. He had won a battle of words, but words alone could not defeat the Primordials. Nor could they stop the House of Draco.

Night had fallen. Despite recent events, Sarim, the old spiritual heart of Yaran country, was still a city of beauty and reverence - the alabaster that covered the walls of the Royal Citadel, taken from the cliffs that overlooked the Great Lunar Basin, shimmered under the light of Anar and Nysa. The Lunar Citadel, the city's crown jewel, stood at its centre - a towering structure of white stone and silver spires, home to the Moon Seers and their sacred texts.

The air within the council chamber of the citadel was heavy with tension. Aran ibn Khalid stood, once more that day, at the head of the crescent-shaped table, his face resolute but strained. Farid had been subdued, the Council of Tribes had just heard his account of the Weaving, and he was determined to face the Primordials. At first his plea was met with doubt, now the tide was beginning to turn. Dialogue between the tribal leaders was beginning to flow. Though some of Aran's strongest supporters were proving hard to convince.

"Aran, you have proven yourself countless times, and have earned my undying trust. But the Primordials?!" Kasim al-Bahir muttered, his deep voice tinged with scepticism. "They are no more than legends, faintly whispered by grandmothers at campfires, not something to base the future of our kingdom upon."

Karim al-Shamar adjusted his spectacles, his sharp features furrowed in thought. "Yet, we cannot dismiss it, Kasim. We know that the Weaving is no trivial phenomenon, but has our king not proven to us that he is capable of revealing truths hidden beneath the surface of our reality."

Zahira, Aran's cousin, spoke next, her voice steady but cautious. "I know our king speaks the truth, so the question is not whether the Primordials are real - because, trust me, they are. The question we should be asking ourselves is what do we do now? We need to consider that we may not be ready for such a powerful threat."

Aran raised a hand, commanding silence. "I am dealing with that threat, and I will resolve it!" His words rebounded through the room, heavy with confidence and authority. "The House of Draco is still our immediate concern - your immediate concern," he emphasized. "As we speak, they watch and wait, looking for weakness. Whether they are connected to the disturbance in the Weaving or not, the threat they pose to our stability is still very real."

Safira nodded and sat beside Aran, her silver robes reflecting the moonlight streaming through the chamber's high windows. "The moons speak of storms on the horizon. We must prepare, not just for what is known, but for what is unseen as well."

At that precise moment, the council chamber trembled. A deep, unnatural rumble - not thunder, but something else. The floor shuddered beneath them. Distant shouts rang through the corridors, followed by the unmistakable sound of steel. A guard burst into the chamber, his face pale with urgency. "My king - Sarim is under attack!"

Everyone shifted in their seats, but Aran didn't hesitate. He leapt to action, faster than they could blink. "Rafiq, Sura - now." Both left the council chamber as swift as the wind.

The chamber erupted into motion, council members scrambling, orders flying. "This is it. The House of Draco is at our doorstep," the king met each tribal leader's gaze, conveying confidence, "Rasha, Bahir, Shamari, Tarek, Ulema, regardless of our differences, it is what unites us that matters most. It makes no difference where we came from, only where we ended up. Here and now - united. We are natives of this land. Let us defend Zarah as one people. Aran swept his gaze across them one last time. "Remember, fight as one." Every tribal leader in the council was inspired by his words, courage blazing through their veins and, in the end, their enemies would learn the true meaning of bravery.

Drathis stood on the bridge of his hovering flagship, the Obsidian Wrath, his scaled armour glinting darkly in the dim light of his command chamber. The Draco had emerged on the horizon, under the cover of night. That desert dreamer, turned king, somehow had defeated his elite assassination team. "No matter," he thought. Aran wouldn't be able to run this time. "Bring the Photon Cannons on-line," He issued the order, his voice low and venomous. "Sarim will fall before these sand dwellers even realise that we are here."
From the fleet's flagship, a beam of concentrated energy lanced through the night, striking the Outer Ward of Sarim with devastating precision. The explosion illuminated the city in an orange glow, sending debris cascading into the streets below.
"Deploy the Chimaeras," Drathis hissed, his slitted eyes narrowing as he watched the chaos unfold. "Let them feel what fear truly is."
The bells of Sarim rang out, their deep tones reverberating through the city. Warriors scrambled to their posts as the streets erupted into chaos.
Aran burst into the citadel's central courtyard, where Sura and Rafiq were already marshalling the defenders. Bahir warriors formed tight formations, their shields locking together as they prepared to hold the gates. Shamari engineers hurriedly set up portable solar disruptors, to counter the Draco's weaponry, their faces grim with determination.
"The Draco are here," Aran said, his voice cutting through the din. "They are targeting the Outer Ward. If they breach it, the city is lost."
Sura strapped on her gloves, her expression fierce. Kasim shouted, "The Bahir warriors will hold the gates. We have faced worse."
"The Shamari can focus on the disruptors," Karim and Rafiq added. "If we can disable their weapons, that should buy us time."
Safira approached, her bow slung over her shoulder, and her quiver filled with both explosive and crescent arrows. "The temple must be protected," she warned. "The Draconians will try to strike at our heart."
Aran nodded. "Then we divide our forces. Kasim, take the Bahir and reinforce the gates. Karim, coordinates the engineers. Safira, take the archers to the battlements and do not be afraid to light them up," he bowed to them, "I will lead a strike team to the temple."
The gates of the Outer Ward shook as the first wave of Chimaera Beasts charged. These grotesque creatures had originally been bred in the Draco's genetic labs back on their home system of Nathair. They were created much in the same manner as the House of Draco had

done when they created the House of Udo. An experiment, where they combined Abraxian DNA with the genetic code from the House of Lyco, a now extinct civilization of The MiddleVerse, in order to create a more powerful Lycan House - one they could control.

These Chimaeras were less evolved creatures, but were, nonetheless, a powerful and towering amalgamations of reptilian strength and unnatural genetic augmentation. Their roars echoed like thunder through the dunes as they slammed into the Bahir shield wall.

Kasim al-Bahir roared back. Despite being past his prime, he wielded his Dune Stalker blade with skill, cutting a wide arc as he cleaved through the neck of a Chimaera. "Hold the line!" he bellowed. "Show these abominations the strength of the desert!" His warriors fought hard, keeping those frightening creatures from invading the streets of Sarim.

Above the city gates, Rasha archers fired volley after volley of Crescent Arrows, a variation to the explosive kind, their glowing tips piercing through the beasts' thick hides.

Safira moved among them, her movements graceful and precise as she fired arrow after arrow. "The moons guide our aim," she said softly, as most of her shots found their mark. Meanwhile, Shamari engineers activated the first of the solar disruptors. Their concentrated beams of light seared through the advancing Draco soldiers, forcing them to take cover. Karim al-Shamar directed the effort from atop the city battlements. "Focus on the flanks!" he shouted. "Do not let them regroup!"

At the temple, Aran's strike team faced a direct assault by Draconian elite soldiers. These warriors, clad in black armour etched with glowing red runes, moved with deadly precision. The king fought at the forefront, his father's blade flashing with moonlight as he parried and struck. Foe after foe fell prey to his deadly dance. Around him, his warriors fought with the desperation of those protecting their home. One of the elite reptilian warriors lunged at him, but Aran was too quick. Sidestepping his opponent's strike, he drove his blade into the gap between the warrior's armour scales.

He turned to Rafiq, who was fending off two attackers at once. "Push them back!" Aran shouted. "We can not let them inside!"

Rafiq dispatched his opponents with brutal efficiency, his eyes blazing with determination. "I will make these reptiles regret ever setting foot on Zarah."

Still, despite their best efforts, a group of Draconian saboteurs managed to breach the temple's outer sanctum. Inside, the Moon Seers huddled around the sacred Lunar Tapestry, an ancient artefact said to hold the wisdom of Anar and Nysa - the seers were using their bodies to protect it from being defiled.

From the other side of the temple, Safira and Sura appeared in the doorway, bow and daggers standing at the ready. "You will not defile this place," the moon seer shouted, her voice like steel. Her arrows found their marks with ease, as Sura flashed her daggers with deadly speed, killing three Draconian warriors before the saboteurs were driven back. However, inevitable and indifferent to their will, as the battle dragged on, tiredness began to set in and the defenders of Sarim began to falter.

The Draco Photon Cannons continued to batter the Outer Ward, showing no signs of relenting, despite the city's archers continuous volleys. Amidst the chaos, Aran caught himself. Recalling the Trials of the Old Kings, he realized that he was making the old mistake of trying to do everything himself - instead of leading and organising his forces. Looking at the bigger picture, it became clear to him that the city's survival hinged on neutralizing Drathis' flagship.

The night hung heavy over the battlefield, the darkened sands of Yaran country, illuminated by the fires of war. Sarim's defenders, though faltering, still stood unbroken, holding firm against the relentless siege of the Draconian forces. Aran, however, knew defence would not be enough. They had to strike back, if they were to stand a chance of winning. He needed to do something - now.

Perched atop the crumbling battlements, sword raised high, his voice cutting through the chaos, he shouted. "Sura, gather the best of the Bahir and Tarek scouts," he commanded. "We are taking the fight to him."

In the shadows of the dunes, cloaked in Nightwing capes, they glided like whispers of the desert wind, weaving through the battlefield. Each heartbeat was a gamble against discovery, the tension thick in the air. Aran's team moved swiftly, unseen beneath the cover of darkness, threading their way through the scattered formations of Draconian forces. Drathis' flagship loomed ahead, a large dark vessel with glowing runes, suspended above the battlefield like a harbinger of doom. Its hull shimmered under the moonlight; its design, ancient and foreign, was a relic of the War of the Shattered Sky - a devastating intergalactic conflict, initiated by the House of Draco, who sought to dominate the House of Abraxas, millennia ago, in the Orionis star system.

Finally, having reached it, they ascended swiftly, barely avoiding the patrols that guarded the ship's perimeter. They reached an access hatch on the lower deck, and Rafiq worked deftly to disable the security seals. The lock hissed open. No alarms. Not yet.

Inside, the air was thick with the scent of ozone and metal, the distant hum of the ship's power cores vibrating beneath their feet. Shadows flickered along the corridors as Aran led the way, his steps silent as the shifting sands. "Move fast," he whispered. Sura, Rafiq, and Safira broke off to plant the charges along the ship's main reactor conduits, their movements precise and methodical.

Aran advanced toward the bridge with the rest of the team, their blades drawn, their breaths steady. Just as they neared the final corridor, the silence was shattered.

An alarm blared, shrill and unforgiving. The corridors erupted into chaos as armoured Draconian sentries stormed their position. Blades clashed, steel sang against steel. Aran met the first warrior head-on, parrying a brutal overhead strike and driving his sword into the gap between his foe's armour plates. He pivoted, dodging another blow, his movements fluid, honed by years of battle. "We are out of time!" he shouted over the melee. "Set the charges and go!"

They pushed forward, cutting through the resistance as they neared the central chamber of the flagship. There, waiting in the gloom, stood Drathis. He was clad in blackened armour, his reptilian features illuminated by the dim glow of the control panels. His golden eyes gleamed with malice, his sword resting lazily in his clawed grip. The air around him crackled with restrained energy, the sheer weight of his presence pressing against them like an unseen force. "You have come far, little king," Drathis sneered. "However, you should have taken my offer when you had the chance."

Aran stepped forward, his grip tightening on his sword. "Your offer was nothing more than a diversion. If I had been foolish enough to accept it, you would have slit my throat the moment I outlived my usefulness. Your House is not known for sharing power."

Drathis bared his fangs in a humourless grin. "You remain ignorant of many things, desert king. But it does not matter. Your vision ends here. Our vision will prevail. Your people are but another civilization waiting to be conquered." He tilted his head, his voice dripping with amusement. "In the end, we always win."

Aran did not falter. His blood burned with the fire of his ancestors, his will as unyielding as the desert itself. "You are mistaken, Drathis. You let your arrogance blind you to our resilience. We are bred by the desert and tempered by its heat. We will never bow to you."

Drathis hissed, his muscles tensing like a serpent poised to strike. Then, in a blur of movement, he lunged.

Their weapons collided in a flash of sparks. Aran barely sidestepped the first strike, the force of it sending shockwaves through the chamber. Drathis was fast - unnaturally so - but Aran was no stranger to battle. He countered, his blade finding an opening, slicing across his enemy's pauldron. Drathis growled, retaliating with a flurry of attacks, each one heavier than the last.

Aran deflected a downward slash, rolling to the side and countering with a riposte aimed at Drathis's exposed side. The Draconian twisted, avoiding the lethal blow, his tail whipping around to strike Aran's legs. He staggered, barely regaining his footing before meeting another strike head-on. Drathis laughed, his blade weaving through the air like a viper. "You fight well, little king. But you will fall."

Aran's breaths came fast, but his resolve did not waver. He met Drathis's attacks with unrelenting force, their duel a storm of clashing steel and raw fury. Twice, Aran nearly sliced his enemy's throat, and twice the Draconian Warlord barely escaped death, fear flickering in his eyes. He snarled, calling for reinforcements, but just as his warriors stormed into the chamber, Sura, Safira, and Rafiq arrived, their weapons gleaming in the dim light. The tide turned instantly. Their combined assault forced Drathis to retreat, his confidence crumbling. Suddenly, the ship trembled. A series of deafening explosions ripped through its core as the charges detonated. Fire and smoke filled the corridors, alarms blaring in desperate warning. "Time to go!" Rafiq shouted. Through the chaos, the small group raced for the escape route. As they neared the edge of the ship, they saw Drathis running, his once-commanding presence reduced to that of a desperate fugitive. Aran and his team leapt overboard just as a secondary explosion tore through the flagship, sending shards of burning metal into the sky. They tumbled through the night air, rolling with the fall, their landing swift and controlled.

Drathis, watching from the wreckage, roared in fury. "I will get you, Aran, son of Khalid! I will prove to your people that you are a fraud - a liar selling them promises you cannot keep!" No answer came his way. Instead, his fleet was met with a volley of explosive arrows, showering them in fire. Realizing his advantage was lost, Drathis ordered a retreat, his fleet vanishing into the night, his war left unfinished.

Aran stood on the dunes, his breath ragged, but his gaze unwavering. The war was not over, but for tonight, Sarim still stood, and the House of Draco had been dealt a blow they would not soon forget.

Chapter XVIII

The King of the Desert Rises

The battle was over, but its echoes lingered long after Drathis' forces had vanished into the desert night. Sarim still stood, defiant under the twin moons, yet the cost of its survival was etched into every stone, every street, and every face that walked its battered paths.

As the first light of dawn crept over the Crescent Cliffs, the ruins of the Outer Ward cast jagged shadows across the sands. Soot blackened and blood streaked the once-pristine white walls of Sarim, marking the sacrifice of both defenders and attackers. Smoke hung in the air, mingling with the acrid scent of burned wood and scorched stone.

Aran walked slowly through the city streets, his boots crunching over shattered tiles and fallen banners. He paused by a toppled fountain in the Lunar Plaza, where children were playing only hours ago. Now, it was filled with rubble and the broken remains of Moonleaf lanterns.

Behind him, Sura approached, her steps deliberate. Apart from her daggers, she now carried a blade in her hand, hanging loosely by her side, its once-bright edge dulled by the night's violence. "Judging by how fierce the battle was, there is not as much destruction as there could have been," she said, her voice calm, but heavy.

Aran nodded, his gaze distant. "We managed to hold them off, but this was only the beginning of their fury. Drathis just wanted to send a message. Sarim may still stand, but the scars he left behind? Those will take time to heal."

They walked together in silence for a moment before Sura stopped, turning to face him. "You are hurt," her face was hatched with worry. "Please allow me to tend to your wounds."

Aran looked at her, as if seeing her anew. After a short moment of silence, he said, "No," his tone was gentle, holding her hands in his. "First, I need to speak to the people. They need to hear from me. They need to know why this happened and what comes next."

The Temple of Anar and Nysa still stood, though its alabaster facade was marred with scorch marks. Inside, the Moon Seers worked tirelessly to restore order, their soft chants filling the air as they repaired the sacred Lunar Tapestry and tended to the wounded who had sought refuge in the temple, as the battle unfolded.

Safira moved among them, her silver robes now streaked with ash and dirt. She paused by a young woman who was scrubbing blood from the temple's marble floors. The girl looked up at her, tears brimming in her wide eyes. "Lady Safira," she whispered. "Did we win?" she asked hesitantly.

Safira knelt beside her, placing a gentle hand on the girl's shoulder. "We won, child. Sarim still stands because of the courage of its people. However, our victory does not represent the end of this conflict. It is a reminder of the strength we must carry forward." A faint smile appeared on the girl's face.

Aran entered the temple, accompanied by Sura, his presence commanding yet sombre. The Moon Seers paused their work to bow their heads, but he raised a hand, bowing to them in turn. "Please, do not mind me, continue your work. This place is sacred because of your efforts, not due to mine." As he turned, he saw Safira.

She approached the pair, her expression grave. "The Draco aimed for more than the walls, Aran. They wanted to break our spirit. The attack on the temple was deliberate. They know the strength we draw from our moons."

He glanced at the partially restored Lunar Tapestry, its intricate silver threads glowing faintly. "Yet, they failed," he said, with a gleam in his eye, "the temple still stands, the moons still shine, and we still endure."

Later that day, Aran convened the Council of Tribes, in the Hall of Unity within the Lunar Citadel.

The room was tense, the air heavy with exhaustion and lingering fear.

Kasim al-Bahir, still clad in his bloodied armour, slammed a fist on the intricately carved table. "Aran is right. This was more than a battle, it was a warning! The Draco did not send their full might. They were clearly testing us, gauging our defences."

Karim al-Shamar, his normally calm demeanour frayed, adjusted his cracked spectacles. "Their cannon technology is far more advanced than we anticipated. If it had not been for our archers and they had managed to focus those weapons entirely on the city, we would not be sitting here right now."

Aran's cousin, Zahira of the Tarek tribe, leaned forward, her voice sharp. "What of their Chimaeras? Those terrifying beasts were so fierce we barely were able to hold them back. If they bring twice as many next time, how will we stop them?"

Aran raised his hand, silencing the room. His voice was steady but carried the weight of the past night's events. "Yes, I am afraid I was right, Kasim - it was a test. Drathis wanted to see if our unity would falter under pressure," he looked around the room, "but we did not break. The Bahir held the gates, the Shamari manned the Solar Disruptors, the Rasha lit the skies, and the Tarek outmanoeuvred them at every turn. We stood together, and that is why Sarim still stands."

Safira added, her tone measured, "The moons have shown me the path forward - our strength lies not just in our defences but in our ability to adapt. Nevertheless, we must anticipate their next move and prepare accordingly, otherwise we might not survive their next attack."

Aran nodded, in agreement. "We will rebuild the Outer Ward stronger than before. The Shamari will enhance the solar defences, the Tarek will map out potential vulnerabilities, and the Bahir will increase their patrols. Still, this cannot be just a defensive effort, for the Draconians must learn that every attack on us will cost them dearly."

Kasim al-Bahir grinned fiercely. "Now you are speaking my language."

At twilight, by order of the king, a solemn ceremony was held in the Lunar Gardens to honour the fallen.

The gardens, though damaged, still carried an air of tranquillity as the people of Sarim gathered under the night sky. At the centre of the gathering, a bonfire burned, its flames surrounded by offerings.

Some warriors left broken blades from their fallen comrades, others left torn banners or other remnants of the battle.

Aran stood before the crowd, his face illuminated by the firelight. "We gather tonight to honour those who gave their lives defending this city. Their sacrifice reminds us that freedom is not given in the desert. It must be earned through courage and unity," he paused, his gaze sweeping over the crowd. "The Draco sought to weaken our defences by dividing us. They have done all in their power to keep us afraid," he could see that fear in their eyes, expectantly awaiting the warmth of light, so he chose his next words carefully. "They sought to break us, to drown us in fear. But fear is only darkness - and we are the light. As long as we stand together, Zarah's flame will never be extinguished." Despite being in mourning, the crowd erupted into a collective cheer, their voices rising into the night like a storm. Anar and Nysa watched, silently, sitting upon their celestial thrones.

Late that night, as the city quieted, Aran stood on the balcony of the citadel, gazing out over Sarim. The city was battered but alive, its streets still buzzing with the energy of survival.

Sura joined him, leaning on the railing. "You did well today," her eyes met his, "and you were right as well, the people needed to hear your voice."

Aran shook his head. "I was only partially right," his eyes watching the city below, "They needed more than me. They also needed each other. That is what saved Sarim, not a king, but a kingdom."

She smiled faintly, placing her hand over his. "Still, having a king helps. Especially one like you."

"I am not special," he said, with a heavy voice, "anyone alive can do astonishing things, if they put their mind and heart into it. You are the ones that keep me going and I live to serve you, not the other way around. I am no more special than any of them. However, together, united, we can become something truly special, perhaps even unstoppable." Sura remained silent, pondering his words.

Safira arrived moments later, carrying a scroll. "My king, the Moon Seers have finished their readings," she said, unrolling the parchment. "Anar and Nysa warned us of another shadow coming our way. This battle was but a prelude to something greater."

Aran exhaled slowly, his shoulders heavy with the weight of her words. "Then we will face it together," he said, his voice resolute. "Whatever comes our way, we will endure."

The three of them stood in silence, the light of the moons bathing the city below, their presence a quiet promise that even in the darkest times, light could prevail.

When the sun came, this time bathing the city in golden light, Sarim's Royal Citadel still stood tall against the morning sky, its domed towers and alabaster walls glistening in the first light of dawn. Though the palace had endured the attack, the scars of battle remained. Entire sections of its outer defences still bore the scorch marks from the Draco's attack, and the scent of charred wood lingered where their Chimaeras had set fire to the southern market district.

It had been three days since Drathis had led his assault on Sarim, and three days since Zarah's warriors, united under Aran's banner, had repelled him. The king himself had fought on the front lines alongside the warriors of the Bahir, the engineers of the Shamari, the archers of the Rasha, the scouts of the Tarek, and the merchants of the Ulema. Their collective effort had kept the Draconian attackers at bay, preventing the streets of Sarim from becoming deadly battlegrounds. The city still stood, and their unity had withstood the test of battle, but the war was far from over - Drathis would return.

Within the Hall of Unity, the Council of Tribes had gathered to determine their next move. The crescent-shaped table, carved from Solarwood, was bathed in light from the sun mirrors above, highlighting its intricate carvings. At its centre, Aran's Banner lay unfurled, a symbol of the kingdom that had survived the storm but still stood on the edge of a greater war. One so complex that none present here could predict its outcome.

The king sat at the head of the table, his expression unreadable, his posture firm. Around him, the leaders of Zarah's six great tribes debated fiercely.

"Drathis will not accept this defeat," Kasim al-Bahir declared, his deep voice filling the chamber. His muscular arms were crossed over his chest, and his crimson war-cloak still bore the stains of battle. "He was humiliated and will not retreat into the shadows forever. Mark my words - he will return stronger, and next time, he will strike at our heart."

Karim al-Shamar adjusted his spectacles, his sharp gaze scanning the reports spread before him. Always analytical, he evaluated outcomes and dissected every possibility. "Our scouts report that his army has withdrawn to the southeastern regions of Zarah, near the mountain ranges," he was looking at the reports as he cleaned his spectacles, "Make no mistake, he is regrouping. The question is, what will his next move be?" Karim's query hung in the air, as the seconds slowly rolled by.

Unexpectedly, the answer came not from a scout nor a strategist but from a moon seer. The air in the hall seemed to still as Safira rose from her seat, her silver robes shimmering in the soft glow of the Sun Mirrors. Her eyes were distant, as if she stood in two worlds at once, the present and some unseen future. "The moons have whispered their warning," she said, her voice barely above a whisper, yet it carried through the hall with unshakable certainty. "Drathis will return within three cycles of the moons. Only, this time, the Draco will not come alone - not if he can help it." A murmur rippled through the council.

"What do you mean?" Zahira asked, her tone heavy with expectation.

Safira looked to Aran, who nodded for her to continue. "The Weaving is still unravelling," she explained. "When our king mended the obelisk at Erythmar, he restored balance, but only partially. There are still fractures and distortions in the tapestry of existence. I have seen shadows gathering beyond the veil of our world, moving alongside the House of Draco - mostly unseen, but not unfelt."

Kasim leaned in, clenching his fists, his eyes unafraid. "So they are bringing something worse with them," he said, cracking his knuckles.

Aran exhaled slowly, his fingers tightening over the edge of the table. He had suspected as much. The Draco were ruthless but even they would not launch a second invasion so soon after their last defeat, unless Drathis thought he held some new advantage.

"There is something else," Safira continued, her gaze never leaving Aran's. "I have seen the northern lands in my visions. The winds of Eltor howl through my dreams, carrying echoes of power. A power buried beneath the ice and stone."

"The next obelisk," Aran said, "Yes, I know. Since my trials in Ryvath, I can sense their presence in the Weaving. Back in Erythmar, when I mended the obelisk in the valley, I felt that the next closest to Sarim is located in the mountains of Eltor."

Safira nodded. "It is. Though I fear that if we do not reach it soon, then Drathis might."

Silence fell over the chamber. The weight of their choices pressed down on them like the silent sun scorching the landscape.

Kasim al-Bahir was the first to break its veil. "So we must divide our forces," he said. "One army to defend Sarim and the other to seek out the obelisk."

Aran turned to face him. "If we send too many warriors north, that will weaken Sarim's defences. Besides, Sura, Rafiq, and myself will be sufficient. Maybe a small group of warriors will help." He looked at Rafiq, who understood his friend's silent nod as a request to gather a skilled group to join them.

Kasim gritted his teeth. "If we send too few, you might be walking into a death trap unprotected." His loyalty shining through.

Zahira leaned forward, her sharp eyes locked onto her cousin's. "What do you think lies ahead?"

Aran's mind flashed back once more to the trials of Ryvath, to the visions of the Primordials, to the sheer power he had felt emanating from them. "Two wars," he finally admitted. "One for the very fabric of our reality, the other for our survival as one united kingdom. Neither can be ignored - to our own detriment."

"No," Karim al-Shamar said urgently, "We must first understand the situation better, before acting."

Surprisingly, a new voice joined the discussion. One that had been silent for far too long. "What if understanding is not enough?" Barash asked, from the corner of the room. All eyes turned on him.

The old man seemed unbothered by this. His weathered hands rested on his lap, his dark robes carrying the faint scent of desert sage and ancient tomes. His face, lined with years of wisdom, bore no emotion, only quiet expectation.

Aran met his gaze. He knew exactly what his old tutor meant by what he said. "Do not let Barash's sarcasm fool you," he explained, "he is merely implying that knowledge without applicability becomes useless. Deep down, he is saying that I must trust my instinct. Use what I have learned thus far and act accordingly to that knowledge - in sum, I know what must be done about the obelisks, and I will see it done." A charged silence filled the chamber, heavy and foreboding.

Kasim spoke first, stubborn as always. "I say, destroy them," he uttered these words as if the matter was already settled, reigniting their old argument. The proud leader of the Bahir continued. "The obelisk in Erythmar nearly killed you, Aran. Besides, these things are connected to the Weaving, and we cannot risk having them fall into enemy hands."

Karim shook his head. "We have spoken about this before, to sheer exhaustion," he adjusted his spectacles. "You should know by now that destroying the obelisks will unravel the Weaving. Who knows what that will bring down upon us."

Safira shifted in her seat. "The moons tell me they are not meant to be destroyed," she added, trying to diffuse the situation, "but neither can they be left untouched."

Zahira steepled her fingers. "I confess to be lost in this matter. What is the solution then?"

Aran's voice was calm, but it carried the weight of finality. "The answer we all seek will not be found in this hall, but instead in the mountains of Eltor." He turned to Barash. "That is the path I will walk!" Aran observed his tutor, who was looking at him with unmistakable pride.

"Then go forth, King of Zarah." Those were his mentor's only words.

The chamber fell silent once more. Some of the smaller tribal leaders exchanged uncertain glances. "If we act too late, we risk everything," Aran continued, "I will not wait for disaster to strike us. I am going north, with or without the council's blessing."

Lady Sylenna, always pragmatic, tapped her nails against the polished Solarwood table. "Then let us ensure you do not fail. The Sylenna tribe will provide scouts to aid you in your quest."

Aran exhaled. "I shall go, but only with a small retinue. We cannot risk removing too many warriors away from the city."

"At least take Sura and Rafiq," Kasim quipped. "You will need them."

Aran smiled and nodded. "I would not go anywhere without them."

The council was silent for a long moment. Then, finally, each tribal leader gave their approval. Some of the leaders from the smaller tribes were reluctant, but the majority of his stronger supporters had total confidence in their king.

Once the council was adjourned, Aran stood upon the balcony of the Citadel, looking out over Sarim, as was his custom. Their city was still standing, still breathing. Yet, he knew that the days ahead would test him in ways far greater than any war ever had. The road to Eltor awaited, so did the next obelisk. In the Weaving, he felt the Primordials stir.

Sura joined him on the balcony. "You are thinking too much again," she whispered, with a smile.

Aran smiled faintly. "That is the burden of my charge."

She nudged his shoulder, affectionately. "Since I know you favour action, let me lighten your load then. I have spoken with Rafiq and the team is ready. We leave at dawn." Aran took a deep breath. Eltor awaited and, with it, the answers he feared most.

After a long but uneventful journey, the cold winds of the northern lands whispered through the ragged peaks of Eltor. As Aran and his small group ventured deeper into the mountains, the chill gnawed at their bones, but the cold was the least of their concerns. The long, arduous journey north weighed on them, each step heavier with the burden of what lay ahead. The council had agreed. Some reluctantly, perhaps, but now their united front would be tested, in ways it had not been before.
Beside him, Rafiq and Sura rode in silence. Rafiq's sharp gaze flickered across the craggy landscape, ever-watchful for threats. Sura's beautiful features were calm but her green eyes were distant. She was deep in thought, likely attempting to attune to the subtle disturbances in the Weaving that had grown more frequent as they drew closer to the obelisk.
She had been speaking less since their departure from Sarim, as though the burden of what lay ahead weighed more heavily on her than she had admitted - perhaps even to herself. Aran suspected that she, like him, had felt the presence of the Primordials growing stronger, more tangible, as they neared their destination.
They had already passed through the lands of several minor tribes, which had abstained from joining his cause, but nonetheless offered them begrudging hospitality. Word of Aran's vision and his quest had spread quickly, and while some saw his actions as necessary, others whispered of madness. There had been no open defiance, but Aran could sense the doubts festering, especially as the unknown weighed heavier on the minds of the people. It was not the armies of rival tribes or even the Draco that concerned them now, but rather the unseen forces that moved through the Weaving, forces they could not entirely comprehend - myths made real.
The trail wound steeply upward, jagged rocks and narrow passes making the journey treacherous. Each mile brought them closer to the obelisk, and with it, a growing sense of unease. As they reached a narrow plateau, the sky above them darkened unnaturally, a heavy cloud cover rolling in from the north. The sun, ever bright in the midday sky, suddenly dimmed behind thickening clouds, casting long shadows over the landscape. The very air pulsed with unseen energy, a tangible sign they were nearing their goal.

"It feels close," Sura said quietly, her voice barely audible over the rising wind. Her eyes flickered with a mixture of awe and trepidation. "I can feel the resonance of the Weaving. It feels stronger here. Perhaps that is why I can also sense it," she paused, "but it also feels...twisted." Aran nodded in approval, though he didn't need her confirmation. He had felt it miles ago. A deep, unsettling distortion in the fabric of the Weaving, as though the ancient pact that held their world together was fraying, slowly pulling apart at the seams. The closer they got to the obelisk, the more pronounced that disturbance became.

That would explain why Sura was able to feel it as well.

Rafiq, ever the pragmatist, glanced around warily. "We are not alone here."

Aran's hand instinctively went to the hilt of his father's sword, not out of fear, but out of an ingrained readiness. These mountains were home to more than just the natural dangers of rockslides and freezing winds. Old legends spoke of creatures that roamed the northern peaks, remnants of a time when the Primordials had first walked the planet, leaving behind echoes of their power.

Though those stories were often dismissed, by most, as myth, Aran had come to learn that myths had a way of bleeding into reality. Especially during times such as this...

As if on cue, the ground beneath them trembled. It was faint at first, a subtle vibration that might have been mistaken for the rumbling of distant thunder. Indifferent to their dismay, the tremor grew stronger. Rocks shifted underfoot as the earth itself shuddered.

"Move!" Aran shouted, pulling his steed to the side as a cascade of rocks tumbled down from the cliffs above.

The group scattered, narrowly avoiding the falling debris. As the dust settled, the trembling stopped, but the silence that followed was more unsettling than the tremors themselves. Rafiq dismounted, his swords drawn, and began scanning the ridges above for signs of movement.

"It was not natural," Sura murmured, her eyes fixed on the distant horizon. "Something is here with us. Watching..."

Aran's mind raced. His visions of the Primordials still haunted him, their immense power and unfathomable motives lingering like a shadow in his thoughts. Were they already active, testing him, or was this something else entirely. Perhaps an ancient guardian, left behind to protect the obelisk?

Before he could voice his thoughts, a deep, resonant hum filled the air, sending a shiver down his spine. It wasn't a sound so much as a vibration that reverberated through his bones, a low, guttural tone that seemed to come from everywhere and nowhere at once. The air itself crackled with energy, and the ground beneath them pulsed in time with the hum. "We are close," he said, looking at the others. "The obelisk is reacting to our presence."

Aran dismounted, his gaze locked on the narrow path ahead. The obelisk was near, but reaching it would not be as simple as walking up to it. The air around them grew thick, heavy with the weight of unseen forces. He could feel the pull of the Weaving here, stronger than anywhere else he had been, and yet, it was not the familiar flow of unseen energy he had come to understand. It was something older, more primal, that resonated with the power of the Primordials.

They pressed onward, moving slowly but deliberately up the steep path. The hum grew louder with each step until it became a deafening roar that seemed to vibrate through the very stone beneath their feet. The obelisk came into view at the top of a ridge, towering above them like a dark sentinel, carved with glowing runes. Its surface was black, obsidian-like, and it pulsed with an inner light, shifting through hues of deep purple and crimson as if it were alive, breathing with the rhythm of the planet itself.

Aran approached cautiously, his heart pounding in his chest. The obelisk exuded an overwhelming presence, its sheer size, and the power it radiated dwarfing everything around it. He could feel the Weaving bending and warping around it, as if the fabric of reality was being drawn toward it, consumed by some sort of gravitational pull.

He quieted his mind and reached out with his senses, feeling the familiar connection he had experienced at the first obelisk he harmonized, in Erythmar. Though, this time it was different, it felt more aggressive and volatile. The obelisk was not offering its power freely - it was demanding something in return.

"We must be careful," he warned. His strong voice was barely audible over the roar of energy being released. "This one is different. The Weaving here is frayed, as though the Primordials themselves have left their mark upon it."

Rafiq and Sura exchanged glances. Aran had a suspicion that this obelisk held the key to stabilizing the Weaving further, but it also held immense danger. The power within it was not meant for mortal hands, and yet, he had to carry on. He had to harness it, or the Weaving would continue to unravel, and with it, the world they lived in.

Taking a deep breath, he stepped forward, his hand outstretched toward the stone monolith. The moment his fingers brushed its surface, the world around him seemed to explode with light. He was no longer standing on the cold, rocky ridge; he was somewhere else, somewhere beyond the physical realm.

The Weaving stretched out before him, an intricate web of light and energy, but it was frayed, torn in places, as though something had ripped through it with brute force.

Then, at the edges of his vision, something stirred. Vast, shifting shadows, moving with purpose, their forms indistinct but menacing.

He did not need to see them clearly - he knew what they were. Their presence was overwhelming, their power suffocating. He could feel their attention shifting toward him, like the gaze of ancient gods who had been disturbed from their slumber.

Aran tried to focus, to reach out and stabilize the frayed threads of the Weaving, but the Primordials' presence pressed down on him, threatening to crush him under the weight of their power. He gritted his teeth, forcing his mind to concentrate on the task at hand.

The threads of the Weaving shimmered before him, and he could feel the obelisk's power surging through his body, a torrent of raw energy that threatened to overwhelm his senses.

Still, he could not stop. If he faltered now, the Weaving would collapse, and the Primordials would be free to reshape the world as they saw fit. He had to push through and had to bend the Weaving to his will, even if it meant risking his own life. "Stand back, just in case…" he shouted.

Aran clenched his jaw, his body trembling under the sheer force of the Weaving's raw energy. Every nerve in his body screamed in protest, his mind teetering on the brink of oblivion. The stone tether's power was definitely not meant for mortals, and yet, he had no choice but to wield it. He reached into the frayed chaos of the Weaving, fighting against an overwhelming force that sought to consume him.

If he failed, it would all come undone.

With a final, defiant roar, he seized the threads and pulled. The energy of the stone needle flowed through him, burning through his veins like molten fire, but he held on, focusing all his strength on repairing the damage and connecting it again to the others.

Without warning, as suddenly as it had begun, it was over. The light faded, and Aran found himself back on the ridge, his hand still pressed against the now cold surface of the obelisk. The hum had subsided, and the air around them was still as though Zarah itself was holding its breath.

Sura and Rafiq stood nearby, their faces pale but determined. Even they had felt it, a shift in the Weaving, the brief moment when it had teetered on the edge of collapse before their king had pulled it back.

As Aran looked up at the darkening sky, he knew, in his heart, that this was not the end. The Primordials were definitely awake now, and they would not be thwarted so easily.

Chapter XIX

Whispers in the Threads of Fate

The storm that had been gathering over the peaks of Eltor showed no sign of dissipating as Aran and his company descended from the ridge. The sky above churned with thick, bruised clouds, and though the rain had yet to fall, the air was thick with the weight of impending deluge. Something that was common, but only in the subtropical deserts, never here in the northern hemisphere.

Beneath this ominous dome, Aran's mind whirled with thoughts of the Primordials. Their presence, vast and indifferent, lingered in his thoughts, an unsettling reminder of the forces at play.

They rode in silence, the gravity of what had occurred at the obelisk weighing heavily on them all. Aran had further repaired the Weaving, but at great personal cost. His body ached from the strain of channelling the obelisk's raw, untamed power. His mind, however, bore the greater burden. The knowledge that the Primordials were awake, that their ancient pact with humanity was fracturing.

Whatever balance had been maintained for millennia was eroding fast, and the task of confronting these forces fell to him alone.

Beside him, Rafiq rode with the quiet vigilance of a seasoned warrior. His eyes scanned the horizon, though Aran suspected that his loyal friend was not looking for mere physical threats. The northern mountains were dangerous enough on their own, but there was something else in the air now. Something darker, and Rafiq had seen too much on their adventures, to dismiss what his heart could feel but his eyes could not perceive.

Sura, on the other hand, remained lost in her own thoughts. It was becoming apparent to Aran that her connection to the Weaving was starting to deepen, and the event they experienced at the last obelisk seemed to be haunting her. He could sense it in the way her hands trembled slightly, in the furrow of her brow, as though she was straining her mind to comprehend something just beyond the edge of her understanding.

Aran could not help but wonder if the Primordials had touched her mind as they had his. The thought alone, unsettled him to his core.

They travelled slowly through the craggy landscape, taking care not to stir any further disturbances in the fragile mountains. The presence of the obelisk had been enough to make the land itself unstable. More than once, they had to navigate around rockslides or narrow paths that had crumbled into ravines. Despite the treacherous terrain, Aran's thoughts kept drifting back to the broader landscape. One not of stone and ice, but of power and politics.

The obelisk had been but one thread in a larger tapestry, and while the Weaving itself may have stabilized for now, the world outside it had not. In Sarim and across Zarah, word of his quest had already spread, fanning the flames of both loyalty and dissent. The Draco, apparently, had been busy, sowing the seeds of dissidence.

His vision of the Primordials and the Weaving had reached the scattered smaller clans throughout the planet, and not all of them were pleased by the implications. Some, no doubt nudged by the Draco, saw it as an affront, others as an opportunity to challenge the authority of the rising House of Aran, while most viewed the Primordials as a myth not worth risking lives and fortunes over.

Aran knew, and not without noticing the irony at play, that fighting the Primordials was one thing. Fighting the ambitions of men? That would prove itself to be far more treacherous.

Even as he faced cosmic forces beyond mortal understanding, his real battle might be waged in the halls of politics, where betrayal was as deadly as any blade.

As dusk began to fall, they made camp in a sheltered alcove beneath the jagged cliffs. The fire they built was small, just enough to ward off the bitter chill that crept in with the night. Rafiq and Sura spoke little as they set about making camp. Aran, too, remained quiet, but his mind was anything but still. He sat at the edge of the firelight, staring into the flickering flames, his thoughts drifting back to the last vision he had experienced at the Eltor obelisk.

The Weaving, in all its intricate beauty, was a fragile thing. Threads of light, and spellbinding energy, bound together the fabric of their world, but those threads had been torn and frayed by time.

At the edges of that fraying, the Primordials had stirred, but their motives remained inscrutable. What had once been a pact between them and humanity, sealed in ancient times, now felt like a tenuous truce at best.

"You are thinking about them?" Sura's voice broke through his reverie, like sandfish through the dunes. There it was again. It astonished him, the ease with which she could read his deepest thoughts.

She sat beside him, her face bathed in the soft glow of the fire. A weariness lingered in her expression, mirroring his own - yet her natural, profound beauty remained undiminished.

Aran nodded, then faced the fire, watching the dancing flames. "I can not shake the feeling that we are being pulled into something much larger than we understand."

"I believe that we are," she said nervously. "The Primordials... they are not like I thought they would be." She, absent-mindedly, ran a hand through her hair, "I have been feeling them more and more," she paused, now looking him in the eyes. "You know I have. I know you felt it happening."

He was truly impressed with her, but since she hadn't asked a question, Aran patiently waited for her to continue. "They are beyond anything I can comprehend," she confessed. "Even the Weaving itself might just be a manifestation of something older, something more... primal."

Aran could sense her unease. He glanced at her, seeing the concern etched into her features. Sura had always been attuned to the mystical forces at play in their world. Maybe not as much as he was, but despite that, even she seemed unnerved, touched by what they had recently encountered.

"Do you think they want to break the pact?" she finally asked.

Aran hesitated, his gaze dropping to the fire. "I am unsure. But one thing I do know is that the balance my forefathers have helped maintain for millennia is shifting. The obelisks are connected to that balance, and someone, or something, is trying to tip the scales."

"Someone?" Rafiq had joined them at the fire, his arms crossed over his chest as he leaned against a nearby rock. His voice was low, but there was a sharpness to it. "Are you suggesting there are other parties at play besides the Primordials? Do you mean Drathis?"

Aran looked up at him, his eyes narrowing slightly. "Yes and no. Drathis might, in fact, be involved, but what I mean is that the art of Weaving is complex. I am sure there are bound to be other ways to manipulate it. The Primordials cannot be the only ones who can command it in its fullness. There are bound to be others, those who know how to bend it to their will. Students of the arcane, perhaps some of the ancient bloodlines. If that is the case, there are bound to be those who will seek to use the obelisks for their own purposes."

Sura frowned. "Wait, just now, you answered both yes and no. Do you think that besides Drathis, one of the other tribes might be involved in this?"

"It is not improbable," Aran admitted. "The obelisks are powerful, too powerful to be left untouched by those who know of their existence. If one of the tribes has found a way to tap into that power, it could explain some of the disturbances we have seen, as well as certain political tendencies during our council meetings..."

Aran noticed the effect his contemplation had on his friends. Trying to lighten the mood, he mused. "Pay no heed to my words. I am just exploring possibilities. I doubt any of the council members are behind this. Unless they are on Drathis' payroll, as Farid once was."

Rafiq scowled. "If it is true that Drathis is behind this, then we are not just dealing with ancient magic. We are dealing with an enemy who knows exactly what he is doing - destroying us from within while he lets the Primordials finish the rest of it, from without."

Aran nodded slowly, the implications of his reverie sinking in. The main six tribes, as well as the smaller kingdoms and clans, had always been rivals throughout Zarah's history, each one vying for control, for influence. Undoubtedly driven to such behaviour, behind the scenes, by the Draco themselves. If, by any chance, one of the tribes had been given knowledge of the secret of the obelisks, that would change everything.

The balance of power would shift overnight and not in his favour.

For a long while, the company sat in silence, the fire crackling softly between them. Sitting around the flames, some of Rafiq's warriors began exchanging stories about their last battle against the Draco. "We showed them," one, called Umar, said. "Did you see our king jumping onto their flagship?" asked another. "I was there with him," answered a third.

The cold wind whispered through the mountains, carrying with it the faint echoes of the storm that was yet to break. Aran's thoughts were torn three ways, the ancient threat of the Primordials, the Draco, and the dangers of political betrayal. All of it had probably been orchestrated by Drathis himself. "We will need to tread carefully," he said, looking at Sura and Rafiq, his voice quiet but resolute. "I truly believe the obelisks hold the key to stabilizing the Weaving, but if the Draco have discovered the rest of them, we could be walking into traps."

Rafiq grunted in agreement. "We should probably assume that they already know. Because if we do not, we might be as good as dead. Remember the ambush he set up for us, on our return from Erythmar."

Aran nodded. He was wary but calm. "There is something else, though. The Weaving. It is not just fraying, it is changing. The way the threads react now, the way they flow, it feels different. It is almost as if the Primordials themselves are reshaping it to their will."

"Reshaping it?" Sura raised both eyebrows in surprise. "To what end?" she asked expectantly.

"I do not know yet," Aran replied, his voice barely more than a whisper. "Whatever the end is, it does not seem to be about balance anymore. The Weaving feels... more alive, like it is preparing for something." He felt that speaking his thoughts out loud, somehow, seemed to amplify them. A cold chill ran down his spine, colder than the mountain wind blowing through their camp.

The thoughts of the Weaving preparing itself, of something ancient awakening within the very fabric of their world, was more terrifying than any foreign army or in House political plotting. His mind turned to the shadows he had seen in the visions he experienced in Ryvath. Of the vast, formless figures at the edge of his awareness. Were they the ones reshaping the Weaving? Or was there something else, something even older and more powerful, stirring within the threads of fate?

As the night deepened and the fire burned low, Aran knew that the path ahead would be darker and more dangerous than any they had walked before. The obelisks, the Weaving, the Primordials, an all out war with Drathis. These were no longer distant, abstract, concepts, they were real, tangible forces, and they were converging.

Standing at the heart of it all was a young king. The weight of his House, his people, and the fate of Zarah pressing down on his shoulders.

Sleep did not come easily that night. When the storm finally broke, rain pattered against the rocky ground, each drop echoing like a distant war drum. Aran lay awake, staring at the swirling clouds. "Unusual geological processes? Random weather patterns?" The threads of fate were unravelling indeed. The Draco would strike again soon - that much was certain. But something else was stirring in the darkness. Watching. Waiting.

Chapter XX

A Covenant Unbound

Dawn broke not with the familiar golden rays of light, but under a thick veil of storm clouds that cast the land in hues of grey and shadow - an unnatural sight in this world. Aran rose early, his sleep fragmented by strange dreams of shifting landscapes and murmuring voices. In his dreams, the Weaving whispered - its threads twisting like silver veins through the void. Somewhere deep within it, something ancient stirred, restless and waiting.

As the rain beat softly against the rocks around them, he took a moment to reflect on the path ahead. His thoughts quickly returned to the cryptic warnings he had given his friends and to the visions he had experienced at the last obelisk.

The Weaving was not just under strain; it felt as though something was actively reshaping it. That thought alone terrified him more than any mortal foe ever could. He was no longer merely a king struggling with political intrigue and war - he was now entangled in a cosmic conflict that transcended his understanding of time, fate, and power.

Aran had always shaped his own fate, bending the world to his will. Now, he was merely a leaf caught in an unseen current, adrift in forces older than time itself. The Primordials were the architects of the world's first binding, perhaps the creators of the Weaving itself.

How was a mortal man supposed to stand against such timeless beings? How could he hope to control, let alone manipulate, forces that had existed since the dawn of creation?

"Aran," Rafiq's voice was steady, a grounding force amid the turbulence in his mind. "We need to move soon. The storm. It looks like it is going to worsen."

Aran looked up, realizing that his companions were already packed and ready. Rafiq was right, as always. This was not the time to wallow in self doubt. The journey to the next obelisk awaited, and every moment of delay could mean the difference between success and catastrophe. The Draco, with their political scheming and opportunistic manoeuvring, were likely to be positioning themselves, leveraging the unrest to their advantage. "You are right, my friend. Let us move." Aran rose to his feet, grabbing his hooded cloak and throwing it over his shoulders. The rain slicked the fabric, the cold bite in the air, a reminder of the greater challenges ahead.

As they continued their descent from the mountains, the terrain shifted from the jagged, rocky outcroppings of the highlands to the rolling oases by the foothills. Aran rode at the front of the group. His gaze fixed on the path ahead, but his mind was elsewhere. The weight of it all, pressing down on him like an invisible shroud, each new step felt heavier than the last.

His thoughts returned to the pact, the ancient covenant between his forebears and the Primordials. In the visions the Weaving had shown him, there had been a moment in time when the two had existed in harmony. When it was shattered, the obelisks set in place by the Old Kings had bound them, sealing their vast power beneath the fabric of the world. Now, that prison was failing.

The Primordials had granted the Old Kings the ability to manipulate the Weaving to shape the world with magic, but the cost of such a power had been too great. The pact had bound the Primordials in a dormant state, forcing them to sleep beneath the surface of reality while thus containing their power within the Weaving itself.

Now, the covenant was breaking. Due to Drathis' actions in the crypt, in the Old Quarter of Sarim, the obelisks, once the anchors of that ancient agreement, had been either destroyed or altered.

By destroying the first obelisk, Aran had set in motion a chain of events with unpredictable consequences. However, the damage he had seen was not random. No matter how he looked at it, he kept arriving at the same conclusion. That, despite his own mistakes, someone, or perhaps something, was deliberately unravelling the ancient bonds, releasing the Primordials from their slumber. Consequently, as the threads of the Weaving unravelled, so too did the very fabric of the world they lived in.

Aran was not alone in this realization. Sura, riding beside him, had sensed it as well. Beyond her natural talent for reading his emotions, her connection to the Weaving was growing stronger. She had been unusually quiet since their departure from Eltor, her normally sharp gaze clouded, as if she were looking at something distant, beyond the normal range of human perception.

"Do you hear it too?" Aran asked her, his voice soft but urgent.

She looked at him, her eyes widening, as if waking up from a dream. "Hear what?" Sura asked, still gathering herself.

"The Weaving," he said. "It keeps changing. Even now, the threads are moving in ways I do not recognize. The Primordials… they are not just waiting. I think they are preparing."

Sura's grip tightened on the reins of her steed. "Preparing for what?" She asked nervously.

"I do not know," Aran admitted, trying to keep his voice calm. "Though I suspect it will be something vast, something that will alter everything we know. The power they hold is not like anything we have ever seen. The Weaving itself is responding to them, alive, shifting in anticipation of their return."

Aran's mind was racing. If the Weaving was reacting to the Primordials' awakening, then the very foundation of the world was unstable. Reality, as they knew it, was being reshaped. His mind turned to the obelisks, those monolithic structures that had once been the safeguard of balance, were now proving to be more dangerous than he had ever imagined. There were still more of them out there, scattered across Zarah, and each one held a piece of the puzzle. They had to find the others, try to understand their purpose, and repair them before it was too late. "We do not have time to waste," Aran's voice was grim with determination. "We need to reach the next obelisk. The Draco are likely moving against us, and they may already be aware of what is at stake."

"What if they attack Sarim while we are away?" Rafiq asked.

"Sarim will hold, like it has before." Although Aran tried, he couldn't completely hide the concern in his voice.

"Yes, but we were there then." Sura remarked. Her words cut through to his heart, like a blade through parchment.

"The more reason for us to move swiftly. I cannot be everywhere at once. I must make choices. Our future depends on it," he said, in a weary voice. Both Sura and Rafiq nodded, their expression hardening. "I can feel its presence. It is located farther south, past the oases of Sarim, near the ruins of Valamar, in the mountains of the same name." Aran uttered, with a heavy heart.

The mention of Valamar sent a ripple of unease through the group. Valamar had once been a thriving city-state, from the time of the Old Kings, a rival to the power of Sarim itself, but it had fallen, many centuries ago, in a cataclysmic event known only as The Great Sundering. What had caused it remained a mystery, but the region surrounding it was now rumoured to be cursed, a place where the Weaving was thin and distorted.

"You are suggesting we go to Valamar?!" Rafiq's tone of disbelief cut through the silence. "That place is a death trap. No one who has gone there has ever returned to tell the tale."

"I know the stories," Aran said, his gaze unwavering. "Unfortunately, we do not have a choice on the matter. The next obelisk is there, and if we do not reach it before Drathis does… the consequences could be far worse than anything Valamar can throw at us." Silence fell over the group once more, as mute as the depths of the Yaran Sea.

Aran remained quiet, weighing their options. The risks were immense, but the stakes were even greater. He could not afford to let fear guide his decisions. If the obelisks were the key to stopping the Primordials' return, they had to act swiftly, and if Valamar was where the next piece of the puzzle was, then that is where they would go.

"It is decided," Aran said finally, his voice steely with resolve. "We make for Valamar. But we will need more than just ourselves if we are going to face what lies there. We will need strong allies."

Rafiq raised an eyebrow. "Where do you plan on finding them? Our list of possible new allies is growing thin, and the council might not exactly welcome us with open arms. Especially now, considering the newest developments with the Weaving and the Primordials become known."

Aran's eyes narrowed. "Not the other tribes. I'm thinking of others. Someone who owes us a favour. A debt from ages past."

Both Rafiq and Sura exchanged glances, confused, unsure of their friend's intent. Aran remained silent on the matter, his thoughts already focused on the journey ahead. There were still forces in the world beyond the kingdoms, the tribes and their political games.

There were ancient orders, old bloodlines, and factions that had withdrawn from the wider conflicts of the world, millennia ago - six thousand years, to be precise.

He had learned much about the old Zarah, since he started studying under Barash, soon after his father's murder - the ancient lore written in stone, rather than parchment. One group, hailing from the ancient world, had pledged their loyalty to his bloodline long ago, during the Wars of the Old Kings.

Four thousand years after those wars took place, they became known as the Wardens of the Shadowed Vale, a secretive order of mystics and warriors who had guarded the borderlands between the world of the living and the realm of shadows for millennia. Though their numbers had dwindled, through the centuries, their knowledge of ancient magics and forbidden arts remained unparalleled. If anyone could help them navigate the dangers of Valamar and the mysteries of the obelisks, it was the Order of the Wardens.

"There is one last thread we can pull," Aran murmured. "A debt long forgotten. A vow bound in shadow and steel."

Rafiq frowned. "What are you talking about?" Aran looked up at his friend, his gaze steely. "The Wardens of the Shadowed Vale."

Rafiq's eyes widened, his scepticism giving way to surprise. "The Wardens? I thought they were nothing more than legend, old stories told around campfires to scare children. Rafiq paused, deep in thought.

"Now that I think of it, I recall Barash mentioning them during one of the council meetings," he mused.

"Yes, they are real," Aran said firmly. "Barash spoke of them to me after we left the catacombs of Sarim, following my destruction of the first obelisk. He told me of legends that speak of an oath, a debt to be paid to my bloodline. One I intend to call in." He placed a hand on Rafiq's shoulder, "If anyone can guide us through the dangers awaiting us at Valamar, it will be them."

Sura still looked uncertain. "If they are real as you say, how do you plan on finding them when they have not been seen by anyone for countless generations?"

"According to the old texts Barash showed me, they are still out there," Aran replied. "They always have been. By the time we make it to the Shadowed Vale, I am hoping they will reveal themselves."

With that, the decision had been made. They would go to Valamar, but first, they would seek the aid of the Wardens.

The path ahead was fraught with danger, but Aran felt a renewed sense of purpose. The obelisks, the Primordials, the sudden unravelling of the Weaving, the part he played in all of it, these could not be just accidental coincidences. Something in his heart kept telling him they were part of a larger pattern, a weaving of sorts, one that had been sown long ago.

At the heart of it, he could feel it, was his bloodline. Its destiny had always been intertwined with the fate of the world. Now, more than ever, that destiny was calling to him - Aran could feel it in every fibber of his body, the legacy of his forbears coursing hot through his veins.

Far away from where Aran was, the desert stretched endlessly before the company. Leander's primary was at the end of its daily decline, though yielding no relief from the heat. Warm fiery light cascaded across burnished dunes, casting molten shadows that rippled like liquid copper. The sand breathed warmth into the approaching twilight as Anar and Nysa prepared to ascend their celestial thrones.

Drathis was studying a holo-map of Zarah, displaying a vast expanse of deserts, mountains, and whispering dunes. They had been travelling for days, and his destination was almost within reach. Beneath the warm twilight sky, his contingent of Draconian warriors and Chimaera beasts marched, in solemn silence, their movements disciplined, their purpose grim - the lost kingdom of Valamar awaited.

That place was mythical, spoken of only in hushed tones among the scholarly institutions his agents had infiltrated. It was a place that had existed since the time of the Old Kings, where some of the oldest texts in Zarah's history were kept, regarding the Weaving, its stone tethers and above all, the Primordials. Those, mighty, unknowable beings that slumbered in the folds of reality were the reason Drathis wanted to dabble with the Weaving in the first place. It was his intention to command them. That had been, if things had gone accordingly, his original plan to begin with.

Back at the crypt, in Sarim's Old Quarter, if Aran had not interfered and inadvertently set in motion the unravelling, Drathis would have surely succeeded in his pursuit. That desert upstart, by sheer accident and blind luck, had turned the Primordials against him.

Drathis had never feared battle, but facing a power beyond time itself had forced his retreat. Once over, Aran had defeated him - and that was too many. "That's twice," he thought to himself, his nostrils flaring, "yet for each, you shall render a heavy toll."

After that 'incident', Aran had devoted himself to studying the ancient texts. He listened to the ramblings of an old mentor and had felt the tremors in the Weaving itself. After all, due to Drathis' actions, the man did unintentionally give birth to the process now in motion. Later, trying to make amends for his mistakes, he learned more about the Weaving and sought to meddle with the obelisks, seeking to mend and harmonize them. "The fool." Drathis thought. The Weaving was not meant to be mended but controlled, and if the Primordials were a force with enough raw power to shift cosmic tides, then he would have them kneel before the House of Draco - before himself.

The wind howled amongst the ruins as the army pressed forward, a storm was rising in the distance. Imminently, they were inside the borders of Valamar.

His first lieutenant, Vhaskar, rode beside him, a hulking reptilian warrior with scales black as obsidian, eyes tyrian purple, and the strength of ten Draconians. "This place," Vhaskar growled, his voice deep and guttural, "does not seem to welcome us."

Drathis did not turn his gaze from the setting sun. "It does not need to. All it needs to do is obey our will," his eyes reflected Zarah's primary. "My will," he thought to himself.

Without warning, the land twisted with their approach, as if the very fabric of reality was bending. The dunes shifted unnaturally, forming jagged ridges that had not been there moments before. The air thickened, growing heavy with an unseen but nonetheless palpable energy. Then they saw it, in the distance, up in the mountains. The city of Valamar. "Forward." Drathis shouted.

"You have come here unbidden!" A disembodied voice echoed across the dunes. Drathis did not flinch or hesitate. "I have come with an offer." Shadows shifted as the sun set. The air trembled. Something vast, something ancient, pressed against the edges of reality - unseen yet suffocating, like the weight of a thousand unblinking eyes.

"You seek dominion where dominance is not yours to claim."

The ethereal voice was not coming from a single source but rather from everywhere. The ruins at the foot of the mountain pulsed with energy, the very stones vibrating with power. A wave of trepidation swept through Drathis' army.

The Draconian warlord, however, stepped forward, unbowed. "I am Kael Drathis, of the House of Draco, and I come to offer an alliance. Due to the actions of Zarah's king, the Weaving is fraying. Because of that, the world is shifting. Now is the time for you to reclaim your place, but for that, you will need one who can act in the realm of the living."

"Fool," the voice bellowed," Did you think there was anything we did not know? Aran ibn Khalid did what he did, in Sarim's Old Quarter, because of your actions, not despite them. If anything, we respect his motives more than we do yours. It was you who first began meddling in things you should have not. You and your kind. Usurpers."

For a long moment, there was silence. Then the sands stirred.

Massive shapes began to surface from the depths of the dunes.

Sand Serpents, their scales glistening like molten glass, their eyes burning with an otherworldly hunger. Twisted by the distortions in the Weaving, they were not merely beasts. These had become avatars of the Primordials' will.

Drathis' warriors reacted instantly. For they were far more afraid of the upper hierarchy of their House, than anything else in the known MiddleVerse. The Chimaeras roared, wild as they were. Feral genetic mutations, lunging toward the serpents, their claws raking against the shifting scales. The Silent Claw, Drathis' special squad within his army, forged in the fires of countless battles, did not hesitate.

Their blades sang the song of steel, and their vibrospears struck true. The sands of Valamar erupted with the force of battle. They slashed through the serpents with minimal casualties for their outfit.

Still, in spite of their best efforts, the enemy was unrelenting. For every Sand Serpent they managed to cut down, two more sprang from the sands, in their stead. The tide of the battle was shifting, and fast.

More and more Draconian warriors were falling, around their leader.

Drathis drew his blade, its sharp edge gleaming in the bright moonlight. Swift and fatal, he moved like a spectre of death, dodging attacks, striking true and severing several serpents' jaws as he danced around them to the tune of finality. Ichor sprayed profusely onto the sands of Valamar. The creatures screeched in pain, writhing on the sands, their bodies convulsing as they collapsed onto the ruins.

Vhaskar, powerful and muscular, tore through another serpent, his sheer strength allowing him to break its spine with a crushing blow of his war hammer.

It was not enough. For no matter how many of these creatures they slayed, more rose from the sands to take their place.

The Chimaeras fell first, their agonized roars cut short as monstrous jaws dragged them beneath the sands. Then came the warriors - their screams lost to the desert, swallowed whole by an abyss that did not spit them back out - forever sleeping beneath the sands of Zarah.

Drathis turned on the spot, searching for a sign of the Primordials themselves. But he saw nothing. Instead, he heard the disembodied voice once more. "Do you still believe yourself to be worthy?" The voice echoed around him - omnipresent.

Drathis snarled. The Draco were too proud, too assured of their House's might, to display any kind of humbleness. "You dare test me?!" His voice was infused with venom. "I am Ka-"

The air shattered and, in what felt to him like half a heartbeat, Valamar vanished. When Drathis opened his eyes, he stood in a void woven from threads of light and shadow. Galaxies unfurled around him, strands of existence tangled in an endless, shifting pattern. He was no longer in a world - he was inside the Weaving itself.

Its energy matrix surrounded him, threads of light and shadow, infinite strands stretching into eternity. Galaxies spread before his eyes. The presence of the Primordials loomed over him, and vast shapes were barely visible beyond the fabric of existence. This place appeared to him to be an energetic representation of the physical world.

"I will grant you this, Kael Drathis. You are strong." The voice spoke.

Yet, it had changed. It was no longer disembodied. Now it was inside him, resonating in his very bones. "Strong enough to stand against the tides, though not strong enough to change them."

Drathis' hands clenched into fists. "We will never bow to anyone."

"Indeed?" asked the voice, its tone sarcastic. A heavy silence followed.

After what felt to Drathis like an eternity, the voice spoke again. "Then your fate is sealed, Kael Drathis, of the House of Draco."

The Weaving surrounding him rippled, casting him out. He fell, not through air but through time and space itself, crashing down into the sands of Valamar, the force nearly shattering his bones. Above him, the serpents still raged, their forms twisting in and out of reality.

His first lieutenant stood at the edge of the battlefield. He saw Vhaskar crushing the skull of a dying serpent with his great hammer. When the hulking warrior saw Drathis, he moved swiftly, breaking through the chaos to reach him.

"We are leaving," Vhaskar growled, seizing him by the arm.

Drathis, bleeding and broken, did not resist. "Call the ship," his voice was feeble.

Vhaskar raised the signal beacon, and moments later, a Draconian anti-gravitational hovercraft appeared from behind the dunes. Drathis boarded just as the last of his warriors fell. When the ship took off, towards the horizon, he looked back in time to watch as the vestiges of the battle sank beneath the sands of Valamar, leaving no trace of the scuffle. Its guardians had returned to their slumber, but the words their masters had spoken to him remained in his thoughts. "Your pride will be your undoing," the voice had whispered to him in the Weaving. "Success remains within your grasp... if only you surrender."

"Surrender?" he mused, "I do not believe we Draco know the meaning of such a word."

The hovercraft, its stealth camouflage engaged, carried them silently through the wilds of Zarah - across the moonlit deserts and toward the southeastern mountain range, where the oldest Draconian temple on the planet lay hidden.

The Temple of Nathair, carved deep into the mountains, had once been a place of worship. Named after the House of Draco's star system, now it was a tomb of forgotten knowledge, the one place where Drathis could regroup and strategize.

In its depths, torches burned with blue fire, casting eerie shadows upon the walls inscribed with the histories of the House's past glories. Its connection to planet Zarah was far older than any of the tribal natives suspected it to be.

Drathis now sat in his chambers, his body wrapped in fresh healing membrane - a synthetic material infused with growth factors and regenerative accelerants.

Around him, working tirelessly, were Draconian medics and nanotech specialists, trying to repair his body as fast as they could.

Drathis' mind, however, was not impaired by the damage his body had sustained. Quite the contrary, it was thinking fast, running recent events, over and over. Analysing every detail.

The Primordials had not killed him. Instead, they had offered him something. "A chance to seize true power," the voice had said.

At that moment, Vhaskar entered, his great form filling the chamber. He approached Drathis, his eyes boring down ominously, his demeanour a reflection of his thoughts.

"What are your plans?" Vhaskar asked. His voice was as guttural and as deep as the chamber they stood in. The medics were removing the layers of healing membrane - its work was complete.

Drathis did not answer. His eyes were unfocused, looking at the burning torches, at the flickering light dancing across the temple walls.

"For now, we wait," he could see a pattern in the flickering shadows on the walls, "Then, Vhaskar, we shall decide whether this world belongs to the natives, to the gods, or to us."

The medical team was done with him. His body was fully recovered. "I am ready. Take me to the war room!" The shadows of the Weaving stirred. The Primordials watched - and they were waiting.

Chapter XXI

Whispers of the Forgotten

The days following Aran's decision to go to the Shadowed Vale were spent in a relentless march toward that ancient place. It felt as if the land itself were watching, aware of the ancient covenant that was about to be rekindled. Each mile toward the Vale brought with it an eerie stillness, as though Zarah was holding its breath, waiting for their arrival at the murky waters of its forgotten history.

For the last six millennia, the Vale existed only in whispered legends and half-remembered tales. Other than the Echo, it was said to be the only other threshold between worlds. A liminal space where the boundaries of the Weaving were particularly thin, allowing those with knowledge of its mysteries to move between realms.

Ten thousand years ago, at the end of Zarah's First Age, after the Wars of the Old Kings, the Wardens became the guardians of this realm, protecting the world from what lurked on the other side. Now, after sixty centuries of silence, the Wardens had faded into myth, their deeds remembered only in ancient carved stone, secret scrolls, and old books.

Aran was one of the few who had access to those archives. He and Barash had spent long nights poring over those faded tomes and scrolls, their writing barely readable, tracing the threads of history that tied the Wardens to his own lineage. It was there he had discovered the debt the Wardens owed to his house, a promise sealed by blood and bound to the Weaving itself.

Though time had obscured the specific terms, the essence remained clear: in exchange for his ancestors' role in binding the Primordials during the Wars of the Old Kings, the Wardens were oath-bound to answer any call for aid from his bloodline, their assistance guaranteed by blood and Weaving alike.

They travelled through the dense oases of the subtropical deserts, where the Kingdom of Shamas would one day rise, but kept pushing deeper into lands long forsaken. The further they went, the more the landscape changed. Ancient Medjool Palms, their gnarled trunks blackened by time, seemed to loom closer, their fronds bent unnaturally, covered heavily with moss and thick vines. Pervasive mist, thick as breath, clung to the ground, its tendrils curling around their feet as though something unseen slithered just beneath the surface.

Nature itself was behaving in unexpected ways, leaving the group on edge, unsure of what to expect next.

"Are you sure this is the way?" Rafiq asked, glancing over at Aran as they moved through the dense undergrowth.

The oases here felt alive in a way that made even the seasoned warrior uneasy, as if the land itself was watching them, silently waiting for them to step too far.

"This feels off," Rafiq added. The weather was completely wrong and he was beginning to feel unsettled.

Aran nodded, though his face betrayed a hint of doubt. "I am certain this is the way. The ancient records Barash showed me, described specific landmarks - the Blackwood Trees, the Stone of Oaths. We should be close now."

Sura, ever more sensitive to the Weaving's ebb and flow, rode behind them, her eyes half-closed as if listening to the hum of the world around her. She had been quiet since they started making their way towards this place, her attention focused on something beyond the physical.

Now, as they moved deeper into the Vale, she spoke for the first time in hours. "There is something here," she said, her voice soft but filled with certainty. "The Weaving is different in this place. It feels…looser, like the threads are not as tightly bound.

Aran acknowledged this, but pressed on. To him, the Weaving had always been a source of mystery, but in this place, it seemed even more unpredictable. Time and space felt malleable, the boundaries between worlds fragile and permeable.

Hours passed, and as the sun began to sink behind the twisted Medjool palms, they came upon the first of the landmarks - The Blackwood Trees. They stood in a perfect circle, their trunks black as night, their bark smooth and untouched by the elements. No birds sang here, no animals scurried among the underbrush. The air was still, unnaturally so, and the mist thickened, swirling around the trees in slow, deliberate patterns.

"We've reached it," Aran said, his voice barely above a whisper. "The Vale of the Wardens." In his heart, a quiet fear stirred - would they deign to reveal themselves to him, to fulfil their oath?

They dismounted, each of them aware that they had entered a place beyond the natural world. The Blackwood trees marked the boundary of the Vale, a place where the Wardens had once stood guard and where Aran hoped they would soon reveal themselves again.

He stepped forward, his eyes carefully scanning the mist for any sign of movement. For a moment, there was nothing but the oppressive silence, broken only by the soft rustling of leaves in the almost non-existent breeze. Every minute that went by felt like an hour.

Then, very slowly, from the dense mist, figures began to emerge.

They were tall, their forms cloaked in dark, hooded robes that blended seamlessly with the haze that enveloped them. Their faces were still obscured, but their presence was undeniable.

A palpable weight hung in the air, and the very ground seemed to tremble beneath their feet.

These were the Wardens of the Shadowed Vale - guardians of the threshold between worlds - those who had helped seal the pact between the Primordials and Aran's ancestors ten thousand years ago, at the dawn of Zarah's Second Age.

"Who enters the Vale unbidden?" The voice came from one of the figures, a low, resonant sound that seemed to echo in the stillness.

Aran stepped forward, his hand resting on the hilt of his father's sword, though he made no move to draw it. "I am Aran, son of Khalid, heir to the bloodline that once stood with the Wardens in the Wars of the Old Kings, and I seek your aid."

There was a pause. The figures stood unmoving, their hooded faces unreadable. Then, the one who had spoken first took a step forward, lowering his hood to reveal a face that was surprisingly young, though his eyes spoke of ancient knowledge, carved by the burden of countless years. "Your bloodline has been silent for millennia. Now, as the world unravels, you seek us. Do you truly understand what you are asking?" He demanded, his tone sardonic.

Aran met the Warden's gaze, his voice steady. "I am here now, seeking your help, precisely for such a reason. Because the old pacts are unravelling, the obelisks are becoming unstable, and despite our best efforts, the Weaving is coming undone. As for the Primordials, those your order once helped to bind, they are awakening. If we do nothing, the world will fall into chaos, and everything we fought for will be lost."

The Warden's eyes narrowed as he studied Aran intently. After millennia of isolation from the world, the thought of the Primordials had clearly disturbed him. "The Primordials?" He mused, the weight of the word hanging heavy in the air. "I wonder why we did not sense it? If what you say is true, then the danger is far greater than any of you can imagine."

Sura stepped forward, her voice quiet but firm. "We have seen the signs. The Weaving itself is changing. The threads are loosening, bending to forces beyond our control and, as Aran has warned, the obelisks that once kept the world in balance are now behaving erratically. We need to stop this, but we do not know how. We have studied everything in our grasp, but the final solution continues to elude us." She waited, expectantly.

The Warden remained silent, his penetrating gaze shifting from Aran to Sura and back again. When he finally spoke, his voice carried a grim finality. "There is still much you do not know about the Primordials and about the true nature of the Weaving. If you are to confront them, you need to understand the full scope of the power you are about to face." With a gesture, he beckoned them forward. "Come. There are things you must see."

The Wardens led them deeper into the Vale, the mist growing thicker with each step. There were trees here that none of them had seen anywhere else on Zarah. They seemed to close in around them, their branches intertwining above to form a canopy that blocked out the light. The air grew colder, and the ground beneath their feet felt soft, as though they were walking on something other than soil.

After what felt like hours, they emerged into a clearing. At the centre stood a stone circle, ancient and weathered, its surface etched with runes that pulsed faintly with a blue light. This was the heart of the Shadowed Vale, the place where the Wardens drew their power from and where the boundary between worlds was thinnest.

The Warden who had spoken earlier turned to Aran. "This is the Stone of Oaths, the place where our ancestors made the pact with the Primordials. As those from your bloodline signed their pact on the black stone altar underneath what is now Sarim, so did our forebears in this place. It was in between these two sites that the Weaving was bound for a second time, and it is here that you will learn further about the truth. Are you ready?"

Aran stepped forward, his heart pounding in his chest. The air around the stone felt charged with energy, a low hum vibrating through the ground. The Weaving manifested here more strongly than anywhere else, its threads visible to him as they shimmered like strands of silver in the air. As he approached the stone, the runes flared brighter, and the air seemed to shift. He felt a tug, a pull on his mind, as though something was calling to him from beyond the physical world. He reached out, his fingers brushing the surface of the stone, and in an instant, his surroundings vanished.

He found himself standing in a vast, endless expanse of light and shadow, the Weaving stretching out before him like a tapestry of stars. The threads pulsed with life, intertwining in patterns too complex for his mind to fully comprehend. Amidst the beauty of the Weaving, there was something else - concealed. A darkness, coiling and twisting at the edges, vast and patient, shifting against the very fabric of existence itself.

Suddenly, as if the threads of what makes up a nightmare were being brought to life, he finally saw them - the Primordials. Massive, primal, incomprehensible beings of pure energy and will, their forms shifting and flickering like flames in the cosmic winds. They were the architects of the Weaving, the creators of this world, but they were also its destroyers. Their power was vast, and as Aran stood before them, he realized the enormity of what they were facing.

The Primordials were not merely bound by the Weaving, they were an intrinsical part of it, their essence woven into the very fabric of reality. To fight them was to fight the world itself, to challenge the very foundation of existence.

When it ended, the vision did not simply fade away - it shattered, small fragments of cosmic truth tearing away as Aran was violently thrust back into his physical form. He stumbled backwards from the stone, painfully collapsing to one knee, his breath coming in ragged gasps that echoed in the sudden silence of the clearing.

For several heartbeats, he couldn't distinguish between the cosmic realm he'd witnessed and the earthbound clearing where his knees pressed against damp soil, reality bleeding back into focus like ink spreading through water. Cold sweat beaded on his brow as the enormity of what he'd witnessed crashed through him like a Yaran tidal wave.

His mind struggled to contain knowledge never meant for mortal comprehension, while his body trembled with the aftershocks of standing in the presence of such vast, primaeval power. The truth of what he had seen weighed on him not just as knowledge but as a physical burden pressing down on his very soul.

It was but a subtle difference between what he had already learned.

A minuscule nuance, but one that made all the difference in the world. The Primordials could not simply be defeated. There was no way to defeat them. They had to be understood, their power was to be either harnessed or contained.

The Warden watched him closely. "Now you understand the magnitude of the task you have ahead of you. The Primordials transcend the concept of enemies to be fought in the conventional sense. They exist as fundamental forces of nature, inextricably bound to the Weaving itself. To stop them, you must first understand them."

Aran nodded, his mind whirring.

Finally, he had seen the truth of the Weaving - and with it, the path forward. Yet the road ahead, indifferent to his newfound knowledge, remained fraught with uncertainty - one that would demand more than mere strength of arms. They would need wisdom, knowledge, and allies more than ever before.

"We will aid you," the Warden said, his voice firm. "But know this." His eyes were alive with pure energy, as if a lightning storm flashed from within. "The Primordials are indeed stirring from their ancient slumber, and once fully unleashed, they may prove unstoppable."

Sura shuddered. Beside her, Rafiq shifted his stance.

The Warden continued, unperturbed. "You were already on the right path, Aran, son of Khalid. Your only hope still lies in the obelisks - in restoring the balance before it is too late. The difference now is that you truly know what you are facing."

Aran turned to his companions, his resolve hardened. "Then we will go to Valamar. We will find the obelisk that lies there, and we will stop this before the world is torn apart." Rafiq and Sura exchanged a glance, both nodding, their expressions shadowed by concern.

As the Wardens prepared to guide them from the Vale, Aran felt in his soul that they were standing on the edge of something far greater than any of them had ever dared to imagine. The fate of the world balanced on the edge of a blade, and his bloodline - woven into the heart of Zarah's history - stood at the centre of the coming storm.

Chapter XXII

Between Worlds

The journey out of the Shadowed Vale was marked by an eerie, expectant silence. As Aran's group, accompanied by the Wardens, made their way through the dense oases, the oppressive mist clung to them - hesitant, as if the Vale itself was unwilling to let them go.

After a couple of hours of travel, the air around them grew lighter, a direct opposite of the weight of what they had learned pressing down upon their hearts.

Aran rode ahead, his thoughts churning. The vision he had experienced at the Stone of Oaths had reshaped his understanding of the task ahead. He now knew, for certain, that the Primordials were not enemies. Not in the traditional sense anyway. They were neither inherently good nor evil, but rather forces of creation, as well as destruction. An inseparable part of the Weaving, of creation itself, their wills were intricately bound to the fate of all things.

He glanced at Sura, riding silently beside him, her face etched with concentration. She had spoken little since they left the Vale, her eyes often distant as though she was yearning for something just beyond the horizon. Aran knew she had felt the same pulse in the Weaving, had glimpsed the same dark tendrils coiling within the fabric of reality. What they faced now was a threat far greater than they could ever foresee. The obelisks had once been the key to balancing the forces of the world, and now, driven unstable, that balance was rapidly eroding. In part because of him. Still, how could he have known how poorly his decision would age?

Rafiq rode behind them. Silent, strong, his hand never straying far from the hilt of his dagger. He had always been a warrior at heart, the protector of Aran's ambitions, but even he seemed more solemn than usual. The Wardens had revealed little about themselves, their movements almost spectral as they guided the group through the Vale's boundaries, but their mere presence was enough to unsettle even the most hardened warriors.

The path toward Valamar, the city of lost secrets, stretched before them. That city had once been the heart of the Old Kingdom's repository of knowledge, a sanctum of ancient wisdom, and the resting place of an obelisk long thought lost. It was there that they expected to find further answers to their questions. Though Aran suspected that the city itself would hold more than just forgotten lore.

For days, they travelled across the ever-bleaker landscape, the distant horizon dominated by unnatural jagged mountain peaks that seemed to be scratching the heavens.

When they neared the domains of the Old Kingdom, the very air seemed to hum with an unstable energy. The closer they came to its borders, the more the Weaving seemed to shift, the threads quivering as though disturbed by something unseen.

They decided to camp for the night, near a small water hole, surrounded by Medjool Palms. The place had a good view of its surroundings - easy to guard - and the following day they would press on. Aran started a fire while Sura and Rafiq went out hunting. The Wardens gathered around the flames, in silence. Soon after, his friends returned with supper, and before long, the night air was filled with the scent of roasted meat. The night was quiet, but the twin moons shone strangely in these lands.

"It feels different here," Sura said as she ate. Her eyes observed the mountains upon which stood the city of Valamar. Her voice was soft, barely more than a whisper, as if she feared the mountains themselves might be listening. "The Weaving is vibrating. I can feel the presence of something old here, something powerful."

Aran nodded, though his gaze remained fixed on the distant outline of the city, built high into the mountains, barely visible in the fading light. Built during the First Age of Zarah, around eleven thousand years ago, Valamar had once been a jewel of that world, its towers reaching toward the skies, its halls filled with the greatest scholars of the age.

Now it stood a ruin, abandoned, shrouded in mystery.

"Barash told me stories," Aran began. "Legends of the fall of Valamar. Some say the city was cursed, after the Old Kings bound themselves to the Weaving, while others say that it was sealed away to protect something too dangerous for the rest of the world to know. Whatever it was, it left the city empty, its gates barred to all."

"The obelisk," Sura said, her eyes still distant. "It was placed here, in the bowels of the city, was it not, Aran?"

"Yes," he was looking at the flames, as if the answers laid there. "Hidden beneath it, protected by whomever once ruled Valamar. If it is still there, we will have another chance to mend the Weaving further, but this might also be our last to stop its unravelling."

Sura said nothing. As silence fell amongst the group, the sound of steel being sharpened filled the night. Rafiq, always the steadfast warrior, was absent-mindedly honing his blades.

Aran remained silent for the rest of the night, his thoughts racing. Valamar's obelisk was indeed their goal, but he couldn't shake the feeling that there was more to this place than the ruins of a fallen city.

The vision he had seen in the Shadowed Vale had shown him glimpses of something deeper, a vast, ancient power sleeping beneath the surface, waiting to be awakened.

The next morning, they resumed their march, the path winding higher into the mountains. The terrain grew steeper, the air thinner, but their resolve only strengthened as they neared the city's gates.

Valamar, in its day, had been built to withstand the ravages of time and war, and though it had long been abandoned, its towering walls remained, their stone blackened and worn, but still standing.

As they approached, the gates loomed before them, a massive, imposing structure of iron and stone, intricately carved with symbols and runes from the time of the Old Kings.

The Wardens, who had travelled silently beside them, stepped forward, their leader raised a hand toward the gate. "We must be cautious," his voice was low and ominous. "Valamar is no ordinary ruin. The wards placed upon this city might still hold and, if they have, they will not be easily overcome."

Aran watched while the Chief Warden traced a pattern in the air, the runes on the gate beginning to glow with a faint, blue light. The symbols pulsed, their energy growing stronger as the Warden chanted in a language that seemed to Aran, older than the sands of the deserts. For a moment, the air around them seemed to thicken, as though the very fabrics of reality were bending, and then, with a deafening crack, the gates swung open.

Beyond lay the silent streets of Valamar, its Minare towers casting long shadows across the ground. The city stood in unnatural silence, its buildings casting skeletal shadows against the darkened sky. No voices, no footsteps - only the wind whispering through hollow streets, as if the city itself was remembering what it had lost. Once, it had pulsed with knowledge and power. Now, it was a tomb where time had forgotten to move on.

They kept going further in, and as they ventured deeper into the city's labyrinthic streets, their sense of unease grew. They were deserted, but there was a strange, pervasive, feeling that they were not alone in this place. The buildings loomed over them, their windows dark and hollow, like the eyes of long-dead giants.

Aran paused, his hand outstretched as he felt the Weaving shift again. "There's something here," he said, his voice low but made louder by the oppressive silence. "Something ancient. I believe it is watching us."

Instinctively, his hand went to his sword, though he knew that steel would be of little use against the forces they now faced. Whatever it was that haunted the city, it was far older than any foe they had ever encountered, and its power felt tied to the very essence of his world.

As they approached the centre of the city, the buildings grew taller, their architecture more elaborate, and the symbols etched into their walls more intricate.

At the heart of Valamar lay the Sanctum of Knowledge, the great library that had once housed the accumulated wisdom of Zarah's greatest minds. It was there, beneath the sanctum, that Aran believed they would find the obelisk.

The sanctum's doors were wide open, and the once-grand entrance now crumbled and overgrown with vines. Inside, the vast hall stretched out before them, rows of shelves filled with dust-covered tomes and scrolls, their pages long since forgotten. However, it was not the knowledge contained within that drew him - it was what lay hidden beneath.

The Wardens led the way, guiding them through the maze of winding bookshelves and corridors until they reached a staircase, hidden in the shadows at the back of the edifice. The steps spiralled downward, deeper and deeper into the heart of the mountain.

The air grew colder as they descended, the walls lined with ancient carvings that seemed to shift and move in the flickering torchlight. Aran could feel the pull of the Weaving here, stronger than ever before, as though the very threads of reality were converging on this point.

A sudden glance passed between him and Sura, laden with unspoken understanding.

At last, they reached the bottom of the staircase, where a massive stone door barred their way. Unlike the gates of Valamar, this door was still untouched by time - its surface smooth and unmarred, save for the intricate runes that glowed faintly in the darkness.

The Chief Warden stepped forward, his voice echoing in the silence as he spoke the words of the ancient incantation. The runes flared to life, the air around them crackling with energy, and slowly, the door began to open.

The Warden met Aran's gaze. "This is where our path ends, Aran, son of Khalid." Before Aran could respond, the air rippled, the Wardens dissolving like mist retreating from the dawn - leaving only the whisper of their presence behind.

"That was helpful." Rafiq jested. Deep down, Aran knew the Wardens had fulfilled their purpose. Their debt had been paid. What laid ahead was his duty to deal with, and nobody else's.

Beyond the door lay a vast chamber, its walls lined with towering statues of the Old Kings and Queens, their stone faces staring down in silent judgement.

At the centre of the room stood the obelisk, the massive pillar of black stone, its surface covered in the same runes that adorned the gates of Valamar. The air around it seemed to shimmer, as though reality itself were bending in its presence.

Aran approached it carefully, his heart pounding in his chest. After all their struggles, this could be it, the key, the final piece of the puzzle.

The moment he reached out to touch the stone, a voice echoed through the chamber - cold and ancient.

The voice hadn't finished its first word before the hairs on the back of Aran's neck stood on end - a visceral reaction to the sheer weight of its presence. Cold drops of sweat trickling down his back. "You seek to restore the balance," the voice said, its tone laced with a cruel and dry amusement. "Another was here, before you, trying to claim our power for his own. An ambitious goal, to be sure. The Primordials, however, do not forget - and they never forgive."

Aran froze, his hand inches from the obelisk. Was the voice speaking of Drathis? Had he been here, where Aran now stood? The shadows in the room seemed to shift, coalescing into a form. Tall, slender, and cloaked in darkness, the figure's face was hidden, but its sheer presence was undeniable. This was no mere apparition. This was a being of immense power, a force tied to the very essence of the Weaving.

Though individual Primordials governed different aspects of existence, when they chose to speak to mortals, their voices merged into one - a collective consciousness that transcended their separate domains.

"Our power is beyond your understanding," the figure continued, its voice echoing in the stillness. "You can not hope to control it, nor can you stop what has already begun."

Aran clenched his jaw. Without realising he was doing it, his hand tightened around the hilt of his father's sword. "We do not seek to control your power," his voice was steady, "We seek to restore the balance to prevent the world from falling into chaos."

The figure laughed. It was a cold, mirthless sound. "You are a fool, Aran of Karash, much like Kael Drathis is. The control he sought or the balance you now seek were never meant to happen, or last. The Weaving is fraying, and soon, all that you know will unravel. You think in the confines of flesh and time," the voice rumbled, filling his skull like a storm. "The Weaving was never made to last. It is not breaking, mortal. It is shedding."

With a flick of its hand, the figure disappeared, leaving behind only the faintest echo of its presence. Aran stood there for a moment, his mind a cobweb of thoughts. The Primordials were aware of his efforts, and they were not willing to help him.

"We must act quickly," he said, his voice urgent. "The Weaving is weakening by the hour. If we can activate this obelisk, we might have a chance to stop this." Sura nodded, her resolve hardening. They had come too far to turn back now.

As Aran stood before the obelisk, grappling with the Primordials' ominous words, far to the south another confronted the aftermath of his own encounter with these ancient forces.

Deep beneath the southeastern mountain range of Zarah, hidden in the labyrinthine tunnels that twisted beneath the craggy peaks, laid the Temple of Nathair. Carved into the very bones of the mountains by the House of Draco, millennia ago, this temple was a place of whispers and shadows, where the secrets of ages past had been locked away from the light of the sun and moons.

The cavernous halls were, as they had always been, illuminated by eerie blue fire, coming from torches, fuelled by alchemical compounds, that flickered in the still air, casting long, restless, shadows against the obsidian walls. Carvings adorned every surface - reptilian figures coiling around ancient Draconic script, their slitted eyes lit by blue torchlight, seeming to follow all who passed. This was a place of old power, and even those who ruled the House of Draco then did not fully understand the depths of its history.

Beyond the great central antechamber, past the large statues of Old Draconian Kings, and through a corridor lined with bone-like pillars, Kael Drathis sat upon a raised black-stone dais, his eyes dark in forbidding contemplation. Before him, Vhaskar, his first lieutenant stood motionless, his great frame eerily illuminated by the glow of the torches.

The silence between them was heavy, broken only by the distant, faint, dripping of water and the slow, ceaseless groan of stone shifting under its own ancient weight.

"The risks you take grow bolder with each venture. That place could have consumed you entirely." Vhaskar said at last, his deep, rumbling voice carrying through the hall like distant thunder. He sometimes felt that his charge took too many unnecessary risks.

Drathis exhaled, his fingers tightening over the armrest of his throne. "You speak as if I had a choice. Still, as you can see, I have returned."

Vhaskar stepped forward, his massive form moving with a predator's grace, despite his sheer bulk. His dark scales bore the marks of countless battles, old wounds that with time turned to hardened scars. Yet his tyrian purple eyes, burning like dying embers, were what betrayed the unease within. "Only barely," he countered. "But at what cost? The warriors we lost in Valamar were some of our finest. Most of the Chimaeras are gone. Slaughtered like prey before a cold, unseen master." Drathis' jaw tightened, memories of the recent battle flashing before his mind's eye.

The sands were shifting beneath them as the Sand Serpents rose. The shrieks of his warriors being devoured whole. Not that he cared for their lives. They were replaceable and, after all, victory was what mattered most to him. No, it was not that. The worst part had been the crushing presence of something vast, something that did not care for their mortal ambition, nor their conquests.

Then came the voice of the Primordials, whispering, not as foes, but as a force beyond all reckoning. "Success is still within your grasp... if only you surrender." Recalling the words once more, he shut his eyes for a moment, banishing the thought. "The cost of their lives was necessary," he finally said to Vhaskar. "Our battle at Valamar was never one we were meant to win. It was a test."

Vhaskar grunted, folding his massive arms over his chest. "Did you pass?" he asked, sarcastically. A dry, humourless chuckle escaped Drathis' lips. "That depends on whether survival is considered victory." Vhaskar's tail lashed once against the stone floor, betraying his frustration. "Survival is not victory. Not for us anyway, and we are no closer to securing the Weaving. No closer to securing Zarah."

Drathis opened his eyes, and for the first time since Valamar, he spoke the truth of what had happened. "The Primordials do not wish to be controlled," he said. "Nor could we do so if we tried. They do not bend, nor break. They do not fear us. They do not recognize us as anything more than fleeting echoes of a reality that will one day fall into silence."

Vhaskar frowned, his purple eyes narrowing. "Then they are our enemies, by default," he straightened up, his frame impressive.

Drathis exhaled slowly. "Perhaps so. If that is the case, then they are enemies we do not yet understand."

Vhaskar did not respond immediately. Instead, he reached into the folds of his battle-worn cloak, retrieving a scroll marked with the seal of the Nathair Sentinels, his personal network of spies and scouts spread throughout Zarah.

"These reports arrived during your convalescence from Valamar," Vhaskar said, tossing the scroll onto the table before Drathis. "Perhaps you should read them yourself," he intoned, his voice like rumbling stone.

Drathis took the scroll, unrolling the parchment. His eyes scanned the contents. His slitted pupils narrowed as he took in the words. His grip on the parchment tightened. "Aran has entered the city." It said, "Is this true?" Drathis asked, infuriated.

Vhaskar nodded. After a short pause, he added. "With the help of the Wardens."

Drathis' claws scraped against the black-stone of the dais. The Wardens were the keepers of the ancient binding, once neutral in the affairs of men and Draco alike. It seemed as though they had broken their silence. Not only that, but they had aided Aran, allowing him passage into the city of Valamar while turning away the rightful rulers of the Draconian bloodline. So, was it betrayal, or something he might have overlooked?

"They have thrown their lot in with the boy-king," Drathis murmured. "A mistake to be sure."

Vhaskar's voice was measured. "Aran is learning. He has seen the obelisks for what they are. He moves with purpose. If he has aligned with the Wardens, then he is no longer simply reacting to our careful warmongering or what he inadvertently started himself, by trying to stop you. He is seeking to end it before it can truly begin."

Drathis rolled the scroll back, placing it aside. "Then we deliver them to the storm. In other words, we bring it to their doorstep."

Vhaskar tilted his head, his slitted eyes narrowed. "You still intend to attack Sarim, even after our last defeat there?"

Drathis stood slowly, stepping down from the dais. His form was tall, powerful, his dark armour reflecting the torchlight. "I do," he said, his tone puzzling. "But not as we have the last time."

Vhaskar watched him carefully. "You intend to unleash something worse upon them then?"

Drathis turned, his expression unreadable. "We have been fighting with mortal weapons, waging a war of flesh and steel against a kingdom that has now aligned itself with forces beyond mortal reach."

"Wait," the hulking warrior shifted on the spot, "I do not think they have aligned themselves with the Primord-" Drathis raised a hand, commanding silence, then took a slow breath.

"You misunderstand me. I merely meant that if the Primordials cannot be controlled by us, then we must turn their wrath upon our enemies instead." Silence settled over the chamber.

Vhaskar's nostrils flared, his massive tail curling as he considered his commander's words.

"You are playing a dangerous game, courting forces that have, without fail, destroyed entire civilizations," he warned. "You seek to wield the storm rather than shelter from it. But what if you are wrong? What if what you summon does not distinguish us from them?" Vhaskar was genuinely apprehensive.

Drathis smirked. "Then we shall find out if we truly deserve their place in history," he turned back to the great stone map of Zarah, carved and embedded in the centre of the room.

His hand moved over the mountains, where the temple of Nathair was, past the ruins of Valamar, and then up, north-west, toward the white sands of Sarim.

"The next battle will not be like the last," he murmured, tracing a clawed finger over the stone map. "This time, we do not march as conquerors," his eyes gleamed in the torchlight. "We march as heralds." Vhaskar exhaled sharply. "What if the Primordials refuse to answer?" Drathis turned, his voice like iron. "Then we teach them how to kneel."

Chapter XXIII

Veil of the Unseen

In the dark, underground chamber, the obelisk stood silent and unyielding. It loomed before him, its dark surface catching the torchlight with an unnatural gleam. Aran felt the weight of centuries pressing down. This was no mere relic of a forgotten age, no monument to the lost glory of Valamar. It was a nexus, a focal point where the very threads of reality converged. This appeared to be the obelisk to which all others were bound and, if that was so, to touch it, to attempt to activate it, was to play with the powers that had shaped the world itself.

Sura's breath was shallow beside him, her eyes fixed on the obelisk with a mixture of awe and fear. "The energy here," she whispered, "it's like nothing I've ever felt, Aran. It is as if the Weaving itself is alive in this chamber."

He nodded, but his thoughts were clouded. The vision he had seen, it seemed like a lifetime ago, in the Echo of Worlds, haunted him still. The sight of the Weaving fraying, collapsing under the weight of forces that even the Old Kings had feared. The Primordials, once held in check by the obelisks, were stirring, and their awakening would tear the very fabric of existence apart.

Rafiq stood guard at the chamber's entrance, ever watchful, his eyes scanning the shadows for any sign of external danger. The encounter with the cloaked figure had left him on edge. "Whatever that was," he muttered, his voice low, "it wasn't human. It felt... wrong, like something from beyond our world."

"It was a remnant," Aran replied. "An echo of a power tied to the very Primordials themselves. They are aware of our presence, of what we are trying to do. I believe that they will not let us do it without a fight."

He brushed his fingers against the smooth, cold surface of the obelisk. Immediately, a pulse of energy surged through him, filling his veins with a strange, tingling warmth. It was as though the obelisk was testing him, probing his mind, his intentions. The Weaving reacted to his touch, the threads trembling and twisting around him, like an ancient loom trying to accommodate a new pattern.

"This obelisk is connected to the Weaving in ways I barely understand," he said, his voice steady despite the sensations he was experiencing and the tension in the air. "If I activate it, I might be able to reinforce the Weaving to repair the damage further. The bigger problem is that the Primordials will sense it, and they will come for us."

Aran exhaled slowly, his mind racing. Every step he had taken in his life had led him to this moment. Every decision, every battle, every loss, it had all been part of a larger design, one that he was only now beginning to comprehend. However, the enormity of the task before him was staggering. The Primordials were forces beyond mortal understanding, and confronting them was not a matter of sword or strategy. It was a battle for the soul of Zarah itself.

"Then we have no choice," Sura said, her voice trembling. "You must activate it. If there is even a chance we can stop the unravelling, we have to take it."

"Yes," Aran locked eyes with her. "But let us unite our efforts. You have learned much about the Weaving since we began this quest. Help me. Let us do it together." Sura's face, though determined, was pallid. She stepped closer, her hand reaching for the obelisk's surface. "Together, then. You are right, this is not something you should do alone. The Weaving requires balance, so I hope it might respond to the harmony of many voices." Her hand joined his.

Rafiq, ever loyal, placed his right hand on the stone as well. "You are not doing this without me." Winking at his best friend, he placed his left hand on Aran's shoulder.

The obelisk began to hum, a low, resonant sound that vibrated through the very bones of the mountain. The runes etched into its surface glowed brighter, their light growing until the entire chamber was bathed in a soft, ethereal glow.

Then the Weaving reacted. The threads of reality swirling around them shuddered and coiled, pulled toward the obelisk as though drawn by an invisible force. Aran could feel the energy building up, a swirling vortex of power that connected them to the very heart of Zarah. It was exhilarating and terrifying all at once, like standing on the edge of an abyss and staring into eternity.

For a moment, he glimpsed it again. The Weaving, vast, intricate and incomprehensible, stretching out in every direction. The threads shone, intertwined, forming the tapestry of existence, but many of them were frayed, unravelling into chaos. In the distance, he saw the Primordials once more. Their forms, somehow, seemed more vast, monstrous, and utterly alien, their presence warping the Weaving around them.

"They are coming," he whispered, his voice filled with dread, but still determined.

The ancient chamber trembled as the obelisk's light intensified, pulsing in rhythm with the Weaving's heartbeat, and Aran could feel the strain now, the immense pressure as the threads of reality fought to hold together. They were pushing the limits of what was possible, trying to force the Weaving to repair itself, to restore the balance that had been lost. The same balance he helped to destabilise by destroying the first two stone monoliths.

Then - a crack like splitting stone. The obelisk's glow stuttered, pulsing erratically before dimming to a faint, dying ember. A shudder ran deep through the Weaving itself. Aran's heart slammed against his ribs.

"What is happening?" Sura demanded, her voice strained.

"The obelisk," Aran explained, his brow furrowed in concentration. "It is…resisting. We are not enough. We need more power in order to restore this stone tether."

Before anyone could respond, a deafening crack echoed through the chamber. The statues lining the walls shuddered and crumbled, their ancient forms collapsing as the ground beneath them shifted. The Weaving itself seemed to warp, the threads bending and twisting as a massive tear opened in the fabric of reality.

From the gaping tear, something emerged - taller than any man, its form shifting like liquid shadow. Eyes like frozen stars burned in the void of its face, watching, waiting. The air itself recoiled from its presence. This was no mere remnant. This was a Primordial, a being of raw, unbridled power that had existed since the dawn of time. Since the very inception of The MiddleVerse itself.

"You meddle where no mortal should tread. The Weaving was never yours to shape. The pact your ancestors forged? A fleeting breath in the endless tide of time. What might seem to you like an age, is to us nothing more than a celestial heartbeat. You seek to restore what was never meant to be permanent."

Aran stood his ground, his hand tightening around the hilt of his father's sword though, deep down, he doubted that a weapon could harm a being such as this. "We seek to protect the world from your destruction. The balance has been shattered, and if we do not repair it, our world will fall into chaos."

The Primordial laughed, a deep, resonant sound that seemed to shake the very foundations of the mountain. "You are but a tiny speck in the vastness of the cosmos. The balance you speak of is nothing more than an illusion. The Weaving was never meant to last forever. Eventually, it will unravel, as all things must."

The obelisk pulsed again, its light flickering as the Weaving buckled under the Primordial's presence. Sura cried out, her hand trembling as she struggled to maintain her connection to the obelisk.

Aran's mind raced. They were losing. The power of this obelisk, though greater than all the others they had encountered, was not enough to withstand the might of a Primordial. Still, there had to be a way. They had always found a way.

As he watched the obelisk's light flicker and fade under the Primordial's overwhelming presence, a memory surfaced - something Barash had mentioned about the network of monoliths, how they were designed to work in harmony. Each obelisk he had encountered had been weakened by isolation, their power diminished without their network intact. His hope that this single stone tether would be enough had been naive.

"The other obelisks," he said suddenly, his voice sharp. "They are still out there. We do not need just this one. If we can awaken the others, unite their power, we might be able to hold the Weaving together."

Sura nodded, her face pale but determined. "It is risky. The obelisks are scattered, and we do not know how many of them remain intact. This obelisk was meant to be their anchor, their central point, but even anchors need a chain to hold anything in place. However, if we can manage to activate the rest, we might have a chance."

The Primordial's eyes narrowed, its form shifting as it seemed to loom even larger. "Foolish mortals. You cannot stop what has already begun. The unravelling is inevitable."

The Primordial's form began to waver, not from weakness, but from apparent disinterest. "Your struggle amuses us, mortal. We will watch as you exhaust yourselves against the inevitable." The tear in reality began to close, the being's presence receding like the tide pulling back from shore. The rift, however, did not fade completely...

Aran didn't question their fortune. Whether the Primordial viewed them too insignificant to bother destroying, or whether some deeper game was at play, he seized the opportunity.

He ignored the foreboding taunt, his mind already racing ahead. "Then we need to act quickly. Rafiq, Sura, we have to leave. There's nothing more we can do here."

Reluctantly, Sura withdrew her hand from the obelisk, the light fading as the connection was severed. Rafiq moved swiftly, already preparing for their retreat. The chamber trembled as the Primordial's presence began to grow stronger, the tear in the Weaving widening with each passing moment.

"We need to find the other obelisks," Aran said as they made their way back up the winding staircase, the mountain shaking beneath them. "We need to restore the balance before the Primordials tear everything apart. Something happened here though," he paused, trying to focus his mind. "A shift in my perception. Despite still being able to sense them, I do not feel the obelisks as intensely as I was able to. Perhaps the Primordial's presence has affected my connection to the Weaving, or perhaps the network itself is more damaged than we thought."

Sura nodded, but her eyes were now filled with doubt. "Well, that will not make things easier. The other obelisks are hidden, scattered across the world. Finding them could take years, decades, even."

"It goes without saying that we do not have that long," Aran smiled grimly. "The Weaving is unravelling faster than I thought it would. We need to move fast."

As they emerged from the sanctum, the city of Valamar stretched out before them, its once-great towers now cast in shadow. The Primordial's influence was already spreading, the very air around them thick with the scent of decay and ruin.

Aran glanced back at the Sanctum, its dark form barely visible through the haze. It had been their last hope, their final chance to restore the Weaving, and now it was beginning to dawn on him that the obelisks alone might not be enough. He decided to keep this thought to himself, for the time being.

The path ahead would be long. Treacherous. But Aran knew now - this was no longer a battle of men and kingdoms. It was a war against time itself. The Weaving was failing, and his bloodline stood at the threshold of its last stand. Whether they prevailed or perished, history would remember this moment. The moment when the fate of all things was decided.

Chapter XXIV

What Lies Beneath Silence

Dawn broke in a sullen haze, the sky bathed in an unnatural, blood-red glow. This was no ordinary sunrise. Zarah's deserts were meant to blaze under golden light, yet here, over the ruins of Valamar, the air felt thick - tainted. The world was shifting, bending under an unseen force.

Aran stood on the edge of a crumbled parapet, watching as the shadow of the Primordial presence crept across the land, a thick and oppressive gloom that seemed to warp reality itself. He felt the weight of countless decisions pressing upon him.

Until the previous night, this obelisk had been a beacon of hope, a tether to the ancient power that had once held the world in balance. That hope had dimmed, and now he was being forced to readapt yet again. Behind him, Sura was poring over ancient texts, scrolls and maps they had recovered from Valamar's hidden libraries, her fingers tracing over the faded lines and runes. Rafiq was oiling his twin swords, his eyes scanning the horizon as he always did, a sentinel in these ever darkening days.

The Primordial they had encountered had been but the first sign of the greater powers stirring. The air thrummed with the residual energy of their encounter, and though the creature itself had retreated back into the tear in the Weaving, its presence lingered like a nightmare that refused to fade.

"We must move quickly," Aran said, his voice breaking the morning silence. "The obelisks are scattered far beyond this place. All are hidden, and each one is tied to a different aspect of the Weaving, to things like time, memory, life, or death for example. If we are to restore the balance, we must understand how they function together."

Sura's face surfaced from an old scroll and she turned to face him, her expression hard. "We have no idea where the others are, and now you are saying that you cannot feel them the same anymore," she sounded weary. "We could spend years searching, only for the Weaving to be completely unravelled by then."

"Not all of them are lost to us," Aran replied, his voice filled with a cautious hope. "Back in the Echo of Worlds, I saw more than just the unravelling of the Weaving. The visions showed me glimpses of places, of sites where the Weaving is stronger, where the Primordials' hold is weaker. Those places could lead us to the obelisks." Aran shook his head, frustrated. "Unfortunately, we do not have the luxury of trial and error. The Primordials are aware of us now. They will be hunting us, trying to stop us from restoring the balance."

"If this is the only path," Rafiq muttered, steel scraping against stone as he sharpened his short blade. "Then we follow it. We either find the obelisks, or we let the world die. That choice was made for us, the moment Drathis meddled with the Weaving in Sarim."

Aran sighed, his gaze drifting back toward the horizon where the Primordial's dark influence spread. He could feel the threads of reality twisting and fraying with each passing hour, every moment bringing them closer to the brink of oblivion.

"Very well," he decided, his voice firm. "We will follow the visions. Sura, gather everything we have on the obelisks. Rafiq, prepare the men. We leave within the hour."

They prepared frantically, for what lay ahead, during the next several days of tense travel. Aran and his companions moved swiftly, gathering supplies, consulting the remaining scholars and dispatching scouts across Zarah.

The political climate in Sarim was deteriorating again. Word had already reached the Yaran capital that Aran kept delving into ancient, forbidden knowledge. Whispers of treachery, of madness, spread like wildfire amongst several of the minor tribes. Although he knew that his main supporters, the larger tribes like the Rasha, the Shamari, the Bahir, the Ulema, the Tarek, would continue to be loyal to him, he also feared that the minor tribes might coalesce into a larger force, bringing chaos from within his House.

However, given the present circumstances, Aran had no time to address any of these concerns. The Primordials were a far greater threat than any political rival. After Valamar, they had begun to corrupt the very fabric of reality, and as the group travelled deeper into the northern deserts, the signs of this corruption became impossible to ignore. Where Oases once thrived, now fields lay barren under strange, twisted skies. Rivers traced different paths across the rugged landscape, and the once-majestic Solarwood Trees stood silent and decayed, their leaves blackened as if scorched by some unseen fire.

Their next destination, the Broken Expanse, was a place spoken of by Barash - but only in whispers, for fear of unfriendly ears. Located in the northern region of Zarah, north-east of Sarim, it was a desolate region where, according to Aran and Sura, the Weaving was now supposed to be at its thinnest.

At their last camp, Sura shared legends that spoke of ancient battles fought there between the Primordials and the Old Kings - of obelisks buried deep beneath the earth and sea, guarding secrets even those ancient rulers dared not unearth. In her recent studies, she had also discovered a long-forgotten link between the House of Draco and the Weaving itself.

"So," Aran mused, "It appears there was more behind Drathis' visit to the Old Quarter of Sarim than we suspected." Though he played it off as unimportant, both Sura and Rafiq could see Aran's mind spinning.

"You do realise this could change everything, right?" Sura asked, her voice trembling.

"Yes I do," he replied, "However, we should not jump to conclusions until we know more." Neither Rafiq nor Sura pressed the matter any further, but both exchanged worried glances.

For Aran, this revelation cast Drathis' actions in an entirely new light. What had once seemed like mere ambition now revealed itself as something far more dangerous: a hereditary claim to power over the very fabric of reality itself.

As they travelled, each day, Sura continued explaining about what she had been studying. About the significance of the obelisks in greater detail. "The obelisks were never just barriers," she said one evening as they camped under a fractured sky. "They were, and still are, the true keystones of the Weaving itself. You were right Aran, about what you told us at Valamar, each obelisk represents a different pillar of creation, bound together by a single, unbroken thread of power."

"That means that if we can reawaken them all," Aran asserted, "we can strengthen the Weaving and stop the unravelling."

Sura nodded, though her expression was troubled. "That is the theory. Though there is also something else," she hesitated, unsure on how to deliver such a devastating blow. "The obelisks do not just bind the Weaving - they also serve as locks that keep the Primordials imprisoned within the confines of the Weaving."

"I already knew that. What are you trying to say?" he asked, confused.

She merely stared at him, her eyes a mix of love and sorrow. "Aran," she said, looking deep into his. "Think." He frowned, his eyes unfocused, his mind putting the pieces together. "Wait," the blow was, to say the least, unexpected. "Does that mean that every time we have thereby reawakened an obelisk, we have been weakening those locks?"

"Precisely," she smiled faintly. "The more we use their power, the more we draw the Primordials' attention. It's a delicate balance. Too much, and we could unleash the very forces we are trying to contain."

Aran felt as if an ice blade had pierced his heart. They were walking a razor's edge, and one misstep could lead to catastrophe. There was no turning back now. The Weaving was fraying, and if Barash was right, the obelisks were their only hope. They would have to be careful, precise in their actions. One mistake could doom them all.

The Broken Expanse was even more desolate than Sura's stories had described. Vast plains of cracked earth stretched out before them, the sky above a swirling mass of storm clouds and unnatural light. It was a place where the Weaving was almost non-existent, where reality itself seemed to bend and twist in ways that defied understanding.

At the centre of the expanse stood the first of the obelisks they sought. An enormous monolith of black stone, half-buried in the sand. It was ancient, weathered by time and the elements, but it still pulsed with a faint, otherworldly energy. Runes covered its surface, glowing faintly in the dim light, like the last embers of a dying fire.

Aran approached it cautiously, his hand resting on the hilt of his father's heirloom - the blade half-drawn, catching the obelisk's otherworldly light as if awakening to the ancient power ahead.

Sura was beside him, her eyes scanning the runes with a mixture of awe and trepidation. "This is it," she whispered. "The Obelisk of Memory. It holds the power to bind time itself to repair the threads of the past."

There was a long pause, during which Rafiq was studying them both, intently. After observing the stone monolith, in detail, Sura glanced at Aran. "How do we activate it?"

He hesitated. "I'm not sure. The runes... they speak of a trial, a test of memory," he leaned in, squinting at the shifting glyphs. "Only those who can endure the weight of their own past can unlock the obelisk's power."

She frowned, her mind racing - but to no avail. "What do you think it means?"

Before Aran could think, let alone respond, the ground beneath them trembled, and the obelisk began to glow more brightly. A deep, resonant hum filled the air, and the runes on its surface shifted, rearranging themselves into a new pattern. Suddenly, the world around them seemed to dissolve, the landscape of the Broken Expanse fading into nothingness. Aran felt a strange, disorienting pull, as if he were being drawn into the obelisk itself.

When the vertigo subsided, he found himself no longer in the Broken Expanse, but standing within the great hall of Sarim. The walls were lined with banners of the House of Aran, and at the head of the hall sat his father, King Khalid ibn Rashid, resplendent in his golden armour.

And yet, this was no memory, for Khalid had never been king. This was, undoubtedly, another vision - the most surreal he had experienced thus far.

The sight of him crowned stirred something deep within Aran - not confusion, but recognition. This was not memory but possibility. A glimpse of what might have been had the man who raised him not turned from power to protect his bloodline from the ancient pacts that bound it to the Weaving.

"You have come far, my son," Khalid said, his voice both strong and commanding. "Only now, you carry the weight of our House upon your shoulders," he paused, his gaze softening as he admired his child. "Do you remember the stories I told you when we roamed the caravan routes together?"

Aran stared at his father, his heart pounding in his chest.

He remembered every word. "You told me that life binds us all - that the strength of a man comes not from power or wealth but from the bonds he shares with the world and its peoples."

Khalid nodded solemnly. "Unfortunately, as we speak, those bonds are fraying. I am sorry that you have been thrust into this, my son, but the Weaving is unravelling fast, and the fate of our world rests in your hands. However, before you can heal it, you must first mend yourself. Be the change you wish to see reflected back at you." He swallowed hard. "My child, you must face your own past once more - fully, and without retreat. Forgive yourself." Aran shuddered at his father's words. "This will not be pleasant," he whispered.

His surroundings shifted again, and now he stood on a battlefield - a graveyard of brothers, their bodies sprawled in the sand like discarded hopes." His own, Amir, lay at his feet, his lifeless eyes staring up at the sky. The memory of that day flooded back to him. It had been the day he failed to save him - months after Amir had marched to war despite their father and mother's pleas.

Still, this pain did not stand alone. Amir had left when Aran was only twelve, and just months later, their father was murdered in the night by Drathis, who came cloaked in another's face - Malik the Vulture. Though Aran never found out his father's murderer true identity, he was there that night - he saw it happen.

These losses, separated by months of grief and miles of desert roads, had carved the same wound into his soul. Yet over coming months and subsequent years, under Barash's guidance, grief had tempered his spirit. Aran no longer clung to vengeance like a blade - he had chosen a harder path. To unite the tribes. To root out the darkness festering in Zarah's heart. To ensure that no more sons and daughters would bury their parents, and no more siblings would fall unheard in the sand.

"You carry our death like a chain around your soul," Khalid's voice echoed. "I trust that now you know that the Weaving does not care for vengeance, nor does it grant absolution. If you are to mend what is broken, then you must first mend yourself."

Aran's grip tightened on his sword - his father's - his knuckles white. He had spent years trying to forget that day, to bury the pain of his brother's death. Now, faced with the obelisk's test, he knew that he could not move forward until he confronted it - once and for all. Kneeling beside Amir's body, his chest tight with emotion, Aran spoke from the heart. "I am truly sorry," he whispered, tears running down his face, "I was too young, and failed you - I will not fail our family. I will gladly give my life in exchange for the safety of our people. Please, brother, forgive me!"

As the words left his lips, the battlefield began to dissolve, and the obelisk's hum grew louder. Aran could feel the weight of guilt leave him, the world solidifying once more.

When he opened his eyes, he was back in the Broken Expanse, the obelisk now glowing brightly, its runes pulsating with renewed energy.

"I believe you did it," Sura said, her voice filled with joy and awe. "You passed the test."

Aran rose to his feet, his gaze fixed on the obelisk. "One down," he said, winking at her, trying to mask his concerns, "but there are more to come. Let us not cry victory, for we are not done yet."

"Good," Rafiq cut in, trying to lighten the mood. "After all, what is a warrior without a battle to fight?"

As they prepared to leave the Broken Expanse, Aran couldn't shake the feeling that something was watching them - his father, maybe? The air was thick with tension, and the sky above seemed to pulse with dark energy. The Primordials were stirring, most likely due to his mending. Then again, why had they allowed him to mend this tether? Or had this vision been caused by something more powerful than them? Of one thing he was sure though, they would not allow the other obelisks to be reawakened without putting up a fight.

Nevertheless, Aran was no longer the man he had been when this journey began. He had faced his past, confronted his deepest fears, faced powerful foes, both from this reality as well as the next, and emerged stronger for it. Presently, as they prepared to seek out the remaining obelisks, he truly understood that his hardest tests were only just beginning. The Primordials were coming, after millennia of slumber, and this time, there would be no way to avoid their reckoning.

Hundreds of miles to the south-east, another player in this cosmic dance was making his own preparations. While Aran sought to heal the Weaving through trials of the spirit, his nemesis had chosen a far darker path - one that would force the very powers that shaped reality to bend to his will.

Leander's primary was blazing down, with its habitual harshness, on the south-eastern largest mountain range on the planet, painting the dunes, extending before its roots, with a golden light.

Carved deep into the mountains, the Temple of Nathair had long been a place of silent worship, a hollowed relic of the old Draconian kings, but tonight it would become something far more terrible, a conduit for forces that even time had dared not erase.

Drathis strode through the cavernous halls, the blue-flame torches flickering in eerie anticipation, his mind a maelstrom of thought. The Weaving had been further mended, repaired by Aran's meddling with the obelisks, and the Primordials had denied Drathis dominion over them. However, that did not mean they were beyond his reach - and no, he would not beg them. He would instead force them to listen.

Behind him, Vhaskar followed, his towering form moving with a measured, deliberate gait. His first lieutenant had stood beside him for countless decades, had bled in his name, followed him into Valamar and saved him from that place. Yet, even Vhaskar had hesitated when Drathis had spoken of this plan.

"You would summon them," Vhaskar rumbled, breaking the silence as they entered the lower sanctum of the temple.

Drathis did not slow his pace. "It will not be the first time. Besides, I would have succeeded in Sarim, if it had not been for that desert dreamer's interference. But no, not summon," he corrected the muscular warrior. "Awaken," he smirked.

Vhaskar's narrowed slitted eyes were burning. "Semantics," he grumbled. "In all seriousness, have you given any thought to the possibility that they might not come as allies? Our ancestors weren't any luckier."

Drathis stopped walking, turning on the spot. The glow of the torches bathed his chiselled features in an ethereal glow, his crimson cloak flowing like liquid shadow behind him, as he pivoted. "Well," his slitted eyes were as cold as the nights of Qamaria, "If they come as foes, then we will teach them fear," he said simply.

Vhaskar studied his friend for a long moment. There was no arrogance in his words, only certainty. That was what made Drathis so dangerous. He did not seek power for the sake of conquest, as some of the lesser Draco warlords, he did so because he truly believed in its inevitability.

The air in the temple grew heavier, as though the very walls could sense what was about to happen. Ahead, the entrance to the Shadow's Divide yawned open. The Divide was a vast circular chasm carved into the lowest depths of the temple where, millennia ago, the old Nathair bloodlines of the House of Draco had tried, and failed, to communicate with the entities beyond time - except one faction.

There, beneath the carved effigies of famed reptilian warriors and old Draconian Gods, a gathering had begun.

The warriors stood in a circle, clad in obsidian armour, their serrated glaives gleaming in the dim light. These were Warlocks of the Nathair Cult, the last remnants of an ancient sect who had once managed to appease the Primordials. They began to move about the great stone platform, inscribing sigils of invocation with a mixture of their blood and sand from the Black Dunes, famed for its high concentration of crystals.

A great pit of molten stone roiled at the centre of the chamber, its surface shimmering with unnatural light. This was the heart of the Divide, one more wound in Zarah's bosom where the Weaving grew thin, where things from beyond the veil could slip through.

Drathis approached the edge of the pit and raised a clawed hand.

The warlocks ceased their work, their masked faces turning toward him in reverence.

"We call upon the Forgotten Ones," Drathis intoned. His voice was pure commandment of will. "We call upon the Lords of the Weaving," the warlocks echoed, their voices rising in a dark hymn. Drathis stepped forward, standing at the very precipice of the molten abyss.

The heat seared his scaly skin, but he did not flinch. He could feel the power shifting, the air trembling with unseen hands. Closing his eyes, he spoke the final invocation in a language as old as time. In fact, it was the same language he used a long time ago, in Sarim's Old Quarter, before the boy-king foiled his plans.

"Shed your slumber, oh Forgotten Lords.
Stir beneath the veil of time.
The world has shifted, and we call to you,
Not as servants. But as masters of the storm."

For a long moment, nothing happened. Then the ground shook beneath their feet, and a deep rumbling filled the chamber, as if the very bones of Zarah were groaning in protest. The molten pit bubbled violently, the sigils on the floor burning with cold fire. The warriors tightened their grips on their weapons, and even Vhaskar's expression hardened in wary anticipation. After all, they were the last line of defence in case Drathis' plan went awry. Suddenly, the air split open.

A sound, not meant for mortal ears, tore through the chamber. A voice so vast it was like the grinding of celestial titans or the shifting of endless dunes. It felt like the exhalation of something older than the stars. "You dare call us again?"

Drathis' breath hitched, but he did not lower his gaze. "Yes," he said, his voice even. "And this time, you will listen." Silence.

The air was thick with anticipation, suddenly it rippled and the flames burnt white-hot as the presence of the Primordials filled the room.

A roar erupted from the Divide. Yet, it was a roar of hunger, not of rage.

In the depths of the temple of Nathair, the atmosphere grew unbearably hot, and from the molten pit, they came - Sand Serpents. Their forms coiled out of the abyss, their glass-like scales glistening, their jaws lined with powerful fangs. Their eyes burned with primordial light, their bodies undulating with the shifting of the Weaving itself. Drathis' warriors braced themselves for battle, but the serpents did not strike - not yet. For the time being they appeared to be in a trance, undulating, hovering above them.

The Primordials spoke again, but this time, their layered voices came not from the air around Drathis but from within his own mind. They were speaking to him directly. "You did not listen before, Kael Drathis. You did not pay heed to our warnings. We do not forget nor forgive."

Drathis clenched his fists. "I do not need to listen to your musings," rage coursed through his veins like molten stone, "I need you to act accordingly with mine. Perhaps it is you who should listen to me."

Behind him, anticipating events, Vhaskar, made a subtle move, reaching for his war hammer. He thought Drathis was pushing things too far.

"Why should we?" The voice asked, in a sarcastic, almost derogatory way.

Drathis felt as if the voice was coming from his very bones, coursing through his veins, mocking his intent and ambition.

His patience snapped. "Because your realm is crumbling, as fast as the Weaving unravels, and because if you do not move, then others will shape your fate for you."

A deep silence followed. It was so intense, it reverberated in Drathis' ear drums. Only to be surpassed by the voice's power. "You misunderstand the situation, mortal. What is happening to the Weaving will only set us free," the voice echoed in his head. Its tone was detached, disparaging. Drathis words, on the other hand, came out through clenched fangs. "That, I can not allow!" Behind him, Vhaskar stood ready.

The Sand Serpents struck, without warning, lunging at Drathis, their massive jaws snapping shut where he had stood seconds before. Faster than a Dune Stalker, their prey had already lept into action, his blade flashing, slashing, carving deep into the hide of the first beast. Ichor sprayed freely onto stone, and as the creature struck the floor, shrieking, its death-throes shook the cavern walls.

The Warlocks of Nathair, now lost in their allegiances, and against their better judgement, in fear for their lives, opted to engage the beasts in battle. Their weapons got to meet the flesh of these avatars, but their battle-cries, however, were swallowed by the Sand Serpents' deafening roars, along with their mortal coils.

Drathis turned on the spot, his breathing ragged, blade at the ready, his gaze locked on the remaining serpents. Were they multiplying?

"You fight," the Primordials taunted, half-amused, half-disappointed. "Yet you struggle to yield, even when you know you cannot win."

Drathis wiped the blood from his sword. "I fight because I choose to fight. Survival is not victory to us. We would choose death, a thousand times, over defeat. We, the House of Draco, are the rightful heirs to all the bounties of creation, and we will not rest until all of it is in our grasp." As Drathis spoke, two more Nathair Warlocks fell to the Weaving's slithering avatars.

Another Sand Serpent lunged at him, but Vhaskar stepped in - his war hammer crashed into its skull, sending the beast reeling backwards. Drathis did not hesitate. Leaping onto the creature's back, he plunged his sword deep into its spine. The beast writhed, its death-screech splitting the air - but Drathis held firm.

The Primordials watched impassively. However, true to their nature, they could not resist to taunt Drathis further, with the promise of a pact. "We offer you greatness, Kael Drathis. We offer you power beyond your reckoning. All you have to do is kneel before us, as Aran's ancestors have - as well as yours." The taunt was too great.

In defiance, Drathis drove his blade deeper into the creature writhing beneath him. "I bow to no one." The Sand Serpents vanished, and silence followed. Heavy seconds went by, then the voice spoke, for the last time. "So be it, Kael Drathis, of the House of Draco."

The Weaving shattered around him, casting him out for the last time.

Drathis collapsed hard against the temple floor, his body battered, his breath ragged.

The Sand Serpents were gone. Perhaps they had been illusions, but the after effects of the battle were as real as the pain he felt. The chamber was in ruins, the sigils scorched away, and the Shadow Divide sealed itself once more. The Primordials were gone, leaving the mortal remains of Drathis' warriors scattered about.

Vhaskar loomed over him, offering a hand. "I hope you are satisfied," he jested, as he lifted his friend to his feet. "What now?"

Drathis, though gasping for breath, let out a low bitter laugh. "Now," he said, smirking, despite the considerable pain he was in, "we will do it differently than our forebears - no fancy tricks, no ancient pacts. We shall fight fire with fire."

Vhaskar raised a brow. "Do you mean?" Finally, his friend was making sense. Drathis' eyes burned. "Enough whispers in the dark," he snarled, his breath ragged but his will unbroken. "No more schemes. No more subterfuges. No more patience. We will take Sarim - and the rest of Zarah - by fire and steel."

"Yes!" the hulking warrior shouted, his voice echoing through stone halls and corridors steeped in the planet's history.

Chapter XXV

A Council in Shadows

The journey back to Sarim was brutal. The land itself groaned under the weight of the unravelling Weaving, fractures spidering through the earth as if reality itself were protesting their passage. Aran felt it in his bones - this was no mere shift - Zarah was resisting its own fate.

With every step, the group felt the lingering presence of the Primordials, as though their ancient eyes were upon them, watching from beyond the veil of reality. The ground trembled beneath them, not with the simple shakes of tectonic activity, but with the rumbling heartbeat of a world fighting against an apparently unavoidable end.

The Obelisk of Memory had been reawakened, but that was only one fragment of the ancient pact that bound their world.

The visions granted to Aran within Valamar's Sanctum of Knowledge had revealed three more obelisks - each bound to a distinct aspect of the Weaving, each the keeper of its own sacred trial. Yet even these were not the full measure of his burden.

If it wasn't enough that the Draco were already a formidable force to contend with on their own, what Sura had told him about them being connected, in their distant past, to the Weaving, brought further consternation to his already burdened mind.

After an arduous journey across shifting dunes and starlit wastes, they at last neared the borders of Sarim. The air grew salt-rich, tinged with the scent of the Yaran sea, and the wind carried with it the distant cries of seabirds and the creaking of distant ships moored beyond the dunes.

Pale mists rose from the coastline each morning, curling through the Moonleaf groves and brushing the outer watchtowers with fingers of fog.

As they passed through smaller settlements - clusters of sandstone homes and moon-tiled courtyards - they began to hear the familiar cadence of Sarimite tongues once more. And with it, the distant echo of politics, growing louder with each passing league.

The marketplaces murmured with rumours, the tea-houses crackled with tension. Whispers moved faster than caravans, and none could ignore them.

The kingdom seemed adrift. In Aran's absence, a vacuum had formed - and into that void, the lesser tribes had gathered, not in concord with his vision, but arrayed in quiet defiance.

The remainder of the council was restless. Rivals within his court had seized upon the uncertainty, and now, whispers of rebellion and betrayal followed them all the way back to the Yaran capital.

He wondered who might have been the one that had led them astray. It could not have been Farid this time - the man was a shadow of his former self, broken and spent.

With each passing league, the tone of conversation shifted. No longer confined to whispered tales of ancient threats few could comprehend, the question had grown heavier: could their king hold the kingdom together long enough to meet the peril he claimed was coming?

At last, when the dunes gave way to firmer ground, the city of Sarim loomed before them, its towering walls and spires rising from the coastal desert like a fortress against the chaos that surrounded it.

The once-proud banners of his kingdom fluttered in the wind, but there was a sense of unease around the city. The fields were quieter than usual, and the people's faces were drawn with fear. Something had shifted in the atmosphere, and even the air itself seemed heavy with foreboding.

As they approached the city gates, Aran noticed a group of heavily armed warriors waiting for him. These were not his men, but rather the personal guard of Lord Ryvan, one of the most powerful men in the council and a man known for his ambition.

Though he spent most of the council's meetings in silence, Ryvan had always been a staunch supporter of his. Yet Aran could not help but feel the chill of suspicion settle into his bones. Something was out of place with the man, like a tapestry woven from threads that did not belong together.

Sura stepped closer, her eyes narrowing at the sight of the soldiers. "Something is wrong," she murmured. "Ryvan's men should not be here, not like this."

"I know," Aran replied swiftly, his voice low. "Be that as it may, we do not have time to deal with court intrigue. Not with the Primordials stirring."

After being granted passage through the city, they began to make their way toward the palace, where the true test of Aran's authority awaited.

Even as they passed through the gates and into the Yaran capital, the sense of unease only deepened. The people of Sarim whispered amongst themselves as they watched Aran's return, their eyes flickering with doubt. News of his involvement with the ancient obelisks and the forbidden magic they held, had spread quickly. Rumours of dark pacts and hidden powers had sown seeds of fear among the populace, and it was clear that many no longer saw him as the hero they had once revered. Whether that was of their own volition remained to be seen.

When they arrived at the palace courtyard, they were greeted by a group of tribal leaders from the smaller clans, each wearing the solemn expression of those who had prepared themselves for a difficult confrontation. At their head stood Lord Ryvan, tall and imposing, his silver hair gleaming in the dim light. He bowed deeply to Aran, but there was a certain coldness in his eyes that did not match the gesture.

So, of all people, it was him that sowed the seeds of doubt amongst the smaller tribes and clans. He was undoubtedly making use of the situation to further his own political agenda.

Apparently, his support had been a well played façade to hide his true ambitions. Aran, however, wondered if Drathis had gotten to him, offering kingship in exchange for his integrity.

"My king," Ryvan intoned, his voice smooth and measured. "Welcome home. We feared for your safety during your prolonged absence."

Aran dismounted from his steed, his gaze locking onto Ryvan's. "You feared for more than my safety, it seems," he let his words linger in the air. "What news do you bring from the council?"

Ryvan straightened, a flicker of irritation passing over his face. "There have been... concerns. Your absence has left the kingdom vulnerable. The council is restless and the people are afraid. They do not understand the threat we face, nor do they trust the measures you've taken to combat it." He let the words out slowly, savouring each one.

Aran's jaw tightened. "The threat is very real, Ryvan. The council spoke about this the last time I was here, why did you say nothing then?" He could barely hide his frustration now. "The Primordials are stirring, and if we do not act, they will consume this world. I have seen, first hand, the destruction they can bring."

Ryvan inclined his head, but his expression remained unreadable. He chose to ignore Aran's question and instead opted for a change in strategy. "I do not doubt your words, my king," his tone carried concern but Aran knew it to be fake. "However, you must understand," Ryvan continued, "the people are not concerned with ancient myths, but with the here and now. They want stability, and many of your advisors fear that your pursuit of these... obelisks may lead us down a dangerous path."

Aran felt a surge of anger rise within him but, with enormous strain, he forced it down. He knew that Ryvan and those that followed his mellifluous discourse could not comprehend the true scope of the danger they faced. They were too caught up in their petty rivalries and political games to see the larger picture.

After that tense exchange in the courtyard, Aran gestured for Ryvan to lead the way inside. The older man's lips twitched - perhaps in irritation at being commanded like a common servant - but he bowed his head slightly and turned toward the Council room.

They ascended the grand staircase in silence, their footsteps echoing against the polished steps. Sura and Rafiq followed several paces behind, their eyes constantly scanning for threats. The marble walls of the corridor were lined with ancient tapestries depicting the founding of Sarim - scenes that once filled Aran with pride now seemed to watch him with judging eyes.

"The council has been in session since dawn," Ryvan said, breaking the silence as they reached the landing. "They await your... explanation." Aran noted the careful pause. "I am sure they are."

As they approached the massive doors of the council chamber, he could already hear the heated voices within - arguments pausing only when the sentries announced his arrival.

Ryvan's hand lingered on the door handle, his rings glinting in the light from the overhead sconces. "Remember, my king," he said quietly, "many here have had months to form their opinions in your absence."

"While you had months to shape those opinions, have you not, Ryvan?" Aran replied, his voice equally low.

A fleeting smirk crossed Ryvan's face before he pushed open the doors to reveal the circular chamber beyond. Sunlight streamed through the high windows, illuminating the solarwood crescent table where the council members now rose to their feet. In certain faces, Aran saw a mixture of relief, suspicion, and poorly concealed hostility.

Sura stepped closer to him, her presence a steady reassurance at his back, while Rafiq positioned himself near the door, his keen eyes cataloguing every face, every gesture, every potential threat in the room. All three took comfort in the knowledge that their principal allies remained loyal, prepared to stand firm in their king's stead.

Kasim stood proud, his powerful arms crossed over his chest, Safira stood up, Karim straightened his spectacles and Zahira was looking at Ryvan with utter disdain.

Many other supporters of the king shifted in their seats, but Aran raised his hand, commanding silence.

"I did not return to dally in games of court," he said, his voice cold. "I did so to save our kingdom from an ancient enemy as well as a current one." Ryvan made an imperceptible move towards the hilt of his sword. A gesture that did not go unnoticed by Aran. "If any of you think you can stop me from doing that, you are welcome to try," he looked at Ryvan, whose eyes flickered with a hint of amusement. "No one wishes to oppose you, my king. We only wish to ensure that you remain," Ryvan paused, "focused on the matters at hand. After all, a kingdom without its king is a kingdom on the verge of collapse," he smiled, holding Aran's gaze.

Ryvan's words hung in the air like a threat, and for a moment, the two men stood in tense silence. Before the situation could escalate further, Kasim al-Bahir got up and stepped forward, his hand making a clear, perceptible move towards the hilt of his long blade.

"We do not have time for this," he growled. "Did you not hear our king? The Primordials are coming, and every moment we waste on this nonsense brings us closer to disaster."

Ryvan glanced at Kasim, his expression cool, then turned to face Aran. "Of course," his voice came out silky, yet dubious, "we will not detain you any further, my liege. The council will await your return once you have... settled things."

Aran nodded curtly, then turned and strode dismissively past Ryvan and his advisors, Sura and Rafiq following close behind. He could feel the eyes of his opposers, on the back of his head, as he walked, their whispers like the distant hisses of Sand Serpents in Zarah's dunes. Regardless of the opposition, he would not be deterred. Not by Ryvan, not by the council, and certainly not by the petty politics of the court. His mind was already focused on the path ahead. Finding the next obelisk.

Back in the privacy of his chambers, Aran stood before the great map of the known world, his fingers tracing the locations where Barash said the Weaving would be weakest. The same, from his visions in Valamar.

Each location pulsed with a faint resonance in his mind - echoes of the awakened Memory Obelisk calling to its dormant siblings. The Sea of Ash location seemed to throb with particular urgency, as if the pillar of life itself was crying out for restoration.

The next obelisk, according to the visions from the Sanctum of Knowledge, lay there, in a vast, treacherous expanse of desert where no life could survive, not even the hardiest of shrubs.

Sura sat at a nearby table, poring over the texts, eyes darting across faded glyphs, searching for anything that could lead them forward. "The Sea of Ash has always been considered cursed," she said, not taking her eyes from her studies, "there are legends of entire cities swallowed by the sands and of travellers who vanish without a trace. If the obelisk is there, it must be well protected."

She traced a finger along the ancient text, her voice growing quieter. "The pillar of life doesn't just govern creation - it maintains the balance between growth and decay. Without it properly anchored, even the living lands we have passed through will begin to wither. The trembling ground beneath our horses' hooves, the fearful wildlife - they sense what we are only beginning to understand."

"Nothing worth doing is easy in life," Rafiq muttered from his place by the window. He polished his swords with slow, habitual precision, though his gaze drifted to some future battle not yet fought. "Still, we are going to need more than just maps and legends. If the Primordials know what we are doing, they will be waiting for us."

"They will be waiting either way," Aran replied, his voice grim. "If we do not mend the remaining obelisks, the Weaving will collapse and, whether we want to or not, the Primordials will end up consuming everything." He paused, the words heavy between them. "They are not merely destroyers," he added quietly. "They are the ends of all things... and perhaps, though I cannot yet say why - what comes after."

Sura was silent for a breath, the weight of his words settling around them. Then she spoke, her voice low but steady. "It would make sense," she confirmed. "The Sea of Ash was once a thriving region, before your ancestors desperately struck their pact with the Primordials. According to my studies - guided in part by Barash - the obelisk that lies there is tied to the pillar of life, representing not just creation, but the full cycle: decay, death, and renewal. If we can restore it, it might slow the unravelling, and buy us time to find the others."

"What of the final obelisk?" Aran's gaze flicked back to the map.

Sura hesitated before answering. "That one... is different. The information in the old texts we found at Valamar is unclear, but it is said to be the Obelisk of Death - the most powerful of them all. It lies somewhere beyond the borders of the known world, in a place where the Weaving no longer holds sway."

Aran's blood ran cold. "Do you mean to say it lies beyond this world? What does that even mean?" His mind reeled.

"It does," Sura said quietly. "It is a realm that exists apart from the Weaving, akin to the Echo of Worlds - a dominion of the Primordials. If we are to fully restore the balance, we will have to venture there."

Rafiq let out a low whistle. "Sounds like a death sentence."

Aran was silent, his thoughts turning like a storm. The idea of venturing once more beyond their world - into the heart of the enemy's dominion - was daunting. And yet, if the obelisks were the key to salvation, they would have to go wherever the Weaving demanded. "Let us deal with the Sea of Ash first," he said at last, his voice resolute. "Then we shall face whatever comes next."

Later that evening, Aran convened a meeting of his closest advisors. The great hall of the palace was dimly lit, casting long shadows over the faces of those gathered. Sura, Rafiq, and several of Aran's most trusted commanders sat around the crescent table, their expressions grim as they discussed the coming journey.

Before they could begin planning in earnest, the doors to the hall swung open, and Ryvan strode in, flanked by several minor tribal leaders.

He moved with the confidence of a man who knew he was in control of his minions, his eyes gleaming with barely concealed arrogance.

"My king," Ryvan voiced, inclining his head in mock respect. "I trust you are preparing for your next venture into the unknown?"

Aran met Ryvan's gaze with cold determination. "We are," he leaned in. "The next obelisk lies in the Sea of Ash, located in Zarah's southern hemisphere, and we will need no short amount of time and resources to reach it."

Ryvan smiled, though it did not reach his eyes. "Of course... if you must," he smirked. "However, in spite of your reveries, there are those in the council who believe that perhaps... we should reconsider this course of action."

Though his fists clenched, Aran's voice held firm. "Reconsider?"

"There are concerns," Ryvan continued smoothly. "Concerns that pursuing these ancient relics may be doing more harm than good. The people are frightened, and the council is growing restless. We fear that by awakening these obelisks, you may be inviting the Primordials to strike sooner than they otherwise would."

Ryvan opened his arms, as if representing the entirety of the council. This presumptuous gesture triggered immediate outrage. "Speak for yourself!" Kasim, Safira and the rest of Aran's most fervent supporters shouted, almost in unison.

The king raised a hand, his eyes narrowing. "So, Ryvan, after all our deliberation, you are of the opinion that we should do nothing?! Let the world fall apart while we idly sit back? Is that what you are suggesting?" Aran's eyes bored down on his opponent's.

Ryvan brought his hands together, in a gesture of false concern. "Caution is a virtue, my king. The obelisks wield unfathomable power, and many fear that in awakening them, we are not preventing disaster, but hastening it. The council," Ryvan pressed, then paused as he surveyed the room, noting Kasim's defiant posture and the other loyal supporters. With a slight smile, he adjusted his approach. "That is to say, I merely wish to ensure that we do not inadvertently hasten our own demise."

Before Aran could respond, Kasim slammed his fist on the table, rising to his feet with a snarl. "Enough of this cowardice! The Primordials are coming whether we awaken the obelisks or not. If we do not act, we will all be doomed!"

Rafiq, who had been silent, took a step forward from behind Aran. "Lord Kasim is right." As a proud member of the Bahir, Rafiq was loyal to his tribal leader, having fought beside him countless times.

Ryvan's gaze shifted from Kasim to Rafiq, his expression icy. "You forget your station, commander. Policy is not decided by those who know only the language of steel - however eloquently they may speak it." Rafiq was about to open his mouth to retort, when Aran held up a hand, gesturing for his friend to remain calm.

He turned to face Ryvan, his voice cold and commanding.

"You seem to be forgetting your place," he intoned, with absolute authority. "I am the king, Ryvan - I will decide what course of action we take. The council's role is to advise, not to dictate." Aran let this last word hang in the air, and its effect did not go amiss.

Looking his political opponent in the eyes, he concluded. "If I am to be blamed for all of my kingdom's failures, then I must also be burdened by the choices that led us there. You would give me leniency on that, yes?" Aran asked, his voice heavy with sarcasm.

Ryvan's eyes flashed with anger, but he kept his voice calm. "Of course, my king. Still, I would caution you not to underestimate the power of the council. There are many who believe that your obsession with these obelisks may be clouding your judgement. Because of that, they may not be so willing to blindly follow you into the unknown."

Aran stood up and stepped forward, his gaze piercing as he stared his opponent down. "Then let them stay behind, as I am sure you will." Ryvan flushed with anger at the comment, but remained silent.

Aran continued, unperturbed. "I will not be swayed by fear or politics. The obelisks remain the key to saving our world, and I will not abandon that path, even if it leads to my death," he locked eyes with Ryvan. "Are you willing to make such a sacrifice yourself?" Aran asked, his voice like steel drawn in quiet defiance. "Would you lay down your life - not for ambition, but for the people you claim to serve?" The question hung in the air like a blade.

For a moment, the two men stood in silence, their eyes locked in a battle of wills. Finally, Ryvan inclined his head, though his expression remained unreadable.

The months of Aran's absence had given him time to plant seeds of doubt - not through lies, but through careful emphasis on uncomfortable half-truths. The king's quest had already cost them resources, allies, and stability. How much more would it demand?

"As you wish, my king. Yet, know this - power does not protect a ruler from those who see clearer paths, for even kings may find themselves walking darker roads than they intended." With that, he turned on his heels and strode outside the hall, his newfound political entourage following close behind.

Aran watched him go, then spoke, his voice clear and unwavering. "The obelisks remain our only salvation, Ryvan," Aran said, his voice like quiet steel. "If you cannot see that, then step aside - there are others who will not falter."

The doors closed behind his opponents with a weight that seemed to echo through the chamber. Aran let out a slow breath, his fists still clenched. He knew that Ryvan and his supporters were a threat but, for now, he had more pressing concerns. The obelisks had to be mended, and time was running out. "We leave at dawn," he said quietly, turning to his companions. "The Sea of Ash awaits."

Chapter XXVI

The Calm Before the Storm

The night air was crisp, carrying faint scents and fragrance from the gardens of the Lunar Citadel, blending with the ever-present aroma of sand and spices that clung to the streets of Sarim. The city stretched below, like a sprawling ocean of sandstone and silver, its domed rooftops gleaming beneath the celestial light of Anar and Nysa, the twin natural satellites watching over Zarah's night skies since time immemorial.

A gentle breeze whispered through the open arches of the royal balcony, rustling the folds of Aran's cloak as he gazed upon the city. From this high vantage point, he could clearly distinguish the winding streets, the bustling markets closing for the night, the distant torches that lined the walls of the Outer Ward, where Kasim's Bahir warriors stood at their posts, their shields reflecting the moonlight.

Yet, despite the serenity of the moment, he could also sense the nervousness beneath the city's apparent veneer of peacefulness. Whispers were spreading throughout the city - the Primordials, the House of Draco.

Aran could not lie to himself either, for shadows also loomed over his thoughts. What would he find at the Sea of Ash? Could he protect his kingdom from the threats looming over it? Since his defeat, Drathis' silence was more than unsettling. The Draconian Warlord had not yet brought full scale war to his doorstep, but Aran could feel it coming.

It was, in every way, ironically similar to the threat the Primordials represented - a storm gathering beyond the dunes, silent but albeit relentless.

Unable to sleep, Sura decided to join him on the balcony. She would have almost taken him by surprise, if not for the soft jingle of the golden bangles on her wrists. "Finding it difficult to embrace the veil of rest?" Aran asked, still gazing at the horizon.

Sura placed her hands on the stone railing beside his, her shoulder brushing his as her eyes swept the sleeping city below.

She studied him in silence. "You are restless," she said at last, her voice quiet - but the concern beneath it did not go unnoticed.

Aran exhaled slowly, his fingers tightening around the edge of the balcony. "According to your spies - the few that survived - Drathis has failed to claim hold of the Primordials with his ancient summonings," he mused, watching, as a caravan of traders made its way toward the city gates below, their desert steeds silhouetted against the flickering torches. "I know him," he rubbed his beard, absent-mindedly. "After his last defeat at our gates, along with your report of his recent setback, you must know that will not sit well with him." His gaze seemed to be lost in the horizon again. "Drathis is too proud and will not so easily accept defeat."

Sura tilted her head slightly, but her gaze never left him. "So, you are absolutely sure he will attack Sarim again?"

Aran was looking at the moons, the expression on his face would have been unreadable to anyone else on Zarah - except to her.

His following words only confirmed Sura's darkest fears. "Use your senses. We both know his nature, therefore we both know his will."

Silence settled over them, but it was a calm silence, a peaceful one, stretching as wide as the dunes that pervaded throughout Zarah.

As soft as the night breeze in Arsian lands, Sura spoke again, her words measured as she clasped his hands. "You know that I will stand by your side, no matter what," her eyes were glistening. "You do not have to carry all of the burden upon your shoulders. I can help you carry some of it, if you wish."

Aran turned to look at her, and for a moment, he saw something unspoken in her gaze. It was something that went beyond loyalty, beyond friendship, even beyond love - a kind of understanding that could only be achieved through battle, through trust, through loss. Only those who had struggled together through life's tribulations could begin to grasp its elusive significance.

He also saw what seemed to be threads of something else in her eyes, but he pushed that thought away - there would be time for that later, if they made it out alive.

"I know," he admitted, moved by her undying support. "Regardless, I must face him head on. It is my duty as king."

Sura studied him for a long moment before nodding. "Then you should prepare yourself for when the time comes." Before either of them could speak further, a distant sound shattered Zarah's night stillness.

A deep, thundering horn. The air shifted as the bells of Sarim rang out in warning, their sonorous toll reverberating through the city streets.

In the distance - ominously - the first fires began to rise.

Within mere moments, the tranquillity of Sarim was gone. Shouts echoed through the streets. The Bahir soldiers guarding the Outer Ward mobilized, their sand serpent scale armour glinting as they rushed toward the gates.

Torches flickered wildly, illuminating the frantic movements of merchants who hurried to secure their goods, of civilians ushering their children into the safety of their homes.

In the courtyard of the citadel, warriors were already assembling. Kasim al-Bahir stood at the forefront, his large curved blade resting over his shoulder, barking orders to his men. His crimson war-cloak billowed behind him as he turned to face Aran and Sura, who had descended from the balcony with swift urgency.

"Scouts spotted movement in the eastern dunes," Kasim reported, his voice steady despite the commotion. "Drathis has arrived!" He stood ready, no matter the odds.

"How many?" Sura asked. She had already removed her bangles and was fastening leather bracers on her wrists. Kasim's expression, despite his bravery, darkened. "Too many, I fear."

At that moment, Karim al-Shamar, his robe dishevelled from being pulled hastily over his armour, rushed into the courtyard, clutching a series of parchment maps. "The Draco are not wasting any time," he shouted, adjusting his silver-rimmed spectacles. "They have siege engines. Catapults. I saw them from the observatory."

Safira appeared from the corner of the courtyard, moving with ghostlike grace, her silver hair catching the wind. She carried her Solarwood Crescent Bow over her shoulder, the silver inlaid carved runes on its limbs, glowing faintly under the light of the moons.

"The stars had foretold this," she murmured, her voice like the whisper of distant sands. "I was warned they would be back. The storm I spoke of has come."

Aran turned, facing his gathered allies, the strongest warriors in Zarah, the ones who had stood beside him through thick and thin. "Then we meet it head-on," he said, his voice calm, unyielding.

As the Draconian war horns echoed across the valley, announcing the arrival of Drathis and his army, the king drew his father's sword. The Battle for Sarim, for Zarah, had begun.

For a moment, time held its breath, the vast desert stretching out beneath the cold glow of Anar and Nysa, the only sound was the wind whispering through the dunes like a warning of what was to come. From the high ramparts of Sarim, Aran stood motionless, his sharp eyes fixed on the darkened horizon. He could see them now, thousands upon thousands of Draconian warriors, their black armour glinting in the moonlight, their banners rippling like the wings of carrion birds.

At their centre, mounted upon his obsidian-scaled war beast, was Drathis, the High Inquisitor and Warlord of the Draco, his crimson cloak billowing behind him like the shadow of death itself.

Beside him, rode Vhaskar, his first lieutenant, a titan clad in blackened steel. His massive war hammer resting against his shoulder, his glowing tyrian purple eyes fixed upon the city like a predator watching wounded prey. Mounted on a formidable warrior beast, he was indeed a force to be reckoned with.

Behind them, the siege engines loomed, their towering forms silhouetted against the night sky, their weapons ready to unleash fire and ruin upon Sarim.

Karim al-Shamar fidgeted with his silver-rimmed spectacles, as he stood beside Aran on the battlements. Looking upon the battlefield, he studied the enemy formations with an analytical gaze, his military mind already racing. "They are positioning their siege weapons," he murmured as he turned to his king - urgency coating his words, as he shouted. "My liege, we await your orders!"

Aran exhaled, his grip tightening around the hilt of his sword. "Drathis is not the kind to waste time, is he?" Instantly, as if the warlord had heard him, the Draconian war horns sounded.

A deep, thunderous roar, rolling across the dunes like the voice of an ancient beast, shaking the stones of Sarim's walls. Time stood still - then came the first strike.

The Draconian siege weapons fired in unison, their synthsteel war catapults launching projectiles wrapped in alchemical fire. From the walls, the defenders watched as the night sky ignited. The first wave of destruction arced toward them like a shower of falling stars, each round carrying death. "Brace yourselves!" Karim al-Shamar shouted. "Impact incoming!"

The first shot struck the eastern watchtower, its massive frame shattering into a hail of stone and fire, sending the defenders stationed there screaming into the depths below.

The walls trembled, dust and rubble cascading down onto the streets of Sarim. Desperate screams echoing across its streets. Another projectile crashed into the lower district, smashing through the Solarwood rooftops of the market square, igniting the stalls, setting the heart of the city ablaze.

The flames spread instantly, engulfing the cactus-silk canopies, the wooden carts and the goods of merchants who had, just an hour ago, filled these streets with life. Civilians who had not yet reached safety, fled through the city's alleys, running for their lives - their terrified screams pierced the night.

From the ramparts, Aran clenched his jaw, watching as the city began to burn. Below him in the artillery section, he spotted Karim organizing the defenders. "Karim," he shouted. "It goes without saying that you have my permission to fire away!"

"Solar disruptors at the ready," Karim ordered his men. "Fire!" His voice resounded through the battlements. The engineers of the Shamari rushed to their bronze-plated artillery, their hands moving with mechanical precision as they activated the golden cores of their solar weapons.

The first disruptors hummed to life, their energy building into a blinding golden glow, illuminating the night. "Target the siege towers!" Karim called. "Send the Draco back where they belong!"

The first defensive shot tore through the night, a beam of concentrated sunlight, striking the front of the closest Draconian siege tower. The synthsteel plating, despite its usual resisting qualities, melted on impact. The concentrated sunlight tore through it and, within moments, the structure exploded from within, sending Draconian warriors plummeting into the sands.

One after the other, the siege towers fell to the power of Sarim's disruptor cannons. The defenders cheered, but their celebration was short-lived, for the enemy had expected this.

Drathis sat atop his war beast, watching as his siege towers collapsed in a fiery ruin, but his expression did not change.

The Warlord turned to his field commander, a scarred Draconian captain, his red-plated armour still stained from the last time they attacked the city - this particular captain was responsible for many of the enemy's casualties during that battle.

"Send in the first wave," Drathis ordered. The disfigured captain nodded once, then raised his clawed hand, signalling to the waiting infantry divisions. "Forward!" his voice was cold as the depths of Zarah's remaining ocean.

Following his command, thousands of obsidian-clad warriors moved in unison, their ranks precise and disciplined, their collective movement resembling a dark, Yaran tide surging toward the city gates.

At the head of the charge were the Chimaera War-Beasts, their twisted reptilian forms thundering across the sand, their serpentine tails lashing, their fangs glistened with venom.

From the walls, Safira, perched atop the highest watchtower, narrowed her eyes. "Archers!" she called, drawing her bow. "Aim for their mutated beasts!"

The Rasha archers loosed their arrows, the projectiles whistled through the air, striking the Chimaeras in their exposed flesh. Most fell, in the first salvo, their massive bodies collapsing into the sand, but quite a few insisted - their hides were too thick, their fury too great.

One of these monstrous creatures, twice the size of a Desert Steed, lunged toward the walls, its claws digging into the stone, climbing the ramparts with terrifying speed.

"Here they come," Sura shouted, drawing her twin daggers. "Let them, we are ready!" Though doubt ate at her, she stood, steadfast.

One Chimaera reached the top of the wall, its glowing eyes locking onto the nearest warrior. Despite the man's best efforts, the beast's massive jaws closed around his torso, lifting him into the air before crushing his body beneath its fangs, blood spraying against the stone.

Aran didn't hesitate. Having escaped death by an inch, as the creature lunged at one of his warriors, he surged forward - his movements precise, his sword flashing, cleaving through the beast's exposed flank, slicing deep. The Chimaera beast shrieked, twisting in pain, but before it could retaliate, an arrow struck its skull, fired by Safira from the upper battlements of Sarim.

The creature collapsed, its massive form slumping over the edge of the rampart, falling back into the chaos taking place below. Unrelenting, more Chimaeras were coming forth, and beyond them, Drathis' legions pressed forward. Large Draconian warriors, of the Varros bloodline, were closing in, with siege battering rams, nearing the gates. Karim al-Shamar, standing near one of the solar disruptors, wiped the sweat from his brow, his mind racing, his spectacles fogging. "We cannot hold forever," he yelled, "our batteries are waning."

Aran, still trying to catch his breath, looked over the battlefield. Not for the last time that night, did he feel the weight of his crown pressing upon his head and shoulders - heavy with unpaid debts.

The walls of Sarim had stood for over three millennia - long before Aran's dreams of a unified Zarah. Its towering sandstone fortifications had been weathered by time and war alike.

The city had repelled invading forces many times over: raiders from the east, warlords from the north, even the House of Draco - once before, and not so long ago, in its storied history.

Still, never had they faced an army like this. The Jewel of the Northeast desperately screamed in pain. Its massive iron-bound gates trembling under relentless assault from Draconian battering rams. These devices, plated in obsidian and reinforced with synthsteel, kept striking with earth-shaking force - each impact sending cracks spider webbing through the ancient Solarwood.

On the walls, Karim al-Shamar, ever the strategist, moved among his engineers, directing the defences with precise calculations and unwavering focus. "Steady!" he called, his confident voice cutting through the chaos. "Wait for them to cluster!"

Below them, the Draco forces surged forward, their formations precise, methodical. One of the remaining siege towers rolled toward the walls, desperately pushed by Chimaera beasts, their mutated forms heaving beneath the weight of the war machine.

Karim's ever watchful eyes narrowed. "Bring it down!" he ordered.

The solar disruptor atop the southern watchtower, manned by Umar al-Shamar - youngest of Karim's engineers - hummed to life, its golden core pulsing with concentrated energy. The weapon let loose a lance of searing light, cutting through the night like a second sun. The beam pierced the Draconian siege tower's core, sending a shockwave through its frame before it exploded in a violent inferno, sending flaming debris crashing onto the battlefield, spreading chaos.

Sarim's defenders cheered, but the enemy did not falter - more siege towers loomed in the distance. The Varros battering rams struck the gates again - the city's walls would not hold much longer.

If Sarim's walls were its shield, then, that fateful night, Kasim al-Bahir became the city's sword. The proud tribal leader, though having passed his younger years, still fought with the spirit of ten men.

The Bahir cavalry, mounted on onyx coloured desert steeds, bred for war, formed a crescent formation within the outer wards, waiting for the precise moment to counter the Draco advance.

Kasim, with his ornate curved blade resting on his back, watched the battlefield with the gaze of a seasoned warrior.

He saw it clearly. The tide of war, the ebb and flow of blood and steel. A formation shift. A moment of hesitation from the enemy. The perfect time to strike. "Ride with me!" Kasim roared, his voice a battle hymn. "For Zarah - for Aran!"

The Bahir cavalry thundered forward, their spears aimed low, their steeds kicking up clouds of sand and smoke. The Bahir cavalry hit the enemy's army flank like a desert storm, shattering the front lines, their blades carving through the black armour of the Draconian legions.

Kasim rode ahead, his blade flashing like fire in the night, cutting down three warriors in a single sweep.

A badly scarred Draconian captain, wearing red-plated armour, lunged at him. His polearm arced toward Kasim's chest, but the experienced Bahir warrior twisted in the saddle, cleaving through the scared enemy's torso, sending the body crashing to the ground.

Kasim's cavalry fought fiercely, though they could not break the enemy's forces. From the dunes beyond the city, more horrors were approaching. A loud, collective roar shook the battlefield. The ground trembled as

Drathis unleashed more Chimaera mutations, their massive, reptilian bodies moving with unnatural grace, their twisted limbs ending in deadly razor-sharp claws.

The beasts charged, fangs dripping from the blood of Sarim's fallen warriors, their glowing red eyes burning with rage. Evolution, meddled with genetically, resulting in pure, insatiable hunger.

One Chimaera, twice the size of his steed, barrelled toward Kasim's cavalry, its claws tearing through steed and rider alike. Kasim pulled hard on his reins, narrowly avoiding the creature's charge. His mount reared back, but the Bahir warlord held firm, his muscles still toned from countless years of battle.

As the beast struck, Kasim reared his steed around, then brought his blade down in a diagonal arc, striking the beast's thick hide - his sword bit deep, but the Chimera did not fall. Instead, it turned on him, its jaws snapping forward. Death was a second away, but before it could sink its fangs into Kasim's throat, an arrow whistled through the night, striking the creature between its glowing eyes.

From Sarim's rooftops, Safira and the Rasha archers fired another volley, their arrows glowing alight. The Chimaera screeched, thrashing wildly before collapsing onto the sand, its final breath escaping in a death rattle.

Sarim's moon seer, perched upon the ruins of a broken Minare tower, whispered a prayer to Anar and Nysa, then nocked another arrow. "Keep firing!" Safira called to her archers. "Either we hold this city, or we die with it!"

At that moment, with a deafening bang, the Varros battering rams broke through the city gates. The scent of burning wood, scorched stone, and blood choked the air as Drathis' forces pushed deeper into the heart of the city. Its once-vibrant streets, filled with traders and merchants under golden canopies, suddenly became a graveyard of fire and shadow. The clash of steel rang like war drums, echoing through the alleyways. Screams of the wounded were mixed with the battle cries of warriors - their voices rising in defiance against the unstoppable tide of obsidian-clad invaders.

At the heart of the bloodshed, Aran ibn Khalid, King of Zarah, fought with the fury of a storm given flesh.

The battle raged on, Sarim's streets running red with the blood of the fallen, both human and Draconian alike.

Sura fought beside him, her twin daggers flashing, weaving between enemy strikes, cutting down warriors with deadly efficiency. "More coming from the east!" she shouted, kicking the legs out from under a Draconian warrior, then driving a blade through his chest.

Aran, standing amidst the carnage, took a brief moment to assess the battlefield. The walls were failing. The defenders were being pushed back - yet, they still stood, defiant.

From the northern passage, Karim and his engineers unleashed another disruptor blast, the golden beam tearing through an advancing siege engine. From the southern square, Kasim and the cavalry continued their relentless assault, their numbers dwindling, but their spirits unbroken. From the rooftops, Safira and the Rasha archers kept raining death from above, holding key vantage points, preventing the Draconian forces from fully surrounding the city's defenders.

In the heart of the battle, Aran stood unyielding, his armour was slick with blood, his father's sword gleaming like dawn itself. Drathis had thrown everything at them - still, Sarim endured.

The air was thick with the stench of blood, smoke, and steel, the distant screams of the wounded merging with the clash of battle. The streets ran red beneath the silver glow of Anar and the pale radiance of Nysa. The twin moons watched in silent judgement as the House of Aran and the House of Draco waged war.

Drathis moved through the carnage like a spectre, his blackened greatblade slicing through warriors with effortless brutality. Beneath his obsidian armour, his muscles tensed with each kill, his movements precise, unforgiving. This was not simply a battle - it was a reckoning. The people of Sarim fled in terror before him, his mere presence filling them with dread.

His crimson cloak billowed behind him, torn and scorched from the fires raging through the city. The silver serpent sigil of Nathair gleamed upon his chest, smeared with blood, both from his enemies and his own warriors. His eyes, dark as a starless abyss, scanning the battlefield, looking for his nemesis, until he found him.

Standing amidst the ruins of a broken courtyard, Aran, Zarah's 'boy-king', awaited him.

Drathis slowed, exhaling a quiet chuckle, his fingers tightening around the hilt of his blade. "Remember the day I offered you power?" he asked, sardonically. "You should have taken my offer, and tonight you should have run for your life," he murmured, stepping forward - his voice, deep, a serpent's hiss. "Or, you should have let the sand swallow you when you had the chance."

Aran did not move. His eyes ablaze, his bearded face set with quiet defiance, his bloodied sword gleaming in the moonlight. His dark hair was matted with sweat and dust and his armour was dented from the battle, yet still he stood, unshaken, unbroken. As he cleaned his father's blade, he looked Drathis in the eyes. "I do not run from cowards who hide behind monsters," he said, his voice calm, but edged with steel.

Drathis smirked. It was a slow, knowing smile. "Then let us see if you can fight like a king."

They clashed. Drathis struck first with a brutal downward slash, meant to split Aran in half. Honed to martial excellence, Zarah's king was faster. Sidestepping the blow, his blade flashed like desert lightning, slicing toward Drathis' exposed side. The Draconian warlord twisted, deflecting the strike at the last moment, their swords colliding with a shower of sparks.

The force of the impact sent a shock wave through the courtyard, the air ripping apart with sheer kinetic energy. Aran pressed forward, his movements fluid, precise. His father's blade danced through the air, in a series of relentless strikes aimed to pierce the armour of the one who sought to tear his kingdom apart.

He met his match, for Drathis was a wall of spinning steel, his blade moving like a black storm, parrying each strike with the calm precision of one who had outlived empires. The longevity of the Draconians had forged him into a master of war. "You fight well, boy." Drathis taunted, his hissing voice laced with amusement. He pushed forward, forcing Aran back, their blades ringing through the empty streets. "But I have crushed warriors greater than you beneath my heel."

Aran slid back, steadying himself. "Then you should have no trouble beating me, should you?" Drathis snarled and lunged again.

They fought like gods made flesh - their weapons colliding in a battle of light versus darkness.

Aran duelled with the grace of the desert winds, his movements precise, fluid, honed. His sword struck like the Nightwing avian diving for its prey, each movement was calculated to exploit a weakness in his opponent's stance.

Kael Drathis fought with unyielding power, his strikes heavy, relentless, meant to break his opponent with sheer force. His blade was akin to an executioner's axe, cleaving through wood, through stone, through air. Through anything that stood in its way.

A ruined fountain crumbled behind Aran as one of Drathis' swings missed him by a hair, the sheer power behind it shattering the ancient marble.

Zarah's king capitalized on the opening, ducking low, his blade tearing through Drathis' shoulder armour, underneath the armpit, drawing upon its edge a thin line of crimson.

Drathis gritted his teeth, staggering back, his left arm now compromised. For the first time that night, the smirk had faded from his eyes. "You do fight like a king," he begrudgingly acquiesced, rolling his shoulders. "However, I do not need you to fight like a king," his slitted eyes darkened, his grip tightening on his blade. "I need you to die like one!"

Drathis surged forward, his strikes heavier, faster, more brutal. He attacked without hesitation, without mercy, his sword crashing down like a tempest made of steel.

Aran struggled to keep up, his breath coming faster, his muscles burning as he deflected each strike. He could feel the sheer strength behind every blow. The raw, unrelenting force of one who had nothing left to lose. Suddenly, without telegraphing his move, Drathis changed his approach. Instead of striking high, he suddenly dropped low, sweeping Aran's legs from beneath him. He hit the ground hard, the impact knocking the air from his lungs.

Drathis loomed over him, his blade raised for the killing blow. "This is the difference between us, boy," he spat, his voice like a death knell. "You fight for an idea," he savoured his next words, "I, on the other hand, fight for a certainty."

He brought his blade down, fast, but Aran rolled to the side, barely escaping the strike as the sword slammed into the stone, splitting the ground where he had just been lying.

As swift as the winds blowing through Kartalia, Aran kicked out, knocking Drathis' knee sideways. The Draco warlord stumbled and, in that instant, Aran struck true.

With everything he had left, he drove his blade into Drathis' side, piercing through the armour, through flesh, through bone. The Draconian grunted in pain, staggering back, blood spilling freely from the wound.

Proud as he was, he did not fall, his slitted eyes burning, and for a brief moment, Aran saw something else in them. Not just rage, not just vengeance, but something unspoken. Something doubtful. "This is not over, boy!" Drathis growled, his wound bleeding profusely. As fast as a Sandfish navigating the dunes, he vanished into the chaos that surrounded them.

Aran remained standing, his chest rising and falling, his fingers tight around the hilt of his father's sword, slick with Drathis' blood.

The city still burned. The Battle of Sarim had raged through the night, the flames of war reflecting off the silver glow of Nysa and the white radiance of Anar. The once-proud city now lay in ruin and chaos, its streets awash with the dead and the dying, the cries of the wounded mingling with the clash of steel and the distant roar of siege weapons tearing through stone.

The city's defenders had fought with relentless fury, but the Draconian legions, bolstered by their Chimaera monstrosities, refused to break, fuelled by the wrath of their warlords.

At the heart of the battlefield, where the firelight cast long shadows over the bloodstained sand, Rafiq stood alone, his twin blades slick with crimson, his breath coming in ragged gasps.

Around him lay the bodies of several Draconian warriors, their black armour glistening with blood drawn by his blades. He was tired beyond belief, and yet, through the inferno of battle, one figure approached.

A large figure, making itself visible through the haze, a giant of a warrior. His form shrouded in black war-plate, his movements were slow, deliberate, like a predator stalking its prey - it was Vhaskar.

His tyrian purple eyes, glowing like smouldering magical embers, locked onto Rafiq with a quiet, unshakable menace. His war hammer, by itself an instrument of raw destruction, rested idly upon his shoulder, its massive head still drenched in the blood of those who had dared stand against him.

Rafiq exhaled, rolling his shoulders, shaking the fatigue from his limbs. He was fast. He was deadly, and he knew it. Still, this hulking mass of Draconian muscle was something else entirely.

"You would be wise to flee, boy," Vhaskar rumbled, his voice deep as the shifting dunes, ancient as the mountains themselves. "You are not ready for me. No man is!" Vhaskar's eyes burned ablaze.

Rafiq tilted his head, grinning through the blood smeared across his face, colouring his beard scarlet. "Then you do not know me at all. Even if I die here, I will make you remember my name," he raised his twin blades, in defiance.

Without warning, Vhaskar moved with terrifying speed for someone his size, his war hammer swinging in a devastating arc, meant to shatter bone and break will.

Rafiq twisted to the side, his blades flashing in unison, from different angles, as he aimed for the gaps in Vhaskar's armour. His steel did meet Vhaskar's flesh, but just barely.

The reptilian goliath turned with inhuman agility. Being able to swing his massive weapon with one hand, he used his free one to grasp for Rafiq, but the swordsman rolled backward, just out of reach. Vhaskar straightened, unamused. "You are fast, I will give you that." He tapped the haft of his hammer against the ground, the vibration cracking the stone beneath him. "However, speed alone will not save you."

Without hesitation, Rafiq lunged again, his swords flashing toward Vhaskar's exposed ribs.

Only this time, the Draconian titan was ready. He sidestepped, pivoting his massive frame with an ease that should have been impossible for a warrior of his size. His hammer came up in a brutal backswing, and Rafiq barely had time to react.

The impact hit his swords, its steel withstanding the blow, but the sheer force of it sent him flying backward, crashing against the ruins of a broken wall. Aside from his bruised back, pain flared through his arms, his fingers trembling from the shock of the blow.

Vhaskar approached slowly, unhurried, the flames of battle reflecting off his eyes, a dazzling combination of amethyst and fire. "You are not like the others," he mused. "You fight like a man who has known struggle. Who has known hunger. I respect that."

Rafiq coughed, pushing himself to his feet. Every part of him ached. "You, on the other hand," he spat blood, "fight like one who does not know what it means to lose, and the lessons one can take from defeat." Gathering his strength, he shouted. "Allow me to teach you!"

Vhaskar's gaze darkened, as Rafiq surged forward, but this time, faster, sharper, more relentless.

His twin swords struck from multiple angles, testing his opponent's defences, seeking the gaps in his footwork, the weak points in his stance. One blade cut across Vhaskar's shoulder, drawing blood. Another grazed his side, leaving a shallow wound beneath the plates of his armour.

Still, the Draconian did not fall. Instead, he laughed out loud. A deep, guttural chuckle, dark and foreboding. "You think you are the first to wound me?" Vhaskar asked, his voice tinged with amusement. "You think you are the first to believe that speed will always beat strength?"

Rafiq ignored the taunt, launching another assault, but this time, Vhaskar caught him mid-strike. His massive hand closed around Rafiq's wrist, the sheer pressure enough to send pain lancing up his arm. Then, with a single, brutal motion, Vhaskar drove his knee into Rafiq's ribs. The impact was thunderous, the sound of cracking armour echoing through the battlefield. Rafiq gasped, his vision blurring from the force of the blow. He staggered back, clutching his side, his breath ragged. Vhaskar did not advance - he was savouring the moment. "You fight well," the Draconian admitted. "But I am simply too much for you to handle."

Rafiq clenched his jaw, refusing to fall to his knees. "Then you'd better kill me, because I will never yield!" Vhaskar tilted his head. "No, I don't think I will. You are too valuable an opponent for that."

From beyond the walls of Sarim, Drathis' retreat horn sounded. Severely wounded, he was calling his waning forces back. Vhaskar glanced toward the outer walls, his expression unreadable.

Rafiq, still breathing heavily, still aching, lifted his swords. "If you are leaving, then you better start running," he taunted, despite the pain he was in. Vhaskar exhaled, the purple light in his eyes flickering. "We shall meet again!" His voice was low. With astonishing speed, he vanished into the retreating army.

Rafiq stood amidst the bodies of the fallen, his chest heaving, his body aching from the wounds Vhaskar inflicted upon him. The city was still burning, but the battle was dying out - Sarim had endured.

As Rafiq looked toward the ruins of the Outer Ward, where his warriors gathered amidst the destruction, where his lifelong friend, his king, stood victorious, he knew one truth above all others - this war was not over yet. He touched his ribs, feeling the deep bruises, the pain still burning beneath his skin. "I will live," he mused jokingly, "but next time, I must be stronger." Rafiq knew, as any experienced warrior would, that this had not been the last he would see of Vhaskar.

Anar and Nysa's pearly radiance washed over the battle-worn city, painting the sky in hues of silver, casting long shadows over the smouldering remnants of war. The streets that had, mere hours ago, thrived with life, bustling with merchants, storytellers, and wandering minstrels, were now choked with the bodies of the fallen. The scent of smoke, blood, and dust clung to the air, mingling with the faint traces of the Lunaris flower that had somehow survived the devastation.

The walls of Sarim, though still standing, bore deep scars from the battle, with massive cracks spider webbing through the stone, remnants of the Draconian siege engines that had battered them through the long night. The great iron gates of the city hung partially open, their wood splintered and blackened, their frame still smouldering from the siege fire.

Atop the ramparts, stood Aran, his eyes scanning the ruins below. His sword was still in his grip, though its edge was dull now, the once-gleaming blade was stained with the blood of countless foes. His armour was broken in places, his cloak tattered, but he stood tall - unbroken. Yet, the weight of victory pressed upon his shoulders. Sarim had endured. But at what cost?

Throughout the city, the survivors moved among the wreckage, searching for the living, mourning the lost. The warriors of the Bahir, the Shamari, and the Rasha worked tirelessly, pulling bodies from the rubble, offering prayers for the departed.

Kasim al-Bahir knelt at the base of the citadel steps, his bloodstained hands resting upon the hilt of his curved sword. His once-proud crimson war-cloak was now ripped and soaked with sweat, his dark eyes shadowed by exhaustion.

He looked up as Aran approached, his voice gravelly from battle. "We held," he said simply, his words carrying the weight of the long night. "Though barely."

Aran exhaled, running a hand through his long, dust-covered, hair, his throat dry. "How many?" he asked, though he feared the answer. The sun made its appearance bathing Sarim in heat.

Kasim glanced toward the rows of bodies being lined along the square, warriors wrapped in white cloth, their names whispered by their comrades as they were carried toward the funeral pyres. "Too many," Kasim murmured. "But not all of them died for nothing."

Aran swallowed hard, his hands curling into fists at his sides. None of the warriors' deaths had been meaningless, but that didn't make their loss any easier to accept.

From behind them, Karim al-Shamar approached, his usual sharp wit dulled by the weight of the morning. His robes were stained with soot, his spectacles cracked, but he still carried himself with the poise of a man whose mind, truly, never stopped working. "The walls will not hold if they attack again," Karim said, rubbing his temples. "We have lost three towers, half the city's water supply is compromised, and the market district..." he sighed, shaking his head. "It is gone, my king." Aran's jaw tightened. Sarim stood, but it was still bleeding.

In the lower districts, the healers of the Ulema Order worked tirelessly, tending to the wounded who lay on makeshift cots beneath torn, burnt canopies. The scent of herbs and incense filled the air, mingling with the coppery stench of blood.

Sura moved among them, her hands stained red, her sleeves rolled up as she pressed cloth to a young warrior's wounds, called Umar al-Shamar. "You were lucky," she told him, her voice calm but firm. "A few inches to the left, and now you would be offering your prayers to the moons instead of lying here complaining about stitches."

The soldier, a boy no older than eighteen, gave a weak chuckle. "I think I prefer complaining."

Sura allowed the faintest hint of a smile, then moved to the next patient. At the far end of the camp, Rafiq sat against a crumbling wall, his sand serpent armour discarded, his bandaged ribs aching with every breath. He watched the healers move, his fingers tapping restlessly against the hilt of his dagger. He had survived his duel with Vhaskar, but the sting of defeat still burned beneath his skin.

Aran found him there, his shadow stretching long in the morning light. "You are lucky to be alive," he said quietly. Rafiq snorted, wincing at the movement. "That makes two of us."
They sat in silence for a moment, both men watching as the city slowly came back to life, as the people of Sarim, though wounded and weary, began to rebuild.
"We held," Rafiq murmured after a long pause, more to himself than to Aran. "But they will be back, will they not?"
Aran's eyes darkened. "Probably. Though I suspect not like they did tonight - we dealt a serious blow to his army. Still," he added, "I doubt we've seen the last of him." Drathis was not finished, he thought - he never seemed to be.
By midday, the fires had been extinguished, and the people of Sarim, battered but not broken, began rebuilding what had been lost. The torn banners of Zarah were mended and raised once more. The surviving warriors stood together, their wounds bandaged, their eyes filled with grim determination. Aran walked amongst them, offering words of encouragement. He looked at his people, at the warriors who had fought beside him, at the citizens who had refused to surrender, and knew that he had to make another hard choice.
The next obelisk awaited, but the Primordials would not wait for him. The Sea of Ash called, yet, to depart now meant leaving Sarim vulnerable. Could he afford to turn his back on his people again and leave them defenceless? Then again, wouldn't staying mean forfeiting the greater battle to come?
That evening, beneath the ruins of the great citadel, Aran gathered his closest allies, Kasim, Karim, Sura, Rafiq, and Safira. Ryvan was nowhere to be seen, his body had not been found. They sat around a war table, the map of Zarah spread before them, the edges still marked with bloodstains from the battle. "As you know, the Sea of Ash holds the next obelisk," Aran began, his voice steady. "If we want to mend the Weaving in time to stop it from unravelling, I must go there." Karim folded his arms. "You are saying that as if you have a choice."
Sura frowned. "You saw what happened tonight. Sarim barely survived this attack. If we leave now, if we take our best warriors with us, what is stopping Drathis from returning and finishing what he started?" Silence fell over them - heavy as a Crystalline Leviathan.
Safira, who had remained quietly observant until now, finally spoke. "The stars have shown me something," she murmured, her eyes distant. "A path filled with darkness. A road that leads to something… ancient. Something waiting." Aran's gaze met hers. "The Primordials?" he asked. She nodded, her eyes grave.

The weight of their journey ahead pressed down upon them. Kasim let out a long breath, rolling his shoulders. "Then I suppose there is only one way we do this." Aran arched his brow. Kasim smirked. "You go to the Sea of Ash and we will stay behind, to protect our people."
A slow, determined smile spread across Aran's lips. "Then, brother, let us finish what must be done."

Chapter XXVII

The Wasteland's Call

The scorching desert held its breath in the aftermath of defeat, silent save for the wind's whispers, which carried along with it the stench of blood, sweat, and burning steel, dragging in turn what remained of Drathis' fighting force.

Once the terror of Zarah, the Draconian army now trudged through the sands like wounded animals, their banners tattered, their war machines smouldering ruins upon the battlefield far behind them.

Kael Drathis led the remnants of his army - though calling it an army now was generous.

Mere hours ago, his obsidian-scaled war beast had stood as a symbol of Draconian might. Now, it limped beneath him, its hide gashed, its breath ragged. As for Drathis himself, he had never felt pain like this.

In the old ways of his House, defeat meant death - better to fall upon one's own blade than endure the shame of survival.

Yet here he lay, breath still filling his lungs, heart still beating its stubborn rhythm. Was this weakness, or was it something else?

His ancestors would have called it cowardice, but perhaps they had never faced an enemy who wielded the very forces of creation itself.

His left arm hung limp at his side, the wound Aran had carved into him burning like molten steel searing his bones. His black armour, once pristine, was shattered and scorched. His crimson cloak was torn, stained so deeply with blood it no longer carried its regal hue.

Yet, the worst of it was not the pain. It was the defeat - the silence. There were no victory songs being sung by his warriors. No boasts of conquest. No sneering declarations of dominance over the weak. Only the sound of boots dragging through the sand.

Unbeknownst to Aran, who was at this very moment back in Sarim dreading their return, the Draconian war machine had been broken.

The Jewel of the Northeast had endured, and the tide of war had turned against Drathis, and against the legacy he sought to carve for his House.

By the time they reached the southern mountain range, located on Zarah's lower hemisphere, as was the Sea of Ash, his once-great Draconian legion had been reduced to a shadow of its former self.

The Temple of Nathair loomed ahead, in the vast distance, an immense underground fortress carved deep into the cliffs, its entrance flanked by massive statues of Draconian kings, long dead now, their expressions cold and merciless in the face of his defeat.

As the wounded filed through the hidden ancient doorway, priests and healers of the Nathair cult rushed forward, ushering the injured deeper into the temple halls. The air was thick with the scent of burning incense, of ritual oils, of old stone that had never known the warmth from Zarah's primary star.

Drathis, barely able to remain upright, slid from the back of his mount. His boots struck the cold stone floor with a dull thud, and for a moment, his vision blurred, the world spinning around him. He clenched his jaw, forcing himself to remain standing, but his knees buckled, and darkness crept at the edges of his vision. The pain was unbearable, but it was not the worst of it - failure was.

The word alone sent a fresh wave of nausea rolling through him. Not just failure on the battlefield, but in his very purpose.

He had called upon the Primordials, and they had dismissed him. He had fought Aran, and the boy had bested him. His warriors, once the unchallenged storm of Zarah, were now broken.

He stumbled forward, catching himself on the stone wall. His own reflection in the polished black obsidian glared back at him, and what he saw sent ice through his veins. This was not the conqueror he had envisioned. This was not the warlord who dreamed he would carve his name into the history of The MiddleVerse.

This was a broken Draconian in shattered armour, a relic of a war he had already lost. He slipped, but before he could fall, a massive hand caught him by his good arm, holding him steady. "Vhaskar, my old friend," he said, feebly.

His first lieutenant, whose eyes burned in the dim light, regarded him with an expression that was neither pity nor concern. Only calculated understanding. "You are too stubborn to die," Vhaskar muttered. "Get inside before you collapse right here. What are you trying to prove?"

Drathis inhaled, swallowing his pride, then exhaled slowly, gathering what little strength he had left. With Vhaskar at his side, providing support, he entered the depths of the temple, where the shadows swallowed them whole.

The Draconian healers stationed at the temple of Nathair, worked tirelessly over the next several days, applying copious amounts of healing membranes to his wounds, along with herbal salves and other alchemical compounds to prevent infection and encourage cellular regrowth. However, no amount of science or primeval magic was enough to heal Drathis' wounded pride.

He now lay within his private chamber, a massive stone hall carved deep into the temple's heart, where blue torches flickered against walls engraved with detailed carvings of ancient Draconian history, dug deep into the very bones of Zarah.

His sword lay against the far wall - within reach, yet untouched.

For the first time in his long life, Drathis felt trapped. Failure had never been an option, and defeat was not something the House of Draco was ever prepared to accept. Yet, it had come for him. Merciless and almost fatal, leaving him to stew in his own shortcomings. Failures that the intergalactic House he was proudly part of, would deem as unforgivable. His warriors were broken, and his war halted. His path to power was shattering before his eyes. Worse still, he had been cast out by the Primordials themselves - thrice over.

Informed by ancient knowledge, gathered by his bloodline, he had tried to dabble with the obelisks in an attempt to influence events to his advantage. He also witnessed their power - hell, he felt it in his bones. He tried bending their power to his will, and for his hubris, had been expelled, discarded like an insect unworthy of their presence or aid. Now, the boy-king walked free, mending the Weaving, defying fate itself.

Drathis clenched his fists. His talons biting deep into his palms, ego getting the best of him until blood beaded at his fingertips. He had lost but, somehow, was not finished. As he sat there, his mind composing the symphony for his redemption, a low rumble of laughter echoed from the doorway. "As always, you are thinking too much."

Drathis turned his head, pain lancing through him - though it would not be the last time. There, in the archway, stood Vhaskar, arms crossed over his broad chest.

The reptilian titan stepped forward, his heavy boots echoing against the stone floor. His wounds were already healing, thanks to his superior genetics, aided by regenerative membranes. His skin had mostly knit itself back together, though scars from his battle with Rafiq still lined his arms. "Glad to see you alive," he uttered as he pulled up a heavy stone chair with ease, lowering himself into it. "Do you know what that means?"

Drathis swallowed his pride - grudgingly, and not for the last time.

"That means you still have choices." The muscular titan rumbled.

Drathis exhaled, closing his eyes for a brief moment. "Choices?" he hissed. His voice was weak and feeble but filled with restrained venom. "What choices do I have left? What options do we have to turn this debacle around?" Drathis spat, his voice low but no less poisonous.

Vhaskar tilted his head, studying Drathis' demeanour. His friend's apparent weakness repulsed him, however he was willing to believe he would recover from this. Hoping to infuse fire into him, he jested. "You could stay here," Vhaskar intoned, as he cracked his knuckles. "Rebuild," crack, "lick your wounds," crack, "regroup what remains of our warriors," crack. "Or maybe, even call upon our House's galactic might for aid," louder crack - his friend said nothing.

Vhaskar's every word was aimed like a blade at Drathis' pride - his ego a battlefield of its own. He was desperately trying to bring the warrior out of him.

He studied Drathis for a long moment, his reptilian gaze unreadable. "Your father would have burned that city to the ground," Vhaskar murmured. He let the silence stretch like a blade drawn slowly from its sheath, watching as the barb found its mark. Vhaskar had learned long ago that the deepest wounds were often self-inflicted - one need only provide the proper knife.

Drathis stiffened - a well-placed dagger between his ribs would not have hurt worse than that comparison. His father - that titan of conquest - who had carved his name across several star systems. What would the old tyrant say to see his heir broken and bleeding in these forgotten halls? "Rise, whelp," came the phantom voice of memory, "or die as you deserve." Perhaps that was what Vhaskar sought to awaken - not just pride, but the ancestral fury that had built their House upon the bones of lesser worlds.

"Yet you live," Vhaskar continued, his voice smooth, deliberate. "Strange, is it not? One who loses a battle and still breathes. That is not how the old ways worked. The weak perished - the strong endured."

Drathis' fingers twitched. "Are you calling me weak?"

Vhaskar grinned, fangs gleaming. "No. I call you alive," he looked at Drathis, "and as long as you live, you can still shape what comes next," he added, with a twinkle in his tyrian purple eyes.

Vhaskar leaned in, lowering his voice. "The boy-king believes he has won. That is his mistake, a fool's mistake. He sits upon his throne, thinking he is safe. Convinced our war is over."

Drathis looked away, jaw clenched. "You think we should march on Sarim again? With what army? We lost."

Vhaskar chuckled. "Not an army. Not this time," he let the silence stretch before adding. "You know what happens when kings are hunted, don't you?"

Drathis opened his eyes, a flicker of interest breaking through his gloom. "Explain."

Vhaskar's snout curled into a faint smirk. "We have lost this war. However, war is not the only way to obtain victory." He leaned back, his massive hands resting on the stone armrests of his chair. After a moment of silence, he finally said it. "Aran bested you. Accept it and move on."

Drathis swallowed hard. Vhaskar's words would not go down easily - sitting like stone in his gut.

The titan's voice rumbled through the chamber. "Yet you lived, and he is still out there, thinking himself untouchable now. Most likely surrounded by his loyal warriors, moving to mend the last obelisks. Aran actually believes he is restoring balance." Vhaskar rolled his shoulders, the joints popping slightly. "Nevertheless, balance is a fragile thing if even kings can be hunted down - and killed."

Drathis' smile widened, his eyes glinting. Vhaskar leaned in. "How about you and I go on the hunt. Like old times." The challenge was set.

Distant memories shook loose, somewhere inside Drathis mind, but he remained still. Pondering. Calculating. Weighing Vhaskar's proposition - kindling the flames.

He still felt his recent failure pressing down on him, but his lieutenant's words had ignited something deep within him. A fire not yet fully extinguished. Not as long as Nathair blood ran in his veins. "If we do this," Drathis murmured, "we do not go after his armies. We do not wage war as we did before."

These were not questions, but rather a complete change in strategy - a departure from the old ways.

"No," Vhaskar said. He could see his inception blossoming in Drathis' mind. "We go after him instead. After his closest companions. We strike at his heart, not his walls." The giant suggested.

Drathis exhaled, a slow, measured breath. He was beginning to feel like himself again. He could clearly see what was ahead of him without any judgement on his failures.

There was no allying with the Primordials anymore. There was no grand conquest awaiting him. However, there was still vengeance, and that was enough for now - it would have to be. Slowly, Drathis sat up, the pain in his body already a distant ache compared to the fury building inside him. He turned to face the Draconian colossus, his gaze dark, but focused. "Then we hunt!" Drathis' eyes were alive again.

Vhaskar grinned broadly. "I was hoping you would say that."

And while Drathis plotted his vengeance in the shadowed depths of the Temple of Nathair, hundreds of leagues to the north-east, beneath the fading stars of Sarim's night, Aran stood upon his balcony - unaware that the hunt had already begun.

The crown's weight had never felt heavier than in these moments of solitude when the voices of advisors fell silent and left him alone with the magnitude of choice. Below, his people moved like ants rebuilding their hill, trusting that their king would shield them from forces they could scarce comprehend. How many rulers throughout history had stood thus balanced upon the knife's edge between salvation and damnation?

Dawn came with a bitter wind, sweeping through Sarim like an omen of what lay ahead and a sombre reminder of what lay behind. As the first rays of sunlight pierced the horizon, the royal palace was already a hive of activity. Steeds were being saddled, supplies being packed, and a select company of warriors hand-picked by Aran's most trusted commanders began their preparations for the long, perilous journey into the Sea of Ash.

The men moved with practised efficiency, yet their eyes lingered upon him with an unease that had not been there before the battle. Where once they had looked upon their king with simple loyalty, now their gazes held something approaching reverence - and fear.

The bulk of the army would remain on Sarim and they were already working hard, rebuilding the city's defences.

Yet, despite the bustle, an air of foreboding, mixed with mourning, lingered over the capital like a dense shroud, thickening the already strained atmosphere.

Aran stood, once more, at the highest balcony of the royal tower. His eyes scanned the horizon, where the remains of the battle still lay scattered. He could see its cost still being paid heavily by those who survived its horrors - Drathis had dealt a murderous blow onto Sarim.

One that would take time to heal. As he observed the city's inhabitants going about their day, as best they could, his mind was divided once more. Stay or leave?

The Sea of Ash was a place spoken of in hushed whispers, where even the most seasoned travellers had disappeared without a trace. The sands were said to swallow people whole, their bones left as relics of forgotten ages. It was a land where no man held dominion, and no law governed the land, except perhaps the forgotten rules of the Old Kings.

Below him, Sarim stretched out in layers of desert stone and flickering banners. The city was, given the circumstances, restless, the people moving like shadows of their former selves across its narrow streets.

After the battle subsided, word of Aran's quest had spread throughout the city like wildfire, as well as rumours of his dealings with forces beyond their mortal comprehension. Because of that, for many of Sarim's inhabitants, their king still remained a figure of fear rather than hope, despite his undying willingness to protect them, displayed splendidly during their last battle.

Sura joined Aran on the balcony, eager to help, to alleviate his grief. Her brow furrowed as she too stared into the remnants of the conflict. She had barely slept, though not because of memories of the recent fighting, for those emotions had already been dealt with. Instead, her mind was consumed by ancient texts she'd spent the night poring over, in search of some lost knowledge that might aid them in mending the next obelisk. She had invested hours trying to unravel this next riddle, but it had proven itself to be almost unsolvable.

Her research had revealed disturbing patterns - ancient expeditions to similar sites, scholars and warriors who had touched the obelisks and been consumed by their promise of power.

The Sea of Ash was a void in the annals of Zarah's recorded history, its secrets locked away in layers of myth and legend. The task ahead of her, of them, remained, at best, a complete mystery

"Are we ready to leave?" Aran's sudden question took her by surprise, his voice low and steady.

"We," Sura brought a hand to her chest, "are as ready as we will ever be," she replied, a kind smile upon her face, though doubts still gnawed at her inner cobwebs. Upon reflecting further, she added. "Yet there is something that still troubles me about the Sea of Ash. About the next obelisk we seek... this one is tied to the concept of life and death. Creation and decay. According to my spies, the sands in that place are not only barren but also corrupted, as if drained of all vitality. Whatever lies there is not just another monolith or artefact of the Old Kings. From what I have gathered from my studies, I fear it might be something far worse than we feared," her tone was foreboding. "We are likely to find something in the Sea of Ash that might end up killing us."

Aran clenched his jaw. He had felt the stirrings of something ancient and malevolent, dwelling in that place, ever since Valamar, since the visions he experienced at the Sanctum of Knowledge. Those visions had shown him glimpses of that obelisks' true purpose, more comprehensive than those he had seen before, and each new revelation seemed darker than the last. Regardless of the challenge ahead of them, at this point, there was no time for hesitation.

The Weaving was unravelling faster than Aran could repair it. Already, strange occurrences had begun to plague the fringes of his domain. Wildfires that would not die, rivers turning to ash, and many of the desert's creatures driven mad by unseen forces.

The balance of their world was teetering on the edge of a blade, and every day Aran delayed was bringing them closer to calamity. "We must press on," he said finally, his voice hardening with resolve. "For reasons that escape me the Primordials have been mostly idle thus far, but we cannot count on them to wait for us to be ready."

Sura nodded, in agreement, though concern shadowed her face. "In the meantime, you should know that Ryvan resurfaced," her eyes unfocused, "wounded, he claims, by Draconian blades."

Aran took a deep breath. "The Snake! Probably already slithering his way towards manipulating the masses," he mused. "That would explain the continuous suspicion, coming from the people."

She took his hands in hers. "The Council still stands with you. Well, those that matter do," she smiled faintly, "but he is watching closely. If we stay away for too long, if we do not return soon, or if something goes wrong... he might use the opportunity to challenge your crown, and try to seize power in your absence. Or worse, start a civil war." Sura's eyes seemed to be lost in the distance. Turning to face him, she confirmed his musings. "You were right. Ryvan's followers are the ones who have been spreading whispers, sowing doubt. If they do seize power, it will fracture our kingdom, and at the worst possible time." Sura's eyes shifted from the distant mountains, in search of his.

A muscle in Aran's jaw twitched, but he kept his gaze on the horizon. "Let them," he tightened his grip on the rail, "If they think they can hold this kingdom together without me, they are welcome to try," his knuckles were turning white. "When the Primordials come, and come they will, Ryvan and his ilk will see how little their scheming matters."

He finally looked her in the eyes. "I can not believe it, Sura. All those hours of council deliberation, for nothing?!" For Sarim to be swindled by another silver-tongued worm?"

She sighed, stepping closer to him, her voice softening. "You must be careful Aran, for we are meddling with powers beyond our ken and comprehension and you are walking a fine line between being a king and something we may not recognize. Listen to yourself," she urged. "Listen to your own words. If you push too hard -"

"I know," he cut her off, his tone quiet but firm. "I know. But I cannot let fear dictate my actions - not now, of all times."

There was a long pause, stretching as vast as Zarah's deserts. The wind whispered between them as they looked at each other, in silence. No more words were required, other than those of acceptance. She placed a hand on his arm, squeezing gently - her eyes, as kind as moonlight. "Then let us finish this together." Aran's eyes answered in silence.

They descended from the tower making their way to the stables, where Rafiq and the rest of their party were already waiting, prepared.

Their march into the Sea of Ash began at sunrise. A journey that, in hindsight, proved itself to be unlike any they had undertaken before. The landscape grew harsher with every passing league, the once-fertile oases of Sarim giving way to a desolate expanse of rocky crags and dead, twisted trees. The very air grew thick and bitter, laden with the dust of ages and the acrid taste of things long dead.

Each breath burned their throats like swallowing ashes from funeral pyres, while the sun's light grew wan and sickly, as though filtered through the shroud of some vast tomb.

The further south they went, the more the land seemed to resist their passage. It was as though the very earth itself had been cursed, twisted by the dark forces that dwelled within the heart of the planet. One night, away from the campfire, as Aran observed the horizon, he glimpsed two silhouettes in the distance. Something about their movement - careful, deliberate, predatory - reminded him of hunters rather than mere travellers. One was massive, the other tall but lean. It couldn't be. Were they being followed? Each time he spotted them, they vanished on second glance, like mirages.

The desert was never truly silent. Even in the dead of night, the wind whispered through the dunes, carrying with it sounds that did not belong. The first time Aran heard it - low, guttural breathing - he dismissed it as the wind against the sand. The second time, he reached for his father's sword.

On the seventh night, it was Rafiq who confirmed his fears. "We are being watched," the warrior murmured, his voice barely audible over the shifting dunes. Aran stiffened. "You saw them too?"

Rafiq nodded grimly. "Two figures. Always distant. Always vanishing when I turn to look." A cold knot formed in Aran's stomach. He had thought, perhaps, that his mind was playing tricks on him. That exhaustion and tension had made him see ghosts in the sand.

Yet, it couldn't have been a coincidence - if Rafiq had seen them as well, then they were not alone.

Two full weeks of frantic travelling passed by, under these conditions, after which they neared the border of the Sea of Ash, and the first signs of decay began to appear. The two figures vanished entirely - perhaps even they feared entering the cursed lands ahead, or perhaps they had found what they were looking for: knowledge of Aran's destination.

The ground cracked beneath their feet, brittle and lifeless. Strange, unnatural formations jutted from the earth. These were blackened spires of stone, their surfaces etched with runes from a language older than most of them had ever seen.

Even their Desert Steeds, born and bred to withstand the harshness of Zarah's deserts, grew uneasy, their eyes wide with fear as they kept refusing to move any further.

On the sixteenth night, while they camped on the edge of a dried-up riverbed, Rafiq approached Aran cautiously, his expression grim.

"I do not like this. Our men are starting to lose their nerve. This place... it feels wrong, tainted, I can feel their resolve waning."

Aran stared into the flickering flames of their campfire, his mind heavy with the weight of his friend's words. He could no longer deny the oppressive atmosphere that clung to them like a second skin.

There was a sense of unnatural stillness in the air, as though Zarah was holding its breath, waiting for something terrible to unfold.

"We have to keep moving," Aran said quietly, though he deeply understood the fear that gnawed at Rafiq and the others following them. "The obelisk is here, somewhere, we have to keep looking. If we turn back now, the Weaving will continue to unravel, and there will be no other way for us to stop it."

Rafiq grunted, his gaze shifting to the dark horizon. "I know that. Still, whatever we find out there... we need to be ready. On our way to this place, it truly felt like we were being followed, and there is no telling what kind of power has been locked away in this place."

Aran nodded encouragingly, though if he was to be true to himself, he was as unsure as Rafiq was, as to what awaited them in the heart of the Sea of Ash. The visions had shown him only fragments, fleeting glimpses of a power so vast and terrible that it defied comprehension.

The following morning, they pressed deeper south-west, into the wasteland, the landscape around them becoming increasingly hostile. The air itself seemed to hum with energy, crackling with an unseen force that set the hairs on the back of their necks standing on end. Strange, distorted shapes appeared in the distance, only to vanish as they drew closer, mirages, leaving behind nothing but the endless expanse of barren sand.

Then, on the seventeenth day, they found the obsidian monolith. It stood at the centre of a vast crater, its dark surface gleaming in the dim light of the sun that barely penetrated the haze.

Taller than the 'memory tether' Aran had encountered in the Broken Expanse, this one stretched into the sky like a blackened pillar of death, its surface covered in intricate carvings that seemed to shift and writhe, as if it were alive. The ground around it was scorched, the very earth charred and broken, touched by a force beyond mortal reckoning.

Sura gasped as she took in the sight, her eyes wide with awe and fear. "I cannot help myself," her voice was but a whisper. "It is both... beautiful, in its own terrible way, and terrifying at the same time."

Aran stepped forward, his heart pounding in his chest as he felt the immense power radiating from the stone needle. It was stronger than anything he had ever felt before. An overwhelming presence that seemed to be pulling at the very core of his being, as though it was trying to draw him closer. "This is it," he whispered, his voice barely audible over the wind that howled through the crater.

Rafiq and the other warriors moved cautiously around the edge of the maar, their weapons drawn as though expecting some unseen enemy to strike at any moment. Yet, there was no movement - no sound other than the wind and the faint, almost imperceptible hum of energy that pulsed from the Primordial prison. As Aran stepped toward it, the very air around it seemed to ripple. The temperature dropped, and a whisper - no, many whispers - began to swirl around them. Faint voices, layered over each other, speaking in a language that made his bones ache to hear. Sura shuddered. "Aran, wait -"

Too late. Even as Sura's warning died upon the wind, Aran's fingertips met the obsidian surface. The stone was neither warm nor cold, but something beyond temperature - a sensation like touching the void between stars. For one heartbeat, the world held perfect silence. Then the carvings blazed to life beneath his palm, and reality shattered like glass cast against stone. The runes pulsed stronger, not just with light, but with something deeper - something alive.

The obelisk's hum grew deeper, no longer the sound of stone, but something that resonated in their bones - the slow, terrible breathing of something that had slumbered since their world was young.

The ground beneath their feet trembled, and the whispers turned to screams. A force alike, yet unlike anything he had ever known yanked him forward, not just in body but also in spirit, and all Aran could see was the dark swirling energy that radiated from the monolith, enveloping him in its terrible embrace.

His next vision came swiftly, in an explosion of light and sound that shattered his senses and sent him tumbling through time and space. Aran saw the Sea of Ash as it had once been - in its heyday.

A thriving kingdom of lush greenery and sparkling rivers, its people living in harmony with the land. Then, unavoidable, came the darkness, cold, hunting for those that struck the pact, creeping in from the edges of the world like a cancer, corrupting everything it touched.

To prevent that from happening, this stone tether had been placed here as a safeguard, a final defence against the encroaching void - too little, too late.

The vision shifted, and Aran saw himself standing at the centre of the Weaving, the threads of the world unravelling around him as the Primordials descended upon Zarah. Once more, he felt their power, their hunger for domination, as well as their fury at being locked away for so long. They were coming, unrelenting, and there was apparently nothing that could stop them.

Aran shouted. "We shall see about that!"

With a gasp, he tore his hand away from the obelisk, his heart racing as he struggled to steady himself. The vision had been clearer this time, more vivid and terrifying than ever before.

He knew now, without a doubt, that the Primordials were not just mere remnants of a forgotten age. They had merely been patient, biding their time, waiting for the right moment to reclaim what they considered theirs. In spite of that, there seemed to be more to the vision, a glimmer of hope buried deep within the darkness. The stone prisons, though very dangerous, held the key to stopping the Primordials. If he could unlock their true power, he might yet have a chance to prevent what loomed on the horizon - but at what cost? A price that now seemed unavoidable.

"Aran," Sura's voice cut through the fog of his thoughts, pulling him back to the present. "What did you see?" She asked, studying every micro expression on his face. Aran did not reply, seemingly, still lost in dark musings.

Guessing the answer to her own question, she pleaded. "Please, do not give into the temptation. That is how they get you!" She reached for his hand.

"Sura," Rafiq asked urgently, "what do you mean by temptation?"

Before Sura or Aran had time to muster a reply, the ground beneath them trembled, a low rumble that sent shivers down their spines.

The obelisk glowed brighter, its runes pulsing with energy as the ground shook violently. Something was coming. Something ancient and terrible, awoken by their presence.

"Move!" Aran shouted, drawing his father's sword as the ground erupted in a shower of ash and stone.

The world around them exploded in a cascade of cinders and dust as the earth heaved open. Aran barely had time to react before a massive shadow loomed over them, the very air growing thick, pressing down like an unseen force crushing his lungs.

What rose from those sundered sands was neither fully of flesh nor wholly of spirit, but something caught between states of being - a paradox given form. Its substance shifted like smoke given weight, like shadow learning to cast light.

A claw - jagged, skeletal, forged from the same dark stone as the obelisk itself - tore its way free. Then another. A body, vast and shifting, coalesced from the sands, its form never settling, shifting between solid and ethereal, caught between worlds. Its eyes burned, twin embers of molten fury, and when it spoke, the words came not through the air but through the very stones beneath their feet, through the marrow of their bones - its voice was not one, but many. "You still think in the confines of flesh and time," the voice rumbled, filling his skull like a storm. "The Weaving was never made to last. It is not breaking, mortal. It is shedding. We warned you before."

Chapter XXVIII

Emberbound

The ground continued to tremble violently beneath their feet as the monstrous form pulled itself free from the ash and rock.

Aran had seen many things, both in his adventures and in the strange visions that had haunted him throughout his life - but nothing had prepared him for this.

The creature that rose from the heart of the Sea of Ash was unlike anything described in the ancient texts that Barash or Sura, or even he had read. Its form was simultaneously alien and strangely familiar, as though it had been born from the very essence of the land itself - or maybe a distant dream from his childhood?

Its body was a grotesque fusion of molten stone and twisting sand, shifting in and out of solidity as though reality itself was struggling to contain it. The sand coiled around its massive frame like living tendrils, its every movement leaving behind trails of black smoke. Where its feet touched the earth, the ground bubbled and cracked, warping under the immense heat. Its voice - if it could even be called a voice - was no mere roar. It was a deep, thrumming vibration, as if Zarah's very bones were screaming in protest.

The creature's eyes, however, were all too real. Two burning orbs of flame that locked onto Aran and his companions with a feral hunger. The air grew hot and heavy as the Primordial beast let out a deafening roar, a sound so deep and powerful that seemed to shake the heavens themselves.

The ground split further, cracks spider-webbing out from its massive feet, revealing the veins of fire that ran beneath the ash.

"Form defensive positions! Watch your flanks!" Rafiq's voice cut through the din, his hands tightening on the hilts of his blades as the combined force of the company scrambled to form a defensive line. Even as Rafiq spoke, it was clear that none of them had ever faced anything like this.

Aran stood at the front of the line, his inherited sword already drawn, the blade gleaming in the strange, sulphurous light that emanated from the beast's form. His heart pounded like war drums in his chest, but fear was a useless emotion now - he had faced death before.

Aran faced visions of his world crumbling, faced the unravelling of the Weaving itself. Yet, nothing - nothing - had ever felt as final as the presence of this creature. This was not just a guardian; it was judgement. A force that did not seek victory but annihilation.

No ordinary foe, no beast of flesh and bone - it was something far older, far more dangerous, a creature that was an echo of the Primordials themselves.

"Aran," Sura's voice was tense but controlled as she moved to his side. The staff Barash had passed on to her was crackling with arcane energy. "I believe it is a guardian," she shouted. "I have read about them. The Primordials must have called it forth, tasked with protecting this place. The old texts spoke of such creatures, but seeing one..."

Aran's jaw tightened as he watched the creature take a slow deliberate step forward. The ground shook beneath its weight.

"Let me guess," he jested, despite the dread that pierced his soul, that icy blade of fear defying the fire that burned in his heart. He gripped his sword tighter. "It will not let us leave without a fight?"

Rafiq, his face set in a grim frown, suggested desperately. "If this thing is tied to the Primordials, maybe destroying the obelisk will -"

"No!" Sura's voice cracked like a whip, her panic momentarily overriding all else. She whirled on Rafiq, her eyes wide with horror. "Do you have any idea what that would do? Destroying it won't kill the creature - it will unmake everything tethered to this land. The Weaving itself would fray, and whatever is left will be worse than death."

Aran nodded curtly to Rafiq. "Calm yourself, brother. Just follow my lead." He had felt the obelisk's power when he touched it. In and of itself a force that connected the very fabric of the world together. "Destroying it is not an option," Aran warned, "unless you want to accelerate the collapse we are trying to prevent?" Rafiq shuddered.

The creature roared again, its molten eyes blazing with hellish fury as it raised one massive arm, its claws glowing with heat as though they had been forged in the heart of a star. With a speed that belied its size, it swung its arm down toward them, the air hissing as the heat seared through the space between them. "This is where we stand!" Aran shouted. "No ground given - no retreat!"

He barely had time to raise his sword, the force of the impact sending him skidding backwards across the ash-strewn ground. His arms trembled from the sheer power of the blow, but he held his ground, his father's sword shimmering with the residual energy of the strike.

"Weapons at the ready!" Rafiq barked, his warriors unsheathed their blades in unison as the creature prepared for another attack.

Time seemed to stretch thin - and in the breath between stillness and fury, Sura remembered her final night in Sarim.

"I am old, but not done yet," Barash said, his eyes glinting. "Trust Aran, but above all else trust in yourself and you shall do fine." She shuddered at these words. Did that mean he wasn't coming with them? Taking notice of her distress, Barash added. "Do not burden yourself unnecessarily, my child. I shall be there by his side when it matters most."

The memory ebbed, replaced by the heat and fury of the battlefield. She blinked, bracing herself anew. The creature's roar tore through the haze and left no room for doubt: the moment had come.

Still unsure of herself, Sura stepped forward. Her eyes narrowed as she raised Barash's staff toward the creature. The air around her crackled with raw power and, with a single motion, she unleashed a torrent of energy toward the beast. It struck its molten chest with a resounding crack, sending shards of stone and sand flying into the air.

For a brief moment, the creature staggered, its form wavering as though it were about to collapse. Then it righted itself, the fissures in its body glowing even brighter as it absorbed the energy, the cracks sealing themselves almost instantly.

"It is drawing power from the obelisk," Sura shouted, frustration clear in her voice, "and we are feeding it!"

Aran cursed under his breath. They were in a deadly stalemate. The creature was too powerful to defeat directly, and any attempt to harm it only made it stronger. Meanwhile, the energy from the obelisk was sustaining it, making it all but invulnerable.

There had to be another way, he thought desperately, as he glanced toward the towering black monolith at the centre of the crater, its surface still pulsing faintly with that ancient energy. The obelisks had to be the key - they always had been. Still, he wondered, how could they manipulate its power without destroying it or, worse, succumbing to its allure?

He turned to Sura, his mind racing. "Might there be a way to sever the creature from the obelisk's energy?"

She paused, her eyes flicking toward the obelisk. "Maybe... If I can disrupt the flow of energy, weaken the link between them..."

She hesitated. "It will take time." Sura didn't voice what they all knew - that time was the one thing they couldn't afford.

The silence that followed between them carried more understanding than a thousand conversations ever could. "Buy me as much as you can!" Her eyes held a promise of a thousand worlds just waiting to be explored. Aran nodded, with a smile, already aware of her intent. "We will keep the creature occupied. Do it!" he shouted.

Rafiq overheard their exchange. He stepped forward, his expression grim but determined. "Do what you can, Sura. We will provide you as much time as possible."

With a quick shared glance of understanding, Aran, Rafiq, the Bahir and the Shamari warriors moved into formation, surrounding the creature on all sides. The beast let out another bone-shaking bellow, its massive limbs thrashing as it sought to crush them under its weight. They fought with the precision and coordination of seasoned warriors, proud sons of the desert, their movements fluid as they dodged and parried the creature's strikes. Rafiq's twin blades wove a deadly pattern, the desert fighting style of his people - strike, withdraw, strike again.

As the beast brought its paw downwards, Aran rolled left, came up in a crouch, and drove his blade upward in his father's signature rising cut. His grip on his sword tightened. The ground beneath them trembled, heatwaves distorting the air as the beast readied another strike. Every instinct screamed at him to attack, to meet its force head-on, but he knew that was exactly what the creature wanted. This was not a battle of strength. It was a war of time. "Sever it!" he shouted.

Sura, meanwhile, had closed her eyes. She was focusing hard, trying her best to remember the knowledge she had absorbed from the scrolls and books they had brought from the Sanctum. Gripping Barash's staff tightly, she began to chant. Her voice, though soft, seemed to echo in the air around them, resonating with the power of the obelisk itself.

The runes on the surface of the black monolith flickered, as if responding to her call, and slowly, ever so slowly, the flow of energy between the obelisk and the creature began to wane.

The process was far from easy. With each moment that passed, the creature's attacks grew more desperate, its movements more erratic as it sensed the disruption in its connection to the obelisk. It lashed out wildly, its molten claws striking the earth with enough force to send tremors through the ground.

Two of Rafiq's warriors were thrown backwards, their swords shattered as the creature's claws cut the air.

Rafiq's jaw tightened as he saw Hakim clutch his broken arm, while young Yasir struggled to rise from where the creature's blow had hurled him against the crater's edge. "Fall back to the perimeter!" Rafiq commanded, his voice carrying both authority and barely contained worry for his men. "Sura, we are running out of time!" he shouted, his swords flashing as he struck at the creature's leg, trying to draw its attention away from her.

Aran moved with practised precision, his blade cutting through the suffocating air as he dodged the creature's increasingly desperate attacks, each movement a dance between life and death.

Yet, even with all his skill, he could feel the strain taking its toll. The heat from the creature's molten body was smothering, and the ash-filled air made it difficult to breathe. They couldn't keep this up for much longer.

"Sura!" Aran called out, his voice strained. "How much more time do you need?"

"I'm close," she replied, her voice tight with concentration.

The runes on the obelisk were now flickering erratically, the flow of energy between it and the creature weakening by the second.

The beast, however, was far from finished. With a final, desperate roar, it raised both of its front paws, preparing to bring them down in a crushing blow that would obliterate everything in its path.

Aran's heart raced. There was no time to think, no time to plan. Only instinct. With a burst of speed, and no small amount of courage, he charged forward, his blade raised as he leapt into the air, aiming for the creature's head. The blade struck true, and as it sank deep into the molten stone of the beast's skull, Aran felt something extraordinary. His father's sword sang - a pure, resonant note that seemed to harmonize with the very essence of Zarah itself. For an instant, he felt his presence, steady and proud, as if Khalid himself guided the strike that would fell this ancient guardian.

The creature let out a deafening scream, its body convulsing violently as it staggered backwards.

At that moment, Sura's chant reached its climax. The runes on the obelisk flared, pulsing in rapid succession, as if caught in a violent heartbeat. A deep, resonant hum filled the air - no, not a hum. A scream. The obelisk did not simply go dark; it fought, as if resisting Sura's interference. The ancient monolith pulsed with what felt almost like indignation - not malice, but the protective fury of a guardian whose charge was being threatened. It had watched over this place for millennia, and it would not yield easily. The energy snapped like a frayed rope, and with a thunderous crack, the bond shattered.

The beast's form began to crumble, stone grinding against stone with a sound like mountains weeping. Its molten eyes flickered once - not with rage, but something almost like relief - before dimming to cold obsidian. The creature's massive frame collapsed inward, dissolving into streams of silver ash that spiralled upward, carried away by winds that seemed to whisper ancient secrets. For a heartbeat, the very air shimmered, as though reality itself was healing from a wound.

Just as quickly as it had appeared, the creature was gone. Only the faint hum of the obelisk remained. Its power mended once more.

Silence descended like a shroud. After the thunderous roars and cracking earth, the sudden quiet was so complete it felt sacred.

Even the wind held its breath. In that moment, suspended between battle and peace, they all felt the weight of what they had just witnessed - the passing of something older than memory.

Aran landed heavily on the ground, his chest heaving as he struggled to catch his breath. The battle had taken everything out of him, but it had been worth it - they had won.

The Sea of Ash itself seemed to exhale, settling into new patterns as ancient energies found fresh balance. Far across Zarah's surface, sensitive souls would pause in their daily tasks, feeling something shift in the world's deep currents.

Aran could feel it now - the Weaving itself, stronger than it was before. Like a wound beginning to heal, the fundamental fabric of reality felt more stable, more whole.

Sura approached him, her face pale but relieved. "It is done. The connection is broken." She swayed slightly, Barash's staff trembling in her grip. The wood felt warm, almost alive, and for a moment, she could swear she felt the old scholar's steady presence flowing through it into her bones. "I managed to mend this one," she said, wonder and sheer exhaustion warring in her voice. "I could feel Barash guiding me - the staff remembers his touch."

Aran nodded, wiping the sweat from his brow as he looked up at the obelisk. "We might have defeated their guardian, but this is not over. The Primordials are still coming, all we managed to do was delay it."

Sura followed his gaze, her expression sombre. "Then we need to find their remaining tethers."

Aran sheathed his blade. Yet even as relief flooded through him, he felt a chill of certainty: their victory here had not gone unnoticed. Somewhere in the ancient places of Zarah, other guardians would be stirring, and beyond them, the Primordials themselves would sense this disruption in their carefully laid plans.

He had seen the possible future in his visions, seen the destruction that awaited them if they failed - but he had also seen a glimmer of hope. The obelisks remained the key, not just to holding back the Primordials, but to understanding the deeper truths of the Weaving itself. If they could fully unlock that knowledge, they might yet have a chance. With renewed resolve, Aran turned to his companions. "Try and rest tonight. Tomorrow we press on."

The battle was won, but the War of the Weaving had only just begun. Aran stared at the now-dormant monument - its dark surface reflecting the storm brewing on the horizon. He had always known the Primordials were coming. Not for the first time, he felt the weight of that truth.

He turned to Sura and Rafiq. "Let us eat - gather our strengths. At first light, we ride."

His thoughts drifted towards the task ahead. No more running. No more waiting. The Weaving would not mend by itself. He thought of all those counting on them - not just his companions, but every soul across Zarah who had no idea how close they stood to the edge of everything. The weight of their hopes settled on his shoulders like a mantle he could never remove.

This guardian had been different from the entities they'd faced before - older, more deeply connected to the Primordials' power. If this was what protected the first of the last obelisks, what would they face when they reached the next?

"No matter," he thought, the blood of the Old Kings, coursing hot through his veins - if the Primordials thought they could dictate the end of this story, they had gravely underestimated the will of mortals.

Chapter XXIX

Following Ghosts

Zarah's deserts were a vast golden ocean, unforgiving to all who dared to cross. By day, the sands shimmered under the brutal sun, mirages luring the weak to their doom. By night, the dunes became an ever-shifting realm of shadows, where the wind carried secrets and the silent hunters reigned. The heat shimmered, unforgiving, relentless, twisting the horizon into a mirage of false rivers, tempting the ambitious into chasing illusions until the relentless sun bled them dry. Still, it was not the day that belonged to the hunters - no, it was the night.

When it came, the planet grew silent, the deserts held their breath. The dunes became shadows shifting beneath the silver gaze of Nysa married to the golden, pale, burn of Anar. Even the wind hesitated, unsure if it should whisper its secrets to the darkness or keep them to itself.

Through this endless silence, two hunters moved swiftly. They travelled without words, their footfalls muffled by the shifting sands, their black cloaks blending with the darkness that stretched across the dunes. They had been following Aran's trail for weeks, watching from a distance and studying the path his company carved through the desert. They saw as the group entered the Sea of Ash, hoping they would not return. Unfortunately for them, they had - now it was time for the predators to stalk.

After managing to enter and leave the Sea of Ash, the boy-king and his dwindling band of warriors thought they were out of danger - alone. Soon, they would find out that they were not.

Drathis' wounds had healed, but his pride remained unassuaged. Each step in the sand was a reminder of his failures - at Sarim, at the temple, in the Shadows Divide, and in the eyes of the Primordials themselves.

He had once commanded large armies. Now, he was little more than a spectre trailing his enemy's footsteps.

He tightened his grip around the hilt of his greatblade, his clawed fingers curling over the worn leather. His breath was slow, steady, but his thoughts churned with a cold, bitter rage.

Aran should have died by his hand, Sarim should have fallen before his army, and the Weaving should have unravelled beneath his grasp. Instead, he had been cast aside by the Primordials, their whispered promises turning to mockery in his ears and the power he had sought was denied to him. His army was destroyed and, now, all that remained was vengeance. Nothing else mattered - nothing else would ever matter.

Vhaskar moved ahead, his massive frame unnaturally silent for a warrior of his size, his tyrian purple eyes gleaming like tanzanite jewels in the moonlight. The titan crouched low, running his fingers through the sand, feeling the faint disturbance where their quarry had passed. "They are slowing down," Vhaskar murmured, his deep voice barely more than a growl.

Drathis watched as his friend studied the ground, reading subtle imprints left behind, the weight in each step, the shift of the dunes, the slightest change in the wind's pattern. Vhaskar had always been more than a warrior - he was a hunter, and Rafiq was his prey.

"They are exhausted," Vhaskar continued, tracing the faint indentation where a boot had sunk too deep into the sand. "Their pace is uneven. The effects from the Sea of Ash still linger upon them."

Drathis exhaled through his nostrils. "Then they are ripe for slaughter."

The hulking Draconian rose to his full height, rolling his broad shoulders. "We could strike now," Vhaskar suggested. "Finish it before they even draw their blades."

Drathis' expression darkened, his eyes fixed on the distant horizon where the oasis waited, its presence marked only by the faintest shimmer of water reflecting under the moons. "No," he spat. "Not yet. I want to savour the chase."

Vhaskar's brow furrowed slightly, but he did not question his friend's decision. "Drathis wants them to feel it," he thought.

Feel the creeping realization of danger, the whisper of fear curling in the back of their minds. Drathis wanted Aran to know he was being hunted, to feel the weight of inevitable death pressing upon his spine. Only when that fear took root, when the certainty of survival began to fray at the edges of Aran's mind, only then would Drathis strike. For there was no death crueller than one that came too late to be stopped.

The desert wind was gentle that night, carrying with it the scent of distant rain, a rare promise in a land where storms came like vengeful gods, carving rivers into the earth only to let them wither away the next day. Drathis paused for a moment, turning his gaze upward.

Nysa hung high, casting her silver light across the dunes, while Anar burned low on the horizon, golden and flickering.

The twin moons had watched him rise, but they had also witnessed his fall. Now, they observed, impartial, as he chased ghosts through the wasteland, a fallen warlord hunting a king who had no right to still be breathing - the irony of it all was not lost on him.

Zarah's moons did not care for the fate of mortals. They had witnessed entire empires rise and burn, had watched kings carve their names into stone, into history, only for their kingdoms to be buried beneath the unforgiving sands of time - soon, they would watch Aran's blood stain the desert red.

He turned back to Vhaskar, his expression unreadable. "Move ahead," he ordered. "Find their camp." Vhaskar nodded once, then disappeared into the night, his form swallowed by the dunes.

Drathis exhaled, his breath curling in the cool air. "One last hunt," he mused. One last kill, and then nothing else would matter. Whatever punishment the House of Draco brought down on him, he would accept it without question.

Vhaskar returned before the hour was out, as Drathis was composing his song of vengeance. "They have made camp near the oasis we saw earlier," he reported, his voice calm but edged with something close to satisfaction. "They think themselves safe."

Drathis allowed himself the ghost of a smirk. "They think the worst has passed," he murmured. "That the battle at the Sea of Ash was their greatest test," he ran his thumb along the edge of his greatblade, feeling the familiar weight of steel, the promise of finality in its sharpened edge. "I nearly had him at Sarim. He was under my blade and I failed. Though, even defeated, they don't understand who they are facing," he continued, voice calm but venomous. "Their worst test was always going to be me."

Vhaskar regarded him for a moment, then nodded. "They are exposed, vulnerable," he observed. "We could strike before dawn."

Drathis considered it. The thought of taking them in their sleep, of swiftly ending the war with nothing but silent steel and moonlight, was tempting - as he had done with the boy's father. But no. That was not how this was meant to end. Not in silence, and certainly not in the dark. "Let them see us," he murmured, tightening his grip on his sword. "Let them feel us coming." Drathis turned his gaze toward the oasis, where their prey waited, unknowing. A broad smile took hold of his face, even his eyes were grinning. Tonight, blood would stain the sands, and the boy-king would know that he had never truly escaped him.

Miles away, through the shifting dunes where their quarry waited unknowing, the oasis where Aran and his friends were camping was a whisper of life in the vast emptiness of the landscape.

By day, it was a hidden jewel, where weary travellers found respite beneath the swaying Medjool Palms, where cool waters reflected the sky like polished glass, and where the air smelled of damp earth and the faint sweetness of desert blooms.

By night, it was something else entirely. A world untouched by time, bathed in the silver light of Nysa, while Anar, hung lower on the horizon, its glow flickering like the last breath of a dying fire. The wind was still, the sands were quiet, and Zarah watched in silence.

Lost in thought, in that silence, Aran ibn Khalid sat by the fire.

For the first time in weeks, the air carried something other than dust and death. The scent of moist earth, of the faintest traces of blooming Lunaris flowers, was almost enough to make one forget the war waiting beyond the dunes. And yet, Aran could not let go - he had seen too many men die, believing in the illusion of safety.

The embers of their campfire glowed softly, casting long shadows against the rock formations that bordered the oasis. The flames danced, sending wisps of smoke curling into the night, their warmth barely cutting through the chill that had settled over the desert.

The journey from the Sea of Ash had been long - too long.

Aran felt it in his bones, in the dull ache of his muscles, in the persistent throb of wounds still healing beneath the wrappings of linen and salve. Every breath he took carried with it the taste of ash and exhaustion. Even so, sleep would not claim him.

His keen eyes, so often alight with quiet intensity, now burned with something else - the weight of memory, of loss, of unspoken burdens. They had survived yet again. Not only that but, somehow, they had defeated the Primordial's Guardian and mended the obelisk. "At what cost?" Aran asked the dancing flames. It would take years for him to get used to the weight of his crown - if he ever could.

The firelight flickered, and for a brief moment, in the shifting glow, he thought he saw the faces of those who had fallen, who had bled for a cause still too far from being won - a war that refused to end.

No matter how hard he tried there was always something else to do.

"Brooding again?" The voice was rough, edged with exhaustion but laced with dry amusement.

Aran glanced up to see Rafiq, reclining against a boulder still warm from the sun, his arms folded behind his head, his broad chest wrapped in tight bandages, a testament to the wounds he had suffered at the Sea of Ash. "You stare at the fire like it owes you something," Rafiq muttered, smirking faintly. "Answers, maybe?" he asked, his eyes twinkling.

Aran exhaled through his nose, a ghost of a smile flickering across his lips. "Well," he paused. "Maybe it does."

Rafiq let out a short chuckle, shaking his head. "Fire doesn't owe anyone anything, my friend. It only knows how to burn."

Aran's smile faded. He turned the words over in his mind. "Fire only knows how to burn," he thought. "Yes - and like fire, war only knows how to consume."

His friend, perhaps sensing the shift in his thoughts, sighed and sat forward, rubbing a hand through his dark beard. "Look, we made it this far," Rafiq said, encouragingly. "We faced that... thing, and we lived. We should take whatever peace we can get before the next disaster finds us."

Aran said nothing, for there was nothing to be said. Because, deep down, he knew that peace would not last - it never had.

Sura sat across from them, at the edge of the fire's glow, with her back to a boulder. Her daggers resting beside her, the gleam of their edges catching the firelight. Barash's staff lay, resting, by her side. She had not removed her armour. Instead, she sat in stillness, her soulful eyes watching the night, scanning the shifting sands beyond the oasis.

Aran had known Sura for many years, since they found each other in the streets of Sarim, and in all that time, he had never once seen her lower her guard. Even now, as exhaustion pulled at their bones, as the empty desert stretched endlessly around them, she remained tense, coiled, waiting. "You should rest," he said at last.

She did not turn to look at him. "You should stop telling me things you know I will not do," her reply came swift, her voice firm, yet kind.

Aran exhaled, shaking his head. "At least let yourself breathe. We made it through the worst. You can close your eyes for a moment." Sura finally turned her gaze to him. The flickering fire reflected in her eyes, making them look like pools of molten bronze, filled with something indistinct, unreadable. She smiled faintly. "I do not think that peace exists for men like you."

Aran arched his brow. "What of you?" he asked. Sura's smile faded, and she looked away, not answering his question. In the distance they could hear the call of the Nightwing - hunting its prey.

Silence descended, and the camp settled into a quiet rhythm. The fire crackled softly, the steeds tethered near the water's edge pawed at the ground, their ears twitching as they listened to the whispers of the night. Even the wind had ceased. No rustling leaves, no more distant calls of nocturnal creatures. Just an unnatural quiet that made the hairs on the back of Sura's neck rise - something was very wrong about this stillness. It was a feeling, not a sound. Not a shadow, just an absence. Her hand moved instinctively to the daggers by her side.

Aran, ever attuned to her, caught the shift in her body language and frowned. "What is it?" he murmured. Sura didn't answer immediately -

she rose slowly, her boots pressing into the sand, her fingers tightening around the hilt of her weapons.

Something was watching them, and she sensed it before she could see it. A presence beyond the Medjool trees. A breath, too controlled, or a shift in the sand, too deliberate. She turned sharply toward Aran, her voice barely above a whisper. "Something is not right."

The fire shuddered, the flames flickering unnaturally, bending toward the darkness as though bowing to some unseen force. A sound broke the silence, but this time it was not the howl of the wind, nor the distant cry of some desert bird. No, this was the sound of metal shifting against metal.

Aran heard the faintest click of armour, and the breath of something monstrous - he leapt into motion, his father's sword in hand, its steel glinting in the firelight, his stance shifting with practised ease.

Rafiq pulled himself upright with the speed of a Dune Stalker - his twin swords already drawn, his expression no longer amused. Like the multi-legged arachnids of the desert, whose exoskeletons refracted light until they vanished from sight, he moved with lethal grace.

Sura's pulse remained steady, her grip sure, her heart playing a quiet drumbeat against her ribs - the tempo of battle.

The presence in the darkness wasn't waiting anymore. A voice emerged, cold and measured, a whisper of death given form.

"You were never supposed to have left the Sea of Ash," Kael Drathis murmured as, from the shadows, he stepped forward, his black war-cloak billowing, his eyes gleaming with the promise of blood.

Behind him, an enormous second figure emerged like a spectre, Vhaskar, a titan of the Varros bloodline, his war hammer resting lightly against his shoulder, his purples eyes gleaming like molten sapphires, beneath the moons.

Sura exhaled slowly, gripping her daggers. Aran's grip on his father's sword tightened, and Rafiq rolled his shoulders, shifting his weight. They had survived the Sea of Ash, defeated the Primordial's Guardian, only to be ambushed in the dead of night.

There, beneath the twin sentinels of night, in the place where the sands met water, death had come for them.

The night shattered, like the breaking of a great glass pane, the stillness of the oasis splintered into chaos. The fire, which had moments before crackled softly in the heart of the camp, guttered wildly in the sudden rush of movement, its golden glow casting long, erratic shadows against the trees.

Drathis struck first, like a viper lunging from the dark, he moved with terrifying speed, his blade carving through the air, aimed directly at his enemy's throat. Steel met steel with a resounding crash, sparks cascading in the night like fallen stars.

Aran had fought Drathis before, had survived by sheer will, but this was different. This was no battlefield clash with warriors at their sides. This had been a hunt, and Drathis was the predator.

Aran barely caught the strike, his muscles screaming as the force of it rattled through his bones - his boots sliding back against the sand as Drathis pressed forward, his face a mask of cold fury.

"You should have died in Sarim," Drathis hissed, his strength bearing down like an executioner's blade - his breath creating frost in the desert air.

Aran gritted his teeth, pushing back, forcing their locked blades to a stalemate. "So should have you," he taunted. "But then, doesn't that mean I must be harder to kill than you thought?"

Drathis' snout curled into something that might have been a smirk, but there was no amusement in his slitted eyes. Only vengeance sharpened with something deadly - the despair of one who had nothing left to lose.

Aran twisted his blade but, using the leverage of their locked swords, Drathis pivoted, his blade sliding down the length of Aran's, redirecting the momentum, and almost catching him. Then the Draconian warlord struck again - fast, brutal and precise.

Aran barely managed to sidestep the blow, but the tip of Drathis' sword still bit into his shoulder, slicing through the layers of sand serpent scales, drawing first blood.

Pain lanced through Aran's arm, hot and immediate, but he had no time to dwell on it, for Drathis was already striking again.

Not far from where they fought, Rafiq met Vhaskar like a storm meeting a mountain. The first strike came from above, Vhaskar's war hammer a blur of blackened steel, crashing down like a meteor falling from Zarah's skies. The experienced Bahir warrior rolled to the side, sand exploding into the air as the hammer struck the ground, shattering the stone beneath. Rafiq sprang up instantly, his twin swords flashing in the firelight as he slashed toward Vhaskar's exposed flank with a clean strike. Or rather it should have been, if Vhaskar was nothing but a common foe.

With inhuman speed, the reptilian titan pivoted, catching one of Rafiq's blades with his gauntlet, twisting it away before bringing his massive fist into Rafiq's ribs. Pain burst through the Bahir warrior's body, his breath torn from his lungs as he staggered back. Vhaskar followed, pressing forward, his hammer swinging in a wide arc.

Rafiq ducked low, feeling the wind of the weapon's passage mere inches from his head, as he picked his blade from the ground.

Before the hulking Draconian could react, he lunged forward, his swords flashing once more and, this time time, they struck true. One blade sank into Vhaskar's side, just underneath the armoured plating. A shallow wound to be sure, but deep enough to remind his opponent that, no matter how strong he was, he bled just like any other warrior.

Vhaskar exhaled sharply, stepping back. He glanced down at the crimson streak along his side, then at his enemy - he smiled broadly. Here, finally, was an opponent worth fighting - here was an opponent worth killing. "As I told you, back on the battlefield of Sarim, you fight well," Vhaskar admitted, rolling his massive shoulders. "However, you will break before I do."

Rafiq wiped the blood from his lip and grinned, despite the ache in his ribs. "We shall see about that." He braced himself for the worst.

The night shattered with the clash of steel and the cries of the dying.

Rafiq's warriors, hardened by years of battle, formed a loose defensive ring around the trio. Their blades glinted under the twin moons, their breath shallow but steady, their bodies battered but unbowed.

They had faced horrors before, though never like this - never against Drathis and Vhaskar.

Idran, a young Bahir warrior, stepped forward to meet the enemy. A man of unwavering resolve, he drew with his twin sabres, his crimson cloak billowing as he lunged at Drathis. Their swords met in a furious exchange. With Idran striking fast, precise, relentless - yet, Drathis was faster. With a flick of his wrist, he knocked aside a blade and drove his blade through Idran's chest.

The young man gasped, blood bubbling at his lips, but he still managed to cry out, in defiance. He fell as warriors of Zarah always had, boldly, reluctantly, with steel in their hands.

More warriors surged forward. Rashid, a muscular fighter from the Tarek tribe, bearer of a Solarwood spear, thrust his weapon toward Vhaskar, aiming for the chink in the titan's armour.

The massive Draconian merely turned, caught the spear mid-strike, and snapped it in two before crushing Rashid's skull with his war hammer - the sickening crack echoed across the dunes.

Sura moved through the battle like a whisper, her daggers flashing in the dark. She had seen Drathis fight before. She was there, standing on the battlements of Sarim, as she watched Aran fight his nemesis. She had memorized his rhythm, the way he controlled the battlefield like a master tactician, forcing his opponent into a fight they didn't want to be in. Analysing their demeanour, she could see how he fought Aran now. Relentless. Efficient. Deadly.

Aran was holding his own, but was bleeding. He was slower than usual, his wounds from the Sea of Ash not yet healed, and she knew what she had to do. Spotting an opening in Drathis' stance, a moment where he had overcommitted to his next strike, his side became exposed, and she took the chance.

Like a shadow breaking from the dark, she lunged forward, her dagger slicing toward the gap in Drathis' armour - she never made it. He moved faster than she thought possible, twisting at the last second and, before she could react, his elbow slammed into her ribs, knocking the air from her lungs. She stumbled back, gasping, clutching at her side, but Kael Drathis didn't even look at her.

"Stay down, girl," he sneered, his voice laced with cold amusement. "This is between kings."

Sura gritted her teeth, gripping her daggers tightly. "Then you don't know a damn thing about me," she spat, and struck again.

The fire kept casting long, flickering shadows across the battlefield, illuminating the chaos, the blood, the clash of steel and flesh. The desert night was a graveyard of echoes, the dying screams of men swallowed by Drathis and Vhaskar's rage.

Umar al-Shamar, a young warrior whose blade had defended the city of Sarim, fought with the grace of a dancer. His curved sword slashed through the darkness. Pivoting, his eyes locked with Vhaskar's terrible gaze - he knew his fate was sealed. The Varros titan lunged, with astonishing speed, grabbing Umar by the throat. With one brutal motion, Vhaskar lifted the young man off the ground. "You fight well," the titan growled. "But not well enough." Umar's body cracked as the Draconian hurled him into the rocks, falling at Rafiq's feet. His blade fell from his lifeless fingers, vanishing beneath the shifting sands. "No!" Sura shouted, her voice breaking. She could still hear him, wounded but laughing after Sarim: "I think I prefer complaining." He would never complain again.

Across the battlefield, Aran's warriors fell one by one. He knew he could not save them all. He had fought beside them, laughed with them, and bled with them. Now, he watched as they died for him. Tariq, an old veteran from the Tarek tribe, who had once taught Aran about the art of war, stood alone against Drathis. His armour was cracked, his left arm hung useless at his side, but his eyes burned with defiance. "I should have killed you when you first set foot in Sarim," Tariq spat, his sword trembling in his grip.

Drathis smirked. "Yet, here you stand, precisely because you did not fight me then." Their duel was swift. Drathis toyed with the old warrior, as Aran watched, dodging his strikes, forcing Tariq to overextend. Then, in one final merciless movement, he drove his blade through his heart. When Aran saw Tariq fall, something inside him snapped - broken.

Drathis was winning, and he could feel it. The weight pressing down on him, the brutal force behind every one of Drathis' attacks.

He had fought this foe before, had seen his ruthless precision, and had bested him by sheer will - tonight, Aran was tired, wounded, and Drathis knew it.

"You are slowing," Drathis taunted, driving him further back, his blade slicing through the night like a scythe through sand whispers. Aran barely caught the strike, his arms screaming from the effort. "You are breaking." The Draconian teased - then he fainted left, but struck right. Aran wasn't fast enough this time, the blade biting into his side, just below the ribs. Not deep, but enough. Pain flared through him, sharp and burning, and he gasped, staggering.

Drathis grinned, for he had his enemy precisely where he wanted him. The end was nigh for Aran ibn Khalid - Zarah's little king.

Without warning, the ground trembled. A low, deep rumble shook the oasis, like the growl of something vast moving beneath the sand. The fire flickered wildly, the very air shuddering with unseen power. At first, it was subtle, a whisper of movement beneath the dunes, the faintest shudder that sent grains of sand trickling down the slopes like an hourglass spilling its last moments. Then, the tremor grew. The oasis, once a sanctuary of stillness, stirred with something ancient. The firelight flickered brighter, its glow stretching and shrinking as the earth beneath it shifted, twisted, and came alive.

Aran felt it before he saw it. A presence, vast, ancient, watching.

His breath caught, his fingers tightening around the hilt of his sword, blood still dripping from his wounds. He turned his eyes to the dunes beyond the trees, where the sand was churning, rippling, rising like Zarah's sea before a storm.

Then the desert erupted. The roar that followed was one Aran quickly recognized - so loud, it tore through the night.

A colossal shape burst from beneath the dunes, its golden eyes glowing like molten suns, its massive, coiling body writhing as it broke through the surface of the world. A Sand Serpent… and yet, something far more ancient, more terrible than the name alone could conjure - this one bore the weight of legend.

Its coils rose into the air, its body stretching toward the heavens, before it came crashing down, sending tremors through the earth, knocking both warriors and steeds off their feet. Its massive, scaled body broke once again through the surface of the world, sending cascades of sand pouring from its shimmering hide, each scale reflecting the glow of the moons like burnished bronze and silver. Rafiq's surviving warriors scattered into the night, and he did not blame them for it. This foe was far beyond their skills - perhaps even his own. Drathis stumbled back, eyes wide, his blade still gripped tight, but for the first time that night he hesitated.

Vhaskar, too, had gone still, his war hammer lowered, his slitted purple eyes watching the monstrous form before them.

To everyone's surprise, the Serpent did not attack. Instead, it coiled its massive body between Aran's company and their enemies, its very presence a wall of living, breathing power. It had chosen a side.

Drathis clenched his teeth, rage curling in his chest. "Not again."

"Fall back!" Vhaskar shouted "We cannot defeat them now, especially with that thing strengthening their side."

Kael Drathis seethed, his fingers twitching around his sword.

"No!" He shouted louder. "I will not have my vengeance foiled, along with the rest of my plans and ambitions." As if it could understand him, the colossal ophidian turned to meet his eyes.

Drathis had faced many horrors in his lifetime - spanning centuries. He had even faced these beasts before, though the ones he fought before were mere flesh avatars, not to mention much smaller.

This one was different - somehow it felt more ancient. This was a true 'god of the sands', untamed, powerful, and extremely dangerous.

For all his power, all his ambition, Drathis was nothing before this creature. A warlord, once feared, now reduced to prey before a force as ancient as the stars themselves. The Primordials had denied him, and now, it seemed, even the beasts of this world had chosen a different fate than the one he had envisioned.

To think that, throughout his long life, he had stared into the abyss of the Weaving, had sought the favour of Primordials older than the stars, had commanded armies that had laid waste to cities and drowned entire civilizations in blood. Yet, as he gazed up at the serpentine colossus, its golden eyes locked onto him, its fanged maw opening wide enough to devour him whole, he felt a strange feeling. One that had never before made an appearance in his life, as the countless decades passed. It was a feeling with which he was becoming more and more familiar with, in recent times. Something he had never allowed himself to feel, but was now constantly present in his heart - an unyielding doubt, gnawing at his soul.

Vhaskar stood beside his friend, his war hammer lowered, his breathing steady and deliberate. He, too, was watching, not in fear, but in steady, calculating silence. "This is not a fight we can win," he muttered.

Drathis gritted his sharp fangs, rage curling in his chest. "Not again," he shouted. "Not again!"

The Sand Serpent moved with unnatural speed, its massive coils unfurling in the air, casting a monstrous shadow over the battlefield. Then it lunged. The world blurred around him as the titan struck toward the duo, its fangs gleaming, its movement so sudden that it seemed to bend time itself. Drathis barely had a moment to react - he twisted fast, dodging just as its long fangs slammed into the ground, sending a shock wave rippling through the oasis, tearing roots from the earth, splitting stone and sand alike.

Vhaskar leapt back, his war hammer raised, his eyes narrowed. "Move!" he barked, but Drathis was already moving, already calculating, already searching for an opening.

Yet, there was none. This was not a battle against men. Not against steel and weak flesh. This was something far older, beyond mortal reckoning, and it definitely had chosen a side - not theirs.

Aran staggered back, clutching his father's sword, his vision blurred with exhaustion and pain. The Serpent's colossal body unfurling between him and his enemies, its massive coils forming an impenetrable barrier of glistening hard scales, separating him, Rafiq, and Sura from Drathis and Vhaskar. It was protecting them.

But why? The Sand Serpents had no allegiance to kings or warriors. They were a force of nature, guardians of the old ways, beings whose existence had long been spoken of in whispers and half-believed myths. Yet, this one had chosen to rise now.

Aran recalled the one they had faced on the road, months ago, driven mad by the obelisk. Had this one sensed the Weaving's unravelling? Had it been drawn by the battle, by the blood staining the sands? Or was it something deeper?

He did not know the answer to any of these questions, but he knew one thing - for the second time since they met, Drathis looked unsure.

The Draconian warlord stood on the other side of the Sand Serpent's coils, his cloak tattered, his greatblade still gripped tightly in his hands.

Drathis' dark eyes flickered between the Serpent and Aran, calculating, measuring the fight that had just turned against him.

"Fate has not been kind to you, has it?" Aran murmured, in pain, his breath ragged. Drathis hissed, his jaw tightening, his clawed fingers flexing against his sword hilt. "You think this is fate?" Drathis spat, voice raw with fury. "This is just another delay. Another interruption," his eyes blazed with something feral, something that refused to accept what was happening. "I will kill you, Aran," he swore. "If not tonight, then tomorrow. Or the day after. It doesn't matter. In the end, you will die by my hand."

Aran said nothing. There was no point, for Drathis' fate had been sealed long before this night. Back in the Old Quarter of Sarim, it had been sealed the moment he had tried to take control of the Primordials.

The desert had fallen silent. Where moments before the air had been thick with the clash of steel and the cries of warriors, where the sands had trembled beneath the weight of titanic forces, there was now only stillness.

The great Sand Serpent, its immense coils half-buried in the dunes, watched with the patience of something ancient, something beyond mortal reckoning. Its golden eyes, like twin burning suns, reflected the dying embers from the fire, casting its gaze upon both the victors and the defeated, as though weighing their worth.

Aran could still hear his own breath, ragged and uneven, his ribs sore, burning with every inhale. Blood, his own and that of others, soaked into the sand beneath his boots, seeping into the veins of the earth, feeding a land that had long been accustomed to the taste of war.

The battle was over, but Drathis still stood - a foreshadow that the war against the House of Draco had not yet ended.

Drathis was still gripping his sword tight. His fingers were taut around the hilt, his knuckles cracking with fury, his entire body vibrating with the rage of some caged beast denied its final kill. His Nathair cloak, once a banner of Draconian authority, now hung in tatters, streaked with blood and dust, whispering against the wind like the shroud of a fallen king who refused to stay dead. This was not how it was meant to end. Not with a monster from the depths of legend interfering in his battle. Not with Aran still breathing, still standing, still defying fate itself.

Drathis' jaw tightened, the muscles in his face twitching as he pushed down the burning rage curling like smoke in his lungs. Pride was, indeed, a hard thing to swallow. "Do you think this changes anything?" His voice, though quiet, carried across the ruined battlefield, hoarse with tempered exhaustion but raw with something deeper than hatred, something closer to obsession.

Aran exhaled, still gripping his own sword - his heirloom - but he made no move to raise it again. Not unless Drathis tried to attack. "You lost," he said, his voice steady, despite the pain he felt. "The battle is over. Take your friend's advice and leave this place."

Drathis' eyes burned, not with defeat, but with something darker, with something that refused to be extinguished. "Do you think that matters to me?" he whispered. His grip on his blade tightened. "Defeat? Do you think any of this matters anymore?"

Drathis sounded deranged. His words were not a confession of despair, nor were they calculated, they were some sort of mad promise.

A desperate curse, trying to disguise the fact that he had already lost everything - the war, his honour, and his place among his own people. Now, he had nothing left but pure, unbridled vengeance.

Vhaskar had been watching him, in silence. He had not spoken since the Serpent had risen, had not moved as the sands had settled, as the reality of their failure set in like the weight of a thousand dying stars. Now, he let out a slow breath, adjusting the grip on his war hammer before shifting his gaze toward Drathis. "It is over," he murmured.

His friend didn't react, so Vhaskar pressed, his tone even. Not cruel, not taunting, just final - accepting. "We lost."

Drathis let out a sharp breath, something between a laugh and a snarl. "You sound ready to surrender."

Vhaskar shook his large head. "Surrender?" Though his voice remained calm, there was something grim beneath it. "No. There's no surrender for those like us."

A beat of silence, then a sigh - long, slow, and weighted with resignation. "Still, there is knowing when to leave a battlefield before you die on it." Vhaskar murmured. Aran wounded, watched in silence.

Drathis turned toward Vhaskar, his expression unreadable, but his fury was clear in the way his breath hitched, in the subtle tremor in his fingers still gripping his sword. "Then leave," he spat.

The words felt hollow in his mouth, because he knew there was nowhere left to go. Not back to their star system of Nathair, nor back to the House of Draco - he would be branded a failure. Their own kind would never forgive him for this defeat. Yet, Drathis could not bring himself to stop fighting, for what was he without a war to wage?

Vhaskar tilted his head, regarding his friend with a gaze that was neither pitying nor cold - just knowing.

After a long silence, he turned. He did not wait for permission, nor did he argue. He just walked away. Drathis watched, powerless, as his oldest companion, his most trusted and powerful warrior, left the battlefield without another word, disappearing into the night as though the dunes themselves had swallowed him whole.

There, for the first time in his life, on the sands of that small oasis, Kael Drathis felt truly alone - an unfamiliar, hollow ache blooming in the chest of a creature who had never known true companionship or love - only conquest. In that silence, so vast and absolute, even his fury had no voice.

The wind had begun to pick up, swirling around the remnants of the battlefield, kicking up the scent of blood and burnt embers. There Drathis stood, staring at the sand where Vhaskar had walked, staring at the ruins of everything he had built, staring at the man who had ruined his ambitions. His fingers ached from how tightly he was gripping his blade. He could still lunge forward. He could still strike. He could still try to kill Aran, here and now. Even with that ancient being watching. Even with his wounds slowing him down.

Drathis did no such thing, because something deep in his soul knew this was not his night. Another situation would present itself, and when it came it would not be an ambush, nor a battle of numbers. It would be him and Aran. A duel. A reckoning. A final act written in blood.

He lifted his sword, pointing it toward his enemy. "You will die by my hand," he whispered. It was not a threat. It was not even a promise. It was simply the truth - the only truth he had left to believe.

Drathis' fingers twitched over the hilt of his blade. One strike - one final chance. However, as the serpent's glowing eyes bored into him, he accepted the undeniable truth - this was not his time. Not yet. Rage coiled inside him, but even he knew when to wait. Revenge was a patient beast, and he would feed it when the time was right. Without another word, he turned, and like Vhaskar before him, he vanished into the dark. Aran and his friends, however, did not lower their weapons until long after Drathis had gone, and even then, they did not relax - they knew that it was not over.

The Sand Serpent remained. Its colossal form dominated the battlefield in silence, eyes aglow with a primeval, unblinking light.

Aran turned to face it fully, weapon still at the ready - not from threat, but from habit, from instinct. The great creature tilted its massive head, its gaze locking with his. For a breathless moment, the world stood still. In that moment, Aran felt it - not words, not thoughts, but something deeper - recognition. Not just of him, but of what he had chosen. A warrior who had stood his ground. A man who had not succumbed to fear.

The serpent blinked once, slow and solemn, then turned away. With a wide ripple of sand and a hiss like thunder, it vanished into the dunes, leaving only the memory of its presence behind.

Aran's grip on his blade eased slightly as he watched it disappear.

He was not sure if the creature was a guardian, a judge, or something older still - yet, it had spared them. Not by chance, but by choice.

It had watched the battle, seen the lines drawn in blood and flame, and had made its decision. Perhaps, Aran thought, some powers in this world still respected courage. Or perhaps it had simply seen the same thing he now understood - that light casts shadows, not the other way around.

Rafiq exhaled, finally dropping to one knee, his twin swords sinking into the sand, his body heaving with the weight of exhaustion. "That was… unpleasant," he quipped, wiping the sweat from his brow.

Sura, standing nearby, rolled her shoulders, wincing slightly as she touched her ribs. "When you think about what just happened, It could have been much worse."

Rafiq arched a brow at her. "How exactly do you mean?"

She glanced toward the distant dunes where Drathis and Vhaskar had disappeared. "They could have stayed," she winked at Rafiq.

Aran remained silent, his mind was already racing, already planning, already bracing for their next inevitable battle - because Drathis would not stop. Not now, not ever. Not as long as he drew breath.

If Aran was to survive this war, if his kingdom was to remain standing, then he would have to finish what had been started, though perhaps not by him. So, no more battles in the dark. No more waiting for fate to decide. Next time, when Drathis came for him, Aran would be ready. The desert wind howled through the oasis, whispering a name across the sands. A name that would not fade. Not yet. Not until the war was over. Until then, the shadows would always follow.

Chapter XXX

Veins of the World

The desert stretched into infinity, the memory of the Sea of Ash fading behind them like a ghost of battles past. Aran and his companions pressed onward, deeper into the uncharted wilds of the south, where no maps guided their path, and no civilisation had dared to linger.

Two weeks had passed since the battle with the molten guardian, and they were five days removed from their battle with Drathis and Vhaskar.

The toll for their struggles had begun to weigh heavily on all of them. The once vibrant company now walked in silence, broken, their faces drawn with exhaustion and their bodies aching from battle and the constant travel. Even Rafiq, ever the steadfast commander, moved with a weariness that seemed to settle into his bones.

The landscape had changed dramatically as they ventured farther from the last obelisk's domain. Gone were the jagged, volcanic plains and the choking ash-filled winds.

Instead, the terrain had become a mixture of barren rock and dry grasslands, the air still and hot beneath the oppressive sun.

And yet, there was something else at work - unseen. Something unsettling that lay just beneath the surface. The ground beneath their feet felt different, as though the earth itself was shifting in subtle, imperceptible ways.

At times, Aran could swear he felt the pulse of something vast and unseen beneath them - an echo of power coursing through the rock, a heartbeat of the world itself. The sensation was neither comforting nor hostile. It simply was, and that was perhaps the most unsettling part of all. He could sense it at a deeper level. His connection to the Weaving had grown sharper the more obelisks they encountered, and now, as they travelled deeper into the unknown, he could feel the flow of energy beneath the ground, like veins of power running through the world. It was not unlike the sensation he had felt when he first touched his first obelisk, but slightly different. This was raw, untamed, and primeval.

"Do you feel it?" Sura asked quietly, walking beside him. The amber at the end of Barash's staff glowed faintly in the dim light of the setting sun, the runes etched into its surface pulsing with a soft, rhythmic energy. "The Weaving is... stronger here. More volatile."

Aran nodded in approval, his gaze fixed on the horizon. "It is as if the land itself is alive. The further south we go, the more it feels like we're walking on the edge of something... vast."

"It must be the Primordials' influence," she said, her voice low. "The closer we get to the heart of their power, the more unstable the Weaving becomes. The obelisks were meant to anchor it, but as they falter, the world around them starts to fray."

Aran didn't need her to explain this to him, but he said nothing.

He had seen the visions, felt the weight of the future pressing down on them. The destruction of the very first obelisk had set something in motion, something that looked like it could not be undone. Now, every step they took brought them closer to the point of no return.

"We need to find the next one," Sura said. "Before the Weaving unravels completely."

Aran nodded, his expression playful. "Thank you for stating the obvious," he said with wry humour. She chuckled involuntarily, though she gave him an admonishing look. A mixture of levity and foreboding settled on his features. "When we find it, we might be able to stabilize the flow of energy. The further we go, the more dangerous it will become - guardians or not."

"More than it has been already?" Rafiq jested.

Aran managed a faint smile, then glanced back at the rest of the group. Rafiq and his surviving warriors began moving with silent determination, their faces hard with resolve. They had all seen the dangers that lay ahead, but none of them had wavered in their commitment to the cause. Aran knew that they would follow him to the ends of the earth if necessary - yet, the burden of that loyalty was taking its toll on them. Every life lost, every sacrifice made, pressed down on his conscience like a crushing mass.

And Aran carried them all - those who marched beside him and those who had fallen along the way. He could still hear their voices in the wind, the echoes of oaths sworn and never fulfilled. With each step taken, he wondered how many more names would be added to the growing list of the lost?

The sun dipped below the horizon as they continued their tired march, casting the world in a deep, reddish hue. Shadows lengthened across the landscape, and the air grew cooler, but the tension remained thick, like a storm waiting to break.

It was just before nightfall when they reached the edge of a vast canyon, its depths shrouded in darkness. The land here was wrong.

It did not feel like erosion or the work of time but rather the aftermath of something ancient and violent - a fracture in the world's very foundation. The canyon yawned before them, deep and hungry, as though it had been carved by a force that did not belong to Zarah. It stretched as far as the eye could see, a jagged scar that cut through the landscape like a wound. It was not the canyon itself that caught Aran's attention, but rather the strange, glowing fissures that ran along the canyon walls, veins of energy that pulsed with an eerie light.

The very air tasted of copper and ancient storms, thick with the memory of powers that predated mortal understanding - powers that had shaped the world's foundation. The same energy that he had felt beneath the ground now flowed visibly, winding its way through the rock like molten fire.

"This is it," Sura whispered, her eyes wide with awe. "What I spoke of the other day."

Aran stepped closer to the edge of the canyon, his gaze fixed on the glowing fissures. The energy that flowed through them was unlike anything he had ever seen or felt. It was alive, pulsing with a rhythm that matched the heartbeat of the planet itself. He could feel the power radiating from the canyon, a deep, primal force that seemed to call to him. "The next obelisk is here," he said quietly, his voice carrying, in the silence. "Somewhere deep within this canyon."

Rafiq approached, his face hard as he surveyed the landscape. "If the obelisk is down there, we need to find a way to descend safely. This place does not look welcoming at all."

"Nothing about this whole journey has been," Aran replied, a wry smile tugging at the corner of his lips. He turned to Sura, as she asked. "Can you sense its location?" her inquisitive eyes boring eagerly into his.

Aran closed his eyes. Stretching his arms wide open, he reached out with his mind. The air around him shimmered faintly, and for a moment, everything was still. Then, slowly, his eyes opened, and he pointed toward a distant point along the canyon's edge.

"There," he said. "There is an entrance, a hidden path that leads down into the heart of the canyon. The energy here is unstable, so the deeper we go, the more dangerous it will become. Besides the obelisk, this place holds the ruins of an ancient city."

"I feel it too." Sura murmured to herself, her breath quickening.

Aran nodded gravely. "Then we must move carefully. Rafiq, have the men prepare ropes and climbing gear. We descend in the morning."

His loyal friend gave a curt nod and moved to relay the orders to the rest of the group. As the warriors moved to their preparations, Aran stood at the canyon's edge, his cloak stirring in the wind, eyes fixed on the glowing veins of energy that pulsed far below - like the lifeblood of the world, laid bare.

The closer they got to the obelisk, the more he could feel, once more, the presence of the Primordials pressing in on him.

It was a suffocating feeling, as though the very air around them was thick with their unbending will.

"They are watching us," Sura said quietly, standing beside him.

She did not require an answer to her question, and Aran did not need to ask who she meant by that. The Primordials had been watching them from the moment they set foot in this land. Their influence was stronger whenever the group got near to an obelisk.

"They know what we are trying to do," Aran said, his voice low. "They will not let us succeed without a fight."

Sura nodded, her expression sombre. "They have waited millennia for this moment. I have been reading one of the smaller books we brought from Valamar. It speaks of the Weaving and its many manifestations throughout history. The Weaving has been fraying for centuries, but now… it's unravelling faster than ever before. If we are not able to stop it -"

"We will be," Aran interrupted, his voice firm. "We must!" He looked at her, determination burning in his eyes, trying to convey confidence.

Sura said nothing, but the uncertainty he saw in her eyes spoke volumes. She was his master spy, and now she was also becoming something else - perhaps even a Weaver - one of the rare few, like Aran, who truly understood the delicate balance that held the world together. Not even she was sure if they could stop the unravelling. Aran saw the doubt in her eyes and did not turn away.

He let it settle in his chest like a weight, then fed it to the fire that burned at his core. If Sura could no longer be certain, then he would be - for her, for all of them. Someone had to believe. If the Weaving itself began to fray, then he would become its last thread - unbroken, defiant, and burning with the kind of hope no storm could ever extinguish.

That night, they made camp at the edge of the canyon, the glowing fissures casting an eerie light across their small encampment. The remaining warriors sat in a small group, speaking in hushed tones as they prepared for the descent into the canyon. There was a palpable tension in the air, a sense of impending doom that none of them could shake.

Aran sat apart from the others, his back against a rock as he stared out at the canyon. His thoughts were a tumultuous storm, a whirlwind of doubts and fears that he could not quite banish. The weight of the responsibility he carried was crushing. Not only was the fate of his bloodline at stake, but the fate of the entire planet, of Zarah, rested on his shoulders.

Yet, despite everything, a strange calm settled over him. His path had been chosen years ago - each step, each sacrifice, had led him here.

There was no turning back now, only forward, into whatever fate awaited.

As the night wore on, the sounds of the camp quieted, and one by one, they all drifted off to sleep. Only the faint crackle of the campfire and the distant hum of the canyon's energy broke the silence. Aran remained awake, his gaze fixed on the horizon, waiting for the dawn.

At first light, the company descended into the canyon. The hidden path that Aran had sensed was narrow and treacherous, barely wide enough for a single person to traverse. The air grew colder the further down they moved, the walls of the canyon rising ominously, high above them, casting long shadows that swallowed the light.

As tangible as a visible constraint wrapping itself around them, the deeper they went, the more oppressive the atmosphere became - its weight pressing down like an invisible force.

The glowing veins of energy continued to pulse along the canyon walls, growing brighter and more erratic the further they descended. It was as if the very fabric of the world was fraying before their eyes, the Weaving unravelling in slow motion.

"This place feels... alien," one of the Bahir warriors muttered, his voice barely audible over the faint hum of the energy.

Aran couldn't find it in himself to disagree. There was something deeply unsettling about this place, something that sent a chill through his bones. Yet, indifferent to his personal feelings, the obelisk was down here, somewhere in the heart of this forsaken canyon, and they had to find it before it was too late.

Hours passed as they made their way deeper into the gorge.

The path grew steeper, more treacherous, and the air became thick with an almost electric tension. Every step felt like a battle against the press of the energy that pulsed through the ground, and even the most seasoned of Rafiq's warriors struggled to keep their footing.

At long last, after what felt like an eternity carved from shadow and stone, they reached the canyon's floor - where silence clung like dust and every breath tasted of ancient earth.

It was a vast, open space, the walls rising high above them like the sides of a colossal stone maw. The ground beneath their feet was cracked and uneven, the veins of energy running through it like molten rivers. Ancient stones lay scattered across the canyon floor - fragments of walls and columns that spoke of a civilization lost to time. The ruins stretched into the mist beyond the obelisk, their broken architecture bearing the same otherworldly runes that pulsed with fading light. There, at the centre of the canyon, stood the obelisk - hidden by the mist.

It was big, far larger than the one they had encountered in the Sea of Ash, its surface covered in intricate runes that glowed with a faint, otherworldly light. The air around it hummed with power, and Aran could feel the weight of its presence pressing down on him, a deep, primal force that seemed to resonate with the very core of his being. "This is it," Sura said, her voice barely above a whisper. "Are you ready?"

Aran stepped forward, his eyes fixed on the stone monolith. This was the moment they had been preparing for, the moment that would decide the fate of the world. As he approached the stone needle, he couldn't shake the familiar feeling that something was watching them. Something ancient, untamed - yet, undeniably powerful.

The obelisk's runes began to pulse with increasing urgency, as though responding to some ancient summons. The canyon itself seemed to draw breath and hold it.

Then, from the shifting shadows at the canyon's edge, the air itself seemed to split apart. A void, deeper than darkness, poured forth, coalescing into something vast and unknowable.

It did not simply emerge - it was, as though it had always been there, watching, waiting. Aran could not believe his eyes. Was this a Primordial?

Rafiq, Sura and the men stepped back in both horror and awe.

It was massive, its form shifting and writhing like smoke and fire, its eyes glowing with a shifting radiance. The very air around it seemed to warp and twist, the energy of the Weaving bending to its will.

Aran drew his father's sword, the weight of the ancient blade comforting in his hand - although it would not be enough. He knew that truth, deep down. No steel could cut through time, no blade could sever fate. Yet, he stood firm, because standing was the only thing left to do - that was what kept the darkness at bay.

Chapter XXXI

The Primordial's Gambit

The canyon trembled beneath its presence, the weight of its being pressing into the very bones of Zarah. Its form, neither solid nor ethereal, writhed like a Sand Serpent trapped between worlds - shadows and molten light coiling, reforming, as though struggling to remain in one shape. The pulsing veins of energy along the canyon walls flared in rhythm with the creature's presence, as though the very land was responding to its call.

A low hum filled the air, a resonance that vibrated through bone and sinew, pressing upon Aran and his companions with suffocating intensity. He felt his pulse quicken, his breath shallow against the weight of the Primordial's gaze. It was as though this ancient being was able to peer into their very souls - unravelling every secret, every fear they had buried deep down. Aran tightened his grip on the hilt of his father's sword, its once-comforting weight now a reminder of how fragile mortal weapons seemed before a force older than time itself.

Behind him, Sura stood motionless, her eyes wide with awe and terror. Barash's staff glowed dimly, but its light seemed a flicker compared to the storm of energy swirling around the Primordial. Rafiq and his brave warriors, those that still clung to life, had drawn their weapons, but there was a palpable uncertainty in the air, for they knew they stood on the edge of something far beyond their comprehension, or experience.

Two of the men lay motionless against the canyon wall, their sand serpent-scale armour blackened by the Primordial's guardian assault. The survivors moved with the careful economy of wounded predators, each step calculated to preserve what strength remained.

The creature's form shifted again, taking on more solidity as it moved forward. Its molten limbs, crackling with veins of fire, seemed to brush the very fabric of reality, distorting the air around it. Its voice, when it spoke, was not a sound but a presence. An unfathomable, nevertheless overwhelming force that pressed against the minds of those who heard it. "You tread where no mortal should, child of dust. Your kind claw at the edges of a design you will never fully comprehend, mistaking old echoes for truths, illusions for dominion."

These words echoed within Aran's mind, a deep, resonant voice that seemed to come from everywhere and nowhere at once. He winced, feeling the weight of each syllable.

The Primordial's presence was not merely physical; it was entwined with the Weaving itself, woven into the very threads of existence. This was no mere guardian of the obelisks, but an embodiment of the power that had shaped this world long before the rise of men.

Aran stepped forward, forcing the fear from his voice. "We seek to prevent the unravelling of the Weaving," he said.

"The obelisks," the voice resounded again, powerful, unyielding. "The obelisks were never meant for you." The Primordial's voice was cold, otherworldly, alien. Its burning eyes fixed on Aran, narrowing as though it studied the mortal before it, weighing his worth. "They were meant to bind what you could never fully grasp. Yet, you have come, thinking you can wield power that does not belong to you."

Sura moved beside Aran, her face pale, but she was determined to stand by his side, no matter what. "The Weaving is fraying," she said, her voice strained. "The balance has been broken. If we do not act, everything we know will be lost."

The Primordial's form shifted, molten limbs crackling with arcs of energy. "Mortal child, you think yourself able to understand what is at stake?" It growled, mockingly, the canyon walls reverberating with its fury. "You continue to meddle with forces far beyond your reach. As we have told you before, the Weaving was never meant to be preserved. It was meant to change, to evolve... or to end."

Aran felt a chill slither down his spine at the Primordial's words.

The unravelling of the Weaving had not been a mere accident. Not a stroke of cosmic misfortune, but something deliberate, something willed. Had he been fighting fate itself?

Every step toward repairing the Weaving, every battle fought, had been a step against an inevitability woven long before his first mortal breath was drawn. These stone monuments were not safeguards; they were shackles - and the Primordials were their restless prisoners.

The realization struck him to the core. For a moment that stretched like eternity, Aran felt the foundations of his understanding crumble. Every prayer offered to the moons, every sacrifice made to preserve the ancient ways - had it all been hubris?

The weight of countless lives lost in battles he had believed righteous now pressed upon his shoulders with crushing certainty. Their journey, if one could even call it that, had led him to believe the obelisks were anchors, great pillars holding the fabric of reality in place. As the journey progressed, with each passing moment the truth sharpened, becoming clearer, yet far more terrifying.

The Primordials had woven this world with purpose, but despite whatever pacts had been forged in Zarah's past, that purpose might not align with the survival of humankind.

"What do you mean?" Aran demanded, his voice sharp. "Do you mean to say that you wish to destroy our world?"

The Primordial's burning eyes flared, its voice rippling through the air like a thunderclap. "The world must change. The Weaving must evolve. The old ways, the ancient pacts, those were all part of a cycle, one that you cannot comprehend. The end of your world is merely the beginning of another. Your kind clings to permanence," the Primordial continued, its voice carrying what might have been ancient sorrow. "Yet you are but a single note in an endless symphony. When the music changes, would you have the composers remain forever silent for fear of disturbing your brief refrain?"

The metaphor struck Aran with unexpected force. If they were merely notes in a cosmic composition, what gave them the right to demand the music never change? Yet what gave the composers the right to silence them without consent? His heart raced as the implications of the words sank in.

The unravelling of the Weaving was not just a threat to his kingdom or the lives of his people, it was a part of a larger plan, a cosmic design that transcended the mortal plane. He felt the weight of his decisions bear down on him more than ever before. His struggle was not just against a force of nature but against the very destiny the Primordials had set in motion aeons ago.

Sura looked at him, her face tight with worry, but also with unbound love and loyalty. "We have to stop it," she whispered. "If the Weaving unravels completely, we will lose everything. Our planet, our people, everything will be consumed."

Aran knew, in his heart, that she was right. They couldn't allow the Primordials to complete their design, not if it meant the end of all they had ever known. Still, how could they fight against a being of such immense power? How could they stop a cycle that had been set in motion before the dawn of time? Before the awakening of all things.

The obsidian monolith loomed behind the Primordial, its massive form pulsing with an eerie, celestial light. The ornate runes etched into its surface flickered with raw energy, and Aran could feel the Weaving's strands inexorably drawn toward it.

The obelisks were the key - they always had been the simple answer, hidden in plain sight all along. If they could somehow sever the Primordial's connection to the Weaving, they might be able to stabilize the flow of energy, or at the very least, buy themselves more time.

"There has to be a way," Aran muttered, more to himself than to anyone else.

"There is no escape from what is coming," the Primordial hissed, its form shifting and writhing like an ophidian of molten stone. "You will fight. You will struggle. Yet, regardless of what you do, in the end, all things must fall to ash." Its form coiled, shifted form again, and with a surge of power, it struck.

It did not move - it unfolded, surging forward in an impossible blur, as if space itself bent to accommodate its will. Its limbs lashed out like whips of molten fire, rending the air with a sound like shattering glass, reality itself recoiling from its touch. Aran barely had time to raise his sword before the force of the blow, softened by Sura, yielding Barash's staff, sent him stumbling back. Even protected, the heat from the creature's attack seared through his armour, and he gritted his teeth against the pain.

Rafiq's voice rang out as he rallied his warriors, their swords drawn, faces grim with determination. They formed a protective line around Aran and Sura, their shields raised as they prepared for the onslaught. Rafiq racked his brain, but no matter how he turned it over in his mind, he couldn't fathom how steel and flesh were meant to stand against such an ancient force.

The Primordial struck again, its molten claws raking across the ground, sending jagged rocks and debris flying. Aran ducked, narrowly avoiding the deadly strike and countered with a swift slash of his sword. The ancient blade glowed faintly, the runes along its edge humming with power. When it met the Primordial's searing form, though the steel remained unscathed, it barely left a mark on the creature.

Sura moved with fluid precision, though uncertainty flickered beneath her calm. Her understanding of the Weaving had deepened through trial and necessity - not the effortless mastery of legend, but something harder-won and more precious. As the Primordial's molten claws tore through the air, she summoned barriers of crystallized energy. Each one trembled beneath the force, barely holding.

For a heartbeat, she feared she might falter - but she did not. Guiding the creature's fury aside, she focused not on perfection but survival. Her face was calm, but not unshaken - this was no inherited destiny fulfilled, but a role she had chosen, arduous and still becoming.

She raised Barash's staff, her voice rising in a chant as she tried to call upon the Weaving. The air around her shimmered, and for the briefest moment, the energy of the canyon seemed to shift in response. A bolt of pure energy shot from the staff, striking the Primordial in the chest. The creature shrieked, its form rippling in pain, but it did not falter. Its voice, almost unbearable to withstand. "Child of dust, do you think your primitive science can harm us?" The Primordial snarled, in a roar of molten fury. "We are the Weaving!"

The ground beneath them shook violently, and cracks began to spread across the canyon floor, veins of molten light spilling out like rivers of fire. Aran could feel the Weaving tearing apart around them, the very fabric of reality fraying under the Primordial's assault.

"We have to touch the obelisk!" Sura shouted over the din of battle. "We must, in order to reach its core, like last time. It's the only way we can sever the connection!"

Aran nodded, his mind racing. But how could they reach it with the Primordial standing between them and their goal?

As if sensing their intent, it surged forward, its form towering above them like a living storm of fire and brimstone. It struck again, and this time Aran barely managed to block the blow. Even with Sura's help, who conjured a temporary energy cocoon to shield her king, the force of the impact sent him sprawling to the ground, his sword clattering out of reach.

The Primordial loomed over Aran, its eyes burning with cold fury. "You cannot win, mortal vessel." Its voice was a whisper now, cold and detached, yet it carried the naked weight of inevitability. Aran's vision blurred, as he struggled to stand, every muscle in his body screaming in protest. The Weaving pulsed around him, a chaotic swirl of energy that seemed to mock his efforts. He could feel the Primordial's power pressing down on him, as if the weight of the entire world rested on his shoulders. Then, amidst the chaos, a voice cut through the storm, pulling at his heartstrings. "Aran!"

Sura stood at the edge of the battlefield, with staff raised high, its light blazing like a beacon in the darkness. In her eyes, Aran saw something he had not expected. Was it hope?

"Do you trust me?" she shouted, her voice steady. Aran didn't hesitate - he scrambled to his feet, his gaze locked on the stone tether behind the Primordial. It was their only chance. "I do," Aran's eyes shifted to meet hers, finding in them the certainty he needed.

Sura began to chant, her voice rising in a powerful conjuration.

Aran focused with all his might. The Weaving around them pulsed in response, the chaotic energy of the canyon bending to their will. The ground trembled as the veins of molten light began to shift, converging on the obelisk like rivers drawn to the Yaran sea.

The Primordial roared in fury, its form writhing as it struggled against the pull of the Weaving. Yet, despite its best efforts, the combined force of Aran and Sura was too strong - two halves of a singular force.

The creature's molten limbs flared with energy as it fought to maintain its form, but the power it drew from the obelisk was slipping from its grasp. "Now!" Sura shouted.

With a final, desperate burst of strength, Aran lunged. His father's sword, now a blazing arc of defiance, carved through the darkness, striking the obelisk with the fury of dying stars. The blade sang as it cleaved the charged air, its ancient steel drinking deep of the Weaving's power. Aran felt the weapon's hunger, felt centuries of dormant purpose awakening as it sought its destined target.

The obelisk seemed to lean toward the approaching strike, as though welcoming its own destruction. The impact was deafening - a resonant thunderclap that split the air, sending shock waves rippling through the Weaving itself. For an instant, time held its breath, as if waiting expectantly for what came next.

The obelisk shattered, its surface cracking open as a wave of energy burst outward, rippling through the air like a storm unleashed. The force of the blast sent the Primordial reeling, its form dissolving into a maelstrom of molten light and shadow. Aran stumbled back, his vision swimming as the world around him seemed to blur. He could feel the Weaving shifting, the fraying threads of reality slowly knitting back together. The Primordial's presence was fading, its power slipping away as its connection to the obelisk was severed.

The canyon was silent, the air still. The Primordial was gone, its form dissolved into nothingness. The obelisk lay in ruins, its once-glowing runes now dark and lifeless. Aran collapsed to his knees, his body trembling with exhaustion. He felt the toll of battle in every fibre of his being, yet beneath the fatigue stirred a muted relief - a fragile sense that, for now at least, they had won. If only temporarily.

The silence that followed was not peace but exhaustion - the kind that settles into bones after witnessing the reshaping of reality itself. Aran's hands trembled not from fear now, but from the aftershock of having, once again touched forces that predated creation itself.

Sura approached, the top of Barash's staff still glowing faintly in the dim light. She knelt beside Aran, her face pale but calm. "You did it," she said softly, her eyes kind, filled with unbound love.

Aran shook his head, his breath ragged. "No," he looked deep into her eyes. "We did it!"

Rafiq staggered over to them, his face still pale from what they had witnessed. The humour that followed was the desperate kind - a man's attempt to convince himself he was still alive to laugh.

"Next time you two decide to challenge an ancient being older than time itself," he winced, dropping heavily beside them, "perhaps we could start with something smaller? A Crystalline Leviathan, maybe? Or just a particularly angry Sand Serpent?" Rafiq let out a pained chuckle. "At least those do not bend reality when they are upset."

Sura and Aran broke out in laughter, followed by Rafiq. Yet, when levity subsided, they sat in silence for a long moment, the weight of what had just happened sinking in.

They had faced a Primordial and lived to tell the tale. In spite of that, as Aran looked out over the ruins of the obelisk, he couldn't shake the feeling that, once again, they were back at the starting line.

For all their struggles, for every battle fought and won, the storm had not passed - it had merely shifted, waiting on the horizon.

The Primordial's final words echoed in his mind, their weight pressing deeper than the wounds on his body. Was victory even possible? Or had they only delayed the inevitable?

The Weaving had been stabilized, but the echoes of the Primordial's words still lingered in his mind. The world was changing. The cycle was continuing, and there was no telling what lay ahead.

Yet even as he pondered these dark possibilities, Aran felt something stirring within the damaged Weaving - not decay, but transformation. The Primordials had spoken of cycles and change. Perhaps the real question was not how to prevent the inevitable, but how to guide it toward mercy rather than annihilation.

Chapter XXXII

The Weight of the Ancients

Aran, Sura and Rafiq stood amidst the ruins, their breath shallow, the air thick with the scent of scorched stone, dust, and the acrid copper taste of spilled blood that clung to the back of their throats - the lingering scent of battle. The Weaving itself trembled beneath his skin, pulsing like a wounded thing, as though reality had barely withstood the ancient force they had faced. The remnants of their confrontation with a Primordial still vibrated through the threads of the Weaving, a deep, slow pulse that danced in time with Aran's heartbeat. In that coursing rhythm, he sensed the immediate threat had passed - but also that the long game was not over yet.

The Primordial's final words echoed in his mind, ominous and cryptic, hinting at greater dangers lying ahead of them, hidden within the dark web of destiny he had stepped into. What if the cycle was not meant to be stopped? What if it was never meant to be broken? What if their struggle was merely another turn in an endless, futile loop - each generation rising only to fall, each king playing a role long ago etched into Zarah's very bones?

His close companions were scattered across the desolate battlefield, each grappling with the aftermath in their own way.

Sura, wan from the draining force of the Primordial, leaned against a shattered pillar, her gaze fixed on the distant horizon beyond the walls of that forsaken place, as if it held the answers she so desperately sought. He felt her pain.

Rafiq, silent and grim, cleaned his blades with methodical precision, the once-radiant steel now tarnished by the ichor of the Primordial they had defeated. The remaining Bahir warriors moved cautiously through the rubble, but each man's eyes betrayed the same weariness and doubt as his brother's. It wasn't just physical exhaustion that weighed on them, but the unspoken realization that they had stepped into a realm beyond mortal understanding - yet, there was no guarantee they would return the same.

Aran's thoughts dwelled on his recent vision - a spiralling nightmare of the Weaving unravelling, cycles of creation and destruction stretching back through untold aeons, and the monstrous force that lurked behind it all.

Then it struck him, not as revelation but as recognition - an epiphany that had always been waiting at the edge of knowing. The ancient pact between the Old Kings and the Primordials was not a covenant of harmony but a desperate bargain. It was never meant to last - only to delay the inevitable. The truth had always been there, plain and terrible, but drowned beneath the noise of pride, politics, and the illusion of control. He finally understood - the pact was nothing but a fragile thread holding the world together, fraying fast in the hands of those who thought it unbreakable.

Just as the weight of the revelation settled in his chest, a voice cut through the silence, pulling him back to the present - Rafiq, ever grounded, ever irreverent. "Surely, it was lying to us," he muttered, steel rasping against polishing stone as he sharpened his swords. "Trying to make us believe there's no hope left. No different from the Draconians," he paused, then scoffed, shaking his head. "Except the Primordials do not need armies - they shape the world itself. Bastards!" Despite the pain, Aran still managed a feeble smile.

Ever since they were children, Rafiq possessed this gift for making light of the heaviest burden - Aran had always taken comfort in that.

Sura, however, was not in a humorous mood. "The Primordials cannot lie," she spoke urgently, breaking the heavy silence. Her voice was low, almost hollow.

She had barely uttered a word since the battle, as if the encounter had drained more than just her energy. "They are bound to truth in ways we mortals cannot comprehend," she paused, catching her breath. "Yet their words are often as deadly as any blade."

The very air around them seemed to thicken with the echo of the Primordial's presence, carrying a metallic tang that made their tongues numb and their skin prickle with unease.

Aran furrowed his brow, her undeniable words pulling him back to reality. "Do you believe what it told us? That we are merely repeating the Old Kings' mistakes? That the Weaving itself is doomed to collapse?"

Sura hesitated, her soulful eyes meeting Aran's. "I don't know. But, I fear that what we faced was only a fragment of a much larger game. One that stretches back further than we can imagine."

Rafiq stood, sheathing his weapons, his voice urgent. "Then what are we to do? We barely survived this battle, let alone our previous encounters," he took a deep breath. "These damned Primordials, tearing at the Weaving like Dune Stalkers at a carcass."

He looked at his brother in arms - his king. "What in all the hells of Zarah are we supposed to do if reality itself starts coming apart at our feet?"

Aran's hand clenched into a fist. His friend's anger only added weight to his kingship, but even that now seemed built on shifting sands. He had been raised to believe a king's duty was to protect his people, to uphold the traditions of Sarim's forebears. Though he could not help but ask himself, what use were traditions against forces that had shaped the world before man had ever drawn breath?

The visions he had experienced, the voices in his head, the whispers of destiny that had haunted him since his father's caravan days - they all pointed to one truth: he was no longer just a man bound by mortal laws. His fate was tied to something far older, something far more dangerous.

"We cannot turn back," Aran said firmly. His voice carried authority, but beneath it was the unmistakable edge of resolve forged in the fires of uncertainty. "We have glimpsed a truth that can not be ignored. If we retreat now, if we abandon this path, we leave the world to fall into chaos," he observed his friends, "Everything we know will be destroyed. I will not allow that to happen."

Sura stepped closer, her eyes softening as she studied him. "You speak as if you already know what must be done."

Aran's mind raced. The Weaving, the obelisks, the ancient pact, it was all connected, part of a larger tapestry that even the Old Kings had only partially unravelled. The destruction of the first obelisk, by his hand, had been only the beginning, a spark that had set the cycle into motion once more. Now, with the Primordial's cryptic warning, Aran received a much needed confirmation that the obelisks had always held the key to understanding the true nature of the Weaving - and perhaps even how to control it.

He stepped closer to the nearest broken pillar, running his hand along its weathered surface. The stone still hummed with residual power, warm to the touch despite the cool air. The Weaving pulsed beneath his palm - a rhythm that matched his heartbeat, confirming what his mind had begun to piece together.

"These obelisks are much more than mere anchors," he said, his voice steady but thoughtful. "They hold the power to reshape reality - the last remnants of a pact older than any kingdom of men. There are still more to be found," he took a deep breath. "The rest are tied to the remainder cycles of the Weaving. If we can find them and understand them, then perhaps we can do more than stop the unravelling - perhaps we can reshape the Weaving itself.

Rafiq frowned. "What if the Primordials stand in our way once more? It's only natural to assume that if they are the keepers of this knowledge, then how do we intend to take it? By fighting them?"

"No, we do not need to fight them all - not yet anyway. However, we must uncover the truth hidden within the remaining obelisks." A flicker of vision crept into Aran's mind, unbidden. "We must succeed, whatever it takes. Our survival depends on that," he added, as his eyes shifted, unfocused.

His thoughts began to drift to the Sanctum of Knowledge in Valamar. Aran had felt something within that liminal space, a presence, or perhaps a consciousness, watching them.

That place was more than just a passage between realms - it was a conduit, a place where the lines between past, present, and future blurred. If they could return there, perhaps they could uncover more than just fragments of ancient lore.

Perhaps they could find a way to alter the very course of history. Or was it a better option to pursue the rest of the obelisks? If that were to be the case, then the dangers of the next stone tethers were not to be taken lightly. Throughout their journey, the obelisks had been warnings in themselves, teachers, ancient seals holding back powers far greater than anything they had faced in their lives.

As if in silent accord, the trio simultaneously realized that each step closer to the truth would lead them deeper into a web of intrigue and danger, testing not only their strength but their very will to survive.

Fleeting as a desert breeze, and as if sensing Aran's thoughts, Sura stood straighter, her voice persuasive. "The first thing we should do is return to Sarim," she suggested cautiously. Rafiq gave Aran a reassuring nod.

Sensing acquiescence in his posture, Sura pressed on. "We need to regroup - gather our strength. The political climate at home could be unstable. If we are to face what lies ahead, we cannot afford to be divided." Her gaze locked with his.

Though a part of him resisted the idea of returning, Aran nodded. The burden of leadership had only grown heavier since they had left Sarim. He knew that some in council would seize on any hint of weakness. The smaller tribes, emboldened by Ryvan's backing, had already shown their willingness to conspire against him - and now, with rumours of his dangerous journey spreading, there would be those eager to exploit his absence, or worse, question his sanity.

Sura was right - there was no avoiding it. If they were to confront the Primordials, uncover the mystery of the obelisks, and prevent the unravelling of the Weaving, they could not do it alone. The Council of Tribes had to be united once and for all - no matter the cost.

Aran turned to face the battlefield one final time, pressing his fist to his heart in the traditional Tarek salute to the fallen - both enemy and ally alike. "May the sands always remember your courage," he spoke quietly, the ancient words carrying across the ruins. His warriors echoed the gesture, their voices joining him in the brief, solemn ritual.

"Prepare the steeds," Aran ordered, his voice resolute. "We return to Sarim."

The long journey back north was marked by a tense silence, as if each step toward the Yaran capital carried them deeper into the unknown. The warriors accompanying Aran, though still loyal, were no longer as eager as they had been at the start of their journey to the Sea of Ash. The encounters with the Guardian, then Drathis and Vhaskar - the Sand Serpent - but especially with the Primordial, had shaken their faith in the world around them. Even the landscape seemed different now, the once-familiar plains and oases of Sarim cast in a pall of unease, as if the very planet sensed the growing discord within the Weaving.

The remains from the battle Sarim fought against Drathis' army had already been cleared from the fields, but the city's walls still bore heavy scars from the conflict. Sections remained missing, though workers could be seen tending to the repairs - slowly restoring it to its former glory.

As they approached the city gates - partially rebuilt - Aran's thoughts turned to the political struggles that likely awaited him. He could already imagine the whispers spreading through the court like wildfire: accusations of heresy, of obsession. Would Ryvan have tightened his grip in Aran's absence? Had the minor clans grown bolder, perhaps even moving to unite against his throne? The thought of returning to find his carefully negotiated treaties in shambles gnawed at him.

He had left to fight for Sarim, but had Sarim already begun to turn against him? His long absence, coupled with rising tensions between the smaller tribes and the six main tribal leaders who supported him, could only have fanned rivalries and stoked ambition.

Yet, despite it all, a strange calm settled over him. The visions he had seen - the terrible truth of the Weaving's fragility - had transformed him, with or without his consent.

Aran was no longer merely a king burdened by courtly concerns. He had become something more, though he could not yet grasp what that truly meant. By the vicissitudes of fate, his destiny was now bound to forces far older and more powerful than any mortal ruler - save perhaps the Old Kings themselves.

As his party passed through the gates and into the heart of the city, Aran's eyes turned toward the palace - the royal citadel where his banners fluttered once more in the wind, repaired - crimson and gold shimmering like sandfish in the setting sun. Yet, beneath the grandeur, he sensed an undercurrent of tension gripping the 'Jewel of the Northeast' like a vice.

Someone in the court would be waiting, ready to test him, to challenge his authority - knife in hand, patience in pocket.

As he ascended the palace steps, he steeled himself, the weight of responsibility pressing down on him. Yet this time, it felt different. With each step, the weight of his crown settled like a familiar mantle. Something had changed - he was no longer just a king fighting for his throne. Aran was a man who had glimpsed the threads of fate itself - and now, he had to decide whether to weave or to unravel.

Fear no longer held power over him. He finally understood, at his core, the difference between destiny and choice - that every decision, every alliance, every sacrifice, would shape not just his kingdom but the fate of the world itself.

He cast his eyes skyward for a moment, where the first stars were beginning to pierce the twilight. Somewhere among those distant lights, the Old Kings had once walked the same path he now travelled. The thought brought neither comfort nor fear - only clarity.

The doors to the council room awaited him. Aran stepped forward, ready to face whatever lay ahead.

Chapter XXXIII

When Shadows Sit at the Table

As he walked to the Council of Tribes, the echoes of battle clung to Aran like shadows, trailing behind him through the marble halls. Every step he took was burdened by the weight of war, by the unseen forces that had shaped his journey and the unseen enemies who now awaited him within. The weight of his mantle suddenly felt heavy again, his crown like an anchor binding him to a realm that teetered on the edge of chaos. The potential majesty of his kingdom stretched out before him, yet the forces arrayed against him, both supernatural and mortal, kept casting long shadows over every step taken.

The council had assembled to greet him upon his return, the tribal banners lined along the hall as though ready to remind him of their power.

He saw the familiar faces of his most fervent supporters. Kasim al-Bahir stood, as he entered. Karim al-Shamar, fidgeting with his spectacles, gave him a worried look. Safira, the moon seer, saluted him though her face bore the semblant of concern.

His cousin Zahira came to meet him in a warm embrace.

As he held her tight, he could see the measuring gazes of some of the other tribal lords and ladies, each measuring the king who kept disappearing, for months at a time, on perilous journeys - who had faced forces they could scarcely comprehend.

The shadows that sat at the table were not just metaphorical - they wore names, titles, and smiles. And beneath their silk and polished words, blades lay hidden. Aran knew these men and women well and knew the ambitions that coiled beneath their courtesies.

Loyalty, especially among the smaller tribes, was a fleeting thing, as fragile as glass and just as easily shattered by the promise of power.

His long absences had given them time to plot, reasons to conspire. They would see his weakened state, his weariness from battle, and doubt his strength. What they did not understand was that he was no longer the man who had arrived at Sarim in pursuit of a dream, through the unpredictability of life reclaimed his throne, only to be thrown into a quest that had its roots dug deep in their peoples history. These very events had led him to face forces older than the stars, witnessed visions of the unravelling of the very fabric of their world, and touched upon truths that would terrify even the boldest among these few dissident, so-called nobles.

The true weight of the crown was not in the battles fought between men but in the unseen war with the ancient powers that sought to claim everything they held dear.

The hall quieted as Aran sat, and his voice rang clear and firm, though within, his thoughts swirled. "My lords, my ladies, I have returned."

There was a murmur among those gathered. Most nodded in deference, while quite a few merely exchanged furtive glances.

It was Zahira who broke the silence, stepping forward from her place beside the throne, her gaze steady and reassuring. Her presence was a balm, a reminder that not all in the court stood ready to betray him. She seemed to have fully embodied her new role in life.

"Your journey has been long, my king," she said, her voice carrying through the chamber, "and much has transpired in your absence. The council awaits your word."

Aran studied the faces around him. The Council of the Tribes had been summoned at his return, though not all in this room remained his allies. The smaller tribes - the Veylan, the Korrath, and others - had once stood with him, but their loyalty now wavered under Ryvan's influence and their own growing fears. His greatest concern, however, lay not with the council but with the undercurrents of tension rippling through the common folk and the city's army, who had heard whispers of the growing unrest. Already paying the price for the battles the city had endured, they now lived in fear.

However, it was Ryvan, tribal leader of the large tribe of the same name, who spoke next, his voice dripping with the kind of feigned solicitude that masked a hidden plan. It had been him, after all, that had coerced the minor tribes to join his dissident cause. "We are, of course, pleased to see you safe, Your Majesty." Every word Ryvan spoke dripped with venom. "However, troubling whispers reach our ears yet again. The people continue to speak of dark forces, of ancient powers beyond mortal grasp. These tales have spread like wildfire, fanning fear and unrest. Tell me, Your Majesty, how much of it is truth... and how much is merely myth?"

The subtle challenge in his tone did not go unnoticed by Aran. Given Ryvan's behaviour before the battle of Sarim, it had become clear he long harboured ambitions of greater influence, and any perceived weakness in Aran's rule would be an opportunity for him.

The smaller tribal leaders watched the exchange closely - like Sand Serpents circling a lost caravan.

Aran's response came with the weight of certainty. "What you dismiss as mere stories, Ryvan, are the warnings of a world on the brink. The forces we face do not belong to the realm of myth - they are as real as you or I, and they are moving against us. We have seen them and survived where others would have fallen," he indicated Sura and Rafiq. "What is more, we fought them." Aran looked around the table. "We have no choice but to meet this threat directly if we wish to preserve what we have built."

A ripple of unease spread through the council chamber. Some minor tribal leaders exchanged wary glances, while others shifted in their seats, discomfort plain on their faces. Whether from disbelief or fear, it was clear that few wanted to accept that the world they had always known was unravelling before them.

Aran continued, his voice hardening as he addressed the unspoken doubts. "The Primordials have awakened. For those of you with weaker memories," he looked Ryvan in the eyes. "They were once bound by a pact made with the Old Kings, but that pact is broken. Their power stirs beneath Zarah's surface, and I fear we stand at the precipice of something far greater than any war fought between mortals on this world."

The silence that followed pressed down on the council like a physical weight. These were not matters of petty politics or the usual machinations of court. This was something that stretched beyond the understanding of many in the room. Yet for all their scepticism, Aran could see his words had planted seeds of fear. After all, they had witnessed the omens themselves - strange phenomena that defied explanation, whispers in the streets, a world that seemed to be shifting beneath their feet.

Kasim, rubbing his thick beard, was the first to break the silence. "We are well aware of the dangers the Primordials represent, it is only these doubters," he pointed at Ryvan and his followers, "that need further convincing. We have witnessed these signs ourselves," he stated, his voice rising with conviction. "Only wilful blindness could deny what stands before us." His hand struck the table with controlled emphasis.

Karim al-Shamar, adjusting his spectacles, spoke up in support.

"Our king always had our best interests at heart. If it was not for him defeating Drathis in the battles we fought here, in this city, Sarim would not be standing."

Ryvan remained silent throughout this exchange, biding his time, waiting for the right moment to plunge his sharp tongue into the conversation.

Aran raised a hand, and found that he still commanded authority within the council, for silence followed his gesture promptly.

He began by giving an account of the events that transpired while he was away: the obelisk's power, the Guardian, and Drathis' ambush.

"He attacked us on the road, accompanied by his lieutenant, Vhaskar," he explained. "We had just left the Sea of Ash, where we fought a Guardian of the Primordials, and we would have died in Drathis' ambush if it had not been for a larger than usual Sand Serpent that came to our rescue."

"Sand Serpent?" Safira asked. "I thought they had no stake in the ongoing progress of our kingdom?"

Aran exhaled. "I find myself at a loss as to why it aided us - but aid us it did. Its actions mirrored precisely those of Uramak, the Sand Serpent from legend." He wondered if the serpent had truly been Uramak, or perhaps a descendant of the legendary beast.

Gathering his thoughts, he continued to recount their tale. "After that battle subsided, Drathis and Vhaskar disappeared into the night. Next, we deliberated as to whether to return here or continue to pursue our quest. We decided to track the next obelisk. Following many weeks of perilous travel, we found it - the largest we ever encountered, and that is where the first Primordial manifested itself," Aran heard gasps amongst those seated at the table. "We fought it," he paused, recalling the horrors of battle. "If it had not been for our team work, we would have all perished in that liminal place."

Ryvan smirked sardonically, making no effort to hide his cynicism.

It was Rafiq who stepped forward this time, his imposing frame cutting through the tension. His voice was steady, as always. "Our king speaks the truth. Sura and I were there, fighting alongside him, when he faced the Primordial. This is not a threat we can afford to dismiss."

Ryvan's eyes flicked toward Rafiq, calculating. "Then what would you have us do, Your Majesty? Shall we wage war against these mythical beings? Or shall we cling to our swords while our people grow ever more uncertain?"

"Your scepticism will not make them disappear, Ryvan. They exist, they threaten us, and we will act." Aran's voice carried the weight of absolute certainty. "Forces exist in this world that seek to undo the very foundation upon which we stand. We have seen them with our own eyes," he gestured toward Sura and Rafiq, "and more than that - we have fought them. Only by facing these powers head-on do we stand any chance of preserving our realm."

Aran paused, locking eyes with Ryvan, letting the silence stretch between them - heavy and deliberate. "Why do you make me repeat myself?" There was no answer, so Aran pressed. "Or has that been your plan all along? To entangle the council in pointless deliberations while you attempt to amass supporters for your claim to my throne?"

Kasim gave Aran a reassuring nod, while Karim winked at him as he adjusted his spectacles.

Ryvan was livid, "That is not..." he trailed off - uncertain of how to reply to such a direct attack by the king, he chose to remain silent, biding his time. A murmur rippled through the council as Aran's words hung in the air like thick incense. Some faces showed clear disbelief, while others betrayed a deeper fear – perhaps not of his words being true, but of what their truth would mean.

"The Primordials have indeed awakened," Aran continued, his voice hardening as he addressed the unspoken doubts in the room. His gaze fixed deliberately on Ryvan, while he cast an understanding look toward Farid, who now sat alone in a corner - broken. "Though I have tried my best to keep doom away from our doorstep, our work is not complete," he held Ryvan's gaze. "My work is not complete." He exhaled deeply.

"I am afraid that I must leave you once more, if we are to survive this."

Ryvan's eyes narrowed. "You speak of matters that reach far beyond the concerns of this council," he paused, for dramatic effect. "All the while you, once again, stand ready to embark on your quest for these relics of the past. I ask, who shall safeguard Sarim? The people grow uneasy. They wonder, they whisper... about a king who is more myth than monarch."

Aran stiffened, aware that Ryvan was pushing for a crack in his rule. "Sarim will not be neglected. I will ensure the city is secure and its people are reassured. In spite of that, we must not remain blind to the greater danger. Besides," his gaze was strong enough to burn, "anything that might put at risk the stability of our kingdom deserves to be discussed at this table. Do you disagree?"

Ryvan's lips curled into a predatory smile. Expertly avoiding Aran's question, he replied. "Indeed, my king. We would not wish to see the kingdom fall into disorder... especially in such uncertain times, when such disorder might benefit those prepared to restore order in their own way." This was a veiled threat, and Aran knew it.

Ryvan, much like Farid and those like them, would use the fear of the unknown to their advantage, manipulating the court's unrest in an attempt to erode his power. They had, however, committed a grave mistake - Aran was prepared now.

He had faced forces far darker than their ambition, and his resolve had been forged in battles more perilous than any council intrigue.

"There will be no disorder," he said, his voice cold. "I will see to it personally. Anyone," he paused, looking around the chamber. Kasim, Safira, Karim and his other supporters gave him nods of approval. "I repeat," his hand moving towards the hilt of his father's sword. "Anyone here who seeks to destabilize this kingdom in my absence will answer directly to me." His eyes blazed.

The objectors to his rule shifted uneasily, and Ryvan's smile faded. Those conspiring against him had expected uncertainty, perhaps even hesitation, but Aran's forceful response had left them momentarily disarmed.

He turned to the assembled tribal lords. "At dawn, the council will convene. We will set our course for the remaining obelisks. Sarim's defences will be strengthened, and I will ensure our people remain protected. Our kingdom will not fall - not to the hunger of forgotten gods, nor to the ambitions of lesser men."

The weight of his words settled over the chamber like dust after a sandstorm. Aran felt the familiar exhaustion that followed such confrontations - not of body, but of spirit. How many more battles would he fight in halls that should offer sanctuary? He looked at Ryvan, who had fallen silent, his followers now avoiding his gaze.

With that, Aran turned and left the hall, leaving the court in silence. His mind raced, but his steps were sure. The political landscape of Sarim was treacherous, and the forces at play were more than mortal greed and ambition. The obelisks held the key to everything, and he had no choice but to keep pursuing their secrets, no matter the cost. Even if that meant forfeiting his life.

He had spoken with conviction - Yet, conviction was not the same as certainty. And Aran knew that the hardest truths were still ahead.

As he walked out of the council room, Sura joined him, her face drawn with concern. "You handled them well. However, that will not stop Ryvan. He seeks to undermine you at every turn."

Aran nodded. "Let him. We have more important things to focus on."

She hesitated. "What of the Primordials? Do you truly believe we can master the Weaving, before they act decisively?" Aran's eyes darkened. "We must. Or there will be nothing left to rule."

He ran a hand gently along the side of her face. Her eyes were truly mesmerizing and, when Aran met them, they held the strength of a promise yet to be fulfilled.

They walked in silence toward the war room, where Sura had arranged for the maps of the ancient world, as well as the scrolls and tomes they brought from Valamar to be assembled for study. Once a decision was reached, the search for the next obelisk would begin.

When they passed by the towering windows of the palace, Aran glanced out at the darkening horizon and could swear he saw the faintest shimmer of the Echo of Worlds, like a mirage of forgotten realms.

The path ahead was fraught with growing peril, but he knew he needed to remain strong, in his people's stead.

The more he reflected on his path, the clearer it became - his choices had never been his own. He was not merely forging his destiny; he was walking a road paved by the echoes of those who came before him. The fate of Zarah, the future of his House, all rested on the decisions he made now. Would he break the cycle… or would history claim him as it had the Old Kings?

Chapter XXXIV

The Threads of Fate

Tension coiled around Sarim like a tightening noose. Aran stood at the centre of a vast web - one spun from politics, war, and forces beyond mortal comprehension. The threads stretched far beyond his palace walls, beyond the reach of his kingdom, into the depths of myth and power, where even the Old Kings had feared to tread. He could feel the weight of each thread, some fraying, others pulling tighter, each representing forces moving against him - the rival tribal lords, the restless populace, the ancient powers that now stirred in the dark.

Yet, for all the myriad forces at play, Aran knew that time itself was the most pressing of his enemies. The Weaving was unravelling fast, and the Primordials would not wait for him to gather his strength.

The war room had become his refuge, a place where the weight of kingship met the weight of the unknown. Spread before him were maps not just of land, but of ley lines, lost civilizations, and cosmic forces older than time. Symbols from a forgotten age littered the ancient parchment, warnings left by those who had glimpsed the abyss before him. At the end of the week, Aran called for a special meeting, their last, to decide their next move.

Around the table stood his most trusted companions. Kasim al-Bahir and Karim al-Shamar stood together near the maps, while Safira the Moon Seer whispered quietly with his cousin Zahira. Sura, as always, was by his side, her keen intellect and intuition helping to unravel mysteries that even Barash was struggling to comprehend. Rafiq, his loyal general and best friend, who would follow him into any battle without hesitation, kept his watchful stance by the door. Sitting quietly in a corner was Barash himself, his father's oldest friend - the old warrior turned scholar and advisor, whose knowledge of the Weaving had proven to be invaluable. Aran could sense that Barash's own fears had deepened, now that they were nearing their goal.

The king's voice broke the silence, his tone measured, though the urgency beneath it was clear. "Let us begin by strategizing our defences back here, at home. Sarim cannot stay unprotected. Drathis might still try to attack you in my absence."

Kasim, ever the proud warrior, spoke firmly, his voice regal and sharp. "My king, go forth with the confidence that the Bahir warriors will keep our walls standing, no matter what comes at them, be it Draconians or Primordials."

Safira spoke with a mixture of calm and warning. "The moons have told me many things. Some were easy to decipher, others too oblique to interpret correctly. Still, be sure of one thing, Aran. No matter what happens, my archers will ensure no enemy will ever cross our outer battlements again. They shall burn before they ever reach us."

"Our Solar Disruptors are ready. I will ensure Sarim still stands upon your return," Karim al-Shamar spoke firmly and confidently, his hands calmly resting on the crescent table.

"Ryvan will not be a problem," Zahira said with a knowing smile. "Politically, so it seems, you shattered his influence at the last council. Should he attempt anything in your absence, he will find himself facing me," she leaned back, the edge of her voice laced with amusement, "and that is a fight he will regret starting."

Aran tried his hardest to suppress a chuckle, but Karim al-Shamar was not so successful, and Kasim al-Bahir broke out laughing, followed by the rest of his supporters.

After a brief, but well-deserved moment of levity, the king's expression darkened. "We have located the next obelisk. According to the old texts, it lies in the Ruins of Kartalis, far to the south, in the shadow of the Blight Peaks."

Sura's brow furrowed as she traced the route on the map. "Kartalis... that place has been abandoned for centuries. The Old Kings built it as a fortress against the Primordials, but when the Weaving was sealed, it was said the land itself turned barren. Nothing grows there anymore."

"Perhaps that is why this obelisk has remained untouched," Barash murmured. "Few would dare venture so close to the Blight Peaks. They said the Primordials' influence still lingered there."

Rafiq grunted in agreement. "Be assured that we will face more than just desolation. The smaller tribes have grown restless. They've been raiding the borderlands, emboldened by the rumours of unrest throughout the deserts."

Aran's eyes remained fixed on the map. "Then we will need to move quickly before word of our journey reaches their ears. They might be on Ryvan's side and if the obelisk truly lies in Kartalis, we cannot afford to delay."

A silence fell over the room as each of them understood the gravity of the task ahead. This was not a simple quest for power. This was a race against time to prevent the Primordials from reclaiming their ancient dominion - for Aran had seen in his visions, without the shadow of a doubt that the consequences of failure would be catastrophic, not just for Sarim, but for the entire world.

"We leave at dawn," Aran said, his voice firm. "Rafiq, assemble a small force but no more than a dozen of our best. We cannot afford to draw attention."

His friend nodded, reassuringly. "Consider it done."

Aran turned to Barash. "I will need you to prepare the necessary wards around the city. If the Primordials' presence is as strong as we suspect, our people will need every protection you can muster."

Barash bowed his head. "I will ensure that Sarim will be shielded from their influence."

As the room cleared, Sura lingered by Aran's side. Her eyes searched his face, reading the tension there, the exhaustion he refused to show to all the others. "Aran," she began softly, "you have carried this burden alone for far too long."

He shook his head, a faint smile touching his lips. "I'm not alone, Sura. You and Rafiq have been with me every step of the way."

She frowned, her gaze steady. "But you have not let me in. Not completely. You are shouldering the weight of the world, and you are too proud to admit how much it is costing you."

For a moment, he said nothing. She was right, of course. As always, she could glimpse, unbound, into his soul. The visions had left their mark on him - more than he had let anyone see. The power of the Primordials, the Weaving's slow collapse, the endless decisions between duty and destiny had hollowed him in ways that even he didn't fully understand. Yet, there was no room for weakness now.

Not when the fate of everything he held dear was at stake.

"There is no other way, Sura," he said at last, his voice quiet but resolute. He touched her hands gently. "If I falter, all of this, my dream, everything we have built will fall with me."

She reached up to touch his face. "That is not true. You have us. I have told you this, over and over again." Her eyes were a pool of light and love. "You do not have to do this alone." Her gaze held his, unwavering.

Aran covered her hand with his own, the warmth of her touch a fleeting sanctuary in the storm of fate. "I know," he murmured. "Still, some burdens must be carried alone, or they might break those who share them."

They stood there in silence for a long while, the weight of what was to come settling between them. When Sura finally left, Aran remained in the war room, staring at the map of Kartalis, his thoughts drifting toward the future. He had seen glimpses of it, long ago, back in the Echo of Worlds - the vastness of the Weaving stretching out before him, the threads of fate intertwining with his own.

There was no turning back then, and there was no turning back now. The path he had chosen was fraught with peril, but it was the only path left to him. The Primordials were rising, and soon, the final confrontation would be upon them.

Dawn broke over Sarim, casting long shadows across the city as Aran and his companions rode southward. The long journey to Kartalis was gruelling, the landscape growing harsher with each passing mile. Several days went by. The lush oases of the equatorial deserts gave way to barren plains, and after twelve days of travel, they could see the jagged silhouette of the Blight Peaks rising in the distance, their summits stark against the sky.

Kartalis lay at the foot of those mountains, a crumbling ruin that had once been a bastion of the Old Kings. Now, it was little more than a graveyard of broken stone and shattered memories. As they approached, the king of Zarah could feel the air grow colder, the weight of the Primordials' presence pressing down on him like a suffocating fog. The silence bore against them, broken only by wind and hoofbeats. Even Rafiq, usually quick with a jest or story, rode in contemplative quiet. The group made camp just outside the ruins, and beneath the twin moons Anar and Nysa, Aran stood at the edge of the firelight, staring into the darkness. His thoughts turned to the obelisk that somewhere within those ruins waited for him. One more key to understanding the Weaving - a weapon against the Primordials. Would it be enough?

Sura joined him, her eyes scanning the horizon. "Do you sense it?" Aran nodded. "The Primordials' presence is stronger here. I can feel it in the air." She glanced at him, her brow furrowing. "Are you sure we are ready for this?"

He met her gaze, a gentle smile touching his lips. "Do we have a choice?" Aran asked. Sura's eyes softened as she looked at him, and she didn't need words to express what lay between them.

The next morning, the group entered the ruins of Kartalis. The stone walls towered over them, their weathered surfaces etched with runes that glowed faintly in the dim light, pulsing like dying stars.

Ancient sigils spiralled across the crumbling stone, telling stories in a language long forgotten. The next obelisk lay somewhere deep within the fortress, buried beneath centuries of dust and shadow, waiting in chambers that hadn't felt a mortal's touch for many ages of this world.

They made their way through the winding corridors. Rafiq took point, his swords drawn, their mirror polished surfaces reflecting the ethereal glow of the runes. Behind him, Barash muttered protective chants under his breath, each word carrying the weight of old knowledge. With each step into the ruins, the air thickened - not just with dust and decay, but with something older. The taste of metal and time lingered on their tongues, as if the fortress itself remembered the blood once spilled within its walls. "How many have walked these halls before us?" Aran wondered, his fingers trailing along the cold stone. "How many never walked out?" The deeper they ventured into Kartalis, the stronger the pull of the Weaving became, tugging at his very soul like an insistent tide. It whispered promises and warnings in equal measure, though he could never quite grasp their meaning.

The passages twisted and turned, some partially collapsed, others eerily intact. Remnants of the fortress's former glory lay scattered about - broken pottery, tarnished metalwork, fragments of old tapestries that crumbled at the slightest touch. Every step taken echoed with hollow reverence, as if the very stones remembered when these halls rang with the footsteps of the Old Kings.

"The power here," Barash whispered, his voice tight with tension. "It's different from the other sites. Older. Rawer." His hands trembled slightly as they traced the air, testing the currents of ancient energy that swirled invisible around them. "Whatever sleeps in this place never truly died."

Rafiq's grip tightened on his swords. "Then let's hope it stays asleep."

Finally, they reached the heart of the ancient fortress. The narrow passage opened into a vast circular chamber that seemed to stretch endlessly upward, its ceiling lost in darkness. There, standing in the centre like a stone spear thrust into the earth, was the obelisk. Unlike many they'd encountered, this one was perfectly intact, its obsidian surface smooth and unblemished.

It radiated an ancient power that made the air hum and crack with vital potential - setting Aran's teeth on edge.

Columns ringed the chamber, their surfaces carved with scenes of battle and triumph, of ritual and sacrifice. The floor was an intricate mosaic depicting what appeared to be a map of the stars - though not of any constellation pattern any of them recognized. Aran wondered if these could be the very stars from which, according to legend, the Old Kings had come. Exchanging looks with Barash and Sura, he saw in their eyes that they were pondering the same thing.

As they stepped further into the room, their footsteps stirred up clouds of dust that danced in the pale light streaming from high, narrow windows. Barash approached cautiously, his eyes wide with a mixture of awe and fear. "This... this is it!" His voice quavered. "One of the nexus points, where several of the planet's ley lines converge. The old texts spoke of them, but I never truly believed..." he trailed off, overwhelmed by the magnitude of their discovery.

Aran stepped forward, his heart pounding against his ribs like a war drum. The Weaving writhed around him, visible now as faint threads of light that twisted and turned in patterns that defied logic and sanity. Could this obelisk finally be the key to understanding it all?

The question burned in his mind, fierce with hope and dread in equal measure. He was almost certain of it - but then, how many other certainties had crumbled to dust in his hands? Every truth he had clung to, every conviction that had driven him forward, had eventually been proved false.

"Yet, this feels different," he mused to himself, studying the obelisk's perfect surface. "This feels final, as if we are almost done."

The chamber seemed to hold its breath as he approached the stone monolith. The air grew thicker, heavier, and charged with promise.

His fingertips tingled as he reached out toward the smooth black stone. Just before his skin made contact, a voice echoed through the chamber - ancient, powerful, and terrifyingly familiar. "You can not stop what is coming, children of clay." Everyone froze in place.

The voice was low and guttural, filled with ancient malice that seemed to freeze the very air. Aran spun around, his hand instinctively finding his father's sword hilt. His mind raced with recognition - he had heard this voice before, many times over, in dreams that had plagued him since childhood. Dreams of darkness. Dreams of unravelling worlds.

"Who's there?" Rafiq demanded, his twin blades already drawn.

The Bahir warrior's usual calm had given way to tension; Aran quickly recognized it in the tight set of his friend's shoulders, the careful way Rafiq placed himself between shadow and kin.

From the abyss at the chamber's edge, something stirred. Shadows thickened, congealing into a form that was neither fully present nor entirely absent - shifting like smoke caught between worlds.

Then, slowly, it stepped forward. Its eyes burned with an unnatural amber light, vast and hollow as the cosmos, staring through flesh into the soul.

It was tall, its outline shifting and indistinct, like smoke caught in an ever-changing wind. "This is what we have been fighting all along," Aran thought, his heart hammering relentlessly against his ribs.

When the figure spoke again, its voice reverberated through the walls, making the ancient stone tremble. "The Weaving will unravel. We are rising!" Its words carried weight beyond their meaning, each syllable heavy with the promise of destruction. "There is nothing any of you can do to stop it."

Barash stumbled back, his face ashen. The old scholar's hands were shaking as he clutched his staff, knuckles white with tension.

"By all the old gods," he whispered, "it's actually here. A true, unbound, manifestation."

Rafiq moved closer to Aran, his voice low. "We have faced worse." He nudged his friend.

"Have we?" Aran replied, elbowing his friend lightly, though he truly appreciated his attempt at comfort. In fact, he welcomed the levity.

Drawing his sword - his father's - with deliberate slowness, Aran stepped forward. He forced steel into his voice, despite the cold fear creeping through his veins. "We shall see about that." The blade caught the ethereal light, its enchanted surface shimming with an inner fire that seemed to push back against the darkness.

The figure remained unnaturally still. Then it laughed. It was a sound in between breaking glass and crumbling mountains - a sound that spoke of epochs passing and worlds dying. "You still cling to your mortal weapons, your fleeting courage." Its form rippled, spreading outward like ink in water. "We are eternal. We are beyond your understanding. The barriers weaken. Soon we shall walk your world as we once did, when your people were young. Your resistance is nothing but the last gasp of a dying age."

"Perhaps," Aran replied, surprising himself with the calm in his voice. "Still, this age is not dead yet." His fingers tightened around his sword hilt as he felt the Weaving surge around him, responding to his will.

"As long as it lives, I will fight for it until my last gust of breath."

The Primordial's form contracted suddenly, its burning gaze intensifying. "You still know very little of what you face, Child of the Last Dawn. The threads you seek to protect are already fraying. The pattern you serve is unravelling before your eyes." Its voice took on an almost pitying tone. "Look for yourself."

With a single motion of its hand, reality warped. The air shuddered, and in its place, the Weaving unfurled before them - a cosmic tapestry stretching across existence. But it was dying. Holes bled through its threads, edges curling like parchment set aflame. The sight made Aran's stomach lurch, a silent horror pressing against his mind, whispering of an unravelling too vast to halt.

"Enough!" Barash shouted, his voice cracking. The old scholar thrust his staff forward, sending a burst of protective energy through the chamber. The vision shattered like glass.

The Primordial's form began to dissolve into the shadows, its laughter echoing through the chamber. "Time grows short, Aran, son of Khalid. When the final thread breaks, you will understand the futility of your struggle."

As the presence faded, Barash stumbled forward, his face drawn and pale. "That... that was no mere manifestation. It was one of the Greater Ones themselves." He leaned heavily on his staff, looking older than Aran had ever seen him. "They must be aware of how close we are to attaining understanding of how to correct the Weaving."

"Then we are still on the right path," Rafiq said grimly, though his blades remained ready.

Aran stared at the space where the Primordial had been, feeling the weight of prophecy and fate pressing down on him. "We need to move quickly." He turned to face Barash, trying his best to keep the urgency from his voice. "Please, old friend, would you activate this one?"

The warrior turned scholar nodded, gathering himself. With a complex gesture and a muttered incantation, he sent a surge of power into the ancient stone. The runes on the obelisk's surface blazed to life, filling the chamber with brilliant light. The Weaving shifted around them, its patterns temporarily stabilizing, granting their minds a fleeting clarity and shared purpose. The monument's power coursed through Aran, and with it, the threads of the Weaving began to align - subtle, intricate paths he had never before perceived

When the brilliance dimmed to a steady glow, he studied the monolith anew. Its surface now carried meanings he had once overlooked. What they had witnessed - what the Primordial had revealed - had changed everything. And yet, in a deeper sense, nothing at all. He would stay on course, against all odds.

With this ancient pillar secured, they began the long journey back to Sarim. The effect of what they had encountered in Kartalis weighed heavily in their hearts, darkening their thoughts and conversations. The desert winds seemed colder now, carrying whispers of ancient threats and impending doom.

"What do you think it meant, by Child of the Last Dawn?" Rafiq asked one evening, as they made camp near a water hole, his voice barely audible over the crackling fire. He was methodically oiling and cleaning his blades, but the tension in his movements was palpable.

Aran stared into the flames, remembering the Primordial's burning gaze. "I have no idea. One more riddle to solve, I suppose."

Yet the title haunted him, stirring something deep in his memories - fragments of old stories his grandmother used to tell, tales of a time when their world was young and the boundaries between realities were thinner.

Barash sat hunched over his scrolls, his weathered fingers tracing the ancient texts. "The Last Dawn appears in several ancient prophecies," he muttered, more to himself than the others. "Always connected to the final turning of an Age." He looked up, his eyes reflecting the firelight. "Prophecies are treacherous things, Aran. Do not put too much heed into them - they show us paths, not destinations."

Aran pondered Barash's words until sleep took hold of him. One by one, the group fell to rest - each consumed by their own musings.

The journey back to Sarim took them through territories that had changed since their last passage. The small oases towns they had passed through mere weeks ago now stood empty - soulless - all their inhabitants fled from some unseen threat. In a village closest to Sarim, doors hung open like mouths frozen mid-scream. Sand had already begun to drift across the abandoned market squares.

The very land seemed to be holding its breath, waiting for something to break.

When they approached the Yaran capital, the 'Jewel of the Northeast', the coastal winds brought Aran the first hints of trouble - the smell of smoke, the distant sound of angry voices. The great port city had always been a crucible of politics and power, but now it felt like a powder keg waiting for a spark.

While Aran prepared for what lay ahead, he felt the threads of fate tightening, pulling him towards something inevitable.

The final confrontation loomed on the horizon - a battle fought not merely over honour and legacy, but for the fabric of reality itself. In that moment, as the desert winds whispered through the city of Sarim, he finally understood the truth that had always lingered at the edge of his awareness. There had never really been a choice to begin with. Only the road - and the storm at its end.

Chapter XXXV

The Crumbling Pillars of Sarim

The winds of Sarim had turned. Where once they carried warm scents of spice and salt through streets of a kingdom secure in its certainty, now they howled with cold edges and whispered unrest.

The city had changed in Aran's absence - its people wary, its council restless. He could feel it in their stares, hear it in their hushed murmurs. Sarim was unravelling, its own 'weaving' fraying at the seams. As he rode through the city's gates, he felt the eyes of his people upon him. They were anxious, their voices filled with hushed tones of unease. The obelisks may have been the key to stopping the Primordials, but Sarim was coming undone in its own way - underneath the heavy weight of its internal divisions, simmering unrest, and the machinations of those who wished to claim the throne for themselves.

In the days since the council had last convened, tensions had risen to dangerous levels. Aran's prolonged absence in pursuit of the Kartalis obelisk had given his rival an opening. Rumours of rebellion had begun to spread through the outer territories. The smaller tribes that had once sworn loyalty to him, due to Ryvan's plotting, were now testing the strength of his rule. Within the heart of Sarim itself, dark whispers spoke of treachery from within his own court.

In his absence, dangers had been allowed to fester, and Aran knew he could no longer ignore them. Zarah was, after all, a realm of mortals, and its people would not wait for their king to finish his celestial quest before tearing it apart. Fear was, indeed, a powerful tool - ready to be wielded by those who cared for nothing but themselves.

As he walked towards it, the throne room felt more distant now than it had before. Its grand pillars loomed like the skeletal remains of some forgotten colossus. Ancient tapestries depicting Zarah's storied history hung between columns of black marble, their golden threads catching the torchlight like captured starfire.

Aran took his seat, the heavy crown resting upon his brow, feeling the weight of both duty and destiny pressing down on him. Rafiq and Sura stood at his side, their faces set with grim determination.

Barash lingered nearby, lost in thought, his mind clearly still fixed on what they had witnessed in Kartalis.

A moment later, the doors to the hall opened, and the gathered tribal leaders - those loyal and otherwise - began to filter in. Their faces were carefully blank, but Aran could sense the tension radiating off them.

There was an unspoken war being waged beneath the surface, one that had been simmering for months on end, and it would not take much to ignite it into open flames.

The council chamber grew silent as Ryvan ibn Farid, one of the most prominent voices opposing Aran's rule, stepped forward. His silvered hair gleamed under the reflected light, and his sharp eyes were fixed on the king with barely concealed contempt.

After the signing of the Great Desert Unification, Ryvan had remained quiet in council - yet Aran had always sensed ambition beneath that silence. This was a man who saw opportunity in the cracks of any foundation. A dangerous ally to keep close - and a far more dangerous enemy to leave unwatched.

"Your Majesty," Ryvan said, his voice measured, each syllable gliding like the edge of a well-honed blade. "At last, you return to us after yet another... well, extended departure. The court has been eager for your wisdom. Though, I must confess, some have begun to wonder - what truly holds your attention?" He grinned. "Our kingdom, or the myths you continue to chase?"

Aran met Ryvan's gaze, his expression unyielding. "I have been ever securing our survival, lord Ryvan."

The irony of being called lord by the king did not go unnoticed. Ryvan bit his lip as the words washed over him.

Aran pressed on. "You play politics while forces beyond your vaunted comprehension stir beneath our feet. This is not a matter of ambition or conquest - it is a war for existence itself. Perhaps you choose not to see it. However, that will not make it any less real."

"Ah, the obelisks," Ryvan responded, feigning interest. "Of course. These ancient stones you have been chasing across Zarah's rugged wilderness." A smirk played on his lips. "Yet, while you seek these stone relics, these tethers as you call them, your kingdom continues to suffer. Our borders grow restless - the smaller tribes divided. How long can the crown afford to chase ghosts when the present demands action?"

Whispers rippled through the chamber after Ryvan's retort, and Aran felt the weight of every eye upon him - evaluating his strength.

He knew Ryvan's game well; the man was still playing on the fears of the council, the populace, using the kingdom's uncertainty to plant more seeds of doubt about their king's leadership. Nonetheless, there was truth in Ryvan's words. Aran had been absent, and Sarim's growing unrest was undeniable.

Indifferent to all of this, the Weaving was still crumbling - and if the Primordials were not stopped, none of it would matter in the end.

"It is not a choice between the present and the past," Aran said, his deep voice cutting through the murmurs. "The obelisks remain our only hope to stop the forces that threaten us all. The Primordials are not myths, I tell you - they are rising, and Zarah's fate, along with our own, rests on understanding the power within these ancient structures." Despite being aware of Ryvan's true intentions, Aran still held out hope the man might yet see reason - rather than remain shackled by his own ambition.

Ryvan, cold and indifferent to Aran's pleas for rationale, raised an eyebrow. "I only ask you this: how long must we wait for salvation, my king? How long until we see results? Sarim bleeds in your absence, while you speak of ancient powers and vanish for indefinite stretches of time. The people grow hungry - the minor tribal leaders grow restless."

This was it, Ryvan thought. His moment had arrived. "You are not the only one with a vision for this kingdom's future."

A collective intake of breath swept through the chamber. Some lords leaned forward, others drew back. The moment crystallized - loyalties becoming visible in posture and glance. Aran held his gaze - until the man, unable to withstand it, was forced to look away.

Kasim al-Bahir slammed his fist against the crescent table. "Traitor!"

The loyal lord appeared to summon every fibber of strength to prevent himself from lunging at Ryvan.

Safira moved to speak, but Aran raised his hand, his eyes narrowing.

"You tread a fine line, Ryvan," he said, his voice low and dangerous. "I suggest you step carefully - and choose your next words wisely."

Ryvan's smile was thin, but his words were pointed. "I would remind you, king, that your crown rests upon your head, not merely by the power of old pacts or bloodlines, but by the will of those gathered here, around you. Should your judgement falter, it is our duty to ensure that we remain strong, with or without you. Am I wrong?"

Zahira looked like she wanted to kill Ryvan. Feelings that had been, no doubt, harboured from previous, unsuccessful, perhaps even violent, arguments with the man. Sura placed a hand on Aran's shoulder, beckoning him to remain calm.

The tension in the room was palpable. Rafiq shifted at Aran's side, his hand inching toward the hilt of his dagger, but Aran held up a hand to sway him. He knew Ryvan's true ambition, and he could see the way his supporters were watching, waiting to see how the king would respond to this challenge.

A show of force would only feed Ryvan's narrative, painting Aran as a desperate monarch clinging to power.

Nevertheless, a decisive blow needed to be struck here, and it needed to be one that would remind the court of who truly held the power to save them all.

"Lords and Ladies of Zarah," Aran said, rising from the throne.

His voice was cold and commanding, echoing across the vast hall. "Do not mistake the urgency of my quest for the absence of rule," he calmly declared. "The power I seek is not for myself, but for the protection of this kingdom and all who dwell beyond its borders. The Primordials are coming, whether you believe me or not, and when they do, they will not care for the squabbles of men and women. Be certain of this. If we do not unite now, once and for all, we will all be swept away by forces far greater than any of you dares to imagine."

His words hung in the air and, for a moment, there was only silence. Aran could see the flicker of uncertainty in the eyes of some of the nobles, but Ryvan's reaction was one of those that mattered most. The older lord's smile had faded, replaced by a calculating look - he had pushed the king, and though he had not succeeded in undermining him completely, the seeds of dissent were already sown.

Aran took a deep breath. This was it, the moment had come for him to fully embody his role as protector and guide for his people. Even if he needed to protect them from themselves.

Aran, son of Khalid, king of Zarah, chose his next words carefully, but he would not spare them of his frustration. When he spoke, his voice was steady and infused with an underlying menace.

"Ryvan, I speak now directly to you, and whomever is foolish enough to pay heed to your musings. I appreciate your concern for the welfare of our kingdom, but I would caution you against mistaking the crown's silence for weakness. My bloodline ruled Zarah for countless, storied generations, from the depths of our peoples' past, and I will continue to do so, with or without the support of those who now fancy themselves kingmakers."

Ryvan inclined his head, but there was no mistaking the tension in his jaw. "Of course, my king, I only seek what is best for our people."

"Then you will support me in the defence of our kingdom, yes?" Aran asked, his gaze unflinching. "Or you will be remembered as one who sought to weaken it in its hour of greatest need." Ryvan felt the blow.

Sensing the shift in the room, Aran pressed on. "Do not forget that Drathis is still out there. He has attacked Sarim twice before, and though we defeated his army, he is bound to attack us again. I seriously doubt we have seen the last of the House of Draco." The king's words were met with utter silence.

In the corner, half-lost in shadow and wreathed in smoke from his pipe, Barash flipped a dagger between his fingers with lazy precision. His knowing smile suggested he had anticipated this confrontation - perhaps even engineered it.

No one knew how to respond to the king, and in that moment of stillness, Aran rose once more from his throne - the Moonleaf silver and sand crystal crown catching the light as he descended the marble steps to the council floor. His loyal tribal leaders parted before him as he deliberately approached Ryvan, stopping only when they stood face to face. Close enough that only those nearest could hear his words. "You believe I chase shadows while the kingdom crumbles," Aran said, his voice low but carrying in the hushed chamber. "Then come with me, Ryvan ibn Farid."

Confusion flickered across Ryvan's face. "What game is this, Your Majesty?" He asked, his left eye twitching.

"No game. An invitation." Aran's gaze held Ryvan's, unyielding as desert stone. "Join me on my journey to the last obelisk - the monolith that embodies death and rebirth. See for yourself what I have seen. Touch the ancient stone and experience the fractures in the Weaving within your own body."

Ryvan's jaw tightened, sweat trickling down his brow. "You would have me abandon my people to chase your visions?"

"I would have you understand the true threat before you undermine our only chance of survival," Aran countered, loud enough now for all to hear. "Unless, of course, your concern for Sarim extends only as far as your ambition." Ryvan blushed.

Kasim al-Bahir stepped forward. "I will gladly go in his stead, my king. If there is truth to be witnessed, let those loyal to your crown bear witness first."

Still, Aran kept his eyes fixed on Ryvan. "I am moved by your unyielding loyalty, Kasim, my brother. But no - Lord Ryvan remains the one who has questioned my path most boldly - the invitation is for him alone."

The tension in the chamber shifted, crystallizing around the two men. Ryvan's supporters exchanged glances, while loyalists to Aran's crown watched with barely concealed satisfaction. The king's dare was no mere political gamble - it was a direct challenge. One that his opponent could not decline without losing face before the council.

Ryvan's shoulders slumped, his silver hair gleaming like polished metal in the chamber's light, as he cowered. "Your Majesty asks much," Ryvan said, his composure cracking slightly. "Such journeys are the burden of kings, not their advisors. I will serve Sarim best by remaining to guard against... more earthly threats."

"Wait," Aran shot. "So now, it is my charge, is it? Am I to understand from this that you lack the courage to sustain your own claims?"

Ryvan diminished - shamed - though not defeated. In his eyes, Aran could still see open defiance. "We shall continue this discussion at a later time," he turned to leave.

"There is nothing more to discuss," Aran retorted, "I believe everyone here is well aware, by now, of the quality of your mettle - or lack thereof." As Ryvan was walking out of the council chambers, he felt all eyes on him.

The council was dismissed soon after, but the undercurrents of Ryvan's dissidence still lingered, swirling through the halls of the palace. Aran was sure that Ryvan was not alone in his ambitions. There were bound to be others who waited in the wings, biding their time, ready to strike when they sensed weakness.

As evening shadows lengthened across the palace marble halls, the weight of the day's confrontation settled upon Aran's shoulders like the crown he bore. Even so, he took comfort in knowing that, for now, they had been reminded: the House of Aran still stood - and its king would not be so easily undermined.

That night, Aran stood alone on the balcony overlooking the city of Sarim. The lights of the coastal capital flickered below, and beyond the walls, he could see the distant expanse of the desert that stretched out to the opposing horizon. It was a vast, complex web of loyalties, rivalries, and ancient traditions, all held together by the thread of his rule. That thread, old as it might have been, in Zarah's past, had never felt thinner.

Sura joined him after supper, her presence quiet but comforting. She didn't speak, but Aran could feel her eyes, waiting for him to share the thoughts that weighed so heavily on his mind.

"It's slipping, Sura," he murmured, his voice quieter than the salty wind. "Not just our kingdom, but our dream. The world we fought for. It is fraying, and I can feel it unravelling through my fingers."

If Ryvan succeeded in fracturing the tribal alliance, Zarah would shatter into warring factions just as the Primordials emerged. The kingdom would destroy itself before the true enemy ever arrived.

"You still have time," she said softly. "The obelisks-"

"The obelisks are only part of it," he interrupted, turning to face her. "Even if we find them all, even if I stop the Primordials... What will be left of Zarah by the end of it? As cold as the depths of the ocean at our doorstep, Ryvan and his supporters are already moving against us. However, they do not understand the danger, and by the time they might, it may prove itself to be too late."

Even though she had already shared her opinion on the matter, Sura felt it necessary to reinstate her stand. "Then you need to ensure that they understand," she said, her eyes fierce. "You need to show them that this is not just about power or politics. It is about survival."

Aran turned to face the horizon, Sura's words swimming in his thoughts. "Show them more than I already have? How blind can they be?" he asked himself.

He nodded back, not wanting to upset her further, though his heart was heavy with doubt. In the last two years of his life, he had faced the ancient powers of the world, seen the vastness of the Weaving, and yet it was the fragility of the visions he was shown that filled him with the greatest fear - how could he protect their world from the Primordials if it was already tearing itself apart from within?

The wind whipped around them. Aran felt the pull of fate stronger than ever. The threads were tightening, and soon, the final choices would be upon him - unavoidable.

Whether he would emerge as Zarah's saviour or join the dust of its forgotten kings would depend on battles yet to come - those within his kingdom's heart and those beyond the Weaving itself.

Chapter XXXVI

Shadows of the Past

Aran stood in the great hall of Sarim's palace, where history itself clung to the air like a ghost. The tapestries lining the walls bore the weight of millennia, each stitch woven with the triumphs and tragedies of his ancestors. Kings, queens, warriors, rulers - figures who had shaped Zarah long before his time. For most of his life, their legacy had been little more than distant echoes, a burden thrust upon him by fate. Now, as he stood beneath their watchful gaze, he felt the fraying threads of his world slipping through his fingers. Would he be Zarah's saviour? Or its final mistake? He could feel the growing tension between the past and the present - between the legacy he sought to protect and the uncertain future that loomed before them all.

Outside, the skies were darkening, the wind howling through the ancient Minare spires of Sarim. It was as though the very elements conspired to mirror the turmoil within his kingdom.

The north was shifting. Reports spoke of banners rising in defiance, of swords sharpened in the dark. Several minor lords - emboldened by Ryvan's insidious whispers - were testing the limits of their oaths.

A rebellion was no longer a question of 'if,' but of 'when'.

While Aran had spent two winters and nearly two springs fighting for Zarah's survival against cosmic threats, his kingdom had begun rotting from within. Rebellion was simmering on the horizon, threatening to tear his House apart, whilst the greater dangers of the Draconians and the Primordials remained unresolved, seeking to destroy it from without.

In the heart of this storm, Aran stood at a crossroads. He had returned to Sarim after countless struggles, so he thought, with a more comprehensive approach to the obelisks and the looming threat posed by the ancient pact. Still, even that knowledge came with more questions than answers. What he and his friends unearthed along the way had revealed several truths about the Weaving, but the true nature of the Primordials remained elusive, locked away in the forgotten corners of time. The next steps he took would determine not only his fate but that of an entire planet.

Rafiq and Sura, along with the rest of his most fervent supporters, were already waiting when Aran arrived in the war chamber. The room, with its circular table filled with scrolls and detailed maps of Zarah, had once been the site of carefully measured strategies and heated diplomatic discussions. Now, it felt like a war room in the truest sense. Sarim was preparing for battle, both within and beyond its borders. After the last council meeting, Ryvan had left the city in great haste, and most of them believed he was gathering fighting forces to oppose Aran's reign.

Rafiq's face was hard, his eyes burning with a quiet fury. "Some of the northern lords are amassing their armies," he said without preamble, pointing to the northern region of the map. "Our scouts have sent word that the Selaran and the Graidan tribes have placed themselves alongside Ryvan, and intend to stand against you. They say that Ryvan has already started consolidating support from the smaller clans. He has amassed quite an army, in the process. If we do not act soon, we will be facing open rebellion."

Aran's jaw tightened. "What about the others?"

Sura stepped forward, her voice steady. "The southern territories remain loyal for now, but even their support is tenuous. Lord Iram al-Yrith is wavering. He is one of Ryvan's supporters, but he is waiting, biding his time, to see who emerges strongest before he declares his allegiance. The coward!" she grunted. "The capital remains under our control, but the people are restless. They fear the growing instability. Word of the Primordials is spreading, though most still dismiss it as myth."

Aran nodded slowly. "They focus on what they understand - war, politics, power. Despite what is happening before their eyes, the ancient threats feel too distant to them, too abstract. Therefore, they chose to ignore them instead of facing their fears head-on. Fools. They do not realize how close they are to losing everything they hold dear."

Rafiq's eyes darkened. "And Ryvan? What does he understand?"

"He understands ambition," Aran said, his voice like tempered steel. "Ryvan does not believe in causes - only opportunities. He knows that fear is the sharpest blade of all. He will cut this kingdom apart if it means placing the crown upon his own head. Unfortunately he, the same as our people, does not understand the true scope of what we are facing. For if he did, he would not be so quick to stoke the fires of rebellion."

Kasim pretended to cough. "You should have let me take care of him before he could bring us more harm." If a gaze were able to bring death upon another, Ryvan would collapse upon facing Kasim's eyes. Kasim al-Bahir was furious with himself. "Just like that rat, Farid. No one knows where he is. Either dead or escaped, who knows. Good riddance is what I say." He slammed his fist on the council table.

"No," Aran's voice gave away no hint of the storm toiling inside his soul. "Killing Ryvan would only bring us down to his level. We are better than that." His voice was calm, despite the doubts gnawing at his resolve.

"Better to have done that than to deal with an enemy on the inside," Karim al-Shamar spat. "As if our outer threats weren't enough to begin with, we also have snakes slithering around our feet?" He was dishevelled but, nonetheless, focused.

Sura met Aran's gaze, her expression filled with quiet determination. "We still have time to turn the tide, but we need a show of strength - something that will remind the dissident tribal lords, the people, and our enemies alike, that Sarim is not so easily vanquishable."

Aran exhaled slowly, running a hand through his long hair. His mind raced, trying to piece together the complex fragments of the puzzle laid before him. The rebellion was a distraction from the main threat, minor by comparison, but one that could not be ignored. Ryvan's actions threatened the very foundation of Sarim, and if the kingdom fell to internal strife, the Primordials would find it ripe for conquest.

Yet, even as Aran weighed his options, his thoughts kept drifting back to the obelisks - the forgotten pillars of power that stretched back to the dawn of the Weaving. He went through them in his mind. He had, inadvertently, destroyed two, and after many struggles and study, he managed to harmonize the rest.

Now, the last one was calling to him. The one where all his hopes lay. Aran could feel its presence tugging at his consciousness, as though it was a living thing, bound to him by a force he did not yet fully understand. The monolith of death. Were the Primordials waiting for him to make a move? Their inaction puzzled him. Were they biding their time? If so, what for? "What of the obelisks?" he asked the room, his voice low. "There is one more left. I can feel it calling to me."

Barash, who had been silent until now, stepped forward. His robes, frayed from travel and the weight of their quest, fluttered slightly as he spoke. "I have spent the last several days, in deep meditation, studying the Weaving, and following the threads that link us to the Primordials. Aside from those who chose to betray us, everyone in this room knows by now that the obelisks are not merely monuments, and their power is no mere myth - they are anchors. Each one held a piece of the power that bound the Primordials to our world. So far, our king has done a splendid job in dealing with them." He scratched the stubble on his chin and looked at Aran. "However, do you remember that they are also keys? I told you this when we encountered the first one, right here, in the bowels of our city. Forgotten by time but not by the House of Draco."

Aran nodded. "I do remember. Why are you mentioning it now?" Barash studied his pupil carefully. The son of his dearest friend just needed a nudge. Aran's eyes were as inquisitive as they had been throughout his life. "Keys, Aran." Barash repeated, his eyes twinkling. "Keys that can open doors... or shut those doors forever."

Aran's eyes sharpened. "Shut them?"

Barash nodded slowly, his expression unreadable. "Consider this: the Weaving might appear stable, but it is not. If we end up destroying the last obelisk, we may sever the Primordials' grip on this world... or we may shatter the balance entirely. Either way, it will not be done without consequence." The room fell into silence, each breath a whisper of uncertainty. "There is no victory without sacrifice," Barash murmured, almost to himself. "The only question is whose sacrifice it will be."

Aran was running all his options in his mind, racing from possibility to probability, without end.

Still, there was another question that gnawed at him, one that had haunted his thoughts since his first encounter with the Echo of Worlds. In that liminal place, he had been faced with the option to try and control the Weaving. If the obelisks could be used to sever the connection to the Primordials, they could also be used to control that power. Unfortunately, that choice came at the peril of losing himself to power and corruption. That was something he had sworn he would never do, even under threat of demise. "Death before dishonour." His father's words branded into his very soul.

This thought burned in his heart, as the question he dreaded to ask left his lips. "What if I wield the Weaving?" he asked, the words heavier than iron. The chamber went still. Karim al-Shamar fidgeted with his silver-rimmed spectacles, his knuckles white. Safira, the moon seer, looked stricken, as if the very air had turned to ice. No one spoke, yet the weight of their silent horror filled the space between them. Aran let the question linger, tasting the enormity of it. Would he become a saviour? Or merely the next in a long line of fools who thought they could command the gods?

Barash hesitated, his eyes narrowing as he considered the question. "The Weaving is delicate and fragile, yet extremely powerful. To tamper with it is to invite chaos. But," he seemed to be struggling to get the words out, "yes, it is possible. The Old Kings, in their ignorance, once wielded the power of the obelisks, a device of their own making, to their own detriment, but if someone could learn to control it..." he looked Aran in the eyes as if to convey something that mere words could not. "They would possess unimaginable strength."

Aran's heart pounded, for he knew well the dangers, as well as the risks of meddling with such ancient forces.

At the same time, the fate of their world was at stake. If he could master the obelisks' power, he could defeat the House of Draco, the Primordials, crush the rebellion, and restore order to his kingdom. That was a lovely theory, but what would be the cost?

That had always been the biggest thorn at his side. Would he be weak as his forebears had been and fall to the temptation of limitless power, or would he rise above his forefathers and achieve something they could never have, even in their wildest dreams?

Was he able to sacrifice himself for the well-being of his people?

The answer was yes, an indomitable and resounding yes. After all, he knew what needed to be done and had been, even without knowing, preparing himself for such a sacrifice since birth.

The chamber was silent as the weight of his thoughts settled over him. Sura exchanged a glance with Rafiq, both of them sensing the conflict brewing within their friend. Perceptive as always, her eyes were filled with tears. "You can't seriously be considering this," Sura met his gaze, and not for the first time, Aran saw not just worry but heartbreak. Not fear, nor sorrow, but something deeper. "You can't," she whispered.

"Not this," her voice was firm, yet fragile, as if speaking the words would make them real. "The obelisks are too dangerous. We felt their power in our blood. We fought it," she shuddered. "Even the Old Kings, despite their wisdom, were consumed by their power, in the end. If you try to wield it..." her voice trailed off, vanquished by her feelings.

Aran, his eyes kind and peaceful, took her hands in his. "We have tried everything else. We have destroyed them, as well as harmonizing them to the Weaving. So far, it helped in delaying the problem, nothing more," he wiped a tear from her face, "I don't know if we have any other choice," he pleaded, his voice low. "If I do not act, Sarim will fall. Either by Drathis' hand or the unravelling of the Weaving. On the other hand, if we take too long to act, if the Primordials rise before we are ready? It will not just be Sarim that falls - it will be the whole of Zarah."

Barash stepped forward, his expression grim. "There may be another way." Both Aran and Sura turned to face him, his brow furrowed, hers expectant. "What do you mean?" They asked, in unison.

Barash's gaze was distant, as though he were peering through the veil of time itself. Only Safira seemed to be able to glimpse what Barash could see. "As you know by now, the Weaving is not a static thing," he said. "It can be manipulated and reshaped -"

Aran cut in. "We already know these things, Barash," he was getting impatient. Sometimes, his tutor's ways bewildered him. "Why are you telling us this again?" Everyone around the table was quiet, expectantly waiting for Barash's next words.

Barash kept going as if there had been no interruptions. He was too focused. Thinking out loud. This helped him to organise his thoughts. "The obelisks are tied to the fabric of reality, but they are not immutable. If we can find the last obelisk, the one that governs both death and rebirth, we may be able to rewrite the Weaving itself - to sever the Primordials' connection without the need for destruction."

Aran's mind raced. The implications were staggering.

To reshape the Weaving would be to change the very nature of existence, to bend the laws of reality to his will. He knew that road led to playing with powers that could take hold of his soul, as it had his ancestors. It was a path where, at its destination, he could lose his essence. That frightened him more than death.

He turned slowly, his fingers brushing the edge of the ancient map spread across the war table, tracing the worn lines that charted a world on the brink. And yet... there was a glimmer of hope, a way to stop the Primordials without risking unleashing their full power. If it went wrong for him, his life would be a small price to pay for their freedom from these ancient historical chains. One he was more than willing to pay. Still, that would require more than just knowledge. It would require courage and no small amount of personal sacrifice.

"How do I do this?" Aran found himself asking, his voice filled with both curiosity and dread. Sura got up and left the room. Aran made a gesture to stand, but Rafiq placed a hand on his shoulder. "Steady yourself, brother. Leave her be, she shall find her peace. Focus on the task at hand." His voice was apparently calm, if not for a small tremble of the chin.

Aran's heart twisted as he watched her retreating form, knowing that each word spoken here carved deeper the chasm between duty and the life he might have chosen, had fate played a different hand.

Barash looked like he had been pulled from a trance. He hesitated before answering. "The Weaving is bound by life. To alter it, to try and manipulate its threads, would require a force equal to that which created it. The threads themselves pulse with the heartbeat of existence - visible as streams of silver light to those who can perceive them, each one singing with the voices of every soul it touches. In essence, to reshape the Weaving," he closed his eyes, for his next words tasted like dread, "someone would have to offer their life to become part of the fabric itself."

Aran felt a chill run down his spine. "A life, you say?" All those sitting at the table held their breath.

Barash nodded slowly, with a heavy heart. "One life to save many. Yet, it must be someone with a deep connection to the Weaving," he paused, trying hard to push the words out. "Someone who has touched the obelisks, who understands the flow of time and power that binds the world together."

The weight of the truth settled over him, cold and final. As for the weight of fate? It settled upon him like an old cloak, familiar yet heavier than ever before. There was only one life the Weaving would accept. His own.
"So be it." Aran's voice was steady, unshaken.
In the silence that followed, he could almost hear the whispers of his ancestors - not in judgement, but in understanding. They too had faced impossible choices. They too had carried the burden of a crown that demanded everything.
Fate had carved this path long before he could walk it. He had spent his life searching for purpose, and in the end, it had been waiting for him all along.
Aran let out a soft chuckle, humourless yet sincere. "Fitting," he thought. "A king, giving himself to the threads that wove him." The sound of his laughter was bitter, yet strangely freeing. "Humour," he mused to himself, "truly is the last shield against the dark."
Now came the harder task - convincing his friends that some prices, however dear, were worth paying.

Chapter XXXVII

The Woven Path

The night was cold - colder than it had been in living memory. Sarim lay beneath a suffocating sky, Zarah's twin moons, Anar and Nysa were swallowed by an ocean of heavy, unrelenting clouds. The salty wind howled through the streets like a lament, a restless murmur that carried whispers of forgotten ages. It felt as though the past itself was stirring, reaching out to the present with unseen hands.

Aran stood alone in the tower chamber, staring into the darkness, his mind a fortress of certainty. Nonetheless, despite his conviction, Barash's revelation weighed heavily on him. The obelisks had proven themselves to be an almost endless source of bewilderment. They had always been the simplest answer to the riddle that was the Weaving, staring him in the face, only to ever remain elusive and enigmatic. They were not just keys to open portals to another dimension, or tethers that bind the primordials to their fragile prison - they were conduits. Physical threads woven into the very fabric of the Weaving. To sever them could save Sarim, could even save Zarah from the Primordials. Yet, the cost... the cost was unthinkable, unpredictable.

The Weaving itself was ancient, older than the kingdoms of men, perhaps even older than the Primordials. It was a lattice of life and death, creation, and destruction. To alter it would require not only immense power but the ultimate sacrifice. One that he was continuously willing to offer. The threads of fate were tightening, binding him in a grip he could not escape. He felt it in his bones, in the marrow of his very soul. For all his strength, all his victories, his life had never been his own. It was not a path he had chosen - it had been carved into the very fabric of the Weaving long before he was born. Now, that path had led to a decision that could ripple across eternity.

Aran closed his eyes, breathing deeply. He thought of his ancestors, the kings and queens of his bloodline, who had ruled Sarim for millennia. He thought of their strength, their wisdom, their struggles. Would they have been able to make this decision? Would they have had the courage to sacrifice themselves for the greater good, or would they have fought for their survival, even if it meant dooming their subjects and the world to the chaos promised by the Primordials? Unfortunately, he did not have the luxury of finding out the answer to that question. Though, giving his forebears choices on the matter, such an answer was not too difficult to hypothesize.

The door creaked open behind him, and Sura entered, her steps soft but filled with purpose. She had been his constant companion throughout this ordeal, her loyalty and love unwavering. She approached him, her face etched with concern, awash with tears.

"Aran," she began softly, "I know what you are thinking. I can feel it."

Aran did not turn to her immediately. Instead, he kept his gaze fixed on the horizon, where the mountains of the north loomed like silent sentinels. "No surprise there," he said, his eyes twinkling.

She managed a feeble smile, as she leaned on his shoulder. Both stood in silence for a long time, observing the city below. Aran could sense the nervousness that pervaded its streets. "You know the choice I have to make," he said at last.

The words tasted like iron - not a lie, but not the whole truth either.

He spoke of choice as if alternatives remained, when his decision had already crystallized into certainty.

She nodded, her voice firm once more. "Yes, I do. Still, it does not have to be a burden for you to bear alone."

Aran finally turned to face her, his eyes shadowed by the weight of his thoughts. "Sura," he began. "It is my burden because I am the only one who can carry it," he replied. "Barash was clear. The obelisks respond to those who have touched the Weaving and, besides the two of you, and Rafiq once, no one has been closer to it than I have, and I am not risking your lives anymore.

She held his gaze in hers. "Why not mine?" Her voice was barely above a whisper, yet it cut through his defences like a well sharpened blade.

Aran exhaled, his fingers brushing against her cheek. "Because I could not bear it."

She looked into his soulful eyes as he spoke, wishing to embrace him, to provide some comfort. "I can take care of myself." Her eyes, soft as Moonleaf petals, were kind as she replied. "I know, but this is different. You could die, Aran." It seemed to her that he was avoiding something. "Anyone can die, at any time, why am I different, in your eyes?" She wanted to hear him say it - she needed it.

"Because," Aran hesitated, unsure if he should say it aloud, "because I-" He broke off, remaining silent for a moment - his eyes shifting towards the horizon.

Deciding this was not the moment to open up his feelings for her, he looked her deep in the eyes and said. "You must understand, the Echo of Worlds, the Trials of the Old Kings, the visions, the stone monoliths themselves - it is all tied to me, Sura. To my bloodline."

She understood why he hadn't said it, why he had avoided it. Stepping closer, her hand resting on his arm, she said. "You are the king. But you are also more than that - you are a man, Aran. A man who has fought for his people, who has stood against impossible odds time and time again. Willing to make the necessary sacrifices to give your people a better future."

Sura looked at him, trying to make eye contact, but he was immersed in thought. Though his gaze was distant, his silence invited her to continue. "You have the strength to make this decision, Aran, but you do not have to make it in isolation."

Little did she know that he had already made it. Aran's chest tightened. He wanted to believe her. He would give anything to believe her. To believe that there was another way, another solution that did not require such a devastating price. Yet he sensed that the Weaving could not be so easily manipulated. He would do what needed to be done, but there was no avoiding the cost.

"I wish there was another way, but there isn't one," he whispered, more to himself than to her. For a moment, the certainty that had carried him this far wavered like a candle flame in the wind.

What if Barash was wrong? What if his sacrifice would be meaningless, his people left defenceless and his death merely the first of countless others?

The doubt clawed at him, cold and sharp, before he forced it down. Some paths could not be walked while looking backward. Sura's hand tightened on his arm, her voice fierce. "Then we will find one!"

Aran remained silent for a few seconds, then shook his head slowly. "No, Sura. The path has already been set. The Weaving is still mostly bound to the obelisks, and those are still bound to the Primordials. We can destroy them and even try to harmonize them, but that will not end the threat. The Primordials will always find a way back unless we sever the connection once and for all. That's what Barash meant when he said the Weaving had to be rewritten. To do that... someone must, willingly, become part of it."

Sura's eyes filled with pain, but she did not release her hold on him. "You mean to tell me that you believe that someone must be you. Right?" Her eyes, though steady, were glistening.

"Sura, it has to be me," Aran pleaded, his voice steady. "Your help has been invaluable, I would not be here now without it. Notwithstanding your unwavering support, I am the only one who has truly touched the Weaving and survived. If anyone else tried to manipulate it, they would be consumed by it. Barash said as much, after you left."

For a long moment, the room was silent, save for the howling wind outside. Despite the tears running down her face, Sura's gaze did not waver from his, though he could clearly see the anguish in her eyes.

Anguish, yes, but also admiration, as well as an undying loyalty. This gave him strength. But more than anything else, her eyes were filled with love, and that had been precisely the reason why he had not expressed his true feelings for her. That would make it final and their goodbyes even harder.

Sura's eyes caught his. "You have always been willing to sacrifice yourself for your people," she said quietly. "But this time... this time the cost is too high." He looked at her, his expression softening. "What other choice do I have? Send someone else in my stead?"

Her jaw clenched, her hands trembling slightly. "We will find another way. We always have. This is not the end."

Again, he wished he could believe her. Though he knew, deep down, that the end was coming - whether he was prepared for it or not. Yet, he could not resist.

Looking deep into her eyes, he asked the question. "Why are you so determined to stop me from doing this?" Sura looked away, her eyes awash with tears - a deep pool of feelings waiting to be unleashed. She took a deep breath and returned his look.

"Because I..." She faltered, her breath catching as the words she had carried for so long pressed against her lips like caged birds desperate for flight. Her eyes searched his face, memorizing every line, every shadow cast by the flickering torchlight.

The silence stretched, heavy with all the things they had never dared to say, until the door to his chambers burst open and Rafiq entered, his expression grim. The spell between them shattered like glass. Aran straightened, his shoulders squaring as he shifted from lover to king in the space of a heartbeat - the transformation so swift and complete that Sura felt the distance between them widen like a chasm.

"Ryvan's coalition is marching," Rafiq announced, his voice clipped, sharp. "Rumours say that he will lead them personally. They will reach the gates of Sarim within days."

Aran's heart sank, though he had expected this news, Ryvan was moving faster than anticipated, rallying the disaffected tribes to his cause. The rebellion was no longer a threat on the horizon - it was here, at the gates of his kingdom. This was an irony written at large. His vision for a unified Zarah was brought to its knees by old curses and petty rebellions. "How many?" he asked. "A few thousands, perhaps more. Ryvan has promised them a new dawn, a kingdom free of your crown's weakness. He has promised them a future." Rafiq's hands were curled into fists.

Aran turned away from the window, his thoughts racing. Ryvan had always been ambitious, but this was something else entirely - a direct challenge to his rule, to his very right to wear the crown. If Ryvan succeeded in fracturing the kingdom, Sarim would fall into chaos, and the Primordials would return to a world already weakened by civil war. "Let us not forget Drathis. Who knows what he is plotting. We can not afford to fight a war on two fronts, let alone three." Aran said quietly, despite the storm brewing inside of him. "If either Drathis or Ryvan breaches the walls, our kingdom is lost."

Rafiq 's jaw tightened. "Then we must make our stand here, at Sarim. We will hold the gates, no matter the cost."

Aran nodded, though he knew the battle would be bloody. Sarim was fortified once more, its walls thick and strong. At the same time, the forces rallying against them were determined, and none would stop until they had torn his kingdom apart. All the while, the eminent threat of the Primordials loomed ever closer, like a shadow creeping across the land.

"We will defend the city," Aran said. "But I must also confront the final obelisk and the Primordials. We do not have time to wait for the war to play out. The Primordials are already rising, and if we do not act now, nothing will stop them from breaking the binding."

Rafiq looked at him sharply. "You intend to leave?! Now? With Ryvan marching towards us?"

"I have no choice," Aran replied. "Regardless of our successes or failures with them, the obelisks remain the key to stopping the Primordials - the key to change everything. If we do not sever their connection to our world, everything we have fought for will have been for nothing. Drathis, the rebellion, the war - it will all be meaningless in the face of their return."

Rafiq's expression hardened, but he did not argue. He knew the truth as well as Aran did. Their kingdom's future did not rest on any single battle, but rather on a much larger struggle.

"We will leave tonight," Aran said. "Barash and I will travel to the final stone tether. With any luck, we can find a way to use it to sever the connection between the obelisks and repair the Weaving before the Primordials are fully awaken."

"What of Sarim?" Rafiq asked, his voice low. "What will we do if you do not return?" His face was stoic, betrayed only by a slight tremble of the jaw.

Aran met his friend's gaze, his voice steady. "Then you fight, brother. You fight and you keep fighting, with everything you have. Represent me, and make sure that the people of Sarim survive, no matter the cost." The silence that followed spoke louder than the words they exchanged.

As the night deepened over the city, casting a pale light over the landscape, Aran prepared for his journey. The obelisks called to him, their power pulsing through the Weaving, pulling him toward them.

He could feel their presence more acutely now, like a steady heartbeat thrumming beneath the surface of his skin - always present.

Barash had already prepared the supplies for their journey, the old warrior's expression solemn as he stood by Aran's side.

The journey to the last obelisk would not be easy - it lay deep within the mountains, in the forgotten lands beyond the north-western borders. A place that had not seen human footsteps in generations. Zahira, Kasim, Safira, and all his main supporters were there, so they could pay respect to the man who was willing to give up his life, in exchange for theirs.

Sura stood beside him, her eyes filled with a mixture of fear and fierce determination. She had fought by his side for years, through every battle, every hardship. Only this time, he knew he would have to leave her behind. "I will return," Aran said softly, though he wasn't sure if he believed that himself.

Sura's lips pressed into a thin line, but she nodded. "You better."

For a moment, they stood in silence, the weight of unspoken words hanging between them. The moment stretched, heavy with unspoken truths, until, with a final glance at the kingdom he had sworn to protect and expand, Aran mounted his steed.

"Wait!" A voice shouted from behind him.

Aran turned to see Rafiq approaching, already mounted and armed for travel. His friend's jaw was set with familiar determination, the same expression he had worn, many times, when they were boys planning raids on the kitchen stores, and later when they had stood together on countless battlefields.

"I decided you are not going anywhere without me," Rafiq declared, though his voice carried a tremor that spoke of the weight of leaving his post. "I have served as your shield-brother through every trial. I will not break that oath now, when your greatest trial awaits."

"Our kingdom needs you here," Aran protested.

"The kingdom needs its king to return," Rafiq replied firmly. "And I intend to make sure that happens."

The two warriors and lifetime friends looked at each other in silence. Then, with a smile, Aran said. "So be it." Barash mounted his onyx steed nearby, offering Rafiq a silent nod of approval.

The gates of Sarim yawned open with the groan of ancient hinges, the wind shrieking like a spectre as Aran and his companions rode into the night. The cobblestones rang hollow beneath their horses' hooves, each strike echoing off the stone walls like a funeral drum.

Cold air bit through Aran's cloak, carrying the scent of distant snow and something else - something that might have been the metallic tang of approaching fate.

The city behind him was a sea of torchlight and whispered prayers. He did not look back. The path before him was set. The last chapter of his story had begun. The end was coming, indifferent to whether he was ready for it or not.

With each step taken toward the final obelisk, he felt the threads of the Weaving pulling tighter around his soul, drawing him toward a destiny that had perhaps been written in starlight before his first breath. The choice he was about to make would determine not only his fate, but the fate of every living thing that drew breath beneath Zarah's twin moons. He was grateful for his friends' presence beside him, and grateful too for the chance to purchase their freedom with his life - a price he would pay gladly.

Chapter XXXVIII

Ashes in the Wind

The desert wind carried with it the scent of blood and failure. It moved in slow, curling gusts across the dunes, whispering through the night like the echoes of forgotten battles. It was a cruel wind, indifferent to the suffering of those who walked beneath - or against - its gaze, scattering the embers of broken dreams into the endless sands.

Vhaskar trudged forward, his steps slow but deliberate, each heavy footfall sinking into the yielding ground. The weight of his armour was nothing compared to the burden of thought pressing upon him. His wounds still ached from the battle, but it was not the pain of flesh that troubled him. It was the pain of knowing that he had followed a dying cause, that the fire of conquest had burned to embers, leaving only the bitter smoke of regret.

The Moons shone high above him - Nysa, pale and watchful, and Anar, smouldering in the horizon like the last remnants of a dying sun. Their light cast long shadows, stretching his form across the dunes, as if trying to pull him back toward the past he was walking away from.

Behind him, lighter footsteps sounded against the shifting sand. A presence he knew well. One he had left behind, but who refused to be left. "You should have let me go." Vhaskar's voice, a deep rumbling, quiet but edged with something final. Still, he did not turn, did not stop.

Drathis was silent for a long moment before he spoke. "You were never mine to let go," he finally said.

Vhaskar exhaled sharply, finally halting. The wind howled between them like an unseen spectre. He turned slowly, meeting Drathis' dark, piercing, unyielding gaze. The Draconian Warlord before him was a shadow of who he once was - leaner now, his cloak torn, his armour scuffed and dented. Yet, the fire in his eyes remained, burning, insatiable.

"You lost," the titan said plainly, his voice devoid of mockery, devoid of anything but truth. "Fate made its choice."

Drathis' eyes flashed, a mirthless smirk barely tugging at the corner of his mouth. "The desert does not choose kings. It only buries them."

A gust of wind swept through, carrying the scent of distant rain. Was it an omen or a lie?

"You can still walk away," Vhaskar murmured, his tyrian purple eyes searching Drathis' for something - some flicker of reason, some faint, smouldering ember of the leader, the friend he once followed. "You don't have to die for this. You can still walk away."

Drathis chuckled softly, but there was no warmth in it, only the brittle sound of one standing on the edge of oblivion. "What, Vhaskar? Tell me, my friend, what would I walk towards?" He spread his arms, motioning toward the endless sea of dunes. "There is nothing left for us here. No conquest. No kingdom. No home. No future." Drathis' words carried the weight of finality.

Vhaskar clenched his powerful jaw. He had always known this about Drathis. He was someone who did not know how to stop. Another Draconian warrior who had never been taught that survival meant more than victory. "Then do not make this your last road," he said, the rumble in his voice quieter now, the plea almost imperceptible beneath the weight of his exhaustion. "Find another."

Drathis shook his head - slowly, deliberately. "This is the only road we know. The only road we were taught to walk," his fingers brushed the hilt of his sword, absent-mindedly tracing the grooves in the leather. The familiar weight of steel was an anchor in the storm of his thoughts. He looked at his companion, in silence - waiting.

Vhaskar studied Drathis for a long time. When he finally spoke, his voice rumbled like distant thunder. "Aran and his warriors will be leaving Sarim tomorrow night. Our remaining scouts say they ride for the last obelisk." He paused, watching the flicker in Drathis' eyes. "One last battle. One last chance?" Purple embers alight with the flames of contest. The fire rekindled in Drathis' gaze, a flame long starved but never truly extinguished. A slow smirk forming in his visage. "One last hunt?" In the silence of the desert, beneath the eternal gaze of the twin moons, they made their choice.

Their pursuit was relentless. Zarah's deserts were vast and unforgiving, an endless expanse of dunes, jagged cliffs, and ancient ruins buried beneath the weight of forgotten time. Even so, there was no path, no matter how carefully tread, that could remain hidden forever. With each passing night they drew closer and closer to their target.

Once more, they followed Aran with the precision of seasoned hunters. The chase took them through canyons, where the wind screeched through towering rock formations like the wails of lost souls. They crossed the flats, where the bleached remains of Crystalline Leviathans lay scattered, relics from a time when this desert had once been Zarah's second ocean.

For days, they followed the trail, reading the land like an open book - a broken twig, a disturbed patch of sand, the faintest hint of hoof prints pressed into the dust.

Drathis spoke little, his mind sharp, focused. He was not merely tracking Aran. He was desperately chasing an ending, some sort of resolution to the fire burning inside him.

Vhaskar, walking beside him, watched him carefully. He saw the raw obsession tightening its grip. "This is different for you," he finally said one night as they rested beneath an overhang, the embers of their small fire flickering in the gloom. Drathis, seated across from him, looked up, his eyes gleaming. "How so?"

"I merely wish to face the man that gave me my hardest fights, but you don't just want to kill Aran," Vhaskar replied. "You need to do it."

Drathis exhaled through his nostrils, a slow, measured breath. "He took everything from me."

The large warrior's purple eyes held his gaze. "Only after we tried to take what was his. Besides, he only took from you what you were not willing to let go." Drathis' jaw tightened, but he did not retort.

The silence between them stretched, heavy as the desert night.

When dawn broke, they resumed their pursuit. After a long while Drathis said. "You should have killed me before you walked away," his voice was sharp as steel against flesh. Vhaskar's massive form came to a halt several paces ahead of him. "I thought about it."

A bitter laugh escaped Drathis's throat. "Yet here we stand."

"Yes, here we stand," Vhaskar agreed, his eyes reflecting the sunlight. "Though you look more like a ghost than a warrior now."

Drathis turned, studying his former brother-in-arms. Despite their defeat, Vhaskar was still an imposing sight - a Draconian titan wrapped in dark battle-scarred armour, his war hammer slung across his broad back. Nonetheless, something had changed in the way he carried himself, as if the weight of their shared past had begun to bow even on his mighty shoulders.

"Do you remember the Battle of Crimson Vale, back home, on the Nathair system?" Drathis asked suddenly, his voice distant. "When we held the line against Malakai's Legion, after his betrayal?"

"Three days and nights we fought," Vhaskar nodded slowly. "Back to back, neither of us slept."

"We were unstoppable then." Drathis said, reminiscing.

"That was centuries ago, we were young then," Vhaskar corrected. "Not to mention, foolish enough to believe we could never lose."

Drathis's hand drifted, once more, to the hilt of his sword, clawed fingers tracing the familiar grooves worn into the leather. "Aran rides for the last obelisk. We have one final prize to claim."

The Draconian titan decided to persuade his companion, one last time. "Let him have it," Vhaskar said, an edge of exhaustion in his voice. "Haven't enough of our people died for those ancient stones?"

"This is not about the obelisks, nor is it about the Primordials." Drathis tightened the grip on the hilt of his blade. "This is about finishing what we started."

"No, this is about finishing what you started," Vhaskar corrected. "I followed you into enough battles. I have seen where this path leads."

Drathis turned fully now, his eyes burning with an inner fire that had never quite died. "Then why are you here? Why follow me after our last defeat?" A long silence stretched between them, filled only by the howling wind.

Vhaskar studied his former charge, and for the first time in years, there was no shadow of respect in his gaze, only resignation. "You followed me, remember?" His deep, resounding, voice sounded detached. Drathis did not reply, so the muscular Draconian concluded ominously. "You will die from this obsession." It wasn't a question.

Drathis' snout curled into something resembling a smile but it was twisted, devoid of joy. "Then let it be a good death," Drathis uttered, his eyes on the horizon, peering over the edges of insanity.

The next three days were a blur of pursuit across the untamed wilds of Zarah. They tracked Aran's company through broken ravines and sun-scorched valleys, past the bones of ancient ruins where only ghosts still walked. Each night brought them closer, and each dawn revealed fresh signs of their quarry.

"They are tiring," Vhaskar observed on the third evening, examining tracks in the cooling sand. "Pushing too hard."

Drathis knelt beside him, running a finger along the edge of a hoof print. "Their steeds' stride is shorter. They are slowing down," the hulking titan said. "I think he knows we are coming." Vhaskar's tone was foreboding.

"Well, that depends on one's perspective. I see it as a good thing." Drathis stood, his armour creaking. "Let him continue to taste the fear of being hunted." He let the words out slowly, savouring each one.

"Like we have?" Vhaskar's voice was quiet but resounding. "When that colossal serpent drove us from the fight?"

Drathis's jaw tightened. "No. That was different."

"Was it?" Vhaskar rose to his full height. "Or have you forgotten too quickly what it feels like to be the prey?"

Before Drathis could respond, Vhaskar raised a hand for silence. In the distance, barely visible through the heat haze, a thin column of smoke rose against the darkening sky.

"There," Drathis breathed, his heart quickening. "In the valley." Finally, as the sun dipped below the horizon, they saw it. Ahead, beneath the crumbling remains of a once-grand archway - a remnant of the Old Kingdoms - Aran's company had made camp.

Three warriors remained: the boy-king himself, Rafiq, and some old man. Their fire was low, their voices hushed with exhaustion.

The pair of hunters approached as darkness fell, using the towering rock formations for cover. Drathis' fingers curled around the hilt of his sword. The satisfaction was impossible to put into words.

His pulse was steady. "We take them now," he whispered, drawing his blade. "While they're -"

"Wait." Vhaskar's massive hand gripped his shoulder. "Look at them, Drathis. Really look."

Below, Aran sat with his head bowed, Rafiq cleaned his twin blades with mechanical precision, his movements betraying exhaustion. Even the old man seemed to move with a newfound weight. "They look finished," Vhaskar said, dispassionately. "Forget about this. Let them go." Drathis shrugged off his large, clawed hand. "No. We end this tonight." The hulking warrior sighed, and grabbed his hammer. Locking eyes with his oldest friend, he said. "Then let us end it."

Their attack was swift and brutal, descending from the ridge like vengeful spirits, their weapons catching the firelight. There were no battle cries, no declarations - only the singing of blade against blade as the night erupted into violence. The first clash of steel shattered the silence of the night, a thunderous echo that rippled across the dunes.

Drathis, wasting no time, lunged for Aran, feinting left before twisting his wrist at the last second. Aran caught the deception and sidestepped, parrying low as sparks flared between their clashing blades.

The Draconian struck again, but Aran countered swiftly, his sword an extension of his will, his eyes locked onto his foe.

He countered Drathis's charges with practised grace, their blades clashing in a shower of sparks. "I wondered when you'd come," Aran grunted, parrying a vicious strike.

"Did you think you could run forever?" Drathis snarled, slowly pressing forward.

"I was not running!" Aran replied fiercely, his movements measured and precise. "I was waiting for you to understand. Since we last fought, you have been chasing me across the sands," he gritted out, blocking yet another strike. "Ironically, you are the one who is lost."

Drathis snarled, pressing forward. "No, Aran!" he hissed. "I am the one who refuses to be forgotten. You buried me once - I will not let you write the ending."

Their duel was a storm of steel and spite, each blow carrying the weight of their shared history. Drathis attacked with the fury of one possessed, while Aran defended with the calm certainty of one who had already accepted his fate - to give his life in protection of his people.

It was a clash of will and history, their blades striking with the weight of every battle they had ever fought. Drathis moved like a tempest, his strikes fuelled by the sheer force of obsession, while Aran remained calm, measured, a tide refusing to break against the storm.

Every strike was a conversation between warriors who had crossed paths too many times, every deflection a silent argument over who fate would favour. Drathis' attacks were ruthless, unrelenting, his greatblade carving vicious arcs through the air, but Aran refused to yield. He had learned the rhythm of Drathis' rage, had tempered himself in the fires of battle, and though his arms ached, he firmly held his ground.

Nearby, Vhaskar and Rafiq engaged in their own deadly dance. The Draconian war hammer swept through the air in devastating arcs, but Rafiq's twin blades found every gap, every moment of overextension. Barash flowed between them all, moving like wind through stone, striking with precision, never remaining still long enough for either Drathis or Vhaskar to land a true blow. His presence shifted the tide, forcing the two Draconians to fight harder, fight faster - fight knowing that time was running out.

"You still battle like you have something to prove," Aran said between exchanges, blood trickling from a cut above his eye. Drathis response was another furious combination of strikes. "No!" He snarled. "I fight to erase you from history."

"History, you say?" Aran laughed, though there was no joy in it. "History cares nothing for us mortals. To it we are just sand in the wind."

Infuriated, Drathis renewed his strikes, the Nathair blade - his heirloom - carved vicious arcs through the air, forcing his nemesis to step back, his feet gliding over the sand with precise, measured control.

In a fraction of a second, Aran adjusted his stance, shifting his weight onto the balls of his feet, his knees slightly bent. He parried, deflected, then pivoted sharply, forcing Drathis to overextend. A flick of Aran's wrist sent his father's sword in a tight, disciplined counterstrike - an attempt to exploit the brief opening - but Drathis twisted at the last second, rolling his shoulder to absorb the impact before retaliating with a fast, ruthless, downward slash.

Steel met steel with a shriek of protest. "I can see in your eyes that you have lost everything," Aran parried a high blow, "but these are the results of your actions, and mine were in reaction to yours." Aran gritted out, stepping into Drathis' guard instead of away.
He locked their blades together, using the leverage to push against his opponent's grip. "So, shall we finish this." Aran taunted.
Drathis snarled, breaking the lock with brute force and a sudden, subtle, deceptive sidestep. His foot dug into the sand, pivoting sharply as he swung his greatblade in a feint toward Aran's ribs - only to flick his wrist at the last second, redirecting the strike toward his foe's exposed thigh.
Aran barely evaded the strike, shifting into a crouch, using the momentum to drive his blade in a low sweep aimed at Drathis' calf. It would have been a precise, crippling cut, but Drathis leapt, twisting mid-air, his blade lashing downward. Aran rolled aside just in time, feeling the wind of the strike graze past his shoulder.
The Draconian landed hard, sand shifting beneath him, but he adjusted instantly, planting his lead foot forward, sword raised in expectation of his opponent's riposte. Aran exhaled. He had fought Drathis too many times to underestimate him.
The battle reached its crescendo as the twin moons reached their apex. The Draco Warlord, driven by pure hatred, finally overextended. Aran, son of Khalid, saw the moment - slow and inevitable - and lunged his father's blade through Drathis' ribs, deep into his heart: the final stroke of a story long overdue.
Drathis did not collapse immediately. He stood, shaking, blood staining his fanged mouth, staring at Aran with eyes still burning - not with pain, but disbelief.
Time slowed as he looked down at Khalid's steel protruding from his chest. His sword slipped from nerveless fingers, striking the sand with a muted thud. "This is not how it ends," he hissed, blood staining his snout. Zarah's king met his slitted gaze, unflinching. "It is!"
Kael Drathis fell to his knees, then forward into the sand - his hopes fading as fast as the light from his eyes. His last sight was of his brave lieutenant, his friend - still fighting, still standing, as he always had been.
"Aran, do not interfere," Rafiq shouted. "You are too important."
Vhaskar, the proud Varros warrior, fought on, even as Rafiq and Barash's combined assault drove him back step by step.
It was a duel of brute strength and unwavering resilience. Vhaskar wielded his war hammer with bone-crushing force, every swing meant to shatter, to end. Rafiq was faster - honed by lessons learned through trials and tribulations, defeats and victories - his twin swords weaving a

dance of death, striking where armour was weakest, where flesh was left unguarded. He was not just fighting to survive - he was fighting to prove that even the strongest could fall.

Vhaskar planted his feet, bracing against the sand as he swung in a devastating arc. Rafiq ducked low, spinning beneath the hammer's path, his left blade flicking out to carve a shallow cut along Vhaskar's exposed flank.

A growl rumbled from the titan's chest. He twisted sharply, using the momentum of his missed strike to send the haft of his hammer lashing backwards like a battering ram. Rafiq barely managed to dodge, but the force of air alone sent him staggering. He adjusted quickly, using the fall to roll over his shoulder and come up onto his feet in a ready stance, twin blades raised.

Vhaskar pressed forward, dragging the hammer's head through the sand before snapping it upward in a sudden vertical strike. Rafiq had no choice but to cross his swords to absorb the impact, the force sending painful vibrations through his arms. "You are slowing," the scaled titan rumbled, his slitted eyes flaring. Rafiq gritted his teeth. "And you are overcommitting," he scoffed.

Vhaskar smirked, feinting another overhead strike - only to suddenly drop the hammer's head, letting gravity pull it down before swinging it sideways, aiming for Rafiq's ribs.

The manoeuvre was unexpected, brutal, and only a last-second backstep saved Aran's friend from having his bones shattered.

Barash flowed between them. He was a spectre, darting between both combatants like wind through stone, striking with precision, constantly moving.

He used the terrain, springing from loose rocks, sliding through the sand to evade the sweeping attacks of his towering foe.

At one point, he lunged for Vhaskar's exposed back, his twin daggers flashing. But the powerful warrior, without even turning, spun his large hammer behind him in a blind defensive arc, forcing Barash to vault backwards to avoid death.

He landed in a crouch, a sharp smirk on his lips. "You still have your instincts." Barash's compliment had, as was his intention, the opposite effect of flattery. Vhaskar hissed but barely spared him a glance. "You will have to try harder." Barash exhaled a laugh, then blurred forward again. His ruse was working. The battle lasted for what felt like hours. In reality, it was only moments. Still, in that short time, destinies were being decided.

Distracted by an attack from Barash, when the end came for Vhaskar, by Rafiq's deep cut across his jugular, it was almost gentle. Dropping to his knees, tyrian purple eyes filled not with rage or fear, but with a quiet acceptance. "Well fought," he acquiesced, his voice a rumbling gurgle, looking up at the one that had bested him.

Rafiq nodded, acknowledging the honour in those final words. There was no need for hatred, no need for mockery. In battle, there should only be respect. Then Vhaskar fell, and the desert wind continued its eternal song, indifferent to the drama it had witnessed.

In the aftermath, Aran stood over Drathis's body, his expression unreadable. There was no triumph in his posture, no satisfaction - only the weary acceptance of a man who had seen too many battles reach their bitter end. Gripping his father's sword tightly, he felt the weight of it all.

Drathis had spent what appeared to be his final breath in defiance, his eyes burning with refusal even as the last of his strength bled into the earth. There would be no peace for Kael Drathis, of the House of Draco, not even in death.

Rafiq, standing over Vhaskar's body, was breathing heavily, his whole body trembling - not out of fear, but from pain. His swords were slick with blood, his arms weak from the endless exchange of blows. The fight had drained him, leaving nothing but exhaustion in its wake.

Barash surveyed the fallen warriors, his gaze lingering on the fading, purple, ember of life in Vhaskar's eyes. The Draconian, ever the warrior, met his end with silent dignity, refusing to cry out, refusing to curse the fate that had claimed him. "At last... I am free," he whispered.

Rafiq, breathing heavily, leaned on his swords. "You're wounded," Barash observed, noting the way his companion favoured his left side.

"Nothing mortal," Rafiq managed a weak smile. "But I will not slow you down. You still have work to do."

They exchanged an understanding look. Aran nodded slowly, his gaze already turning toward the horizon where the last obelisk waited. "Go back to Sarim, my friend. Barash and I will finish this."

"Here," the old man said, while he took something from his pouch, passing it to the wounded Bahir warrior. "Apply this to your gash, before going back to Sarim. It will make the riding smoother."

As Rafiq began the long journey home, Aran and Barash continued onward, leaving behind two Draconian warriors who had finally found their rest beneath the eternal watch of Anar and Nysa.

The desert sighed under the weight of the past, carrying with it the story of Drathis' last stand - a tale of obsession, ambition, and the price of refusing to let go.

Somewhere in the distance, the obelisk of death waited, holding inside it that which would determine the fate of a planet that had seen too many warriors fall in pursuit of glory and destiny. The sands drank deep of their struggle, as the stars above bore silent witness to their final reckoning.

Chapter XXXIX

The Loom of Fate

The farthest north-western mountains of Zarah, named in the old tongues as Paligenis, loomed like the ribs of a fallen god, their jagged peaks clawing at a sky swollen with the weight of an impending storm.

As Aran and Barash climbed higher, the world below faded into a vast, empty silence - only the whisper of the wind remained, carrying with it the secrets of an age long past. The journey had been arduous, a constant battle against both the elements and the unseen forces that seemed to conspire against their every step. With each passing day, the air grew thinner, colder, the wind biting with an unnatural ferocity that chilled not only the skin but the spirit. Yet it was not the weather that troubled Aran most - it was the Weaving.

The threads of fate, once modestly distant, whispers at the edge of his consciousness, now pressed against his mind like an endless chorus of voices clamouring for attention. The Weaving was no longer a close whisper - it was a constant and unavoidable presence, a pulse beneath Zarah's surface, breathing in time with his own heartbeat.

It did not merely surround him; it enveloped him, it watched, it waited, it hungered.

The obelisk they sought, the last of the ancient anchors that bound this world to the will of the Primordials, was getting close - the one linked to death. Its presence tugged at him, a dark beacon in the twisted fabric of reality.

Barash walked in silence beside him, his expression inscrutable beneath the hood of his cloak. The mysterious figure had been both guide and enigma throughout Aran's life, his knowledge of the ancient world invaluable but his motives ever unclear. The pupil had long since stopped questioning his tutor's methods, for Barash's actions had always spoken louder than his cryptic words.

Yet, as they approached the culmination of their quest, doubt still gnawed at the edges of Aran's resolve. Could he fully trust Barash when the fate of their world hung in the balance? Was his father's close friend as free from the Primordials' influence as he claimed to be, or could he inadvertently be another piece in their grand, inscrutable design?

The path ahead narrowed as they entered a steep pass, the Paligenis mountains rising like walls of stone on either side.

The wind howled through the crags, carrying with it the scent of frost and something else - something very ancient and ominous.

Aran's hand instinctively went to the hilt of his sword, though he knew that its steel, though well tempered, would offer little protection against what awaited them. His gaze flickered to Barash, who gave a slight nod, his eyes gleaming with a knowing light - twinkling, as always.

Both climbed in silence, their breaths coming in visible clouds as the temperature suddenly plummeted. The higher they ascended, the stronger the pull of the final stone monolith became. It was as though the mountains themselves were alive, their heartbeat synchronized with the Weaving, drawing them ever closer to the closest source of its power. Each step they took was heavier than the last, not from the weight of their packs or the biting cold, but from the sheer gravity of the energy that saturated the air around them. After a considerable amount of time and effort, they crested the last ridge and saw it.

The valley below them was a barren expanse of rock and ice, framed by towering cliffs that seemed to rise endlessly into the sky.

At the valley's heart stood the tether of death and rebirth - a wound in the fabric of reality itself. It was impossibly vast, a monolith of obsidian midnight, its surface too smooth, too perfect, as if untouched by the passage of time. Ornate runes adorned its sides, some that, with time, Aran had become familiar with, others that were still alien to him.

They pulsed like dying stars along its length, whispering secrets in a cosmic language beyond mortal comprehension.

The air around the stone monument shimmered with energy, a distortion in the fabric of reality that made it difficult to look at for too long. It was as if this obelisk existed in multiple dimensions at once, its presence both there and elsewhere.

Aran felt a chill that had nothing to do with the cold that bit into his bones. This stone prison was a thing of terrible beauty, a relic from an age before the world as they knew it had been shaped. It was ancient, older than the mountains that surrounded it. Perhaps older older than the stars themselves? He wondered. Within it, Aran could feel the power of the Primordials - vast, hungry, and patiently waiting.

Barash came to stand beside him, his gaze fixed on the carved obsidian tether with an intensity that bordered on reverence. "We have arrived at the heart of the Weaving," he said quietly, his voice barely audible over the wind. "This is where, on our planet, the threads of fate are most tightly bound. This rock column is both anchor and conduit, the final node in the vast tapestry of existence." Aran's hand clenched around the hilt of his father's blade. "The connection between it and the Primordials must be destroyed, right?" Barash's eyes flickered with something unreadable. "Not destroyed, Aran. Severed."

The wind howled furiously, bringing whispers of an unfulfilled promise - a crescendo counterpoint to Aran's beating heart.

He turned to Barash, frowning. "Is there a difference?"

"The Weaving is fragile," Barash explained, his gaze never leaving the obsidian monolith. "It has been corrupted by the Primordials, yes, but it is still the fabric of reality itself. To destroy it outright would be to tear a hole in that fabric, to risk unravelling the very threads that hold our world together. No, we cannot destroy it. We must re-form the Weaving itself." Barash inhaled deeply - his next words tasted like ash in his mouth. "You must sever the Primordials' influence upon it, and weave its threads anew."

Aran's heart pounded in his chest as he processed Barash's words.

Re-form the Weaving? He had no such knowledge, no understanding of how to manipulate the intricate tapestry of fate. Yet, deep down, he knew that Barash was right. The obelisks were not merely physical objects - they were linchpins in the metaphysical structure of reality. "How do we sever its connection?" Aran asked, his voice hoarse.

Barash turned to him at last, his eyes gleaming with the weight of ancient knowledge.

Yet, when he spoke, the burden in his voice was measurable. He looked at his charge, his best friend's son, with a heavy heart. "There is only one way. The Weaving must be touched by one who has been marked by it. You, Aran. Only you, with your bloodline, have the power to reach into the Weaving and re-shape it."

In spite of being willing to sacrifice himself to save their world, Barash's words still struck Aran like a physical blow. Unsure on how to proceed, he asked. "I understand that it has to be me. I accepted my fate a long time ago. Still, I've barely begun to comprehend the complexities of the Weaving. How can I -?"

"It is not a matter of understanding," Barash interrupted, his voice soft but firm. "It is a matter of being. The Weaving has already chosen you, Aran. Your life, your fate, has been bound to it since before you were born. Every step you have taken, every choice you have made, has brought you here, to this moment in time. You are the only one who can re-form the threads because you are already part of them."

Aran stared at the obsidian monument, his breath shallow.

The truth settled over him like a familiar funeral shroud. This was not a battle to be won with steel, muscle or strategy. To sever the Weaving from the Primordials was not an act of strength - it was an act of pure surrender. Of becoming something more. Or... something less. He finally understood, with a sickening certainty, that this would cost him everything. "If I do this?" His voice barely a whisper. "What will happen to me?" The wind howled, in response.

Barash's expression was unreadable. "You will become one with the Weaving. Your essence will be bound to it, just as the Primordials have bound their power to the obelisks. However, unlike them, you will not remain an individual. Once you repair its broken threads, and use your essence to weave them anew, you will cease to exist as you are now. You will become... something else."

Aran's throat tightened. He had faced death before, many times over. He had faced battles, betrayals, and the crushing, inevitable weight of responsibility.

But this? This was something different. This was not just the end of his life; it was the end of his very self. To become part of the Weaving was to lose everything that made him who he was, to vanish into the endless tapestry of fate.

He thought of Sura, of Rafiq, of Zahira, of the people of Zarah who had followed him, who had believed in him. He thought of his bloodline, a lineage stretching back through millennia of history, and the legacy he had fought so hard to protect. If he made this choice, there would be no one left to carry that legacy. No king to rule, no name to remember. But the alternative...

Aran closed his eyes, the weight of his decision pressing down on him like a physical force - unrelenting. The Primordials were waiting. Their power, ancient and terrible, was poised to reclaim the world. If he did nothing, if he walked away from this moment, the Weaving would be consumed by their corruption. Their world would fall into chaos, and all that he had fought for would be lost forever.

"I can not ask you to make this choice," Barash said quietly. "No one has that right. It is yours alone to weigh. But know this - whatever you decide to do, the world will change regardless. For better or worse, the Weaving will not remain as it is. That much is clear."

Slowly, Aran opened his eyes, staring once more at the ornately carved obsidian obelisk. He could feel the threads of fate pulling at him, urging him forward - beckoning him to join them.

The Weaving was alive, vibrant, and it needed him. "I will do it," he said, his voice steady. "I will re-form the Weaving."

Barash's expression softened, and not for the last time, Aran saw something like respect in the old man's eyes.

"Then let us begin," the king of Zarah uttered, his voice firm.

The two of them descended into the valley, the stone prison towering above them like a dark sentinel. The air around it crackled with energy, and as Aran approached, he could feel the Weaving stirring, reacting to his presence. The threads of fate reached out to him, invisible but tangible, wrapping around him like a web of energy.

Barash stepped back, giving his charge space. "Place your hand on the obelisk," he instructed. "Feel the threads. Let them guide you." Aran took a deep breath and reached out. His fingers brushed the cold stone, and the world around him dissolved.

He stood at the heart of the Weaving - not a place, but an endless expanse of time itself, where past, present, and future twisted together in a dance of impossible beauty. Threads of golden light wove through darkness, stretching into infinity, forming patterns beyond his mortal comprehension. He was no longer Aran ibn Khalid, no longer king of Zarah - he was part of the loom, part of the fabric of fate itself. Each thread held a life, a choice, a moment in time. They stretched out in all directions, forming a tapestry that was both beautiful and terrifying in its intricacy.

At the centre of it all, pulsing with a dark, malevolent energy, were the corrupted threads. These were the threads that had been touched by the Primordials, twisted and tainted by their influence. They spread through the Weaving like a cancer, their darkness infecting everything they touched.

Barash was right, he knew what he had to do - moreover, he knew how to do it. He had to sever those tainted threads to cut away the corruption, without destroying the Weaving itself. It was delicate and strenuous work - more precise than anything he had ever done. One wrong move, one misstep, and the entire tapestry could unravel.

Aran took a deep breath, his mind sharp and focused - with a single thought, hand outstretched, he reached out to the Weaving.

Unsurprisingly, the threads responded to his will, shifting and bending as he guided them. He concentrated his efforts on the corrupted strands, tracing them back to their source. They led to the other obelisks, to the ancient pacts made by the Old Kings, by his own ancestors, with the Primordials.

One by one, Aran began to sever the threads, carefully weaving new ones in their place. A piece of himself left behind in every entwine. The process was very slow, painstaking, but with each cut, he could feel the Weaving healing. The dark power of the Primordials began to wane, their influence over the Weaving - over Zarah - diminishing.

As he worked, Aran could feel himself slipping away - floating.

The longer he remained part of the Weaving, the more difficult it became to hold on to who he was, to where he belonged.

His memories, his identity, began to blur, to slowly fade into the vast tapestry of existence. Still, he pressed on. He had made his choice. Or rather, he had been chosen. "I will willingly give my life as mitigation for the mistakes of my forebears!" He shouted into the night.

In the vast distances of Zarah, Aran could feel the presence of the other obelisks, their power still strong, binding the Primordials to the planet. He knew that to fully extradite their influence, he would have to sever all from the Weaving. That act, according to his studies, and confirmed by Barash, would mean giving up his own life, to serve as the final thread.

Perhaps it would come to that, he thought, but for now, he focused on the task at hand, on his planet, on the people he had sworn to protect. Pushing his mind to its limits, beyond anything he had attempted before, he began to weave new threads, those of hope and resilience, binding the fates of his people to a future free from the Primordials' grasp, the Draco's, or anyone else's. With one final thought, before losing consciousness, Aran severed the last of the corrupted threads and wove the final, mending, strand into place. It was done - his destiny complete.

The Weaving pulsed with new life, the threads of fate vibrating with a resonance that was both familiar and utterly new. The power of the Primordials had been severed, their influence shattered. The world would go on, free from their control - free to chart its own path.

As Aran's rethread settled into place, he felt himself fading, as if his essence was dissolving into the fabric of reality. He could become more than a king, more than a man, even.

He was dissolving, unravelling into the very essence of the Weaving. He could feel eternity stretching before him, calling him to let go, to become something greater, something eternal. In the distance, a single, solitary, thread remained unbroken - a tether pulling him back to the world of men. Sura. The choice was his, after all. His final thoughts, before losing consciousness, were of her, of Zarah, of the people he loved and fought for.

Chapter XL

A New Dawn

The city of Sarim had never seen a night so radiant, nor a people so united. The air was thick with the scent of the Lunaris flower and burning Solarwood, their fragrance mingling with the salt-kissed winds from the Yaran shores.

At the entrance to the Lunar Citadel, along the great colonnades, thousands stood, draped in the colours of the many tribes - gold for the Shamari, crimson for the Bahir, silver for the Rasha, green for the Ulema and dark blue for the Tarek - their voices rising like the dawn itself.

At the heart of it all, beneath the great obsidian arch of the six kingdoms, stood Aran - the saviour of Zarah, the king who had walked the edge of oblivion and returned. His name, once whispered in the dark as a lost hope, now thundered across Sarim's streets, sung in unison by a sea of thousands of voices who came to pay respect.

His gaze swept over the throngs of his people, their upturned faces radiant with devotion, their hands raised in salute. Beside the king stood Sura, the woman who had been his anchor through the trials of the Weaving's unravelling, the Primordials' fury, and Drathis's malevolent grasp. Tonight, the golden embroidery of her robes caught the torchlight like liquid fire, but it was her green eyes - deep as the night sky, fierce as the desert winds, that captivated him most.

Kasim al-Bahir stood to his right, muscular arms crossed, his stance the same unshakable foundation that had anchored the king through many battles. Rafiq, his brother in everything but parenthood, ever watchful, stood a pace behind, his sharp eyes scanning the crowd with the wariness of a guardian who had seen too much to trust a moment of peace. Karim al-Shamar, adorned in the golden sash of his people, nodded respectfully as his gaze met Aran's, a silent acknowledgement of what had been overcome. Zahira, her braids woven with threads of midnight blue, whispered something to Sura and smiled - perhaps a jest, perhaps a blessing.

Barash stood apart, wreathed in contemplative smoke, his weathered eyes fixed upon Zarah's future - and its king. The flames from the nearest torches, playfully casting shadows, as the smoke he was exhaling danced around him.

Safira al-Rasha, stepping down as High Priestess of Sarim but still its Moon Seer, draped in her tribe's ceremonial silver, raised her hands in silence. The cacophony of the gathered multitude quickly softened into an expectant hush.

Though barely past her thirties, Safira's voice carried the gravitas of ancient knowledge, resonating with the force of a desert gale. "Before Zarah's dawn, we were but dust, scattered and bound to the whims of fate. After its first light, we were divided, still blind to the threads that wove us as one. After millennia came the fire, the unravelling, the unavoidable storm. Yet, from the void, from the claws of despair, a man rose - and from ruin, a new path was forged. Aran ibn Khalid, son of the dunes, heir to the trials of Zarah - tonight, we honour not just the victory you have delivered, but the strong spirit that carried you through the darkness."

The people erupted into thunderous applause, thousands of voices rising to the heavens in chants of praise - their king had saved them.

Aran stepped forward, raising a hand, and the clamour ebbed into reverent stillness.

The weight of the moment pressed against his ribs, yet he stood tall, the memories of war and sacrifice carved into his very being.

When silence fell like a benediction over the gathered thousands, Aran's voice carried across the night air. "I am no more than the desert's son," he began, his voice steady as stone, though his heart bore the weight of shifting sands. "After the murder of my father, Khalid ibn Rashid, I have walked the burning sands, crossed the abyss to unite us all, and stood against the storm - from this world, as well as the next," he felt the Weaving vibrate, in accordance. "Still, I have never walked alone. You, the people of Zarah, have carried this fate alongside me. Sura, who never wavered in the face of despair. Rafiq, whose blades cut paths where none existed. Kasim, whose strength never faltered. Karim, who stood even when his people's blood darkened the sand. Safira, our moon seer, who turned whispers of doubt into roars of defiance. It is not I who should be honoured - it is you!"

The crowd exploded, in a deafening roar - Zarah was free at last.

Sura reached for Aran's hand, and he felt the warmth of her fingers entwine with his. In that moment, the ache of battle, the scars of sacrifice, the shadows of all they had endured - they faded beneath the luminous certainty of what they had built together.

Safira al-Rasha stepped forward, bearing a golden circlet adorned with desert sapphires, each stone a reflection of the night sky. "Then let this be the symbol not of a ruler's triumph, but of a people's resilience. Protector of the desert realm, bearer of the sun's light - may this crown rest upon you not as a weight, but as a promise."

As Safira placed the circlet upon Aran's brow, the city erupted once more, voices swelling in celebration. The drums of Sarim beat a song of victory, of remembrance, of renewal.

Aran turned to Sura, finding in her gaze the quiet promise of all that was yet to come. In his corner, enveloped in smoke, Barash smiled.
Tonight, they did not stand in the shadow of war, nor beneath the weight of destiny. Tonight, they stood beneath the open sky of a world reborn. However, the work of a king never ends in victory; it merely transforms into the quieter battles of governance and foresight.
Even in triumph, Aran knew: the true test of victory lay not in celebration, but in the quiet work that followed.

A year had passed since the Primordials had been silenced. Beneath the low-hanging rays of the Leander system's primary star, Aran gazed across the crystalline sands of Qamar, where he was about to rewrite history once more.
Zarah's sun was painting the sky in hues of gold and crimson as its dying light stretched long shadows across the desert.
Aran stood at the pinnacle of the Great Temple of Qamaria, gazing over the endless sands that had shaped his people for countless generations. The wind whispered through the high arches, carrying the scent of Moonleaf incense and sun-warmed stone, as if the desert itself had come to bear witness to the momentous decrees that would forever alter the course of this planet's history.
The king was not alone with his closest friends beside him. Sura, her eyes shining with a promise of a future together, and Rafiq, who stood stoically by his side, awaiting his moment. Barash, with a twinkle in his eyes, stood behind Aran, watching intently.
Also, arrayed before the king, in solemn silence, stood the elders, the tribal leaders, the scholars, and the mystics - all those who had helped guide the House of Aran through its trials and triumphs.
Facing him, Amara al-Rasha, recently appointed High Priestess of the Sun, knelt upon the sacred dais, her silver robes shimmering like the twin moons above. Aran raised a hand, and the hush that fell upon those gathering at the Great Oasis of Qamar was deep and expectant, as though the very stars in the firmament had ceased their celestial course to listen in.
The king closed his eyes for a fleeting moment, feeling the pulse of the land beneath his feet - the Weaving pulsating under his skin.
Despite having defeated Drathis and surviving the mending of the Weaving, the House of Draco would not, so easily, give up on Zarah. Aran had seen the visions in his dreams - the coming days of reckoning, the peril that would befall his people if they did not prepare. The Draco, undoubtedly disguised, still lurked in the shadows, their thirst for utter dominion never truly quenched.

The sands would continue to shift, as they always did, but only the very wise could foresee the storm before it struck.

At last, the king spoke, his deep voice carrying over those assembled like a decree etched in stone. "The sun has guided us since the first footsteps of our ancestors upon this sacred land. Its unbound light is both a sword and a shield, a force of creation and destruction, a herald of wisdom. Long have we walked its path, but now we must forge its will into something greater - a beacon to guide the lost, a fire to temper the unworthy, a sanctuary for those who seek the truth."

Zarah's king turned to Amara, his gaze steady. "New High Priestess, as the flame of our star burns eternal, so too must its keepers endure. I command the formation of the Priesthood of the Sun - a Sacred Order to guard the knowledge of the cosmos and preserve the balance between us and the desert. Let them be the keepers of wisdom, the arbiters of justice, and the shepherds of those who seek enlightenment."

A murmur of assent swept through the gathered council, for they knew that such an order had long been foreseen in the prophecies of old. Amara al-Rasha bowed her head, her voice a melody of reverence. "By your will, my king, the Priesthood of the Sun shall rise. We shall forever walk the path of the sun and ensure its light never dims."

The king nodded, though his heart bore the weight of a greater task yet. He turned to the warriors among them, to the men and women who had bled for the House of Aran, to those who had known the taste of battle and the burden of duty.

"Wisdom alone is not enough. Knowledge without strength is as fleeting as the desert winds. Our sun gives away light, but it also casts shadows. In those shadows - unwatched - dangers grow. Despite their defeat, our enemies watch, waiting for weakness, ready to undo all that we have built. Thus, we must forge a new order that does not stand upon thrones or within temples - but moves unseen, protecting the land from threats before they rise. An order of the sacred desert itself."

A ripple of tension passed through the gathering. Every warrior knew what was coming - they were all eager to join.

"I decree the founding of the Order of the Sacred Desert," the king continued, his voice firm with conviction. "These warriors shall not be bound to thrones or temples, but to the land itself. They shall be the watchful eyes upon the dunes, the silent blades in the night, the guardians of the people when the walls of our cities cannot hold. Let them be our last line of defence, the unseen force that ensures our survival." Aran made a gesture for his best friend to step forward.

A stir of agreement rose among the gathered warriors. Rafiq took a step and knelt, his voice strong as a lion's roar. "We will be as the shifting sands, my king. Unyielding, ever-moving, unseen until the moment of reckoning." When he finished speaking, Rafiq winked at his friend, a broad smile illuminating his face. They looked into each other's eyes - the unspoken bond between the two warriors stronger than any words could ever convey.

The king's gaze swept the assembled warriors, seeing in their faces the understanding that he was asking them to become something new - guardians not of throne or temple, but of the very soul of their world. His House's twin pillars of wisdom and strength, the sun's light and the desert's shadow - both now woven into the fabric of the planet's destiny.

As the final echoes of his decree settled into the marrow of those present, Aran turned his gaze once more to the horizon, where the first stars now pierced the darkening sky - Sura by his side, as always.

The future of their House had been forged that day, tempered by the wisdom of the Priesthood and the future vigilance of the Order of the Sacred Desert. The sun had set upon the old Zarah. A new dawn awaited - one of unity, of wisdom, and of a House prepared for the storms yet to come.

Epilogue

The Final Thread

The sky over Qamaria hung heavy with the weight of twilight, a vast expanse where the stars hesitated to emerge, as if they, too, were waiting. The city, so often vibrant with the bustling heart of an empire, had grown quiet, hushed by the solemnity of what had transpired in the wake of the Weaving's final surge. The palaces and citadels, once teeming with the intrigues of politicians and warriors, seemed now like monuments to an age that had burned brightly - and whose light would echo through the Ages.

In the grand hall of the Qamarian Throne, amber light poured through high windows, casting long shadows across the ancient stone. Dust motes danced lazily in the air, indifferent to the currents of time that had swept through these hallowed chambers.

Where once the Council of Tribes quarrelled, now there was peace and understanding, a solemn reflection of the transformation that had reshaped the very fabric of the House of Aran - becoming a monument not to conquest, but to unity.

King Aran ibn Khalid, now in his middle years, sat upon the throne - not as a ruler holding court, but as a man reflecting on a legacy far greater than himself. One that would outlast him.

His beard, once dark and vibrant, had become streaked with the grey of wisdom and burden. It framed eyes that had seen both glory and loss - and had learned to bear them. The lines upon his brow were deep, carved by the countless battles - both internal and external - that he had waged. His hands rested upon the armrests of his throne, calloused and worn, but still steady and strong. The weight of the crown atop his head felt somewhat heavier, not because of its gold and jewels but because of the choices it symbolized.

For two decades, his House had known peace.

The Order of the Sacred Desert had kept the Draconian threat at bay, and the Primordials, those ancient forces that had once threatened to tear the very fabric of existence apart, had receded into the mists of legend, sealed by the pact that Aran had forged in the heart of the Weaving. In the end, it was his willingness to give up his life that had saved it.

The Obelisks, now mere sentinels of forgotten power, stood silent across the lands, their once ominous glow dimmed to an eerie hum, felt rather than seen. The cost had been great, but the reward had been worth it.

The Council of Tribes, once rife with ambition and intrigue, stood united. The six main tribes of his House had been transformed into keepers of the six kingdoms they represented; Qamaria, Shamas, Arsian, Sayf, Kartal and Yara - their names remembered in the dusty tomes of scholars.

Sarim itself had grown back to its ancient glory, its streets filled with historians, merchants, artists and travellers.

After the Weaving's mending, it was as if his entire kingdom had drawn a deep breath and exhaled slowly, careful not to disturb the tenuous balance that Aran's victory had wrought. Yet there was still work to be done.

Aran had never sought to master the Primordials. That path, fraught with the allure of absolute power, had tempted him, but in the end, he had chosen prevention over domination. He had walked a fine line, one that had required not only strength but sacrifice. One he had been willing to pay for with his life, and though the Primordials slept, Aran knew that the forces they represented - the chaos, the untamed wildness - could never truly be extinguished.

They were part of the Weaving itself, as essential to existence as the stars that watched over Zarah, or the ocean-deep waters that kissed the shores of Sarim, now part of the new Kingdom of Yara.

From the shadows of the grand hall emerged a figure. Sura, his queen, former spymaster and his dearest love, approached the throne. Her hair, once black as night, was now adorned with strands of silver, but her presence was as commanding as ever, and her beauty was still breathtaking. In her hands, she carried a scroll, the weight of its knowledge as profound as the burden of their reign.

"Another missive from the High Scholars?" Aran asked, his voice rougher than it was in his youth, though its strength and warmth had not diminished, in the slightest.

Sura nodded, her eyes soft as she approached him. "They continue to unravel the mysteries of the Weaving. The Echo of Worlds has yielded more than we could have ever imagined. There are layers upon layers of existence, Aran, realities that brush against our own like threads in a loom." He leaned back in his throne, his gaze drifting toward the high windows, where the first stars were now beginning to blink into view. "Yet, despite all their knowledge, the simple truths remain the most elusive."

Sura smiled gently, kissed him tenderly, and placed the scroll upon a nearby table. "The Weaving is vast. Even with all our understanding, we are but a single thread in its infinite design. The more we learn, the more questions we have. Perhaps the mystery is the point."

He looked at her, and for a moment, the weight of the years seemed to lift. "Perhaps," he murmured, "but I cannot help wondering if we have done enough. If what we fought for, what we sacrificed, will always be remembered."

She moved closer, her hand resting lightly on his shoulder. "Legends are not built on monuments or battles alone, my love. They are built on the choices we make, the lives we touch, and the hope we leave behind. Our House will endure, not because of your victories, but because of the way you carried the weight of the world and never faltered."

Aran closed his eyes, feeling the warmth of her hand, the quiet reassurance in her words. "The weight of the world," he repeated softly. "I fear that is a burden our son will one day bear."

Sura's smile faltered for just a moment, a flicker of worry crossing her features, but soon it was replaced by her broad, beautiful smile. "He will," she caressed his face, "but he will not bear it alone. Just as you did not."

In the years since the Weaving had been stabilized, their son, Khalid ibn Aran, had grown into a capable leader. The boy who had once watched from the shadows of the throne had become a man in his own right, wise beyond his years yet still carrying the fire of youth. Khalid understood the delicate balance of power and the responsibilities of leadership, but he also carried within him the dreams of a new generation - dreams that, perhaps, could transcend the legacies of old.

The future was not without its uncertainties, but Aran had come to accept that uncertainty was the nature of life. The Weaving, with all its complexities and mysteries, mirrored the very nature of existence. There would always be threads that frayed, destinies that unravelled, but there would also be those moments where everything aligned, where the pattern of fate revealed itself in breathtaking clarity.

He stood from his throne, the weight of the years having no bearing in his muscled body. He took Sura's hand, and together, they walked to the high windows that overlooked the kingdom.

Below, the streets of Qamaria stretched out in a labyrinth of light and shadow, a city built as the foundation of an empire that had survived the impossible. Beyond the city walls, the plains stretched out toward the horizon, where the remainder of the obelisks stood sentinel.

As they gazed out upon the land, Aran felt a sense of peace he had not known in many years. The stars above twinkled, their light distant yet eternal, reminding him of the vastness of the cosmos, and his place within it. "Do you think they will remember us?" Aran asked, his voice

barely above a whisper. Sura turned to him, her gaze steady, her love unwavering. "They will. Not as rulers, nor as warriors," she looked at the horizon. "As the ones who stood at the edge of the abyss... and refused to let the darkness win."
With those words, the twilight deepened into night, Anar and Nysa rose in the night sky, and the first star of evening shone brightly above the House of Aran - a beacon, not of power, but of hope.

The End

Appendices to the Book of Aran and the History of Zarah

Appendices

I. Key Figures

II. The Tribes of Zarah

III. Locations of Importance

IV. The Obelisks & Their Mythology

V. Creatures & Natural Wonders

VI. Genealogies & Timelines

VII. Historical Accounts

VIII. Tales From Myth and Legend

IX. Lost Dialogues

X. The Chronology of Legends and Legacy

Each section will be detailed with:
Historical origins
Mythology and folklore
Cultural and political influence
Strategic importance in Aran's journey

Taken from the *Echoing Archives of the House of Tempus
Planet Chronaxis, the Kronos System.*

Appendix I: Key Figures

<u>Aran ibn Khalid – The Visionary King</u>

"A man is not shaped by the sand beneath his feet, but by the storm he chooses to walk through." *(Qamaria - 266 years ago)*

Born in the oasis town of Karash, Aran ibn Khalid was raised in the traditions of the Tarek tribe, a once-great nomadic people who had long since faded into obscurity. Though his father, Khalid, was a modest trader, whispers spoke of a deeper lineage - one tied to the forgotten rulers of Zarah's ancient past. From a young age, Aran displayed an unusual depth of intellect, preferring to listen rather than speak, to observe rather than act. While other boys revelled in the art of war, he sought the wisdom of the desert itself - its rhythms, its secrets, and the way it tested those who dared to cross it.

Despite being already on his way to uniting the tribes of Zarah, Aran's true journey began when he encountered Kael Drathis, a shadowed warlord of the House of Draco, who revealed secrets he was never meant to know. With the destruction of the first obelisk, Aran awakened something within himself - a power buried in his bloodline, tied to the legacy of his ancestors. This revelation set him on a path not only to fully unite the fractured tribes of Zarah but to confront the hidden forces that sought to unravel his world.

His leadership was defined by diplomacy and wisdom rather than brute force. Unlike the Zarahan leaders before him, Aran did not conquer the tribes - he persuaded them. He learned from their elders, adapted their technologies, and presented unity not as submission but as an elevation of their strengths. This approach won him allies but also earned him powerful enemies, particularly among those who profited from division.

Yet beneath his growing legend, Aran carried a personal burden - the loss of his older brother and father. Wounds that never fully healed but cemented his desire to unify the tribes of Zarah under one banner. Though he rarely spoke of it, the pain shaped his every decision, reminding him that every life, every alliance, was a fragile ember that could be extinguished in an instant.

Aran's destiny was inextricably tied to the obelisks. The War of the Weaving was not just a battle against an ancient enemy - it was a battle against the fate imposed upon him. As the secrets of his bloodline continued to unfold, Aran had to decide whether he was the master of his destiny or merely a player in a game far older than himself.

Sura – The Shadow in the Sand

"A sharp blade in the dark is worth ten raised in the light."
(Sarim - 279 years ago)

Where Aran rules through diplomacy and Zahira through foresight, Sura rules in silence. As head of Aran's intelligence network, she was the unseen force that moved through Zarah's underbelly, gathering whispers, uncovering secrets, and eliminating threats before they could take root. Despite her ancient bloodline, whose roots are now almost lost to history, little did she know that her future held the weight of rule.
Her old lineage was scattered in the wind, and she lost her father and mother at a young age, forcing her to fend for herself. Once a thief and street survivor in Sarim's Old Quarter, Sura learned early that the world belonged not to the strongest but to the most invisible. She mastered the art of blending into the background, her presence barely noticeable even in the most crowded of rooms. This skill caught the attention of Aran's growing movement. When their eyes met, fate intervened. Rather than deliver her to the authorities, he offered her a purpose - to be his eyes where he could not see and his ears where he would not hear. In private, she became his confidant.
Because of her rough upbringing, Sura became pragmatic to the core. She did not believe in visions, destiny, or the will of the gods - only in what could be seen, heard, and acted upon. While she respected Aran, she did not fully share his idealism, believing that unity must be maintained not only by words but by swift, precise action against those who would undermine it.
Though she, at first, dismissed the legends of the obelisks, she was not blind to their effects. After all, she also carried an old legacy in her veins, and she had seen people driven mad by their power, gaining a deeper understanding that something ancient stirred beneath Zarah's sands. She did not fear it - she only wanted to know how to kill it.
Her loyalty to Aran was unwavering, not because of prophecy or kinship, but because he had given her a place in a world that had abandoned her. She never asked for praise, and she never sought recognition. When night fell and daggers were drawn in the dark, it was Sura who ensured Aran lived to see another sunrise.

Rafiq – The Lion of the Sacred Desert

"Give me a reason not to strike, and I will give you ten reasons why I should." *(Sarim - 279 years ago)*

Rafiq was Aran's most trusted warrior - his blade-arm, his battle-brother, and the shield that stood, many times, between him and death. Where Aran wielded diplomacy as fiercely as he did his blade, Rafiq only wielded steel. He was a man of few words, but sharp wit, preferring action to discussion, and his presence alone on the battlefield turned the tide of many conflicts.

Descendant from the lost tribe of Khazraj, but born of the Bahir tribe, he was a former commander in their warbands. Rafiq was raised in a culture that valued strength, endurance, and honour above all else. He fought and bled for his people, surviving battles that would have killed lesser men, earning him the respect of even the fiercest warriors. Yet despite his skill, he was no warmonger - he fought not for conquest but for a future worth defending.

Rafiq followed Aran, not out of blind loyalty, but because he believed in his vision. He had seen what war did to men - how it turned leaders into tyrants and heroes into ghosts. He understood that Aran's path was the only way to break the endless cycle of bloodshed that had plagued Zarah for millennia. However, his greatest challenge was not battle, but restraint. He did not share Aran's patience for diplomacy, and he often questioned whether mercy was a luxury they could afford. His most heated debates were with Zahira, Aran's cousin, who argued that he was too quick to draw his sword, while he countered that she was too willing to let their enemies scheme in the shadows. Beneath his unshakable exterior, Rafiq carried his own burdens. He saw comrades die, watched leaders betray their own people, and wondered if the desert would ever know peace. As long as Aran fought for that possibility, Rafiq would stand beside him - blade in hand, ready to carve a path forward

<u>Zahira – The Watchful Flame</u>

"A kingdom is not forged in steel, but in the choices of those who refuse to kneel." *(Karash - 288 years ago)*

Zahira was more than Aran's trusted ally - she was his kin, the daughter of his mother's sister. Raised within the intricate politics of the Rasha tribe, she learned early that words could be sharper than swords, and silence deadlier than war. Where Aran relied on diplomacy, Zahira relied on calculated foresight - trying to anticipate danger before it struck.

Her belief in the importance of the obelisks placed her at odds with many tribal leaders. While others saw them as remnants of a forgotten past, she saw them as the key to Zarah's survival. She knew that unity alone would not be enough - there were forces at play beyond mere warlords and kingdoms.

Unlike her cousin, Zahira carried no illusions of mercy when it came to their enemies. She understood that the House of Draco did not negotiate; it consumed. While Aran sought to outmanoeuvre them, Zahira believed they must be eliminated before their influence spread too far. This pragmatic ruthlessness is both her greatest strength and her greatest weakness - her willingness to do what must be done sometimes lead her down paths Aran refused to walk.

Despite their differences, her loyalty to Aran was absolute - not because of blood, but because she believed in the world he envisioned - a world where the people of Zarah were no longer pawns in a game played by unseen masters.

Barash – The Silent Mountain

"strength does not solely lay in words, but in how you choose to carry yourself." *(Karash - 288 years ago)*

Barash was a fortress in disguise - lean, unshakable, and fiercely loyal to Aran's father. He did not speak often, but when he did, his words carried the weight of stone. A warrior among warriors, he moved with the patience of one who understood that true power lay not in reckless force but in knowing when to strike.

Once a gladiator forced to fight for the entertainment of the Draco elite, Barash's body was a living testament to a lifetime of battle. Scars crisscrossed his thick, weathered skin, each one a silent record of an enemy he faced, a wound he endured, a battle he survived. Yet, unlike many warriors who revel in the thrill of combat, Barash never fought for glory or bloodlust. He fought because he had to. Because someone had to stand between the innocent and the monsters that sought to devour them.

Despite his fearsome presence, Barash was not cruel. He did not take pleasure in destruction, nor did he seek unnecessary bloodshed. His strength lay not only in his raw power but in his discipline, his endurance, and his ability to outlast forces that would break lesser men. He was not just a warrior - he was a guardian, a man who carried the burdens others could not bear.

But there was more to Barash than the battlefield. Though he was forged in combat, he was also a student of Zarah's ancient lore. Throughout his life, he delved into the forgotten histories of their people, unearthing knowledge that most had long abandoned. In time, he became a scholar in his own right, learning of Aran's family curse, the hidden obelisks, the ancient Primordials, the lost pacts, the Wardens, and The Weaving itself. His wisdom was not just in war but in the unseen forces that shaped the world.

As a close friend of Aran's father, Barash had always been more than a warrior - he had been a mentor, a guide, and a silent protector, watching over the boy long before he ever picked up a sword. He understood Aran's lineage before the boy himself did, and he had spent years, at Khalid's request, preparing him - not just to fight, but to lead. To become more than a warrior. To become a king.

As the events of Aran's story unfold, where Rafiq was the blade and Sura the fire, Barash was the immovable wall - the unyielding shield that would not break, no matter the storm that raged around him.

His loyalty to Khalid as well as his son was absolute, but it was not blind. Though his bond with Aran's father ran deep, he followed Aran not out of duty or nostalgia, but because he believed in the boy's vision - a world where strength was no longer the only path to survival, where wisdom and justice guided the future instead of fear and conquest. He fought not to preserve the old ways but to forge something new, something better.

Barash did not argue, nor did he raise his voice. When he spoke, his words were few, but they were final. When he fought, enemies trembled. To his foes, he was a beast of war, but to his allies, he was the pillar that held the flame alight. To Aran, he was more than his father's closest companion, more than a warrior, a friend or a teacher - in time, he became family

Kael Drathis – The Shadowed Hand

"You see the desert as your ally. I see it as a graveyard waiting to be filled." *(Zarah - 310 years ago)*

A high-ranking warlord of the House of Draco, Drathis moved in both whispers and battle, shaping events from the darkness and the battlefield alike. He was both a leader, a warrior and a manipulator, his influence felt in every conflict, every betrayal, and every moment of doubt.

Drathis' true goal remained a mystery, even to those who served him. He did not act out of loyalty to the House of Draco - he acted for something greater, something beyond even their ambitions. He spoke of a larger plan of conquests that were only a piece of a much greater design. One he never saw to fruition.

Unlike most of his kin, Drathis did not seek conquest alone. He sought understanding. To him, power was never an end, but rather the means, and the obelisks were not mere weapons - they were keys, and he intended to unlock the doors they hid.

Drathis was not an enemy to be defeated in battle, for he was never where the blade struck. He was the voice that turned allies against each other, the shadow in the corner of a council room, the unspoken fear that perhaps the world was not as simple as Aran believed. His final words before vanishing from the underground crypt, in Sarim's Old Quarter, lingered in Aran's mind. "The obelisks are not what you think they are. Neither are you."

Varros Vhaskar – Drathis' Warhammer

"If you see me on the battlefield, you have already lost."
(Nathair System 400 years ago)

Vhaskar was Drathis' first lieutenant - a hulking Draconian warrior of unmatched brutality and precision. Unlike many of his kin, who relied on sheer strength alone, Vhaskar was both a tactician and a warrior, wielding his massive warhammer with terrifying speed and efficiency. Cold and calculating, he feared no man, no beast, nor god. He was not just Drathis' right hand - he was his executioner, the hammer that broke kingdoms and crushed hope.

Standing taller than most Draconians, Vhaskar's body was a fortress of muscle and scale. His burnished bronze skin gleamed under the sun, his slitted purple eyes carried the quiet menace of a predator who knows exactly when to strike. Every movement was measured, efficient - deceptively fast for his size. He did not waste breath on threats; his presence alone was enough to silence a room.

On the battlefield, he was a force of nature. His warhammer, Maul of the Eclipse, being only one of its many monikers, was a monstrous weapon, heavy enough to break bone and shatter steel. He moved with unnatural speed, closing the gap between himself and his enemies before they even had time to react. His strength was overwhelming to most foes, capable of bringing down warriors in a single blow. Vhaskar was not just a warrior - he was a living weapon, shaped by the House of Draco, for a singular purpose: to bring ruin to those who opposed them.

Unlike other Draconian warlords, Vhaskar was not consumed by arrogance or ambition. He did not seek power, nor did he hunger for conquest. He existed to fight. To him, loyalty was absolute - but not blind. He followed Drathis not because of words or ideology but because Drathis had proven himself worthy of being followed. He did not fight for glory. He fought because he was made to fight. His voice was deep, guttural, controlled, and devoid of emotion - he spoke only when necessary. To those who stood against the House of Draco, he had only one warning: "Kneel, or break."

<u>Kasim al-Bahir – The Warlord of the Black Dunes</u>

"Strength is not given. It is taken."
(Sayf - 290 years ago)

Kasim al-Bahir was the living embodiment of war. During Aran's rise to kingship, he was the undisputed ruler of the Bahir warbands. Born into a culture that valued strength above all else, he rose to power not through bloodline but through sheer force of will. Where Aran sought unity through diplomacy, Kasim believed in domination through might - to him, the only lasting peace was one enforced by the blade.

He was a man of unshakable resolve, whose presence alone could command an entire army. Believing that the weak existed to serve the strong had been the philosophy that had kept the Bahir powerful for generations. He respected warriors who proved themselves in battle but despised leaders who relied on words, hiding behind them, rather than take action.

When Aran sought to unite the Bahir, Kasim did not greet him with negotiations - he challenged him. The Trial of the Scorpion, an ancient Bahir rite, was meant to have broken Aran. Instead, the future king had passed with flying colours.

For the first time, Kasim saw a leader who did not bend or break, a man whose strength came not just from battle but from something deeper. Though he begrudgingly accepted Aran's rule, he did so with a warning: "If ever you show weakness, Aran ibn Khalid, I will be the first to cut you down." He later served as Aran's greatest warrior - but also as his most loyal servant.

Karim al-Shamar – The Scholar-Lord of the Shamari

"The mind is the greatest weapon. Yet fools waste it on war."
(Shamas - 300 years ago)

During Aran's time, Karim al-Shamar was the leader of the Shamari, the most advanced and technologically gifted tribe on planet Zarah. Unlike Kasim al-Bahir, he detested war, believing that knowledge and innovation were the keys to true power. Though he respected Aran's vision, he feared that uniting the tribes would weaken Shamari's dominance.

He was highly intelligent, calculating, and pragmatic. He saw battles as games of strategy, not strength. He was a man who distrusted idealists, believing that most visions of unity end in corruption and ruin. He preferred science over prophecy, diplomacy over war, and saw the Obelisks as dangerous artefacts of an age best left forgotten.

Initially, Karim refused to support Aran or his father before him, fearing that a united Zarah would force the Shamari to share their advancements. When Aran, Khalid's son, offered him knowledge in return - Bahir storm-watching techniques, Rasha water-harvesting methods - he realized unity was an opportunity instead of a burden. Still, he remained wary, often questioning Aran's decisions, and served as both an advisor and a sceptic. His greatest fear? That Aran's quest for the Obelisks would awaken something that should remain buried.

Safira al-Rasha – The Moon Seer of Sarim

"The moons do not choose sides, but they see all that will come to pass." *(Sarim - 284 years ago)*

Safira al-Rasha was the High Seer of Sarim, the spiritual leader of the Rasha tribe and keeper of Zarah's most ancient prophecies. It was said that she was born under a full moon eclipse, a sign that she would one day shape the planet's destiny. She did not rule with laws or armies, but with visions - and the people of Sarim followed her because her predictions were seldom wrong.

She spoke in riddles and visions, never revealing more than what she felt should be known. She believed in fate above all else - that Aran's rise, the fall of the Obelisks, and the return of The Primordials - were all foreseen. Though she always supported Aran, she tried to warn him that his journey would not end as he expected, trying to prepare him for the hardest choice of his life.

Aside from Shara, Zarah's first moon seer who lived over three thousand years ago, Safira was the second to predict Aran's rise, years before he was even born. When he came to Sarim in search of the Draco, she greeted him not as a guest but as a prophecy fulfilled. Yet when he asked if destroying the Obelisks was the right path, she only gave him one answer: "There is no right path besides the one you have already chosen."

Farid al-Rasha – The Shadowed Politician of Sarim

"Power is not taken with the sword. It is taken in whispers, in deals, in moments of hesitation." *(Sarim - 280 years ago)*

Farid was a high-ranking politician and a member of the Rasha Council in Sarim, known for his sharp tongue, calculated decisions, and quiet ambition. He was once a respected diplomat, but behind closed doors, he aligned himself with the House of Draco, believing their influence would secure his own rise to greater power. Unlike warriors like Kasim or Ryvan, Farid waged war with words, alliances, and manipulation.

He was a master of political intrigue who preferred subtlety over direct confrontation. Believing Aran's vision of unity was dangerous, fearing it would disrupt the power structures of Sarim and, by consequence, his own, he did everything he could to undermine him. He was self-serving but not foolish - he did not openly betray Zarah but worked in the shadows to ensure his own influence.

Before Aran's arrival to Sarim, he initially supported him publicly but secretly opposed him behind closed doors, using his position in the Rasha Council to delay Aran's policies and weaken his alliances, to spread the Draco's influence among influential nobles in Sarim, as well as convincing neutral factions that Aran was too radical to be trusted.

When his dealings with the Draconian envoys were discovered, he denied everything, but Aran knew the truth - Farid had already chosen his side. Yet even when exposed, Farid was too skilled to be easily removed, for he survived by shifting blame, redirecting anger, and always staying one step ahead.

As the quest for the Obelisks escalated, he began to realize the House of Draco had its own agenda - one that did not include him and his ambitions. When the time came, he would be forced to choose between his own survival or betraying the very empire he tried to build.

<u>Ryvan – The Rebel Lord Who Nearly Took the Throne</u>

"Aran ibn Khalid speaks of unity. But I ask you - unity for whom? For us? Or for his own empire?" *(Sarim - 278 years ago)*

Ryvan was not merely a warlord - he was a ruler in his own right. As the tribal leader of the Ryvan Tribe, one of the large and influential factions on planet Zarah, he was a man born to lead.

To him, Aran was not a liberator - he was a usurper, a pretender who was using the myth of the obelisks to take what was rightfully his.

Unlike the Bahir, who sought dominance through war, or the Shamari, who pursued knowledge, Ryvan believed in his own destiny - that he alone was meant to be Zarah's true king. Therefore, he did not simply oppose Aran, but challenged him at every turn, turning the people against him and painting himself as Zarah's true saviour.

He was a masterful orator capable of rallying crowds and swaying even a few of Aran's own allies against him. Being cunning and opportunistic, he played both the council and the battlefield to his advantage, and saw diplomacy as a weapon, using it to weaken his enemies before ever drawing a blade.

Along with Farid, Ryvan was Aran's greatest political adversary, and unlike the Draconian warlords who opposed the king on the battlefield, Ryvan waged war in the council chambers, using words as his weapons. During the tribal council sessions, he repeatedly defied Aran in front of the assembled leaders, using rhetoric, half-truths, and passionate speeches to turn the crowd against their king. He questioned Aran's legitimacy, claiming that no man had the right to unite Zarah.

Even going as far as to accuse him of being a tyrant, warning that once the tribes surrendered their independence, they would never be free again.

Deception was, after all, his greatest weapon - not steel, not war, but the power to make men question what they once believed. However, Ryvan was not content with words alone.

As Aran's rule grew stronger, Ryvan worked in the shadows, forming a coalition of rebel tribes who feared losing their power under the new rule. He worked tirelessly to convince minor warlords to rise against Aran, promising them wealth and freedom. He secretly undermined Aran's supply lines and disrupted trade, weakening his ability to rule. He went as far as to gather an army in the desert, waiting for the right moment to strike, and when the moment came, Zarah stood on the brink of civil war.

Appendix II: The Tribes of Zarah

For millennia, the tribes of Zarah existed in a delicate balance - sometimes allies, most often enemies, but always independent. Each tribe adapted to the deserts in its own way, forging unique technologies, customs, and philosophies suited to their lands. However, this fractured existence also made them vulnerable - to famine, to war, and to foreign powers seeking control over their lands. Though the arrival of Aran ibn Khalid heralded the possibility of unity, not all welcomed it. Some saw it as strength, others as submission, and others still as a threat to the old ways. In the epoch of Aran's ascendancy, these were the five major tribes of Zarah, their history, culture, and their role in the unification.

The Shamari – Masters of Solar Energy & Water Purification

"The sun does not belong to any man. And yet, it is our greatest weapon." *Karim al-Shamar (Shamas - 295 years ago)*

The Shamari were the engineers of the desert, a people who had mastered the harshest subtropical climates through their command of solar energy, metallurgy, and water purification. Their capital, Shamaris, was a city of golden spires, its lifeblood sustained by colossal sun mirrors that generated energy, heat, and irrigation.
They were aristocratic people, governed by a council of scholar-warlords, each responsible for a different aspect of their civilization - military, technology, commerce, and diplomacy. Unlike other tribes that relied on survivalist traditions, the Shamari saw science and progress as the key to mastering the desert.

They were the most technologically advanced of the tribes, having developed:
- Solar mirrors that harnessed and focused sunlight into powerful beams, used in forges, agriculture, and defence.
- Despite living in areas where water was not too scarce, they developed water condensers that extracted moisture from the air, providing a nearly self-sufficient water source.
- Heat-reflecting armour made from a unique alloy known as Sunsteel, allowing them to fight even in the harshest sun.

Cultural Beliefs & Rites

The Shamari worshipped the sun, but not as a god - rather, as a force of power and knowledge.

The Rite of the First Sun demanded that young Shamari crafted their own solar artefact, a test of skill and ingenuity that marked their passage into adulthood.

To them, the greatest sin was wastefulness - to waste water, food, or knowledge was to invite ruin upon the tribe.

The Shamari Tribe & Aran's Unification

Like his father before him, Aran sought to ally with the Shamari early in his campaign, recognizing that their technology and infrastructure could transform the desert into a thriving land. However, their leader, Karim al-Shamar, refused, as he had refused his father before him. He believed unity would dilute their strength, forcing them to share their hard-earned innovations with weaker tribes.

Following his father's example, Aran did not fight the Shamari. Instead, he presented them with knowledge, sharing techniques from the Bahir sandstorm predictors and Rasha moon diviners. In doing so, he proved that unity was not weakness - but an opportunity to evolve beyond each tribes' limitations. Karim agreed, but reluctantly. In his heart, he feared unity was a gilded cage - one where the strength of the Shamari would be diluted by the burdens of lesser tribes.

The Bahir – The Desert Warriors & Keepers of the Black Dunes

"A blade is only as strong as the hand that wields it."
Kasim al-Bahir (The Black Dunes 293 years ago)

The Bahir were the fearless warriors on Zarah, dwelling in the Black Dunes, a region where the sands shifted unpredictably and the winds howled like the voices of the dead. They were a people forged in conflict and endurance, known for their ruthless martial discipline and unbreakable loyalty to their clans.

Unlike the aristocratic Shamari, most of the Bahir lived in tight-knit strongholds, each led by a Warlord-Chief chosen through combat and strategy. Their society was built on meritocracy - the strong rose, the weak served, and the cowardly perished.

The Bahir were masters of battle, having perfected:
- A technique that allowed them to predict and use sandstorms as natural cover in battle, called Storm-watching. Although that proved to be of no avail, during the unnatural Great Sandstorm Crisis.
- An aggressive fighting style using one large blade, inspired by the deadly Sand Scorpion.
- Desert armour crafted from the hardened shells of creatures that roam the desert.

<u>Cultural Beliefs & Rites</u>
The Bahir tribe believed in the law of the blade - justice was served through combat, not words.
The Trial of the Scorpion was a trial where warriors must retrieve a sacred stone from beneath a venomous scorpion without being stung
Victory was worship - they believe the spirits of the desert favoured those who took what they desired through strength.

<u>The Bahir Tribe & Aran's Unification</u>
Of all the tribes, the Bahir were the most resistant to Aran's vision. To them, unity was a leash - an attempt to weaken the strong by tying them to the weak. Their warlord, Kasim al-Bahir, challenged Aran to the Trial of the Scorpion to prove his worth.
Aran did not fight with force alone - he won through patience and precision, retrieving the stone not by meeting the scorpion with brute strength, but by understanding its nature and applying precision. This act earned him Kasim's respect, and the Bahir swore their allegiance - but with a warning:

"If ever you become weak, we will cut you down ourselves."
Kasim al-Bahir (Sayf - 280 years ago)

<u>The Rasha – The Lunar Mystics & Navigators of the Crystalline Deserts</u>

"The moons do not answer to kings, nor do they bow to war. Yet they have watched every empire that ever rose and fell beneath them."
Safira al-Rasha (Sarim - 285 years ago)

The Rasha were the mystics of Zarah, a people who lived in the crystalline deserts where the night reigned longer than the day.

Unlike the sun-worshipping Shamari or the war-driven Bahir, the Rasha looked to the twin moons, Anar and Nysa, believing they held the secrets of fate, time, and destiny.

They were master navigators, capable of reading the stars, mapping the dunes, and predicting great changes before they came. Their home, Sarim, was a fortified city of moonlit towers and celestial observatories, where scholars and seers studied the heavens, searching for omens.

Their knowledge was ancient and deep, making them the keepers of Zarah's lost histories, forgotten myths, and prophetic visions.

Cultural Beliefs & Rites

- The Moon Seers: A caste of mystics who claimed to receive visions from Anar and Nysa, interpreting their cycles as signs of coming change.
- The Rite of Eclipse: Once in a generation, when the moons aligned, a Rasha heir had to endure a trial of isolation in the desert, seeking a vision of their people's future.
- The Forbidden Stories: Certain legends - especially those concerning the obelisks - were known only to the oldest Seers, locked away because of their dangerous truths.

Strengths & Contributions

- Masters of celestial navigation, allowing them to cross the desert faster than any other tribe.
- Ancient knowledge of the desert's hidden places, including long-lost ruins and buried cities.
- Powerful diplomacy - many rulers sought their wisdom, giving them influence across Zarah.

The Rasha & Aran's Unification

The Rasha did not resist Aran with war but with silence. They refused to involve themselves in what they saw as the petty conflicts of men, believing the desert's fate was already written in the stars.

However, Aran gained their loyalty, at a young age, when he survived the Moon Seers' Trial of the Eclipse. Unlike past warriors who sought power, he asked only for the truth - and in doing so, proved himself worthy. The Rasha joined him, but with a warning:

"The moons have seen your path, Aran ibn Khalid. It does not end where you think it does."
Safira al-Rasha (Sarim - 281 years ago)

The Ulema – The Guardians of the Hidden Oases

"The desert takes. We protect what little it leaves behind."
Sayf al-Ulma (Qamar - 287 years ago)

The Ulema tribe were the keepers of Zarah's most sacred resource - water. Hidden across the desert were secret oases, some natural, others shaped by forgotten civilizations. The Ulema tribe were sworn to protect them at all costs, ensuring that water was never wasted, hoarded, or used for war.

Unlike the other tribes, the Ulema did not seek power, expansion, or battle. They were reclusive people, governed by the Ulema Elders, a council of scholars, healers, and desert priests. They followed the Old Laws, a strict code of conduct that forbade unnecessary war, treachery, or waste. To outsiders, they were seen as strange, even dangerous, for they did not recognize the rule of kings - only the rule of nature.

Cultural Beliefs & Rites

- The Oasis Pact: Water is sacred. To steal, poison, or hoard, it was punishable by death.
- The Sandkeepers' Oath: Every Ulema child swore to never reveal the locations of their hidden wells, even under torture.
The Trial of the Dying Sun: A dangerous rite where young Ulema had to survive for seven days with no supplies, proving they were worthy of guarding the desert's secrets.

Strengths & Contributions

- Masters of desert survival, possessing knowledge of edible plants, hidden springs, and natural medicine.
- Neutral peacekeepers, often acting as mediators between feuding tribes.
- Custodians of lost knowledge, including texts and maps that predate even the oldest settlements in Zarah.

The Ulema & Aran's Unification

The Ulema did not trust Aran. To them, all rulers eventually turned to greed, seeking to control what should belong to all. They believed he would destroy what he sought to unite.

However, Aran proved himself when he refused to claim an oasis for his army, even as his men were dying of thirst. Instead, he negotiated a water-sharing agreement between multiple tribes - something never done before.

Seeing that he valued balance over conquest, the Ulema agreed to support him, offering their maps, healers, and wisdom. But they remained watchful, reminding him:

"Should you ever take more than you give, we will not be the only ones to rise against you." *Sayf al-Ulma (Yara - 283 years ago)*

The Tarek – The Forgotten Tribe & The Lost Historians of the Sands

"Our people did not vanish. We were erased."
Khalid ibn Rashid (Karash - 307 years ago)

The Tarek were the ghosts of Zarah, a tribe that once ruled over all others, but mysteriously vanished centuries ago. Some say they fled to the mountains, others that they were cursed for their arrogance. But in reality, the Tarek were systematically erased, their knowledge stolen, their history buried. Few remember their name, and fewer still speak of what truly happened to them.
What is known is that they once built cities greater than any in Zarah today. That they possessed knowledge of the obelisks, their purpose, and their creators. Their disappearance coincides with the rise of the House of Draco's influence on Zarah. Amongst most scholars, it is now speculated that Drathis, disguised as Malik the Vulture, was responsible for the death of Aran's father.

Cultural Beliefs & Rites
- The Last Historians: A secret group of surviving Tarek who still passed down their lost history in whispered songs and coded messages.
- The Sand Veil Ritual: A rite of concealment, allowing them to erase their presence from the records of men.
- The Forbidden Name: Tarek survivors never spoke their true names, believing it tied them to a past they needed to protect.

Strengths & Contributions
- Hidden libraries and ruins containing knowledge lost to all other tribes.
- Advanced pre-tribal engineering, including ancient aqueducts and forgotten cities beneath the sand.

- A bloodline that connects directly to Aran's past, suggesting he may be one of them.

The Tarek & Aran's Unification
Having left his tribe at an early age under Barash's tutelage, Aran did not seek the Tarek when he reached manhood. Still, they found him - an old wanderer, cloaked in rags, came to him one night and spoke a single phrase: "You are searching for the past, my boy. But the past has also been searching for you, Aran ibn Khalid."
Through them, he found a lost city buried beneath the dunes, where the last of the Tarek endured in shadow. There, among the echoes of a forgotten empire, he unearthed a truth that shattered everything he thought he knew. The House of Draco had tried to erase them. Even so, the sands do not forget, and the lost would rise once more.

Appendix III: Cities & Locations of Importance

Zarah is a world shaped by both the cruelty of its deserts and the will of those who dare to call them home. Its cities rise from the sands like jewels, testaments to human perseverance, while its sacred sites and ruins whisper of civilizations long forgotten. Each location carries a history steeped in legend, whether through the rise of kings, the fall of empires, or the echoes of battles that shaped the fate of the world.
From the silver domes of Sarim, where rulers and scholars alike weave the destiny of the kingdom, to the haunted ruins of Valamar, where the past lingers in shadowed corridors, Zarah is more than a mere collection of settlements - it is a tapestry of power, faith, and mystery. The shifting sands do not merely conceal - they do not forget.

This section details the most vital cities, fortresses, and sacred places that define the planet's desert kingdoms, illuminating the stories behind their foundations and the roles they play in the grand saga of the Weaving. For in order to understand Zarah, one must know its cities, walk its streets, stand before its obelisks, and listen to the silent voices carried upon the desert winds.

Sarim – The Lunar Capital of the Rasha

"Sarim is not built of stone and sand - it is built of time and stars."
Sura al-Rasha (Sarim - 285 years ago)

Sarim is the oldest continuously inhabited city in Zarah, home to the Rasha tribe and their legendary Moon Seers. It is a fortified city of silver domes, celestial observatories, and moonlit gardens, where the cycles of the twin moons, Anar and Nysa, govern all aspects of life.

Historical Significance
- Built over 3,000 years ago upon the ruins of an ancient city on the shores of Yaran country, still is to this day a renowned centre of learning and prophecy, drawing scholars from distant lands.
- The city is home to the Grand Archive of the Rasha, also known as the Royal Library of Sarim, containing the oldest maps, myths, and astronomical charts on Zarah, with the exception of the city of Valamar.

- Legends say the first Moon Seer, a woman named Shara, received her visions there, leading to the reformation of the Al'Shara tribe into the Rasha.

Cultural & Political Role
- Ruled by the High Seer, a figure chosen through prophetic visions, not bloodline succession.
- A place of spiritual pilgrimage, where rulers and warriors seek the guidance of the Moon Seers before making great decisions.
- The twin moons determine the city's calendar, rituals, and even its leadership - when a rare lunar eclipse occurs, the ruling High Seer must undergo the Trial of Eclipse, which can either reaffirm their rule or lead to their exile.

Strategic & Mystical Importance
- The Moon Seers possessed knowledge of the obelisks, but they have hidden the full truth for centuries. Patiently awaiting, through the generations, for the arrival of the one that would unify Zarah.
- It is said that one of the moons is not just a celestial body, but something far older - a remnant of the past before men ruled the sands.
- Sarim was the key to unlocking Zarah's forgotten history, but the Seers only reveal what they believe the world is ready to hear. So it was when Aran was king.

Sarim & Aran's Journey
When Aran arrived in Sarim seeking answers about the House of Draco, the High Seer did not greet him as a saviour - but as a man walking toward an inescapable fate. She told him:

"You do not seek the truth, Aran ibn Khalid. The truth has been waiting for you. But beware, for once you know it, you will never again be free."
Safira al-Rasha (Sarim - 281 years ago)

The Hall of Kings – The Forgotten Throne

"A throne left empty for too long is no longer a throne - it is a grave."
Safira al-Rasha (Sarim - 286 years ago)

Built deep beneath Sarim's Royal Palace, the Hall of Kings was a forgotten wing of Zarah's history, a chamber that had remained sealed for countless generations. Within it stand statues of rulers long erased from memory, some names worn away, their deeds unrecorded.

Historical Significance
- Once the throne room of Zarah's last great empire, before the age of warring tribes.
- The statues suggest that Zarah was once united under a single lineage but someone tried to erase this history.
- Aran was connected to this lost dynasty, even though, at first, he did not understand how.

Cultural & Political Role
- The Hall of Kings was a forbidden place, known only to a few scholars and even fewer members of the Rasha. In later years, Barash managed to uncover the truth.
- The House of Draco feared this place, suggesting that what lied here could undo their influence over Zarah.

Strategic & Mystical Importance
- An inscription in the Hall of Kings spoke of "the first obelisk", hinting that they were not just prisons, but something greater.
- It was here that Aran began to suspect his role in the fate of the obelisks was no coincidence.

The Hall of Kings & Aran's Journey
Just as it was in the underground crypt, below Sarim's Old Quarter, when Aran first steps into the Hall, he is struck by a terrible feeling of familiarity - as if he had been there before. Then he sees one statue left unfinished, its face uncarved. Yet beneath it, an inscription reads:

"The Last King of Zarah. He will return when the sands are ready."
Al'Shara (3477 years ago)

The Old Quarter – The Underground Crypts

"There are places beneath this city where even the dead whisper in fear." *Barash ibn Sulaym (Sarim - 280 years ago)*

The Old Quarter was a forgotten district beneath Sarim, buried by centuries of construction and neglect. Once a thriving part of an older city, at the time of Aran it existed as a labyrinth of abandoned halls, collapsed streets, and sealed crypts that few dared to enter.

Historical Significance
- Originally the oldest part of Sarim, built before the Rasha became a great power.
- It contains the Tomb of Al'Shara, the First Moon Seer, an ancient resting place where legends claim a prophecy was hidden away.
- Some claim the House of Draco once held secret experiments here, though evidence of this is scarce.

Cultural & Political Role
- Considered off-limits to most citizens, as many believed the Old Quarter was haunted.
- A refuge for outcasts, criminals, and seekers of forbidden knowledge.
- Controlled by a shadowy faction known as the Silent, who traded in secrets and lost artefacts.

Strategic & Mystical Importance
- The underground crypts contain runes matching those found on the obelisks, suggesting a connection to their origins.
- Some claimed that something unnatural stirred beneath the Old Quarter, awakening after centuries of silence. This proved to be the first obelisk that King Aran I encountered.
- The Silent know paths beneath the city that proved to be vital in times of war.

The Old Quarter & Aran's Journey
Aran descended into the Old Quarter, seeking answers about the Draconians. Instead, he found more questions - and a warning carved into a crumbling wall, though in a language he had not yet learned:

"If you stand before the obelisk, do not speak its name. Some doors are meant to remain closed."

Qamaria – The Future Seat of the House of Aran

"A city built in the sands will fall. A city founded in the hearts of its people will endure." *Aran ibn Khalid (Qamaria - 277 years ago)*

At the time King Aran I created Qamaria, it was not yet the great capital it was destined to become. At the start of his journey, it began as a struggling oasis settlement, a place of refuge for those fleeing war, drought, or oppression. Under Aran's leadership, it would grow into the first true city of united Zarah, a beacon of hope where all tribes stood as one.

Historical Significance
- Built around the Great Oasis of Qamar, the largest freshwater source in that desert.
- Starting as a meeting place for the Council of the Tribes, in time, it became a symbol of unity when Aran chose it as the Royal City.
- It was said that long before the tribes, the Old Kings built structures beneath the oasis - ruins that remained undiscovered for millennia.

Cultural & Political Role
- A city where all tribes have a stake - Shamari engineers, Bahir warriors, Rasha mystics, and Ulema waterkeepers all contribute to its survival.
- Governed by the House of Aran, but with a council of tribal representatives, ensuring no single people dominate the city.
- After the reset of the Weaving, it symbolized the end of tribal isolation - with Qamaria's success, Aran proves that Zarah's peoples could truly be united as one.

Strategic & Mystical Importance
- The oasis is vital to Zarah's survival, making it the target of both diplomatic intrigue and military threats.
- Beneath Qamaria, something ancient sleeps, waiting for the right moment to be uncovered.
- The city would stand or fall based on Aran's leadership - if he failed, the dream of unity would die with it.

Qamaria & Aran's Journey
When Aran chose Qamaria as his capital, many doubted him. Some called it a fool's dream. Others saw it as a challenge to the old ways. Kings Aran's simple answer was:

"I do not build for today. I am building for tomorrow."
Aran ibn Khalid *(Qamaria - 280 years ago)*

The Black Dunes – The Bahir's War-Torn Lands

"There is no peace in the Black Dunes. Only war, and those who survive it." *Kasim al-Bahir (Sayf - 281 years ago)*

The Black Dunes are a vast and deadly desert. They were home to the Bahir for centuries, before the rise of Aran. Unlike the golden sands of southern Zarah, the dunes here are dark, shifting, and treacherous, with violent windstorms that can bury entire armies

Historical Significance
- The site of countless tribal wars, where warriors are forged or buried beneath the sands.
- Once home to an ancient fortress, now lost beneath the ever-moving dunes.
- The battlefields here have been soaked in so much blood that the sands themselves are said to thirst for more.

Cultural & Political Role
- The Bahir warbands roamed the dunes, ruling through combat and strength.
- Dune Stalkers, deadly six-legged predators, lurk beneath the sand, making travel dangerous.
- Only the strongest warriors can cross the Black Dunes unscathed.

Strategic & Mystical Importance
- Some believed the Black Dunes hid the remains of a lost obelisk, shattered long ago. At a later time, that obelisk was proved to be in the Sea of Ash.
- The ever-shifting sands make it nearly impossible for armies to invade or hold territory here.
- It is said that the spirits of fallen warriors still walk the dunes, seeking revenge.

The Black Dunes & Aran's Journey
To prove himself to the Bahir, Aran crossed the Black Dunes, surviving the storms, the predators, and the visions of the dead that plague

travellers here. When he finally emerged, just before the Bahir warriors surprised his party, an elder warrior tells him:

"The dunes did not kill you. That means the desert wants you to live. For now." *(Sayf - 280 years ago)*

The Oasis of Shadows – The Cursed Sanctuary

"Water is life. But in this place, it also means death. You will die here tonight, Aran ibn Khalid." *Kael Drathis (278 years ago)*

The Oasis of Shadows is one of the largest oases in Zarah, yet no tribe dares to claim it. Though it never runs dry, it is said that those who drink from its waters are never the same again.

Historical Significance
- Legends say the oasis was once a thriving city, but something erased it overnight.
- Ancient carvings near the oasis depict a monstrous being, bound by chains of light.
- Some claim the Tarek knew the truth about this place, but their knowledge was lost with them.
- It is said that it was here that Uramak himself resurfaced to protect King Aran I and his companions, from Kael Drathis and Varros Vhaskar, of the House of Draco.

Cultural & Political Role
- Considered forbidden ground - no army could march through it, and no ruler could claim it.
- Used as a meeting place for secret negotiations, as its neutrality was respected by all. Well, almost all…
- Some outcasts and exiles still live here to this day, whispering of things that move beneath the water.

Strategic & Mystical Importance
- The water is unnaturally pure, yet those who drink it experience intense visions.
- Rumours persist that one of the lost obelisks lies beneath the oasis, its power seeping into the waters.
- Others believe that something ancient watches from the depths, waiting for the right moment to rise again.

The Oasis & Aran's Journey
When Aran arrives at the oasis, he finds a single inscription carved into stone:

"The water remembers."

The Crimson Cliffs – The Edge of Destiny

"That is where men go to become legends - or to be forgotten forever."
Barash ibn Sulaym *(Karash - 300 years ago)*

The Crimson Cliffs are towering red rock formations located on Zarah's south pole, marking the last boundary before the endless sands begin moving northwards.

Historical Significance
- The cliffs have been the site of many gruesome battles, where warriors made their final stand against impossible odds.
- It is said that long ago, a large, ornate, stone gate stood here, leading to another world. It is speculated by scholars to be the same gate that Queen Amara, of Ryvath, crossed 2475 years ago.
- The blood of fallen warriors has stained the cliffs red, giving them their name.

Cultural & Political Role
- The Bahir consider it sacred ground, a place where only the most honourable warriors may be buried.
- Many seek visions here, believing the winds carry whispers of fate.
- Some say that when the war from the stars begins, the Crimson Cliffs will be the battlefield where the first battle will take place.

Strategic & Mystical Importance
- Those who meditate here often experience visions, though sometimes their meaning remains unclear.
- The cliffs hold ancient markings, suggesting they may have once been part of a lost city.
- It is said that whoever stands upon the highest peak at the right moment will see their true destiny.

The Cliffs & Aran's Journey
After the War of the Weaving, Aran stood at the edge of the cliffs and asked himself:

"Is this where my story ends? Or is it only the beginning?"
Aran ibn Khalid (The Crimson Cliffs - 276 years ago)

The Hidden City of the Tarek – The Buried Past

"Our people did not vanish. We were erased."
Khalid ibn Rashid (Karash - 307 years ago)

Jawhara, the Hidden City of the Tarek was one of the greatest mysteries of Zarah - a lost metropolis buried beneath the sands, where the last remnants of the Tarek tribe still guarded their secrets.
Legends speak of a time when the Tarek ruled not just Jawhara but the whole of Zara - a civilization whose knowledge surpassed even that of the Shamari. Then, something happened. Their cities were abandoned, their people scattered, their name nearly erased from history.
During King Aran's time, few knew the city still existed. Fewer still had seen it and returned to tell the tale.

Historical Significance
- Once the greatest city in Zarah, known then as Ishkandur, home to the most advanced scholars, architects, and thinkers of its time.
- It was said to contain a library that held knowledge predating even the first Moon Seers.
- Something or someone destroyed it - but the truth remains buried. Some claim it was a great war, others that it was a betrayal from within. There are, however, a few Zarahan historians that suggest that the Tarek were systematically eliminated by the House of Draco.

Cultural & Political Role
- The last survivors of the Tarek lived in secrecy, guarding the final remnants of their history.
- They possessed forbidden knowledge - secrets of the obelisks, the lost kings of Zarah, and the forces beyond the desert.
- Though most tribes believed the Tarek were gone, some whispered that they still guided events from the shadows.

Strategic & Mystical Importance
- Hidden beneath the ruins of Ishkandur were records of the obelisks, suggesting they were not just prisons, but something more.

- The city was guarded by ancient traps, coded messages, and illusions, making it nearly impossible to be found, unless by those with prior knowledge.
- The few amongst his inner circle knew Aran was tied to the Tarek Warden bloodline, making him the only one who could unlock the last of their secrets.

The Hidden City & Aran's Journey

One night, Barash approached Aran and spoke the words. "You seek the past. But the past has been waiting for you." Following his tutor, Aran embarked on a journey deep into the desert, where he would uncover truths that shook the very foundations of his belief system. In the heart of the hidden city, he stood before a revelation that changed everything he thought he knew about the obelisks.

Valamar – The Lost City of the Old Kings

"Valamar is not dead. It sleeps, hidden in the mountains, waiting for the day its name is spoken once more."
Barash ibn Sulaym (Sarim - 279 years ago)

Deep within the southeastern reaches of Zarah, hidden amongst jagged mountains, surrounded by shifting dunes, lies Valamar, the forsaken city of the Old Kings. Once the heart of an empire that spanned the deserts of Zarah, its towering spires and grand colonnades stood in eerie silence for countless years, swallowed by time. The city was said to be cursed, untouched by human hands for centuries, its gates sealed by forces older than memory. Yet, those who had glimpsed it from up close, claimed that on certain nights, when the twin moons hang heavy in the sky, lights flicker in its abandoned halls and whispers echo through its broken streets.

Historical Significance

Built over eleven thousand years ago, Valamar was the seat of the Old Kings, a dynasty that ruled before the formation of the modern Zarahan tribes. It was the first great city of the desert, a beacon of knowledge, power, and sacred authority.
The city fell during the Binding of the Primordials, when its rulers attempted to harness the power of the obelisks and paid the price for their hubris. Its name was erased from history, its location lost to all but the most dedicated seekers of forbidden knowledge.

Some believe that Valamar never truly fell - that its people vanished into the Weaving itself, becoming something more than mortal, waiting for the day their city would be reborn.

<u>Cultural & Political Role</u>
- Even today, the Priesthood of the Sun forbids all who seek it, warning that those who enter do not return. Whether this is due to lingering sorcery or something more sinister, none can say.
- Legends speak of a hidden chamber beneath the ruins, where the last king of Valamar still sits upon his throne, waiting for a ruler worthy enough to awaken him.
- The few mystics who have entered Valamar claim that the city is not empty but filled with shadows of the past, fragments of time that replay endlessly - ghosts trapped in the final moments before the city's fall.

<u>Strategic & Mystical Importance</u>
- Beneath Valamar lies one of the most ancient obelisks of the Weaving, a monument tied not only to life and death but to the very fabric of reality itself. If reawakened, it could reshape the balance of Zarah.
- Some claim that Valamar is not a ruin but a prison. That its gates remained sealed to prevent something from escaping rather than to keep explorers out.
- In the time of King Aran I, there were whispers that Valamar held secrets that could rewrite history, that within its halls lay knowledge that could either restore the balance of the Weaving - or shatter it beyond repair.

To this day, Valamar remains untouched, a city both forgotten and waiting. It does not beckon travellers, yet it lingers in their dreams. It does not speak, yet its silence demands to be heard. The Lost City of the Old Kings is not truly lost. It simply waits - for the one who will call its name.

Appendix IV: The Obelisks & Their Mythology

The Obelisks were not merely relics of the past - they were the keystones to Zarah's fate. Their presence predated the rise of the human tribes, predating even the oldest legends whispered by the Moon Seers of Sarim. Who, themselves, are descendants of the original Seers from the Al'Shara tribe, three thousand years ago.
Some named them prisons. Others deemed them barriers. Yet, there were those who believed they were something far older, far more dangerous.

<u>The Obelisks – Pillars of the Forgotten Age</u>

"Stone does not whisper. Yet these do. They have been whispering for far too long."
Safira al-Rasha Moon Seer of Sarim (279 years ago)

The Obelisks are all the same and, at the same time, different from one another. Each is linked to a separate part of creation. Massive, black monoliths, towering structures scattered across Zarah's most ancient sites, they are adorned with runes of a forgotten age, pulsating with an energy neither wholly natural nor entirely arcane.
They have stood for more than ten thousand years, resisting the passage of time, impervious to wind, sand, and even the fiercest storms. However, more than their durability, what terrifies those who stand near them is their presence. People say they are alive - that these tethers are not wrought of dead stone. For they breathe, they whisper, and when one is destroyed, the desert itself seems to recoil, as though some vast, unseen force has been disturbed.

<u>Origins & Builders</u>
- No tribe claims to have built them. No living tribal record speaks of their construction. Those records that exist are scarce with information about them.
- The Rasha Moon Seers say they were forged before the first kingdom of men, left behind by those who came before, from the stars…
- The Tarek scrolls, King Aran I found in their hidden city, described them not as prisons but as anchors, holding something in place.
- In fact, the obelisks were built by the Old Kings and Queens, in order to bind the Primordials, so they could control the Weaving.

<u>Their Purpose</u>
Through the ages, generations of scholars believed the Obelisks were prisons - hiding some ancient horror beneath the sands. But the truth was far more terrifying. The Tarek records were correct, and the Obelisks were not simply keeping something in... They were holding something out.

<u>The Obelisks & Aran's Journey</u>
When Aran destroyed the first Obelisk, he felt it - not relief, but absence. As though a door, long locked, has begun to open. In that moment, he heard a voice he never shared with anyone, not even Sura, his future wife. The voice was not his own, nor was it human. It whispered from the depths of his mind:

"One is gone. The others will follow. Join me, and when the last one falls... we will reshape the world anew."
Kael Drathis (Sarim - 280 years ago)

<u>The Whispering Mist – The Curse Within</u>

"It does not see you. It does not hear you. It feels you, for it only remembers what was lost."
Barash ibn Sulaym (Sarim - 280 years ago)

When an Obelisk is damaged, it haemorrhages - not in blood, but in mist. This mist moves as though it is alive, twisting, and recoiling from the light. It clings to the ruins, lingers in the air, and sometimes... it devours those who venture too near. Those who breathe in the mist experience visions, nightmares, and, in some cases, madness. These were considered the lucky ones. Some claimed it was a curse. Others believed it was a memory of something long forgotten, seeking a vessel to speak through.

<u>Origins of the Mist</u>
- The Shamari scholars believed it is a form of ancient energy, bound to the Obelisks.
- The Rasha Seers claimed it was the remnant of those who once walked the world but were erased from it. Unbeknownst to them, they were the tribe closest to the truth.
- The Tarek texts contain a single phrase, repeated multiple times: "It is not a thing. It is a thought."

Effects of the Mist
- Short exposure: Voices, whispers, fleeting hallucinations.
-Extended exposure: Dreams of a world before Zarah, strange symbols, and an overwhelming sense of loss.
- Erasure: The most common effect is that those surrounded by the mist dissolve or, as some say, are swallowed.
- Possession: Rare, but recorded - when the mist does not simply whisper but speaks through the living.

The Mist & Aran's Journey
After destroying the second Obelisk, Aran begins to hear fragments of a forgotten language, spoken in his own voice. In his dreams, he sees a city, standing beneath twin moons - but not the moons of Zarah. Something else. Something older. Something waiting to be remembered. He never shared these dreams with anyone.

The First Obelisk – The Key to Everything

"You think they are prisons. You are wrong. They are locks. And you are breaking them."
Rafiq al-Bahir (280 years ago)

The First Obelisk is different. Connected to water and the passage of time. Ancient, and unlike the others, it is not buried in the desert. Well, that depends on the point of view... It stands in an old crypt, located in the bowels of Sarim's Old Quarter, but close to the ocean, as though it were never meant to be seen.

Historical Clues
- The Tarek texts described it as the 'Pillar of water', suggesting it predated even the formation of the Yaran desert.
- The Ulema waterkeepers believed it affected the entire region's climate, subtly controlling the flow of water beneath the sands.
- The House of Draco feared it. Besides Drathis' claim, they have never tried to look for it, or sent forces near it.

The Final Revelation
Aran's journey leads him to the First Obelisk, where he discovered something impossible: The runes on the Obelisk matched those inscribed onto the stone he was given by Ashir, the Draconian trader he met in his youth, and those etched in the black throne, within the Hall of

Kings. He learns that the forgotten Old Kings of Zarah did not just rule the desert, they were part of whatever came before it. If Aran had destroyed more than two obelisks, he would not free something trapped beneath the sands. He would have quicker brought back something that was locked away. Something that was never meant to return before its time.

The First Obelisk & Aran's Choice
Standing before the First Obelisk, Aran was faced with the ultimate question.
If the Obelisks were indeed locks, then what would happen when those locks were opened? After Barash told him to destroy the first one, as he placed his hand upon the stone, he heard a whisper:

"You are not destroying us. You are waking us."
(Sarim - 280 years ago)

The Forgotten Gods & The Cosmic Forces Beyond Zarah

"The records call them gods. But gods demand worship. These beings do not care for prayer, nor for mortals. They only remember what was stolen from them."
Barash ibn Sulaym (Sarim - 279 years ago)

The Obelisks were not built to imprison monsters nor to contain mere energy. They were meant to seal away something that should never have been forgotten. But forgotten they were. Now, they were awakening.

The Forgotten Gods – The Beings Beyond the Veil of the Weaving

Legends across Zarah speak of great forces that once walked the sands before it belonged to the Old Kings or, after them, to men. They were called many names - Titans, Watchers, Forsaken Ones, the Nameless - but most scholars throughout history dismissed these stories as myths. Yet the ruins, the Obelisks, and the warnings inscribed in the oldest texts suggested otherwise.
There was a time when Zarah was not a desert.
It was a place of vast oceans and rivers, towering cities, and wonders beyond imagination. The First Civilization did not fall to war or famine. It was erased - its name was stripped from time itself. The Obelisks were

not built by mortals. They were placed by something else, something greater, to hold back the ones who once ruled.

<u>The Three That Were Lost</u>
Ancient inscriptions, found by Barash, in the ancient Tarek city buried beneath the sands, referenced three beings, three Primordials, each bound by an Obelisk - entities that existed before humanity, before the sands, before even the moons of Zarah took their place in the sky.

<u>I. *Ithakar*, the Mind That Never Sleeps</u>

"They did not kill it. They could not. So they broke it into a thousand thoughts and scattered them across the winds."
The Wardens of the Weaving (9,800 years ago)

- The whispering mist that seeped from the broken Obelisks was not just a curse.
- It was Ithakar's fragmented mind, seeking to pull itself back together.
- Every vision, every nightmare, and every lost memory brought it closer to awakening.

<u>II. *Xir'vaneth*, the Maw Beneath the Sands</u>

"The deserts were not always deserts. In Zarah's ancient history, some were oceans. Then, they became graves. Then they became something worse."
The Wardens of the Weaving (9,800 years ago)

- Beneath the Oasis of Shadows, something stirs.
- Xir'vaneth is not a creature - it is hunger given form, an endless void that consumes and never ends.
- The legends of the Sand Serpents may be distorted memories of its influence, creatures twisted by its will. Others claimed they were offspring of Uramak, and yet others suggested they were the guardians of the Weaving in the physical plane.

<u>III. *Orannis*, the Veiled One</u>

"It was never seen. It was never heard. Yet all who knew its name trembled. When it was forgotten, the world was made safe again."
The Wardens of the Weaving (Shadowed Vale - 9800 years ago)

- The Tarek believed there was a third moon, one that did not shine, cursed by the Primordials themselves. Where one of their own was ostracised.
- The First Obelisk, beneath the city of Sarim, was found to not be sealing something beneath the earth but rather blocking something from ascending.
- Orannis is the greatest unknown of all - if it was hidden, it was hidden for a reason.

Prophecies & Legends

"The stars are not what they once were. Soon, neither shall we be."
Shara, the first Moon-Seer (3477 years ago)

Every culture on Zarah has stories of what would come when the sands shifted for the last time. Some believed in a saviour. Others, in a reckoning. History showed that the Moon Seers from the Al'Shara tribe were the first to have foreseen it during the planet's Third Age (3500 years ago)

The Prophecy of the Final Eclipse
Throughout Zarah's history, the Moon Seers have long recorded celestial events as omens. But there is one event that has never occurred, one that has only ever appeared in their visions - the Black Eclipse. In their dream-records, it is written: "If all the obelisks are sundered, the twin moons will align in darkness, the veil shall break, and what was locked away shall step forward once more." No such eclipse was ever recorded, but the Moon Seers have kept a watchful eye.

The House of Draco's True Fear
The House of Draco has ever hungered for dominion, control, and conquest, but before Drathis, there was one thing even they did not dare touch - the obelisks. Zarahan historians have wondered why, for centuries.
Only recently, in the last three hundred years, has the answer been found. Long ago, their ancestors tried and failed, with most ending up lost to the Weaving and the Primordials.
Drathis, however, found a hidden Draco archive, deep within the temple of Nathair, containing records of an ancient war - a war not fought between tribes but between something greater.
At the end of that war, the victors did not destroy their enemies. Instead, they sealed them away. Unlike Drathis, the Draconian Lords suspected

that if the Obelisks fell, Zarah would not simply belong to them, for it had always belonged to those who were locked away.
Drathis, on the other hand, believed he could control such beings...

<u>The Choice Before Aran</u>

"You did not come only to unify Zarah, Aran ibn Khalid, son of my dearest friend. You came to awaken it."
Barash ibn Sulaym (Karash - 288 years ago)

Aran believed he was fighting for a future free from tribal wars, a future of unity. The truth, however, was far greater. He was heir to something older than Zarah itself - a lineage tied to the last rulers who stood before the First Obelisk. Those who had come from the stars. Faced with his charge, he had only two choices before him. Either fade away, along with Zarah or rise above his forebears and save the planet and his people.

Appendix V: Creatures & Natural Wonders of Zarah

<u>Creatures of the Deserts</u>

<u>The Sand Serpent (Uramaki)</u>
A mythical colossus said to be as long as the dunes are vast, the Sand Serpent is a creature of legend and fear. Revered as a guardian of balance by some and a harbinger of doom by others, this massive serpent burrows beneath the sands, striking unseen. Its shimmering, scale-like hide reflects the golden hues of the desert, allowing it to vanish within the landscape. The most famous of these creatures, the mythical Uramak, was said to have saved an entire caravan by shielding them from an eternal storm, proving that these beasts are more than mindless predators - they are the sentinels of the desert.

<u>The Dune Jackal</u>
A cunning predator, the Dune Jackal moves in swift, calculated strikes, using the cover of shifting sands to stalk its prey. Known for its eerie howl that echoes across the dunes at night, many Zarahan tribes believe the jackal is an omen - either a warning of impending disaster or the presence of unseen forces watching from the void. With fur the colour of burnt ochre and piercing yellow eyes, these creatures are not just scavengers but masterful hunters. Their numbers have dwindled over the centuries, with sightings being less and less frequent.

<u>The Desert Nightwing</u>
A rare and elusive nocturnal predator, the Desert Nightwing is a majestic avian that soars through the Zarahan skies under the cover of darkness. With wingspans reaching up to seven feet, these creatures possess an uncanny ability to navigate the night with unparalleled grace and silence. Their feathers are unlike any other in the natural world - deep, iridescent red and blue that absorb moonlight rather than reflecting it, rendering them nearly invisible against the star-strewn sky. This adaptation makes them supreme hunters, striking their prey with swift, lethal precision before vanishing into the night like living shadows.

The Sand Scorpion
A creature of both fear and fascination, the Sand Scorpion is a relentless predator that thrives in the most desolate corners of Zarah. With an armoured exoskeleton the colour of obsidian, it blends seamlessly with the night, lying in wait beneath the sand for unsuspecting prey. Its pincers can crush stone, and its venom - called Night's Kiss - induces a slow, paralysing agony that ends in a merciful sleep. The largest of their kind, known as the Ashen Scourge, is said to grow large enough to rival a small child, its stinger capable of piercing even the strongest Zarahan steel. Many tribal warriors whisper that the Sand Scorpions are not merely beasts, but remnants of an ancient curse, their endless hunger a punishment woven into the Weaving itself.

The Dune Stalker
This creature is a spectral terror of the Zarahan wilderness, a creature that exists on the edges of sight and legend. Some specimens reach a considerable size, their elongated limbs allow them to glide effortlessly across the deserts. Along the dunes, its presence is betrayed only by the fleeting shimmer of its chitinous hide, which shifts with the sand, making it nearly imperceptible to the unwary. Its piercing golden eyes, burning like embers in the twilight, are said to see through both sandstorms and deception, marking its prey long before it strikes. With razor-edged claws capable of slicing through armour and flesh alike, the Dune Stalker is whispered to be more than mere beast - it is a hunter woven from the desert's own wrath, a spectre that walks unseen until the moment it decides to claim its next victim.

The Sand Fish
A marvel of desert adaptation, the Sand Fish is a small, elusive creature that moves beneath the dunes as effortlessly as it does through water. With its smooth, scale-like plating, it burrows deep to escape the scorching heat of the day, surfacing only under the cool embrace of night. Despite its fragile appearance, the Sand Fish is a staple in nomadic diets, its flesh rich in minerals and hydration. Some Zarahan mystics claim that the Sand Fish can sense disturbances in the Weaving, vanishing entirely before great calamities strike, making their sudden disappearance an omen of misfortune.

The Crystalline Leviathans

Deep beneath the surface of the Yaran ocean, the last of these colossal beings known as Crystalline Leviathans slumber in the darkness. These ancient, slithering behemoths are said to be formed from living glass, their bodies shimmering with iridescent hues as they move beneath the waves. Their very existence defies logic - some scholars believe they are remnants of a forgotten age. Legends tell of rare moments when one breaches the surface, its translucent body catching the sunlight like a fallen star. To see a Crystalline Leviathan is said to be an omen of great change, for they surface only when the balance of the Weaving is disturbed.

Natural Wonders of Zarah

The Sea of Ash

A desolate and lifeless expanse where the sand is no longer golden but black as night, the Sea of Ash is a place of death and rebirth. Formed by an ancient calamity lost to time, the sands here are sharp like glass, and the air carries a bitter, acrid taste. No life grows within its borders, save for the creatures that have forsaken the light of the sun. Mystics believe that the Sea of Ash was the site of a battle between the Old Kings and the Primordials, leaving behind a wound upon the world that never fully healed, along with an obelisk .

The Crescent Dunes

Endlessly shifting, the Crescent Dunes are a sea of golden waves sculpted by the eternal breath of the wind. Their beauty is mesmerizing, but their danger is unmatched. Many travellers have wandered into their embrace, only to find that the dunes are never where they once were. Some scholars claim that an ancient force moves beneath the sands, guiding the landscape into an ever-changing labyrinth that no man can truly map.

The Gilded Oasis

A paradise hidden among the sands, the Gilded Oasis is a place spoken of in hushed reverence. Said to be veiled by powerful magic, it is a place where the water is purer than crystal and the air carries the scent of forgotten flowers. It is rumoured that only those deemed worthy by the desert itself may ever find it, and those who do are forever changed, marked by the blessings of the unseen. Some believe it to be the last remnant of the Old Kings' final sanctuaries.

The Dune Serpent's Spine
Lying deep within the desert east of Sarim, the Spine is a jagged ridge of fossilized bones - the remains of a creature so massive that entire villages could be built upon its ribs. Whether the bones belong to a lost ancestor of Uramak or something even more ancient, none can say. The Priests of Solkara believe the Spine is sacred, a reminder that even the greatest beings can be swallowed by time. However, some fear that what lies buried beneath may one day awaken once more.

The Shadow Divide
A place of unfathomable darkness and ancient heresy, the Shadow Divide is a vast circular chasm hidden within the lowest depths of the Draconian Temple of Nathair, a place where the old bloodlines of the House of Draco once sought to pierce the veil between the mortal world and the realms beyond time. In Zarah's distant past, the most ambitious of the Draconian Warlords gathered here, their rituals drenched in blood, in an attempt to commune with the forgotten entities that existed before the Weaving itself was spun. They failed, and in their failure, they unknowingly brought doom upon their own lineage. The Divide did not answer with knowledge, but with hunger. Kael Drathis was the first, in many centuries, to attempt to control such entities. After the Draconian Wars, the Priesthood of the Sun forbade all from seeking the Shadow Divide, declaring it an open wound, a scar left behind by hubris. Yet, for those who still honour the Draco, the Divide still calls, still waits - for the right soul, for the right offering, to finally reveal what lies beyond the veil.

The Shadowed Vale
Hidden deep within the western expanse of the Talon Mountains, the Shadowed Vale is a realm spoken of only in ancient scrolls and whispers - a place where the Wardens of the Weaving withdrew from the world, awaiting the day when balance would be restored. Shielded by perpetual mist and looming cliffs, the vale is a land where time seems to slow, untouched by the chaos of the deserts beyond its borders. Its forests, an anomaly in the kingdom of Zarah, are said to have grown from the Weaving itself, their leaves humming with unseen energy, their roots entwined with forgotten power.
Once, the Wardens of the Weaving were the keepers of balance, their wisdom surpassing even the Priesthood of the Sun. They helped King Aran's ancestors bind their own pact with the Primordials.
When the Weaving began to fray, they foresaw a future where they could no longer intervene - only prepare.

Those in possession of the old knowledge claimed they retreated into the Shadowed Vale, vanishing from history, leaving behind only echoes of their teachings and the promise of a return when Zarah's need was greatest.

Through the centuries, few ever found the vale, and fewer still returned. Those who did return spoke of stone monoliths covered in shifting glyphs, of guardians who did not age, and of voices in the wind that called to those who listened. It has been debated, amongst the Priesthood of the Sun, that within the vale lies the final archive of the Weaving, a sacred vault containing knowledge long thought lost.

Appendix VI: Genealogies & Timelines

<u>Aran ibn Khalid – The Unifier of Zarah</u>

Aran's genealogy traces a lineage that intertwines with the Old Kings, the Wardens of Zarah, and the keepers of the Weaving. His bloodline carries both the burden and the destiny of those who came before him, ensuring that the fate of Zarah would always rest upon his shoulders. Below is the full genealogy, from the time of the Old Kings to Aran's reign and marriage to Sura.

The first list, included in this section of our archives, represents a chronological summary of Aran ibn Khalid's genealogy, followed by the historical recount of his bloodline.

I.   <u>The Age of the Old Kings (12,000–10,000 years ago)</u>

- *King Maelor, the First Warden* (12,000 years ago) – The first ruler of Zarah to commune with the Primordials.
- *Queen Ithara the Starlit* (11,800 years ago) – A ruler and seer who strengthened the bond between mortals and the oceans. It is said that she heard the voices of the Primordials in her dreams. Her daughter, *Layla the Last Light*, led the binding of the Primordials.
- *King Harun, the Titan-Slayer*, great grandson of *King Maelor* (11,500 years ago) – Defended Zarah from the Colossi of the Deep Sands, great beings that emerged after the first fractures in the Weaving.
- *King Khalif the Silent*, son of *Queen Sylthia* (11,200 years ago) – Known for the First Exodus, when all of Zarah's tribes scattered throughout the land, fearing the return of the Primordials.
- *Queen Layla the Last Light* (11,000 years ago) – Daughter to *Queen Ithara*, she, along with her kin, gave up her essence to the Weaving, to fully Bind the Primordials and thus ensured the Old Kings' knowledge kept being passed to their descendants before the turn of the age.

II.　　The Age of the Wardens (10,000–6,000 years ago)

- The Wardens of the Weaving (10,000 years ago) – A lineage separate from the ruling kings formed to protect the knowledge of the Obelisks.
- *Zafir the Keeper* (9,500 years ago) – The first of the Wardens who studied the Obelisks after the fall of the Old Kings.
- Malith the Sun-Warden (8,000 years ago) – Preserved the knowledge of the Weaving through oral traditions when written records were lost.
- *Asiya the Shadowed* One (7,200 years ago) – Attempted to repair the fraying Weaving but vanished into legend.
- *Jalil the Last Guardian* (6,000 years ago) – The final Warden before the bloodline retreated to the Shadowed Vale, and the rest were lost into the sands of time.

III.　　The Forgotten Age (6,000–2,500 years ago)

- Lost Bloodlines of the Wardens – After *Jalil*, knowledge of the Weaving faded, the bulk of the order moved to the Shadowed Vale, and the rest of their descendants lived as warriors, mystics, and desert wanderers, disappearing into the various tribes.
- *Queen Amara the Celestial* (2,500 years ago) – Reignited the old knowledge, guiding her people toward balance before vanishing on her final journey.
- *Ishaq the Wanderer* (2,200 years ago) – A scholar who sought the lost temples of the Wardens and revived their teachings.
- The Bloodline Fragments – Over the next 1,500 years, many descendants carried traces of the Warden lineage but lived as nomads, rulers, or warriors.

IV.　　The Age of the Shattered Thrones (800–300 years ago)

- The warrior-merchants of Karash – a powerful, forgotten, noble line that unknowingly carried Warden blood, influencing the course of Zarah's history.

- *Ashira of the Sands* (800 years ago) – A legendary figure whose survival instincts and cunning shaped her descendants when she merged with the Zafiri tribe.
- *Malik ibn Rahim* (500 years ago) – A warrior-scholar who pieced together fragments of the Weaving's lost history.
- *Khalid ibn Rashid* (333 years ago) – warrior-merchant of Karash and Aran's father, who knew about his lineage's true purpose and worked in secrecy to prepare for the coming struggle.

V.   <u>The Rise of Aran ibn Khalid (300–282 years ago)</u>

- *Aran ibn Khalid* (300 years ago) – Born to *Khalid ibn Rashid* and his wife *Zahara al-Tarek*, raised in Karash, and trained in both war and wisdom.
- *Iram ibn Khalid* (308 – 288 years ago) – Aran's older brother, killed in battle against the Halithar tribe.
- Unification of the Tribes (282–278 years ago) – Aran united the warring factions of Zarah, reclaiming his ancestors' legacy.
- The War of the Weaving (280–278 years ago) – Fought against Drathis, the Draconian warlord, while Aran sought to mend the fractures in the Weaving.
- The Reshaping of the Weaving (278 years ago) – Aran's final act in the war, ensuring the Primordials would never rise again while maintaining the balance of power.

VI.   <u>The Marriage of Aran and Sura (277 years ago)</u>

- *Sura al-Rasha* – An intuitive spy, who walked alongside Aran in his trials and, in time, helped him mend the Weaving.
- Marriage to Aran (277 years ago) – After the war, Aran and Sura ruled together, blending their strengths - his legacy of kingship and war, and her wisdom of the unseen forces.
- The Legacy of Their Bloodline – Their child, *Khalid ibn Aran*, and his descendants inherited both the strength of warriors and the sight of the wind, ensuring the Weaving's protection for generations to come.

Historical Recount of Aran ibn Khalid's Bloodline

I.   The Age of the Old Kings (12,000–10,000 years ago)

The Age of the Old Kings was a time of legend and might, when the rulers of Zarah were more than mere men - they were architects of fate, wielders of power drawn from the very fabric of existence. It was an age where the world had yet to forget its primordial roots, where the vast dunes of Zarah were not merely land, but living history - a place where star travellers, gods, spirits, and mortal rulers stood side by side in an uneasy balance.

The Rise of the First Kings

Before the great cities of Zarah rose from the sands, the desert was a vast and untamed expanse, home to nomadic tribes that wandered beneath the watchful eyes of the twin moons, Anar and Nysa. They followed the rhythms of the dunes, shaping their lives around the whispers of the wind and the movements of the stars. But in the heart of this desert planet, something ancient stirred - an awakening that would reshape the world.

The first to answer the call was *Ilyas the First Warden*, a man whose origins were shrouded in mystery. Some say he came from the stars, others that he was born beneath an eclipse. Others still, that he emerged from the dunes themselves, shaped by the will of the desert. Regardless of his beginnings, his destiny was undeniable.

Ilyas did not seek to rule by conquest, but by understanding. He was the first to recognize the deeper forces woven into this land - the Weaving, a cosmic thread that bound all things together. Through years of meditation and communion with the unseen, he learned to hear the echoes of those who came before, the spirits of the desert who whispered of power long forgotten, in The MiddleVerse.

Under his guidance, the first great city, Ryvath, was built - a city carved from obsidian stone, steel and sand, rising like a jewel amidst the northern mountains. It became a seat of knowledge, where scholars studied the stars, where warriors trained not only in the art of war but in the discipline of the mind. It was here that the first Warden Kings ruled, not just over men, but over the unseen forces that shaped the world. Yet power never goes unchallenged.

The War of the Titans
As the Old Kings sought to harness the power of the Weaving, they unknowingly disturbed something far older than themselves. Beneath the mountains, in the forgotten caverns where no light had touched for aeons, the Colossi of the Deep Sands stirred. These primordial titans, remnants of a time before men, were beings of immense strength and will, creatures whose existence defied mortality itself.

The greatest of these was *Rhazak, the Devourer*, a being of shifting obsidian and fire, whose body was said to be composed of the very essence of Zarah's fury. When he emerged from the depths, the sky itself darkened, and the sands turned to glass beneath his feet.

For decades, war raged between the Colossi and the Old Kings of Zarah. The cities burned, the land trembled, and the stars themselves seemed to weep.

King Harun, the Titan-Slayer, Maelor's great-grandson, led the charge against these ancient horrors. Clad in armour woven with sigils of the Weaving, wielding a blade forged from the heart of a fallen star, he stood against *Rhazak* in a battle that lasted seven days and seven nights.

In the end, *Harun* struck the final blow, shattering the Devourer's form, binding his spirit to the deepest well of the desert, where his essence would be locked away for eternity. But victory came at a cost. The war had drained the Old Kings, leaving the balance of the Weaving fragile, vulnerable to forces they had yet to comprehend.

The Binding of the Primordials
With the Colossi vanquished, a greater truth was revealed - the Weaving was never meant to be wielded by mortals alone. Hidden within its depths were the Primordials, ancient entities who embodied the fundamental aspects of existence: Life and Death, Creation and Decay, Time and Fate.

The Old Kings had long drawn upon the Weaving's power, but they had not understood its cost. The more they pulled upon it, the more they frayed its delicate threads, and in doing so, they roused the Primordials from their slumber.

It was *Queen Layla, the Last Light*, descendant of *Queen Ithara*, the final ruler of the Old Kings, who saw what was coming. She understood that the balance could not be maintained by force alone. To prevent the Primordials from unravelling the world in their awakening, she called upon the greatest sages, warriors, and mystics of her time, forging a desperate pact - a binding of power, a sealing of fate.

Twelve Obelisks were raised across Zarah, each carved from a single massive stone, each inscribed with runes that tied them to their particular aspect of existence, as well as its very fabric. They would act as conduits, stabilizing the Weaving, ensuring that the Primordials could never rise in full force again. Unbeknownst to them, this binding came with a price.

To anchor the power of the Obelisks, Ithara's daughter and her most trusted kin sacrificed themselves, offering their own essence to seal the balance. Their names were wiped from secular history, their deeds whispered only in secret, but their sacrifice ensured that the world would endure.

<u>The Fall of the Old Kings</u>
With the Binding complete, the Age of the Old Kings came to an end. The knowledge of the Weaving, once freely wielded, was hidden away, passed only to those who were deemed worthy. The cities of the Warden Kings began to crumble, their once-great halls reclaimed by the sands. Time, ever merciless, buried their legacies beneath the weight of forgetfulness. As one Era moved into the next, the Wardens exiled themselves into the Shadowed Vale, becoming almost untraceable in the records of Zarahan history. But the deserts are flawless, and Zarah never truly forgets.

The bloodline of the Old Kings endured, though fractured and scattered. Some became wanderers, others scholars, their heritage hidden in the names of nomads and warriors who knew not the ancient power they carried in their veins. Thus, the world moved on, the echoes of the past fading into legend.

Legends, as all things, are bound to the Weaving. Therefore, they are never truly lost. Somewhere, buried beneath the sand, the stories of the Old Kings still whisper in the wind, waiting for those who would listen. Waiting for those who carried the bloodline in their veins.

II.   <u>The Age of the Wardens (10,000–6,000 years ago)</u>

When the last of the Old Kings vanished into the annals of history, they left behind more than ruins swallowed by time and sand. Their legacy was a wound - a world forever altered by their ambition, their wars, and their final desperate act to bind the Primordials.

The Weaving had been sealed, the great Obelisks, hidden away, standing like silent sentinels across Zarah, but with that sealing came an undeniable truth. Those who did not understand the past would doom the future by repeating it in a seemingly endless cycle. So, from the ashes of the fallen dynasties, the Wardens of the Weaving arose.

The Birth of the Wardens

With the sacrifice of the Old kings, the last of the ruling bloodlines fractured. The great cities that had once stood proud, with their towers gleaming beneath the twin moons, crumbled as power fell into the hands of tribal warlords, mystics, and those who sought to claim the remnants of the Old Kings' dominion.

In the midst of this chaos, a council was formed - not to rule, but to protect. The Wardens of the Weaving were not kings nor warriors but guardians of knowledge. They were those who had witnessed the Primordials' Binding, who understood what had been locked away, and who swore an oath that the mistakes of the past would never be repeated. Though, with time, they tended to focus too much inward, closing themselves off to the world.

Nonetheless, it was *Zafir the Keeper*, a scholar who had walked the halls of Ryvath before it fell into the corners of history, who gathered the first of the Wardens in the shadow of the ruined city. "The world must not forget," he had said, his voice carrying across the obsidian stone. "The Weaving is not a chain to be broken, nor a tool to be wielded without wisdom. It is a river. Its appealing waters will draw many to its depths, but most will drown in them." He looked around at those assembled. "We must be its stewards."

Under *Zafir's* guidance, the Wardens became more than mere scribes. They were seekers, wanderers, and whisperers of truths too dangerous for common folk. They studied the Obelisks, ensuring that their power remained undisturbed, that the bindings remained strong. They travelled across Zarah, moving between the nomadic tribes and fledgling city-states, teaching the old ways to those willing to listen and erasing knowledge from those who sought to misuse it.

"Blessed be the creators because the cosmos is never kind to those who carry the burden of knowledge." *The House of Tempus*

For centuries, the Wardens operated in secrecy, their influence woven into the very fabric of Zarahan society. But not all who walked the desert sought balance. There were those who still coveted the power of the Old Kings, who longed to break the chains that bound the Primordials.
One such faction arose in the city of Nahir, located in Zarah's southeastern hemisphere, what is now called the Sea of Ash, a once-great kingdom that had survived the fall of the Old Kings but had grown bitter in its isolation. Its rulers, believing themselves to be the true inheritors of the lost dynasties, sought to reclaim what they saw as their birthright - the full, unfettered power of the Weaving. They called themselves the Scions of the First Dawn.
Under *Malith the Sun-Warden*, the order discovered the Scions' plot to unearth one of the buried Obelisks in Valamar, believing that by doing so, they could reclaim the lost power of the Old Kings. *Malith* led a band of Wardens to Nahir, hoping to reason with its rulers...

"Since the birth of creation, reason is a brittle thing, and power is a language that requires few words."
The House of Tempus
Echoing Archives, Chronaxis, the Kronos System

The Scions struck first, and the sands of Nahir ran red. The war that followed was not one of armies, but of the darkest shadows - assassins against scholars, hidden knowledge turned into whispered death. The Wardens fought, not for conquest, but for silence - to ensure that what had been locked away remained forgotten. Darkness was upon them. Faced with inevitability, they were forced to make a terrible choice. To prevent the Scions from reaching the Obelisk, Malith and his followers collapsed the tunnels, leading to it - burying themselves alive in the process. With their deaths, the first of the Wardens' strongholds fell, and the weight of their task grew heavier.
As the centuries flowed through the passageways of time, the Wardens realized that secrecy alone would not be enough. For knowledge could be stolen, twisted, and reforged into weapons. The temptation of the Weaving would always remain, lurking in the hearts of those who sought to wield it for their own gain. They had arrived at a crossroads. In order to protect that which was most sacred, they decided to erase their own history.

The cities that had once housed their libraries were abandoned. Their literature was either scattered to the winds or sold to the highest bidder. The names of their greatest sages were stripped from the records, their teachings reduced to myths.

Even the Obelisks themselves were 'hidden' - not through physical means, but through the Weaving itself.

For only those who bore the blood of the Wardens could see them for what they truly were. Still, father-time remains inexorable, and so, the world forgot.

Yet, the Wardens remained. They walked unseen through the great cities, watching, whispering, waiting. No longer known as kings or scholars, they became something else entirely - ghosts of the desert, keepers of an oath sworn to a dying age. Vows bound to the Stone of Oaths.

By the time of *Jalil, the Last Guardian*, the Warden's ranks had dwindled considerably. For time will always be the silent sculptor that shapes what we become while erasing what we were.

Time, that most elusive of fractions, had worn them thin, and the world had moved on. The city-states of Zarah had grown strong again, their rulers dismissing the old legends as nothing more than fables.

Jalil, aware of the shifts in the Weaving, saw what his predecessors had refused to accept - that nothing lasts forever. Their bloodlines were thinning, their knowledge slipping beyond the reach of even their most devoted followers. If they continued as they were, they would vanish, and with them, the last remnants of the Old Kings. Faced with oblivion, he made a choice that defied everything his ancestors had believed. Time was upon them to scatter through Zarah while maintaining a stronghold in the Shadowed Vale.

He took the last of the Wardens and sent them into the world - not as sages, but as warriors, as merchants, as common souls to exist as men and women who would live and die without ever speaking of their true heritage. Most of them, not even aware they possessed it. Facing the fading of his kind, he placed the final pieces of their knowledge in the blood of his people, ensuring that if one fell, another would rise to take their place. This was not preservation. It was survival.

With enough time gone by, as quietly as he had lived, *Jalil* vanished into the desert, his fate unknown. With his passing, the Wardens ceased to exist as an order within the secular world. Their lineage became scattered whispers, their purpose, an unspoken promise passed down through the generations.

However, blood is powerful, and it works in mysterious ways. Blood remembers, and so does the desert.
Though they had been forgotten, the Wardens' legacy endured, buried within the veins of those who carried out their purpose, either knowingly or unknowingly.
The day would come when the Weaving would call upon them once more, and at that time, their descendants would rise again. For the desert forgets many things, but it never forgets blood.

III.   The Forgotten Age (6,000–2,500 years ago)

When *Jalil*, the last of the Wardens of the Weaving, vanished into the annals of forsaken history, his people left behind no banners, no grand tombs, nor written records to mark their depart. Nevertheless, he had succeeded in his purpose - for the Order to be forgotten.
Yet, the desert does not forget. Instead It whispers through the sands, carrying memories in the wind and keeping watch over those who bear the blood of ancient oaths. Though history moved on, scattered across the shifting dunes were remnants of a forgotten time, carried unknowingly by those who bore the silent legacy of the Wardens in their veins.
This was later called The Forgotten Age, a time of lost truths and fractured destinies, when the knowledge of the Weaving had faded to myth, and the last embers of the Old Kings flickered in the darkness.

The Fracturing of the Bloodline
Outside of the Shadowed Vale, where the remnants of the order resided, and without its guidance, the scattered Warden descendants lived as wanderers, warriors, and mystics, their heritage reduced to whispers in the night and dreams they did not understand. Most married into the various tribes, unaware of their legacy. Others became nomads, their lives entwined with the shifting dunes, carrying pieces of lost knowledge in their oral traditions, as well as in their veins. They spoke of places unseen, of hidden pathways in the sands, of whispers carried by the wind that only the wise could hear.
A small number settled in cities, blending into the rising kingdoms that flourished in the absence of the Old Kings. They became merchants, scholars, and some even rulers - unaware that in their very blood rested the remnants of a once-great purpose.

Amongst them were those who still felt the echoes of what had come before.
In the depths of the desert, far from the reach of kings and warlords, a few remained who remembered. They were called, by history, the Silent Keepers, those who had devoted themselves to safeguarding what little remained of the Weaving's knowledge. They passed down teachings in secret, training their children in the ways of the lost Wardens, though even they had forgotten their true origins. To them, it was not history. It was something more powerful - it was instinct, a duty buried so deeply in their souls that even time itself could not erase it.

<u>The Kingdoms of Sand and Stone</u>
With the Wardens gone, the world was left to forge its own destiny. The great cities of Zarah, once bound by the silent wisdom of the Weaving's stewards, now warred among themselves.
The Kingdom of Valamar, once a place of enlightenment and study, became a nation of warlords, cursed, its rulers obsessed with the remnants of power hidden beneath the dunes. They sent expeditions deep into the desert, seeking the lost Obelisks, believing them to be the key to dominion over the known world.
To the west of Valamar, the City of Eruthis rose to power, a beacon of trade and influence. Its rulers dared to claim divine right, believing themselves chosen by the gods to rule. They outlawed all mention of the Weaving, branding those who spoke of the past as heretics, burning scrolls, and executing mystics who still carried traces of the old knowledge.
The lands of Erythmar, a once-mighty province of scholars, descended into ruin. The scholars who had once chronicled the stars now wandered the desert as exiles, their libraries reduced to ash, their wisdom lost to the winds.
Beyond Erythmar stood those who had stolen the world for themselves. They watched with silent amusement as the peoples of Zarah tore themselves apart. For these rulers had long since abandoned the Weaving, instead forging their strength from steel, conquest, and the will to endure.

<u>The Return of the Forgotten</u>
For centuries, the Weaving remained quiet, buried beneath layers of history and neglect. But the desert does not sleep - it waits.
So it was that in the bowels of Valamar, the first signs of the awakening stirred. An excavation, ordered by an unbridled king, uncovered something that should probably have remained lost - an Obelisk.

Humming with an energy that had not been felt in millennia. At that moment, the Weaving trembled.

The Silent Keepers, sensing the shift, abandoned their hidden sanctuaries and began to move across Zarah once more. The bloodline of the Wardens, long scattered, began to stir in those who carried it unknowingly. Strange dreams came to wandering warriors, visions of places they had never seen. Merchants found their hands tracing symbols they did not recognize yet somehow understood. Children whispered in their sleep of voices calling from the deep places of the world. The time of forgetting was coming to an end, but with it, so too would come the return of those who had long waited in the shadows. For if the Weaving stirred, then so did its enemies.

The Twilight Before the Storm
By the end of The Forgotten Age, the world was on the precipice of change. The descendants of the Wardens, scattered and unaware of their shared legacy, stood poised to be either the saviours of balance or the instruments of its unravelling. Most were common men and women, unaware that the smallest action could shift the course of history.
In the 'eye of the storm,' a boy would be born in the desert town of Karash. His bloodline, known to his father, was tied to the oldest of kings.
In the distant mountains of Yara, a Rasha Seer felt something stir beneath her feet, something vast, something waking, and in the depths of Zarah's history, a nameless scholar uncovered a truth long buried beneath time - a truth that could either restore the Weaving or shatter it forever. For the past was no longer content to remain forgotten. It was coming back, and the world would never be the same again.

IV.   The Age of the Shattered Thrones (800–300 years ago)

By the time the Age of the Shattered Thrones began, the lands of Zarah were already a shadow of what they had once been. Sand and time had covered most of its history. The great cities of the past had either crumbled into dust or stood as fractured echoes of their former glory, their rulers locked in an endless cycle of war and treachery. This was an era not of star empires, but of broken kingdoms, of thrones won and lost with the shifting of Zarah's sands.

The Weaving, once tended by the Wardens and balanced by the Old Kings, had become a thing of myth, whispered only by desert mystics, thieves, and mad scholars. The people no longer remembered the names of those who had bled to protect them, nor the purpose of the Obelisks that still stood - silent, waiting.

Yet, through the chaos, the blood of the ancients endured. Scattered. Hidden. Waiting for the moment when fate would demand its return.

<u>The Rise of the Tribal Warlords</u>

With no star-ancestry left to govern Zarah, the land became a battlefield of ambition. From the western dunes to the highland citadels of the north, clan lords carved out dominions with fire and steel.

In the ruins of Valamar, once a kingdom of wisdom and learning, the first of these new tyrants rose, though briefly. *King Dirash the Bloodied*, a man as ruthless as he was cunning, claimed dominion over the tribes of Zarah through sheer brutality. His warriors rode under banners of black and gold, their swords forged from the shattered remnants of fallen asteroids. *Dirash* had no interest in history or prophecy - only in conquest. He waged war against his neighbouring city-states, toppling dynasties that had ruled for centuries, and though quite a few were descendants from the old lineages, he did not care. He conquered, leaving only ashes in his wake.

Therefore, it should come as no surprise that during these turbulent times, *Dirash* was not the only warlord to try and reclaim the old powers.

Just to the south, beyond the Kartal Highlands, a kingdom unlike any other emerged - the Kartalis Dominion, ruled by the enigmatic *Empress Laleth*.

No one outside her closest circle had ever seen her face, for she ruled from behind a mask of polished Crystalline Leviathan bone, her words carried through ministers and envoys. It was whispered that she knew secrets buried beneath the dunes, that she could speak to spirits and command the loyalty of the wind itself. Some scholars have speculated that she was an offspring of the stars, others that she was a descendant of the old bloodline. While tribal warlords in the south fought for land, *Laleth* fought for knowledge, sending expeditions into the ruins of the Old Kings in search of something lost.

To the east, where the Sea of Ash met the great riverlands, a new power stirred - The Shadows Maw. This hidden force, spoken of only in hushed tones, did not seek to conquer through open battle, but through subterfuge, infiltrating the courts of Zarah's rulers, turning brother against brother. It was said that the Shadows Maw did not fight wars. They simply ensured that their enemies destroyed each other. It is now apparent to historians that they were, undoubtedly, the first signs of the House of Draco operating on Zarah.

It was a time of shifting allegiances, of whispered betrayals, of rulers who wore their crowns uneasily, knowing that each sunrise might be their last.

The War of the Five Thrones

Inevitably, the fragile balance between these warlords and rulers shattered. The War of the Five Thrones began with a single assassination - the sudden, violent death of *King Dirash the Bloodied*. His throat was slit in his own palace, his body left as a message scrawled in crimson across the marble floors. No kingdom claimed responsibility, for all had reason to see him dead. The power vacuum that followed set the land ablaze.

The Kartalis Dominion marched north, hoping to claim Valamar and the surrounding territories before another warlord could rise to take *Dirash's* place. But their ambitions were met with fierce resistance, for *Dirash's* bastard son, *Amir the Ghost*, emerged from the shadows, wielding his father's banner and seeking vengeance for his murder.

In the east, the Shadows Maw struck silently, its agents poisoning wells, burning granaries, and sowing dissent among rival courts. No one saw their warriors upon the battlefield, yet their enemies fell all the same.

This war raged for nearly a century, consuming generations. Cities were taken, lost, and taken again. Bloodlines that had ruled for centuries were extinguished in a single night. Temples were turned to rubble, their sacred knowledge lost forever. In the end, after all that destruction, none of the Five Thrones claimed true victory.

The war had broken the land and weakened its people. The rulers who survived were left ruling over ruins, their wealth spent, their armies thinned. The Age of Warlords had come to its bitter end, not through conquest, but through exhaustion.

The Lords of Karash and the Hidden Bloodline

While the great powers fought and bled, one small desert town remained untouched by the tides of war - Karash, the City of the Oasis.

Nestled deep within the desert, protected by the natural barriers of shifting dunes and treacherous ravines, Karash did not seek war, nor did it invite it. Its rulers, the Tarek, were known not for their ambition but for their patience. They traded with all, made enemies of none, and above all else, they listened. For within Karash, hidden beneath centuries of careful lineage, the last remnants of the Warden bloodline still flowed.

Though they did not know their full history, the tribal lords of Karash carried the instincts of those who had come before them. They understood the Weaving in ways they could not explain, sensing its ebb and flow, knowing when to act, and when to wait.

It was in Karash, in the final years of the Age of the Shattered Thrones, that a child was born. His name was *Khalid ibn Rashid*, and he was *Aran ibn Khalid's* father.

Though he did not yet know it, he would set the wheels of destiny into motion, preparing the way for the one who would finally break the cycle of war. The Age of the Shattered Thrones was coming to an end.

V.   The Rise of Aran (300–278 years ago)

The warlords, kings, and merchants who carved their fleeting dominions into the land believed themselves the masters of fate, but the desert knew better.

The sands of Zarah had long whispered of a coming change. The Seers of the distant past had foretold of his arrival. Beneath the ruins of fallen empires and the echoes of forgotten bloodlines, something ancient stirred, waiting for the moment when the past and future would converge once more. That moment arrived with the birth of Aran ibn Khalid.

He was born in Karash, the City of the Oasis, under a sky heavy with stars, to the Tarek tribe. They had once been powerful and respected as masters of the dunes but had fallen into obscurity by the time of his birth. Their shamans, who once communed with the sands, were now old and scattered, their influence waning.

Karash, at this moment in time, had no more than a few hundred souls living in it. His father, *Khalid ibn Rashid*, aware of his bloodline, was a merchant and a leader, unlike those that dominated the age - he was a patient trader, a scholar, as much as a warrior. He was a man who understood that true power was not taken with the sword but earned through wisdom. Aran's mother, *Zahara*, was descended from a long line of desert healers and mystics, women who had, for generations, spoken to the wind and read the shifting dunes like a tapestry of fate.

It is said that on the night of his birth, the winds ceased their howling, and the desert stood still. The old mystics of Karash, the ones who still could, saw this as a sign - one of both promise and warning. For a child born in silence was a child who would one day command the voice of the world itself.

Aran grew beneath the watchful eyes of his father and the careful teachings of Barash, one of the last true sages of Obelisk Lore.

While other boys learned only the sword, Aran was taught the deeper laws of the land - the unspoken currents that governed not just men but the unseen forces that still lingered in the forgotten places of the desert. However, no amount of wisdom could shelter him from the destiny that awaited.

The Unification of the Tribes

For years, Aran wandered the sands, gathering strength, wisdom, and allies. He did not seek war - war had already found him. Instead, he sought unity.

The tribes of Zarah had been scattered for centuries, each ruled by its own chieftains, bound by blood feuds older than the stones themselves. But Aran was not like the warlords who had come before him. He did not seek to rule by conquest, but by purpose.

The first to follow him were the Bahir, the Ulema, and the Shamari, as well as those who had kept the old ways alive in the deepest corners of the deserts. Then came the warriors of the High Cliffs, from the future Kingdom of Kartal, the remnants of shattered armies who saw in him something greater than a mere tribal leader. Even nomads hailing from the various deserts, long untouched by the affairs of kings, bent the knee. By the time Aran had completed his unification, he was not leading an army. He was leading a worldwide nation.

The War Against Drathis and the Mending of the Weaving

Through the centuries, Drathis had not been idle. He had been covertly working with powerful Zarahan politicians, such as Farid al-Rasha from the city of Sarim. He sought to break the seals that held the Primordials at bay and claim their power for himself. Aran was plunged into a conflict he had no idea existed, but he quickly learned that if Drathis had succeeded, there would be no war to win nor would there be a world left to rule.

The war that followed was unlike any fought before. It was not just men against Draconians, but forces beyond mortal comprehension clashing in the heart of Zarah. The conflicts were many, some fought out in the open, while others were conducted in secrecy.

The Dawn of a New Era

With the Weaving restored, the desert exhaled a breath it had held for millennia. The war was over. The world, now repaired, endured.

Aran was not simply a king anymore. He was the final Warden, the last guardian of Zarah's fate. At his side stood Sura, his partner in both war and wisdom, his queen in all but name. Together, they did not merely rule. They rebuilt. And so, the Age of the Shattered Thrones ended, and the Kingdom of Qamar was born.

VI. <u>The Marriage of Aran and Sura (277 years ago)</u>

The desert had known war. It had known bloodshed, the rise and fall of local kings, the whispers of the Weaving, and the echoes of forgotten gods. But on the eve of Aran's ascension, it knew something else - a moment of peace, a promise fulfilled, and a love that had endured trials beyond mortal reckoning.

<u>The Union Foretold in the Wind</u>
The legends had spoken of it long before the war, long before Aran had raised his banner against Drathis before the Weaving had been mended. A union not of politics, nor necessity, but of balance.
Sura, though born to the Rasha tribe, was the last descendant of the ancient Al'Shara. She had been by Aran's side through battle, through loss, through the very reshaping of Weaving. Where Aran was the wildfire, Sura was the wind that guided it. Where he wielded strength, she wielded wisdom. Where he fought, she listened, often being his close confidant. By the time he stood as a king, she walked as one who understood the language of the unseen and the unspoken.
Their marriage was not just the sealing of a bond between two souls but of two forces - one forged in the weight of duty, the other carried by the currents of destiny. The wedding took place under the moonlight of Anar and Nysa, shining brighter than they had in a generation. The desert was still, as if it, too, held its breath for what was to come.
The ceremony was unlike those of the great kings before him. There were no vast halls of stone, no grand tapestries telling the stories of war. Instead, it was held beneath the open sky, in the very sands that had borne witness to their journey. A great circle was drawn in the sand, marking the sacred space of the ceremony - one not enclosed by walls but open to the endless horizon.
At the heart of the gathering stood an obelisk - one of the twelve, no longer a symbol of broken fate, but of a world healed. The Weaving, which had once been frayed, hummed softly through the night as if blessing the union.

Sura stood dressed not in the heavy finery of queens but in robes woven from the threads of the desert itself - from cactus-silk, the colour of twilight, embroidered with the sigils of the Al'Shara. Her dark hair was braided with silver, and in her eyes, there was no doubt. Only certainty.

Aran stood before her in garments that bore no crown, no weight of conquest - only the simple adornments of a warrior who had found peace. His father's sword, which had known war for too long, was sheathed, bound in cloth, untouched beneath the starlit sky.

The ceremony was conducted by Barash, the last of the great sages, the man who had watched over them both since their youth. His voice carried like the whisper of the dunes, steady, ancient, unyielding. "Before the Weaving, before the sands, before the stars themselves, there was balance. And in that balance, there was harmony." He turned to Aran. "You have walked the path of kings, not for power, but for duty. You have carried the weight of a world that was breaking, and you have mended it, not alone, but with those who stood beside you. Do you stand now, not as a warrior, nor as king, but as a man, bound by choice?"

Aran's voice, quiet yet unwavering, filled the desert air. "I do."

Barash turned to Sura. "You have walked the path of the unseen, carrying the wisdom of those who listen. You have tempered the storm, guided the lost, and spoken for the wind when none could hear it. Do you stand now, not as a spy, nor as a guide, but as a woman, bound by choice?"

Sura smiled broadly, looking at Barash. "I do." she spoke confidently, her eyes reflecting the moonlight. There were no grand pronouncements, no need for elaborate rites. There were only the four of them, for Rafiq had earned the right to be present. They stood before the endless horizon, bound by something far older than the kingdoms of men.

Barash raised his hands, palms facing the sky. "Then let the desert bear witness. Let the wind carry your names beyond the sands of time. Let the Weaving, which you have restored, hold you as one." With that, they were bound - not just as husband and wife, but as two halves of a greater whole that had finally come together.

The celebrations that followed were not those of opulence or excess but of joy. The people of Zarah, weary from war, sang songs of the desert, of the stars, of the journeys taken and the ones yet to come. Elders from the farthest reaches of the land came to offer blessings. Warriors who had once fought on opposing sides now drank from the same cup. For the first time in its history, Zarah was not divided by war but united in hope. As the dawn broke over the dunes, Aran and Sura stood at the edge of the gathering, watching the first light of their new life together.

She turned to her husband. "What now?" Aran could not help but marvel once more on just how beautiful she was.

Ever the weaver, he closed his eyes for a moment, listening to something that she could now also hear. When he opened them, she smiled. "Now, we build." He said, returning the smile. For though their journey had been long, and though the war had been hard-fought, their greatest task was only beginning. Together, they would forge something that had not been seen on Zarah since the birth of its civilizations. A kingdom not built on conquest, nor on fear, but on balance. The Royal Kingdom of Qamar had begun.

Historical Recount of Sura al-Rasha's Bloodline

Sura al-Rasha's lineage is one of resilience, wisdom, and fire - a bloodline forged in the heart of Zarah's shifting sands, shaped by rulers, warriors, and seers who carried the weight of destiny upon their shoulders. Though history remembers her as the first queen to rule all of Zarah, her roots run deep into the forgotten ages, woven with the echoes of those who came before.

Her ancestry traces back to the great tribes of the desert - a union of bloodlines from nomadic warlords, priestesses of the celestial order, and rulers of the fragmented city-states that once vied for control of Zarah's vast expanse. Each generation before her shaped the path that would one day lead to the unification of the desert under her reign beside Aran ibn Khalid.

I. <u>The Dawn of the Bloodline: The Al'Shara tribe, Keepers of the Silver Flame (3,500 years ago - 2,000 years ago)</u>

Long after the rise and fall of the Old Kings, when the shifting sands of Zarah were carved into warring dominions, there existed an early tribe whose power did not originally stem from the blade, but from the heavens themselves. Ancestors to the Rasha tribe, the Al'Shara, Keepers of the Silver Flame, were not born of conquest, nor did their lineage flourish through the sword.

Their bloodline endured through wisdom, through prophecy, through a sacred connection to the celestial forces that governed the fate of mortals. Humans brought to these lands from the stars.

The blood of Al'Shara was touched by the light of the twin moons, Anar and Nysa, at the dawn of their rise. The first of their line, Shara the Moon-Seer, was a star-child of the desert, born beneath an eclipse that turned the sky to silver and the sands to shadow. From the moment she took her first breath, the seers of her time whispered that she was destined to see beyond the veil of time itself.

As she grew, Shara's visions became legend. She spoke of winds that would reshape the dunes and of rivers that would dry before their time. She spoke of future rulers who would fall to their own ambition. The dispersed nomadic tribes sought her counsel, and warlords bent their knee before her wisdom.

But she never sought power - instead she looked for balance. She could see it in the centuries yet to come.

Therefore, to those closest to her, she spoke of the distant future. She foretold the coming of one that would unite the tribes of Zarah. One that would mend the Weaving and bring balance to the world.

It was she who gathered the first Circle of Moon-Seers, a council of sages who read the heavens like a map, deciphering the fates of men in the shifting constellations. Under her guidance, the Silver Flame was kindled - a sacred fire that was said to be a reflection of the Weaving itself, its embers never fading so long as the balance of Zarah remained intact.

The people came to know the Seers of Al'Shara as more than just prophets. They were the silent hand upon the course of history, the voices in the wind that steered rulers away from ruin. Their knowledge of the desert was unmatched - they knew the secret oases, the paths the dunes would soon swallow, the places where the sky touched the sand with divine purpose. Yet, time does not favour those who guide from the shadows, and the world hardly ever listens to those who whisper.

Still, for a time, the Al'Shara flourished. Their wisdom helped shape some of the great cities of the desert, their guidance woven into the edicts of leaders and the laws of the land. They became advisors to rulers, keepers of ancient lore, protectors of the unseen threads that bound Zarah together. Yet with influence came enemies, and with power came fear.

The warlords who ruled through steel and blood began to see the Seers not as guides but as a threat. Their visions unsettled those who sought dominion, their warnings an obstacle to unchecked conquest. Some claimed their prophecies were manipulations, fabrications designed to keep rulers in the Seers' grasp. Others, more ambitious, sought to claim the Silver Flame for themselves. Much like the Old King's binding of the Primordials, they fooled themselves into believing it held the key to dominion over fate itself.

Thus began the Silent War - a conflict fought not on battlefields but in the corridors of power in the whispered betrayals of rulers who had once sought their counsel. There was little doubt amongst the Seers that the House of Draco was having its presence felt on Zarah.

Perhaps due to that influence, the temples of Al'Shara, once revered, were burned in the dead of night. The Seers, once honoured, were hunted like fugitives. The Silver Flame, once thought to be eternal, was extinguished by treachery. But their bloodline endured.

Before the final temple fell, the last High Seer, Layla Al'Shara, gathered the remnants of their people and fled into the deep desert, where the sands swallowed their presence from the eyes of their enemies.

She carried with her the last embers of the Silver Flame, vowing that one day, the Seers would rise again, planting their seed to watch it grow. Like many, many tribes before them, the Al'Shara faded from the annals of Zarah's history, though their bloodline did not entirely vanish. Due to Seers only marrying warriors, who are by nature devoid of true foresight, it fell upon their daughters to carry the lineage forward, their gifts passed from mother to child. Their fathers protected them, keeping them hidden from those who would see them destroyed. In time, they began marrying beyond the warrior clans, into the merchant tribes, into the lineages of kings - but always, the gift remained.

By the time Sura was born into the Rasha tribe, few remembered the name Al'Shara. But in her veins, the sight of the Moon-Seers still lingered. In her dreams, the whispers of prophecy stirred. In her heart, the fire that had once burned eternal flickered anew.

Therefore, when she rose to stand beside Aran, helping him unite the fractured tribes and broken kingdoms into a single House, when she helped him fight the Draco and the Primordials, it was not only the destiny of her people she fulfilled, but the promise of her ancestors - the Keepers of the Silver Flame.

II. <u>The Blood of Warriors: The Ishkari, Lords of the Crimson Spear (2,000 years ago - 500 years ago)</u>

If House Al'Shara was the guiding hand of the desert, House Ishkari was its clenched fist. Where the Seers had shaped the course of history through wisdom and prophecy, the Ishkari forged their legacy in the crucible of war, their names written in the blood of those who stood against them.

Theirs was a lineage of conquest, their warriors the scourge of the fractured city-states, their crimson banners fluttering over the ruins of their enemies. For nearly fifteen hundred years, the name Ishkari struck fear into the hearts of those who dared oppose them.

They were rulers not by divine right but by the weight of the steel in their hands and the fire in their souls.

The origins of House Ishkari can be traced back to a time of great unrest, when the desert was divided among warring clans, each vying for control over the scarce oases and trade routes that kept their people alive.

The first Ishkari, Sahir, the Crimson Blade, was not born into nobility. He was a warrior of no great tribe, no noble lineage - only a blade for hire, a sellsword who had grown weary of fighting for the ambitions of lesser men. However, the deserts did not belong to those born into power. They belonged to those strong enough to seize them. Therefore, Sahir did not wait for fate to carve his name into history - he carved it himself in the flesh of his enemies.

With a band of ruthless warriors, he laid waste to the great citadels, taking cities not by siegecraft, but by swift and brutal assaults, cutting through the ranks of his foes like a storm tearing through the dunes.

He took no prisoners, and those who knelt before him were given one choice - swear the oath of the Ishkari or perish beneath the Crimson Spear. Thus, the foundation of House Ishkari was laid, not in the halls of diplomacy, but upon the smoking ruins of a dozen fallen lords.

Centuries passed as the Ishkari dominated the shifting power struggles of Zarah. Their warriors were unparalleled - trained from childhood, their blood tempered like steel, their loyalty absolute. But power breeds enemies, and House Ishkari was surrounded by those who would see them fall.

It was Rashad Ishkari, the Blood-Tyrant, who ensured that their dominion did not crumble beneath the weight of ambition. Where his forebears had conquered with the sword, Rashad ruled with fear.

He established the Trial of the Spear, a brutal test that determined the worth of every heir to House Ishkari. Only those who survived the trial - which often meant killing their own kin in single combat - were deemed worthy of leadership.

Under his reign, the Ishkari became more than just warlords; they became legend. Their crimson-clad warriors stood as an unbreakable shield against the endless tide of challengers.

The annals of time reveal this truth: power seized by the sword must ever guard against the sword, and for all their might, House Ishkari made one fatal mistake. In their arrogance, the Ishkari believed they could not be undone. That their rule would last for eternity, as unyielding as the deserts. They committed the sin of forgetting one truth - the deserts do not tolerate stagnation.

Like many other tribes before them, the downfall of the Ishkari did not come from a great war or a rival kingdom. It came from within.

For generations, the Trial of the Spear had ensured that only the strongest ruled, but strength alone is not wisdom, and brutality is no substitute for leadership.

In the end, the warlords turned on one another, brothers spilling each other's blood for the right to a throne built upon bones. As they fell, the sands reclaimed their empire.

The last of the Ishkari rulers, Kasim the Black Spear, was slain not by an enemy army but by his own kin. His stronghold, once a fortress of power, was abandoned, its halls filled with nothing but ghosts and the echoes of past glories. The name Ishkari faded from the tongues of men. Their banners, once feared, became nothing more than forgotten relics buried beneath the dunes.

No matter what the sands of Zarah bury in their depths, its deserts do not forget. Though their empire had crumbled, the blood of the Ishkari did not vanish. Their descendants carried their legacy forward - not as rulers but as wanderers, mercenaries, and exiles. So, their bloodline endured, waiting for the day when the fire of the Crimson Spear would burn once more.

One such descendant was Khalim al-Ishkari, the father of Sura. Though he was born into the Rasha tribe, and his lineage had long since lost its kingdom, he carried the strength of his ancestors within her veins, the dormant power of sight. He did not rule from a throne, nor did he lead armies into battle - but he raised his daughter, Sura, with the fire of their ancestors, with the spirit of those who had once held their foresight over Zarah.

When the time came, it was his daughter that would rise - not as a mere warrior or a spy, but as a queen.

A queen who would unite what her ancestors had once divided. A queen who would wield their strength not for conquest but for the birth of a new age.

III. <u>The Lost Princess of the Sands: House Rahmani, Heirs of the Forgotten Oasis (500 years ago - Present Day)</u>

As the last embers of Ishkari's rule flickered and died, the deserts reclaimed what had once been theirs. The great halls of the warlords stood empty, their banners tattered ghosts swaying in the wind. The mighty warriors who had once ruled with steel and fire became little more than wandering remnants, their names whispered in half-remembered tales by ageing nomads beneath starlit skies.

Notwithstanding their predicament, blood remembers, even when history forgets, and from the ruins of war and exile rose the Rahmani tribe, a line descended from the scattered remains of once-great rulers. Unlike their forebears, they did not seek conquest, nor did they long for the days of bloodshed. Instead, they turned inward, carving out a new life within the shifting sands, hidden from the eyes of the warring world.

It is said that Rahim the Exile, the first patriarch of the Rahmani line, was guided by the stars and the whispered wisdom of his ancestors to a place that should not have existed - an oasis untouched by war, veiled beneath dunes that shifted to conceal its entrance. This sanctuary, known only as Karash, became a refuge for those who sought peace, including the Tarek tribe, a hidden kingdom among the dunes where the weary could rest and rebuild.

The Rahmani did not raise armies, nor did they forge empires of stone. They built their legacy in knowledge, in diplomacy, in the careful balance of power that allowed them to survive while greater tribes fell.

They became masters of the desert's unseen paths, keepers of lore that others had long abandoned. They knew the secret wells that never ran dry, the winds that foretold storms, the silent footprints of merchants and warlords alike. In later years, quite a few amongst their numbers joined the Ulema tribe.

In time, their influence grew, not through battle, but through quiet control. Kings came to seek their wisdom. Nomads swore oaths in their name. Traders flourished under their guidance. Yet, for all their power, they remained in the shadows - never rulers, never conquerors. But the blood of warriors still ran in their veins, and in the heart of their line, the fire of forgotten queens still burned.

<u>The Last Heir: The Birth of Sura al-Rasha</u>
Born to Khalim al-Rasha and Miryam al-Rasha, both descending from the Ishkari, Sura was the culmination of generations of wisdom and strength. From her mother, she learned the quiet cunning of the Rahmani sages, and from her father, she inherited the unbreakable will of the Ishkari warriors.

She was raised in the hidden oasis of Karash and was taught the ways of the desert by those who had spent centuries mastering it. She walked the dunes with the elders, studied the stars, and learned the art of negotiation at her father's side. Though she was born in the same year and place as Aran ibn Khalid, the two never crossed paths until much later, in the streets of Sarim.

Yet, from an early age, it was clear that Sura was not meant to live in the shadows. She was restless, fierce, filled with the kind of fire that could not be contained by tradition. Where others sought refuge, she sought purpose. Where others whispered, she spoke with a voice that carried over the sands.

The Rise of a Queen

When war returned to Zarah, when the balance of power teetered upon the edge of a blade, Sura did not stand aside. She walked into the fire, afraid but determined, her ancestors' blood singing in her veins. It was she who stood beside Aran ibn Khalid, not as a mere consort, but as his friend, his strategist, his confidant. She did not simply inherit the legacy of the Rahmani - she redefined it.

With Aran, she forged a House where there had been only scattered tribes and kingdoms, a future where there had been only ruin. When the desert finally bowed before its new rulers, it was not only Aran's name that was spoken in reverence but hers as well.

She was the last heir of the lost princesses of the sands, the daughter of warriors and seers, the unbroken flame of a lineage long thought extinguished. Through her, the blood of her forebears lived on.

Queen of the Desert, Keeper of the Weaving

Sura's journey to the throne was not paved with luxury or privilege. She fought for every grain of respect, every ounce of authority, against a world that had never known a queen to rule outright since the time of the Old Kings, with the exception of Empress Laleth of the Kartalis dominion. For the last eleven thousand years, Zarah's deserts had been lands of warriors, where men carried the banners of power, where women were mostly seen as consorts, advisors, or mystics, but never rulers. Sura defied them all. From her father, Khalim al-Rasha, she inherited a warrior's heart - the relentless discipline, the skill with the blade, the unyielding will to shape destiny rather than be shaped by it. From her mother, Miryam al-Rasha, she learned patience, diplomacy, and the quiet art of seeing the tides of power before they shifted.

Even the most precious gifts may desert us in our hour of greatest need. Sura, who had developed abilities to protect others, failed to foresee the death of her parents, murdered by a Warlord-Chief called Malik the Vulture. Orphaned at a young age, she found herself in Sarim's Old Quarter, where she, later in life, met Aran.

Other than what they saw in each other's eyes, when they met, it was these gifts that had failed her so poorly, that made her indispensable to Aran vision. In the wars that defined her husband's reign, she became more than a voice at his side - she was a warrior in her own right. She led men, negotiated fragile alliances, and when battle came, she fought alongside Aran, her blades flashing beneath the twin moons. Through her veins, unbeknownst to her, ran the last vestiges of the first Moon-Seers of Al'Shara.

When the Weaving began to unravel, when the fabric of reality threatened to collapse, Sura stood beside Aran in his greatest trial, finding within herself the strength to rise to the occasion, not as an observer, but as a weaver of destiny itself. The Priesthood of the Sun called her the Hand of Fate, the Keeper of the Weaving, the Queen Who Sees, but she dismissed their titles. "I am only Sura," she would say. "Only a woman who refuses to let the desert fall into ruin."

She ruled as she had lived - with fire in her spirit, steel in her hands, and wisdom in her heart.

Thus it has ever been that those who flee from power prove most worthy to bear it, for she was not a ruler of extravagance.

She walked among her people, dressed in simple robes, her hands calloused from war, her eyes sharp with the weight of responsibility. She listened to the merchants who gathered in the markets, the nomad tribes that wandered the endless dunes, the elders who carried the weight of forgotten centuries. Her justice was swift but never cruel. Her wrath was fierce but never reckless. She was beloved, but not because she sought love but because she had earned it.

When the wars ended, when the land was finally unified, she did not grow complacent. She helped her husband build roads where none had dared carve a path before. Like him, she forged alliances not with steel but with trust, ensuring that the sands of Zarah would no longer be a battleground of endless bloodshed but a kingdom where its peoples could thrive.

Sura ruled for decades, alongside Aran, through prosperity and hardship alike, and when the time came for the next generation to take their place, she did not cling to power. She let go, knowing that true legacy is not in holding a throne but in ensuring that the kingdom endures beyond you.

<u>Queen Sura's Legacy</u>
To this day, the stories of Sura are told beneath the desert stars. Not as a queen of mere lineage, nor as a consort to a great king, but as a ruler who, along with her king, forged a new age from the bones of the old world.

She was the warrior who fought with the strength of the Ishkari, the seer who guided fate, like the lost daughters of Al'Shara, and the diplomat who shaped kingdoms with her words, like the Rahmani sages before her.

In the end, she was more than all of these things. She was Sura, Queen of the Desert, Keeper of the Weaving. And through her son, Khalid ibn Aran, the blood of the desert flowed unbroken - carrying with it her fire, her vision, and the echo of a queen who walked with shadows and shaped the fate of empires.

<u>**Historical Recount of Barash ibn Sulaym's Bloodline**</u>

Barash's lineage is one of warriors, mentors, and protectors, stretching back to the very heart of Zarah's history. Unlike the great tribes that sought to rule through conquest or bloodline alone, his ancestors were the hidden keepers of balance, warriors who shaped destiny not from thrones, but from the battlefields, from the sacred halls of wisdom, and from the very sands themselves.

I. <u>The Keepers of the Unyielding Blade: House Al-Zahir, Defenders of the Crescent Sands (3,500 years ago - 1,500 years ago)</u>

Zarah's deserts are cruel and merciless expanses, vast and shifting worlds where the unprepared are swallowed by the sands, and the weak are forgotten by time. Yet, for those who understand their whispers, for those who respect their ever-changing nature, the deserts are the greatest teachers of all.

This was the lesson upon which the Al-Zahir tribe was founded - a tribe that did not seek to conquer, but to preserve; a lineage that did not lust for power, but for balance.

It was said that the first of their line, Zafir Al-Zahir, was not born in the halls of kings, nor was he raised among the high towers of Zarah's early rulers. He was born in the wilderness, in the heart of the Crescent Sands, where the dunes rose and fell like the breathing of the world itself.

From an early age, Zafir understood a truth that few tribal leaders cared to acknowledge - strength alone was never enough to rule the desert. Those who sought to dominate the sands through force alone were doomed to fall, for the land had never been tamed, and it never would be. Only those who walked in harmony with the desert, who understood its language, could truly endure.

Thus, he did not build castles, nor did he raise legions. Instead, he formed a brotherhood of warriors who would dedicate themselves to the art of protection - not as mercenaries, but as sentinels of balance, warriors who would intervene only when the land itself called for their blades.

The Al-Zahir warriors lived by a single vow, an unbreakable code passed down from generation to generation: "To wield the blade is to bear the burden of its weight. To stand in defence is to carry the weight of all who cannot. We are the watchers of the horizon, the hands that hold the balance. We do not seek war, but we do not flee from it."

This philosophy set them apart from the power-hungry warlords of Zarah. They did not fight for crowns, nor did they spill blood for the sake of conquest. Instead, they acted as protectors, their swords drawn only when chaos threatened to consume the land.

Their mastery of the Serpent's Flow, a fighting style inspired by the movements of the great Sand Serpents, made them nearly invincible in battle. They did not rely on brute force but on precision, patience, and adaptability.

Through the centuries, though, in a different manner from the Khazraj tribe - Rafiq's ancestry - they became the hidden force that shaped Zarah's fate.

When rulers sought dominion over all, it was the Al-Zahir who whispered warnings in their ears. When wars threatened to consume the land, it was their warriors who ensured that devastation never tipped beyond repair.

Unfortunately, for those they ruled, Zarah's regents were not fond of those who stood against unchecked ambition. The desert, however, does not tolerate arrogance.

For nearly two thousand years, the Al-Zahir served as Zarah's unseen protectors, the silent sentinels who stood against the tide of destruction. Their very existence was a threat to those who sought absolute rule.

The warlords feared them, for their power lay not in armies but in knowledge. The rulers despised them, for they could not be bought or swayed. So, as greed and corruption festered in Zarah's tribal houses, a secret pact was forged in the shadows. The rulers of the desert, tired of the Al-Zahir standing in their way, much as they had done with so many others, turned against them in a single, devastating act of betrayal.

On the Night of the Sundering, the great fortresses of the Al-Zahir were set ablaze. Their warriors, who had spent lifetimes in service to balance and justice, were cut down in their sleep, slaughtered not by enemies, but by the very rulers they had once protected.

If it had not been for the shifting sands of the desert, almost all of their sacred libraries - where the wisdom of a thousand years had been preserved - would have been burned to ash. Their weapons were melted down and reforged into the blades of their betrayers. The survivors, few and scattered, fled into the desert, their names stricken from records, their legacy erased.

Though the Al-Zahir tribe had been shattered, its teachings were not lost. Its knowledge lived on in the hearts of those who had escaped the massacre, passed down in whispers, hidden in the bloodlines of those who would one day remember their purpose.

One day, the line of Al-Zahir would rise again - not as rulers but as unseen guardians, walking the same path as their ancestors before them.

That bloodline would continue, unseen and unbroken, until it found its way to Barash ibn Sulaym - the last son of the Unyielding Blade.

II. The Betrayal and the Sundering of the Blades (1,500 years ago - 700 years ago)

The Al-Zahir warriors had long stood as silent sentinels of Zarah's balance, defending not thrones but the fragile peace that existed between the desert's warring factions. They were the whisper in the wind, the unseen blade that struck down ambition before it festered into tyranny.

For centuries, they had been operating outside the ambitions of kings, answering only to the land itself. In time, they committed the sin of forgetting that power does not suffer those who stand in its way.

The rulers of Zarah had grown weary of the Al-Zahir. Their presence was an inconvenience, a check upon the ever-growing hunger of men who sought dominion over all. The warlords had watched for generations as these warriors refused to bend, defying kings and conquerors alike, always speaking of 'balance' when rulers only desired control. So, in the heart of their greed, the lords of Zarah conspired against them.

The Pact of the Five Thrones

It was in the shadows of the palace of Qadeth, in the lands of Qamar, that the Pact of the Five Thrones was forged - a secret council of rulers, warlords, and nobles who had grown tired of the Al-Zahir standing between them and total supremacy.

Under the guise of peace, as their forebears had done to other tribes before them, they invited the Al-Zahir to the great city, proclaiming that the age of war had ended, that the rulers of Zarah wished to forge a new covenant of unity, one where the Al-Zahir would no longer need to police the land but could instead serve as honoured protectors.

Many within the tribe were wary, for history had taught them that peace was often the mask of betrayal. They were, nonetheless, in a difficult position, for refusing the invitation was to brand themselves as enemies of the throne.

The Al-Zahir, who had never sought war against Zarah's rulers, came.

A thousand warriors, the greatest masters of the Serpent's Flow, walked into the palace as honoured guests. They entered not as conquerors nor as supplicants but as guardians who believed they were finally being given the respect they had long been denied.

As the sun dipped below the horizon, the city of Qadeth burned. The warriors of the Al-Zahir, unarmed in the halls of false diplomacy, were slaughtered where they stood. Their hosts, having broken sacred law, drew hidden blades and struck them down at the feast tables, turning their wine to rivers of blood. Those who attempted to fight back found the palace gates sealed and the streets crawling with mercenaries hired by the five rulers. The assassins of the court descended upon the visiting warriors, felling them before they could even call upon their legendary skills. The city's great bell tolled - a signal not of warning, but of execution. All across Zarah, the other strongholds of the Al-Zahir came under coordinated attack. The libraries of Al-Ruham, where generations of their wisdom had been preserved, were set alight, their scrolls turned to ash. The training halls of Maqir, where the youngest warriors learned the dance of the Serpent's Flow, were reduced to rubble.

However, the hidden sanctuaries in the Crescent Sands, where their elders had meditated for centuries, were buried beneath the weight of shifting sand, as if Zarah itself was protecting its history.

Despite this fortuitous event, by the time Leander's prime shone bright, the name Al-Zahir had been stricken from the records of the largest tribes, its warriors declared 'traitors to the peace' by the very rulers who had orchestrated their slaughter. But not all of them had died.

A handful of warriors escaped the massacre, fleeing into the wilds of the deep desert. They had no banners, no strongholds, no brothers left to fight beside them. The great tribe they had sworn their lives to was gone, its legacy shattered beneath the weight of betrayal.

Some of the survivors wandered, seeking exile among the nomadic clans. Others swore vengeance, turning their blades against the rulers who had betrayed them. But the true remnants of Al-Zahir did not seek war, for they knew that such a battle could never be won. Instead, they chose the path of the Hidden Blade.

The last great masters of the Serpent's Flow scattered across Zarah, abandoning their names, hiding their knowledge in secret lineages, and forgotten sanctuaries. They whispered their teachings to only a chosen few, ensuring that their way would never truly die.

For centuries, they faded into legend, becoming nothing more than a story told by ageing desert nomads beneath the stars - a tale of warriors who had once held back the tide of destruction, only to be undone by those they had sought to protect.

Despite the world having forgotten their name, the blood of the Al-Zahir still ran through the veins of their scattered descendants. In time, that bloodline would produce a child who carried the same fire, the same discipline, the same unbreakable code as the warriors of old. A child named Barash ibn Sulaym.

He would not be raised in a fortress, nor would he grow up surrounded by warriors. His father, Sulaym ibn Kadir, was one of the last true Keepers of the Hidden Path, a master of the old ways who had forsaken all titles, disappearing into obscurity to ensure that the teachings of Al-Zahir would not vanish completely.

Barash was trained from childhood not just in the ways of the blade but in the understanding of why the blade must be wielded at all. Though the rulers of Zarah no longer feared the Al-Zahir, the desert had not forgotten. The desert never forgets, and when the time came for fate to shape the destiny of Zarah once more, it would be Barash - heir to a forgotten house, guardian of a lost oath - who would stand beside Aran ibn Khalid, not as a servant, not as a follower, but as the last protector of an unbroken legacy. He stayed true to the promise he made to his oldest friend. For the true warriors of the Al-Zahir had never been erased. They had only been waiting, and through Barash, the watchful blade would rise once more.

III. <u>The Wanderers and the Keepers of Forgotten Knowledge (700 years ago - 400 years ago)</u>

The fall of the Al-Zahir did not erase their teachings, nor did it extinguish the flame of their legacy. The warriors who had once served as guardians of balance had become ghosts, their names lost to history, but their purpose unforgotten. Scattered across the shifting sands, the last remnants of the Al-Zahir did not seek vengeance. They did not march upon the great cities to reclaim their honour, nor did they raise armies in their name. Instead, they vanished into the vast expanse of the desert, embracing the silence, becoming more myth than men.

They took new names, adopting the customs of the nomadic tribes, moving unseen through the marketplaces of Zarah's great cities, and hiding in the ruins of lost civilizations. They did not seek to rule, nor to destroy, but to preserve.

For centuries, the descendants of Al-Zahir became the Keepers of Forgotten Knowledge - watchers who carried the wisdom of the old ways in whispers, passing their teachings from master to apprentice, ensuring that the blade remained sharp, even in exile. The last warriors of Al-Zahir did not seek students; those who were worthy sought them. To carry their teachings was to bear the weight of an entire lost tribe. Not all were strong enough. Fewer still were wise enough.

Thus, for every century that passed, only a handful of new Keepers were chosen in all of Zarah. They were not born into privilege. They were not noble heirs. They were wanderers, orphans, and warriors who had nothing left but their will to endure. The training of a Keeper was brutal, lasting many years, sometimes decades. They were taught not just to wield the blade but to understand it - to know when to strike and when to stay their hand, when to shape history, and when to let it unfold. They learned the Serpent's Flow, the legendary fighting style of the Al-Zahir, kept alive through the generations. But more than that, they learned patience. They learned how to move unseen, how to listen to the desert's whispers, and how to survive when the world had forgotten them.

To be a Keeper of the Hidden Path was not to seek glory. It was to become a shadow, a protector unseen, a force that influenced history without ever claiming its triumphs.

As more centuries passed, the Keepers became more than warriors. They became seekers of knowledge, preservers of the truths that the rulers of Zarah had tried to bury. They mapped the ruins of civilizations long forgotten, finding the remnants of kingdoms that had risen and fallen before Zarah had even been named. They gathered the last of the old scrolls, preserving the wisdom of their ancient scholars in hidden vaults beneath the sands, far from the reach of those who would misuse them.

They studied the Weaving itself, the threads of fate that connected all things, searching for the moments where history could be shaped without bloodshed.

Their influence was felt, though no one knew their names. When a tyrant sought to burn the last temple of the Moon-Seers, it was a Keeper who ensured that the sacred texts were spirited away before the flames could consume them. When warlords planned their conquests in secret, their messengers would sometimes disappear into the night, their plans never reaching their allies.

At times when the rulers of Zarah grew complacent, forgetting the lessons of history, it was the Keepers who ensured that history would not forget them in return. As time kept its inexorable march, the number of Keepers dwindled. The old ways were fading, and the world no longer sought the wisdom of the past.

Fewer and fewer warriors were chosen to bear the title, and by the time of Khalid ibn Rashid's birth, only a handful remained on the whole planet. They were no longer a hidden order but scattered individuals, waiting for the moment when Zarah would need them once more.

Among them was Sulaym ibn Kadir, the last master of the Hidden Path, the man who would one day father and train the boy who would change Zarah's fate forever. Sulaym had spent his life searching for a worthy heir, knowing that the teachings of the Keepers could not die with him. As fate would have it, he found that heir in his own son - Barash.

From the moment he could walk, Barash was trained in the ways of his ancestors, carrying the full weight of a thousand years of knowledge upon his shoulders.

He was taught that the blade was not a tool of destruction but a symbol of responsibility. That history was a river, and those who understood its currents could change its course without damming its flow. He was also told that the time of the Keepers was ending. The world was changing, and the Hidden Path could not remain concealed forever. Soon, the balance of Zarah would shift once more, and the last of the Al-Zahir would have to choose - remain in exile or step into history once more.

Barash did not yet know his place in this great cycle. But fate had already chosen for him. The time of watching was over, and soon, the last heir of the Keepers of the Unyielding Blade would stand beside the one man who could bring balance back to Zarah - Aran ibn Khalid.

Through Barash, the legacy of the Al-Zahir would not fade into dust. Through him, the Hidden Path would walk in the light once more.

IV. <u>Barash ibn Sulaym: The Guardian of the Future (400 years ago - ?)</u>

Barash ibn Sulaym was born into a lineage that no longer existed in the eyes of history. The world had forgotten the name Al-Zahir, but the desert had not. The blood of warriors, sages, and silent sentinels ran through his veins, though he would not know the weight of that inheritance until much later in his life.

His father, Sulaym ibn Kadir, was one of the last Keepers of the Hidden Path, a man who had abandoned his true name to ensure the survival of his ancestors' teachings. He did not raise his son in luxury, nor did he allow him to believe the world owed him recognition.

Instead, he raised Barash in the solitude of the dunes, beneath the watchful eyes of the twin moons, where the only laws were those of the shifting sands.

From the time he could walk, Barash's life was shaped by discipline. His father taught him not just how to wield a blade, but how to see beyond it - to understand that a sword was not a weapon, but a question, and that every man who held one was responsible for the answer he chose to give.

"A warrior who fights for himself is already lost," Sulaym told him. "A warrior who fights for others becomes something greater." This had been a lesson Barash would carry for the rest of his days.

While other boys learned to read in great city libraries, Barash learned from the whispered wisdom of his father and the wind-carved runes of the ancient ruins. He was taught the secrets of the desert, the stories hidden in the stars, the old ways that had long since faded from the minds of rulers.

His father took him deep into the Crescent Sands, where the last of the true Keepers still gathered in secret. There, he was trained in the Serpent's Flow, the fighting style of their ancestors, long thought lost to time.

His masters did not go easy on him. Every lesson was earned in sweat and blood, every skill honed through trial. By the time he came of age, Barash was more than just a fighter - he was a living extension of a forgotten tradition, the embodiment of a code that the world believed had died with his ancestors.

Yet for all his strength, his father kept him hidden from the world. Sulaym feared what would happen if his son revealed himself too soon. The rulers of Zarah still carried the blood of those who had betrayed the Al-Zahir, and though centuries had passed, power never forgets the enemies it has wronged. Fate, on the other hand, had other plans for Barash.

Barash was not a young man when he first crossed paths with Aran's father, Khalid ibn Rashid, the man who would change the course of his life forever. Khalid was not like the other warriors of Zarah. Where others saw power as a throne to be claimed, Khalid saw it as a responsibility. Where others built walls to keep their enemies at bay, Khalid sought to unite his people. Their friendship was unexpected, but it was also unbreakable. Khalid saw in Barash a strength that was not just physical but spiritual - the strength of a man who understood what it meant to protect, not just to rule.

Likewise, Barash saw in Khalid a potential leader unlike any other. He was not arrogant nor blinded by ambition. He was a man who understood the burdens of power, a man who sought to build rather than destroy.

Because of that unexpected friendship, Barash swore himself not to a throne, but to a man - a man who he believed could finally bring the balance that his ancestors had fought and died for.

He remained at Khalid's side for many years, acting as his closest confidant and protector. He taught him the ways of the Hidden Path, guided him in the wisdom of the Keepers, and ensured that his vision for Zarah remained untarnished by the corruption of power. Notwithstanding, history has proved, time and time again, that even the greatest men are not beyond the reach of fate.

Khalid, ever aware of the shifting currents of destiny, knew that his time was drawing to an end. Malik the Vulture, the warlord who was in truth Drathis in disguise, was closing in, and Khalid had foreseen his own demise. So, he turned to Barash, not with a command, but with a request. "My son will walk a path darker than mine," Khalid told him. "And I will not be there to guide him. Will you, my friend?"

To take care of a fatherless child was not an easy burden to accept. Barash had never seen himself as a teacher, nor as a father to another man's son. However, despite his hesitation, he had sworn himself to Khalid, and in doing so, he had sworn himself to Aran, by extent.

When Khalid fell, as he himself had foreseen, Barash did not weep. He did not seek vengeance. He did what he had always done - he protected. Patiently awaiting the boy's return from his self-imposed exile, he prepared himself to become a teacher.

When Aran returned from the desert, he took the child under his wing, training him not just to fight but to understand the weight of leadership. He became not just a mentor but a second father, ensuring that the boy who would one day rule Zarah would do so with wisdom as well as strength.

Barash's role in Aran's rise to power was not written in the histories of kings. He did not seek titles, nor did he ask for recognition. He stood in the shadows, guiding when needed, watching when necessary, and always ensuring that Zarah's destiny remained on the right path.

During Aran's rise to power, uniting the tribes and taking the throne, Barash didn't always sit beside him. Instead, he often returned to the desert, disappearing as his ancestors had before him. Spending those absences travelling and further studying the secrets of the desert. To those who knew him well, he was more than a warrior. He was more than a mentor. He was the last of the Keepers, the guardian who had shaped the future without ever claiming it for himself.

Though, in time, he left the courts of kings behind, the desert kept whispering his name, carrying it in the winds across the sands he had once walked.

Some say he still wanders, watching over the land from afar, while others believe he faded into legend, his story becoming one with the sands. However, to those who study the tides of history, we all agree on one thing. Without Barash, there would have been no Aran, and without a unifier, Zarah would have remained forever divided. His work was never for himself. It was for the future. In the end, due to his vision, there was one.

<u>The Mentor and the Oath</u>

The wind howled through the halls of Karash, carrying with it the scent of the desert - a mixture of sun-baked stone, distant rain, and the ever-present dust of time. Barash stood in silence, his gaze fixed upon Khalid ibn Rashid, the man who had been his brother in all but blood. The noble legacy of his forebears left behind him, there were no lavish banners hanging from the sandstone walls, no golden thrones, or indulgent feasts. The rulers of Zarah who had come before had drowned themselves in excess, but Khalid had always been different.

Now, as they sat across from one another in the dim glow of an oil lamp, they both knew that this would be the last conversation they would ever share.

Khalid's voice was quiet yet resolute. "He is not ready." His fingers traced the rim of the earthen cup before him, the tea inside untouched. "He will not be ready for years yet. But I will not have years, will I?"

Barash inhaled sharply, his jaw tightening at the weight of the words. He had known Khalid too long to deny the truth. Malik the Vulture - Drathis in disguise - was closing in. The enemy had worn many faces over the years, but Barash had never seen him more dangerous than he was now. The shadows stretched long over Zarah, and Khalid was wise enough to see that his time was running out.

"I will stand at your side," Barash said, his voice unwavering. "I will fight with you until my last breath, if that is what it takes."

Khalid smiled, but it was a tired smile, one filled with the acceptance of a man who had long made peace with his fate. He shook his head. "No, old friend. My war is already lost."

Barash wanted to protest, to argue that no battle was lost until the last blade fell. But deep inside, he understood. Khalid had always seen further than most men - he had glimpsed the currents of fate long before others could recognize the tide.

The time had come when those currents were pulling him toward an ending that could not be undone. "Then what would you have me do?" Barash asked, his voice heavy.

For the first time in his life, he felt unmoored. If Khalid was lost, then what remained? What purpose was left? His friend's gaze hardened, the fire of distant rulers flickering behind his eyes. "Aran." He said, simply.

The name alone carried the weight of an unborn empire. Khalid's son, the boy upon whom all the hopes of Zarah now rested. A child who had been born not just of blood but of prophecy.

"He will grow into a great man," Khalid continued, his voice firm. "He will become more than even I could have been. But he will need you, Barash. He will need someone who will tell him the truth when others seek to mould him into something he is not."

Barash exhaled slowly, rubbing a hand across his beard. He had watched Aran grow and had seen the fire in the boy's eyes, the same fire Khalid had carried when he was young. But the path ahead would be anything but easy.

"What if he does not listen?" Barash asked. "What if he rejects the teachings of an old warrior?"

Khalid smirked. "Then, you have my permission to knock him to the ground until he does." A long silence stretched between them, filled only by the distant rustling of the wind through the courtyard beyond. Finally, Barash leaned forward, resting his forearms on the wooden table. "If I do this, it will not be as his servant. It will not be as his shadow. If I am to guide him, he must see me as an equal." Khalid nodded. "I would not ask it of you otherwise."

Barash studied him for a long moment before exhaling through his nose. He had fought many battles and spilt blood across countless battlefields, but this? This was the greatest burden he had ever been asked to bear.

At last, he reached across the table and clasped Khalid's forearm in a warrior's grip. "I swear it," Barash said, his voice like stone. "You have my word, that I will watch over him. I will finish shaping him into the man he must become. When the time comes for him to walk the path alone, I will make sure he does not falter." Khalid smiled, and in that smile, there was true relief.

The two men sat in silence for a long while, listening to the desert wind sing its mournful tune.

Unbeknownst to both men, this was to be the last night they would ever share. Khalid departed that night, with Aran, in a caravan route, and by the time the sun rose, his oldest friend would be gone, taken by the same shadows he had fought so hard to defy.

What of Barash? He would remain. Not as a ruler nor as a warlord, but as a mentor. A guardian. The last keeper of an unbroken oath. For Aran's destiny was no longer just his own. It was the destiny of Zarah itself. And Barash would see it through, no matter what it would cost him.

<u>The Eternal Guardian</u>
Barash ibn Sulaym had never been a man of titles. He had never sought a throne nor longed for a place in the chronicles of kings. His purpose was not to rule but to shape the one who, someday, would.

Yet, in the long years that followed the death of Khalid ibn Rashid, his name became a legend among those who knew the truth. He was remembered not as a warrior or a merchant but as something far greater - a guardian of Zarah's future, an unshakable presence in the storm that threatened to consume it. Those who studied history celebrated him as the unseen hand in Aran's rise

The hard truth was, Khalid was no longer by his son's side, so as Aran grew from a grieving boy into a warrior, it was Barash who stood beside him.

He was not a soft tutor who coddled his charge. He was the storm against which Aran would sharpen his blade. He did not hold back, nor did he offer easy wisdom. Every lesson was hard-earned, every strike a test, every failure an opportunity to grow.

Where others, in the circle of truth, saw a boy destined for greatness, Barash saw a youth unprepared for the trials ahead. So, he forged him in fire. There were nights when Aran collapsed in exhaustion, his hands bloodied from wielding the sword, his body bruised from endless sparring. And yet, Barash never once relented, for he knew that no ruler - no true ruler - could afford weakness. "Do you think that the desert will pity you?" he would say, standing over Aran as he struggled to rise. "Do you really believe that fate will grant you kindness? Get up. Again."

However, for all his harshness, there was no cruelty in his teachings nor the tone of his voice. He was never needlessly unkind. His hands, though rough, were steady. His words, though sharp, were true.

Therefore, when Aran finally stood his own ground, when he struck with precision, when he carried himself with the weight of the king he did not know he was meant to be, Barash was the first to nod in quiet approval.

During the years when Aran was uniting the tribes, when he rode into battle against Drathis and the Draco, when he finally took his place as ruler of a kingdom reborn, many expected Barash to take his place beside him - to be named a general, a minister, an advisor. Barash, to the surprise of everyone besides his charge, asked for nothing. He did not seek wealth. He did not seek power.

When the war was won, when the banners of Zarah flew high and the cities stood stronger than they ever had before, Barash did what no one, but the king, expected. He left.

The halls of kings were not for men like him. He was not meant for courts and councils for the weight of politics and the games of rulers. Finally, the oath to his lineage had been fulfilled. Aran was the leader Zarah needed. The future was secured.

So, one night, without ceremony, without farewells, he took his blade, his staff and cloak, walked to Sarim's gates, disappearing into the dunes. Returning, at last, to the place that had shaped him, to the sands that had whispered his name long before any king had spoken it aloud.

For many years, after his disappearance, there were stories. Tales of a lone warrior who walked the deserts, protecting the lost, defending those who could not defend themselves. Merchants spoke of a shadow that appeared when bandits struck, a swordsman whose movements were like the shifting sands, swift and deadly, who left only silence and justice in his wake.

Nomads whispered of a figure who stood upon the highest dunes at sunset, watching over Zarah as if waiting for the day it would need him once more. Some claimed he had become more than a man, that the desert itself had taken him, making him one with the winds, an eternal guardian of the land. Others believed he had simply found peace at last, that he had laid down his blade and allowed the world to move forward without him.

<u>The Last Oath</u>
Though he had left the city behind, one final promise remained. On the night of his departure, beneath the pale glow of the twin moons, he left behind a single message, carved into stone at the gates of Sarim.
It read: "When the storm comes again, I will return."
And so, even in his absence, Zarah knew that it was never truly without its guardian. For Barash ibn Sulaym was not just a warrior. He was not just a mentor. He was the last of the Hidden Path, the keeper of an unbroken legacy. He had been the silent watchman of Zarah's destiny. Its Eternal Guardian.

Historical Recount of Rafiq al-Bahir's Bloodline

Rafiq's lineage is one of warriors, wanderers, and protectors, a bloodline forged in the crucible of battle and bound by an unbreakable oath to the desert. Though history remembers him as Aran's most loyal friend and the first Head Warrior of the Order of the Sacred Desert, his ancestry stretches back to the very roots of Zarah itself. He was not born to nobility, nor did his bloodline rule from gilded halls. His ancestors were the shield of Zarah - the warriors who bled so that others could live, the outcasts who found purpose in the endless sands.

I. The Sons of the First Spear: The Khazraj tribe, Guardians of the Eastern March (3,000 years ago - 1,000 years ago)

Long before Zarah was a unified kingdom, before its cities rose from the desert's embrace, while the blood of conquerors stained its sands, there was the Khazraj tribe.

They were not rulers, nor were they conquerors. They were the guardians of the shifting frontier, the shield against the horrors that lurked beyond the Great Divide, where remnants from the Old Kings resided. Their legacy was not written in ornate tomes but carved into the bones of those who dared trespass upon the lands they swore to protect.

The First Spear and the Birth of the Oath

The origins of the Khazraj tribe can be traced to Jibran Khazraj, the First Spear, a warrior whose name was spoken in hushed reverence across the desert. Born of the sands, raised by the blade, he was the first to forge a path against the old ways where none dared tread.

In his youth, Jibran was a lone wanderer, a sword-for-hire who sold his skill to the warring city-states that dotted Zarah's eastern frontier. He fought in countless battles, but with every warlord he served, he saw the same cycle - cities rising only to fall to greed, alliances forged only to be broken by ambition.

Beyond the walls of these warring states, beyond the comforts of civilization, Jibran saw the true enemy.

The barbarian hordes that descended from the Great Divide were not mere raiders - they were the harbingers of the old ways , pillaging and destroying all in their path, not for conquest, but for annihilation. And yet, the ruling tribes of Zarah, blinded by their petty rivalries, did nothing.

It was then that Jibran Khazraj made his choice. If the rulers of the desert would not defend their own land, then he would.
He gathered warriors not from noble houses, not from great armies, but from outcasts, exiles, and the forsaken - those with nothing to lose and everything to prove. With them, he formed a brotherhood bound not by blood but by oath.
Thus, the Khazraj tribe was born - not of lineage but of purpose.

For nearly two millennia, the Khazraj warriors held the eastern border, their fortress-settlements the only barrier between Zarah's heartlands and the endless tide of invaders. They asked for no gold, no lands, and no titles. They lived and died by the spear, their only reward, the knowledge that the desert tribes endured because of them.
Legends tell of the Battle of the Blackened Sky, when an army of one thousand Khazraj warriors held the Pass of Tura against ten thousand raiders from the Divide. For seven days and nights, they fought without rest until the sands ran red and the sun itself was veiled by the storm of blood and steel. Not a single warrior retreated, and when the last of them fell, their bodies became the foundation of the pass itself. Their names were never recorded, for among the Khazraj, honour was not found in glory. As in most of Zarah, it was found in sacrifice.
In time, the planet's rulers came to rely upon the Khazraj tribe, trusting them to guard the frontier while they played their endless games of politics and power. Yet, for all their service, the Khazraj were never welcomed into the halls of kings. Through egotistical, ruling eyes, they were seen as necessary but expendable, their purpose acknowledged but never truly honoured. Thus, they remained in the shadows, neither seeking recognition nor demanding it.

As the centuries passed, the rulers of Zarah grew complacent. The Khazraj had defended the borders for so long that the kings and warlords began to believe the threats beyond the Great Divide had been vanquished.
When a new war broke out among the city-states, the ruling lords saw an opportunity. They accused the Khazraj tribe of holding too much power of being a force that could not be controlled. They claimed the warriors of the frontier had grown arrogant, that they might one day turn against the cities they had sworn to protect. In an act of treachery, the ruling tribes of Zarah turned on their own defenders.
Much like the Al-Zahir tribe, under the promise of peace and recognition, they called the Khazraj leaders to the capital, offering them a place among the ruling tribes.

Unaware that they were walking into a trap, when the warriors arrived, they were ambushed and cut down in the streets like common criminals. Their fortresses were burned, their names erased from the records. The few who survived fled into the desert, hunted like beasts. Tribe Khazraj was no more. Although their story did not end there.

Though the name Khazraj was lost, their legacy lived on in the hearts of those who refused to forget. The survivors took new names, hiding among the nomadic tribes, passing their skills and traditions in secret.
Some became mercenaries, their loyalty bound not to any ruler, but to their own unbreakable code. Others vanished into legend, their bloodlines scattering into the sands, waiting for the day when the desert would call them back.
Among those scattered remnants, across the centuries of exile and silence, one bloodline remained unbroken. The blood of Rafiq ibn Azim, a forebear to Rafiq al-Bahir. Born of warriors who had once stood as the first and last line of defence for Zarah, he carried their spirit within him - the fire of the First Spear, the unyielding will of the defenders of the Eastern March. Though the world had forgotten the Khazraj, the desert had not, and through Rafiq, the legacy of the lost house would rise again.

II. <u>The Exiled Sons: House Al-Raheem, The Forgotten Warriors</u> <u>(1,000 years ago - 400 years ago)</u>

When the Khazraj tribe fell, its warriors scattered like grains of sand upon the wind. As these annals elsewhere attest, some fled to the deep desert, vanishing into the shifting dunes where no ruler's law could reach. Others took refuge among the nomadic tribes, becoming part of them, living as wanderers, their past spoken only in whispers. Though there were those of the bloodline who refused to fade into obscurity. Among them were the men who would one day become tribe Al-Raheem, the remnants of the warriors of the March. They still did not seek revenge, nor did they crave any power. They sought only to preserve what had been stolen from them - their honour, their purpose, their way of life. Their legacy.

The Al-Raheem tribe did not possess a kingdom in the traditional sense. They had no great fortresses, no noble banners, and no vast armies.

Instead, they were bound by an unspoken pact - a silent agreement carried from father to son, from master to apprentice.

They became swords-for-hire, but they did not serve warlords. They protected the weak, guarded the lost, and fought only for causes they deemed just. They moved unseen through the desert cities and wilds alike, their identities known only to those who needed them most.

In the great trade hubs of Zarah, merchants and commoners alike would speak in hushed voices of the "Ghosts of the Dunes," warriors clad in veils of sand-coloured cloth, appearing only when the balance of justice had been broken.

It is said that during the Siege of Qamar, when the ruling tribe sought to raze an entire settlement to the ground for harbouring his enemies, the Al-Raheem appeared in the dead of night. By dawn, the leader's personal guard had vanished, his war camp turned to ruin. The city was spared, and the warriors disappeared once more. They did not take credit. They did not stay to be praised. They kept moving like the wind - felt but unseen, shaping the course of Zarah's history from the shadows.

To be born of the Al-Raheem bloodline, one of the few descending tribes of the Khazraj was to inherit more than just a name. It was to be tested.

Boys were not raised in noble courts or trained in the lavish halls of royal academies. They were sent into the desert alone, armed with nothing but their wits, to survive against the land itself. Those who returned became apprentices, trained by elders who carried the last remnants of the Khazraj teachings. They learned the art of swordplay, but also the art of restraint. They were taught not only how to kill but also when not to.

A warrior of Al-Raheem was not judged by his victories in battle, but by the wars he prevented, by the innocents he saved, by the burdens he bore without complaint. Because of that, among their most sacred teachings was the belief that a blade without purpose is a blade already broken.

They did not fight for coin. They did not kill without reason. They served only the desert, only the unseen threads of fate that bound their people together.

For centuries, the Al-Raheem continued their silent work, neither growing nor diminishing. They existed as a whisper, a myth, a shadow that flickered upon the edge of history. As the years passed, Zarah continued to change.

Its rulers, once blinded by greed, were now beginning to turn their eyes toward unity. The wars that had once torn the land apart became fewer, the city-states forging uneasy alliances in pursuit of greater prosperity. It was a time of change when Zarah's tribes were, unbeknownst to themselves, preparing for the arrival of the one that would unify them. During such times, with no great conflicts, there was no need for exiled warriors. And so, the Al-Raheem began to fade.

When Rafiq's great-grandfather was born, only a handful of true Khazraj warriors remained. The once-sacred trials were abandoned, and their purpose became fractured. Most that remained sought new lives, blending into the cities they once watched from afar. Others wandered aimlessly, unable to find meaning in a world that no longer needed them. However, a few still clung to the old ways, passing their teachings in secret, waiting for the day when the desert would call them back to war. Rafiq al-Bahir was one of their kind.
He was the last of his line to inherit the full weight of his ancestors. The last to be trained in the way of the Wandering Blades. The last true son of the Al-Raheem, the true descendants of the original Khazraj tribe. Through him, their forgotten legacy would be reborn.

III. <u>The Last Warrior: Rafiq ibn Azim, The Lion of the Sacred Desert (310 years ago - ?)</u>

By the time of Rafiq ibn Azim's birth, the name Khazraj had all but faded from the annals of Zarah's recorded history, and the name Al-Raheem was barely remembered, except in campfire conversations. The Al-Raheem tribe had long ago been integrated into the larger Bahir tribe, and the rulers of Zarah no longer feared the exiled warriors, nor did they seek their aid. The city-states had grown fat in their prosperity, convinced that the wars of the past would never return. In their arrogance, they forgot that the desert remembers all.
Rafiq's father, Azim ibn Qadir, was a simple hunter, a man of quiet strength who carried the last whispers of the Al-Raheem legacy in his blood. His mother, a healer, taught him the ways of patience, the value of mercy, and the delicate art of tending to wounds - lessons that would shape him as much as any blade. But the desert does not allow its chosen sons to live in peace. Rafiq's early years were spent in the deep desert, where life was dictated by the shifting sands and the harsh whims of the sun. He learned to track prey through barren wastes, to read the stars as his ancestors once did, to listen to the whispers of the wind for signs of coming storms.

His father was his first teacher. From him, Rafiq learned the old ways - not just how to fight, but when to fight. "A blade is not power," Azim told him. "A blade is a question. What matters is the answer you give when you draw it." These words would stay with Rafiq for the rest of his life. Unfortunately, the peace of his childhood was short-lived.

When Rafiq was only twelve years old, his home was burned to the ground.

A band of warriors, from a dying kingdom, seeking to claim what little wealth remained beyond the borders of their lands, descended upon their village in the dead of night, taking everything.

Rafiq watched as his mother was struck down before his eyes, as his father fought until his last breath to protect the people he had called kin. He fought, too, though he was only a child, his hands wrapped around a blade too large for him, his heart filled with rage too vast for words. He survived, but barely. Left with nothing but the clothes on his back and the scars of that night, Rafiq wandered the desert alone.

For years, he lived as an outcast, surviving on the fringes of civilization. He worked as a sellsword, a caravan guard, a fighter in the sunbaked pits where men bet their lives for coin. But he never forgot the lessons of his father. He did not fight for sport. He did not kill for pleasure. He fought because it was the only path left to him, the desert had stripped him of everything else.

It was in these years of wandering that he began to hear whispers of another boy who had lost everything. A warrior, a future king, a man who sought to do what none before him had achieved - to unite Zarah, to break the cycle of endless war. That man was Aran ibn Khalid, and when their paths finally crossed, Rafiq knew that his destiny had found him at last.

From the moment they met, Rafiq and Aran were like fire and steel - separate forces but bound together by fate and friendship.

They fought side by side through the bloodiest battles of the war for Zarah, their bond forged in fire and sharpened by hardship. Rafiq was more than Aran's sword - he was his shield, his right hand, the brother this future king never thought could possibly replace his own.

There was no battlefield where Rafiq did not stand at Aran's side. No war was waged without his presence. No battle won without his blade cutting through the darkness. They were two halves of the same soul - one bound to the destiny of a kingdom, the other to the duty of its defence.

When the war for Zarah was won, when the Draco were vanquished and the weaving finally mended, Rafiq did not seek riches, nor did he ask for titles.

Aran knew his friend had but one path left to walk, so in the wake of victory, he entrusted Rafiq with the greatest responsibility of all.

He made him the Head Warrior of the Order of the Sacred Desert, a brotherhood sworn to protect Zarah from the shadows that still lingered beyond its celestial borders.

They were not an army. They were not rulers. They were the chosen blade-bearers of the sacred covenant, bound neither to earthly throne nor mortal ambition, but to the eternal pact between crown and sand. An oath that was passed down through generations of unborn sons.

Rafiq, the last heir of the Khazraj bloodline, took up this duty without hesitation, and when the warriors of the Sacred Desert looked to him, they did not see a forgotten name. They saw a leader. A fighter. A man who had been tested by fate and still stood unbowed. They saw Rafiq, the Lion of the Sacred Desert.

Through him, the bloodline of the lost warriors of Zarah would endure.

<u>The Order of the Sacred Desert: The Final Legacy</u>

With the war won and Zarah united under Aran's rule, many believed the time for warriors had passed. The great battles had ended, the tyrannical Draco had been cast down, and the land could finally heal from millennia of division. Yet, Aran and Rafiq both knew the truth - peace was never permanent, and the shadow of the House of Draco was never truly banished. Though their forces had been shattered and their leaders driven into the abyss, the scars they had left upon Zarah ran deep. The Weaving had been disturbed, the balance of the world fractured by their dark influence. Across the land, whispers of unseen threats still lingered - adherents to the fallen darkness dwelling hidden within the great settlements, while bands of the scattered enemy wandered the empty places beyond civilization's reach, corrupt nobles scheming in secret, seeking to undo what Aran had built.

Zarah needed guardians, warriors who answered to no throne, bound only by duty to the land itself. So, Aran called upon his brother-in-arms once more. Not as a mere warrior, not as his right hand in war, but as the first leader of something greater.

Thus was born the Order of the Sacred Desert - a hallowed brotherhood within the ancient Priesthood of the Sun. Warriors, unlike any before, sworn to root out the remnants of the House of Draco's influence, to protect Zarah from enemies both within and beyond, and to ensure that no force, mortal or otherwise, would ever again threaten its people.

The Order of the Sacred Desert was not an army. Not in the usual sense. They had their banners, but no grand citadels, and no legions marching in lockstep. It was a multitude moving in shadow.

A whisper upon the wind, a shadow at the edge of the dunes.

To become one of the Sacred, a warrior had to abandon all personal ambition, all ties to kingdoms or political power.

They swore an oath that bound them not to kings or councils, but to the desert itself - to protect its peoples, to uphold its balance, to remain ever vigilant against the return of the darkness that had once threatened to consume it. This oath was not spoken lightly, and once taken, it could never be undone, for to break it was to become an exile. To dishonour it was to meet dishonour at the hands of one's own brothers.

<u>The warriors of the Sacred Desert lived by three sacred tenets:</u>

I. <u>The Desert Claims No Master</u> - They served no ruler, owed allegiance to no throne. Their duty was to the land itself, to the protection of peoples who walked it.

II. <u>By Steel We Swear, Not Slay</u> - They did not kill for sport, nor for conquest. Every strike had purpose, and every battle had meaning.

III. <u>The Shadows Must Never Rise Again</u> - The Draco's corruption was not vanquished with their fall, but the Sacred Blades would ensure that it would never take root again.

These tenets set them apart from any order that had come before. They were not warriors bound to the crown, nor were they mercenaries. These were something more, something deeper - keepers of the land's forgotten truths.

Under Rafiq's leadership, the Order spread across Zarah, its warriors walking unseen among the cities and the sands. No citadel of stone contained them, no fortress of mortal making could hold their purpose. They lived among the people, their identities known only to those they trusted, yet their presence was always felt. When corruption stirred in noble hearts and armies gathered in shadow, dawn would find only silence where treachery had whispered, the would-be usurpers claimed by the desert's justice. When Draconian loyalists gathered in secret within the ruins of a lost temple, they vanished without a trace, their banners left to be swallowed by the dunes.

When a forgotten warlord attempted to raise an army from the nomadic clans, the sands themselves rose against him in the form of a lone guardian, bearing but one blade yet carrying the weight of the desert's wrath - a warrior of the Sacred Desert, who left his body where it fell as a warning to all others who would dare to rise against peace and prosperity.

They did not fight wars but were called upon to prevent them. They did not seek glory. Nonetheless, their legend grew.

Rafiq led the Order for many years, his name becoming a whispered legend among the people of Zarah. To his enemies, he was a ghost, a force that kept the balance without ever seeking power for himself. To those who knew him - to the warriors who had fought by his side, to the people he had sworn to protect - he was something more.

He was the last son of a forgotten house, the heir to an oath that had never truly died. In his blood lived the embodiment of the warriors who had once stood at the edge of the old world, guarding it against destruction. He had become the Lion of the Sacred Desert. When the last of his battles had been fought, when the desert called him to his final rest, when his blade was finally laid to rest, the Order did not end with him. For their oath was eternal. The sacred warriors remained, their purpose unchanged, their vow unbroken. The desert endured, and so did they.

Genealogy of Kael Drathis & Varros Vhaskar's Bloodline

Kael Drathis and Varros Vhaskar's genealogy trees are deeply rooted in the dark legacy of the House of Draco, a lineage forged in the fires of conquest, genetic manipulation, and an insatiable thirst for power. Their bloodlines, though intertwined with the House of Draco's oldest ruling castes, were shaped by different paths. Drathis became the master of deception and war, while Vhaskar emerged as the beast of the battlefield - a warrior born of savagery and brutal discipline. Below is the full history of their lineages, told in a manner befitting the grandeur of their legacies and their tragic ends. The first list, included in this section of our archives, represents a summary of both Drathis and Vhaskar's genealogies, followed by the historical recount of their bloodline.

Kael Drathis' Lineage

I. *Zyrr-Kael Nathair, The Subjugator* (Ancestor, 5,000 years ago) - The Draco who first inhabited the Leander System, founding the dynasty that would bear his name. His reign began the tradition of subjugating species not by war but by cultural erosion - slowly replacing rulers, traditions, and beliefs until nothing remained of the original civilization.

II. *Sakarath Nathair, The Whispering Warlord* (Ancestor, 3,200 years ago) - A ruler known for perfecting the art of infiltration. His assassins moved unseen, his enemies fell without knowing they had been at war. Under his rule, five entire planetary systems changed allegiance to the Draco without a single battle.

III. *Kael-Zyrr the Harbinger* (Father, 1,000 years ago – 320 years ago) - The last great mastermind of the Draco before their downfall. He was a distant descendant of one of the architects of the War of the Shattered Sky, against the House of Abraxas, and the one who placed Drathis in power before the Draconian Empire began to crumble.

IV. *Selvaris Nathair, the Veiled Fang* (Mother, 980 years ago – 280 years ago) - A zealot priestess, a master of genetic alchemy. She ensured that Drathis would be the pinnacle of his lineage, enhancing his mind and body beyond natural limitations.

Varros Vhaskar's Lineage

I. *Varro-Thaskar the Red Tyrant* (Ancestor, 6,000 years ago) - A warlord who led several Draconian planetary genocides, wiping out entire species simply to prove the might of his legion. His methods became the foundation of Draco war tactics.

II. *Vhaskor the Unchained* (Ancestor, 3,500 years ago) - A warrior who fought in the Great Slave Rebellions, crushing uprisings and carving his name into the history of The MiddleVerse, through the ritualistic execution of a thousand traitors.

III. *Kraathis the Maw* (Father, 800 years ago – 350 years ago) - A commander of the House of Draco's last great armies. A beast of war, known for leading charges that tore through entire cities.

IV. *Vhaskar the Blackened* (Son, 505 years ago – 278 years ago) - The last warhound of his lineage. Loyal to Drathis, but truly loyal only to the art of war.

Historical Recount of Kael Drathis' Bloodline

<u>The Ancestry of Drathis the Usurper</u>
Kael Drathis was the last scion of a bloodline steeped in deception, war, and an unyielding thirst for dominion. His ancestry was not merely one of strength, but of insidious influence - a lineage that shaped the House of Draco's rise and, in a manner, its fall, in ways both seen and unseen. While the warriors of the Draco had crushed worlds beneath their claws, Drathis' forebears had done something far more dangerous - they had bent civilizations to their will, manipulating and watching empires crumble from within before taking the shattered remains for themselves. This was the Nathair legacy: Not conquerors of stone, but of minds. Not warlords, but puppet masters. Kael Drathis was meant to have been their masterpiece.

I. <u>The First Whisper in the Dark: Zyrr-Kael Nathair, The Subjugator (5,000 years ago)</u>

The Draco had been feared for their brute strength for aeons of time, due to their ability to crush those who stood in their way. But Zyrr-Kael Nathair understood something his kin did not - true power was not taken by force, but by quiet, patient corrosion.
Unlike the warriors of his time, who measured victories in the number of skulls claimed, Zyrr-Kael measured his by how many rulers he could turn into his unwitting servants. His campaigns were not waged with armies alone, but also with whispers in the halls of power, with carefully placed alliances, with rulers who, without realizing it, woke up one day and found themselves to be the House of Draco's vassals in all but name.
His conquest of several star systems was legendary - not because he took them in a storm of fire but because they surrendered without a single battle.
By the time the ruling families of those systems realized what had happened, they were bound by debts, treaties, and pacts they could not break. Their armies were loyal to the House of Draco. Their people worshipped them as saviours, and in certain cases, as deities. By the time Zyrr-Kael finally revealed his true face, there were no rebellions - only quiet, bitter resignation.

It was this philosophy that became the foundation of the Nathair bloodline: The sharpest blade is the one never drawn. The strongest chains are those that can not be seen.

III. The Whispering Warlord: Sakarath Nathair, Master of Infiltration (3,200 years ago)

If Zyrr-Kael had built the foundation, Sakarath Nathair perfected it. He was a warlord in name only - his true battlefield was in the courts of kings, in the backrooms of merchant guilds, in the quiet exchanges between those who thought themselves safe from the House of Draco's grasp.

It was Sakarath who pioneered the art of subversion, crafting the first true Draco infiltration networks that would later make the House of Draco not just a force of war but a shadow empire throughout The MiddleVerse.

Under his direction, five planetary systems fell to Draco rule without ever realizing they had been conquered. By the time their rulers uncovered the truth, it was too late - their most trusted generals were Sakarath's agents, their people had already embraced the House of Draco's rule, their economies were bound to Nathair-controlled trade. It was said that Sakarath never lifted a weapon, yet entire empires fell at his feet.

IV. The Harbinger of Ruin: Kael-Zyrr Nathair, The Architect of War (1,000 years ago – 320 years ago)

Drathis' father, Kael-Zyrr the Harbinger, was the first of the Nathair bloodline to deviate from its traditional path. Where his ancestors had ruled from the shadows, Kael-Zyrr sought to do so in the open.

He believed that the time for secrecy had ended. That the House of Draco, after millennia of hiding behind politics and subterfuge, had grown weak. He envisioned an empire that no longer whispered but roared.

Thus, it were Kael-Zyrr's distant forebears who orchestrated the War of the Shattered Sky, a conflict meant to bring the Draco to true, undeniable dominance, trying to overcome their nemesis - the Abraxians - one of The MiddleVerse's Guardian Houses.

Kael-Zyrr became, in his own right, a master of both deception and strategy, using the old ways of his lineage to weaken his enemies before crushing them with overwhelming force.

For a time, it worked. The Draco surged across the stars, seizing worlds, shattering fleets, making stellar-kings kneel. But they had made a fatal miscalculation - they underestimated the resilience and the resourcefulness of the Abraxians. The war did not end in victory but in ruin. The House of Draco suffered a great defeat, and in the aftermath, Kael-Zyrr was slain by his enemies, his empire shattered. Yet, his legacy did not die with him. For he had already crafted his successor.

V. Selvaris Nathair, the Veiled Fang: Kael Drathis' Mother, Priestess of the Dragon Lords (980 years ago – 280 years ago)

While Kael-Zyrr sought power through war, Selvaris the Veiled Fang sought something far greater: ascension beyond mortality.

She was a high priestess of the Cult of the Dragon Lords, a sect that believed the Draco were not mere conquerors but destined gods-in-the-making. She saw the restoration of the House of Draco as not just a political necessity but a divine mandate. She truly believed they were destined to rule The MiddleVerse.

It was Selvaris who ensured that Drathis would be the greatest of his lineage.

Through ancient rites and genetic alchemy, she shaped him before he was even born - enhancing his mind, his body, his very essence.

She whispered to him in the womb, of his destiny, of the greatness that would be his, of the empire he would reclaim in the name of their kind. When he was born, she raised him not as a child but as a weapon.

Kael Drathis, The Last Nathair (606 years ago - 278 years ago)

Drathis was meant to be the pinnacle of his bloodline, the culmination of centuries of carefully cultivated power. He was to be the mind that rebuilt the Draco Empire, the hand that crushed those who had defied his kind. In the end, his fate was no different from those before him.

His obsession led him to the deserts of Zarah, where he spent centuries trying to undermine the planet's political institutions. He sought to bend the Weaving to his will to harness the power of the Primordials and carve a new age from the ashes of the old. Yet, fate had other plans.

After a war with Aran, one he lost, he hunted Aran, Rafiq, and Barash, believing them to be the last obstacles to his dominion. That hunt did not end in conquest. It ended in blood.

On the sands of a sunken city, beneath the twin moons, Drathis met his end at the blade of Aran ibn Khalid. With his dying breath, he whispered not a curse, not a plea for mercy, but a warning. "You do not understand… You have only delayed the inevitable." Then, the last Nathair-Kael fell. Unbeknownst to Aran, he planned to use his last breaths on a desperate vengeance…

The bloodline that had once shaped the fate of entire worlds ended with a single stroke. Yet time is a wheel, and the House of Tempus sees all turnings. And the desert remembers… There still were other Draconian Warlords out there, amongst the stars, and though Drathis' name faded from history, the echoes of his ancestors still linger in the void, waiting for the moment when the House of Draco might rise once more.

Historical Recount of Varros Vhaskar's Bloodline

The Ancestry of Varros-Vhaskar the Blackened

In the annals kept by the House of Tempus, few bloodlines burn as brightly in war as the Nathair-Varros. Where Drathis was the product of careful manipulation, selective breeding, and political intrigue, Vhaskar was forged in fire, tempered in blood, and shaped by war itself. His was a lineage of warriors, conquerors, and executioners - those who ruled not by subterfuge but by force alone. If Drathis represented the mind of the House of Draco, Vhaskar was its fist, its unyielding instrument of destruction.

The Warbreed of the Kael-Varros Line

The Kael-Varros were an ancient strain of the Draco, bred for one purpose: to be the perfect warlords of a ruthless empire. Unlike the Nathair bloodline, which valued control through manipulation, the Varros line believed that only raw strength could ensure dominance. From birth, their sons and daughters were hardened by cruel rites, their bodies moulded into living weapons, their minds conditioned to see weakness as an abomination. They did not fear pain. They did not fear death. They only feared dishonour - the failure to be worthy of the Draco name. It was said that no Kael-Varros warrior ever died in bed.

Vhaskar, the last of his lines, embodied this legacy. His blood was the culmination of generations of warriors who had forged their reputations in the carnage of the battlefield. His ancestors had fought, bled, and conquered more than any other lineage within the House of Draco, their names etched into The MiddleVerse's history, in fire and ruin.

I. The First Butcher: Varros-Thaskar the Red Tyrant (6,000 years ago)

The first true warlord of the Kael-Varros bloodline, Varros-Thaskar, was a monster among monsters, a conqueror whose campaigns left entire planets lifeless.

He was not content with mere subjugation. He did not believe in vassals or tributes. When he conquered the Thyssian Worlds, he did not accept their surrender. He had their cities razed, their rivers poisoned, their rulers burned alive upon pyres of their own people. Entire civilizations now lay extinct because of him.

Their planets turned to living cemeteries due to Varros-Thaskar's insatiable thirst for destruction.

It was not enough for him to defeat his enemies. He had to erase them. The Varros line's philosophy was born from this brutal doctrine: Mercy is weakness. Fear is a weapon. Only the strong are fit to rule.

Varros-Thaskar's proclivity for slaughter earned him the name "The Red Tyrant", for it was said that the worlds his empire swept through ran red with the blood of his victims.

II. The Chainbreaker: Vhaskor the Unchained (3,500 years ago)

Varros-Thaskar's descendant, Varros-Vhaskor, embodied the same philosophy but wielded it differently. He was not merely a butcher - he was an executioner of rebellions. When the Draco's enslaved worlds revolted, it was Vhaskor who was sent to crush them. Which he did with such efficiency that it horrified even his own kind. His most infamous act must have been during the Great Slave Rebellions of Nerrath, where the entire planetary system rose against their Draco masters. Vhaskor led his warriors into the heart of the rebellion and executed every captured insurgent with his own hands.

Not content with merely ending the rebellion, he made an example of their leaders. Their bodies and armies were stripped, burned, and displayed along the rings of the Nerrath Star System's capital moon so that any who looked to the heavens would see their failure carved in fire. For his brutal nature, he became a legend. The name "Unchained" was not a title given, but a title taken. More than that, it was a warning, for wherever Varros Vhaskor went, hope died.

III. The Maw of the Draco: Varros-Kraathis the Devourer (800 years ago – 350 years ago)

Kraathis, the father of Vhaskar, was not so much a warlord as he was a predator. While his ancestors had ruled through slaughter, Kraathis took it a step further. His warriors did not fight battles in the traditional sense. They did not march in grand legions. They did not need to, for they took pride in their elite stirp.

His nonpareil warriors would descend upon their prey like beasts - tearing, rending, consuming. He was the commander of the Dread Legions, the House of Draco's elite berserker forces.

Where he walked, there was no strategy, no politics - only war in its rawest form.

His largest massacre came at the Siege of Karaz-Torr in the Devasa Star System, home to the House of Cawr, where, rather than accept the surrender of the defeated army, he ordered his soldiers to burn their enemies alive. Such a cruel act was not done out of necessity, nor hunger, for it was a message. A declaration. There would be no prisoners. No survivors. No memory left behind but horror.

The House of Draco had revered him. The MiddleVerse had feared him. Yet, it was his son, Vhaskar, who would carry his legacy to its ultimate end.

IV. <u>Vhaskar the Blackened, The Last Warhound of the Draco (505 years ago – 278 years ago)</u>

If Kraathis was a beast, Vhaskar was something far worse. Born in the final age of the Draco's subversion of Zarah, he knew only war. His father raised him not as an infant but as a weapon. Pain was his tutor, steel his cradle. By the time he had seen twenty of Nathair's sun cycles, he had fought and killed more foes than most warriors faced in a lifetime. He was the same as his kin, yet unlike any who came before him, Vhaskar fought not out of conquest, nor duty. He fought because he knew nothing else. Despite being friends with Drathis for centuries, his loyalty to him was not because he believed in his vision but because Drathis gave him what he craved - war without end. So, he became his shadow, his executioner, his enforcer. Where Drathis schemed, Vhaskar killed. Where Drathis spoke of destiny, Vhaskar carved it into flesh. They fought countless battles, side by side, back to back, always emerging victorious. But war, like all things, must end.

The Last Duel and the End of the Kael-Varros Bloodline
When Drathis fell, Vhaskar did not run. He could have disappeared into the wilds, faded into history, and waited for another chance to carve his name into the stars. That was not in him, though. He did not seek survival but rather an ending worthy of his bloodline, and in his final

battle, he faced Rafiq and Barash in the endless dunes of Zarah. He fought like a demon. Like a Draconian Warlord.

He did not yield. He did not falter. For he had never known how. In spite of his bravery, the desert does not bow to beasts. Neither did Rafiq al-Bahir.

When the final blow came, Vhaskar did not curse fate. He did not rage against death. Instead, he laughed. As he fell and his body broke, Rafiq could swear he heard Vhaskar utter these words. "At last, I am free." And with that, the Kael-Varros bloodline was almost spent. A legacy of blood and conquest, buried beneath the sands of Zarah.

Appendix VII: Historical Accounts of the Orders of the Sun & the Sacred Desert

The Birth of the Order: Aran's Vision and the Founding of the Priesthood

The birth of the Priesthood of the Sun did not come as a sudden decree nor as a mere extension of the faiths of old - it was a culmination of wisdom, necessity, and destiny, brought forth by Aran ibn Khalid, the unifier of Zarah. His triumph over the forces that sought to unravel the Weaving had left Zarah whole once more, but the scars of war and division ran deep. Balance had been restored, but balance, as Aran knew, was fragile. Without guidance, the cycle of chaos would begin anew. It was with this knowledge that he stood upon the Sunlit Terrace of the Citadel of the Sun, overlooking the vast expanse of desert as dawn broke across the dunes. The golden light bathed the sandstone walls of Sarim, illuminating the wounds of a land still healing from its recent past. The people needed more than a ruler - they needed a foundation, something that would endure long after kings had turned to dust.

Summoning the greatest minds and spiritual leaders of the age, Aran convened what would later be called the Council of the Dawn - a gathering of sages, warriors of the Sacred Desert, and Barash who had studied the Weaving and its cosmic threads. Among them were the first Moon Seers of Qamar, the elder scholars of the Temple of Solkara, and warriors who had fought at Aran's side in the great war against Drathis and the House of Draco.

The meeting took place within the Halls of Illumination, a sacred chamber in the heart of the Citadel where only the most profound deliberations were held. There, beneath the vast dome where the constellations had been inscribed in ancient times, Aran spoke of the path ahead. "We have fought. We have bled. We have won. But war is a fire that consumes itself, and victory without wisdom is a fleeting thing. I did not mend the Weaving so that it may unravel again. We must be the hands that hold it together."

The gathered council listened as he laid out his vision - not of a kingdom ruled by steel and law alone, but one anchored in enlightenment, in faith, and in the eternal balance of the Weaving.

The people of Zarah needed guidance, not just in governance but in spirit.

As deliberations continued, the gathered scholars and seers spoke of Solkara, the Sun Goddess, whose light had guided Zarah in the time of the Old Kings. Her flame represented both creation and destruction, wisdom and wrath, renewal and retribution - all aspects of the cycle of the Weaving. At the height of the council's debates, Safira al-Rasha, moon seer of Sarim, stood and uttered a prophecy long hidden within the sacred tomes of the Moon Seers. An ancient text she had revealed to no one save the king.

Her voice was mellifluous, like the soft silver light of Anar and the ember glow of Nysa. "When the Weaving is torn, when the sands burn and the stars weep, a new fire shall be lit, not to consume, but to guide. From the hands of the Restorer shall rise a flame eternal, a priesthood of the sun that shall stand against the night." Both Aran and Safira knew that this prophecy would settle the matter. The Order was to be dedicated to Solkara, not as a mere deity of worship, but as a manifestation of the cosmic balance that Aran had restored. The Priesthood of the Sun was thus named, not to rule as kings, but to stand as keepers of wisdom, watchers of the Weaving, and guardians of Zarah's fate.

Aran also knew that for this order to endure, it had to be built upon unshakable tenets, not shifting allegiances or mortal ambition. Thus, he and his council established the first laws of the faith, later inscribed upon the walls, inside the Temple of Solkara.

First: The Sun Rises for All – No ruler, tribe, or warrior would hold dominion over the Priesthood. It would remain neutral in the affairs of men, a beacon of wisdom for all, regardless of allegiance.

Second: The Light Must Be Guarded – Knowledge of the Weaving was sacred. The Priesthood would safeguard its secrets and ensure its teachings were not twisted for selfish gain.

Third: Fire is Both Sword and Shield – The priests were not mere scholars; they would be trained to defend the balance, should darkness rise again.

Fourth: The Blade that Walks in Light – The Order of the Sacred Desert, though separate from the Priesthood, would serve as its sword and shield, striking against corruption, hunting the remnants of the House of Draco, and ensuring that the balance of the Weaving endured.

With these tenets in place, the first initiates were chosen. Warriors laid down their swords to take the Oath of the Eternal Flame. Scholars abandoned their earthly pursuits to seek enlightenment. Healers, seers, and mystics flocked to Sarim, drawn by the promise of something greater than themselves.

<u>The Birth of the Order</u>
The official ceremony would be held at a later date, at the recently built Great Temple of Qamaria, in the Kingdom of Qamar, but to mark the birth of the Priesthood of the Sun, Aran led his followers to the Temple of Solkara.
Located deep within the heart of Zarah, the temple had become, once more, a beacon of divine power, wisdom, and balance. It still stands to this day as one of the most significant spiritual and historical sites in Zarah's history, holding immense influence over its past and present rulers.
In the chronicles of the House of Tempus, it endures as one of the oldest, human built, edifices on planet Zarah.
The temple was constructed over 11,000 years ago, during the Age of the Old Kings, when they sought to unify their people under a single faith. The Old Kings, fearing the growing chaos and the whispers of the Primordials, dedicated the temple to Solkara, believing that the Sun Goddess could guide them in their quest to maintain order and balance.
Millennia later, inside the same walls, Aran knelt before the sacred fire, his voice carrying through the halls. "May this flame burn so long as Zarah endures. May its light guide the rulers who shall one day replace me so that they may never walk in darkness."
The gathered priests, warriors, and scholars knelt beside him, each offering their vow to the Weaving. As the ritual came to a close, a sudden gust of wind swept through the temple, causing the flames to flare higher than ever before. The assembled priests took it as a sign - a blessing from Solkara, the sun Goddess herself. Thus, the Priesthood of the Sun was born, its mission clear, its purpose eternal.
From that day forward, the Priests and Priestesses of Solkara walked among the people not as rulers but as keepers of wisdom and balance. The House of Aran had found its guiding light, and though the years would bring trials and divisions, the Order would remain strong - watching, teaching, and protecting. The dawn of the Priesthood had begun, and the sun would never set upon its flame.

I. <u>The First Era of the Priesthood (277 – 200 Years Ago)</u>: <u>Guardians of Balance</u>

By the reckoning of the House of Tempus, the years following the consecration of the Priesthood of the Sun were marked by a profound transformation across Zarah. The tribes, once fractured by war and distrust, had been unified under one rule, and now the House of Aran had a new guiding force - one that was neither bound to a single ruler nor entangled in the ambitions of warlords. The Priesthood of the Sun, with its scholars, warrior-priests, and healers, became the cornerstone of a new era.
From the halls of Sarim's Grand Library to the distant crystalline dunes of Qamar, the Priesthood's influence expanded, not through conquest, but through wisdom. Temples were raised, not as fortresses, but as sanctuaries for knowledge and balance. The High Priests and Priestesses, guided by the original tenets set forth by Aran, ensured that their teachings reached every corner of the planet.

"The sun does not favour kings over beggars, nor warriors over healers. It rises for all, as must we." *High Priestess Amara al-Rasha* *(Sarim - 278 years ago)*

This philosophy led to the establishment of three great centres of learning and spiritual practice, each devoted to one of the Threefold Paths of the Sun:

<u>The Citadel of Illumination (Path of Knowledge & Wisdom)</u>
Built on Sarim, two hundred and fifty years ago, under the supervision of Prince Khalid Ibn Aran, Queen Sura and King Aran's son. This grand structure became the heart of the Priesthood's vast archives, preserving texts from the time of the Old Kings and expanding upon the mysteries of the Weaving. Philosophers, astronomers, and historians gathered here to study the cosmic order and divine balance.

<u>The Fortress of the Eternal Flame (Path of Guardianship & Warfare)</u>
King Aran and Rafiq al-Bahir oversaw its construction. Built deep in the Talon Mountains, near the Sea of Ash, this was the sole monastery that trained the Sacred warrior-priests. Those who swore to defend the Order's sacred sites and the House of Aran from those who would seek to corrupt or destroy it. Here, recruits underwent the Trial of the Burning

Sands, where they proved themselves worthy of wielding both sword and knowledge.

<u>The Temple of Dawn and Dusk (Path of Healing & Balance)</u>
Built near the Royal Oasis of Qamaria by King Aran I, this sacred retreat became a haven for the sick and the weary. Here, the Priesthood worked in tandem with the Moon Seers of Sarim, training generations of healers in the arts of solar and moon alchemy, developing medicines infused with both essences.

With these institutions, the Priesthood of the Sun ensured that its mission would continue for generations, but although the Order had been established, its path was not without opposition. Many of the old cities and small oasis towns spread throughout Zarah, still clung to the traditions of their ancestors, seeing the rise of the Order as a challenge to their worship of the Serpent Gods. Chief among them was the Warlord of the Sea of Ash, whose allegiance to the remnants of the House of Draco had not been entirely extinguished. For years, this warlord had maintained power in the eastern reaches of Zarah, where the sands ran red with iron and rebellion.
The Priesthood, guided by its principles, sought diplomatic resolution rather than war, urging them to accept the new order of balance. In an attempt to explain that the old ways brought only war and destruction, they sent emissaries. Those warriors never returned. Their deaths, marked by burned sigils of the old Draco clans, were a declaration of defiance. An attempt to reclaim the old ways by those who desperately yearned for the return of their reptilian masters. Nevertheless, their message was clear. They would not kneel to the Priesthood's wisdom, nor would they allow its influence to take root in their lands. Thus began the Silent War of the Ashen Sands - a conflict fought not on open battlefields but in the shadows, in whispers, and in the clash of light against darkness.
The Sacred Desert warriors were dispatched to the eastern frontier. Not yet as conquerors, but rather as protectors of the innocent villages caught between warlord rule and the Priesthood's ideals. For years, they engaged in strategic skirmishes, defending settlements from raids, breaking the influence of Draconian loyalists, and slowly turning the tide in favour of peace. When the discord turned to open warfare, one of the greatest victories of the Order was the Siege of the Obsidian Hold. This was a fortress dug deep within the mountains near the Sea of Ash, where one of the last of the warlords had made his final stand. The siege lasted twelve days and nights, with neither side willing to yield. On

the eve of the longest night, the Order of the Sacred Desert lit the sky with flames, unleashing fire that illuminated the fortress like a second dawn.

The defenders, believing it to be the arrival of their Draconian gods, surrendered at sunrise. These rebels were brought before the High Priestess, where they knelt in the sacred halls of the Temple of Solkara.

"The sun does not demand worship. It simply rises, and all who live beneath it must choose whether to walk in light or remain in shadow." *High Priestess Amara al-Rasha*, upon accepting the surrender of the warlords

With the war won, the next half-century became known as the Era of the Golden Sun - a time of unprecedented peace, learning, and prosperity. The teachings of the Priesthood of the Sun were embraced across Zarah, guiding the people not just in matters of spiritually but also of philosophy, science, and governance.

The Codex of Light was written, collecting the combined wisdom of the greatest scholars of the age. The High Priests and Priestesses of Solkara became advisors to the rulers of the six main kingdoms, ensuring that the House of Aran remained aligned with the cosmic balance of the Weaving. For the first time in millennia, Zarah stood unified - not through fear, nor through conquest, but through understanding.

Thus do the chronicles of the House of Tempus record the first flowering of the faith.

II. <u>The Golden Age of the Priesthood (200 – 100 Years Ago):</u> <u>Keepers of the Weaving</u>

The Golden Age of the Priesthood of the Sun was not merely an era of peace but a time of unparalleled enlightenment. With the last remnants of the House of Draco being hunted down, and Zarah united beneath the wisdom of Aran's son, King Khalid Ibn Aran, the Priesthood became more than a religious institution - it became the living heart of Zarah's culture, governance, and pursuit of cosmic knowledge. Because of that the House of Aran flourished, and the deserts, known only for their harshness, became lands of prosperity.

The wisdom of the Weaving, long hidden in scattered scrolls, forgotten oral traditions, was meticulously gathered, studied, and preserved by the scholars of the House.

In this era, the Priesthood of the Sun truly became the keepers of balance. With stability secured, they sought to consolidate all knowledge of the Weaving into a single sacred tome.

Thus began the Great Codification, a century-long endeavour to record the deepest mysteries of existence, divine law, and the cosmic forces that governed Zarah.

The task fell to the most esteemed scholars and mystics of the House of Aran, who worked tirelessly within the Vaults of Radiance, a hidden chamber beneath Solkara's Temple. Every surviving text from the Age of the Old Kings, every fragment of wisdom from the Moon Seers, and even the first-hand account of the War of the Weaving, by King Aran himself, were compiled into a singular work - the *Codex of Light*.

This tome, bound in gold-etched leather, was more than a book. It became the soul of the Priesthood itself, containing prophecies, divine laws, astrological charts, healing techniques, and even the sacred rites for maintaining the balance of the Weaving.

"Knowledge is the flame that must never be extinguished. As long as the words endure, so too shall the light of Zarah." *High Scribe Tariq ibn Harun*

Copies of the Codex were painstakingly transcribed by the Scribes of the Eternal Flame, with each great temple across the planet housing a protected copy. However, the original remained sealed within the Sanctum of Illumination, where only the highest in the order were permitted to read its pages in their entirety.

The completion of the Codex marked the zenith of the Priesthood's influence. For the first time throughout its history, all of Zarah's spiritual and intellectual knowledge was unified into a single, unbroken lineage of wisdom.

With the unrelenting march of time, as the reach of the Priesthood grew, so too did the weight of its responsibilities. Though the House of Draco had been defeated and the old dishonest warlords had sworn fealty, whispers of corruption still lingered in the hidden corners of the kingdom. To combat this, the Order of the Sacred Desert, originally formed after the Draconian Wars, continued to be a highly disciplined elite force of warrior-priests. Their sole purpose being to root out any remnants of Draconian influence, ensuring that the darkness that had once threatened Zarah would never return. Clad in ceremonial black desert-armour, these warrior-priests were both feared and revered. In honour of Rafiq al-Bahir, original head of the Order, they wielded dual blades imbued with sacred carvings. In most situations, their mere presence was enough to drive out those who sought to unravel the balance.

The greatest test the Order ever came under was the Night of the Ashen Blades, when a secret cabal of Draconian loyalists, long thought extinct, attempted to desecrate the Temple of Solkara.

The Order of the Sacred Desert engaged in a brutal midnight battle within the temple's hallowed halls, ensuring that the eternal flame was not extinguished. Though the battle was won, it served as a reminder that the forces of darkness could never truly be forgotten.

With the cabal defeated and the six kingdoms at peace, the influence of the Priesthood of the Sun truly extended throughout Zarah. Rulers, from Kartal to the kingdom of Arsian, sought audience with the High Priests, hoping to learn from them the wisdom of the Weaving.

Pilgrims from across the planet travelled to the Temple of Solkara, seeking enlightenment, healing, or divine purpose. Trade routes flourished as merchants transported sacred spices, cloths, scrolls, relics, and artefacts in between all the kingdoms. To accommodate the influx of scholars, travellers, and seekers of knowledge, Solkara's Beacon - a grand structure located on the cliffs by the shores of Sarim - was erected. Here, the Priesthood established a vast observatory, where astronomers studied the movements of celestial bodies, seeking a deeper understanding of the Weaving's cosmic flow.

"The Weaving does not end at the edges of Zarah. It stretches across the stars, binding all things in harmony." *Grand Seer Anira al-Yara*

For nearly another century, the Priesthood stood unchallenged, its wisdom unquestioned, its influence unparalleled. Unfortunately, as history has shown, time and time again, even the brightest light casts its shadows.

As the priesthood's power expanded, so too did differences in ideology. Some within the Order believed that the Priesthood should remain purely spiritual, guiding rulers but never interfering in governance. Others saw the Priesthood as the rightful rulers, believing that the kings of Zarah had become reliant on their wisdom and should defer to them entirely. This tension, though minor at first, grew like a slow-burning ember. Disagreements began to arise among the High Priests. Should the Priesthood involve itself in matters of state? Should it remain neutral, even in times of political turmoil? Was knowledge to be shared with the people, or safeguarded only by the faithful?

These questions would not be answered in this age, but their presence marked the beginning of a great divide. For a time, however, the light of Solkara still burned brightly, and the Priesthood of the Sun remained the strongest force for wisdom and balance in all of Zarah. Yet, as another age drew to a close, the first whispers of dissent hinted at the storm to come...

III. <u>The Schism of the Twin Suns (100 – 50 Years Ago): Faith in Turmoil</u>

As the Golden Age of the Priesthood reached its zenith, the cracks that had long been forming beneath the surface began to deepen. What had once been a unified order dedicated to balance and wisdom became a house divided, torn apart by differing interpretations of its purpose. The Schism of the Twin Suns was not a war of swords but a battle of ideology - a rift that would shape the destiny of the faith for generations.

For more than two centuries, the Priesthood of the Sun had served as the spiritual heart of Zarah, advising kings, preserving sacred knowledge, and maintaining the balance of the Weaving. Still, as the *Codex of Light* spread across the land and the Order's influence extended throughout the six kingdoms, a fundamental question arose. Should the Priesthood remain advisors, or should they take a direct hand in ruling the kingdom? As an answer, two opposing factions emerged, each claiming to uphold the true path of Solkara's will. They were the Followers of the Pure Flame and the Seekers of the Burning Dawn.

The Pure Flame was led by *High Priestess Samira al-Qamar*, whose scholars and seers believed that the Priesthood's role was to remain above worldly politics, serving only as spiritual guides. They feared that direct involvement in governance would corrupt the sanctity of their teachings and turn the Order into just another ruling power. *The Burning Dawn* was led by *Grand Master Tariq ibn Rafiq*, a descendant of *Rafiq al-Bahir*, whose warrior-priests argued that the kings of Zarah had grown too reliant on their wisdom while still holding absolute power. They believed that the Priesthood should rule alongside the monarchs, ensuring that no ruler could act against the cosmic balance of the Weaving.

What began as philosophical debates in the Halls of Illumination soon turned into something far more dangerous. Both leaders presented their arguments:

"The sun does not merely watch over our world - it governs and shapes it. If we are its chosen voices, should we not do the same?"
Grand Master Tariq ibn Rafiq, addressing the Council of Elders

"Fire that is forced into the hands of men becomes a weapon. We are not kings, nor should we seek to be." *High Priestess Samira al-Qamar's* response

With each passing year, the division grew deeper. Temples aligned themselves with one faction or the other, and the whispers of civil unrest began to spread among the faithful.
The conflict reached its peak during the Great Convocation of Sarim, where all high-ranking members of the Priesthood gathered within the Temple of Solkara to decide the fate of their order. The debate lasted for days, neither side willing to yield. The halls that once echoed with wisdom now trembled with shouted accusations and impassioned pleas. Then, on the fourth night, as the council sat beneath the temple's great sun disc, the Eternal Flame flickered.
For the first time since it had been relit, by King Aran I, the sacred fire - the very symbol of Solkara's divine presence - dimmed. Some saw it as a sign of impending catastrophe, while others believed it to be a warning against hubris. Rather than unite the council, the event only deepened the divide.
Enraged, Tariq ibn Rafiq declared that Solkara's will was clear - the time for neutrality was over. His followers, the Seekers of the Burning Dawn, stormed out of the temple, declaring that they would establish a new council, one that would wield power as Solkara intended. At that moment, the Priesthood of the Sun was officially fractured.
Though there was no outright war, the Schism of the Twin Suns led to decades of silent conflict. Cities divided between those who followed the Pure Flame and those who supported the Burning Dawn began closing their temple doors to rival factions, fearing that violence would spill into their sacred halls. Heated debates in courtrooms and town squares turned into bitter rivalries as kings and nobles were forced to choose sides. Some priests abandoned the faith entirely, believing that the Weaving had already been broken beyond repair.
The greatest tragedy of this schism was not bloodshed or civil war, but the loss of unity. For nearly two centuries, the Priesthood had been a

beacon of guidance, a force of clarity, and now, it had become a house of discord, its light obscured by ambition and pride.

As the conflict threatened to permanently unravel the Priesthood, one final effort was made to restore balance. In the fifty-first year after the schism, the most respected elders of both factions met in secrecy in the abandoned city of Valamar, an ancient site from the time of the Old Kings, where Aran ibn Khalid once met a Primordial, during the War of the Weaving. Here, under the open sky and the watchful gaze of the twin moons, a new accord was written.

They called it the Covenant of the Twin Suns, and though this did not fully unite the two factions, it did set forth a compromise.

From that day forth, the Followers of the Pure Flame would remain the spiritual and philosophical heart of the Priesthood, ensuring that their guidance remained untainted by political ambition,

and the Seekers of the Burning Dawn would be allowed to advise rulers more directly, but only as part of a council, ensuring no individual priest wielded unchecked power.

The Sanctum of Illumination became a neutral ground, where both sides could meet in debate, but never in conflict. Most importantly, the Eternal Flame would remain untouched, a reminder that no man, no matter his beliefs, could claim to fully understand the will of Weaving. With the advent of this covenant, the worst of the schism had ended, and the Priesthood of the Sun was saved from collapse. Though tensions lingered, and the two schools of thought remained separate, the flame of faith endured.

IV. <u>The Priesthood Today: Guardians of a Changing World</u>

Through the centuries, the Priesthood of the Sun has endured war, schism, and the trials of time itself. Once an institution built upon the visionary ideals of Aran ibn Khalid, it has evolved into something far greater than its founders ever imagined. Though the flames of division have dimmed, planet Zarah continues to shift, and with it, so too must the faith that has guided its peoples.

In this current age, the Priesthood stands at a crossroads, maintaining its sacred duty as the keepers of the Weaving while confronting new challenges that threaten the delicate balance they have sworn to protect. Zarah no longer moves in the same ways it once did - old enemies have faded, new powers have risen, and the role of faith itself is questioned by those who see the Priesthood as a relic of an ancient time. Yet still, the sun rises, and so too must the Priesthood.

Since the Covenant of the Twin Suns, the Order has remained split into two ideological factions, though they now coexist in relative harmony.

The Followers of the Pure Flame remain the spiritual and philosophical heart of the faith. They tend to the sacred sites, maintain the ancient texts, and serve as advisors to those who seek wisdom in the Weaving. Their influence is strongest in Sarim, Qamaria, and the Crescent Sands, where scholars and mystics alike gather to study the divine mysteries. On the other side, the Seekers of the Burning Dawn continue their active involvement in the governance of Zarah, advising rulers and noble houses, ensuring that power is never wielded without balance.

They have established diplomatic ties with the remainder five kingdoms beyond Qamaria, the Royal City, spreading the teachings into Zarahan lands that once viewed the faith as nothing more than desert superstition.

Though tensions between the two factions still exist, a greater understanding now binds them, for both know that their survival depends on unity rather than division. The eternal flame, once nearly extinguished by ambition, now burns as a reminder that no single path holds all the answers.

Among the most revered groups within the Priesthood remains the Order of the Sacred Desert, the warrior-priests who have stood guard against darkness since the days of Aran and Rafiq. Though open war against the House of Draco ended long ago, the Order continues its sacred hunt for those who seek to unravel the balance of the Weaving.

In the modern era, their duties have expanded beyond simple warfare.

They also serve as protectors of ancient sites, ensuring that no relics of the old wars fall into the hands of those who would misuse them. They root out corruption within Zarah's nobility and religious institutions, preventing the mistakes of the past from repeating themselves. In certain special occasions, they act as emissaries and spies, monitoring distant lands where whispers of forgotten forces grow louder with each passing season.

The Order remains headquartered at the Fortress of the Eternal Flame, hidden within the Talon Mountains. There, the initiates continue to undergo the Trials of the Burning Sands, a series of sacred tests designed to prove their devotion, strength, and wisdom before they are deemed worthy of taking the Oath of the Sun.

"The world forgets, but we remember. The old wars may have ended, but the shadows remain. So long as they remain, so too shall we." *Grandmaster Saif ibn Rafiq*, High Warden of the Order of the Sacred Desert

V. <u>A Shifting World: The Challenges of the Present Age</u>

Despite its resilience, the Priesthood faces new challenges unlike any before:

<u>The Rise of Secular Power</u> – As Zarah advances, so too does the idea that governance should exist separately from faith. Many of Zarah's kingdoms, once loyal to the Priesthood, now view it as an outdated institution, useful only for tradition and ceremony.
Foreign Influence – With trade routes expanding and new alliances being forged, old kingdoms - some of whom worshipped the old pantheons - began to challenge the idea of Solkara as the sole divine force. Missionaries from distant lands brought old gods and their old beliefs, leading to tensions in cities once unified under the sun's light.

<u>The Lost Prophecies</u> – Recent discoveries of ancient scrolls hidden within the Ruins of Valamar suggested that the Priesthood's understanding of the Weaving was incomplete. Some high-ranking priests feared that there are truths they were never meant to uncover, while others believed this is an opportunity to reshape their faith for a new era.

<u>The Waning of the Eternal Flame</u> – Though the Eternal Flame of Solkara still burns within the great temple, some claim that it is not as bright as it once was. The Moon Seers of Qamar whisper of a coming change, a great turning of fate, but none can yet say what it means.

<u>The Road Ahead</u>
In the end, the fate of the Priesthood of the Sun lies not in its past, nor even in its present, but in what it chooses to become. Will it cling to the traditions of old, maintaining its ancient role as the keepers of balance? Will it evolve, embracing the changes of the world while holding fast to its core beliefs? Or will it fracture once more, its divisions too deep, its foundation too worn by time to endure?
These are the questions that weigh upon the High Council of the Twin Suns, who now govern the faith in the wake of the schism. They gather

within the Sanctum of Illumination, debating the future of the faith as the sun sets upon the silver domes of Sarim. One thing, however, remains certain. As long as Leander system's primary star rises over Zarah, so too shall its light endure.

The Priesthood of the Sun has weathered centuries of change, standing as both a pillar of wisdom and a force of unwavering vigilance. From its humble beginnings under Aran ibn Khalid and Rafiq al-Bahir, to its struggles in the modern age, it remains the heart of Zarah's spiritual and intellectual life.

Whether the faith shall remain a guiding force or fade into obscurity is a question only time will answer. In the *Echoing Archives of the House of Tempus*, the priests, scholars, and warrior-saints of Solkara continue their sacred duty, ensuring that the light of their sun never dims and the balance of the Weaving endures.

Historical Account of the Tale: "The Night of the Ashen Blades"

The air in Sarim that night was thick with an unnatural stillness, a silence so profound that even the desert winds hesitated in their eternal dance across the dunes. The moonlight bathed the golden domes and alabaster walls of the Temple of Solkara in an eerie silver glow, casting elongated shadows that stretched like ghostly-fingers over the sacred courtyards. The streets beyond were quiet, the city's heartbeat slowed to the steady rhythm of slumber, yet something unseen stirred beneath the veil of night.

Deep within the temple, the Eternal Flame of Solkara burned with its ever-present brilliance, its golden light flickering against the marble pillars of the sanctum. The air inside was perfumed with sacred incense, the scent hanging heavy like a whispered prayer to the goddess whose light had guided Zarah once more for almost a century. Priests and Priestesses moved through the great hall in silent reverence, their robes of white and gold trailing over polished stone as they performed their nightly devotions. Yet despite the serenity, an unease coiled in the air like an unseen serpent.

At the far end of the temple, seated upon the Sunlit Terrace, Grandmaster Saif ibn Rafiq watched the distant horizon with an expression carved from stone. His weathered features, lined from years of battle and discipline, were set in deep contemplation as his keen gaze traced the city's silent rooftops. Being an admirer of King Aran,

Saif was a man who had spent his life studying not just the art of war, but the language of the unseen - the whispers of the wind, the shifting of the sands, the omens that spoke in the spaces between words. Tonight, the desert had fallen too quiet.

Footsteps approached. Ayla al-Arsian, his second-in-command, stepped onto the terrace, her hands resting lightly on the hilts of her twin swords. She was a warrior in both body and spirit, her eyes sharp beneath the hood of her deep crimson cloak. A flicker of concern shadowed her face, an expression Saif did not miss. "You sense it too," he said, his voice a low murmur. Ayla nodded.

"The Weaving stirs," her voice was calm. "Something moves within the threads, just beyond our sight." For a moment, she turned her gaze toward the temple's great entrance, where the twin bronze doors stood sealed beneath the watchful carvings of the sun goddess. The engravings shimmered in the moonlight, their golden etchings glowing faintly as if whispering an unspoken warning. "The air is too thick," she continued. "The city is asleep, yet it does not rest."

Saif inhaled deeply, his senses sharpening. It was true. There was a weight in the air, a presence that did not belong. It was not fear, nor was it the anxious uncertainty of approaching war - this was something older, something patient, something that had waited in the shadows for a long time.

He rose to his feet, his long crimson robes shifting like the last embers of a dying fire. He had felt this presence before, many years ago, in the days of the last great hunt. When the remnants of the House of Draco had been driven into exile, broken and scattered across the desert. But embers, left untended, sometimes found a way to reignite. "Call the Watch," Saif commanded. "Triple the guard at the temple gates. Have the initiates remain inside the temple and let no one enter without my word."

Ayla did not question him. She knew him too well for that. Saif ibn Rafiq was never one to act on mere superstition, so if he was giving orders, then the danger was real. As she turned to leave, the distant sound of metal striking stone echoed through the temple halls. It was faint, barely noticeable, yet to those trained in the ways of war, it was unmistakable. Then, Ayla heard another sound - a blade being drawn.

Saif, unconsciously, found the hilt of his sword, his pulse steady, his mind already forming the possibilities. He decided not to alarm her further. "I could have been wrong. It is probably nothing," he said, though his worried demeanour betrayed his words. "Are you certain?" Ayla asked, her eyes focused on Saif, who did not answer. Instead, he sat on the stone steps. The desert winds picked up, howling softly through the corridors of the great temple, as if the very sands were whispering a warning. Beyond the sacred walls, in the deepest shadows of Sarim, figures moved unseen.

An hour had passed by, and now the low hum of chanting filled the grand hall of the Temple, voices layered in harmonious devotion. The flickering golden light of the Eternal Flame danced upon the polished marble, casting shifting patterns of radiance across the towering columns. The priests, draped in robes of white, yellow, and crimson, moved in rhythmic procession, their hands raised in solemn reverence as they carried out the sacred rites of the night. Yet beyond the hallowed sanctum, the air trembled with an unseen weight - a tension unspoken, yet felt by those attuned to the Weaving.

High above, within the chamber of the Sanctum of Illumination, the temple's highest-ranking priests had convened. They sat in a circle of ornate stone chairs, the ancient symbols of the sun and stars meticulously etched into their surfaces. At the head of the gathering, Elder Harun ibn Ryvan furrowed his brow. He was a descendant of the tribal lord that opposed King Aran I at the end of the War of the Weaving. A man whose wisdom was said to span nearly a century. His gnarled hands clutched his ceremonial staff, the golden sigil of Solkara embedded at its peak.

Across from him stood Grandmaster Saif ibn Rafiq, his crimson cloak billowing slightly as he moved to speak. His presence commanded the room, yet his voice was measured, his words weighed with the precision of a man who did not waste them. He felt in his chest that this was a moment for truth, not wordplay. "The winds whisper of something unnatural," he looked at those assembled, reading their reactions, "the silence of the city is not a comfort - it is a warning." The elder priests exchanged glances, some shifting uneasily in their seats. "Your instincts have served us well in the past, Grandmaster," Elder Harun acknowledged, his voice aged but unwavering. "Yet what proof do you have of this coming storm?"

Saif exhaled slowly, the warrior blood of his forebears boiling in his veins, his gaze drifting to the great open balcony that overlooked the temple courtyards. The twin moons bathed the land in silver light, and though the city appeared at peace, his senses told him otherwise. "Proof?" He echoed. "I feel the weight of it in my chest. I have listened to the silence that has fallen upon Sarim like a shroud. I have heard the Weaving itself whispering its disquiet."

Elder Rashid ibn Ghazi, a man known for his scepticism, interrupted. "What you have, Saif, is fear." His sharp gaze held no malice, but neither did it hold patience. "Fear clouds even the keenest of warriors," he nodded at Saif.

A shadow of frustration flickered across Ayla ibn Rahim's face as she stepped forward, her hand resting lightly on the pommel of her dagger. "I apologise for my bluntness, but tell me, Elders," her voice was laced with quiet steel, "why have our sentinels not returned from the outer walls? Why does the wind not move as it should? Why does the Weaving tighten, as if bracing for a blade to strike?"

Silence settled upon the chamber. Elder Harun studied her carefully. His expression remained unreadable, but in the depths of his ancient eyes, there was something - a flicker of recognition, of unease he dared not voice. As if fate were knocking, suddenly, the first bell tolled. A single, piercing chime.

Every head turned toward the massive bronze doors of the sanctum as a second chime followed, then a third. The alarm of the temple.

The gathered priests rose to their feet, confusion and alarm washing over them. What they thought to be inconceivable was happening right under their noses. "That is impossible," Elder Rashid murmured, his disbelief wavering. "No enemy has breached these halls in generations."

Saif had already turned, his steps swift, his body a taut coil of discipline honed over decades. "Then you have forgotten history, Elder," he said over his shoulder. "For there is no fortress that cannot be breached - especially when the enemy has already found its way inside."

The first scream cut through the temple's solemn halls like the wail of a dying star. It came from beyond the grand doors of the inner sanctum, where the temple's outer courtyards stretched beneath the watchful gaze of the twin moons. The sound was brief - a sharp cry of warning swiftly silenced - but it was enough. The silence that followed was not peace, but the last gust after the plunge of a dagger.

A distant crash resounded through the temple, the unmistakable sound of iron colliding with stone. Then another, and another. The heavy bronze doors at the entrance shuddered under some unseen force, their great hinges groaning in protest. Saif ibn Rafiq was already moving. "To arms!" he roared, his voice carrying through the sacred halls like the call of a war horn. "The temple is under attack!" The Priests and students, many of whom had never known war beyond whispered stories, stood frozen in shock. The warriors of the Order of the Sacred Desert, however, did not hesitate. Blades sang as they were drawn, torches flared to life, and the great doors of the inner sanctum were barred.

Ayla moved to Saif's side, her twin swords already glinting in the light of the Eternal Flame. "They move too quickly," she murmured. "They were waiting for this moment." Saif's eyes narrowed as another impact sent tremors through the stonework. The enemy was inside the temple grounds. "Then let them come," he said. "And let them break themselves against the light." The great bronze doors did not hold for long, and with a final, deafening crash, they buckled inward, torn from their hinges as if struck by a titan's fist. The temple guards standing closest were flung backward by the sheer force of the impact, their bodies colliding against marble pillars. Smoke and darkness poured through the breach like a living thing, coiling and hungry.

From the blackness, unbidden, they emerged. The Ashen Blades.

They wore robes of midnight and armour black as onyx, their faces hidden behind masks sculpted in the likeness of dragons. Each bore the insignia of a forgotten age, a sigil that had, not three centuries ago, commanded fear in every corner of Zarah. The sigil of the House of Draco.

Their leader stepped forward, his presence alone enough to chill the air. Clad in a flowing cloak that seemed to drink in the torchlight, he bore a blade of dark steel, its edges whispering with hunger.

"Burn it all," the figure commanded, his voice like the distant growl of an oncoming storm. Within seconds, the temple had ignited. The first clash of steel rang out as the warriors of the Order of the Sacred Desert met their foes, which moved with unnatural speed, shadow, and fire given form. Their attacks were precise and relentless. These were not mindless raiders, nor were they mere assassins, but rather disciples of an old vengeance, trained in the arts of war and sorcery alike.

Saif met the first of them head-on, his sword flashing in the firelight. The clash sent sparks cascading like falling stars, his blade carving through the dark steel of his opponent's weapon. The Ashen Blade reeled, but another was upon him before he could finish the strike. Saif sidestepped, raising his sword to meet his attacker. With his left hand, he plugged a dagger in the first.

Ayla, well trained by Saif, moved like a wraith, her twin blades weaving an intricate dance of death. One blade deflected a strike, and the other opened a throat. She twisted through the chaos, her movements fluid, never lingering in one place long enough to be struck. The warriors of the Order fought beside her, their discipline honed through years of gruelling trials. "Hold the sanctum!" Saif bellowed, even as he parried another vicious blow. "We must not let them reach the Eternal Flame!" Yet the enemy came prepared. From the depths of their ranks, a figure emerged, draped in flowing black robes, hands raised in invocation. The air crackled with unnatural energy as he used an old Draconian device, releasing a wave of darkness, erupting outward, swallowing the torches, and plunging the hall into chaos. "They seek to extinguish the light!" Ayla shouted, slicing down an opponent even as another lunged at her flank.

The sacred warriors adjusted swiftly, closing ranks, forming a defensive line before the steps of the inner sanctum. The sacred flame burned just beyond the doors behind them, its glow the last beacon of hope in the encroaching storm. Relentless, the Ashen Blades pressed forward.

As the warriors of the Order of the Sacred Desert fought with all their might, a lone figure ascended the central dais within the great hall. He stood before the Eternal Flame, its golden light illuminating the bloodstained marble at his feet.

It was Elder Harun ibn Ryvan, the eldest of the Priesthood. Though his hands were frail with age, his voice carried with the strength of a hundred generations. "Solkara's light does not dim!" Harun's words rang out like a prayer, and a battle cry alike, a call to the faithful, a defiance against the dark.

Saif felt the fire of his forebears stirring in his chest, the words igniting something deep within him. He lifted his sword high, its blade glowing with the reflection of the eternal flame. "Drive them back! Do hot falter!"

The warriors of the Order roared as one, their voices shaking the very foundations of the temple, and with renewed strength, they surged forward. The battle was far from over, but the Ashen Blades would soon learn what it meant to fight against those who carried the fire of Solkara in their hearts.

The Eternal Flame, the sacred heart of the Temple of Solkara, burned defiantly against the encroaching darkness. Its golden light flickered, casting shifting patterns upon the bloodstained marble floors, illuminating the desperate battle that raged within the sanctum. The warriors of the Order of the Sacred Desert fought with unwavering resolve, but the enemy's numbers seemed endless.

Then, through the storm of blades and fire, they came. From the shattered entrance, the Ashen Blades' inner circle emerged - clad in armour dark as obsidian, their robes billowing like liquid shadow. At their helm strode the Master of the Unseen Flame, his presence seemed to drink in the temple's sacred light. He was taller than the others, his helm adorned with twisted Draconic runes, a relic from a time long before the Weaving had been mended. In his right hand, he bore a black sword, its edges rippling as though forged from living steel. His left hand remained raised, closed in a fist, as if holding something.

Saif ibn Rafiq, bloodied but unbowed, stood at the base of the Eternal Flame's dais, his sword gripped tight in both hands. He had seen many foes in his time, but this one was different. There was no arrogance in the way this master of darkness carried himself - only certainty. "You have fought well," the enemy leader said, his voice smooth as polished stone. "But all things must bow before the inevitable." Saif's jaw tightened. "Nothing is inevitable but the dawn."

The Ashen Blade tilted his head as though amused. Then, with a single motion, from his left hand, he flung a handful of black powder into the Eternal Flame. The temple gasped as one, as the fire sputtered, its brilliant gold shifting to a sickly, unnatural crimson. The heat of it twisted, warping the very air, as though the Weaving itself recoiled in protest. A suffocating pressure settled over the sanctum, pressing into the lungs of all present.

The sacred flame - the symbol of Solkara's eternal light - was faltering. A terrible whisper rippled through the chamber, a voice that did not belong to this world. "Balance is a lie. Light is a fleeting thing. All flames must die. Only darkness will remain king."

The Weaving trembled, and the temple's foundations groaned as if in agony. The murals depicting the Old Kings cracked, golden dust flaking from their once-pristine surfaces. The very air had turned against them.

Saif felt it - a pull at the edges of his soul, an unseen force trying to drag him into the abyss. Around him, some of the younger ones faltered, their knees buckling as though gravity had grown heavier. The desecration was not just of stone and fire - it was of the very faith that bound them together.

Ayla, struggling to keep her footing, turned to him, eyes wide with fury. "We must rekindle the fire!"

"The Weaving does not break so easily," Saif growled, shaking off the creeping weight of despair. "As long as we stand, the flame still burns."

He surged forward, blade flashing, striking at the enemy leader with all the force left in his body. His foe met his assault effortlessly, their blades clashing in an eruption of golden sparks and dark mist.

Ayla, wasting no time, rushed toward the brazier, weaving through the chaos of battle. A Draconian warrior lunged at her, but she twisted mid-stride, severing his arm in one fluid motion before planting a dagger deep into his throat. She leapt onto the dais, reaching for the sacred Sunfire Oil stored in golden vials near the brazier. But the Draconian Warlord had seen her.

He lashed out with his free hand and threw a device that detonated when it hit the ground. Ayla barely had time to react before she was hurled backwards, her body crashing against the steps. Pain exploded in her ribs, and she cried in pain.

Saif ibn Rafiq roared, redoubling his assault, pushing the Draconian Warlord back with a flurry of strikes. Yet his foe did not falter. He flowed like water, meeting each attack with precise counters, his footwork impossibly smooth, as though he fought within the Weaving itself. The battle raged, the clash of steel against steel resounding like the final echoes of a dying world. The Eternal Flame continued to darken. And then - A new light.

Ayla, despite the pain lancing through her body, had reached the sacred oil. With trembling fingers, she uncorked the vial and hurled it into the brazier. The golden liquid struck the corrupted flames, and for a heartbeat, nothing happened.

Then the fire roared to life. A column of pure, radiant sunfire surged upward, consuming the dark tendrils that had tried to smother it. The temple walls shook, but this time, it was not in despair - it was in defiance. The sacred fire did not just burn; it erupted, expelling the taint that had threatened to extinguish it.

The Warlord staggered back, raising his arm to shield his eyes. For the first time, his certainty wavered. Saif did not hesitate. He drove forward, his sword flashing in the golden glow, and with one final, mighty strike, he severed the enemy leader's helm from his shoulders.

The battle did not end in that instant, but the tide had turned. The Ashen Blades, sensing their master's fall, began to retreat, their dark forms vanishing into the corridors, leaving behind only the bodies of their fallen. The flames burned away the last remnants of their sorcery, returning the temple to its rightful state.

Saif stood over the fallen Draconian Warlord, chest heaving, his blade still glowing with the reflected light of the rekindled fire. The temple was scarred but standing, its sacred heart unbroken.

Ayla rose slowly, clutching her ribs but offering a weary smile. "You took your time," Saif exhaled, allowing himself the ghost of a laugh. "Next time, don't wait for me to do all the work." The Eternal Flame burned, brighter than ever, as if in silent approval.

The first light of dawn spilt over the horizon, its golden rays kissing Sarim, and the domes and spires of the Temple of Solkara. The battle had ended, but the scars it left behind ran deeper than the cracks in the temple's once-immaculate marble floors.

Smoke still lingered in the air, curling in ghostly tendrils through the shattered archways. The scent of burning incense and charred flesh intermingled, a stark reminder of the violence that had nearly extinguished the sacred flame. Priests and students moved through the halls in solemn reverence, gathering the fallen, tending to the wounded, and whispering prayers for those whose voices would never rise again.

Saif ibn Rafiq stood at the base of the Eternal Flame, his hand resting on the hilt of his sword. His armour was battered, the once-pristine black and crimson cloak draped over his shoulders now tattered and singed. He bore wounds - deep gashes across his arms, a bruise swelling over his ribs - but he did not falter. His gaze was steady, fixed upon the flame that had nearly been snuffed out. As a result of the Order's combined effort, it burned brighter than ever.

Ayla approached, her steps slow, careful. She held herself with her usual unshaken confidence, but Saif could see the pain in her stance, the exhaustion in her breath. Blood, not all of it her own, stained the edge of her blades. "We held," she said at last, voice hoarse from the night's ordeal.

Saif nodded, exhaling slowly. "This time." He turned his gaze toward the bodies of the fallen Ashen Blades, their blackened armour reflecting the dim morning light. Their leader lay among them, his obsidian helm severed from his shoulders, his snout still twisted in defiance even in death.

The sigil of the House of Draco was engraved into his gauntlet, a reminder that though their empire had crumbled, its shadow still lingered. "They were not mindless zealots," Ayla murmured. "They fought with purpose."

Saif's grip tightened on his sword's hilt. "Purpose alone does not make one righteous."

The doors of the sanctum creaked open, and the surviving elders of the Priesthood stepped forth, their robes heavy with ash and soot. Among them was Elder Harun ibn Ryvan, his aged face lined with sorrow, his hands trembling slightly as he surveyed the devastation.

He walked toward Saif and Ayla, pausing before the rekindled flame. For a long moment, he said nothing. Then, he closed his eyes, whispering a prayer in the old tongue. When he spoke, his voice was heavy with unspoken grief. "We were wrong, and this victory does not belong to us. Due to your bravery, the temple still stands," his hands were trembling, "but at great cost."

Saif turned to face him, his expression unreadable. "This, is the cost of vigilance." He emphasised the first word to further his position on the matter.

Harun exhaled, then nodded, conceding the point, his eyes drifting toward the dead. "So, this was not an isolated attack. Do you believe it was a message?"

Ayla nodded. "Do you not see?" she did not wait for an answer. "They came not just to kill - but to desecrate, to break the will of the faithful."

Saif sheathed his sword. "And they failed," his voice sounded like quiet thunder. "For the Eternal Flame still burns." Harun studied him carefully. "So," he asked hopefully. "Do you truly believe this is over?"

Silence fell between them. In the distance, the priests chanted their morning hymns, their voices rising against the dawn, but beneath the melody of devotion, there was an unshakable note, playing within their harmony. This had only been the beginning.

Saif turned to the temple doors, where beyond them, the world awaited. The House of Draco had been defeated almost three centuries ago, yet their shadows still moved in the dark corners of Zarah. The Weaving was whole, but there were always those who sought to unravel it. "The enemy does not rest," he said at last. "Neither can we." Ayla sheathed her blades, her eyes glinting golden in the firelight. "Then let them come again. We will be ready."

The Eternal Flame flickered, its glow, steady, unwavering. Its light symbolising both a warning and a promise.

End of "The Night of the Ashen Blades"

The Order of the Sacred Desert: An Historical Account

<u>The Founding of the Order</u>
When Aran ibn Khalid restored the balance of the Weaving and brought peace to Zarah, he knew that peace was not the same as safety. The House of Draco had been defeated, but its tendrils had long since buried themselves deep within the institutions of Zarah. The Draconian Warlords had been scattered, but their whispers still lingered in the shadowed corners of the great cities, their corruption poisoning the minds of the ambitious. So, Aran turned to the one man he trusted most - his closest friend and most loyal brother-in-arms, Rafiq al-Bahir.
Rafiq had fought beside Aran through every battle and had bled for Zarah as much as he had bled for his friend. He was not only a warrior but a man of faith, a man who understood that while the body could be struck down, it was the spirit that had to be safeguarded.
On the true night of the founding, Aran and Rafiq stood upon the silvered sands of the Sarai Dunes, the twin moons of Zarah casting their light upon the desert. There, surrounded by the most trusted warriors of their cause, who had fought in the war with the Draco, who had lost homes, families, and everything to them - the Order of the Sacred Desert was born.

"The Sacred Oath": A Tale From the Order of the Sacred Desert

The night was deep, and still, the sky stretched wide and vast over the dunes. The twin moons cast their pale glow upon the endless expanse of the Sarai Dunes. The wind whispered through the sands, carrying with it the echoes of a world that had long been at war. The Weaving had been restored. The battle against Drathis had been won. However, peace was never the end of a story - only the beginning of another. The official ceremony, that took place in Qamaria, was over. The official titles had been addressed, and the celebrations were done with. This was different, though. This was personal, private, something that needed to happen confidentially, between the warriors and the desert.
Aran ibn Khalid stood at the crest of a dune, his silhouette stark against the celestial sky, his embroidered cloak billowing in the desert wind.
Around him, gathered in solemn silence, were warriors of the War of the Weaving, who had fought beside him, bled beside him, and now found themselves standing in the twilight of their battles.
Their weapons, scarred and stained with years of conflict, were sheathed - but their purpose had not yet faded. At the centre of the

gathering, Rafiq al-Bahir knelt, his head bowed, his hands pressed into the still-warm sands of Zarah. The man who had been Aran's shadow in war, his blade in the darkest hours, his brother not of blood but of bond - it was to him the king turned with one final task. He had already sworn his allegiance during the official ceremony, but this was between brother-in-arms and the desert.

Aran drove his father's sword into the sand between them, the steel gleaming beneath the moonlight.

The gathered warriors inhaled sharply, for it was not merely a gesture - it was a declaration. "Everyone gathered here knows the war is not over," Aran intoned, his voice steady but edged with a weight that none could deny. "Even though we have defeated our enemies, their shadow lingers. For the House of Draco does not simply vanish overnight. They are far too ambitious for that. If need be, they will recede into the darkness once more, festering in the hearts of men, twisting them with poison and promises of power. If we do nothing, their corruption will take root once more."

Rafiq lifted his gaze, his eyes meeting Aran's. He had always known this to be true. Even in their hardest-won victories, he had seen it - the lingering influence of the Draco, the way their whispers never truly faded, only found new ears to seduce. They might have killed Drathis and Vhaskar, but the rest of the House would not so easily give up on Zarah. Their history ran too deep, entwined with the planet's long past.

Aran's hand found Rafiq's shoulder. "I have fought with you, bled with you, and you have placed your faith in me. Now, I place the future of Zarah in your hands." A hush fell over the gathered warriors. "Will you take up this task?" Aran asked, solemnly. Rafiq exhaled slowly, the weight of it settling over him. But he did not hesitate.

He pressed his palm against the hilt of Khalid's sword, his fingers tightening over the steel. "By my own blades and blood, I swear it."

One by one, the warriors followed. They stepped forward, kneeling in the sands, pressing their hands to the weapon that bound them together in purpose. Their voices rose in unison, a solemn oath beneath the gaze of the twin moons.

"We are the storm upon the dunes, the blade in the shadow. We do not seek power. We seek only to preserve what is just. The serpent shall never rise again."

The Order of the Sacred Desert was truly born that night, not with ceremonies nor with titles, but with the unbreakable will of those who refused to let the darkness take root in their home again.

As the wind carried their vow across the dunes, Aran turned to Rafiq, and in that moment, their bond was no longer just one of brotherhood but of duty. The battle was not over, it had simply changed.

The war against Kael Drathis had been fought in the open, upon blood-soaked battlefields where steel met steel, and the cries of the fallen echoed across the dunes. The war that followed - the one fought in the shadows - was far more insidious, far more dangerous. For the enemies of Zarah no longer wore the banners of conquest; they now wore the faces of its own people.

The first signs of corruption were subtle. Whispers in the markets of Qamar, merchants with sudden wealth beyond measure, nobles whose allegiances had once been clear but now turned murky.

Rafiq had seen this before, during the War of the Weaving.

The House of Draco did not simply fight battles against them - they were infiltrated, manipulated, or corrupted from within. The fall of a city rarely came from siege engines battering down its gates, but from the slow, insidious turning of its rulers' minds. With the Weaving restored and the Draco seemingly defeated, their influence had begun to slither back into the halls of power.

Rafiq gathered his warriors, the first of the Order of the Sacred Desert, and divided them into small, elite groups. They were not an army. They were hunters.

Their mission was clear: root out the remnants of the Draco. Destroy them before they could take hold. What made matters worse was that they were not facing warriors on the battlefield. They were facing ghosts, wearing the faces of their people.

The first true strike came in Eruthis, located south-west of Sarim. Eruthis had once been a beacon of trade and culture, but beneath its golden towers, Rafiq uncovered a nest of vipers.

For years, a secretive council had ruled from the shadows - merchants, aristocrats, and scholars who had once served the Draco and had continued to do so long after their masters had been slain. After many weeks of investigation and several unsuccessful attempts, Rafiq finally uncovered that they were called the Whispering Court. This organisation was actively working with the House Draco, and their goal was not conquest but subversion.

They did not seek to raise armies. They sought to control those who did.

At night, Rafiq and his warriors approached their meeting place. A large, isolated house, on the outskirts of Eruthis. They waited in the shadows and struck as the moons shown brightest. Cloaked in the desert's silence, they infiltrated the great halls of the Whispering Court, cutting down its members before they could scatter like insects. It was a bloodless victory, with no losses for his people, or so Rafiq had thought. History has shown us that the Draco are nothing, if not cunning, for even in death, they had laid their traps. The next morning, the people of Eruthis awoke to find their water poisoned. Hundreds died before the sun had reached its zenith. The message was clear. The House of Draco would not go away quietly.

The Purge of the Whispering Court was only the beginning. For every Draco sympathizer Rafiq's warriors cut down, more seemed to rise in their place. Some were true believers, coming from families that had long served the enemy, still devoted to the old masters of the Draco, waiting for their return. Others were simply opportunists, those who had grown fat and powerful under the House of Draco's corruption and did not wish to see their influence fade. The most dangerous, however, were those who did not even realize they had been corrupted. Men and women who believed themselves free yet carried the words of their enemy in their hearts.

This, however, is not a phenomenon particular to Zarah. The House of Draco has perfected its craft across a thousand worlds in The MiddleVerse. They understand that the most elegant chain is one the bearer does not feel. The most perfect prison is the one where the captive believes themselves to be free.

This cosmic truth repeats itself with such regularity that one might mistake it for natural law - a gravitational force pulling societies toward intellectual homogeneity. Whether through golden words or iron fists, the few who orchestrate reality find fertile ground in minds that crave certainty over truth.

Unfortunately, for most societies, this type of mindset constitutes the majority of their populations. Therefore, the Order's fight became more than just a hunt - it became a war of shadows, deception, and patience.

Rafiq and his warriors moved unseen through the cities and outposts of Zarah. They rooted out hidden cults, silenced traitors before they could spread their poison, and eliminated those who sought to resurrect the House of Draco in secret. Yet, even as they struck down their foes, the corruption persisted. For the Draco did not forget, and they did not forgive.

One night, beneath blood-red moons, the Sacred Desert suffered its first great loss.

In the mountains on the outskirts of the Sea of Ash, the fortress of Ashen Valley, one of the hidden outposts where the Sacred Desert trained its warriors, was found and destroyed. When Rafiq arrived, his heart turned to stone.

The air was thick with the scent of burning flesh. The walls, once white as bleached bone, were blackened with soot. The warriors who had stood watch over the fortress had not simply been killed. They had been left as warnings. Bodies strung upon the gates, the sigil of the House of Draco carved into their chests. This had not merely been an attack. It was a message.

As a consequence of this, Rafiq gathered the remaining warriors of the Sacred Desert and made them swear a new oath. "No more shadows," he said, standing among the burnt ruins. "No more waiting. We will not simply silence the Draco - we will hunt them to the ends of Zarah."

Thus began the next stage of the war. No longer were they simply the hidden hand, striking only when necessary. Now, they would be the storm that swept the desert clean. The Draco had openly declared war on the Sacred Desert, and Rafiq had no intention of losing.

The war against the remnants of the House of Draco had been waged in the shadows for years, but there came a time when darkness alone would not suffice. There came a time when the hunters of the Sacred Desert had to step into the open and face their foes beneath the full light of the sun. That moment arrived with Blackfire Hold.

Nestled deep within the Kataran Mountains, Blackfire Hold was an ancient stronghold of the House of Draco, once thought lost to time. It had been recently found by a Sacred Warrior, during an investigation. Its halls had seen the rise and fall of kings. Its walls had stood against sieges that had broken entire kingdoms. For years, it had lain dormant, little more than ruins swallowed by the mountains. Or so it was believed.

Though the stronghold stood, apparently derelict, through whispers and intercepted messages, Rafiq al-Bahir uncovered the truth - Blackfire Hold had never been abandoned. Deep within its halls, the last warlords of the Draco, on Zarah, had been gathering their strength, consolidating their forces, preparing for the moment to rise again. They had been watching. Waiting. Biding their time. Now, they were ready to strike.

Upon learning this crucial information, Rafiq did not hesitate. He sent a warning to the King and began gathering every warrior of the Sacred Desert who could wield a blade. When the company was ready, Aran, Sura, and Rafiq led them into the mountains. The march was long and arduous, the path treacherous, but none faltered. Each warrior who followed them into the mist-shrouded peaks knew what was at stake. If the Draco were allowed to reclaim their power, the planet would bleed once more.

The assault began beneath a sky thick with storm clouds, a roiling canvas of black and grey that seemed to mirror the conflict about to unfold below. Lightning cracked across the heavens in jagged arcs of brilliant white, illuminating the landscape in staccato flashes - as if the gods themselves had turned their gaze upon the battlefield, casting their judgement upon mortal affairs.

Sura stood beside Aran on the ridge overlooking Blackfire Hold, her eyes narrowed against the rising wind. "The storm works in our favour," she murmured, pulling her hood tighter. "Their sentries will be distracted, their visibility compromised."

Aran nodded, his face betraying nothing of the storm of emotions within. This fortress had once been, in Zarah's distant past, a bastion of hope, then corrupted, defiled by the Draco presence. "The Sacred Desert strikes first," he said, his voice carrying to the warriors assembled behind them. "Move like the wind. Strike like thunder. Remember what we fight for."

The warriors of the Sacred Desert moved like wraiths through the craggy cliffs, their bodies wrapped in dark cloth that melded with the shadows cast by the lightning's intermittent glow. Aran and Sura, rulers of Zarah, led the first wave, his muscular frame and her lithe form scaling the outer wall with practised ease. Behind them, a dozen of Rafiq's best, who had learned to kill with the efficiency of desert vipers.

The first sentry died without a sound - Sura's blade across his throat, a silent apology in her eyes as she lowered him to the ground. The second managed half a shout before Aran's blade silenced him. The third reached for his horn, fingers brushing its surface before an arrow from the darkness pinned his hand to the wooden bannister. "Quietly now," Rafiq whispered to his followers, moving deeper into enemy territory. "We must secure the gate before-"

A war horn sounded from deep within the fortress, its mournful wail echoing across the stone corridors of Blackfire Hold. Sura cursed under her breath. "They know."

From within the heart of the stronghold, Rhaskar smiled as the horn's call reached his ears. He had been waiting - no, hoping - for this moment. The Draconian warlord, of the Varros bloodline, ran a calloused hand across the blade of his massive war axe, feeling its familiar weight. "Here they come," he growled to his lieutenants, his voice like rocks grinding together. "Prepare the gifts we have made for them." Outside, Aran heard the horn and gave the signal. "The Draco are alerted! All forces advance!"

Warriors of the Sacred Desert poured from their hiding places, a tide of determined flesh and forged steel flowing toward Blackfire Hold's massive gates.

Archers loosed volleys that soared into the sky before descending upon the fortress walls, forcing defenders to seek cover.

Rafiq, already inside with Aran and Sura, led the inside attack, his twin swords already drawn, reflecting the lightning that continued to splinter the sky above. "For Zarah!" he roared, and outside the walls, two hundred voices echoed his cry.

The first gate fell easily - too easily. As the warriors of the Sacred Desert pushed through the breach, Sura felt a chill that had nothing to do with the storm winds. "Aran," she called out, "this is wrong. They are letting us in."

Before he could respond, the mountain itself seemed to roar. War horns blared from a dozen different positions within the fortress, and suddenly, the narrow passages of Blackfire Hold vomited forth nightmares. "May the gods preserve us," whispered a young Bahir warrior at Rafiq's side, his face draining of colour. "What are those things?"

These were not the Chimaeras they had faced at the Siege of Sarim. No, these were something far worse - twisted creatures born of ancient rites and foul alchemy. Humanoids with scaled skin that gleamed like metal in the lightning flashes, their eyes burning with inner fire. Beasts that walked like men but tore through warriors with the strength of ten, their claws shredding armour as if it were parchment. "Stand fast!" Rafiq shouted, stepping forward to meet the first of these abominations. "I am sure they bleed like any other!"

To prove his point, he ducked beneath the creature's swipe and drove both swords into its abdomen. The beast howled - a sound all too human from such an inhuman throat - before collapsing onto the ground. All around them, the battle transformed from a measured assault to desperate close-quarters combat. The narrow passages of Blackfire Hold became killing grounds, where the Sacred Desert warriors fought not just for victory but for survival itself. "They have been breeding these... things," Aran said, cutting down an enemy, his voice tight with disgust as he joined Rafiq in the front lines. "The House of Draco continues to delve too deep into forbidden knowledge."

"Talk less, fight more," Rafiq jested, pulling his blade from another fallen monster. His eyes scanned the chaos. "Rhaskar is here. I can feel it. He's the head of the serpent - cut him down, and these abominations lose their master." Aran caught his friend's arm. "I beg you not to go alone. These passages are a maze of -"

"I know the way," Rafiq interrupted, his face set with grim determination. "You, contrastingly, are needed here, my friend. You are the king, and our men look up to you." A smile flickered across his battle-stained face. "Besides," he gave his brother-in-arms a reassuring nod, "I have been waiting for this reckoning."

Before Aran could protest further, Rafiq plunged deeper into the fortress, cutting a path through any who stood in his way. His mind was clear, focused on a single purpose. The teachings of his father coupled with his King's - the philosophy of fighting not for glory but for protection - had forged him into something more than a mere skilled warrior. Each strike of his blades was more precise and economical. He no longer fought with rage but with conviction.

"The Draco must fall," he thought, sidestepping a scaled monstrosity and hamstringing it with a backwards slash. "For all they have done. For all they will continue to do if left alive."

The inner sanctum of Blackfire Hold rose before him - a cathedral of stone dedicated to war, its walls adorned with the weapons of fallen enemies. There, upon the steps leading to the altar, stood Rhaskar.

The Draconian warlord was a mountain of a warrior. Clad in armour black as the abyss, with pauldrons sculpted to resemble dragon heads, he seemed more statue than flesh. His war axe - a brutal instrument large enough to cleave a steed in two - rested casually on one broad shoulder.

"Rafiq ibn Azim," Rhaskar's voice rumbled through the chamber, a sound that belonged in the depths of Zarah rather than from a living being. "I wondered which of you would come for me. The king? The shadow? No... the Sacred Blade." His scaled lips peeled back in what might have been a smile, revealing teeth filed to points. "How fitting."

Rafiq stepped into the chamber, his twin swords held low at his sides. "You have crippled us for too long, Rhaskar. Your House has twisted nature itself, fallen victim to its own hubris. And for what? For vengeance?" he needed to understand the madness.

"Revenge?" Rhaskar laughed, the sound echoing from the stone walls. "You mistake me, desert dweller. This is not vengeance. We do not mourn our dead. No, this is reclamation. My House ruled these lands when your ancestors were still learning to make fire. Here, we were gods among insects."

"I know my history. You were tyrants, no different than the Old Kings." Rafiq countered, slowly circling, measuring the distance between them. "Now you are a relic - the last gasp of a dying line."

Rhaskar tilted his head, wondering if Rafiq knew that he was, in fact, the last warrior of the Varros Line, on Zarah. His eyes narrowed, the tyrian purple glow within them intensifying. "You have been striking back since the day you drew breath. But tonight," he hefted his massive axe with surprising speed, "it ends!"
"For once," Rafiq smirked, raising his twin blades, "we agree on something."

The two warriors clashed with a sound like thunder. Rhaskar's axe swung in a devastating arc that would have cleaved Rafiq in two had he not twisted aside at the last moment. The blade missed him by a hair's breadth, striking the stone floor with such force that sparks erupted from the impact.
"Fast," Rafiq thought, "too fast for his size." He countered with a flurry of strikes, his twin swords seeking gaps in Rhaskar's armour. The hulking warlord blocked most with the haft of his axe, but one blade slipped through, drawing first blood from his forearm. Rhaskar bellowed - more in rage than pain - and launched a counterattack. The massive axe became a blur in his hands, forcing Rafiq to give ground, to focus entirely on defence. Each impact against his swords sent shockwaves up his arms.
"You fight well," Rhaskar growled between strikes. "But can you match this?" With fluid motion, he suddenly kicked a nearby brazier, sending burning coals scattering across the floor toward Rafiq. In the moment of distraction, Rhaskar closed the distance, his axe sweeping low.
Rafiq leapt over the strike, but Rhaskar had anticipated this. The Draconian titan's armoured fist smashed into Rafiq's chest in mid-air, sending him crashing into a pillar with bone-jarring force. Stars exploded behind Rafiq's eyes as he slumped to the floor, struggling to breathe.
"Get up," he commanded himself. "Get up or die right here, right now."
Rhaskar approached, twirling his axe. "Where is your king's philosophy now, blade of the desert? Does it comfort you to know you die for a noble cause?"
Rafiq used the pillar to pull himself up, "Do not worry yourself about me," he looked his foe in the eyes and spat blood on the ground, "I do not plan on dying tonight."
Rhaskar took a step forward. "No one ever does," the hulking warrior mocked.
Rafiq launched himself forward, feinting with his left blade while the right sought Rhaskar's exposed neck. The reptilian warlord parried the feint - exactly as Rafiq had hoped - but the true strike was blocked at the last moment by Rhaskar's vambrace. The two warriors separated, circling

again, each reassessing the other. "You have improved since our last encounter," Rhaskar admitted, rolling his massive shoulders.

"Last encounter?" Rafiq frowned, trying to recall if they had met in battle before.

"The Battle of Sarim," Rhaskar's eyes glittered. "I was there, though we did not cross blades. I watched you fight Vhaskar. I studied you. Though you lost that night, word has reached me that you killed him. Congratulations," his eyes were ablaze, "but I seriously doubt that you will get lucky twice." Rhaskar caressed his axe.

"He's trying to unsettle me," Rafiq realized. "Stay focused."

Lightning illuminated the chamber through the high windows, casting their shadows in stark relief against the walls. In that moment of brilliant clarity, both warriors charged. What followed was a dance of death, each movement precise, each strike potentially lethal. Rafiq moved like the desert wind - fast, relentless, slipping past Rhaskar's guard to land, glancing blows before retreating from devastating counterattacks.

Rhaskar fought like a mountain avalanche - both speed and overwhelming force channelled into calculated destruction.

Rafiq's twin blades wove patterns of silver light in the air, seeking weaknesses, creating openings. A cut here, a thrust there - a combination of small wounds that began to accumulate as the duel stretched on.

Rhaskar's axe crashed against pillars when Rafiq dodged, shattering stone. The warlord, in desperation, used everything at his disposal - furniture, wall hangings, even the bodies of fallen warriors who had tried to intervene in their duel.

"You cannot win," Rhaskar panted, blood seeping from a dozen minor wounds. "I am the future of this world. The House of Draco will rise again."

"No," Rafiq countered, his own breathing laboured, a gash across his forehead dripping blood into his left eye. "You are the past. Like a nightmare that refuses to fade away."

Rain began to fall through the shattered ceiling, mingling with blood on the stone floor. During their clash, the sounds of battle elsewhere in the fortress had grown distant, as if the world beyond this chamber had ceased to exist.

Rhaskar suddenly changed tactics, abandoning his measured approach for a berserker fury. His axe became a whirlwind of death as he charged forward, pushing Rafiq back step by step.

"He's tiring," Rafiq realized. "Making one final effort." A mistake - a slight overextension on a wide swing - was all Rafiq needed. He ducked beneath the axe and drove both swords into Rhaskar's side, finding the gap between breastplate and backplate. The hulking Draconian roared in pain but did not fall.

He dropped his axe and seized Rafiq by the throat with one massive hand, lifting him off the ground. "If I die," he snarled, blood bubbling from his scaled lips, "you die with me."

Rafiq's vision began to darken as Rhaskar's grip tightened. Before losing consciousness, with the last of his strength, he pulled one sword free and drove it upward, beneath Rhaskar's chin, through his mouth, and into his brain.

The warlord's eyes widened in shock. His grip loosened. For a moment that stretched into eternity, the two warriors stared at each other - one in triumph, one in disbelief.

Then, with a final guttural shriek that seemed to contain centuries of hatred, Rhaskar fell. His massive body tumbled down the steps of the sanctum, each impact a thunder of metal on stone, his blood mingling with the rain that poured through the broken roof.

Rafiq collapsed to his knees, gasping for breath, his swords slipping from numb fingers. Around him, the battle for Blackfire Hold continued, but something fundamental had changed. With Rhaskar's death, the tide had turned.

Outside the sanctum, the twisted creatures of the Draco suddenly faltered as if a puppet master had released their strings. The warriors of the Sacred Desert pressed their advantage, pushing deeper into the fortress.

Aran and Sura found Rafiq still kneeling beside Rhaskar's body, silent and contemplative. "It is done, then," Aran said quietly, placing a hand on his friend's shoulder.

Sura watched, in silence, as Rafiq nodded, his eyes still fixed on the fallen warlord. Victory felt righteous, though it had come with a heavy toll. "But at what cost?" He demanded from the heavens. Then, facing Aran, he asked for the price of his choices. "How many did we lose today?" It cost him dearly to utter these words. Every syllable burned like fire in his throat.

"Too many," Aran admitted. "But they died protecting our world from... this." He gestured to the chambers beyond, where the Sacred Warriors had discovered laboratories filled with evidence of the House of Draco's foul experiments.

The choices one makes for one's charge are never easy, and Rafiq's next was, undoubtedly, his hardest. To burn the Draco away from this place, including his students, those nameless sons of Zarah, who dared stand for its survival.

"We shall burn it all," Rafiq said, slowly rising to his feet. "Cleanse this place with fire."

As dawn broke over Blackfire Hold, the fortress burned - a beacon visible for miles across the desert. A necessary sacrifice, but they would rebuild, they always did. The surviving warriors of the Sacred Desert stood in silence, honouring both their victory and their fallen comrades. Their eyes rested upon their commander, Rafiq, 'The Lion of the Sacred Desert'.

He watched the flames, his twin swords wiped and sheathed across his back. The battle had been won, but the war - the eternal struggle against those who would twist nature and enslave others - continued.

Rafiq, the Grandmaster of the Order of the Sacred Desert, looked at his king and queen, his friends. "What now?" Sura asked, although she knew the answer.

"Now?" Rafiq drew one sword. "If they dare to return, we strike back," he whispered, echoing Rhaskar's words but giving them new meaning.

Throwing a wink at Aran, he added. "We will always strike back."

When dawn broke over the Kataran Mountains, Blackfire Hold was no more.

The Draco's, supposedly, last stronghold had been reduced to ruins, its warlord slain, their forces scattered to the winds. Yet, as Rafiq, Aran, and Sura stood atop the highest tower, looking down at the destruction they had wrought, they felt no triumph. For they knew the truth. The House of Draco had always been patient, and they wouldn't give up on Zarah so easily.

The sands of Zarah shift, ever-changing, but some things remain. Though the great war against the House of Draco has long since faded into legend, the echoes of their corruption still linger in the hidden places of this world. So, too, does the Order of the Sacred Desert, its warriors still walking unseen paths, their blades still honed, their oaths unbroken.

The Order does not march in armies unless at times of the utmost need. It has no banners, no cities, and no grand temples in its name. It does not stand as a kingdom or a nation, for its purpose is not to rule.

Thus, the Order of the Sacred Desert exists as a whisper, a force unseen, its members scattered like grains of sand across Zarah.

They are not an open brotherhood, such as the one they belong to, for their work demands secrecy. To be known is to be hunted, and to be hunted is to risk failure. Instead, the Order survives in fragments - small enclaves hidden within the labyrinthine alleys of ancient cities, in sanctuaries carved deep into canyon walls, in the profound silence of the desert where few feet dare tread.

Only those deemed worthy find their way into the Order. There are no formal invitations, no open initiations. A recruit is chosen only after they have proven themselves - not through battle, for many can do that, but through conviction. Only those who understand the weight of the Order's purpose may take its oath.

However, when the pledge is taken, they cease to be of their former life, becoming part of something older than any kingdom, something beyond name and bloodline. They become the last line of defence against the ever-returning shadow.

Nowadays, the House of Draco no longer holds dominion over Zarah, but its remnants persist in secret. There is always the odd Draconian Warlord seeking to rekindle the old ways, and those who whisper of ancient powers best left undisturbed. In the shadows, the Order listens.

In the courts of every kingdom in Zarah, from Sayf to Yara, in the alleys of merchant cities, in the distant outposts where few dare venture, the warriors of the Sacred Desert move unseen.

When a noble grows too ambitious, whispering of power beyond mortal reach, a shadow falls upon them. When an underground cult dares invoke the rites of the old serpent gods, their temple is reduced to ruin before dawn. When rumours of the House of Draco's bloodline resurface, the Order ensures that such blood never reaches a throne. They do not seek war, but at times when it seems unavoidable, they end it before it can begin.

Though they are warriors, the Sacred Desert is also a keeper of knowledge.

After the War of the Weaving, under Aran's teachings, Rafiq finally understood that the greatest threat coming from the House of Draco was not its strength but its knowledge. The way they twisted truth, how they bent history to their will, how they hid in plain sight. So, the Order of the Sacred Desert became more than just a blade. It became a vault.

There are still places in Zarah where no traveller walks, where only the wind stirs the dunes. In those places, the Order has hidden what must never be found.

Scrolls of the old Draconian sorceries, writings of their forbidden arts, knowledge too dangerous for any ruler to wield, but too precious to be destroyed - all locked away in sanctuaries known only to the King, and those highest among the Order.

Even among their own ranks, there are secrets that remain veiled. Only the Grandmaster of the Sacred Desert knows where every vault lies, and such knowledge is never written. For if the House of Draco ever returns in force, it will not be with an army. It will be with knowledge.

Though they are spectacular warriors, they have learned long ago that most cunning of lessons - that lies will get you farther and faster than weapons.

With the passing of the centuries, the rulers of the House of Aran no longer call upon the Sacred Desert as their forefathers once did. In the current Age, most believe them to be a relic of the past, a tale told by merchants to frighten the greedy into caution. Others even doubt they ever truly existed.

The Order of the Sacred Desert allows these rumours to spread. For as long as the world forgets, their enemies grow bold. Boldness breeds recklessness and in their foes' moment of weakness. They will reveal themselves.

The warriors of the Sacred Desert do not seek recognition, nor do they seek gratitude. They seek only the promise their predecessors made so long ago, beneath the twin moons, when their blades were first drawn from the sand.

A promise they hold true to this day. That the Draco shall never rise again, and Zarah shall nevermore fall into the serpent's grasp. That when the serpent slithers, there will always be a blade in the night to cut it down.

For as long as Leander's primary rises over the dunes, the Order of the Sacred Desert shall endure.

End of "The Sacred Oath"

Appendix VIII. Tales From Myth and Legend

The history of The MiddleVerse, is written not only in stone and blood but in the whispers of legend and the echoes of myth.

What follows, in our *Echoing Archives*, are the Tales of Zarah, stories passed down through generations, chronicling the deeds of kings, warriors, and the forces that shaped the fate of its deserts. These tales, such as The Tales of the Old Kings, the legend of Uramak, the saga of Ashira of the Sands, of Amira of the Qarr, the reign of Queen Amara, and the harrowing account of The Great Sandstorm Crisis, serve as both history and prophecy, immortalizing the struggles and triumphs that shaped Zarah's destiny.

Beyond these ancient chronicles lies one of the most guarded sections of our archives - The Lost Dialogues, a small collection of private conversations between Barash ibn Sulaym and Khalid ibn Rashid, father of King Aran I. Long withheld from the main narrative, these exchanges unveil hidden truths, unspoken fears, and the quiet wisdom of those who foresaw the gathering storm, long before Zarah's fate was sealed. And yet, even these spoken memories give way to the greater pattern - the Chronology of Legends and Legacy, where the echoes of all things converge.

"The Tale of the Old Kings and the Binding of the Primordials" (12,000–10,000 years ago)

The Realms of the Old Kings

Before Zarah was shaped by the hands of men, before its cities rose from the sands, there were the Old Kings. Hailing from the stars, they ruled over their Seven Realms on the planet. Each domain was a reflection of their strength, their wisdom, and their deepest desires. Legends say that these kings were not born of flesh alone but were touched by something older, something beyond mortal comprehension - a fragment of divinity, a tether to the forces that shaped the cosmos itself. Whispers among the oldest scholars speak of a Divine Experiment from which they derived, though such tales are seldom spoken aloud.

Their realms were not simply kingdoms of men, but living extensions of their sovereigns' will, realms woven into the very fabric of the planet's Weaving, bound by ancient science that mirrored their rulers' essence.

Each kingdom thrived under its sovereign's might, but beneath the grandeur, there was an ever-present shadow - the knowledge that such power came at a cost, that the very forces they ruled over would one day seek to reclaim what had been borrowed.

The Seven Realms and Their Kings

The Realm of Eternal Flame – *King Varuth the Incandescent*
The land of *Varuth* was a domain of ceaseless fire, where the very ground burned with molten rivers that carved their way through obsidian valleys. His cities, sculpted from blackened stone, stood resilient against the inferno, towering monuments of a kingdom that thrived in heat where no others could. His people were forged like the metal of their weapons, hardened by flame and unyielding in battle. It was said that *Varuth* himself was born of fire, that he carried the embers of the first forge within his heart, and that no mortal blade could pierce his flesh. He was both a king and a god-smith, and in his realm, no war was fought without his hand shaping the steel that would spill blood. After Aran's unification of the tribes, these lands would later become the *Kingdom of Shamas*.

The Realm of the Endless Tide – *Queen Ithara the Drowned*
In an age when Zarah was blessed with twin oceans instead of the single one it bears today, *Ithara* ruled over both their boundless expanses. She was a queen whose will was as unpredictable as the tides she commanded. Her kingdom was no mere collection of coastal islands, but an empire that sprawled beneath the waves, where the ruins of her long lost civilization lay hidden, beneath the deep water of the Yaran ocean. It was whispered that her people did not drown, for the ocean had embraced them as its own, binding their souls to its depths. To outsiders, the sea was a cruel mistress, swallowing fleets whole and dragging sailors to watery graves, but to those who belonged to *Ithara*, it was a cradle, a kingdom where the ocean sang in whispers and the tides obeyed only one voice. After Aran's unification of the tribes, these lands would later become the *Kingdom of Yara*.

The Realm of the Shadowed Vale – *King Nathair the Veiled*
The land of the Vale was a kingdom unseen, a place where shadows moved of their own accord and whispers slithered through the air like unseen serpents. It was a place where the sun dared not linger, where the moon cast only half-light, as if fearing to illuminate what should

remain in darkness. It is whispered that *Nathair* was a Draconian in disguise.

His cities lay hidden beneath the earth, vast labyrinths carved into the bedrock, guarded by those who spoke in hushed tones and walked unseen. It was said that *Nathair* knew every secret ever spoken, that even the wind conspired to whisper its truths into his ear. He was the architect of conspiracy, the silent watcher, the unseen hand behind every war waged in the name of ignorance. This realm was where the Wardens of the Weaving went to live in exile after they were betrayed by the rulers of Zarah. On that fateful night, most of their order were either killed, or they scattered throughout the planet's deserts.

<u>The Realm of the Wailing Winds</u> – *King Aerion the Soaring*
Aerion's domain was not of the land but of the sky, a kingdom built upon floating citadels that drifted with the wind. His people were born into the clouds, their homes anchored to great spires of rock that pierced the heavens. The winds carried their voices, their prayers, and their armies, for they alone commanded the storm. It was said that *Aerion* himself could fly upon the wings of the tempest, that his eyes burned with the fury of the storm, and that no arrow loose from mortal hands could find its mark upon him. His kingdom was unreachable by the armies of men, for the winds themselves turned against those who sought to claim what belonged to the sky. After Aran's unification of the tribes, these lands would later become the *Kingdom of Kartal.*

<u>The Realm of the Verdant Throne</u> – *Queen Sylthia the Rooted*
In the heart of the ancient Medjool oasis, where Solarwood Trees touched the heavens and roots burrowed deep into the bones of the earth, *Sylthia* ruled. Her kingdom was no mere woodland, but a living entity, an expanse where nature itself was sentient, its will bound to hers. The trees whispered her name, the rivers carried her voice, and the beasts of the land knelt in her presence. Her people did not carve cities from stone but grew them from the very lifeblood of the oases. It was said that she could hear Zarah's heartbeat, that the very essence of life pulsed through her veins, and that no blade could strike her down so long as a single root remained unbroken. After Aran's unification of the tribes, these lands would later become the *Kingdom of Arsian.*

<u>The Realm of the Ivory Sands</u> – *King Korvath the Unyielding*
He ruled from the mountains, where the desert stretched beyond the horizon, where Leander's primary had little strength and cold reigned supreme, the dunes shifting with the will of the wind.

His was a kingdom carved from the bones of fallen empires, built atop the ruins of those who had dared to claim dominion over these crystalline sands.

His people moved like phantoms, unseen until it was too late, striking from the veil of the desert's embrace. Legend tells that he did not bleed as mortal men did, that the sun had burned weakness from his bones, leaving behind only a king made of gold and stone. His empire was eternal, for the sands remembered all, swallowing those who defied him and preserving the names of those who swore loyalty in whispers carried upon the wind. After Aran's unification of the tribes, these lands would later become the *Kingdom of Qamar*.

<u>The Realm of the Silent Depths</u> – *King Maelor the Pale*
In the realm of *Maelor*, death was not an ending but a beginning. His kingdom was a vast necropolis, where the spirits of the dead walked as freely as the living. His people did not fear the end, for they knew that he watched over them even beyond the veil of mortality. His city of bone and silver stood eternal, where the echoes of lost souls lingered, whispering of truths forgotten by time. It was said that *Maelor* himself did not draw breath, that his body had long since withered, but his will remained, bound to the thin thread between life and death. He did not rule through fear, but through reverence, for all who lived would one day come to kneel before the Pale King. After Aran's unification of the tribes, these lands would later become the *Kingdom of Sayf*.

Each of these realms stood as a pillar of power, a testament to the sovereignty of those who ruled them. Nevertheless, the Star-Kings and Queens knew that power was not given freely. It was borrowed, and one day, the debt would come due. With the passage of time, the world kept turning, the Old Kings reigning in majesty, unaware that their time would soon come to an end. For the Primordials had begun to stir.

<u>The Binding of the Primordials</u>
The Primordials were not beings of flesh and bone but of pure, unbound essence - forces of creation and destruction that predated even the stars. They were the architects of existence, entities older than time, who wove the foundations of the cosmos with neither order nor reason, only instinct and ceaseless renewal. They were neither benevolent nor malevolent, for such concepts were foreign to them. They simply were, and when they turned their gaze upon Zarah, the Seven Realms trembled.

They descended upon the kingdoms like an unrelenting tide, unmaking and reshaping as they pleased. *Varuth's* eternal flames dimmed as the Primordial of Ash sought to consume the fire's heart. *Ithara's* tides turned against her, rising in monstrous waves under the will of the Primordial of Depths.

Nathair's shadows, once loyal to their master, slithered with a will of their own as the Primordial of Night whispered forbidden secrets into the dark.

The Old Kings, despite their might, were but leaves before a storm. They fought, and they faltered. Their will could not harm the formless. Their technologies were swallowed by the abyss. For the first time, they learned the meaning of fear.

The Council of Kings

In the ruins of the Celestial Spire, the Old Kings gathered, their great banners torn, their armour stained with blood not their own. The sky above them was split with colourless fire, and the echoes of the Primordials' might rang through the heavens. Their kingdoms were crumbling, and with them, the very fabric of the world. *Ithara*, Queen of the Endless Tide, her armour crusted with salt, spoke first. "We cannot fight the tide. We must shape it."

Varuth, wreathed in the embers of his fading flames, struck the table with a gauntleted fist, molten sparks dancing from his fingertips. "Then we must forge their essence into form. Bind them before they unravel all that we have built."

Aerion, his wind-touched cloak in tatters, folded his arms. "What of the cost? Even if we succeed, we will not walk away unchanged."

Maelor, pale and silent, the whisper of the dead clinging to his form like mist, finally spoke. His voice was but a breath, yet it carried across the chamber with the weight of prophecy. "We must become the chains. To seal them, we must give of ourselves."

The Kings knew the truth of it. They knew that to shackle the Primordials, they would have to offer more than their power, more than their lives. They would have to bind their very souls to the task, sacrificing their claim to the Weaving so that balance might be restored. One by one, they gave their solemn oaths. One by one, they surrendered to fate.

The Obelisks and the Blood Price

The Kings, in their final act of defiance against the Primordials, fashioned twelve obelisks, each a prison meant to hold a fragment of a cosmic force that refused to be tamed.

For these were not simple stones nor mere artefacts of enchantment, but towering monoliths of raw power carved from the obsidian bones of the planet itself.

The obelisks were constructed not with mortal hands alone but through the very life essence of the Old Kings, imbued with their will, their suffering, and their unyielding duty. Each obelisk became more than a cage - they were scars upon the world, a testament to the terrible price of balance. The Kings did not simply create these prisons. They became those same prisons.

<u>The Ritual of the Twelvefold Binding</u>
On the eve of the final battle, the Kings gathered one last time atop the Celestial Spire, where the Weaving was strongest. There, under a sky split with cracks of unearthly light, they spoke the first words of the Twelvefold Binding, a ritual so ancient and powerful that the very stars above seemed to dim in its presence.

The air grew thick, charged with a force beyond mortal reckoning, as the Old Kings and Queens each stepped forward, each in a different part of Zarah. Their bodies were already beginning to wane, their flesh fading as they offered themselves to the eternal struggle. The star rulers bound themselves to seven tethers. The remaining five obelisks were bound to aspects of creation: life, death, time, space, and fate.

Led by *Layla*, daughter of *Queen Ithara*, one by one, from wherever they stood on Zarah, they cast their bindings:

Varuth, his body wreathed in dying flame, summoned forth the Forge of Eternity, a furnace of unquenchable fire. As he uttered the final words of sealing, his form was consumed in a great inferno, his very essence fused into the molten veins of the world. His obelisk, a pillar of obsidian laced with fire, stood deep within the heart of the mountains, where the Primordial of Flame raged within its unbreakable crucible.

Ithara, standing upon the abyssal precipice of the world's deepest trench, called forth the Tomb of the Abyss. With a final breath, she cast herself into the fathomless depths, her body dissolving into the dark embrace of the sea. Her obelisk, a towering column of black obsidian, was placed in the depths of what is now called the Old Quarter of Sarim. This is where the Primordial of Tides would remain locked in eternal slumber.

Nathair, veiled in shadows, stepped into the eternal void beneath the world. There, he whispered his own name into the blackness and, in doing so, erased himself from history. His obelisk, a monolith of shifting darkness, was buried beneath the forgotten ruins of Valamar, where the Primordial of Night lay coiled in the unseen depths.

Aerion, standing atop the highest peak of the world, let the storm take him. The winds howled as his form shattered into the sky, becoming one with the tempests he had once commanded. His obelisk was left atop the mountains of Eltor, where the Primordial of Storms raged, bound by the whispers of his lost king.

Sylthia, the heart of the oases, knelt before the Great Solarwood Tree, her body sinking into the ancient roots. The earth trembled as the very essence of nature claimed her, transforming her into the lifeblood of the land itself. Her obelisk stood in the heart of the last untouched glade, where the Primordial of Growth slumbered beneath the roots of the world. This was the second obelisk Aran destroyed.

Korvath, standing in the endless dunes, bled into the sands, offering his final breath to the desert. His warriors watched in silence as his form disintegrated, the wind carrying away his name, his past, his presence. His obelisk was left in the Sea of Ash, amongst the endless shifting dunes, keeping the Primordial of Earth locked away beneath the very land it sought to command, protected by a guardian.

Maelor, the last to stand, stepped beyond the veil of life. He did not speak, did not fight, and did not rage against his fate. Instead, he embraced it. His soul left his body, slipping into the unseen world of the dead, becoming the eternal warden of what lay beyond. His obelisk, Aran's last, stood upon the threshold between life and death, in the mountains of Paligenis, where the Primordial of Decay was sealed within the void that even time dared not touch.

When the final binding was complete, the world fell silent. The sky no longer burned. The waters no longer raged. The winds stilled, the shadows retreated, and the earth quieted. The Primordials were defeated but not destroyed. They were bound but not gone. For what had existed before time itself could never truly die.

And so began the age of mortals, walking unknowingly upon ground sacred with sacrifice, living their days under the watchful presence of prisons built from the souls of gods. The obelisks remained silent sentinels across the face of Zarah - their true purpose forgotten by most, remembered only in the oldest tales. Yet with each one that Aran would later destroy, the ancient bindings weakened, and somewhere deep within the fabric of existence, the Primordials stirred once more in their eternal slumber, awaiting the day when all chains would break and the world would know their touch again.

<u>Aran's Forebears and the Unfinished Oath</u>
The world had long since forgotten the names of the Old Kings, their sacrifice buried beneath the sands of time, their deeds reduced to whispered myths carried on the desert wind.
The great cities of the Seven Realms crumbled into dust, their towering monuments worn smooth by the hands of centuries.
Though the Kings had vanished from the annals of Zarah's history, their legacy endured - not in stone or scripture, but in blood and sand.
The chronicles speak of when the Old Kings gave their final sacrifice, the Weaving took something from them in return. Not all of them were wholly erased. A fragment of their essence, a lingering ember of their immortal souls, was passed on - not into temples or relics, but into a single bloodline. A lineage meant to bear the burden of their unfinished oath.
Many centuries before Aran's birth, this bloodline was no longer royal nor noble. It did no more sit upon thrones or wear crowns of gold. Instead, it wandered the world unseen, drifting like autumn leaves upon the river of fate.
It lived in scholars, traders, and warriors, in poets and prophets, in the hearts of those who carried the weight of destiny without ever knowing its full measure.
The first of Aran's ancestors were called the Watchers, those who walked unseen in the world, their duty passed from father to son, from mother to daughter. They did not build kingdoms nor seek glory, for their purpose was far greater than conquest or rule. They were the silent keepers of the obelisks, bound by an oath older than any kingdom, sworn to guard the sacred prisons lest the bindings fail.
Over the centuries, the bloodline thinned, and the knowledge faded. What had once been an unbroken chain of duty became fractured. The Watchers became wanderers, their purpose lost to the erosion of time. Some abandoned the oath entirely, choosing to live as ordinary men and women, blissfully unaware of the old legacy carried in their veins. Others, sensing the old magic in their blood, sought the path of scholars and mystics, yearning for knowledge they could not name.
By the time Aran ibn Khalid was born, the Watchers were nothing more than ghosts of a forgotten age, their purpose lost, their numbers

scattered. Yet, as the House of Tempus knows, fate is not so easily unwound.

Precisely for that reason, to fully understand how deeply steeped in ancient history his birth was, one must travel back to Zarah's distant past. For it was long ago, in the ruins of an ancient city, beneath a sky heavy with storm clouds, that the prophecy was first spoken.

The Al'Shara tribe began roaming the planet around three thousand, five hundred years ago, and through the ages, they became part of the Rasha tribe.

Sura al-Rasha, Aran's wife, was direct descendant of that tribe. In those ancient days, a woman named Shara, one of, if not the first moon seer on Zarah, was able to pierce the veil of years.

She sat, surrounded by members of her tribe, gazing into the embers of the dying fire and saw what was to come.

Her voice deepened, and her eyes glazed with silver light as words poured forth that were not her own. "The Weaving frays. The chains weaken. The slumbering ones stir. The last son of the forgotten kings shall walk the path of shadow and fire. Blood shall call to blood, and the world shall tremble."

As the final words left her lips, the fire before her flared with unnatural brilliance, then died to ash in an instant. Many dismissed it as ramblings, while a few, those who still held faith in the old ways, listened in solemn silence, knowing the time would come when Shara's words would bear terrible truth.

<u>Aran ibn Khalid's Inheritance</u>

Aran did not grow up in a palace, nor was he raised with the knowledge of his true ancestry. He was a warrior, a leader forged in the fires of hardship, his destiny unfolding before him like the shifting dunes of the desert. But the blood of the Old Kings ran in his veins, whether he knew it or not.

He had always felt it - the unseen force that pulled him forward, the whisper of something greater lingering at the edge of his thoughts. He had been drawn to places he could not explain, felt the weight of choices he did not understand. The first time he touched an obelisk, he felt it awaken - not in the stone, but in himself.

His dreams, already frequent for years, soon after became more intense and recurring. Visions of fire and water, of storm and shadow. Of kings whose names had long since faded, yet whose eyes burned with the same golden fire that flickered in his own. They spoke to him, not in words, but in memories, fragmented thoughts of a battle fought before time itself. A choice made at the cost of everything, accompanied with a warning - the seals are breaking, the Primordials are stirring, and you must finish what we began.

He never shared these dreams with anyone, not even Sura or Rafiq, for at the time, he did not understand them himself. However, he knew something was coming. He could feel it in the bones of the world, in the air before a storm, in the whispers that curled through what he yet didn't know was the Weaving, like unravelling threads. After the death of his brother, he was the last of his bloodline, the final heir to an oath made in a time before memory, and the burden now rested on his shoulders alone.

Would he rise to meet it? Would he forge a new path where the Old Kings had fallen? Or would he too be swallowed by the tide, another name lost to time, another broken link in a chain that had stretched across eternity?

There was no answer, only the path ahead, winding through the sands of Zarah, toward an end he could not yet see. Beyond that path, the shadows clouded everything.

<u>The Whisper of the Old Kings</u>
The night was thick with silence. Not the quiet of peace, nor the gentle hush of a resting world, but a silence that pressed upon the soul, that spoke of something waiting beyond the veil of reality. The air was heavy, thick with the scent of old stone and lingering echoes of voices long past. The company had just returned from Ryvath back to Sarim, after Aran faced the trials of the Old Kings.

Deep underground, in the ancient crypt below the Old Quarter of Sarim, he stood alone before the remnants of the first obelisk. Its towering, though shattered, form was etched with ancient glyphs that pulsed with a faint, ghostly light. The stone was cold beneath his fingertips, but as his hand rested upon its surface, a shiver ran through his bones - not from the chill but from the presence that stirred within. Even though it was broken, he could feel them watching. Not with eyes, but with something deeper, something woven into the very fabric of existence. The Old Kings had not truly faded.

A gust of wind curled through the ruins, carrying with it a whisper, soft as dying embers. It was not the wind that spoke. It was something older, something bound to the world long before men had given names to the stars.

"You stand where we once stood." The voice was as deep as the earth itself, resonating through Aran's very bones. In fact, it was not one voice, but many - layered upon each other, woven together like strands of fate. He swallowed, his pulse steady but his breath uneven. He had heard whispers before but never like this. Never with such weight. "The binding is failing."

The words were not spoken in anger or fear. They were a warning, an undeniable truth etched into the foundation of reality itself. Aran had been responsible for the destruction of two obelisks, and now the others were weakening. The seals that held the Primordials at bay had begun to unravel, their ancient chains fraying like threads pulled too tight for too long.

A second voice joined the first, like the tide pulling against the shore, an echo from the depths of time. "You carry the burden of our sins."

Aran's fingers curled against the stone. "I did not ask for this." His voice was steady, but beneath it lay the weight of a man who had spent his life running after a destiny he did not fully understand. "Neither did we," came the reply, this time like the sighing of wind through forgotten halls. "And yet we bore it. As must you."

A presence stirred within the obelisk, a flicker of something vast and distant, a great shadow cast from an unseen light.

Then, another whisper - barely more than a breath, yet it sent a tremor through Aran's soul.

"Will you finish what we began? Or will the world burn?"

The question was not a challenge, nor a plea. It was simply the last truth that remained.

Aran closed his eyes. He could feel the weight of the ages pressing down upon him, could hear the echoes of those who had come before. The Kings who had given everything of themselves. The Watchers who had faded into dust. Now, it was his turn.

For so long, he had fought against this, had clung to the idea that he was free to choose his own fate. But fate did not bargain. It did not bend to the will of men. It called, and in the end, all must answer.

Around him, the air began to shimmer with ethereal light. The broken obelisk pulsed with renewed energy, casting long shadows that seemed to move of their own accord. In those shadows, figures began to take shape - translucent silhouettes crowned in fading glory. The Seven Kings and Queens stood in a spectral semicircle, their features blurred by time, but their presence undeniable.

Varuth's form flickered with inner flame, his eyes two embers in the darkness. *Ithara's* silhouette rippled like water disturbed by a stone. *Nathair* was little more than a shadow among shadows, his outline constantly shifting. *Aerion's* presence stirred the air into gentle currents that whispered through Aran's hair. *Sylthia's* form seemed woven from strands of living light, as if the very essence of nature had taken shape. *Korvath* stood solid as mountain stone, his phantom gaze fixed upon Aran with the weight of judgment. *Maelor*, pale even in spirit form, watched with eyes that had witnessed the birth and death of countless generations.

They spoke not with lips but with thoughts that echoed in Aran's mind, their voices blending into a chorus of ancient power. "We gave what we could, but it was not enough. The bindings weaken. The Primordials stir. What was once sealed may soon break free. You are the last of our line, the final thread in a tapestry woven across the ages. The choice is yours, as it once was ours. But know this - should you fail, all that is, all that was, and all that could be will fall into the void."

Aran opened his eyes, his breath steady now. He was no longer just himself. He was the last of a broken lineage, the final strand in a tapestry woven by hands long since turned to dust. After their trials, he could feel them now - not just the voices but their presence, lingering just beyond the veil. They were waiting for his answer. He straightened his shoulders, his hand still upon the obelisk. The blood of kings flowed in his veins, but it was the heart of a warrior that beat in his chest. He would not run from destiny any longer. "I am not you," he said, his voice gaining strength with each word. "I am not bound by your mistakes or your regrets. But I will not let this world fall to chaos."

The spectral kings watched in silence, their forms wavering like candles in a breeze. "I will find a way to strengthen the seals," Aran continued. "Not through sacrifice alone, but through unity. Not through binding, but through understanding." A murmur passed through the ethereal gathering, a ripple of surprise - or perhaps hope.

The wind whispered once more, carrying the weight of the past, the sorrow of what had been lost, and the hope of what might yet be. Aran inhaled deeply, then stepped back from the obelisk. He turned his gaze upward towards the surface, where the path ahead lay in shadow and fire. Then he spoke, not a whisper but a vow that echoed through the ancient chamber like thunder.

"I will finish it. Not as you began it, but as it must end. Not through death, but through life. The Primordials will be contained, but I will find a way that does not demand the price you paid." As the final word left his lips, the spectres of the Old Kings and Queens began to fade, their forms dissolving into motes of light that spiralled upward and vanished into the darkness of the vast cave. Before they disappeared entirely, Aran felt something pass from them to him - not a burden but a blessing, not a chain, but a key.

In that moment, as the last echoes of their presence faded from the world, Aran understood what had always been true. He was not merely the inheritor of an ancient doom but the harbinger of a new beginning. The end of one tale and the dawn of another.
He walked from the old crypt alone but not unburdened. The weight of the world rested upon his shoulders, yet his step was light. For the first time since the dreams began, his path was clear. The Tale of the Old Kings had ended, but Aran's story had only just begun.

End of the "Tale of the Old Kings."

<u>"The Tale of Amira, of the Qarr" (10,000–6,000 years ago)</u>

A long time ago, before the great crimson and gold banners of the House of Aran fluttered over the alabaster citadels of Zarah, millennia before the name of Aran ibn Khalid was etched in the very fabric of the Weaving itself, there was born a child beneath a blood-moon sky in the remote lands of the Dahmiran Reach - an arid crescent of desert that swept along the western cliffs like the curved blade of an ancient sword, carved by merciless winds and the relentless chisel of time itself.

She was named Amira al-Qarr, daughter of Shael al-Qarr, chieftain of the Qarr tribe - an elusive and enigmatic people who drifted like living shadows across Zarah's dunes. These nomads lived at the edge of myth and memory, said to commune with the whispering spirits that dwelled deep within the ever-shifting sands. The Qarr were known throughout the deserts for their faces forever hidden behind veils of midnight blue, their haunting songs that mimicked the desert wind's lament, and their absolute, unwavering refusal to bind themselves to the blood-soaked politics of the greater tribes. They lived by one law only, passed down through generations uncounted - that the desert speaks to those who possess the patience and wisdom to listen.

Amira was born on a night when Nysa, the greater moon, turned crimson as freshly spilled blood, and the stars, in reverence or perhaps fear, veiled themselves behind a shroud of obsidian clouds. The tribe's clairvoyant, a blind woman named Tayhira whose milky eyes had witnessed visions beyond mortal comprehension, placed her ancient, trembling hands upon the infant's brow and proclaimed in a voice that seemed to rise from the depths of Zarah itself: "This child is marked by forces beyond our understanding. The very sands will test her mettle, and she will answer their call with either triumph or oblivion. May she endure what is to come, for her path shall shape the fate of more than just our people."

No one fully comprehended what Tayhira meant, not even Amira's father, who held his swaddled daughter tightly against his chest with arms still bearing the fresh scars of battle against Bahir raiders - though they were not known by that name at the time. When Shael ibn Sahal gazed down at his child's face, illuminated by the blood-moon's glow, he whispered, "Whatever comes, my daughter, know that you carry the wisdom of the Qarr in your blood. We bend like the Sand Whispers in the storm, but we do not break."

Amira grew, resilient as the Sunbloom Cactus, and curious as the Dune Jackal.

From her earliest days, it was clear she was unlike the other children of the tribe - where boys and girls played, danced, and chased one another through the dunes, their laughter carried away by the wind, Amira sat apart, perfectly still, her young face a mask of intense concentration. She listened. Always listened. To the sigh of the dunes as they shifted in their eternal dance, to the soft crackle and whispered secrets of the fire, to the distant, mournful wail of the dune jackals as they called to their kin under the twin light of Anar and Nysa.

"They are not mere sounds," she once told Tayhira as they sat together beneath the constellation of the Water Bearer, the old woman weaving complex patterns into a prayer rug while Amira watched, with fascination. "They are voices, are they not?" she asked, but did now wait for an answer. "The desert speaks to us, just as our elders have always claimed." There was a light in her eyes that went beyond mere reflections.

Tayhira's gnarled fingers paused in their work, and a smile like cracked parchment spread across her weathered face. Her blind eyes, clouded like glass caught in a sandstorm, seemed to look beyond Amira, perhaps into the girl's very future. "Then speak back, child," she said, her voice soft as a desert breeze yet weighted with significance. "Still, do so only when you are ready to be changed by the answers it gives. For the desert's truths are ancient and unforgiving, and those who hear them are never the same again."

Amira pondered these words often in the years that followed, as she grew from a curious child into a young woman of uncommon beauty and even less common wisdom. Her eyes, the colour of amber held to firelight, seemed to hold secrets gleaned from her solitary communions with the desert. Her long, raven-black hair was often adorned with small tokens she found in her wanderings - a perfectly preserved Sand Scorpion claw, a stone polished to gleaming smoothness by sand and wind, a feather from a bird no one else had ever seen. The other young men and women of the tribe both admired and feared her, for there was something in her gaze that spoke of knowledge beyond her years.

Time flowed onward like water through a wadi after the rare desert rains, and eventually, as Tayhira had foreseen, the day of reckoning came.

It was in Amira's sixteenth summer, when the heat rose from the dunes in shimmering waves and even the hardy desert creatures sought shelter from Leander's primary merciless gaze, that the Trial of Winds was called.

This sacred ritual, older than the oldest stories told around the Qarr night-fires, was both feared and revered.

Each couple of years, a youth chosen by methods known only to the tribal elders, was sent alone into the deepest reaches of the desert with nothing but a water skin, a curved ceremonial dagger of sand-forged steel, and a single set of flint and steel. They were told to survive for three days and three nights, alone with the desert and whatever secrets it might choose to reveal. Most returned, changed in ways both subtle and profound. A few did not return at all, mostly the women, their bones becoming one with the eternal sands. Though all who did come back were forever altered by what they had experienced.

That year, despite his impassioned pleas before the Council of Elders and his best efforts to prevent it through every means at his disposal, Shael ibn Sahal watched in silent anguish as his beloved daughter's name was drawn from the sacred urn.

The night before her departure, father and daughter sat together beside a small fire at the edge of the camp, the vast expanse of stars stretching endlessly above them. Shael's face was lined with worry, his eyes reflecting the dancing flames. "I could still appeal to the Council," he said, his face rough, veiling his emotions. "The bloodline of a chieftain should grant some privilege-"

"Father," Amira interrupted gently, placing her hand upon his. "The desert does not recognize privilege or bloodline. It knows only the truth. If I was chosen, then I must go."

He looked at his daughter, seeing not just the woman she had become but the memory of her mother, lost to a wasting sickness when Amira was but a child, barely into puberty. She possessed the same quiet strength, the same unflinching acceptance of fate as her mother.

"I have always felt this day would come," Amira continued, her eyes reflecting not fear but a strange anticipation. "I have heard the desert calling to me all my life. Now I must answer."

Her father closed his eyes, a single tear tracing a path down his rough, bearded face. "Then go with my blessing, daughter of my heart. But know this - should you not return, I will search for you until my own dying breath."

Amira embraced him tightly, breathing in his familiar scent of leather and Solarwood incense. "I will return," she whispered. "This, I promise you, father."

As dawn painted the eastern sky with fingers of gold and crimson, Amira stood at the edge of the encampment, dressed in the traditional garb of the Trial - simple robes of undyed cloth, a veil of the deepest blue to protect her from the sun's wrath, and sturdy sandals laced to her calves. Around her neck hung a small amulet of polished bone, a gift from her mother that she had never removed.

The entire tribe had gathered to witness her departure. Children watched with wide, solemn eyes. Women offered silent prayers to the ancient spirits. Men stood tall, their faces impassive save for the concern in their eyes, which happened every time a woman was selected to take the trial. At the front stood Tayhira, her blind gaze somehow finding Amira unerringly.

The old seer approached, her walking staff tapping a rhythm against the hard-packed sand. She reached out, her fingers finding Amira's face with uncanny precision. "The storm comes for you," she said, her voice carrying to all present despite its softness. "When it finds you, remember - do not fight against it, but neither surrender to it. Be as the sand itself, yielding yet eternal."

"I will remember," Amira replied, her voice steady despite the flutter of her heart.

With a final embrace from her father, a touch of blessing from Tayhira, and a water skin filled from the tribe's precious stores, Amira stepped into the vastness of the desert.

Leander's primary was already a molten disc climbing in the eastern sky, casting long shadows across the dunes. Her veil flapped like a broken sail behind her, and her footprints stretched back toward the safety of the camp, soon to be erased by the ever-present wind. She felt no fear, only a strange expectancy that had been building within her for as long as she could remember. As the sounds of the camp faded behind her, she whispered into the growing heat, "I am listening," and the dunes replied with a profound silence that seemed to press against her very soul.

The first day passed with painful slowness. She walked until her legs trembled with exhaustion, rationing her water with the discipline instilled in every child of Zarah. When the sun reached its zenith, she sought what little shade she could find beneath an outcropping of sun-bleached stone. As she rested, she observed a small Desert Scorpion making its deliberate way across the sand, its movements precise and purposeful. "We are not so different, you and I," she murmured to the creature. "Both testing ourselves against the desert's will."

The scorpion paused, its pincers raised as if in acknowledgement, before continuing on its journey.

When the worst heat of the day had passed, Amira continued her trek, guided by nothing but instinct and the whispered tales of those who had undergone the trial before her. As dusk approached, she found herself in a small valley between towering dunes, where the skeletal remains of a Desert Ash tree stood in mute testimony to a time when water had been more plentiful. Its limbs reached toward the darkening sky like grasping fingers turned to stone by some ancient curse.

She made camp beneath its twisted branches, kindling a small fire with her precious flint and steel, and what dead wood she could gather. That night, as the temperature plummeted in the way only desert nights could, she wrapped herself in her robes and gazed upward. The stars bloomed across the firmament like scattered diamonds on black velvet, so close it seemed she might reach up and pluck one from the heavens if she dared. It seemed they might speak if she asked the right question, which might reveal the secrets they had witnessed through countless ages of watching the world below. Still, she remained silent, knowing that the time for questions had not yet come.

On the second day, her water was half gone, carefully measured by cautious sips. Her skin burned despite the protection of her veil, and her lips had begun to crack in the relentless dryness. Her thoughts grew heavy with the weight of solitude, and doubt crept into her mind like a chill despite the day's heat.

"What am I truly looking for out here?" she wondered as she trudged up the slope of a particularly steep dune. "A voice? A sign? Some miracle that will transform me into the person Tayhira believes I can become?"

She shook her head, sending droplets of precious sweat flying from her brow. "No. I'm not here to look for anything. I'm here to listen. As the Qarr have always done."

It was at dusk on the second night, as she huddled beside the smallest of fires to conserve her dwindling supply of gathered wood, that she saw it coming. The sandstorm rose in the distance like a black wave against the star-strewn sky, a churning wall of darkness that devoured the horizon. She could hear its approach long before it reached her - a deep, primordial roar punctuated by shrieks that might have been the wind or might have been something far older and more terrible.

Most desert travellers, faced with such a sight, would seek shelter or dig themselves into the lee of a dune, covering themselves with cloth to filter the choking sand. Amira, guided by some instinct she could not name, stood and faced the oncoming tempest. She extinguished her fire and secured her few possessions, then walked to the crest of the nearest dune, her form silhouetted against the last light of day.

As the storm bore down upon her, she remembered Tayhira's words: "Be as the sand itself, yielding yet eternal." With calm deliberation, she unwrapped her veil and let it fly free from her fingers, a streak of midnight blue quickly swallowed by the advancing darkness. Then she wrapped her arms around herself, not in fear but in a kind of embrace, and knelt in the sand. "I am not here to command," her words were immediately torn away by the rising wind. "I am not here to run. I am not here to conquer or to cower. I am here to listen. To understand. To change."

The storm swallowed her then, a maelstrom of sand and wind and primal fury that obliterated all sense of direction, all sense of time and self. The world narrowed to the stinging impact of countless grains of sand against her exposed skin, the roaring in her ears, and the struggle for each breath. Time fractured into disconnected moments of sensation - pain, disorientation, the taste of grit between her teeth, the complete and utter isolation.

Yet, in the heart of that chaos, where the elements seemed to conspire to scour her very existence from the face of Zarah, Amira experienced something utterly unexpected - not a vision, precisely, but a presence. A vast consciousness, ancient beyond reckoning, that existed within and throughout the storm itself. It was neither cruel nor kind in its assessment of her; it simply was, as the desert itself simply was - a fundamental force, indifferent to mortal categorizations of good or evil. Yaran scholars have speculated that this was not the last the Primordials would show themselves to her.

The storm was not separate from this presence - the storm was it, a physical manifestation of its being. The howling wind was its breath, the stinging sand its touch, the darkness its gaze. In that moment of connection, Amira understood what the Qarr had always known but could never fully articulate: the desert was indeed alive, aware, and eternal in a way that transcended sentient understanding of these concepts.

The presence seemed to take notice of her then, this tiny speck of mortal consciousness that neither fled nor fought against its might. There was a sense of curiosity, of evaluation. Then, like a breath held and finally released, the storm began to subside. The winds grew less violent, the darkness less absolute, until at last there was only the soft whisper of settling sand and the first faint light of dawn breaking over the transformed landscape.

When Amira regained full awareness, she found herself buried to her chest in a soft drift of sand, as if the desert had sought to embrace rather than destroy her. Her water skin was empty, punctured by some unknown impact during the night. Her limbs ached with cold and fatigue. Her lips were cracked and bleeding, her eyes gritty with sand despite her tightly closed lids.

Yet, against all logic... she was not afraid. Not anymore. Something fundamental had shifted within her during the storm, some new understanding that defied ordinary explanation. She felt strangely connected to the vast emptiness around her, as if invisible threads now bound her to the very substance of the desert itself.

With effort, she freed herself from her sandy cocoon and stood on trembling legs. The landscape had been completely transformed by the storm - dunes shifted, landmarks erased, all signs of her previous passage wiped clean. She should have felt lost, disoriented, desperate.

Instead, she felt a pull, a certainty that came not from her mind but from somewhere deeper, more instinctual. Without conscious decision, she began to walk, her steps carrying her not back toward the safety of the Qarr encampment but deeper into the heart of the desert. She walked through the morning hours, stubborn, pushing her body beyond what should have been possible given her lack of water, the ordeal of the night before, and her own physical limitations, when compared to her tribe's male counterparts.

By midday, when the heat's wrath should have forced her to seek shelter, to her surprise, she found herself energized rather than depleted, as if drawing strength from the very air around her. Her thoughts grew quieter, her sense of purpose stronger with each step.

It was on the third day, as Leander's primary began its descent toward the western horizon, that the quality of light around her changed. The harsh glare softened, taking on a golden hue that painted the landscape in otherworldly beauty. Ahead, the dunes parted to reveal a perfect crescent of sand that curved like Nysa's most elegant form, untouched by wind despite the previous night's storm. At the base of this crescent, nestled in sand that glittered with unusual crystalline formations, a sight awaited that caused Amira's breath to catch in her throat.

There, between two pale Lunaris flowers that should not - could not - have bloomed in such heat, such aridity, lay a smooth, black stone shaped like a teardrop. It rested as if placed with deliberate care, its surface gleaming with an inner light that seemed to pulse in rhythm with her own heartbeat. Around it, the sand was arranged in intricate patterns that reminded her of the sacred geometries woven into the Qarr's prayer rugs - whorls and spirals that spoke of old cosmic order and ancient wisdom.

Amira approached slowly, her steps careful and deliberate, as if entering a sacred space - which, she understood with sudden clarity, she was. The stone pulsed more strongly as she drew near, emanating a gentle warmth like that of a living thing, as if it had been recently held in a great hand and still retained the heat of that touch.

She fell to her knees before it, her parched lips forming words she had not consciously chosen. It was more an uncontrolled torrent of feelings and emotions, than a cohesive thought out process. "I hear you. I see you. I accept your gift, whatever it may be." With trembling fingers, she reached out and touched the stone. The world... stopped.

The wind, which had been a constant companion throughout her journey, stilled completely. The sun's light dimmed as if veiled by an invisible cloud.

The subtle sounds of the desert - the whisper of sand against sand, the distant call of the dune jackals, the creaking of heat-stressed stone - all ceased at once. For the briefest of moments, the entire desert was utterly, impossibly silent.

In that stillness, more profound than anything she had ever experienced, Amira heard a voice. It didn't come through her ears but rather resonated directly within her mind, within her very being. It was neither young nor old but contained multitudes of existence within its simple utterance. "You listened when others would have spoken. You endured when others would have faltered. You embraced what most would have feared. Take this gift, Child of Dust, and dream. Remember always the silence that speaks louder than all the noise of civilization, all the clamour of ambition."

The voice was gone as suddenly as it had appeared, leaving her with a sense of loss that was almost physical in its intensity, reminding her of the loss of her mother. Still, the stone remained, warm beneath her fingertips, its surface now subtly altered. Veins of silver had appeared within its obsidian depths, tracing patterns that reminded her of rivers seen from a great height, or perhaps the branches of some cosmic tree.

Amira pressed the stone to her chest, cradling it as one might a precious infant. Tears trailed down her sunburned cheeks, cutting clean paths through the dust that coated her skin. These were not tears of sorrow or even joy, but of profound understanding - the weeping that comes when one has glimpsed, however briefly, the true nature of existence. "Thank you," she whispered to the empty air, to the Lunaris flowers that should not exist in this place, to the desert itself. "I will never forget it."

With renewed strength that belied her physical condition, she rose to her feet, the stone clutched tightly in her hand. Then, with a certainty that came from beyond herself, she turned back toward the lands of the Qarr, her path as clear to her now as if it had been marked with flaming beacons.

The journey back was arduous, taking her two full days with no water save the morning dew she managed to collect on her outer robe. By all natural laws, she should have perished, another victim claimed by the desert's merciless embrace. Yet she walked with steady purpose, her steps unwavering, the stone a comforting, warm weight in her hand.

When she finally appeared on the horizon, walking like a mirage across the shimmering dunes toward the temporary settlement of her people, the lookout's cry of recognition spread through the camp like wildfire. The Qarr poured from their tents, abandoning tasks and meals to witness the return of one they had begun to mourn as lost.

Shael ibn Sahal pushed through the gathering crowd, his face a mask of disbelief that finally, after much suppression, cracked into naked emotion when he confirmed it was indeed his daughter approaching. With a cry that held all the anguish of the past days and all the relief of this moment, he ran to her, his chieftain's dignity forgotten in the face of paternal love.

He fell to his knees before her, not in obeisance but in gratitude to whatever forces had returned his child to him. "Amira," he said, his voice breaking slightly. "My daughter. I thought the desert had taken you from me forever." Amira smiled, her cracked lips bleeding slightly with the movement, and bowed in turn, placing her father's hand on her head. "The desert takes nothing that is not freely given," she said, her voice rough from thirst yet somehow carrying a new authority. "And it gives much to those who truly-"

"-listen," her father finished, a flash of understanding crossing his weathered face as their eyes met.

That night, after she had been given water and food, after her wounds had been tended and her body bathed and clothed in fresh garments, the elders gathered in Shael's tent to hear her account of the Trial. Tayhira sat closest to her, the old seer's unseeing eyes fixed upon Amira's face with unnerving accuracy.

Amira spoke little of what had transpired in the heart of the storm or at the crescent dune. She described the physical journey in brief terms, noting landmarks and conditions as was traditional, but of her deeper experience, she said only, "The stone was given to me by the desert itself, a token of understanding between us."

Some of the elders exchanged sceptical glances. A grizzled woman named Kasifa who had never approved of the chieftain's daughter's unusual ways, scoffed openly. "Given by the desert? The sun has baked your mind, girl. You found a pretty rock and have woven a child's fantasy around it."

Before Shael could rise to his daughter's defence, Tayhira raised her hand, silencing the gathering. She turned her clouded eyes toward Amira, a smile of profound satisfaction spreading across her weathered features. "So," the old woman said softly, "you spoke back." It was not a question but a confirmation.

Amira looked at the blind seer with new understanding, suddenly certain that Tayhira, too, had heard the voice in the silence, perhaps many years ago, on her own journey into the deep desert. For the first time, she could swear that the old woman was truly seeing her, not with physical eyes but with some deeper, more fundamental sense. "Yes," Amira replied simply. "And it answered." She extended the palm of her hand, where the stone lay.

That night, as the camp settled into sleep, Amira sat alone at the edge of the firelight, examining the stone that had not left her possession since she had found it.

In the dancing light of the flames, its surface seemed to shift and flow like liquid, the silver veins within it pulsing with a life of their own. When she held it up to the light of the rising moons, she discovered another wonder - the silver threads shimmered only in moonlight, forming patterns that seemed to depict scenes from times long past or perhaps yet to come, somewhere, in the vastness of the firmament.

As the seasons turned to years, the stone's properties became gradually known among the Qarr. It was warm to the touch even on the coldest desert nights, and when held during dreams, it was said to reveal visions of things long past - ancient cities buried beneath the sands, civilizations risen and fallen, old kings and conquerors whose very names had been forgotten by history.

Some dreamers saw what seemed to be glimpses of times not yet come to pass, or perhaps were happening somewhere else in the cosmos - strange vessels sailing not on water but through the very firmament itself, people speaking across vast galactic distances through devices small enough to hold in the palm of a hand, great battles fought with weapons that hurled light and death.

Amira herself became both seer and shield of her people, taking Tayhira's place when the old woman finally passed into the embrace of the desert. Her wisdom guided the Qarr through drought and plenty, through conflicts with neighbouring tribes and the slow encroachment of the settled kingdoms that viewed the vast desert not as a living entity but as an obstacle to be conquered or a resource to be exploited.

She lived a long life, even longer than was common among the peoples of Zarah, her face lined with the passage of years but her amber eyes still bright with the knowledge imparted to her on that fateful day. Though many sought her hand in marriage, including chieftains of powerful tribes and even warlords from distant lands who had heard tales of her beauty and wisdom, she chose to remain unwed, saying simply that she had already given her heart to the desert itself.

When at last she died, peacefully in her sleep as the twin moons reached their fullness in the night sky, the stone - by then known among the Qarr as "the Desert's Tear" - was kept as their most sacred relic. It passed from one keeper to another, always cherished, always protected, its powers neither flaunted nor forgotten.

The Qarr themselves, however, grew fewer with each passing generation. The settled kingdoms expanded, merging with other tribes, bringing their stone walls and steel weapons, their temples to gods of mountain and sand who had no understanding of the desert's ancient voice.

Trade routes shifted, wells dried up, and the old ways began to fade like mist beneath Leander's primary relentless gaze.

In time, as the chronicles kept in the Royal Library of Sarim tell it, the Qarr disappeared entirely from the knowledge of the settled peoples. Some say they were destroyed in war, others that disease claimed them, still others that they simply integrated into the growing cities at the desert's edge, abandoning their nomadic traditions. The oldest stories whispered still by those who have ears to hear Zarah's voice, tell a different tale. They say the Qarr did not perish but chose to return to the source from which they had come, walking together into the deepest desert led by the last keeper of the Desert's Tear, vanishing from the sight and record of the outer world.

For countless centuries, the stone was thought lost, a relic of legend rather than historical fact. Yet, as the wheel of fate turned, it emerged once more into the annals of recorded history when it was discovered in an ancient, sand-filled temple by Zahira al-Rasha, who recognized its significance from childhood tales told by her grandmother - a Tarek woman of unusual features who claimed distant Qarr ancestry.

Zahira brought the stone to the court of her cousin, King Aran ibn Khalid, ruler of Zarah, founder of the House of Aran, and master of the Weaving, whose wisdom kindled by Barash ibn Sulaym, led him to understand its true nature and importance.

Aran had it enshrined in the Royal Citadel of Qamaria atop a pedestal of white salt-stone, protected behind crystal glass, and watched over by an unbroken line of scholars, mystics, and sovereigns.

He called it Amira's Blessing, this gift from the desert to a girl who dared to listen when all others spoke. They say that once every hundred years, when the celestial alignment matches exactly that of the night Amira first held it in her hands, the wind shifts in the chamber where it lies, though no window stands open, no door ajar. The faintest whisper is heard, a voice neither young nor old, speaking words that remain forever secret to any but the single listener chosen to be present.

None can say with certainty what message the stone conveys, but all who have experienced this phenomenon agree on one thing - it is the desert itself, remembering. Remembering a girl who heard its voice, who carried its gift, who understood what so many have forgotten: that the most profound truths are often found not in the clamour of civilization but in the deep silence of places untamed by sentient hands.

So her tale remains, etched not in ink but in sand and silence, in the memory of the desert itself and the relic that bears her name. A testament to all who dare to listen, to endure, and to learn the wisdom that can only be found when one stops speaking and starts hearing the voices in the wind.

End of "The Tale of Amira, of the Qarr"

"The Tale of Uramak, Guardian of the Sands" (5,000–4,500 years ago)

The desert of Zarah is a land of shifting fate, where the dunes whisper secrets to the wind, and the bones of forgotten empires lie buried beneath golden sands. Those who traverse its vast, merciless expanse do so knowing that the desert is both a giver and a taker, a realm where the will of man is as fleeting as the dust caught in the breeze. It was upon these treacherous sands that the Caravan of the Moonlit Path undertook its fateful journey.

They were over a hundred strong. Merchants, travellers, scholars, and warriors - each bearing the burdens of their trade and the hopes of distant lands. Their steeds, laden with bolts of silk, chests of rare spices, and jars of perfumed oils, trudged dutifully beneath the weight of commerce. Their route was well-worn, guided by the wisdom of generations who had braved the sea of dunes before them.

At the head of the caravan rode Jalal ibn Samir, a man whose name carried weight in every market from Sayf to Qamar. His face, carved by the sun and wind, bore the hard-earned wisdom of a thousand journeys. He knew the language of the sands - the way they whispered of danger before it arrived.

On that fateful day, Zarah's sands spoke of ruin. The first sign was the silence. The deserts are never truly still; they sing in the rustle of shifting grains, in the distant calls of carrion birds, in the murmur of wind weaving through stone. That day, Zarah held its breath.

The air thickened, pregnant with something unseen, and the very dunes seemed to stand still, as if listening.

Jalal pulled the scarf from his mouth and exhaled slowly. His eyes traced the horizon, where the sky had begun to darken - not with the soft hues of twilight but with something denser, more oppressive. A storm.

His insides clenched. He had known storms before, had weathered their tempers, had seen men swallowed whole by their fury. But this was different. The wind did not gust - it loomed. The clouds did not gather - they devoured.

A shudder ran through the caravan as riders approached him, their expressions grave. "Master Jalal," one of his scouts called, his voice tight with unease. "The tempest moves too fast. It is as if the desert itself rises against us."

Jalal narrowed his eyes. It was unnatural. A thing beyond mere weather.

He turned in his saddle, raising a hand to silence the growing murmurs among the caravan. Panic was the true killer of men in the desert. The storm would swallow those who ran first.

"No one strays from the path," he ordered, his voice steady. "No one panics. We move together, and we move now."

Already, the first tendrils of sand licked at their feet, curling around their legs like a predator testing its prey. The sky deepened to an ominous shade of bronze, and then, in the span of a single breath, the world vanished. The storm had arrived.

It struck with the fury of a vengeful god, a wall of howling wind and blinding sand that devoured the horizon in an instant. What had once been a vast and open desert became a churning abyss, a chaos of dust and darkness where the very air turned to stone.

The first wave hit like an ocean swell - a force that sent men and steeds alike staggering, their cries lost beneath the unrelenting howl. The grains of sand, carried at impossible speed, tore at exposed skin like daggers, biting into flesh, seeking to strip them down to nothing.

Jalal ibn Samir braced himself against the force of the wind, his cactus-silk keffiyeh wrapped tightly around his face, but even the thick cloth did little to keep the storm's wrath at bay. It found its way into his mouth, his nose, his eyes - filling his lungs with dust, stealing his breath.

He turned to his people, but the storm had already begun to rip them apart - not by death, not yet, but by fear. The desert was a cruel mother, and those who did not heed her laws would perish within her embrace.

"Stay together!" he roared, but his voice barely carried beyond his own ears.

A merchant stumbled past him, blinded, his hands clawing at the air. "I can't see! I can't-" The wind caught him, and before Jalal could reach him, he was gone, swallowed by the storm.

This one was not merely wind. It was alive. It sought them. It toyed with them, shifting the sands beneath their feet, burying their sense of direction beneath layers of golden oblivion.

The beasts fared no better. The Desert Steeds, those ships of the desert, neighed in terror, their muscular legs struggling to hold steady in the shifting tide of sand.

Some reared back, breaking from their tethers, vanishing into the maelstrom with pitiful cries that ended too soon.

Jalal turned, scanning for the heart of the caravan - where the children, the elders, and the sick had been placed in the most sheltered position. He had promised them safety. Now, he was watching them drown in a sea of sand.

A child's scream cut through the wind, thin and terrified. Jalal rushed toward the sound, each step a battle against the gale. The sand pulled at his boots, clawing at him as if the desert itself sought to claim him.

Through the storm, he saw her - a girl, no older than seven, clutching at the remnants of a broken tent.

Her tiny hands were bloodied, raw from the wind's cruelty, her wide eyes searching desperately for a face she knew.

Jalal lunged, grasping her before the storm could. He wrapped his cloak around her, shielding her frail body from the cutting winds, and lifted her into his arms.

"Hold on to me," he rasped, his throat raw, his voice barely a whisper beneath the storm's scream. The girl buried her face in his chest, her sobs lost in the deafening fury. There had to be shelter. There had to be a way to survive.

Jalal turned, forcing himself forward, his vision a blur of shifting shadows. His warriors were out there, somewhere. His people were fighting to stand against the storm's wrath.

Even as he struggled forward, a terrible truth settled in his bones. The gale would not break. Not in an hour. Not in a day.

This was no passing fury of the deserts. This was annihilation. Suddenly, beneath the howling winds, beneath the screams of man and beast alike, Jalal felt something.

The ground trembled, and a new sound rose through the chaos - not the voice of the storm, nor the cry of the dying, but something deeper. A rumble, ancient and resonant.

The girl in his arms gasped, her fingers digging into his robes. She had heard it too. Then, the dunes shifted. Not with the wind, but with something beneath. Something immense.

Jalal turned his gaze toward the swirling darkness, his breath caught in his chest. Beyond the storm, something stirred.

A shadow. A shape. A force older than the desert itself.

The guardian of the sands had awakened once more. The tremors rippled through the earth like the heartbeat of something colossal. A force neither born of man nor storm, but something older, something eternal.

The very dunes shuddered, shifting like waves upon a restless sea. The sands split apart, and jalal ibn Samir, holding the trembling child against his chest, turned just in time to witness a legend rising from the heart of the storm.

From beneath the veil of wind and dust, a shape emerged - vast, undulating, and terrible in its majesty. Its form was like the dunes themselves. Shifting with an eerie grace, scales the colour of midnight gleaming beneath the fractured moonlight. The twin golden eyes of Uramak, the Sand Serpent of legend, burned like twin suns in the chaos. The storm howled, but Uramak's voice was deeper, a rumbling that echoed through the very bones of Zarah. "Who dares disturb the breath of the desert?"

Jalal, still shielding the girl, could do nothing but stare. His mind reeled, caught between awe and terror.

The stories had spoken of Uramak as a myth, a guardian unseen but always watching, a spirit woven into the fabric of the planet's shifting sands. Yet, here he was - colossal, towering, ancient - as real as the desert.

The caravan's survivors huddled together, some falling to their knees, some whispering prayers, others frozen in fear. To behold, a being such as this was to stand in the presence of something beyond mortal understanding.

Jalal forced himself to move, to take one uncertain step forward. The child whimpered in his arms, burying her face into his robes. "Great Uramak," he called, though his voice was hoarse from the storm's wrath. "We are travellers caught in the storm's fury. If you do not aid us, we will surely perish."

Uramak regarded them, his golden eyes narrowing. The sands whispered as his great coils shifted, his presence alone parting the storm around him.

"The desert owes men nothing," the serpent rumbled. "It is the will of the sands that only the strong endure."

Jalal clenched his jaw. He had heard these words before, from those who ruled with cruelty, from those who believed mercy was a weakness. But Uramak was not a warlord. He was the desert itself - merciless, yes, but not without purpose.

He met the serpent's gaze and spoke with the conviction of a man who had spent his life walking Zarah's dunes. "If strength alone determined fate, then even the greatest would fall. It is not strength that has brought us here, but the will to endure. We do not ask for deliverance. We ask only for the chance to survive."

For a long moment, Uramak was silent. The wind howled around them, but within the circle of his presence, the storm seemed distant, as though it dared not touch what the serpent had claimed. Then, he laughed.

It was a deep, reverberating sound, like thunder rolling across the endless dunes. Not cruel, not mocking - but knowing. "You speak as one who understands the desert," Uramak said, lowering his massive head so that his golden eyes were level with Jalal's.

"Tell me, traveller, do you know the cost of my protection?"

Jalal's fingers tightened around the child in his arms. He did not need to ask what the cost might be. All things in the desert came with a price.

"If I must give my life so that my people may see another dawn," he said, voice unwavering, "then so be it." Another silence. Another rumble in the depths of the sand.

Then, Uramak exhaled, a great gust of warm air that sent the sand dancing like embers. "Brave words," the serpent murmured, "but unnecessary. Your life is not what I seek."

Jalal frowned. "Then what do you ask of us?"

Uramak's gaze flickered, unreadable. "I want you to remember."

Jalal blinked, perplexed. "Remember?"

The serpent shifted, his body coiling around the caravan like a fortress of living stone. "Men forget. They cross the sands, they take from it, they shape it to their desires, and they believe themselves masters of it. The desert is older than all things. It does not bow. It does not serve. It only endures."

Uramak's voice became softer, yet no less powerful. "If I shelter you, if I shield you from the wrath of the storm, you will carry more than goods to distant markets. You will carry my story - not as merchants carry merchandise, but as priests carry sacred flame. You will tell my tale in every oasis, every city gate, every caravanserai where weary travellers gather. You will teach your children the words, and they will teach theirs, until my name becomes woven into the very language of Zarah's winds."

The serpent's eyes flared brighter. "For its sands remember all things, but men forget. And in forgetting, they lose the wisdom that keeps them alive. Promise me this, and know that your words will echo through ages yet unborn - and when the time comes for the desert's children to stand united against a greater darkness, I shall remember your faithfulness."

Jalal felt the weight of those words settle upon him. A story. A truth carried across generations. And he understood.

He bowed low, pressing his forehead to the sand. "By the moons, by the winds, by the blood of my people, I swear it."

Uramak let out another low rumble, satisfaction curling through his voice. "Then I shall ensure that you live."

With that, the great serpent began to move. His massive body shifted, forming an unbreakable shield against the storm, his scales hard as the bedrock beneath the dunes. His coils encircled the caravan, his vast frame rising above them like the walls of a forgotten citadel. The wind screamed, the storm raged - but within Uramak's embrace, the people of the caravan were kept safe.

Jalal sat back on his heels, holding the child close, his heart hammering in his chest. He had bartered not with gold, nor with blood, but with memory itself. He would tell this story, and the desert would remember.

The storm raged on, howling through the dunes like the lament of forgotten gods. It twisted and churned, striking against the coiled form of Uramak, seething like a caged beast denied its prey.

The Serpent did not move. He remained - a monolith against the storm, an unyielding fortress of ancient power. His massive body, coiled in protective rings, formed a living citadel around the caravan, shielding them from the fury of the wind and the suffocating torrents of sand.

Within his sheltering embrace, the storm became a distant nightmare - its deafening roar reduced to a whisper against the vastness of the serpent's form.

Jalal ibn Samir sat in the hush of the protected space, his arms still wrapped around the shivering child. He could hear the muffled cries of his people - some murmuring prayers, others whispering in awe, their voices hushed as if afraid to disturb the guardian who had come to their aid.

His own heart pounded with a mixture of relief and wonder. He had lived his life by the laws of the desert, respecting its cruelty as much as its beauty. Never had he believed he would look upon one of its most ancient legends with his own eyes.

The caravan members huddled together, their fear slowly being replaced with quiet reverence. No one spoke above a whisper. To do so would have felt sacrilegious, as though they were trespassers in a sacred place not meant for mortal feet.

Jalal turned his gaze upward, peering through the shifting veil of sand beyond Uramak's great coils. The sky had vanished, consumed by the storm, but even so, he could see the faint glow of the serpent's golden eyes, watching.

He swallowed hard, then, gathering his courage, stepped forward, careful not to disturb the sand beneath his feet. "Great Uramak," he called softly, his voice measured, respectful. "You have given us shelter when none else would. We are forever in your debt."

Uramak did not move, did not blink. When he spoke, his voice rumbled through Zarah's very bones. "There is no debt." Jalal furrowed his brow, confused. "Then why save us?"

The serpent exhaled, the breath of a creature who had seen ages come and go like grains of sand slipping through fingers. "Because once, long ago, I was as you are now."

Jalal's eyes widened in surprise. "You were a traveller?"

Uramak's coils shifted slightly, the sand beneath him rippling in gentle waves. "A wanderer." The words were spoken slowly, as though they carried the weight of forgotten memories. "One who sought something beyond the horizon, who longed for a place where the wind did not call him away."

The great serpent's voice grew distant, as if speaking across the vast gulf of ages. "I swam through Zarah's sands when they were young, when those who came from the stars built cities that rose like mirages from the dunes. I sought the Eternal Oasis, the place where all wanderers find rest." His golden eyes dimmed with ancient sorrow. "I followed every star in the firmament, traced every wind-carved path, listened to every whispered legend. Still, the desert called me back, again and again, until I finally understood - I was not meant to find home, but to become it for others. A heavy silence followed. To hear a being as eternal as Uramak speak of longing… It was humbling.

The men and women of the caravan sat frozen in quiet awe, hanging onto every word. "Did you find it?" Jalal asked at last, his voice barely more than a whisper.

For the first time, Uramak's golden eyes flickered, dimming slightly - not from weakness, but from something deeper, something ancient. "No." The single word was like a sigh lost to the sands.

Jalal's throat tightened. He had spent his life believing that the desert belonged to no man, that it could be crossed but never tamed. And yet, here stood the oldest of its children, a being of immeasurable power who sought what all mortal souls seek - a place to call home.

The concept marvelled him, but the more he thought about it, the more it unsettled him. If even Uramak had never found rest, what hope did any man have?

Before he could speak, the great serpent stirred, his body shifting like the dunes in the moonlight. "Sleep, wanderers. The storm will pass, and with it, you will be free to walk your path once more."

Jalal bowed low, his forehead nearly touching the sand. He had never bowed to a king in his life, for he had never met one. But he bowed to Uramak.

One by one, the caravan members followed his example. Some pressed their palms to Zarah's sandy skin, and others whispered silent words of gratitude.

The storm howled beyond the guardian's coils, but within his embrace, they were safe.

As a reverse behaviour to his prior conduct, for three days and three nights, Uramak did not move. Not for them to quench his thirst, but for the storm to satisfy its own against his body. He stood against it like the pillars of an ancient temple, his presence alone enough to defy the wrath of the desert. When the fourth dawn broke, the storm was gone.

The sands lay still once more, their inner fury spent. The sky, once an endless void of dust and shadow, now stretched vast and brilliant above them, painted with the colours of dawn.

Jalal rose to his feet, blinking against the light. His people stirred beside him, murmuring in disbelief. They had survived. As he turned to offer his respects to the great serpent, he found that Uramak was already moving. The massive coils that had shielded them unwrapped, shifting with a slow, deliberate grace. The sand rippled in waves as the guardian of the desert prepared to return to its depths.

Jalal stepped forward, heart pounding. "Will we see you again?" Uramak paused. For a long moment, he simply regarded the caravan, his golden eyes unreadable. Then, at last, he spoke.

"So long Zarah endures, so too shall I. Spread my tale, and when the time comes, I shall return the favour."

The great serpent began to sink then, not in defeat but in a slow, stately withdrawal. As his coils disappeared beneath the surface, the sand rippled outward in perfect circles, like drops of water falling into a still pond.

Uramak's head resurfaced, his golden eyes were the last to vanish, holding Jalal's gaze with an intensity that seemed to burn the promise into his very soul. Then, silence - but not emptiness.

The desert felt different now, not just vast but watchful, not just ancient but also aware. Where Uramak had rested, the sand bore a different texture, finer and more golden, as if touched by divinity. The ripples of his passage faded, leaving behind only the memory of his presence.

The desert was still once more. Once a raging tempest of wrath and ruin, now it fell silent. At first, it was subtle - the howling winds no longer shrieked like dying spirits, the suffocating darkness of the storm lightened, and the suffocating pressure upon their chests began to lift. Then, like a beast retreating after a failed hunt, the storm relented. Its fury had spent itself against the immovable might of Uramak, the Guardian of the Sands.

Jalal ibn Samir, his body weary but his spirit unbowed, stirred from where he sat. Around him, the remnants of his caravan, once terrified and clinging to one another, blinked in stunned silence at the transformation of the world.

The sky, which had been a monstrous churning bronze, began to pale, taking on the first hues of dawn. The first tentative rays of the sun pierced the veil of dust, illuminating the battered survivors with its golden embrace. Shadows stretched across the dunes, no longer swallowed by the abyss.

A murmur rose among the caravan, hushed and awed, as men and women slowly began to rise, brushing sand from their robes, looking to one another as if to confirm they were truly alive.

For days, they had known only blindness, only the endless churning sea of dust and fear - but now, they could see clearly once more.

Jalal turned his gaze to the sand where Uramak had vanished through, but the shifting dunes bore no sign of his presence, no disruption in the endless golden expanse.

It was as if he had never been there at all - save for the fact that they had survived due to his mercy.

Jalal exhaled, the enormity of what had transpired settling into his bones. He stepped forward, turning to face his people. "We live." His voice, though raw from the storm, carried through the morning air. "We live because the desert has shown us mercy."

The caravan stirred, heads bowing, hands pressed over hearts in silent gratitude.

They did not need to speak Uramak's name aloud - his presence was intrinsically woven into the fabric of their survival, his legend forever etched in their souls.

In the days that followed, as they resumed their journey, the caravan moved differently. Where once they had cursed Zarah's heat, now they walked with reverence. The merchants no longer haggled over water rations with bitter words, but shared with quiet generosity. Warriors, who had boasted of conquering the sands, now spoke of partnership with them.

Even the children played different games - not of battle and conquest, but of guardians and protection. They had been touched by something greater than themselves, and it showed in every step they took, every shared meal, every evening when they gathered to hear Jalal retell the tale, each telling adding new details as memory crystallized into legend.

The child Jalal had shielded from the storm, tugged at his sleeve. Her small fingers clutched a handful of golden sand, her wide eyes reflecting the endless horizon.

"Was he real?" she whispered, as if afraid that speaking too loudly might dispel the magic that had saved them.

Jalal knelt before her, brushing the sand from her face. He smiled, though his heart still trembled from all that had passed. "Yes," he said. "And we will remember his tale."

The girl nodded, clutching the sand tighter as if it held a piece of the guardian himself. She, too, would carry the legend forward.

The caravan did not linger. They knew better than to question the will of the desert.
With solemn purpose, they began their preparations, tending to the wounded, securing their remaining supplies, adjusting the harnesses on their weary steeds. The journey was not over, but they had been given the chance to continue it.
Jalal stood at the crest of a dune, looking out over the vastness of Zarah. The storm had passed, but the desert was eternal. He had sworn to remember, and so he would. Uramak's name would not be forgotten.
As the first full light of the morning spilt over the dunes, painting the sand in hues of fire and gold, the Caravan of the Moonlit Path set forth once more.
And behind them, carried by the wind, the desert whispered a name. Uramak.
Jalal exhaled, placing a hand over his heart. He had made a vow that night - to remember, to tell this tale, to ensure that Uramak's kindness would never be forgotten. That is what he did.
Being a traveller himself, Jalal spread the story, carried by other merchants and wanderers, whispered in the halls of kings and the tents of nomads. A tale of the guardian of the desert, the ancient serpent who had defied the storm.

End of "The Tale of Uramak"

"The Tale of Queen Amara" (2,500–2,000 years ago)

Zarah's desert winds carried whispers long before her birth, murmurs of a queen yet to come, a ruler who would walk between worlds. Amara, daughter of the moons and heir to the forgotten throne. She was born on a night unlike any other in recent memory, when the heavens themselves seemed to hold their breath, and the stars burned brighter than the torches of a thousand caravans. The air over the great city of Ryvath shimmered with an eerie stillness, as if the cosmos itself was poised to witness the arrival of one foretold in ancient song and scripture.

As the first cries of labour echoed through the palace halls, the city's elders gathered upon the towering terraces, their aged faces illuminated by the celestial glow that bathed the desert in silver fire. It was no ordinary night - comets streaked across the sky in spectral arcs, constellations shifted, aligning in patterns unseen for millennia. Some called it an omen of divinity, others a harbinger of doom. But all knew that something beyond mortal reckoning was at work.

In the highest chamber of the palace, Queen Lysara, last of the Moon-Blessed Queens, lay upon a bed of cactus-silk cushions, her breath laboured but her gaze unyielding. The royal midwives whispered prayers to the old gods, their hands steady but their voices trembling. For this was no ordinary birth. The prophecy had spoken of a child who would reshape the course of destiny, who would stand upon the threshold of worlds. A child of silver fire and boundless wisdom.

Then, she came, crying her existence, for the cosmos to hear, and when Amara finally entered the world, the air itself seemed to still. Her first breath was a sigh upon the wind, her first cry a whisper that carried through the mountain beyond the city walls. The very foundations of the palace trembled as if acknowledging her arrival, and the torches in the chamber flickered violently, bending toward her as if drawn by an unseen force.

The gathered nobles and scholars stepped forward in reverence, but it was the High Priestess of the Lunar Order, veiled in robes of deep indigo, who moved first. She alone had read the oldest texts and traced the lines of fate written in the heavens above. She approached the newborn's cradle with cautious awe, her gnarled fingers trembling as they reached toward the child's delicate brow.

There, beneath the flickering candlelight, she saw the mark. Silver eyes, luminous and unblinking, reflecting the very stars that had heralded her birth.

A murmur swept through the chamber, a ripple of realization and fear. No queen had ever been born with eyes like these.

The High Priestess turned slowly to the assembly of nobles, her voice low but carrying the weight of prophecy fulfilled. "The child bears the mark," she whispered, her words reverent, yet edged with something deeper. "The mark of the Starborn."

A silence followed, deep as the void between the stars. The prophecy was no longer mere myth - it had been made flesh and blood.

In the years to come, the people of Ryvath would whisper of that night, of the child born beneath a sky aflame, whose very presence seemed to bend fate itself. Some would say she was a gift from the heavens, others that she was a storm given form. All would come to know that Amara was unlike any ruler before her. For the stars had called her into being. And the stars would never let her go.

During that Age, the halls of Ryvath's palace were unlike any others on planet Zarah, with the exception of Sarim's. Built from alabaster and obsidian, carved with inscriptions so ancient that even the most learned scholars of the time could not decipher them all, they stood as a testament to an empire that had endured for millennia.

It was within these walls that Amara, the Starborn Queen, was raised - growing up to be not merely a ruler but a force of destiny.

From the moment she could walk, Amara defied expectation. Where other princesses might cloister behind silk-draped chambers, she wandered the moonlit gardens, tracing constellations with her fingertips, whispering their names as if she had known them all her life.

She was not satisfied with mere beauty or etiquette; her hunger was for knowledge, for purpose, for the vast mysteries that stretched beyond the desert and into the infinite sky.

Both her father, King Tarash, and her mother, Queen Lysara, watched with a wary pride. "She is not like the others," they murmured to their chief advisor, Kharim al-Faris, a man who had served Ryvath's royal line for decades and, seasoned by life's vicissitudes, had seen more rulers rise and fall than he cared to count. Kharim bowed his head in quiet understanding. "No, my King. She is not."

Even among her tutors, Amara was an enigma. She devoured scrolls of ancient lore with the same fervour that her male counterparts honed their blades. She was interested not only in history but also in the movements of the stars, the cycles of Anar and Nysa, and the patterns hidden in the shifting dunes.

She did not merely wish to learn - she needed to understand.

One evening, as her astronomy master mapped the constellations upon a great canvas, he paused when Amara's voice broke the silence. "The Path of the Wandering Star is wrong."

The old scholar raised a grizzled brow. "How so, my princess?"

She stepped forward, her silver eyes gleaming in the torchlight, and with a single stroke of charcoal, she corrected the path of a celestial body. The scholar frowned, opened his scrolls, and traced her calculations. His breath caught in his throat. Amara was right. A child of ten had undone centuries of recorded celestial study. The stars whispered their secrets to her, and she listened.

Yet, her knowledge, however vast, would not be enough to rule.

As she grew, so too did the weight of her destiny. The council of nobles, wary of her unorthodox nature, sought to mould her into something more palatable - a ruler of soft words and subtle diplomacy. They had misread the signs of her birth.

During an assembly of advisors, a dispute arose between two noble houses over the rights to an oasis on the outskirts of the kingdom. Voices grew heated, hands clenched into fists. Water, in the desert, was more valuable than gold and sometimes more precious than blood.

Amara, barely fifteen, listened in silence as the nobles bickered. Then, without warning, she rose from her seat. "Enough." Her voice was firm, certain, as if the stars themselves had spoken.

The hall fell into stunned silence. Never before, in Zarah's deep history, had a princess interrupted a council of men twice her age. Her gaze swept across the chamber, not with defiance but with something far more potent - certainty.

"You both claim dominion over something that belongs to no one," she said, stepping forward. "The oasis does not exist for your houses. It exists because the gods willed it so. And yet here you stand, speaking of it as if it were a trinket to be bartered." Her words cut deep, for men were proud in those days, allowing their egos to rule their kingdoms.

The lords, red-faced and indignant, began to protest.

Amara raised a single hand and, inexplicably, they fell silent again.

"You will share the waters, under the guardianship of the temple priests, who will see that neither greed nor thirst dictates its use. If either of you break this pact, the punishment will not come from me, but from the desert itself."

A murmur rippled through the chamber. Kharim, standing in the shadows, smiled faintly. She had not just ruled - she had wielded wisdom as a blade. None in that room dared challenge her judgment.

The shaping of a true queen is not merely a matter of law and learning. A ruler must understand both power and peril. On her twelfth birthday, Amara was sent to train with the Warriors of the Crescent Moons, an elite order sworn to protect the royal lineage. For the first time, she held a blade not as an ornament but as an extension of her will.

After arduous years of training, her last duel before graduation was against Commander Rashid, a veteran of countless battles, his face lined with the stories of war.

According to legend, he did not treat her as a fragile thing. His training was thorough and relentless. In every lesson before that duel, he gradually came at her with the full force of his strength, his curved blade flashing, from sunrise to moonrise.

Amara scarcely flinched, as if guided by the stars themselves, she danced to the cosmic rhythm.

With each lesson, each strike, she learned to move like the wind across the dunes, weaving between his attacks, not with brute strength but with grace and speed.

She was, by far, not the strongest warrior, but she was a fast learner and willing to fail and learn from her mistakes.

After years of training, during a late lesson, she finally found an opening, and her blade kissed the edge of Rashid's shoulder.

The commander exhaled slowly, stepping back. Then, to the astonishment of all in attendance, he knelt before their Queen. "You fought as our moons fight the Yaran tides," he said. "With patience and wisdom, but also with inevitability."

She sheathed her blade and bowed in respect. "A queen must learn how to command," she said softly, "but she must also learn when to yield. If it had not been for that lucky strike, you would have beaten me, like always."

"Do not try to be something you are not, my Queen, you have fought splendidly. I see that my teachings have not gone amiss. You have made me proud." Rashid bowed in turn.

The warriors of the Crescent Moons swore fealty to her that very night.

At twenty-three, she stood at the threshold of destiny. Her mother, Queen Lysara, grew ill, her once-fierce spirit dimming like the last embers of a dying fire.

One evening, as Amara sat beside her, the elder queen took her hand, her grip weak yet firm. "Listen to your father," she said, "he has something important to tell you."

The King held her gaze. With heavy eyes and a father's heart, he said. "The stars chose you," Tarash whispered. "Not because you are strong.

Not because you are wise. For there will always be others better than us. But because you will seek what others fear to know - truth."

Tears welled in Amara's silver eyes. "What if I fail, father?"

Lysara smiled, brushing a trembling hand over her daughter's cheek. "Then the stars shall guide you home."

A mere week later, Queen Lysara passed into legend. Because Tarash had no male offspring, the weight of the throne fell upon Amara's shoulders.

The people wept for the royal couple, but in their sorrow, they looked upon their future queen and saw something more than grief.

They saw a ruler who walked with the wisdom of the past and the fire of the future. With King Tarash's blessing, Amara ascended, not merely as a monarch, but as a legend in the making.

The desert winds carried her name, and the stars above - silent, eternal - watched with knowing light.

The Twilight War

War does not always come like a sudden storm. Most times, it builds like the shifting sands, unseen until it is too late to escape.

For years, tensions had simmered between Ryvath and the Bahir clans, their disputes over water rights and trade routes growing sharper with each passing season.

When Queen Lysara passed and King Tarash ascended his young daughter to the throne, the rulers of the Bahir saw an opportunity. They saw weakness, and they did not send emissaries nor looked to negotiate. They sent war.

It began in the borderlands, where the caravans that once travelled freely between the two regions were waylaid by armed riders, mounted on desert steeds. Silk and spice became plunder, merchants became corpses, and the sands ran red long before the first war banners were raised.

King Tarash was too old to rule, so it fell to Amara to take over the reigns of the kingdom. And so, Queen Amara was barely twenty-four when the first messengers arrived, their tunics torn, their lips cracked from days in the desert. They spoke of forts set ablaze, wells poisoned, villages razed in the dead of night. The council of Ryvath convened in the great marble hall, their voices rising in frantic debate.

"We must retaliate at once!" barked General Rashid, his hand clenched upon the pommel of his sword. "We should march upon our enemies before they bring their full force to bear."

"You would send our people to their deaths?" countered Lord Kasim, an elder statesman with ink-stained fingers. "We must negotiate - find a way to restore peace. That is how King Tarash ruled."

As the chamber descended into argument, Amara sat in silence. Her silver eyes flickered with thought, her fingers lightly tracing the engraved armrest of her father's throne. Then, with a quiet authority that commanded the room, she spoke. "Peace can not be made with a blade at one's throat." The voices fell to a hush.

"The Bahir believe that because I am young, we are weak." She stood, the hem of her robes whispering against the polished floor. "But we will not give them the satisfaction of proving their warlords right."

She turned to Rashid. "We will not march blindly into war, but we will not sit idle as our people suffer. Ready the scouts. I want to know where they strike from, how they move, and what weaknesses they hide."

Then, she addressed Lord Kasim: "Send envoys under the banner of peace. Not because we expect mercy, but because history will remember that we did. That is what my father would have done." From behind the throne, Tarash gave his daughter a nod.

A heavy silence followed. Then, slowly, Rashid bent his head in acknowledgement. "As you command, my Queen." And so, quietly, the Twilight War began.

The first true clash came at Dune Pass, a narrow stretch of land between two towering cliffs, the only viable path for an army to cross into Ryvath lands from the west.

The scouts had returned with dire news - Bahir forces had gathered there, their warbands amassing under the banners of their High Warlord, Khavar the Red Serpent.

Amara chose to ride out with her warriors, not behind the safety of their ranks, but at the forefront, clad in sand serpent scale-armour that caught the desert sun, her sword glimmering with the light of dawn.

On the morning of battle, as the enemy camp loomed beyond the ridgeline, Rashid urged her to stay behind. "A queen's place is not upon the battlefield," he said, his voice tight with worry.

She met his gaze. "A ruler's place is where their people stand."

And so, when the horns of war sounded, Amara led the charge.

The clash of steel rang through the canyon as Ryvath and Bahir warriors met in a tide of violence.

Arrows darkened the sky, blades sang against one another, and the cries of the dying echoed between the cliffs.

At the heart of it, Amara fought - not as a sovereign, but as a simple warrior fighting for their people, her movements swift as the desert winds.

Then, from the midst of chaos, came Khavar. The Bahir Warlord was a towering figure, his armour painted in the blood of his enemies, his great curved blade glinting with the deaths of a hundred men. When he saw Amara upon the battlefield, he laughed - a sound like cracking bone.

"A child dares stand before me? And a woman, no less."

Amara did not answer. Instead, she raised her father's sword.

Their duel was a storm unto itself, a dance of steel and fury. Khavar struck like an avalanche, but Amara moved like the moonlit tide, swift and unyielding.

Being physically weaker, she dodged, parried, countered - not with brute force, but with precision, with intelligence. And, in the end, it was not strength that felled the Red Serpent, but wisdom.

Khavar, enraged by his failure to strike her down, overextended in his final attack.

Amara sidestepped, her blade finding the gap beneath his raised arm, sinking deep into his ribs.

Khavar's body fell to the sand. And with their leader slain, the Bahir army faltered. The Battle of the Dune Pass was hardly won.

During the twilight war, there were victories, and there were losses. There were nights when Amara stood upon the ramparts of the city of Ryvath, watching the fires burn in the distance, knowing that with every sunrise, more of her men would fall.

Still, she never wavered. Heeding her father's counsel, she adapted, and she learned.

She did not rule through fear. She ruled through strength of will, through strategy, through the trust she had built with her people.

When the final siege was broken, when the last of the Bahir warbands were pushed from Ryvath's borders, a message was sent to their rulers:

"This war has ended not with annihilation but with wisdom. We need not be enemies. Choose peace, and Ryvath will answer in kind. Choose war, and you will find that our vengeance does not falter."

The Bahir tribe's answer came not in steel but in silence. They did not dare to test the kingdom of Ryvath any further.

Thus the twilight war ended. Not with a massacre, but with a queen who had proved her worth - not through bloodshed alone, but through wisdom, through resilience, through the fire that burned not only in her inherited sword, but in her very soul.

The people of Ryvath called her the Dawnfire Queen, for she had brought them through the longest night and led them into the light.

Amara knew in her heart that peace was never eternal. The stars in the firmament still whispered, and destiny's hand had not yet played its final move.

The fires of war had dimmed, leaving behind a kingdom that still stood but bore its scars. In the months that followed, Amara found herself restless in ways that troubled her. Victory parades gave way to the mundane duties of rebuilding - arbitrating disputes over grain stores, overseeing the repair of watchtowers, listening to merchants haggle over trade routes. These were indeed noble tasks, necessary work, yet her spirit chafed against their earthbound nature.

The kingdom of Ryvath had weathered the storm, yet Amara knew that victory was but the first step toward a greater destiny. The cosmos stretched vast beyond Zarah's sands, and the stars kept whispering secrets she could no longer ignore.

Even as her city rejoiced in the newfound peace, Amara walked alone upon the palace terraces, gazing up at the constellations that had watched over her since birth.

They gleamed in the deep, endless sky, their patterns shifting ever so slightly, revealing shapes she alone seemed to perceive. She had studied them since childhood, traced their movements, and pondered their meanings. In those moments, they called to her with an urgency she had no name for.

One evening, as she stood upon the highest tower, lost in thought, a voice broke the silence. "You look at them as if they might speak."

She turned to see Zael, the Astronomer-King, a wanderer from the distant isles of the east, on the coast of the Yaran ocean. He had arrived at court weeks prior, a guest of the scholars who tended the celestial archives, but Amara had felt his presence long before they had spoken.

"Perhaps they do," she replied, her silver eyes reflecting the starlight. "Perhaps they always have, and we have simply failed to listen."

Zael tilted his head, intrigued. "And what do they tell you, Queen of Ryvath?"

Amara hesitated. She had spent years unravelling the mysteries of war, the intricacies of rule, the burdens of sovereignty. But this? This was something deeper. She could not explain how. But it was something written into her very being. "They tell me that I am not yet where I must be," she admitted. "That my kingdom is only the beginning."

Zael studied her for a long moment, then turned his gaze skyward. "Then it seems we have much to discuss."

Under Zael's tutelage, Amara's understanding of the stars deepened. He spoke of celestial cycles lost to time, of worlds beyond Zarah's night sky, of ancient knowledge carved into the very fabric of the cosmos.

By day, she ruled her kingdom, ensuring that the peace hard-won in war did not falter. By night, she pored over maps of the heavens, tracing the patterns of constellations unseen by ordinary eyes. She learned of the

Veil of Moons, a cluster of stars whose alignment foretold the rise and fall of leaders. She studied the Eclipse Codex, an ancient text that spoke of rulers who could harness the power of the Weaving. Though most of this ancient tome remained a mystery to her, she could not help but be fascinated by its pages. Images of distorted suns that, to her surprise, brought her the shivers.

She learned and accepted the Path of the Wanderer - a celestial route mapped only in legend, a path that no ruler had dared to walk.

Zael watched her with quiet admiration. "You are different from the kings and queens who came before you," he said one evening as they stood atop the tower. "Most look to the stars for omens. You look to them for answers."

Amara did not turn from the sky. "Is there a difference?" she asked, with a twinkle in her eyes. "Besides, they have never led me astray."

Zael smiled broadly. "Then follow them."

This had been a moment of revelation for her. Because of it, neither her father nor the court was prepared for her decision.

When she gathered the council and announced her intent to leave Ryvath and seek the hidden truths of the Weaving, the chamber erupted into protest.

"But you are our Queen!" Rashid implored, his brow furrowed with worry. "Your duty is here, not chasing myths among the stars!"

"And what is duty," Amara countered, "if not the pursuit of truth?"

Lord Kasim shook his head. "My Queen, Ryvath needs you."

Amara met his gaze. "Then Ryvath will endure. It is not my presence that makes this kingdom strong. It is yours. It is our people's. They will not crumble because I seek that which has called to me since the day I was born."

She turned to Kharim, her voice taking on the measured cadence of her father's. "The Council shall govern in my absence, with Lord Kasim as ruler by birthright, and General Rashid commanding our defences, by equal measure. Our ancient laws shall guide you into the future, as they have guided my forebears across Zarah's history. Should our kingdom ever face peril, seek wisdom from your own council. After all, you have served Ryvath's crown since before my birth. And you have served it well."

The room fell into uneasy silence.

At last, Kharim - the man who had counselled her since childhood - spoke. "It is clear to everyone here that you have always walked a different path, my child." His voice was low, knowing. "If this is your will, then it is not my place to stop you."

One by one, the council relented. They did not yet understand, but had bared witness to her wisdom since childhood and knew better than to stand against the weight of destiny.

In the days that followed, Amara met with each in private counsel, ensuring that the structures of governance would endure long after her departure - for a true ruler's greatest achievement is a kingdom that thrives without them. With her rule in trusted hands, Amara prepared for the greatest journey of her life.

On the night of her departure, the city gathered at the gates, torches illuminating the roads as they watched their queen ascend the steps of her waiting vessel. A full-grown Nightwing, majestic, regal in its stance, its blue and red feathers absorbing the moonlight.

She was clad not in the robes of a monarch, but in the garb of a traveller, her sword strapped to her side, her silver eyes reflecting the stars above. Zael stood beside her, his own cloak billowing in the desert wind. "Are you afraid?" he asked. Amara did not answer immediately. She gazed at her people - at the faces of those who had fought beside her, who had placed their faith in her. "No," she said at last. "For the stars will guide me home."

The night was windless, the sky a boundless sea of silver fire. The stars hung heavy over the desert, their cold light casting long shadows upon the dunes.

Ryvath slept, but the queen did not, for she stood at the threshold of destiny, gazing out from the highest terrace of the palace she had ruled, her silver eyes reflecting the heavens above.

Behind her, the city she had built and protected for years stretched in silence, its towers standing proud against the dark mountains. But even the strongest walls could not contain her fate.

A voice broke the stillness. "It is time." Amara turned to find Zael, his cloak billowing in the faintest desert breeze. He studied her with the quiet patience of a man who had spent his life watching the skies, his own gaze carrying the weight of distant worlds. "Are you ready?" he asked. She exhaled softly. "I have been ready since the day I was born."

And so, without another word, she descended the ivory steps, walking not as a queen weighed by duty but as a traveller answering the call of the cosmos. The gates of Ryvath opened one final time for her, and beyond them, the desert stretched vast and endless, waiting. Into the Unknown. With that, the Queen of Ryvath flew into the night.

The Nightwing took them far beyond the borders of her kingdom, beyond the lands known to the cartographers of men. They travelled beneath the burning gaze of the sun and the cool embrace of the moons, guided only by the silent whispers of the stars. At night, as they rested, Amara sat upon the dunes, tracing constellations in the sand.

Zael watched her in quiet reverence. "You still listen to them," he observed one evening. She smiled faintly. "They have never led me astray."

"What do they say now?" he asked, gazing into the heavens.

Amara hesitated, tilting her head as if hearing something just beyond the veil of reality. "That I must keep going." Zael said nothing more. He understood. Some callings could not be ignored.

Weeks passed, and the journey led them to the Veil of Suns, a canyon whispered of only in myth. Here, the air hummed with ancient power, the very rocks inscribed with sigils older than the kingdoms of men. It was said that this place marked the boundary between the known world and the unseen realms beyond.

The Nightwing flew gently, in the warm breeze, over mountains and valleys it took them. As they approached, Amara felt the weight of unseen eyes upon her. Not of men, nor gods, but of something older, something vast. The stars above seemed to pulse, as if in recognition of her arrival. Zael stepped beside her. "This place..." he murmured. "It should not exist." But it did. And it had been waiting for her.

At the heart of the canyon stood a great stone archway, its surface etched with glyphs that shimmered like captured moonlight. It was not merely a gate - it was a threshold. A passage into something beyond mortal comprehension. A gate to the other side...

Amara reached out, her fingers brushing the cold surface of the arch. A deep vibration ran through her bones, a silent whisper threading through her mind.

Zael tensed. "Amara..." She turned to him, her expression unreadable. "I must go." His jaw tightened. "There is no telling what lies beyond."

She nodded, hoping he would understand. "That is why I must go."

Silence stretched between them, heavy with unspoken words. Then, Zael did something he had never done before - he took her hand.

"You do not have to walk this path alone," he said, his voice low. "Not all who seek the stars must leave everything behind."

For the first time in a long while, Amara wavered. She had ruled a kingdom, led armies, and deciphered the language of the heavens - but she had never been asked to stay.

She searched his face, then the night sky above. The stars shimmered, waiting.

Finally, she smiled - a quiet, knowing thing. "I was never meant to stay."

Zael exhaled, then, with the smallest of nods, released her hand. Not in surrender, but in understanding. And with that, Queen Amara of Ryvath stepped beyond the veil.

None but us, the House of Tempus, know what lay beyond the gate. Some mortals say she walked into a realm untouched by time, where the cosmos stretched vast and infinite before her. Others whisper that she ascended, shedding her mortal form to become something more - a light that burns eternal among the stars she so loved, now shining upon Zarah's landscapes.

The people of Ryvath mourned her departure, but they did not weep. For she had not been lost. She had simply gone where she was always meant to be. Back with their star-forebears.

In Zarah's current Age, according to the *Echoing Archives*, during certain nights, when the sky is alight with silver fire, travellers claim to see a lone figure walking across the dunes, her eyes glowing like twin moons, taking flight in a blue and red Nightwing.

Others claim that when the wind sighs through the canyons, it carries her voice, soft as a dream: "A ruler must not only lead - they must also seek."

Thus, the legend of Queen Amara lives on. For the stars, never forget their own.

End of "The Tale of Queen Amara"

"The Tale of Ashira of the Sands" (800–600 years ago)

The wind howled across the dunes, a voice older than kings, older than time itself. It carried the scent of spice and storm, the whisper of lost empires, the sighs of forgotten gods. The desert was endless, merciless, yet within its vast and shifting heart, legends were born. Among the greatest of these was the tale of Ashira of the Sands - the thief, the warrior, the ghost who walked between shadows.

She came into the world on a night where the sky was black as onyx, absent even the glow of the twin moons. The sands outside the tent where her mother laboured stirred restlessly, as though the desert itself could sense what was to come.

It was an ill-omened night, the kind the elders feared, the kind that marked the arrival of those who would shake the world.

Her mother, Samira the Windseer, was a woman of whispers and wisdom, a mystic who could hear Zarah's voice in the rustling palms and shifting dunes. Her father, Jalal ibn Rashid, had once been a ruler of men, a leader whose name carried weight across the trade routes of Zarah.

By the time Ashira's first cry filled the night, her father's name had been reduced to a bitter curse.

Betrayal had come as all betrayals do - from within. Those who had once sworn fealty to him had turned, their knives quick, their loyalty fleeting as the desert wind.

His allies abandoned him, his people scattered to the far reaches of the dunes. Once, he had commanded a thousand riders, his banners flying high over the caravan roads.

Now, he was a fugitive, a man with only shadows for company. Because of this turn of fate, Ashira was born not into wealth, not into power, but into exile.

Despite his fall from grace, Jalal never spoke bitterly of those who had betrayed him. Instead, he would sit with young Ashira beneath the stars, teaching her the old stories of honour and nobility, even as they lived like outcasts. "A man's true worth," he would say, his weathered hands tracing constellations in the sand, "is not measured by those who follow him in prosperity, but by how he bears himself when all else is lost."

These lessons would stay with her, though she would learn to apply them in ways her father never intended.

Her mother, though broken by loss, did not give in to grief. Instead, she took her newborn daughter into her arms and whispered words not of comfort but of prophecy.

"You will become the storm itself, my child. No person shall hold you. No walls will ever cage you. You will be as the deserts themselves. A Child of Sand and Stars."

Zarah's deserts never nurtured the weak. They do not pity those who cannot bend with the winds, who cannot listen to the voices of the shifting dunes.

Ashira learned these lessons before she could speak. When she was five, she could tell the difference between a viper's hiss and the sigh of dry grass. She could taste the air and know if rain would come, could dig deep into the sand to find the hidden wells her mother spoke of in stories.

By twelve, she was able to outrun the swiftest of Dune Jackals, climb the sheerest rock faces, and vanish into the dunes like a mirage at dawn. Still, survival was never enough for her.

Her mother, Samira, wove her stories at night beneath the vast desert sky, where the stars burned like scattered embers. Tales of the Sandspeakers, who could hear the voice of the world itself.

Legends of the Lost City of Jawhara, buried beneath the dunes, where golden domes still hid beneath the sands. Tarek myths of the Blade of Truth, a sword that could cut through lies and deception, revealing the heart of all things.

Ashira listened. She listened, out of love for her mother, but she did not truly believe the tales.

"Stories are not food," she replied to her mother once, at the age of twelve, when their fire was low, their bellies emptier than they had ever been. "Stories do not put silver in our hands."

Her mother merely smiled, tucking a strand of windblown hair behind Ashira's ear. "No, my love. Still, tales can help shape the world. Maybe one day, yours will as well."

Ashira continued to listen diligently, yet her mother's words did not satiate her hunger.

At the age of thirteen, the child decided she would be a thief.

"If riches do not find their way to me, then I will find my way to them." Her eyes gleamed at the thought.

The years that followed were lean ones. Samira's health began to fail, her visions growing dim as the desert's hardships wore upon her spirit. Ashira watched her mother grow frailer with each passing season, and hunger became their constant companion.

It was then, with her mother's cough echoing through their threadbare tent and their water running low, that necessity carved its lesson into her heart.

When Samira finally succumbed to the fever that had wracked her body for weeks, Ashira did not weep. She sat beside her mother's still form through the night, listening to the wind howl across the dunes as if the desert itself mourned. In the morning, she wrapped Samira in the finest cloth they possessed - a scarf of faded blue silk that had once belonged to better days.

As she laid her mother to rest beneath the shifting sands, Ashira whispered the old prayer her progenitor had taught her, her voice steady despite the hollow ache in her chest.

"May the wind carry your stories to the stars, Mama. May Zarah remember your voice when mine is forgotten." Only then, with the last handful of sand scattered over the grave, did she allow the tears to flow - not of grief, but of farewell.

The city of Dakarai was an ancient jewel of the desert, its walls rising high above the golden sands, its streets filled with the scent of tea and roasted Moonmelon. Merchants bartered beneath great awnings of silk, their voices sharp as the blades they sold. The black steeds neighed as they trudged through the crowded alleyways, their burdens heavy with spices, rare gemstones, and gold-lacquered trinkets destined for the far corners of the world.

It was a place of fortune and folly, where a keen mind and a quicker hand could turn misfortune into opportunity. In these streets, no hands were quicker than those of Ashira.

She moved like a whisper between stalls, her feet light as drifting sand. The crowded market was her hunting ground, a symphony of movement and sound where she was both composer and conductor.

She did not steal out of greed. She stole to survive. Bread from the carts of careless vendors, coins from the silk-robed nobles too drunk on honeyed mead to notice her touch, a golden ring plucked from a merchant's display before his eyes could catch the motion.

To her, it was a game of survival - one where losing meant starvation. Because of her parent's influence, her greatest prize was neither gold nor jewels, but knowledge itself - though she used it for her own benefit.

She learned the way guards moved, the weight of their steps on cobbled streets. She knew which gatekeepers took bribes and which were too proud to betray their posts.

She listened in tea houses as foreign traders spoke of distant wars, as scholars whispered of lost relics buried beneath the sands.

She collected secrets as easily as she lifted purses. But the people of Dakarai took notice. Whispers began spreading through the alleyways, growing into tales spoken by firelight.

"Did you hear? The Phantom of Dakarai stole from the king's own coffers!" In other parts of the city, one could hear. "They say she moves unseen, that the wind itself carries her away before the guards can grasp her shadow."

In the busy market district, the conversation wasn't much different. "A noble once felt a tug at his belt, only to find his dagger gone - and a single date left in its place."

The House of Tempus's records attest that legends are dangerous things, and even the swiftest of shadows cannot run forever...

One night, beneath the silver and yellow dance of light, coming from Anar and Nysa, Ashira stood on the roof of the House of Golden Veils, the most lavish estate in the merchant quarter.

Below her, the great garden stretched wide, perfumed with the scent of flowering Lunaris and Sunbloom cactuses.

A feast was taking place within, the laughter of nobles mingling with the soft notes of a distant lute.

Ashira exhaled slowly. A noble's vault, left unwatched while the house feasted - too tempting a prize to ignore. She slipped through an open window, her bare feet making no sound upon the marble floors. The vault was behind an iron door, thick and proud, but locks were only puzzles, and Ashira had never encountered one she could not solve.

Within, chests of gold gleamed in the dim torchlight, but she did not reach for them. Instead, her eyes sought something far more valuable: a blade, its hilt inlaid with lapis, its curved edge whisper-thin - a dagger said to have belonged to a prince long forgotten. As her fingers brushed the hilt, a blade touched her throat.

"Move, and we will find out how well your blood stains silk." The voice was like crushed stone, deep and measured. A warrior's voice.

Ashira did not flinch, nor did she startle. Instead, she smiled. "Well," she murmured, as she turned slowly, letting her presence speak for her, "that depends. Do you prefer crimson or gold?" she replied with dark humour.

There was a pause, then laughter. The dagger withdrew, though not far enough to give her an opening.

She kept turning slow and deliberately to face the man who had caught her. Khalid ibn Faris, captain of the king's guard.

Khalid was a warrior of quiet strength, his eyes like burning embers beneath his hooded brow. A man who had seen battle, who had carved his way through the ranks of enemies and stood victorious. Now, in this moment, he stood before her. "You move well, little thief," he said, sheathing his dagger. "But not well enough."

She tilted her head, considering. "Then kill me quickly, so I might haunt your dreams."
Another laugh, quieter this time. "A sharp tongue. I like that."
Ashira folded her arms, her eyes hypnotic. "Are you going to turn me in?"
He studied her for a long moment before shaking his head. "No." She frowned. "No?" A slow smirk curled at the edges of Khalid's lips.
"No. But you have only two choices, girl - my dungeons or my service."
She raised a brow, curious. "What kind of service?" she asked, her curiosity overriding her caution.
Khalid studied her, quietly, before replying. "Your kind," he said simply. "You know these streets better than the vermin. You hear whispers that never reach the ears of the court. I need eyes that can see what lurks in the dark."
Ashira exhaled, rolling her shoulders. "What do I get in return?"
Khalid's smile deepened. "Gold. Protection. And the chance to steal something greater than treasure." She frowned at this. "What is that?" Khalid's gaze turned sharp. "Power."
Ashira considered the offer, the weight of it settling on her shoulders like a cloak she did not yet know if she wished to wear. Then she thought of the alleyways, the nights spent running, the empty stomach and the ever-present hunger that no amount of stolen bread could fill.
She extended her hand. "I suppose it was only a matter of time before I stopped running."
Khalid clasped her wrist, his grip firm. "Then let us see what you are truly capable of." There and then, the thief became a spy.

For two years, Ashira walked the line between shadow and steel. No longer merely a thief, she became a whisper in the halls of power, a blade hidden in the folds of silk. Khalid had made good on his promise - she had stolen more than wealth. She had indeed stolen power.
The king's court was a place of opulence and deception. Gilded arches stretched high above perfumed halls, where nobles clad in embroidered silks played their games of politics over goblets of honeyed mead. Every smile concealed a blade. Every word was laced with sweetened poison.
Ashira listened. She watched. She learned to read the shifting tides of loyalty, to slip unnoticed through guarded doors, to pry secrets from lips too careless with their liquor.
She became the eyes in the dark, the ears in the silence, the hand that struck before a knife could find the king's back.

Khalid trained her not just in combat but in strategy, deception, and survival. He drilled her in the art of war and taught her how to read an enemy's stance and how to anticipate their strike before it came.

"A blade is not power," he told her one night as they sparred beneath the torchlit courtyard. "Knowing when to use it or not to use it - that is power, Ashira. That is power."

Through hardship, she proved to be a quick study. By the age of eighteen, she had infiltrated enemy strongholds, uncovered treason within the palace itself, and silenced those who sought to overthrow the king before they could act. But loyalty, sometimes, is a fickle thing.

As months turned into years, Ashira began to notice small things - hushed conversations that ended when she approached, meetings Khalid attended without her, a tension in his jaw when the king's policies were discussed. She told herself it was nothing, that loyalty was not always meant to be questioned.

Yet the desert had taught her to trust her instincts, and her instincts whispered of storms gathering on distant horizons.

One evening, beneath the amber glow of lanterns in the King's Great Hall, Ashira stood at the edge of a gathering, unseen but ever watchful. The air was thick with the scent of roasted meats and spices, the murmur of voices weaving a tapestry of half-truths and veiled threats.

She saw Khalid standing near the high table, his expression unreadable as he spoke with councillor Rashan, the king's most trusted advisor. There was something in the way they stood, the way their words curled too carefully around each other. Some sort of game was being played. One she had not been invited to.

Thus, later that night, she decided to follow Khalid.

Through the winding corridors of the palace, past the marble columns where the statues of long-dead rulers stood sentinel, she moved like a ghost. Khalid was cautious, but he had taught her too well. He did not hear her as she pressed herself into the shadows listening to the conversation that would change her life forever.

A plot against the king. A betrayal from within, as history keeps showing us, over and over again. And at its heart - Khalid himself.

Ashira's breath stilled. She had been called many things in her life - thief, spy, ghost of the sands - but never had she been called a fool. And yet, she had trusted him.

When she confronted him beneath the great Moonleaf tree in the courtyard, her hand resting on the hilt of the dagger he had given her, he did not deny it. "Sayyid is a fool," he said, his voice as steady as it had always been. "He squanders the wealth of our city on feasts while his people starve. He must be removed from power."

Her grip tightened. "And what of loyalty?" she demanded, her voice cutting through the night air.

Khalid exhaled, tilting his head as though she were a child asking a foolish question. "Loyalty is an illusion, Ashira."

She had no words for him. Only a blade. The moment stretched, the silence between them vast as the desert beyond the palace walls. Then, in the space between breaths, he moved.

Steel met steel as Khalid's blade flashed through the air, striking where her heart would have been had she not twisted away at the last moment.

They danced beneath the Moonleaf tree, steel singing against steel in a deadly symphony. Khalid's blade carved through the air with practised precision, each strike meant to end her life swiftly - the mercy of a teacher to his student.

But Ashira had learned his lessons too well. She flowed around his attacks like desert wind, her movements fluid and unpredictable.

When he lunged with a powerful overhead strike that would have cleaved her in two, she spun aside, her dagger tracing a shallow line across his ribs. He pivoted, bringing his blade up in a vicious arc that she barely deflected, the force of it sending vibrations up her arm. For a heartbeat, they stood locked, blade against blade, their faces inches apart. In his eyes, she saw regret - not for his betrayal, but for what he was about to do.

"You were the finest student I ever trained," he whispered, then drove his knee toward her stomach. She twisted away, but not fast enough. The blow caught her hip, sending her stumbling backward. As Khalid's blade arced toward her in what would have been the killing stroke, she let it graze her shoulder - a calculated sacrifice for the opening she needed.

Pain flared through her, but in that same instant, she drove her sword forward with all her strength, slipping past his guard and sinking the blade deep between his ribs, finding the gap in his leather vest with deadly precision.

His breath caught. His knees buckled. And Khalid ibn Faris fell.

Ashira did not watch as he crumpled to the ground. She did not stay for his last breath. She turned, her bloodstained blade still clenched in her hand as she walked away from the palace, away from the city that had tried to make her something she was not. She walked into the desert, where the stars burned cold and unfeeling above her. And she did not look back...

The desert does not forget. The wind carries whispers long after voices have fallen silent, and the dunes remember every footprint, every drop of blood spilt upon their shifting skin.

And so it was with Ashira - the thief who had walked through the gates of kings, the blade that had struck down her own master, the woman who had left a city of stone behind to return to the only home she had ever truly known.

But no kingdom would claim her after that night. No city would welcome her. She had walked away from Dakarai, but her name had not. It travelled in hushed voices among the merchants, in the fearful murmurs of guards who had seen the shadow of her dagger in their dreams. She had become a legend, a ghost, a storm that moved where no walls could hold her.

For weeks, she wandered the vastness of Zarah, the sands stretching endless before her. The heat curled in waves against the horizon, the stars above burning with an eerie, watching silence. She hunted as her ancestors had, tracking the swift-footed animals through the dunes, drawing water from hidden wells only the oldest nomads remembered. She was alone, but she was not lost.

Then, one night beneath the cold silver of the twin moons, she saw the firelight on the horizon.

The scent of roasted meat drifted on the wind, the soft hum of voices rising from a gathering unseen beyond the ridges. Ashira moved like a spectre, her steps soundless as she crested the dune. Below her, a caravan rested - dozens of tents arranged in a loose crescent, their banners fluttering with the symbols of a tribe she did not recognize.

They were nomads, but not the kind she had grown up among. Their garments were not the flowing silvers of the Yarans, nor the deep greens of the southern tribes, like the Ulema. These were warriors, their cloaks cut short for swift movement, their belts lined with knives of bone and steel. They were people who did not stay in one place for long, who lived not by the mercy of the desert, but by the strength of their blades.

Ashira watched from the shadows, but shadows were not always silent.

"You wear the sands well for an outsider." The voice was low, unhurried. A man stood not three paces from her, wrapped in a cloak the colour of storm-touched sand. His face was marked with faded scars, his eyes dark as the depths of a well.

Ashira did not reach for her dagger. A blade was useless when drawn too late. Instead, she straightened, meeting his eyes with her own steady gaze.

"And you move well for a man who should be watching his fire."

The man chuckled, but it was not an unkind sound. "There are those who say the fire watches itself," he tilted his head. "But few dare to come so close without an invitation."

"I was not looking for one," she answered coolly, her eyes wary. "Perhaps," he studied her a moment longer, then gestured to the camp below. "Come. Break bread with us." Ashira hesitated.

Trust was a luxury she could no longer afford. But the hunger in her belly was real, and the desert was cruel to those who denied its offerings. So she followed.

The tribe called themselves the Zafiri - wanderers who claimed kinship with no kingdom, sworn to no lord save the endless sky.

In centuries to come, they would join with greater tribes in wars yet undreamed, but in that moment, they were simply a people caught between the shifting sands of fate.

They were mercenaries, traders, scavengers - people who belonged nowhere and everywhere. Their leader, a man called Sahirrus, ruled by listening more than he spoke, but when he did, others listened in turn.

"You carry the look of someone who has killed before," Sahirrus observed, studying Ashira across the fire that night. "Of someone who does not yet know what to do with that." She did not answer, and Sahirrus did not press her.

The Zafiri welcomed her as one of their own, but they did not coddle her. She earned her place not with words but with skill.

Ashira fought beside them, rode with them when they raided slaver caravans in the east, and tracked the trails of lost traders who had vanished into the dunes.

She did not seek belonging, but she found it nonetheless. When the time came, when a warlord from the city of Khadesh sent men to claim the heads of the Zafiri for disrupting his trade, Ashira did not run. She stood at the frontlines, her sword gleaming beneath the rising sun. She moved like the wind, struck like the storm, and when the battle ended, it was her blade that found the warlord's throat. The sands had claimed another secret. And the desert did not forget. A Name in the Wind.

Years passed, and Ashira's tale grew. To some, she was a saviour. To others, a curse. Traders swore she could move through walls like mist, that she had stolen the heart of a king only to vanish with the dawn. Slavers feared her name, whispering of a shadow that cut their bonds before they could wake. She became more than a person. She became a legend. Suddenly, one day, she was gone.

Some say she walked into the dunes alone, disappearing as all legends do. Others claim she left with a caravan that sought the lost city of

Jawhara, chasing the stories her mother had once told beneath a sky full of stars.

If you stand in the desert beneath a moonless sky, if you listen as the wind moves through the dunes, you may still hear her laughter upon the breeze.

For ghosts do not truly die - they become the stories we tell, the whispers that ride the desert wind, the shadows that dance at the edge of firelight. And in the vast silence of the dunes, where only the stars bear witness, some say Ashira of the Sands still walks, a legend made flesh, a promise that the desert never forgets its own.

End of the "Tale of Ashira of the Sands"

"Tale of the Great Sandstorm Crisis" (275 Years Ago)

The wind had always been the desert's voice, carrying secrets through the shifting dunes, whispering warnings only the wise could hear. It was the breath of Zarah itself, sometimes soft as a lover's sigh, other times fierce as a war cry. But on the eve of the Great Sandstorm Crisis, the wind was something else entirely. It did not whisper. It howled.

For days, the nomad tribes of the southern reaches spoke of unease - a strange stillness in the air before dawn, a heaviness in the planet's soul, as though the sands themselves waited for something unseen. The skies, once the deep blue of a Zarahan summer, had begun to shift into unnatural hues, painted in streaks of burnt copper and crimson, as though the heavens themselves had been set ablaze.

The first true sign came when the desert's oldest water wells, untouched for centuries, began to run dry. At first, it was thought to be misfortune, a cruel turn of fate that forced the caravans to seek water elsewhere. But then, the oasis of Tamr, an eternal sanctuary amidst the dunes, simply... vanished.

One morning, where the lush Medjool palm trees had stood, where traders had refreshed their weary steeds, where the turquoise waters had mirrored the heavens, there was nothing. Just endless dunes, as though the oasis had never existed at all. The desert had swallowed it whole. The people of Zarah that lived, or travelled around that area, took this as a sign - an omen of something far worse than mere drought.

In the streets of Sarim, the Yaran capital, the soothsayers spoke in hushed tones of a great unravelling. The scholars in the Grand Archive pored over brittle scrolls, searching for precedent in history, but found only scattered mentions of an age-old calamity, one so ancient that even its memory had turned to dust.

Then came the windstorm. It arrived without warning, a monstrous gale that descended upon the city at dusk. The palace towers trembled beneath its force, market stalls were torn from their moorings, and the streets became rivers of swirling sand. This was not an ordinary storm - it carried voices, echoes of something vast and unseen, something ancient and hungry.

In the heart of the storm, those who dared listen swore they could hear whispers threading through the air - words in a language older than stone, voices not of men nor women, but of the desert itself. Then, just as suddenly as it had come, the storm ceased.

A dreadful silence followed. The air smelled of scorched earth, of something wrong. The sands had been disturbed, not by nature, but by something far older, something stirring beneath the surface.

It was this silence, this unnatural stillness, that drove the people of Zarah into fear. And it was this fear that led to the summoning of the High Council, a gathering not held in years.

For if the wind itself had turned against them, then the very balance of the world was at stake.

The Council of Sarim had convened many times over the centuries - to settle disputes, forge alliances, to command armies. But it had been three years since they gathered in fear.

The Great Hall of the Citadel, an edifice carved from the desert's very bones, stood tall over the city, its domes gleaming even in the shadow of the encroaching storm. It was here that the rulers, warlords, mystics, and scholars of Zarah came together to decide the fate of their people.

The chamber flickered with torchlight, casting long, restless shadows over the gathered council. The air was thick with the scent of burning incense, an offering to the gods of sand and sky - but there was little faith left in offerings.

At the head of the table sat King Aran I, his eyes dark with concern. His hands, steady even in battle, clenched against the polished Solarwood of the council table. He was no stranger to war, to hardship, but this was something else - something familiar. A force of nature, a force beyond men.

The first to speak was Safira, the Moon Seer, wrapped in robes of deep silver, her bangles whispering against each other as she moved. "There is something wrong with the natural order," she said, her voice neither high nor low, but measured, as if she spoke not from opinion but from the knowledge of the stars themselves. "The balance has been disturbed, and the storm is its consequence." Across the table, Rafiq, Head of the Order of the Sacred Desert, frowned. "Then we must move the people. If the storm does not break, the city will be swallowed. We cannot wait for fate to decide our survival."

A murmur of agreement rippled through the council until Barash raised a single hand, commanding silence. His robes, once dark with sun embroidered motifs, were stained with sand and ink, a testament to years spent unravelling the mysteries of the past. "No ordinary storm consumes oasis and stone alike. No mere wind speaks with voices from the void. This is not nature's wrath. This is a wound upon our world. One left by those who refuse to leave." A hush fell over the chamber.

"A wound? Leave?" Aran repeated.

Barash nodded gravely. "Something has disturbed the Weaving. Perhaps it is something that has long slept beneath the sands, or perhaps something left by the recently departed. But if we do not act, this storm will not be the last." Silence stretched taut, the weight of his words pressing upon them all.

Then, from the back of the chamber, a new voice rose - Queen Sura. She stood with arms folded, her quiet beauty affecting the room, her eyes sharp as a blade's edge. "If the Weaving is still torn, then we must find the tear. We must mend it," she finished, her voice firm.

Aran looked his queen in the eyes. He saw there an understanding a thousand words could not explain. He then exhaled slowly, letting the weight of the moment settle upon him. With the clarity of a man who had faced fate before and won, he spoke.

"Then we ride into the storm." The council erupted in protest.

Karim al-Shamar, ever the strategist, fidgeting with his glasses, spoke firmly. "This is madness! To walk willingly into death without knowing what you are facing?"

"Why not?" Aran replied. "I have done it before."

Kasim al-Bahir stood up, his deep voice, usually firm, wavered with concern. Through the years, he had grown to fiercely respect Aran. "You would risk the throne on a fool's errand?"

Aran did not waver. "No city will stand if the storm does not end. No army will matter if the Weaving unravels once more. We have all faced this before, and we do not have the luxury to waste time on fear when action is required." His words carried the weight of a king, and slowly, the protests died.

At last, Barash leaned forward, his eyes shadowed. "If we are to do this, we must prepare. We must go where the storm is strongest. And we must find what lies at its heart." And so, it was decided. The greatest expedition in the House of Aran's history would march not away from the storm but into its fury.

The desert was never a forgiving place, for it does not cradle the weary, nor does it grant mercy to those who walk its sands unprepared. To enter the storm willingly was an act of defiance against nature. Against life itself.

For three days, the city of Sarim stood in uneasy preparation. The War with the Draconians, just a few years removed, the Primordials only recently appeased, and they were being thrown once more into the maws of destiny. The new city-gates, carved from the bones of ancient titans, remained closed against the approaching stormwinds. Inside, artisans and smiths toiled under the weight of urgency - forging stronger armour, reinforcing the caravan wagons, weaving protective garments that might shield them from the biting sands. Every movement carried a quiet desperation, for none knew if the King's expedition would return.

At dawn on the fourth day, the Expedition into the Maelstrom assembled beyond the city walls. A proud company of two hundred strong, composed of warriors, mystics, scholars, and trackers.

All stood clad in desert-worn cloaks, their faces wrapped against the wind.

The finest breed of Desert Steeds had been gathered, their saddles weighed with provisions, their eyes restless as though sensing the unnatural storm beyond the horizon.

At the head of the column, as was his desire, sat King Aran, his cloak billowing, his gaze fixed upon the distance. He had led armies into war, faced foes that wielded both blade and sorcery, and this was just one more time he would ride into the heart of something that could not be fought. Beside him stood Sura, his spy, his queen, his love. Her hands brushed lightly over the air as if feeling its shifting moods in the Weaving. She had spent her life listening to the voice of the desert, and it was screaming.

The silence of the morning was broken by the deep, resonant call of a war horn.

By midday, the first signs of the storm revealed themselves. The sky darkened, shifting from the deep blue of the Zarahan expanse to the ashen gold of a sky choked by rising sand. The air grew thick, dense with grains that stung exposed skin and turned breath, though protected by a layer of cloth, into labour.

Rafiq rode ahead, his sharp eyes scanning the horizon. "It is worse than we thought," he muttered, his voice muffled behind the cloth that covered his face. "This is no ordinary sandstorm. The wind... it is moving unnaturally."

Sura nodded grimly. "The Weaving has been disturbed here. The storm is not just wind - it is something else, something restless."

The further they rode, the heavier the air became. The dunes, once familiar, had been reshaped into new, jagged forms.

The desert itself seemed foreign, as if being rewritten by unseen hands.

By nightfall, they were forced to halt. No stars were visible in the night sky. Anar and Nysa, the twin moons, were veiled behind a swirling veil of dust. Fires sputtered in protest against the wind as the warriors huddled together beneath reinforced tents.

Aran sat with Barash. The old warrior-sage was tracing symbols in the sand with a weary finger. "When you offered your essence to the Weaving, the obelisks were meant to keep the balance," Barash murmured. "But something has unsettled them."

Aran exhaled. Concentrating, he felt the Weaving around him. "Drathis," he whispered in disbelief. The name alone carried weight, even in death.

The warlord's ambition had led him to tamper with the Weaving, and though Aran had slain him, his final act had left a scar upon the world. As the wind howled outside the camp, Aran clenched his fists. He had ended Drathis, but the war was not over. Not yet.

On the second day within the storm, they encountered the first of the disappearances amongst their company. A scout, sent ahead to map a clearer path, did not return.

His tracks led into the dunes and simply... vanished. No sign of struggle, no remnants of his presence. It was as if the desert had consumed him whole. A whisper of unease passed through the ranks.

By nightfall, two more men had vanished. No screams, no warnings. Only silence played to their disappearance.

That night, as Aran sat watch near the central fire, a sound drifted through the wind - a low, resonant hum. He rose to his feet, scanning the darkness. The sand moved unnaturally, twisting in spirals that defied the wind's chaotic motion.

Then, in the swirling sands, he saw them. What were they? Figures? No, they were more like shadows, standing at the edge of the dunes, barely visible through the storm's haze. They did not move. They did not breathe. They only watched. Aran's fingers tightened around his father's sword. "We are not alone," he spoke softly, alerting the group.

Rafiq, already awake, followed his gaze. "What are they?"

Sura stepped forward, eyes narrowed as she extended a hand into the wind. For a moment, the storm bent around her, parting like a veil. In that brief moment, the figures became clear.

They were not men. They were shapes formed of dust and wind, their faces shifting, their bodies flickering like mirages.

Barash inhaled sharply. "They are echoes."

Aran turned to him. "Of what?" But he already knew the answer.

His tutor's voice was hollow. "Of those the storm has already taken." The silence that followed was heavier than the storm itself.

After the sands subsided, Barash spoke first. "Do not fear. The only power over us here is that which we give away."

By the third day, they reached the heart of the storm. The dunes had flattened into a vast, endless plain of swirling sand, and at its centre stood something unnatural. A structure, half-buried, pulsing with an eerie glow. A forgotten obelisk.

Aran dismounted, his boots sinking into the shifting ground. This was it. The source of this unnatural storm. A forsaken wound in the Weaving.

He stepped forward, the wind screaming around him. As his fingers brushed the surface of the obelisk, a familiar jolt of energy surged through his body, and for an instant, another vision assaulted his senses.

He saw the past, the moment Drathis had fallen. The warlord's final breath had not been in defeat but in sacrifice. His dying hands had touched an obelisk, not to destroy it, but to twist it, to break the balance in his last, spiteful act.

How was this possible? He had seen Drathis die. Or had he?

Three years had passed since that victory, yet here was proof of his enemy's final spite.

After their victory against Drathis and Vhaskar, Aran and Barash had hastened towards the final tether, and Rafiq, wounded, had returned to Sarim. Was it possible that Drathis, mortally wounded, had dragged himself to this obelisk?

Aran staggered back, breathless. The storm was not just an after-effect. It was Drathis's vengeance. The wind roared, the ground trembled, and from the shifting sands, something began to rise. Something stirred. Something awoke.

The obelisk pulsed with unnatural energy, the air thick with the scent of scorched sand and something different - something corrupt.

Aran had seen many horrors in his time - Draconian wars fought in moonlit valleys, the dying screams of warriors, the dark memories of fighting a Primordial. But this was different, as if the storm's wrath had been made flesh.

From the shifting sands, shapes began to rise - first as formless columns of swirling dust, then solidifying into monstrous forms, their bodies forged from wind and shadow, their eyes burning with the embers of the storm itself. Sura gasped, her breath hitching in awe and terror. "The Weaving is giving them form." Barash, his expression carved from stone, whispered a name long forgotten to the tongues of men. "The Efreetu. Creatures from the other side."

The creatures - if one could call them such - towered over the expedition. Their bodies, vast and serpentine, shimmered like mirages, shifting from solid to ethereal with each gust of wind. Some bore the twisted forms of great beasts - Dune Jackals with elongated jaws, Sand Scorpions whose stingers dripped with molten glass. Others walked on two legs, mockeries of men, their eyes empty voids that swallowed the torchlight.

The largest among them stepped forward. Its form was regal yet grotesque, a towering figure wrapped in flowing shrouds of sand, its head crowned with jagged horns of black stone. When it spoke, the storm itself carried its voice. "You do not belong here, flesh-bound ones."

Aran did not flinch. He spoke, fearless. "We seek to mend what has been broken."

The Efreetu's laughter was a hollow echo, rattling through the bones of the desert. "You are the ones who broke it," the creatures spoke in unison, "You are the inheritors of ruin. Now, you will be its sacrifice." With a single, thunderous motion, the Efreetu, summoned by Drathis's sacrifice, raised its arms, and the storm answered.

The storm howled, and the desert became a battlefield. The creatures surged forward, their forms shifting, unbound by the laws of flesh and stone. Blades clashed with wind-forged talons. Arrows, loosed into the maelstrom, found nothing but air.

Aran's sword burned with the power of the Weaving as he met the first beast head-on, his strike carving through its shifting form.

It did not bleed. Instead, it reformed, laughing as though it had never been struck at all.

Sura, standing at the eye of the chaos, raised Barash's staff. The wind obeyed her. It bent to her will. She called upon the spirits of the desert, commanding the storm to turn against itself. For a brief moment, the winds faltered. The storm recoiled. But the Efreetu did not fall.

Barash gripped the ancient runes at his belt and jumped behind Aran. "They are bound to the storm. As long as it rages, they cannot die."

Rafiq, locked in combat with a towering, jackal-headed monstrosity, growled between clenched teeth. "Then we must end the storm. Though I do not know how." He locked eyes with Aran.

The obelisk still pulsed, feeding the storm, fuelling the creatures' existence. It had to be severed from the Weaving.

Aran turned toward the obelisk, its inscriptions glowing with malignant light. He could feel the weight of it - the raw, untamed force bleeding into the world. Drathis's vengeance. He had been here before, and there was only one way to stop it. He gritted his teeth, forcing his will upon the storm. The Weaving shuddered beneath his command. The obelisk cracked, its power resisting, lashing out with arcs of wild energy that burned across his skin. This one did not want to be undone.

The Efreetu sensed his intent, their voices overlaid. "You do not have the strength, mortal child."

Aran snarled, gripping his sword tighter. "Then I will take it." With one final, desperate act, he drove his father's blade into the heart of the corrupted obelisk. The world split apart.

The storm screamed as it unravelled, its energy collapsing in upon itself. The Efreetu howled in rage, their forms twisting, caught between existence and oblivion. One by one, they dissipated, their bodies breaking apart like grains of sand scattered to the wind. Then, silence. The storm was gone.

Aran staggered back, his vision blurring, his limbs trembling with exhaustion. The desert lay still once more, but the scars of what had transpired remained.

Silence fell over the desert. A silence so profound it pressed against the skin like the weight of a thousand unseen hands. The storm was dying, and these were its death rattles.

Where there had once been an unrelenting maelstrom now stood only the vast, endless dunes - still shifting, still breathing, but no longer screaming. The sky, for the first time in weeks, was visible once more. Twin moons hung pale and distant, their silver light bathing the battlefield in an eerie glow.

Still, the world was not unchanged. The land bore the scars of what had transpired. Where once there had been ridges of soft, golden sand, there were now gaping scars - blackened earth where the storm had burned the very soul of the desert. These scars would take time to heal, and time is all the desert has.

At the centre of it all, amidst the ruins of the great obelisk, knelt Aran.

His father's blade still lay buried in the shattered stone, its edge dull from the strain of severing what was never meant to be severed. His breath came slow, heavy, the weight of exhaustion bearing down upon him. He had fought battles before, but never had he felt so utterly spent. Could it be father time? Already?

Soft footsteps approached from behind. A voice, edged with both relief and concern, broke the silence. "Aran?" Sura placed a cautious hand on his shoulder, but he did not move. His eyes remained locked on the remnants of the obelisk, watching as the last tendrils of its unnatural energy faded into nothingness. The wound in the Weaving had been closed, but he could still feel its phantom pain beneath his skin.

"It is done," Barash murmured, stepping forward, his aged face lined with both wisdom and weariness. "The storm will not return."

Rafiq, bloodied but unbroken, surveyed the land with narrowed eyes. "Then why does it not feel like a victory?" No one answered. Because he was right.

They gathered what remained of their forces. More than a third of the expedition had been lost - some swallowed by the sands, others taken by the storm-born beasts, their fates left unspoken.

As the survivors stood amidst the wreckage, a realization settled over them like a funeral shroud. The storm had not been the true enemy.

It had been the consequence of something far greater, something beyond any war they had fought before. A reminder that the Weaving was fragile, that the balance of the world was never guaranteed.

Aran looked at his hands. They trembled - not from weakness, but from something deeper. He had touched the raw edges of existence itself. He had felt the pull of the abyss, the weight of the unseen forces that held the world together. Not for the first, nor last, time in his life, he understood how small they truly were - but also how precious.

That night, as the campfires flickered in the renewed stillness, Sura stood alone at the edge of the dunes. It wasn't only Aran. She could feel them too - the echoes of those who had perished. Not just in this battle, but long before, across the endless history of Zarah. The spirits of warriors, wanderers, and kings whose names had been swallowed by time.
One by one, they faded, carried away by the wind. Their purpose fulfilled. Their duty complete. She closed her eyes and whispered a single word into the night. A word she learned from Barash. A word older than any tongue still spoken. "Rest." And the wind, for the first time in a long while, reposed.
The desert was silent. Though it was not the silence of peace, nor the quiet of a world at rest. It was the silence of something wounded, something vast and unspoken that had only just begun to heal. The air, once thick with the cries of the storm, now carried nothing but the whisper of shifting sands. And yet, that whisper was enough to remind them all of what had been lost.
Aran stood at the edge of the ruined battlefield, his boots sinking into the sand still warm from the storm's wrath. The shattered remains of the obelisk lay before him, half-buried, its inscriptions burned away by the force of its collapse. Whatever ancient power had fuelled it, whatever remnants of Drathis's last defiance had lingered there, were now gone.
He exhaled slowly, watching as the wind began its slow work of erasing the footprints, the remnants of battle. The desert, in its own way, mourned as it always had - by trying to forget.
Behind him, the survivors moved among the dead. Some searching for familiar faces, others standing motionless, caught between grief and disbelief.
Sura sat upon a dune, her fingers tracing patterns in the sand, eyes unfocused. The storm had spoken to her, in its final moments, in a language only the weavers could hear. And its words had not been kind.
Rafiq paced near the remains of the expedition's camp, his knuckles bloodied, yet white, from gripping his swords too tightly. He had lost men. Good men. Sacred Desert Warriors who had followed him into countless battles, believing that strength and will could triumph over any foe. But

how does one fight a storm? How does one protect their people from something beyond steel and blood?

Barash, his robes still heavy with dust, knelt by the remnants of the obelisk, fingers tracing the fractured stone. His face was unreadable. When he finally spoke, his voice was quiet, heavy with something beyond exhaustion.

"The balance has been restored," he added ominously. "For now."

Aran turned to him, his expression foreboding. "And for how long?" The old sage did not answer because he did not know.

The wounded were gathered, their numbers too many. Some would live. Others would not make it through the night.

The storm had not only taken lives - it had taken certainty. The men and women who had ridden into the maelstrom as warriors, as scholars, as seekers of truth, returned not as heroes but as survivors. And survivors carried burdens.

As the fires burned low that evening, Aran found himself standing alone on the outskirts of the encampment. He did not know how long he had been staring at the dunes before Sura's voice broke through the quiet. "We did what had to be done." He did not answer immediately. His fingers curled at his sides, nails pressing into his palms. "And yet, it does not feel like a victory," he intoned, echoing Rafiq's words.

Sura stepped beside him, her gaze following his. "Because it was not."

He turned his head slightly regarding her. She was watching the horizon, where the sky met the endless sea of sand. "We stopped the storm. We sealed the wound. But we did not undo what was done. Not this time."

Aran's throat tightened. She was right.

Nothing could bring back the lives lost. Nothing could erase the scars left upon the Weaving, upon the land, upon those who had faced the wrath of something beyond mortal comprehension. The desert would heal, as it always did. But those who walked upon it would carry the memory of the storm long after the last grain of sand had settled.

"And what of us?" Aran asked at last, his voice quieter than he intended. "What do we do now?" She smiled faintly, though there was little warmth in it. "We do what the desert has always done." Sura let the wind carry the rest of her words away, but Aran understood. "We forget to remember," he whispered.

At dawn, they departed. The banners of Sarim fluttered weakly in the early light as the caravan began its slow journey back. The dead had been burned, their ashes returned to the sand. Their names would be remembered, etched into the halls of the Yaran capital, carried on the tongues of those who lived.

The desert watched them go, impassive as ever. The wind whispered farewell, or perhaps only farewell for now. For Zarah was eternal. And the storms would come again. They always find a way back.

End of the "Tale of the Great Sandstorm Crisis"

Appendix IX: The Lost Dialogues

Not all of The MiddleVerse's history is written in grand libraries or etched into stone - some of it is whispered between friends, carried by the wind, and lost to time - but not to the House of Tempus…

These are two chronicled conversations between Khalid ibn Rashid, father of King Aran I, and Barash ibn Sulaym.

The first conversation took place in Karash, Aran's birthplace, when he was still a young boy, as his father struggled with the burden of preparing his son for a fate neither of them could escape.

The second, their last exchange before Khalid's death - or rather, his murder - a quiet but fateful moment that would shape the destiny of Zarah forever. Though, a glimpse from it has already been addressed elsewhere in our *Echoing Archives.*

These dialogues reveal fears left unspoken, oaths made in secret, and the heavy weight of fate upon those who tried to defy it. They are the last echoes of a father's love and a warrior's final stand, preserved here so that their truth may never be forgotten.

Dialogue I: During Aran's Childhood

The sun hung low over Karash, its golden light casting long, wavering shadows across the sandstone walls of the small oasis town. The desert wind whispered through the ancient streets, carrying the scent of spiced meat, incense, and the faint metallic tang of heated steel from the blacksmith's forges. Karash was a city of survivors, traders, and warriors, nestled at the edge of the great dunes, where the desert met the stone.

Within the courtyard of the House of Rashid, two men sat beneath a canopy of woven silk. The air was thick with the warmth of the dying day, and the scent of herbs wafted from a nearby brazier. A stone table lay between them, worn by time, its surface etched with old Zarahan script - verses from the ancients, speaking of fate, duty, and the unbreakable bond between ruler and realm.

Khalid ibn Rashid, former warrior and guardian of the obelisks, reclined with the ease of a man who had fought many battles and survived them all. His face bore the marks of time and war, his dark beard flecked with silver, his eyes sharp, calculating, yet carrying the weight of something deeper - concern, perhaps even fear, though he would never voice it.

His fighting days were behind him, and now all his sons knew of him was that he was a trader, peddling the caravan routes to put food on their table. His wife knew of his past, but that was their secret. They both hoped that maybe this way, their children would be spared their father's fate. Khalid, however, also believed that his son should be ready, should his fate come to meet him.

Opposite him sat Barash, also a former warrior, turned scholar of the Obelisks. He was older, his skin weathered by time and wisdom, his robe heavy with the dust of countless journeys. His presence was like that of the ancient stones themselves - immovable, unyielding, and infinitely patient.
Between them, a single cup of black tea steamed, untouched. Barash exhaled slowly, his fingers tracing the rim of the cup. "You know why I have come."
Khalid's gaze did not waver. "I know." A silence stretched between them, as wide as the desert itself. Barash tilted his head, watching Khalid closely. "The boy must be prepared."
Khalid's jaw tightened. "He is only a child."
The older man observed his closest friend intently. "Maybe, but he is also more than a child." Barash's tone was kind, but he could see his words stung his friend.
Khalid leaned forward, his fingers pressing against the stone table. "And yet, that is what he is now." His voice was calm, but there was steel beneath it. "A boy, not yet a man. Not yet ready to carry the weight of the Weaving on his shoulders."
Barash sighed. "The Weaving will not wait, Khalid." Though his words were harsh, his eyes were kind, as if he was saying, "I understand your pain, brother."
Khalid's eyes flickered, the flames from the brazier reflecting in their depths. "Neither does a father's duty."
Barash studied him for a moment before speaking again, his voice softer but no less firm. "Perhaps you shelter him too much."
Khalid smirked, though there was no amusement in it. "And you, if I understood correctly, would throw him into the storm before he understands the wind. Does that sound like a good plan to you?"
Barash leaned back, exhaling.
The shadows deepened around them as the last light of Leander's primary kissed the rooftops of Karash. From beyond the walls, the distant hum of the town's night traders stirred - coins exchanging hands, quiet negotiations spoken in hushed tones, the shuffle of the desert steeds being led to their evening rest.
"If he is not prepared," Barash said at last, "the storm will consume him." It pained him to say this to his oldest friend, his brother-in-arms, but he must.

Khalid's hands tightened into fists, resting on his knees. He had seen storms, both of nature and of men. He had fought battles where the sand ran red, had watched kingdoms rise, and crumble. But none of it compared to the war he feared would one day come for his younger son, or perhaps his eldest.

Khalid's voice was quiet, but laced with an intensity that made even Barash pause. "Do you think I do not know this? That I do not wake each morning knowing what he must become?"

Barash's expression softened, but his resolve did not. "Then why do you resist?"

Khalid sighed, rubbing a hand over his beard. "Because he is still mine to protect."

Barash was silent for a long moment. Then, with the patience of old stones, he said, "By sheltering him, you are doing him a disservice. Instead of protecting him, you are delaying the inevitable."

Khalid met his gaze, and in the dimming light, the weight of years, of choices made and yet to be made, passed between them.

At last, Khalid spoke, his voice quieter. "You would have him learn as you did - through suffering. Through fire."

Barash inclined his head. "He must know pain if he is to understand sacrifice. He must know loss if he is to hold the Weaving together."

Khalid looked away toward the far end of the courtyard, where beyond the latticed archways, the first stars had begun to emerge. "And yet, I believe in something greater than suffering." Khalid replied, his eyes unfocused.

Barash arched a brow, as he always did when presented with such challenges. "And what is that?" he asked, eyes twinkling.

Khalid's lips pressed together, as though weighing the words before giving them shape. "Understanding."

Barash's fingers drummed lightly on the stone table. "You think wisdom alone will prepare him for what's to come?"

Khalid shook his head. "No. But neither will cruelty." The brazier crackled, a single ember breaking free and drifting into the night air before fading.

"Then how?" Barash asked, genuinely curious now.

Khalid's expression was unreadable, but there was something there - something unbreakable, unyielding, yet filled with an infinite depth of love.

"You shape steel by striking it," he lifted his gaze, meeting Barash's fully. "I shape my son by showing him the hand that wields the hammer."

A slow smile, barely perceptible, ghosted across Barash's lips.

"A poetic way to say you coddle him."

Khalid chuckled, the sound low and rough. "And you are as relentless as ever."

They both shared a well-deserved laugh. After all, there weren't that many to have in these troubled times. When the laughter faded, silence settled between them - comfortable, familiar, the kind only shared by those who had weathered storms together.

Barash leaned forward, resting his forearms on the table. "You cannot stop what is coming, Khalid. One day, he will have to stand alone."

Khalid nodded, his fingers brushing the rim of the untouched tea. "But not yet."

Barash exhaled through his nose, knowing there was no argument left to win. Khalid ibn Rashid had been and still was many things - a warrior, a leader, a man of unshaken conviction, a trader... and above all else, a father. Something Barash had never been fortunate enough to achieve.

The city hummed around them, the desert breeze carrying with it the scent of the distant dunes, the spice of the night market, the faintest trace of the Lunaris flower.

For now, the storm could wait, and they spent the night reminiscing about their past deeds.

Dialogue II: Barash and Khalid's Last Conversation

The streets of Karash were quieter at night but never silent. The city, nestled at the crossroads of Zarah's great trade routes, pulsed with life even as the moons hung low in the sky. From the high walls to the winding alleys, the scent of the desert mingled with the aromas of roasted spices, black tea, and the distant perfume of the Lunaris flower.

But in The Hollow Fang, a small, dimly lit inn at the edge of the merchant district, the air was different - thicker, heavier, laced with the unspoken weight of danger. The inn was old, its wooden beams darkened by years of smoke and quiet dealings. Shadows clung to the corners like wary travellers, and the flickering lanterns did little to drive them away. It was a place where secrets were whispered, where men met to speak of things that were best left unspoken.

At a table near the back, two men sat across from each other, speaking in voices just above a murmur.

Barash leaned forward, his fingers wrapped around a small brass cup of bitter tea. The candlelight flickered against the deep lines of his face, his expression unreadable, save for the slight furrow of his brow. Khalid ibn Rashid sat opposite him, his cloak draped over his broad shoulders, his eyes shadowed beneath the hood he wore despite the warmth of the room. His fingers tapped absently against the rim of his untouched cup, but his gaze was distant, his thoughts elsewhere. He exhaled softly. "He is hunting me, Barash."

Barash did not blink. "Then he has already lost."

Khalid gave a quiet chuckle, low and rough. "I admire your confidence, old friend. But Drathis is patient. He will not strike until he is sure."

Barash let the silence settle between them before he spoke. "You are certain that Malik the Vulture is him?" Khalid's fingers curled into a fist on the table. "As certain as I am of the sands beneath my feet."

Malik the Vulture - a name whispered through the desert like the hiss of a serpent. A warlord, a killer, a man whose presence was always followed by ruin. But now, Khalid saw what others had not. There was something unnatural in the way he moved, something that did not belong to the sons of Zarah.

He had watched him, studied him, and he knew. Drathis. The Draconian Warlord. Shape-shifter. Deceiver. A shadow wearing a man's skin.

Khalid took a slow breath. "He knows about Aran."

Barash stiffened. The air in the room seemed too thin, as if the very walls were listening. "How much?" Barash asked, voice barely containing the dread he felt.

Khalid's eyes met his, dark and unwavering. "He knows enough."

Barash's fingers tightened around his cup. This was no ordinary war. This was not about swords and banners. This was something deeper - an old struggle, one written in Zarah's bones, in the Weaving itself.

Khalid exhaled, glancing toward the entrance, where the shadowed figures of travellers huddled over their drinks. "If he is here, it means he is done waiting."

Barash took a slow sip of his tea, tasting the bitterness, letting it ground him. "And if you are right, then your life is forfeit."

Khalid nodded as if he had already accepted the words as truth. "Perhaps."

Barash studied him carefully. There was no fear in his friend's eyes, only the measured resolve of a man who had lived long enough to understand the nature of fate.

Finally, Khalid spoke again. "If I fall, Barash, you must swear to me - swear on the sands, on the Weaving itself - that you will watch over my son."

Barash inhaled slowly, the weight of the request settling upon him. "My friend," his eyes were glistening, "You know that you do not need to ask."

Khalid's lips curved into something resembling a smile. "And yet, I must hear you say it." Barash set his cup down with deliberate care. "By our friendship, I swear it!"

Aran's father nodded, his grip loosening, as if some great burden had been lifted from his shoulders. "Thank you, old friend. Thank you, because my son will need you."

Barash's gaze did not waver. "And you, old friend, will need to fight as though the gods themselves are watching." Khalid's smile was small but true "I always do."

For a moment, they sat in silence, two men who had seen too much, who understood each other in ways few ever could. Outside, the desert wind howled through the streets of Karash, carrying with it the scent of dust and secrets.

Khalid finished his tea, rising to his feet. He pulled his cloak tighter around him, casting one last look toward Barash. "If this is our last meeting, old friend, then let me say this - Thank you, Thank you, Thank you!"

Barash nodded once. "The road does not end here, Khalid. Only this chapter."

Khalid smirked, the shadow of a warrior's defiance still lingering in his expression. Then, without another word, he turned and disappeared into the night. Barash watched him go, his hands resting lightly upon the table, his mind already turning toward the path ahead. Outside, beyond the city walls, the desert waited. And so did Drathis.

End of "Lost Dialogues"

Appendix X: The Chronology of Legends and Legacy

Time weaves its own stories, binding myth and history into an unbroken thread. What follows is a complete and detailed account of the Tales of Legend, tracing the years in which these fabled events unfolded - the rise and fall of kings, the shaping of the Weaving, and the echoes of those who walked before.

From the Old Kings to the age of Aran ibn Khalid, this section also chronicles his journey - from Aran's rise to power, his battles, and his reshaping of the Weaving - to the lasting legacy he left behind.

The final entry marks the Great Sandstorm Crisis, the last great test of balance in Zarah's history.

From the dawn of time do the chroniclers of the House of Tempus record - the past is set in stone, ensuring that the deeds of heroes and the echoes of legend are never lost to the sands of time.

The historical dates for The Realms of the Old Kings, the Binding of the Primordials, and the Pact Aran's Forebears made with the Primordials fall into the most ancient epochs of Zarah's history. These events are foundational to the myths, shaping the very nature of the world and its balance between mortals and the cosmic forces that once ruled over them.

I. The Realms of the Old Kings & The Binding of the Primordials – The Age of the First Kings (12,000–10,000 years ago)

- This era, known as the Age of the First Kings, marks the time when the great rulers of old carved their kingdoms from the chaos of the untamed world.

- The Realms of the Old Kings were established around 12,000 years ago, with mighty cities rising across Zarah; their rulers were believed to have travelled from the stars themselves.

- During this time, the Primordials still walked the land, vast and incomprehensible beings that governed reality itself - Life and Death, Creation and Decay, the Endless Weaving of Fate.

- Around 11,500 years ago, war erupted between the Old Kings and the Primordials, as humanity sought dominion over the world, while the Primordials resisted the changing order.
- The Binding of the Primordials took place roughly 10,500 years ago, when the Old Kings, in an act of great sacrifice, forged the Obelisks - structures of immense power that would chain the Primordials to the fabric of existence itself, but also themselves.
- The Binding was not a victory, but a desperate truce, ensuring that the Primordials would neither rule nor destroy the world, but instead be locked within the Weaving, their influence scattered and their power diminished.

II. <u>The Pact Aran's Forebears Made with the Primordials - The Weaving's Accord (10,000–5,500 years ago)</u>

- Over time, the peoples of Zarah forgot the true nature of the Primordials, and the Old Kings passed into legend. Still, the obelisks endured, hidden, their power waiting to be claimed.
- Around 9,500 years ago, the ancestors of Aran rediscovered the ancient knowledge of the Binding and the truth of the Weaving. These were the First Wardens of Zarah.
- Unlike the Old Kings, who sought to chain the Primordials, Aran's forebears chose a different path. They sought to understand and bargain with these ancient beings, for they knew the Weaving was fraying and the balance of existence itself hung in peril.
- Around 9,300 years ago, they made the Pact of the Weaving, an agreement that allowed mortals to harness the obelisks without shattering the bindings that held the Primordials at bay.
- This pact came at a cost - blood and sacrifice, the First Wardens offering their own lineage to uphold the balance, ensuring that only those with their bloodline could wield the obelisks' power.
- By 5,500 years ago, the Wardens had fully taken up their role as keepers of the Weaving, a duty that would pass down through generations, leading to the time of Aran's birth and the rekindling of the struggle between order and chaos.

<u>Legacy and Impact</u>

- The Age of the First Kings is the most ancient of all remembered histories, shaping the myths of the world and establishing the cycle of power, sacrifice, and destiny.
- The Binding of the Primordials is seen as the moment Zarah truly became mortal, forever severing the rule of beings beyond comprehension.
- The Pact of Aran's Forebears is the reason why only his bloodline can mend the obelisks, setting into motion the conflict that would eventually bring Aran to his fate.
These moments are the foundation of Zarah's history, where gods and mortals clashed, and where the fate of existence itself was sealed.

<u>Tales Of Legend and Myth</u>

The historical dates for the tales of Amira, Uramak, Queen Amara, and Ashira of the Sands fall within the mythic and legendary cycles of Zarah's history. Each tale belongs to a different Age, marking the rise and fall of empires, the shaping of the planet's deserts, and the forging of legends. Four great tales stand as pillars of these legendary Ages, each marking a different epoch in Zarah's mythic cycle.

<u>I. The Tale of Amira, of the Qarr – The Age of the Wardens (10,000–6,000 years ago)</u>

- Amira's legend reaches back to the twilight of the Age of the Wardens, a time when the memory of the Old Kings began to fade into sand and folklore, and the great spirits of the world still walked unseen among mortals.
- Most Qamarian scholars place her Trial of Winds some 9,400 years before the rise of King Aran I, in the early centuries of the Wardenic era, when desert and silence still held dominion over the ambitions of mortal empires.
- The Gift of the Desert, known today as 'Amira's Blessing', was first recorded nearly four millennia later, at the beginning of the Third Age of Zarah, though Qarr oral tradition claims it was bestowed during her communion with the storm - an encounter believed by some to mark one

of the last known manifestations of a Primordial presence, before the time of King Aran I.

- Her disappearance from the chronicles is dated to an unknown point in the late Wardenic period. Whether she perished, passed into the deeper desert, or transcended the bounds of mortality remains the subject of spirited debate. Qarr lore says only this:

"She walked beyond the horizon, and the wind remembers her still."

II. The Tale of Uramak - The Age of Titans (5,000–4,500 years ago)

- Uramak's legend predates tribal written history, belonging to an age when the Primordials still whispered in the wind, and the great sand serpents ruled the deserts.

- His tale is often placed around 5,000 years ago, in an era known as The Age of Titans, also known as The Forgotten Age, when the balance between mortals and ancient beings was still shifting.

- The Bargain of Stories with Jalal ibn Samir is believed to have taken place around 4,700 years ago, though its exact date is debated by scholars.

- By 4,500 years ago, Uramak had vanished beneath the sands, and his name became more legend than reality. Although scholars continue to debate, to this day, if the Serpent that aided Aran against Drathis and Vhaskar, was indeed Uramak as he had himself prophesied.

III. The Tale of Queen Amara - The Dawnfire Era (2,500–2,000 years ago)

- Queen Amara's reign is placed around 2,500 years ago, during a golden age known as the Dawnfire Era, a time of vast learning, celestial discovery, and great wars. When the Kingdom of Ryvath was at the height of its power.

- The Twilight War, where Amara defended Ryvath against the Bahir, took place roughly 2,480 years ago.

- Her departure to seek the Veil of Suns and the unknown mysteries of the cosmos occurred around 2,475 years ago, marking the end of her

reign and the beginning of a new age of myths. Some say she went in search of the Old Kings star origins.
- About 2,000 years ago, Amara and her Nightwing had fully transcended into legend, her name spoken in reverence by star-seekers and desert wanderers alike.

IV. <u>The Tale of Ashira of the Sands - The Shadowed Age (800–600 years ago)</u>

- Ashira's exploits are set in a much later time, around 800 years ago, during a period known as The Shadowed Age, or Age of the Shattered Thrones, when empires crumbled and city-states vied for power.
- Her years as a thief in Dakarai, her rise as a spy, and her fateful betrayal of Khalid occurred around 780–770 years ago.
- Her time with the Zafiri and her transformation into the Ghost of the Dunes took place between 770–750 years ago.
- By 700 years ago, she had disappeared from recorded history, becoming a name spoken only in hushed tones by those who still believed in spirits that walked the sands.

Each tale exists within its own chapter of history, their echoes shaping the myths, fears, and destinies of Zarah's people.

<u>Aran Ibn Khalid's Story</u>

Aran's story unfolds in the most defining era of Zarah's history, marking the transition from the age of fragmentation to the forging of a new House, in The MiddleVerse. His rise to power, his war against Kael Drathis, of the Nathair Draconian Bloodline, and his reshaping of the Weaving take place within the last millennium, leading to an age where destiny was rewritten.

I. Aran's Rise to Power – The Age of the Shattered Thrones (800–300 years ago)

- The world before Aran's rise was one of fractured kingdoms, weakened by endless conflict and the slow unravelling of the Weaving.
- Around 300 years ago, Aran was born into a land divided, raised as the heir of an ancient but fading bloodline - the last remnants of the First Wardens of Zarah.
- As a young leader of men, he united the tribes of Zarah, forging alliances that had not existed for centuries. Unbeknownst to him, continuing his father's secret work.
- In a bloody battle against the rebelling Halithar tribe, Aran's older brother, Iram inb Khalid, died in battle (288 years ago)
- 279 years ago, Aran inb Khalid became the recognized leader of Sarim, the largest and most powerful city-state on Zarah, at the time. Not long after, he was crowned by majority, King of Zarah, though not all accepted his rule.

II. The Quest for the Obelisks - The War of the Weaving (280–278 years ago)

- Just before securing his kingdom, Aran uncovered the growing fractures in the Weaving, the result of the long-dormant Primordials stirring once more.
- Around 280 years ago, he began his quest for the obelisks, later learning they were the key to stabilizing the Weaving and preventing the return of chaos.
- He travelled across Zarah, facing great trials - including the Trials of the Old Kings in Ryvath, where he proved himself worthy of wielding the obelisks' power.
- Each one he encountered held a different aspect of existence - Life and Death, Creation and Decay, Order and Chaos, as well as the souls of the Old Kings - forcing Aran to confront his own nature as much as his enemies'.

III. <u>The Wars with Drathis – The Crimson Campaigns (280–278 years ago)</u>

- Drathis, a feared Draconian warlord and the last great general of the Nathair Bloodline, sought to control the Weaving for himself, believing it could grant him dominion over life itself. Thus fulfilling his parents' dream.
- As Aran journeyed to mend the Weaving, Drathis waged war upon his cities, sending spies and agents to undermine his kingdom whilst waging open war against the peoples of Zarah.
- The conflict, known to history as the Crimson Campaigns, raged for nearly two years, with great battles such as:
    - The Siege of Sarim (278 years ago) – Drathis' forces attempted to break the city of the moons but were repelled. Kael Drathis himself was severely wounded by Aran ibn Khalid and forced to call the retreat of his already broken army.
    - The Battle of the Shadows Divide (278 years ago) – Drathis summoned the Primordials, aiming to control them, but was handed a devastating loss, being fully expelled from the Weaving, leaving him aimless, lost.
    - The Final Duel (278 years ago) - Aran and Drathis met in combat one last time near a hidden obelisk's location, where both Drathis and Vhaskar fell, bringing an end to their ambitions, as well as the final conclusion of two of the oldest, and most pure Draconian bloodlines. Vhaskar fell to Rafiq's swords and Barash's strategic strikes.

IV. <u>The Reshaping of the Weaving - The Reckoning of Fate (278 years ago)</u>

- With Drathis defeated and the final obelisk in his grasp, Aran faced his greatest choice - to give up his life to keep the Primordials at bay, hoping they would spare Zarah, or to take control of the Weaving's power, bend it to his will and forever change the fate of mortals.
- He chose to be the caretaker of balance.
- The Reckoning of Fate (also called, by some scholars, the Reshaping) occurred 278 years ago, when Aran mastered the Weaving, repaired the fractures in the Weaving, and thus ensured that the Primordials could live in harmony with humans - but also that their power would not be lost

entirely. By doing so, he ensured that each plane of existence would keep learning from the other.
- By being willing to bind part of his own essence into the Weaving, Aran ensured that the balance would hold, though at great personal risk.
- Some academics claim that in that moment, he transcended mere mortality, becoming something more than a king - a guardian of the unseen forces of the desert.

V. The Legacy of Aran - The Age of Balance (278–Present)

- After the Reshaping, Aran ruled for many decades, but he was no longer just a king - he became a legend.
- The world had changed. The balance of power between mortals and the unseen was forever altered. Through the centuries after his death, his name was spoken as both saviour and enigma.
- Aran moved Zarah's capital from Sarim to Qamaria (276 years ago)
- He lived a long life with Sura, his queen, and they had an offspring (Khalid ibn Aran- Born 275 years ago)
- Some, amongst the Priesthood of the Sun, say that after a very long life, both Aran and Sura vanished into the desert, seeking the last great truths hidden within the Weaving.
- Others claim that they live still, watching from the unseen places of the world, waiting for the day when the Weaving will be tested once more.
- Their legacy lived on in their son and wife, who kept the House of Aran on the path of harmony.
Aran's story marks the end of one age and the beginning of another, a time where the Weaving itself was reforged, ensuring that the fate of the world would never again be left solely in the hands of gods or mortals - but in the balance between them.
Little did he know that fate had one more calamity in wait...

VI. The Great Sandstorm Crisis (275 Years Ago)

- Three years after the Reshaping of the Weaving, Zarah was struck by an event unlike any in recorded history - a sandstorm of unnatural scale and power, one that devoured entire settlements and reshaped the very dunes of the desert.

- Portents of doom preceded the great calamity: the oldest wells in Zarah ran dry overnight, and oases that had existed for millennia simply vanished, swallowed by the shifting sands as if they had never existed. The skies darkened to unnatural hues, streaked with burnt copper and crimson, as though the heavens themselves had caught fire.
- The wind changed. The nomad tribes spoke in hushed whispers of a new voice in the desert - one that did not whisper but howled. A voice of warning. A voice of wrath.
- When the storm finally arrived, it descended upon Sarim without warning, a monstrous gale that shattered rooftops, overturned market stalls, and left the city buried beneath an ocean of swirling sand. The air was thick with something more than just dust - those who listened carefully swore they could hear voices carried upon the wind, speaking in a language long forgotten.
- The High Council of Sarim was summoned, an event not held in years. King Aran, Queen Sura, the mystic Barash, and Rafiq of the Order of the Sacred Desert, gathered with the city's scholars and elders. The Moon Seer, Safira, confirmed their worst fears
- this was no ordinary storm. It was a wound in the Weaving, left behind by something that refused to be forgotten.

Thus speak our chronicles…
The House of Tempus, Echoing Archives, Chronaxis, the Kronos System

Acknowledgements

Writing a novel is, they say, a solitary endeavour. I respectfully disagree. While the act of sitting before a keyboard (or glaring at it in existential dread) is often done alone, the journey itself is far from solitary. It is forged in the presence, and with the patience, of those who walk beside us, often quietly, often heroically, always indispensably.

To my parents, who taught me that imagination is not something to grow out of but something to grow into. Thank you for always making room for wonder, and for never once suggesting I do something "more practical" with my time.

To my wife, whose love, endurance, and capacity to tolerate long, one-sided conversations about fictional politics and metaphysical obelisks is nothing short of legendary. Thank you for being my anchor and my sail.

To my children, who remind me daily that magic is real, and that bedtime stories have the power to ignite galaxies - thank you for being the brightest stars in my universe. Without all of you, I would never have found the peace of mind - or the persistent background noise - that somehow allowed me to take on such a behemoth task.

To Ricardo, my steadfast companion through life's labyrinth, thank you for your undying friendship. You've been both compass and torch throughout my life. Your loyalty is of the kind epics are written about - usually involving dragons, but for the time being, I'll take a Sand Serpent.

To Mike Rawson, a man who challenged me to go further than I thought I could, and then stood back with a knowing grin as I did - thank you. Your belief in me has the gravitational pull of a black hole, except far more positive and significantly less destructive.

To Cindy Toscano, for always believing in me and for being one of my most fervent supporters. Thank you for cheering from the sidelines, even when the game looked unwinnable.

To you, dear reader. Without you, this story would simply drift - unread, uncelebrated - in the silent vacuum of space, like a noble starship with no destination. It is your willingness to embark on this voyage with me that brings the tale to life. Thank you for acquiring the book, for flipping (or swiping) through its pages, and for giving your precious time to the world I dreamed into being.

May your journey through The MiddleVerse be filled with awe, wonder, and just the right amount of danger.

With all gratitude,
Michael P. C. Rocha

"True unity is not the silence of difference, but the harmony of remembered truth" Khalid ibn Aran, Qamaria 255 years ago

www.ingramcontent.com/pod-product-compliance
Lightning Source LLC
Chambersburg PA
CBHW070148310726

48976CB00001B/28